ITALO CALVINO

Fantastic Tales

Italo Calvino's works include *The Road to San Giovanni, Numbers in the Dark, Six Memos for the Next Millennium, The Baron in the Trees, If on a Winter's Night a Traveler, Invisible Cities,* and *Mr. Palomar.* Calvino died in 1985.

ALSO BY ITALO CALVINO

Baron in the Trees

Cosmicomics

Difficult Loves

If On a Winter's Night a Traveler

Invisible Cities

Italian Folktales

Marcovaldo

Mr. Palomar

The Nonexistent Knight

Numbers in the Dark

The Road to San Giovanni

Six Memos for the Next Millennium

Under the Jaguar Sun

The Uses of Literature

Fantastic Tales

Fantastic Tales

*

VISIONARY AND EVERYDAY

EDITED AND WITH AN INTRODUCTION BY

ITALO CALVINO

VINTAGE INTERNATIONAL

VINTAGE BOOKS

A DIVISION OF RANDOM HOUSE, INC.

NEW YORK

FIRST VINTAGE INTERNATIONAL EDITION, NOVEMBER 1998

 Published in the United States by Vintage Books, a division of Random House, Inc., New York, and simultaneously in Canada by Random House of Canada Limited, Toronto. Originally published in Italy as two separate volumes as *Racconti Fantastici Dell'Ottocento: Volume Primo, Il Fantastico Visionario* and *Volume Secondo, Il Fantastico Quotidiano*, by Arnoldo Mondadori Editore, Milan, in 1983. Copyright © 1983 by Arnoldo Mondadori Editore S.p.A., Milano. First published in hardcover in the United States by Pantheon Books, a division of Random House, Inc., New York, in 1997.

Italo Calvino's introduction and headnotes were translated by Alfred MacAdam, as were the following stories: "Autumn Sorcery" by Joseph von Eichendorff, "The Eye with No Lid" by Philarète Chasles, "The Enchanted Hand" by Gérard de Nerval, and "The Holes in the Mask" by Jean Lorrain.

Permissions acknowledgments are on pp. 587–588.

The Library of Congress has cataloged the Pantheon edition as follows:

Racconti fantastici dell'Ottocento. English
Fantastic tales: visionary and everyday / edited and with an introduction by Italo Calvino.
p. cm.
ISBN 0-679-41526-2
1. Fantastic fiction—Translations into English.
2. Fiction—19th century—Translations into English. I. Calvino, Italo.
PN6120.95.F25R3313 1997 93-12824

Vintage ISBN: 0-679-75544-6

Book design by Chris Welch

www.randomhouse.com

Printed in the United States of America
10 9 8 7 6 5 4 3 2 1

Contents

II. The Everyday Fantastic of the Nineteenth Century 305

Introduction by Italo Calvino

The fantastic tale is one of the most characteristic products of nineteenth-century narrative. For us, it is also one of the most significant because it is the genre that tells us the most about the inner life of the individual and about collectively held symbols. As it relates to our sensibility today, the supernatural element at the heart of these stories always appears freighted with meaning, like the revolt of the unconscious, the repressed, the forgotten, all that is distanced from our rational attention. In this we see the modern dimension of the fantastic, the reason for its triumphant resurgence in our times. We note that the fantastic says things that touch us intimately, even though we are less disposed than the readers of the last century to allow ourselves to be surprised by apparitions and phantasmagoria. We are inclined to enjoy them in another way, as elements in the spirit of a bygone era.

The fantastic tale arises between the eighteenth and nineteenth centuries in the same ground as philosophic speculation: its theme is the relationship between the reality of the world we live in and know through perception and the reality of the world of thought that lives within us and directs us. The problem with the reality of what we see—extraordinary things that are perhaps hallucinations projected by our minds, or common things that perhaps hide a second, disturbing nature, mysterious and terrible, beneath the most banal appearances—is the essence of fantastic literature, whose best effects reside in an oscillation between irreconcilable levels of reality.

Tzvetan Todorov, in his *Introduction to Fantastic Literature* (1970), holds that what distinguishes "fantastic" narrative is precisely our perplexity in the face of an incredible fact, our indecision in choosing between a rational, realistic explanation and an acceptance of the supernatural. The character of the incredulous positivist who often appears in this kind of story, seen with compassion and irony because he must surrender when confronted by something he does not know how to explain, is not completely negated. According to Todorov, the incredible event the fantastic story tells must always allow for a rational explanation, unless it happens to be a hallucination or a dream (a fail-safe device that sanctions just about anything).

On the other hand, the "marvelous," according to Todorov, is different from the fantastic in that it presupposes our acceptance of the implausible and the inexplicable, as in fables or *The Thousand and One Nights*. This distinction is faithful to French literary terminology, where *fantastique* almost always refers to macabre elements, such as ghosts. The Italian sense of the term, on the other hand, more freely associates the idea of the fantastic with fantasy. In effect, we Italians speak about the *fantastic* in Ariosto (in *Orlando Furioso*, for example), but according to French terminology we should be talking about the *marvelous* in Ariosto.

The fantastic story is born at the beginning of the nineteenth century with German Romanticism, but during the second half of the eighteenth century the English Gothic novel had already explored a repertory of motifs, settings, and effects (especially macabre, cruel, and horrifying effects) which the Romantics employed profusely. And since one of the first names that stands out among them (because of the achievement of his *Peter Schlemihls*) belongs to a German author born a Frenchman, Adelbert von Chamisso, who brings to his crystalline German prose a lightness typical of the French eighteenth century, we see that the French component is also essential from the first. The French eighteenth century makes a twofold bequest to the Romantic fantastic story: first, the spectacular pomp of the "marvelous tale" (from the *féerique* at the court of Louis XIV to the oriental phantasmagorias of *The Thousand and One Nights*, discovered and translated by Galland), and second, the linear, direct, and cutting style of the Voltairean "philosophic tale," where nothing is gratuitous, and everything tends toward a single end.

If the eighteenth-century philosophic tale had been the paradoxical expression of Illuminist Reason, the "fantastic tale" is born in Germany as the open-eyed dream of philosophical idealism, with the declared intention of representing the reality of the interior, subjective world of the mind, the imagination, giving to that world a dignity equal to or greater than that of the world of objectivity and of the senses. For that reason, it too presents itself as a philosophic tale, and here one name stands out above all others: E. T. A. Hoffmann.

An anthology should delineate its own limits and impose some rules on itself. This one has adopted the rule of including a single text by each author: this rule is particularly cruel when it becomes necessary to choose one story to represent all of Hoffmann. I've chosen his best-known tale because, we might say, it's an "obligatory" text: "The Sandman," where the characters and images of tranquil bourgeois life metamorphose into grotesque, diabolical, and terrifying apparitions, as in nightmares. But I could also have oriented my choice toward other texts by Hoffmann that almost completely lack the grotesque, "The Mines of Galun," for example, where Romantic nature poetry attains the sublime by means of the fascination of the mineral world.

The mines young Ellis sinks into, to the point where he prefers them to sunlight or the embrace of his wife, constitute one of the great symbols of Ideal interiority. And here we see another essential point that any discussion of the fantastic must take into account: attempts to clarify the meaning of a symbol—Peter Schlemihls's lost shadow in Chamisso, the mines where Ellis becomes lost in Hoffmann, the street of the Jews in Achim von Arnim's "Die Majoratsherren"—do nothing more than impoverish their rich suggestiveness.

Hoffmann excepted, the great works of the fantastic genre during German Romanticism are too long to be included in an anthology that seeks to offer the widest possible panorama. A length of fewer than fifty pages is another limit I have imposed on myself, and it forces me to give up some of my favorite texts, which have the dimensions either of a very long story or a novella: Chamisso, about whom I've already spoken, and his short novel *Isabel of Egypt*, the other beautiful works of Arnim, and Joseph von Eichendorff's *Memoirs of a Lazy Man*. To have offered a selection would have involved contravening the third I'd established: to offer only complete tales. (I made one exception: Potocki. His novel, *Manuscript Found in Saragossa*, contains tales which, despite being rather interconnected, enjoy a certain autonomy.)

If we consider the diffusion of Hoffmann's acknowledged influence on the various European literatures, we can be confident that at least for the first half of the nineteenth century, the "fantastic tale" is synonymous with "tale in the style of Hoffmann." In Russian literature, Hoffmann's influence produces such miraculous fruit as Gogol's *Saint Petersburg Tales*, but we should note that even before any European inspiration, Gogol had written extraordinary tales about witchcraft in his two collections of stories set in the Ukrainian countryside. From the outset, the critical tradition has studied nineteenth-century Russian literature from the perspective of realism, but the parallel development of the fantastic tendency—from Pushkin to Dostoevski—is clearly visible. It is precisely in that line that an author of the first rank like Nikolai Semyonovich Leskov acquires his proper dimension.

In France, Hoffmann has tremendous influence on Charles Nodier, on Balzac (on the self-avowedly fantastic Balzac and on the realist Balzac in his grotesque, nocturnal suggestions), and on Théophile Gautier, from whom we can derive a branching out from the Romantic tree that will play an important role in the development of the fantastic tale: aestheticism. With regard to the philosophic aspect: in France, the fantastic is tinged with the esoteric from Nodier to Nerval, or with Swedenborgian theosophy, as in Balzac and Gautier. Gérard de Nerval creates a new fantastic genre: the dream tale (*Sylvie*, *Aurélia*) more supported by lyrical density than by plot structure. As for Mérimée and his Mediterranean stories (and also his Nordic stories: the suggestive Lithuania of *Lokis*), with his skill at capturing the light and soul of a country in an image that instantly becomes an emblem, he opens the fantastic genre to a new dimension: exoticism.

England takes special pleasure in playing with the macabre and terrible. The most famous example is Mary Shelley's *Frankenstein*.

The pathos and humor of the Victorian novel leave a certain margin so the "black" or "gothic" imagination can carry on its work with renewed vigor: the ghost story is born. Its authors perhaps make a point of ironic winks, but in the meanwhile they put something of themselves on display, an interior truth that is not part of the conventions of the genre. Dickens's propensity for the grotesque and macabre finds a place not only in his great novels but also in his minor productions, such as the Christmas stories and tales about ghosts. I say "productions" because Dickens (like Balzac) programmed his work with the determination of someone involved in the industrial or commercial world (and his best works are born in just that way) and published serials filled in the main with narratives he wrote himself but conceived to open the way to the collaborations of his friends as well.

Among the writers in his circle (which includes the author of the first detective novel, Wilkie Collins), there is one who stands out in the history of the genre: Joseph Sheridan Le Fanu, of an Irish Protestant family, the first example of a professional ghost story writer, since he wrote practically nothing else but tales of ghosts and horror. It was at that time that a "specialization" in the fantastic tale appeared which has developed considerably in our century (both in popular and highbrow literature, but often between those extremes). This is not to imply that Le Fanu should be taken as a mere artisan (which is what Bram Stoker, the creator of Dracula, would later be). To the contrary: the drama of religious controversies gives life to his tales, as do the popular Irish imagination and a grotesque, poetic, and nocturnal vein (see "Judge Harbottle") in which we recognize once again the influence of Hoffmann.

What all the very different authors I've named up to this point have in common is the placing of a visual suggestion in the foreground. And this is no coincidence. As I said at the outset, the true theme of the nineteenth-century fantastic tale is the reality of what we see: to believe or not to believe in phantasmagoric apparitions, to glimpse another world, enchanted or infernal, behind everyday appearances. It is as if the fantastic tale, more than any other genre, were destined to make its entrance through our eyes, to become concrete in a succession of images, to entrust its power to communicate to the ability to create "figures." It is not so much a mastery in the manipulation of language, or a pursuit of the brilliancy in abstract thought that is narrated, as is the clarity of a complex and unusual scene. The theatrical element is essential to fantastic narrative: no wonder movies have nourished themselves so much on it.

But we cannot generalize. If in the majority of cases, the Romantic imagination creates around itself a space populated by visionary apparitions, there also exists the fantastic story in which the supernatural is invisible. Rather than seeing it, we feel it. It comes to form part of an interior dimension, as a mood or a conjecture. Even Hoffmann, who takes such delight in evoking anguishing and demonic visions, has stories in which he deploys a tightly knit economy of spectacular elements, where images of everyday life predominate. For example, in "The Abandoned House" (*La casa deshabitada*) the closed windows of a ruined old house amid the rich palaces of Unter den Linden, a glimpse of a woman's arm or a girl's face are sufficient in themselves to create an expectation full of mystery, one that is all the greater because those movements are not observed directly but reflected in an ordinary mirror that takes on the function of a magic mirror.

We can find the clearest examples of these two directions in Poe. His most typical tales are those in which a dead woman, bloody and dressed in white, emerges from a coffin in a dark house whose magnificent furnishings exude an air of dissolution. "The Fall of the House of Usher" constitutes the richest elaboration of this kind. But take "The Tell-Tale Heart," where visual suggestions, reduced to a minimum, are concentrated in an eye opened wide in the darkness, while all the tension concentrates in the murderer's monologue.

To compare the distinctive features of the "visionary fantastic" to those of the "mental," "abstract," "psychological," or "everyday" fantastic, I first considered selecting two stories from each author that would represent the two tendencies. But I quickly noticed that at the beginning of the nineteenth century the visionary fantastic clearly predominates, just as at the end of the century the everyday fantastic prevails, reaching the apex of the incorporeal and the ungraspable in Henry James. I concluded that with having to give up only a minimum with respect to the original project, I could unify both the chronological order and the stylistic classification by calling the first part, which includes texts from the first three decades of the nineteenth century, "the visionary fantastic," and calling the second, which reaches the dawn of the twentieth century, "the everyday fantastic." Inevitably, things become a bit forced in operations like this, which take their point of departure from opposed definitions. Actually, the labels are interchangeable, and a story from one group could just as well be transposed to the other. The important thing is that it remain clear that the general direction is toward the gradual interiorization of the supernatural.

After Hoffmann, Poe is the author who has had the greatest influence on the European fantastic genre. Baudelaire's translation must have functioned like the manifesto of a new formulation of literary taste. The result was that Poe's macabre, *décadent* effects were taken up more easily than his lucid power of ratiocination, which is his most important distinctive feature. I spoke first about his reputation in Europe because in his own country Poe's figure did not become so emblematic that it was identified with a concrete literary genre. Contemporary with him, even a bit earlier than Poe, another great American achieved extraordinary intensity in the fantastic tale: Nathaniel Hawthorne.

Among the authors represented in this anthology, it is certainly Hawthorne who goes deepest into a moral and religious conception, both in the drama of the individual conscience and in the relentless representation of a world forged by a thwarted religiosity, like that of Puritan society. Many of his tales are masterpieces (both of the visionary fantastic—the witches' Sabbath in "Young Goodman Brown"—and of the introspective fantastic—"Egotism, or the *Bosom* Serpent"). But not all. When he leaves his American settings behind (as in the all-too-famous *Rappaccini's Daughter*), his powers of invention indulge in more foreseeable effects. But in his best works, his moral allegories, always based on the indelible presence of sin in the human heart, have a power to make interior drama visible that will be equalled in our century only by Franz Kafka: there can be no doubt that an antecedent of *The Castle* is one of Hawthorne's best and most anguishing stories: "My Kinsman Major Molineaux."

It's important to point out that before Hawthorne and Poe, the fantastic in the literature of the United States already had its tradition and its classic author: Washington Irving. And we must not forget an emblematic tale like William Austin's "Peter Rugg, the Missing Man" (1824). A mysterious divine condemnation obliges a man with his daughter at his side to race forever onward in a two-wheeled carriage never able to stop, driven by a hurricane through the immense geography of the continent. The story, with elemental obviousness, expresses the components of the nascent American myth: the power of nature, individual predestination, adventuresome intensity.

So what Poe—unlike the Romantics at the beginning of the nineteenth century—inherits is an already mature fantastic tradition, which he transmits to his followers, who often are nothing more than inferior imitators and affected stylists (some of them, like Ambrose Bierce, rich in the spirit of the age). Until, with Henry James, we find ourselves face to face with a new line of force.

In France, it was not long before Poe, who became French through Baudelaire, created a school. And the most interesting of his adherents in the specific area of the short story is Villiers de l'Isle-Adam, who in "Véra" offers us an effective mise-en-scène of the theme of love that continues beyond the grave. In "Torture with Hope" we have one of the most perfect examples of the purely mental fantastic. (In their own anthologies, Roger Callois chooses "Véra"; Borges "Torture with Hope." Both excellent choices, especially the second. If I propose a third story, it's because, more than anything else, I don't want to repeat the selections of my predecessors.)

Toward the end of the nineteenth century, especially in England, the paths are blazed that will be followed by the fantastic genre in the twentieth century. In England there appears a kind of refined writer who likes to disguise himself as a popular writer. The disguise works because he doesn't use it condescendingly but with ease and professional zeal, something possible only when we recognize that without professional technique artistic wisdom is powerless. Robert Louis Stevenson is the happiest example of this spiritual disposition, but along with him we should consider two extraordinary cases of inventive brilliance as well as complete control of craft: Kipling and Wells.

The fantastic in Kipling's Hindu tales is exotic, not in the aestheticist, decadent sense but because it derives from the contrast between the religious, moral, and social world of India and the English world. Often the supernatural is an invisible presence, even if it is terrifying, as in "The Mark of the Beast"; other times, the workaday setting, as in "The Bridge-Builders," is torn open and, in a visionary apparition, the ancient divinities of Hindu mythology are revealed. Kipling also wrote many fantastic tales with an English setting where the supernatural is almost always invisible (as in "They") and where the anguish of death dominates.

With Wells, science fiction makes its debut, a new horizon for the imagination, one that will undergo a huge development in the second half of our century. But Wells's genius is not limited to the formulation of marvelous hypotheses and terrors of the future, or to vexing us with apocalyptic visions. His extraordinary tales are always based on a discovery made by the intelligence that can be very simple. "The Case of the Deceased Mr. Evelsham," for instance, is the case of a young man who will be named sole heir of an unknown old man on condition that he take on the old man's name. He accepts; he wakes up in the old man's house and looks at his hands: they are wrinkled. He looks in the mirror: he is the old man. Only then does he realize that the old man has taken his identity and his person and is living his youth. Externally, everything is identical to the normal appearance of before, but reality is a horror without limits.

An author with great facility in combining the refinements of the literary man of quality with the brio of the popular narrator (among his favorite authors he always mentioned Dumas) was Robert Louis Stevenson. In his short, invalid's life, he managed to create many perfect works, from adventure novels to *Dr. Jekyll and Mr. Hyde*, as well as numerous fantastic narratives that were very short: "Olalla," a story of female vampires in Spain during the Napoleonic era (the same setting used by Potocki, though I do not know if Stevenson ever read him); "Thrown Janet," a Scottish tale of witchcraft; the *Island Nights Entertainments*, where with a light touch he shows the magic of the exotic (and also exports Scottish motifs by adapting them to Polynesian settings); "Markheim," which follows the path of the interiorized fantastic like Poe's "Tell-Tale Heart" with a more marked presence of the Puritan conscience.

One of Stevenson's staunchest followers has nothing of the popular to him: Henry James. With James—we don't know whether to call him American, English, or European—the fantastic genre of the nineteenth century has its final incarnation. Better put, its disincarnation, since it becomes more invisible and impalpable than ever: a psychological emanation or vibration. We must take into account the intellectual environment in which Henry James's work is born, especially the theories of his brother, the philosopher William James, about the psychic reality of experience. We can say that at the end of the century, the fantastic tale again becomes a philosophic tale, as it was at the beginning of the century.

The ghosts in Henry James's ghost stories are very evasive: they can be incarnations of an evil with no face or form, like the diabolical servants in *The Turn of the Screw*, or very visible apparitions that give sensible form to a dominant thought, like "Sir Edmund Orme," or illusions that unleash the true presence of the supernatural, as in "The Ghostly Rental." In one of his most suggestive and moving stories, "The Jolly Corner," the ghost the protagonist barely glimpses is the very person he would have been if his life had taken another road; in "The Private Life" there is one man who exists only when other people look at him (when they do not, he vanishes), while there is another who exists twice, because he has a double who writes the books he would never know how to write.

This essay ends with James, chronologically of the nineteenth century, but a writer who belongs to our century because of his literary taste. I've left out Italian authors because I did not like the idea of having to include them merely out of obligation: the fantastic is a minor element in nineteenth-century Italian literature. Special anthologies (*The Poetry and Tales of Arrigo Boito* and *Racconti neri della scapigliatura* (*Dark tales of the Bohemian life*), as well as a few texts by writers better known for other aspects of their work, from De Marchi to Capuana, provide precious discoveries as well as interesting documentation concerning the taste of the era. Among the other national literatures I've omitted, Spanish writing has one very well known author of fantastic tales, Gustavo Adolfo Bécquer. But this anthology does not pretend to be exhaustive. What I've wanted to present is a panorama based on a few examples and, above all, a book that would be easy to read.

Authors Cited in the Introduction

Arnim, Achim von (1781–1831). German Romantic.
Austin, William (1718–1841). American.
Balzac, Honoré de (1788–1850). French.
Baudelaire, Charles (1821–1867). French.
Bécquer, Gustavo Adolfo (1836–1870). Spanish.
Bierce, Ambrose (1842–?1914). American.
Boito, Arrigo (1842–1918). Italian.
Capuana, Luigi (1839–1915). Italian.
Chamisso, Adelbert von (1781–1838). German.
Collins, William Wilkie (1824–1889). English.
De Marchi, Attilio (1855–1915). Italian.
Dickens, Charles (1812–1870). English.
Dostoevski, Fyodor Mikhailovich (1821–1881). Russian.
Dumas, Alexandre ("Dumas père") (1802–1870). French.
Eichendorff, Joseph, Freiherr von (1788–1857). German.
Gautier, Théophile (1811–1872). French.
Gogol, Nikolai Vasilyevich (1809–1852). Russian.
Hawthorne, Nathaniel (1804–1864). American.
Hoffmann, Ernst Theodor Amadeus (1776–1822). German.

Irving, Washington (1783–1859). American.
James, Henry (1843–1916). Anglo-American.
Kafka, Franz (1883–1924). Czechoslovakian.
Kipling, Rudyard (1865–1936). English.
Le Fanu, Joseph Sheridan (1814–1873). Irish.
Leskov, Nikolai Semyonovich (1831–1895). Russian.
Mérimée, Prosper (1803–1870). French.
Nerval, Gérard de (1808–1855). French.
Nodier, Charles (1780–1844). French.
Poe, Edgar Allan (1809–1849). American.
Potocki, Jan Hrabia (1761–1815). Polish.
Pushkin, Alexandr Sergeyevich (1799–1837). Russian.
Shelley, Mary Wollstonecraft (1797–1851). English.
Stevenson, Robert Louis (1850–1894). Scottish.
Stoker, Bram (Abraham) (1847–1912). English.
Villiers de l'Isle-Adam, Jean Marie Mathias Philippe Auguste, Comte de (1828–1889). French.
Wells, Herbert George (1866–1946). English.

I

*

The Visionary Fantastic of the Nineteenth Century

JAN POTOCKI

*

The Story of the Demoniac Pacheco

(Histoire du démoniaque Pacheco, 1805)

The macabre, the spectral, the demonic, the vampiric, the erotic, and the perverse: all the ingredients (hidden or manifest) of visionary Romanticism appear in this extraordinary book, the Manuscrit trouvé a Saragosse, *published in French by the Polish count Jan Potocki (1761–1815). Mysterious in origin and literary fortune and just as mysterious in terms of its content, this book disappeared for more than a century (it was, of course, too scandalous to circulate freely), and only in 1958 was it reprinted in its original form, for which thanks must be given to Roger Callois, a great connoisseur of the fantastic no matter what its historical period or country of origin.*

An ideal prelude to the century of Hoffmann and Poe, Potocki could not be left out of this anthology: but since his is a book in which stories are interpolated into each other (a bit like The Thousand and One Nights*) to form a long novel from which it is difficult to separate one tale from another, I was forced to make—and right at the outset—an exception to the rule the rest of this anthology tries to respect. I am* *including here a chapter from Potocki's book, while the norm will be to offer complete and independent stories.*

The text starts just after the beginning of the novel (the second chapter). Alphonse van Worden, an officer in Napoleon's army, is in Spain, where he sees a gallows and two hanged men (the de Zoto brothers). Then he finds two extremely beautiful Arabian sisters who tell him their story, which is replete with a disturbing eroticism. Alphonse makes love to both, but during the night he has strange visions, and at dawn finds himself embracing the cadavers of the two hanged men.

This theme of the embrace of two sisters (and occasionally with their mother) is repeated in the book several times in the stories of different characters, and it always happens that the man who thinks himself the luckiest of lovers wakes up in the morning under the gallows amid corpses and vultures. A charm linked to the constellation Gemini is the key to the novel.

Still in the early phase of the development of a new literary genre, Potocki knows exactly where to go: the fantastic is the exploration of the obscure zone where the most unrestrained passions of desire and the terrors of guilt mix together. It is an evocation of ghosts that change form just as they do in dreams—with ambiguity and perversion.

Eventually I really did awaken. The sun was burning my eyelids. I opened them with difficulty. I saw the sky. I saw that I was out in the open. But my eyes were still heavy with sleep. I was no longer sleeping, but I was not yet awake. A succession of images of torture passed through my mind. I was appalled by them. Jerked out of my slumber, I sat up . . .

How shall I find words to express the horror that seized me? I was lying under the gallows of Los Hermanos. The bodies of Zoto's two brothers were not strung up, they were lying by my side. I had apparently spent the night with them. I was lying on pieces of rope, bits of wheels, the remains of human carcasses and on the dreadful shreds of flesh that had fallen away through decay.

I thought I was still not properly awake and was having a bad dream. I closed my eyes again and searched my memory, trying to recall where I had been the day before . . . Then I felt claws sinking into my sides. I saw that a vulture had settled on me and was devouring one of my bedmates. The pain of its grip awakened me fully. I saw that my clothes were by me, and I hurriedly put them on. When I was dressed, I tried to leave the gallows enclosure, but found the door nailed shut and made vain attempts to break it open. So I had to climb those grim walls. I succeeded in doing so, and clinging to one of the gallows posts, I began to survey the surrounding countryside. I easily got my bearings. I was actually at the entrance to the Los Hermanos valley, and not far from the banks of the Guadalquivir.

While I continued to look around, I saw two travellers near the river, one of whom was preparing a meal and the other holding the reins of two horses. I was so delighted to see these men that my first reaction was to call out to them, *"Agour, agour,"* which means "Goodday," or "Greetings," in Spanish.

The two travellers, who saw the courtesies being extended to them from the top of the gallows, seemed undecided for a moment; but suddenly they mounted their horses, urged them to the fastest gallop, and took the road to Alcornoques.

I shouted at them to stop, to no avail. The more I shouted, the more they spurred on their mounts. When I lost sight of them, it occurred to me to quit my position. I jumped to the ground, hurting myself a little.

Hunched low and limping, I reached the banks of the Guadalquivir and found there the meal that the two travellers had abandoned. Nothing could have been more welcome, for I felt very exhausted. There was some chocolate that was still cooking, some *sponhao* steeped in Alicante wine, some bread and eggs. I set about restoring my strength, after which I began to reflect on what had happened to me during the night. My memories were very confused, but what I well recalled was having given my word of honour to keep it secret, and I was strongly resolved to abide by my promise. Once having decided on this, it only remained for me to consider what I needed to do for the moment—in other words, which road I should take—and it seemed to me that the laws of honour obliged me more than ever to go via the Sierra Morena.

People will perhaps be surprised to find me so concerned with my reputation, and so little concerned with the events of the previous day, but this way of thinking was again a result of the education I had received; this will be seen from the continuation of my story. For now, I return to the account of my journey.

I was extremely curious to know what the evil spirits had done with my horse, which I had left at Venta Quemada, and since in any case it was on my way, I determined to go by there. I had to walk the whole length of the Los Hermanos valley and that of the Venta, which did not fail to tire me and to make me greatly wish to find my horse. I did indeed find it; it was in the same stable where I had left it and seemed groomed, well cared for, and well fed. I did not know who could have taken this trouble, but I had seen so many extraordinary things that this in addition did not for long detain me. I would have set off straight away, had I not had the curiosity to visit the inside of the tavern once more. I relocated the bedroom where I had slept, but no matter how hard I looked, I could not find the room where I had seen the beautiful African women. I tired then of looking for it any longer. I mounted my horse and continued on my way.

When I woke up under the Los Hermanos gallows, the sun was already half-way through its course. It took me two hours to reach the Venta. So when I had covered another couple of leagues, I had to think of a shelter for the night, but seeing none, I rode on. Eventually I saw in the distance a Gothic chapel, with a hut that appeared to be the home of a hermit. All this was off the main road, but since I was beginning to feel hungry, I did not hesitate to make this detour in order to come by some food. When I arrived, I tied my horse to a tree. Then I knocked at the door of the hermitage and saw a monk with the most venerable face emerge from it. He embraced me with fatherly tenderness, then he said to me:

"Come in, my son. Quickly. Do not spend the night outside. Fear the temptor. The Lord has withdrawn his hand from above us."

I thanked the hermit for his goodness towards me, and I told him that I was in dire need of something to eat.

He replied: "O my son, think of your soul! Go to the chapel. Prostrate yourself before the Cross. I will see to the needs of your body. But you will have a frugal meal, such as one would expect from a hermit."

I went to the chapel and prayed sincerely, for I was not a freethinker and was even unaware there were any; this again was a result of my education.

The hermit came to fetch me after a quarter of an hour and led me to the hut, where I found a place laid for me (everything was reasonably clean). There were some excellent olives, chards preserved in vinegar, sweet onions in a sauce, and rusks instead of bread. There was also a small bottle of wine. The hermit told me that he never drank any, but that he kept some in the house to celebrate the Mass. So I drank no more wine than the hermit, but the rest of the supper gave me great pleasure. While I was doing justice to it, I saw a figure, more terrifying than anything I had yet seen, come into the hut. It was a man. He looked young, but was hideously thin. His hair stood on end, one of his eyes was gouged out, and there was blood issuing from it. His tongue hung out of his mouth and dripped a frothy spittle. His body was clad in a fairly good black habit, but this was his only garment; he wore neither stockings nor shirt.

This hideous individual said not a word, and went and crouched in a corner, where he remained as still as a statue, his one eye fixed on a crucifix he held in his hand. When I had finished my meal, I asked the hermit who this man was.

The hermit replied: "My son, this man is possessed of the devil, and I am exorcising him. His terrible story is good evidence of the fatal power that the Angel of Darkness is usurping in this unhappy land. His experience might be helpful to your salvation, and I am going to instruct him to give an account of it."

Then, turning towards the possessed man, he said to him: "Pacheco, Pacheco, in the name of your Redeemer, I command you to tell your story."

Pacheco gave a horrible cry and began with these words:

THE STORY OF THE DEMONIAC PACHECO

I was born in Córdoba, where my father lived in more than comfortable circumstances. My mother died three years ago. My father seemed at first to miss her a great deal, but after a few months, having had occasion to make a trip to Seville, he fell in love with a young widow, called Camille de Tormes. This person did not enjoy a very good reputation, and several of my father's friends tried to stop him from seeing her, but despite the trouble they were prepared to go to, the wedding took place two years after the death of my mother. The ceremony took place in Seville, and a few days later my father returned to Córdoba with Camille, his new wife, and a sister of Camille, whose name was Inesille.

My new stepmother answered perfectly to the poor opinion in which she was held, and started out in my father's house by trying to win my love. She did not succeed in this. Yet I did fall in love, but with her sister Inesille. Indeed, my passion soon became so great that I went and threw myself at my father's feet and asked him for the hand of his sister-in-law.

With kindness, my father raised me to my feet, then said to me: "My son, I forbid you to think of this marriage, and I do so for three reasons. First, it would be unseemly for you to become, as it were, your father's brother-in-law. Secondly, the holy canons of the Church do not approve these kinds of marriages. Thirdly, I do not want you to marry Inesille."

Having given me his three reasons, my father turned his back on me and left.

I retired to my bedroom, where I gave way to despair. My stepmother, whom my father immediately informed of what had happened, came to find me and told me I was wrong to torture myself; that if I could not become Inesille's husband, I could be her *cortejo*, that is to say, her lover, and that she would see to it; but at the same time, she declared her love for me and made much of the sacrifice she was making by yielding me to her sister. I listened only too avidly to these words that flattered my passion, but Inesille was so modest it seemed to me impossible that she could ever be persuaded to respond to my love.

Meanwhile, my father decided to journey to Madrid, with the intention of securing the post of *corregidor* of Córdoba, and he took with him his wife and sister-in-law. He was to be away for no more than two months, but this time seemed very long to me, because I was separated from Inesille.

When the two months were almost over, I received a letter from my father, in which he instructed me to go to meet him and wait for him at Venta Quemada, where the Sierra Morena began. It would have been no easy decision to travel by way of the Sierra Morena a few weeks earlier, but as it happened, Zoto's two brothers had just been hanged. His gang was disbanded and the roads were supposed to be fairly safe.

So I set out for Córdoba at about ten o'clock in the morning, and I spent the night at Andujar, where the landlord was one of the most talkative in Andalusia. I ordered a lavish supper at the inn, of which I ate some and kept the rest for my journey.

The next day I dined at Los Alcornoques on what I had saved from the day before, and that same evening I reached Venta Quemada. I did not find my father there, but as he had instructed me in his letter to wait for him, I determined to do so, all the more willingly since I was in a roomy and comfortable hostel. The innkeeper who ran it at that time was a certain Gonzalez of Murcia, quite a decent fellow although a big-talker, who, sure enough, promised me a supper worthy of a Spanish grandee. While he busied himself preparing it, I went for a stroll along the banks of the Guadalquivir, and when I returned to the hostel, there I found a supper that was indeed not at all bad.

When I had eaten, I told Gonzalez to make up my bed. Then I saw that he was flustered: he said things that did not make a great deal of sense. Finally he confessed that the inn was haunted by ghosts, that he and his family spent every night at a small farm on the banks of the river, and he added that if I wanted to sleep there too, he would have a bed made up for me next to his own.

This proposal seemed to me quite unwarranted. I told him that he could go to sleep wherever he wanted to, and that he should send my men to me. Gonzalez obeyed, and withdrew, shaking his head and shrugging his shoulders.

My servants arrived a moment later. They too had heard talk of ghosts and tried to urge me to spend the night at the farm. Responding to their advice rather churlishly, I ordered them to make up my bed in the very room where I had supped. They obeyed me, albeit reluctantly, and when the bed was made, again they beseeched me, with tears in their eyes. Genuinely irritated by their admonitions, I allowed myself a display of emotion that put them to flight, and since it was not my custom to have my servants undress me, I easily managed without them in getting ready for bed. However, they had been more thoughtful than my behaviour towards them merited: by my bed, they had left a lighted candle, an extra candle, two pistols and a few books to read to keep myself awake; but the truth is I was no longer sleepy.

I spent a couple hours alternately reading and tossing in my bed. Eventually I heard the sound of a bell or a clock striking midnight. I was surprised, because I had not heard the other hours strike. Soon the door opened, and I saw my stepmother enter. She was in her nightgown and held a candlestick in her hand. She tiptoed over to me with her finger on her lips, as though to impose silence upon me. Then she rested her candlestick on my bedside table, sat down on my bed, took one of my hands and spoke to me in these words:

"My dear Alphonse, the time has come when I can give you the pleasures I promised you. We arrived at this tavern an hour ago. Your father has gone to sleep at the farm, but since I knew that you were here, I obtained leave to spend the night here with my sister Inesille. She is waiting for you, and preparing herself to refuse you nothing. But I must inform you of the conditions I have laid on your happiness. You love Inesille, and I love you. I am willing to bring you together, but I cannot bring myself to leave you alone with each other. I shall share your bed. Come!"

My stepmother gave me no time to reply. She took me by the hand and led me along corridor after corridor, until we reached a door where she set about looking through the keyhole.

When she had looked long enough, she said to me; "Everything is going well, see for yourself."

I took her place at the keyhole, and there indeed was the lovely Inesille in her bed, but she was far from showing the modesty I had always seen in her. The expression in her eyes, her agitated breathing, her flushed complexion, her posture—everything about her was clear evidence she was awaiting a lover.

After letting me have a good look, Camille said to me: "My dear Pacheco, stay at this door. When the time is right, I shall come to let you know."

When she had gone in, I put my eye to the keyhole again and saw a thousand things I find hard to describe. First, Camille undressed with some deliberation, then getting into bed with her sister, she said to her:

"My poor Inesille, is it really true that you want to have a lover? Poor child, you do not know how he will hurt you. First he will flatten you, press himself upon you, and then he will crush you, tear you."

When Camille considered her pupil sufficiently indoctrinated, she came and opened the door to me, led me to her sister's bed, and lay down beside us.

What shall I say of that fateful night? I exhausted its pleasures and crimes. For a long time I fought against sleep and nature, the more to protract my diabolical gratification. At last I fell asleep, and I awoke the next day beneath the gallows on which Zoto's brothers were hanged, lying between their vile corpses.

HERE THE HERMIT interrupted the demoniac and said to me: "Well now, my son! What do you think of that? I believe you would have been very frightened to find yourself lying between two hanged men?"

I replied: "Father, you insult me. A gentleman must never be afraid, and still less when he has the honour of being a captain in the Walloon Guards."

"But my son," said the hermit, "have you ever heard tell of such an adventure befalling anybody?"

I hesitated for a moment, after which I replied: "Father, if this adventure befell Signor Pacheco, it might have befallen others. I will be better able to judge if you would kindly tell him to continue his story."

The hermit turned to the demoniac, and said to him: "Pacheco,

Pacheco! In the name of your Redeemer, I order you to continue your story."

Pacheco uttered a dreadful howl and continued in these words:

I WAS HALF dead when I left the gibbet. I dragged myself off without knowing where I was going. At last I met some travellers who took pity on me and brought me back to Venta Quemada. There I found the innkeeper and my servants, who were greatly worried about me. I asked them if my father had slept at the farm. They replied that no one had come.

I could not bear to stay any longer at the Venta, and I set out again on the road to Andujar. I did not arrive there until after sunset. The inn was full, a bed was made up for me in the kitchen, and I lay down in it. But I was unable to sleep, for I could not banish from my mind the horrors of the night before.

I had left a lighted candle on the kitchen hearth. Suddenly it went out, and at once I felt what seemed a deathly shudder that made my blood run cold.

Someone pulled off my blanket. Then I heard a little voice saying: "It is Camille, your stepmother, I am cold, dear heart. Make room for me under your blanket."

Then another little voice said: "And this is Inesille. Let me get into your bed. I am cold, I am cold."

Then I felt an icy hand take hold of my chin. I summoned up all my strength to say out loud: "Avaunt, Satan!"

Then the little voices said to me: "Why are you chasing us away? Are you not our darling husband? We are cold. We are going to make a little fire."

Sure enough, soon after I saw flames in the kitchen hearth. The flames became brighter and I saw not Inesille and Camille but Zoto's two brothers, hanging in the fireplace.

This sight scared the life out of me. I leapt out of bed. I jumped through the window and started to run through the countryside. For a moment I was able to cherish the fond belief that I had escaped these horrors; but I turned round and saw that I was being followed by the two hanged men. I started to run again, and I saw that the hanged men were left behind. But my joy was short-lived. These detestable creatures began to cartwheel and in an instant were upon me. I ran on, until finally my strength deserted me.

Then I felt one of the hanged men seize me by the heel of my left foot. I tried to shake him off, but his brother cut in front of me. He appeared before me, rolling his eyes dreadfully, and sticking out a tongue as red as an iron drawn from the fire. I begged for mercy; in vain. With one hand he grabbed me by the throat, and with the other he tore out the eye I am now missing. In the place where my eye had been, he stuck his burning-hot tongue. With it he licked my brain and made me howl with pain.

Then the other hanged man, who had seized my left leg, also wanted to leave his mark on me. First he began by tickling the sole of the foot he was holding. Then the monster tore the skin off it, separated all the nerves, bared them, and set to playing on them as though on a musical instrument; but since I did not render a sound that pleased him, he began to twist them, as one tunes a harp. Finally he began to play on my leg, of which he had fashioned a psaltery. I heard his diabolical laughter; while pain wrung dreadful howls out of me, the wailings of hell joined voice. But when it came to my hearing the damned gnashing their teeth, I felt as though they were grinding my every fibre. In the end I lost consciousness.

The next day shepherds found me in the countryside and brought me to this hermitage, where I have confessed all my sins and here at the foot of the Cross I have found some relief from my ills.

AT THIS POINT the demoniac uttered a dreadful howl and fell silent.

Then the hermit spoke and said to me: "Young man, you see the power of Satan, pray and weep. But it is late. We must part company. I do not propose that you sleep in my cell, for Pacheco's screams during the night might disturb you. Go and sleep in the chapel. There you will be under the protection of the Cross, which triumphs over evil spirits."

I told the hermit I would sleep wherever he wanted me to. We carried a little trestle bed to the chapel. I lay down on it and the hermit wished me good-night.

When I was alone, Pacheco's story came back to me. I found in it a great deal of similarity with my own adventures, and I was still reflecting on it when I heard the chimes of midnight. I did not know whether it was the hermit ringing the bell, or whether I was again dealing with ghosts. Then I heard a scratching at my door. I went to the door and asked: "Who goes there?"

A little voice answered: "We are cold, open up and let us in, it is your darling wives here."

"Yes, yes, of course, you damnable gallows' fodder," I replied, "return to your gibbet and let me sleep."

Then the little voice said: "You jeer at us because you are inside a chapel, but come outside a while."

"I am just coming," I instantly replied.

I went to fetch my sword and tried to get out, but found the door locked. I told the ghosts, who made no response. I went to bed and slept until it was light.

JOSEPH VON EICHENDORFF

⁂

Autumn Sorcery

(Die Zauberei im Herbste, 1808–1809)

Eichendorff (1788–1857), who wrote both prose and poetry, is one of the most brilliant authors of German Romanticism. He is best represented by the novella Memoirs of a Lazy Man *(1826). The novella I include here was his first, which he wrote at the age of twenty, though it was published posthumously. In it, Eichendorff gives us a Romantic version of a famous medieval legend: Tannhäuser's sojourn in the pagan paradise of Venus, presented as the world of seduction and sin. This legend—which Wagner would later transform into an opera—would also inspire another tale by Eichendorff,* The Marble Statue *(1819), which has an Italian setting. But here the land of sin is a kind of twin of our own world, a parallel world that is sensual and anguishing at the same time. To pass from this world to the other is easy, and to return to our world is not impossible. But after having suffered being bewitched and having escaped, the man who wanted to expiate his guilt by becoming a hermit ultimately chooses the enchanted world and succumbs to it.*

One tranquil Autumn afternoon, when he was hunting, the knight Ubaldo found himself separated from his company. Riding through the thickly forested, lonely mountains, he saw coming towards him a man dressed in strange clothes. The unknown stranger did not notice the presence of the knight until he was standing before him. Ubaldo was shocked to see that while the man was wearing a magnificent, richly adorned doublet, it was faded and out of fashion. His face was handsome but pale and covered by a thick, unkempt beard.

Mutually surprised, the two men greeted each other, and Ubaldo explained that—unfortunately—he was lost. The sun was hidden behind the mountains, and they were far away from any inhabited place. The stranger invited Ubaldo to spend the night with him. The next day, he added, he would show him the only way out of those forests. Ubaldo accepted and followed him through the deserted canyons.

Soon they came to a high peak, at the foot of which there was a spacious cave, at the center of which was a stone, and on the stone a wooden crucifix. In the back of the cave was a rough bed of dry leaves. Ubaldo tied his horse at the entrance while his host silently brought some bread and wine. After he sat down, the knight, to whom the clothing the stranger wore did not seem appropriate for a hermit, could not keep from asking him who he was and what had brought him there.

"Do not inquire into who I am," the hermit replied dryly, and his face became somber and severe. Then Ubaldo noticed that the hermit listened attentively and fell into deep musings when the knight began to tell him about some of his journeys and the glorious jousts he'd been in in his youth. At last Ubaldo was exhausted and lay down on the bed of dry leaves his host had offered him. He immediately fell asleep, while the hermit sat on the ground at the entrance to the cave.

In the middle of the night, Ubaldo, upset by disturbing dreams, awakened with a start and stood up. Outside, the moon bathed the silent outline of the mountains in clear light. He saw the stranger pacing back and forth outside the cave under the great trees. In a deep voice, he sang a song of which Ubaldo managed to understand only these words:

Fear pulls me out of the cave.
Old melodies call me.
Sweet sin, leave me
Or leave me prostrate on the ground.
Before the magic of this song,
Hiding me in the bowels of the earth.

God! I would beseech you with fervor,
But the images of the world always
Always come between us,
And the noise of the forests
Fills my soul with terror.
Severe God, I fear you!

Oh break my chains too!
To save all men
You suffered a bitter death.
I am lost at the gates of Hell.
How forsaken I am!
Jesus, help me in my anguish!

When he finished his song, he sat on a rock and seemed to whisper an imperceptible prayer that resembled a confused magic incantation. The noise of the brook near the mountains and the light whistle of the fir trees united in a single melody, and Ubaldo, overcome by sleep, fell back on his bed.

Barely had the first rays of the morning sun begun to shine through the treetops when the hermit appeared before the knight to show him the path towards the canyons. Ubaldo joyfully mounted his horse, and his strange guide galloped silently beside him. Soon they reached the top of the mountain and contemplated the dazzling plain that suddenly appeared at their feet, with its rivers, cities, and fortresses in the beautiful morning light. The hermit seemed especially surprised: "Oh, how beautiful the world is!" he exclaimed, clearly moved. He then covered his face with both hands and hastened to bury himself again in the forests. Ubaldo, shaking his head, took the familiar road that led to his castle.

Curiosity led him to seek out those solitary places again, and, with great effort, he managed to find the cave, where the hermit this time received him somberly and silently.

Because of the song the hermit had sung the night of their first meeting, Ubaldo knew he sincerely wanted to expiate grievous sins, but it also seemed that his spirit was struggling in vain, against the enemy, because his behavior lacked the joyful confidence of a soul truly submissive to the will of God. Also, it frequently happened that when they were speaking seated next to each other, a restrained earthly anxiety would explode with a terrible force in the restless and fiery eyes of that man, transforming his features and giving him a savage air.

That impelled the pious knight to visit more frequently—to help that vacillating spirit with all his strength. Nevertheless, the hermit never mentioned his name or previous life during all that time, and seemed fearful of his past. But with each visit he became more affable and trusting. At last, the good knight managed to convince the hermit to accompany him to his castle.

Night had already fallen when they reached the fortress. Ubaldo ordered a beautiful fire and the best wines he possessed. It was the first time the hermit seemed at his ease. He took careful note of a sword and other arms hanging on the wall that reflected the flashes of light, and then silently contemplated the knight.

"You," he said, "are happy. And I behold your strong and gallant figure with true fear and deep respect. You live unmoved by either joy or grief, and you dominate life with serene tranquillity, like a sailor who knows how to use the tiller and doesn't let himself become confused by the marvellous song of the sirens. Next to you I've often felt like an idiotic coward or a madman. There are people drunk on life. How terrible it is to become sober again!"

Ubaldo, who did not want to miss his chance to take advantage of his guest's unusual behavior, vigorously insisted he reveal the story of his life. The hermit was pensive.

"If you promise me," he said finally, "to keep what I tell you a secret forever and allow me to omit the names, I'll do it."

The knight raised his hand to signal his oath and immediately summoned his wife, whose silence he vouched for, so that along with him she could hear the story they so anxiously awaited.

She appeared with one child in her arms and leading another by the hand. She was tall, with a handsome figure, and in the flower of her youth, silent and as sweet as the dawn, her own beauty reflected in her charming children. The guest became deeply confused when he saw her. He abruptly opened the window and stared pensively at the darkened forest for a few seconds. When he'd calmed down, he came back to them, and they all sat down around the fire. He began to speak in the following way:

"The tepid autumn sun was rising over the blue mist that covered the valleys near my castle. The music had faded, the festivities were coming to an end, and the lively guests were leaving. It was a farewell celebration that I was offering to my dearest friend, who that day, along with his followers, had put the Holy Cross on his arms to join the Christian army in the conquest of the Holy Land. Ever since our earliest youth, that undertaking had been our only goal, our only desire, and the only hope of our adolescent dreams. Even today, it is with indescribable nostalgia that I remember those times as tranquil.

"I wandered for a long time until I finally found I was lost in an unknown part of the mountains. With my hawk on my arm, I rode pensively across a marvelous meadow caressed by the oblique rays of the setting sun. The autumn clouds moved quickly in the blue air, and above the mountains could be heard the farewell songs of the migratory birds.

"Suddenly, the sound of several hunting horns that seemed to be answering each other from the peaks reached my ears. Some voices were accompanying them in a song. Until then, no melody had ever moved me in such a fashion, and even today, I remember a few stanzas that reached me, carried by the wind:

High above, in yellow and red waves
The birds fly away.
My thoughts wander without consolation,
Oh woe is me! They find no refuge!
And the dark complaints of the horns
Pierce the solitary heart.

Do you see the outline of the blue mountains
As it rises in the distance over the forests
And the streams that in the silent valley
Go their way whispering?
Clouds, streams, noisy birds:
All join together there in the distance.

My golden curls wave
And my young body sweetly flowers.
Beauty soon succumbs;
Like the splendor of summer that fades,
Youth should bow its flowers.
All the horns fall silent.

Slim arms to embrace,
And red mouth for the sweet kiss,

The refuge of the white breast,
And the warm greeting of love,
The echo of the hunting horns offers you.
Come sweet love, before they fall silent.

"I was dazed by that melody which had moved my heart. My falcon, as soon as it heard the first notes, became unsettled and then disappeared into the air, never to return. Nevertheless, I was unable to resist; I went on listening to the seductive melody that, confusedly, sometimes went away while others, carried by the wind, seemed to draw near.

"Finally, I left the forest and saw, right before me, a majestic castle on the crest of a mountain. Stretching from above down to the forest smiled a most beautiful garden, replete with all colors, surrounding the castle like a magic ring. All the trees and hedges, afire with the violent hues of autumn, seemed purple, the yellows gold and the reds flame. Tall asters, the last stars of summer, glittered there in multiple flashes. The setting sun poured its last rays on that delightful summit, reflecting its dazzling flames on the windows and fountains.

"I realized then that the sound of the hunting horns I'd just heard came from this garden. I was shocked to see, amid such magnificence, that under the arbors was the damsel of my dreams, who was strolling and singing that same melody. When she saw me, she fell silent, but the hunting horns continued to blow. Handsome boys dressed in silk came to me and helped me dismount.

"I passed through the light, golden archway at the entrance and went directly to the garden esplanade where my beloved was standing. I fell at her feet, overcome by so much beauty. She was wearing a dark red dress; long transparent veils covered her golden curls, which were held in place by a diadem of precious stones above her forehead.

"She lovingly helped me to my feet, and in a voice broken by love and grief, said to me: 'How I love you, handsome and unfortunate young man! I've loved you for a long time, and when autumn begins its mysterious festival, my desire awakens with new and irresistible force. Poor wretch! How have you come to the sphere of my song? Leave me and go away.'

"When I heard those words, I was seized by a great tremor and begged her to speak to me, to explain. But she did not answer, and we silently paced through the garden, side by side.

"Meanwhile, it had grown dark, and the damsel's mien became grave and majestic. 'You must know,' she said, 'that your childhood friend, who this very day bade you farewell, is a traitor. I've been forced to betroth myself to him. Only out of jealousy did he hide his love from you. He has not departed for Palestine: tomorrow he will come to take me to a distant castle where I shall be hidden from the gaze of others forever. Now I must leave. We shall only see each other again if he dies.'

"Having said that, she kissed me on the lips and disappeared into the dark galleries. A gem from her diadem froze my gaze, and her kiss shook my veins with a trembling delight.

"Terrified, I pondered the horrifying words of her farewell, which had poured a poison into my blood. Pensive, I wandered for a long time along solitary paths. At last, weary, I stretched out on the stone stairs at the castle gate. The hunting horns were still blaring, and I fell asleep, buffeted by strange thoughts.

"When I opened my eyes, the sun had already risen. The doors and windows of the castle were closed, and the garden was silent. In that solitude, with the new and beautiful colors of the morning, there awoke in my heart the image of my beloved and all the enchantment of yesterday's sunset. And I felt happy knowing myself to be loved and reciprocated. At times, when I recalled those terrible words, I wanted to flee far from there, but her kiss still burned on my lips, so I could not do it.

"The air was hot, almost suffocating, as if the summer wanted to retrace its steps. I wandered through the neighboring forest in order to distract myself with hunting. Suddenly I saw on a treetop a bird whose plumage was more marvelous than any I'd ever seen. Just when I pulled the string back and was ready to shoot the arrow, it flew to another tree. I pursued it avidly, but the bird continued to jump from treetop to treetop, while its golden wings reflected the sunlight.

"Finally, I came into a narrow valley flanked by sheer cliffs. The cool breezes did not reach there, and everything was still as green and flowering as in summer. From the center of the valley arose an intoxicating song. Surprised, I parted the branches of the tangled shrubbery, and my eyes were blinded by the enchantment that revealed itself before me.

"Amid the high rocks, there was a still lake surrounded by ivy and reeds. Many maidens were bathing their beautiful bodies in the warm water. Among them was my most beautiful beloved, without veils. Silently, while the others sang, she stared fixedly into the water that covered her ankles, as if she were enchanted and absorbed in her own beauty reflected in the water. I stood there for a time, staring from a distance, immobile and trembling. Suddenly the beautiful group left the water, and I scurried away so I wouldn't be discovered.

"I took refuge in the deepest part of the forest to calm the flames that consumed my heart. But the further I fled, the more sharply the vision of that youthful body danced before my eyes.

"Night caught me in the forest. The sky had darkened, and a huge storm appeared over the mountains. *We shall only see each other again if he dies*, I repeated to myself, while I fled as if chased by ghosts.

"At times, I seemed to hear on my flank the din of horses, but I was fleeing from all human eyes and any noise that seemed to come near. Finally, on reaching a ridge, I saw my beloved's castle in the distance. The hunting horns echoed as usual, the splendor of the lights shone like a tenuous moonlight through the windows, magically illuminating the surrounding trees and flowers, while everything else in the area struggled in the storm and the darkness.

"Finally, almost losing control of my senses, I scaled a high rock with a noisy creek running beneath it. From the top I could make out a dark shadow, silent and motionless, which, seated on a stone, seemed also to be made of stone. Ragged clouds fled through the sky.

A blood-colored moon appeared for an instant, and I then recognized my friend, my beloved's fiancé.

"As soon as he saw me, he hastily got to his feet. I trembled from head to foot. Then I saw him grasp his sword. Enraged, I threw myself at him and seized him. We fought for a few seconds, and then I threw him from the crag.

"Suddenly the silence became terrible. Only the creek roared more loudly, as if it were burying my past in the din of its turbulent waters.

"I ran quickly from that horrible place. It was then I seemed to hear behind me high-pitched, perverse laughter coming from the treetops. At the same time, in the confusion of my senses, I thought I saw the bird I had chased a short while before. Filled with horror, I rushed through the forest and leapt over that garden world. I banged on the castle door with all my strength: 'Let me in!' I shouted, out of my senses, 'open the door, I've killed the brother of my heart! Now you are mine, both on earth and in hell!'

"The door opened, and the damsel, more beautiful than ever, threw herself against my breast, crushed by so many torments, and covered me with burning kisses.

"I shall not speak of the magnificence of the halls, of the fragrance of exotic and marvelous flowers among which sang beautiful maidens, of the torrents of light and music, of the savage and ineffable pleasure I tasted in the arms of the damsel."

At that point, the hermit stopped speaking. Outside, we could hear a strange song. Just a few notes: now it resembled a human voice, now the high tone of a clarinet, when the wind blew over the distant mountains, shriveling the heart.

"Be calm," said the knight. "We've been used to that for quite some time now. They say that in the neighboring forest there exists a sorcery. Very often, on Autumn nights, that music reaches our castle. But to the same degree as it draws near, it drifts away, and we don't worry about it."

Nevertheless, a tremor shook Ubaldo's heart, and only with effort was he able to control himself. We could no longer hear the music.

The guest, still seated, fell silent, lost in thought. His spirit wandered far. After a long pause, he recovered himself and went back to his story, though not with the same calm as before.

"I observed that from time to time the damsel, amid all that splendor, would fall into an invincible melancholy whenever she saw from the castle that Autumn was going to bid us farewell. But all she needed was a deep sleep to calm down, and her marvelous face, the garden, and the entire setting seemed to me, at morning, fresh and as if newly created.

"Once, as I stood next to her at a window, I noted that my beloved was sadder and more silent than usual. Outside, in the garden, the winter wind was playing with the fallen leaves. I noticed that as she stared at the landscape she became pale and trembled. All her ladies had gone; that day the hunting-horn songs were echoing in an infinite distance, until finally they fell silent. My beloved's eyes had lost their brilliance, almost to the point of being extinguished. The sun hid behind the mountains and illuminated the garden and the valleys with its final resplendence. Suddenly, the damsel clutched me in her arms and began a strange song I had not heard until then and which echoed throughout the room with melancholy notes. I listened, astonished. It was as if that melody were pushing me downward together with the setting sun. My eyes closed involuntarily. I fell asleep and dreamed.

"When I awoke, it was night. A great silence ruled throughout the castle, and the moon shone very brightly. My beloved was sleeping at my side on a silk bed. I observed her with astonishment: she was pale, as if dead. Her curls fell in disorder over her face and breast, as if tangled by the wind. Everything else around me remained the same, just as it was when I fell asleep. Nevertheless, it seemed to me that a great deal of time had passed. I went over to the open window. Everything outside seemed different from what it had always been. The noise of the trees was mysterious. Suddenly, next to the castle wall, I saw two men muttering obscure phrases, bowing to each other and leaning toward each other as if they wanted to weave a spiderweb. I understood nothing of what the two men were saying: I only heard them speak my name. I again looked at the image of the damsel, who was even paler in the bright moonlight. She looked like a stone statue, beautiful, but as cold and immobile as death. On her placid bosom shone a stone similar to the basilisk's eye, and her mouth was strangely disfigured.

"Then I was possessed by a terror the likes of which I'd never felt. I fled the chamber and sped through the deserted halls, where all splendor had been extinguished. As I left the castle, I saw the two strangers stop what they were doing and stand stock-still, rigid and silent as two statues. At the foot of the mountain there was a solitary lake on whose shore some maidens in tunics as white as snow were marvelously singing and at the same time seemed to amuse themselves by stretching strange spiderwebs out over the meadow in the moonlight. That vision and that song increased my terror. I quickly leapt the garden wall. The clouds were scudding rapidly across the sky, the leaves on the trees were whispering behind my back, and I ran breathlessly.

"Little by little, the night became warmer and quieter; the nightingales were singing in the bushes. Below, in the depth of the valley, human voices could be heard, and old, forgotten memories came to light again in my extinguished heart, while before me, over the mountains, a beautiful spring dawn appeared.

" 'What is all this? Where am I?' I shouted in astonishment. I did not know what had happened to me. The fall and winter had gone by. Spring once again illuminated the world. My God, where have I been for so long?

"Finally, I reached the top of the last mountain. A splendid sun was rising. A tremor of pleasure rippled through the earth; the rushing streams and castles shone; tranquil and lighthearted men were preparing for their daily tasks; myriad larks jubilantly soared. I fell to my knees and wept bitterly for my lost life.

"I did not understand and still do not understand how it all happened. I resolved not to return to the joyful and innocent world with this heart full of sin and unrestrained anxiety. I decided to bury myself alive in a desolate place, invoke the forgiveness of heaven, and not to see the houses of men ever again until I'd washed away with tears of sincere repentance all my sins—all there was in my past that was clear to me.

"Thus I lived for an entire year until I met you. Every day I raised up ardent prayers, and at times I thought I'd overcome everything and found the grace of God, but it was a false illusion that quickly faded. Only when the Autumn spread its marvelous net of colors over the hills and valleys did very familiar songs come again from the forest. They penetrated my solitude, and dark voices within me responded to them. The sound of the bells from the distant cathedral horrifies me, when, on clear Sunday mornings, it flies over the mountains and reaches me, as if it were seeking in my breast the ancient and silent kingdom of God of childhood, which no longer exists. Know then that in the hearts of men there is an enchanted and dark realm where crystals, rubies, and all the precious stones of the depths shine with a loving, moving gaze, and you don't know whence it comes or where it is going. The beauty of earthly life is shiningly filtered like the dawn, and the invisible fountains, whirling around, melancholically whisper, and everything pulls you down, eternally down."

"Poor Raimundo!" exclaimed Ubaldo the knight, who had listened to the hermit with profound emotion, absorbed and immersed in his tale.

"For the love of God! Who are you that you know my name?" asked the hermit as if struck by lightning.

"My God," answered the knight, affectionately embracing the trembling hermit. "Don't you recognize me? I am your old and faithful comrade in arms Ubaldo, and this is your Bertha, whom you loved in secret and whom you helped onto her horse after the party in the castle. Time and a happy life have blurred our features from that time. I only recognized you when you began to tell your story. I have never been in a place like the one you describe and never fought with you on a cliff. Immediately after that party, I left for Palestine, where I fought for several years, and when I returned, the beautiful Bertha became my wife. She too never saw you after that party, and everything you've told is an idle fantasy. My poor Raimundo, an evil charm that awakens every Autumn and then disappears has held you for many years. The days have been months for you. When I returned from the Holy Land, no one could tell me where you were, and we all thought you lost."

Because of his own joy, Ubaldo did not realize that his friend was trembling more and more strongly with each of his words. Raimundo stared at him and his wife with wild eyes. Suddenly, he recognized his friend and the beloved of his youth, illuminated by the flickering flame of the fireplace. "Lost, all lost!" he exclaimed tragically. He pulled free of Ubaldo's arms and fled quickly into the night toward the forest.

"Yes, everything is lost, and my love and all my life are nothing more than a long illusion," he said to himself as he ran, until the lights of Ubaldo's castle disappeared behind him. Without realizing it, he went in the direction of his own castle, which he reached at daybreak.

He entered the garden. It was deserted and ruined. Only a few late flowers shone here and there over the yellowish grass. On a branch, a bird was singing a marvelous song that filled the heart with great nostalgia.

It was the same melody he'd heard at the windows of Ubaldo's castle. Terrified, he recognized as well the beautiful and golden bird of the enchanted forest. Standing at a window in the castle was a tall, pale man, stained with blood. It was Ubaldo's image.

Horrified, Raimundo cast his eyes from that vision and fixed them instead on the brightness of the morning. Suddenly, he saw advancing through the valley the beautiful damsel, riding on a spirited stallion. She was in the flower of her youth. Silvery threads of summer floated on her back; the gem in her diadem cast from her brow rays of green gold on the plain.

Raimundo, driven mad, left the garden and followed the sweet figure, preceded by the bird's strange song.

The further he advanced, the more the song transformed into the old melody of the hunting horns, which in another time had seduced him.

My golden curls wave
And my young body sweetly flowers.

He heard, as if it were an echo in the distance:

And the streams that in the silent valley
Go their way whispering . . .

His castle, the mountains, and the entire world all sank behind him.

And the warm greeting of love,
The echo of the hunting horns offers you.
Come sweet love, before they fall silent! . . .

resounded once again.

Overcome by madness, poor Raimundo followed after the melody through the depth of the forest. From that day on, he was never seen again.

E. T. A. HOFFMANN

The Sandman

(Der Sandmann, 1817)

Hoffmann's most famous story, "The Sandman," was the principal source for Offenbach's opera and the point of departure for an essay by Freud on the unheimlich. *To choose one story from the many Hoffmann wrote is difficult: if I choose "The Sandman" it is not to confirm the most obvious choice, but because to me this tale seems to be the most representative of the greatest author in this genre in the nineteenth century (1776–1822), the richest in terms of suggestiveness, and the one with the most narrative content. The discovery of the unconscious takes place here, in Romantic fantastic literature, almost 100 years before the first theoretical definition of it appears.*

Nathanael's infantile nightmares are still with him as an adult: he identifies the bogeyman his nanny evoked to threaten him into falling asleep with Coppelius the lawyer, a sinister friend of his father, and convinces himself that Coppelius is the ogre who plucks out the eyes of children. While a student in the city, he thinks he discovers Coppelius in Coppola, a man from the Piedmont who sells barometers and eye-

glasses. His love for Professor Spalanzani's daughter Olimpia, who is not a girl despite what everyone thinks and is in point of fact a mannequin (this theme of the automaton, the doll, will frequently reappear in fantastic literature), is upset by new appearances by Coppola-Coppelius until Nathanael's madness runs its course.

Nathanael to Lothair

I know you are all very uneasy because I have not written for such a long, long time. Mother, to be sure, is angry, and Clara, I dare say, believes I am living here in riot and revelry, and quite forgetting my sweet angel, whose image is so deeply engraved upon my heart and mind. But that is not so; daily and hourly I think of you all, and my lovely Clara's form comes to gladden me in my dreams, and smiles upon me with her bright eyes, as graciously as she used to do in the days when I used to associate daily with you.

Oh! how could I write to you in the distracted state of mind in which I have been, and which, until now, has quite bewildered me! A terrible thing has happened to me. Dark forebodings of some awful fate threatening me are spreading themselves out over my head like black clouds, impenetrable to every friendly ray of sunlight. I must now tell you what has taken place; I must, that I see well enough, but only to think of it makes the wild laughter burst from my lips. Oh! my dear, dear Lothair, what shall I say to make you feel, if only in an inadequate way, that what happened to me a few days ago could thus really exercise such a hostile and disturbing influence upon my life? I wish you were here to see for yourself! But now you will, I suppose, take me for a superstitious ghost-seer. In a word, the terrible thing which I have experienced, the fatal effect of which I in vain exert every effort to shake off, is simply that some days ago, namely, on the thirtieth of October, at twelve o'clock at noon, a peddler of weather glasses and thermometers came into my room and wanted to sell me one of his wares. I bought nothing, and threatened to kick him downstairs, whereupon he went away of his own accord.

You will conclude that it can only be very peculiar relations—relations intimately intertwined with my life—that can give significance to this event, and that it must be the peddler himself who had such a very unpleasant effect upon me. And so it really is. I will summon up all my faculties in order to narrate to you calmly and patiently enough about the early days of my youth to put matters before you in such a way that your keen sharp intellect can grasp everything clearly and distinctly, in bright and living pictures.

Just as I am beginning, I hear you laugh and Clara say, "What's all this childish nonsense about?" Well, laugh at me, laugh heartily at me, pray do. But, good God! my hair is standing on end, and I seem to be entreating you to laugh at me in the same sort of frantic despair in which Franz Moor [in Schiller's *Die Räuber*] entreated Daniel to laugh him to scorn. But to my story.

Except at dinner we, i.e., I and my brothers and sisters, saw little of our father all day long. His business no doubt took up most of his time. After our evening meal, which usually was served at seven o'clock, we all went, mother with us, into father's room, and took our places around a round table. My father smoked his pipe, drinking a large glass of beer at the same time. Often he told us many wonderful stories, and got so excited over them that his pipe would go out; I used then to light it for him with a spill, and this formed my chief amusement. Often, again, he would give us picture books to look at, while he sat silent and motionless in his easy chair, puffing out such dense clouds of smoke that we were all as it were enveloped in mist.

On such evenings mother was very sad; and as soon as it struck nine she said, "Come, children! off to bed! Come! The Sandman is come, I see." And I always did seem to hear something trampling upstairs with slow heavy steps; that must be the Sandman. Once in particular I was very much frightened at this dull trampling and knocking; as mother was leading us out of the room I asked her, "O mamma! who is this nasty Sandman who always sends us away from papa? What does he look like?"

"There is no Sandman, my dear," mother answered; "when I say the Sandman is come, I only mean that you are sleepy and can't keep your eyes open, as if somebody had put sand in them." This answer of mother's did not satisfy me; nay, in my childish mind the thought clearly unfolded itself that mother denied there was a Sandman only to prevent us from being afraid,—why, I always heard him come upstairs.

Full of curiosity to learn something more about this Sandman and what he had to do with us children, I finally asked the old woman who acted as my youngest sister's nurse, what sort of man he was—the Sandman?

"Why, 'thanael, darling, don't you know?" she replied. "Oh! he's a wicked man, who comes to little children when they won't go to bed and throws handfuls of sand in their eyes, so that they jump out of their heads all bloody; and he puts them into a bag and takes them to the half-moon as food for his little ones; and they sit there in the nest and have hooked beaks like owls, and they pick naughty little boys' and girls' eyes out with them."

After this I formed in my own mind a horrible picture of the cruel Sandman. When anything came blundering upstairs at night I trembled with fear and dismay; and all that my mother could get out of me were the stammered words "The Sandman! the Sandman!" whilst the tears coursed down my cheeks. Then I ran into my bedroom, and the whole night through tormented myself with the terrible apparition of the Sandman. I was quite old enough to perceive that the old woman's tale about the Sandman and his little ones' nest in the half-moon couldn't be altogether true; nevertheless the Sandman continued to be for me a fearful incubus, and I was always seized with terror—my blood always ran cold, not only when I heard anybody come up the stairs, but when I heard anybody noisily open the door to my father's room and go in. Often the Sandman stayed away for a long time altogether; then he would come several times in close succession.

This went on for years, without my being able to accustom myself to this fearful apparition, without the image of the horrible Sandman growing any fainter in my imagination. His intercourse with my father began to occupy my fancy ever more and more; I was restrained from asking my father about him by an unconquerable shyness; but as the years went on the desire waxed stronger and stronger within me to fathom the mystery myself and to see the fabulous Sandman. He had been the means of disclosing to me the path of the wonderful and the adventurous, which so easily find lodgment in the mind of the child. I liked nothing better than to hear or read horrible stories of goblins, witches, dwarfs, and so on; but always at the head of them all stood the Sandman, whose picture I scribbled in the most extraordinary and repulsive forms with both chalk and coal everywhere, on the tables, and cupboard doors, and walls.

When I was ten years old my mother removed me from the nursery into a little chamber off the corridor not far from my father's room. We still had to withdraw hastily whenever, on the stroke of nine, the mysterious unknown was heard in the house. As I lay in my little chamber I could hear him go into father's room, and soon afterwards I fancied there was a fine and peculiar smelling steam spreading itself through the house.

As my curiosity waxed stronger, my resolve to make the Sandman's acquaintance somehow or other took deeper root. Often when my mother had gone past, I slipped quickly out of my room into the corridor, but I could never see anything, for always before I could reach the place where I could get sight of him, the Sandman was well inside the door. At last, unable to resist the impulse any longer, I determined to conceal myself in father's room and wait there for the Sandman.

One evening I perceived from my father's silence and mother's sadness that the Sandman would come; accordingly, pleading that I was excessively tired, I left the room before nine o'clock and concealed myself in a hiding place close beside the door. The street door creaked, and slow, heavy, echoing steps crossed the passage towards the stairs. Mother hurried past me with my brothers and sisters. Softly—softly—I opened the door to father's room. He sat as usual, silent and motionless, with his back towards the door; he did not hear me; and in a moment I was in and behind a curtain drawn before my father's open wardrobe, which stood just inside the room. Nearer and nearer and nearer came the echoing footsteps. There was a strange coughing and shuffling and mumbling outside. My heart beat with expectation and fear. A quick step now close, close beside the door, a noisy rattle of the handle, and the door flies open with a bang. Recovering my courage with an effort, I take a cautious peep out. In the middle of the room in front of my father stands the Sandman, the bright light of the lamp falling full upon his face. The Sandman, the terrible Sandman, is the old lawyer Coppelius who often comes to dine with us.

But the most hideous figure could not have awakened greater trepidation in my heart than this Coppelius did. Picture to yourself a large broad-shouldered man, with an immensely big head, a face the colour of yellow ochre, gray bushy eyebrows, from beneath which two piercing, greenish, cat-like eyes glittered, and a prominent Roman nose hanging over his upper lip. His distorted mouth was often screwed up into a malicious sneer; then two dark-red spots appeared on his cheeks, and a strange hissing noise proceeded from between his tightly clenched teeth. He always wore an ash-gray coat of an old-fashioned cut, a waistcoat of the same, and nether extremities to match, but black stockings and buckles set with stones on his shoes. His little wig scarcely extended beyond the crown of his head, his hair was curled round high up above his big red ears, and plastered to his temples with cosmetic, and a broad closed hair-bag stood out prominently from his neck, so that you could see the silver buckle that fastened his folded neck-cloth. Altogether he was a most disagreeable and horribly ugly figure; but what we children detested most of all was his big coarse hairy hands; we could never fancy anything that he had once touched. This he had noticed; and so, whenever our good mother quietly placed a piece of cake or sweet fruit on our plates, he delighted to touch it under some pretext or other, until the tears stood in our eyes, and from disgust and loathing we lost the enjoyment of the tit-bit that was intended to please us. And he did just the same thing when father gave us a glass of sweet wine on holidays. Then he would quickly pass his hand over it, or even sometimes raise the glass to his blue lips, and he laughed quite sardonically when all we dared do was to express our vexation in stifled sobs. He habitually called us the "little brutes"; and when he was present we might not utter a sound; and we cursed the ugly spiteful man who deliberately and intentionally spoilt all our little pleasures.

Mother seemed to dislike this hateful Coppelius as much as we did; for as soon as he appeared, her cheerfulness and bright and natural manner were transformed into sad, gloomy seriousness. Father treated him as if he were a being of some higher race, whose ill manners were to be tolerated, while no efforts ought to be spared to keep him in good humour. Coppelius had only to give a slight hint, and his favourite dishes were cooked for him and rare wine uncorked.

As soon as I saw this Coppelius, therefore, the fearful and hideous thought arose in my mind that he, and he alone, must be the Sandman; but I no longer conceived of the Sandman as the bugbear in the old nurse's fable, who fetched children's eyes and took them to the half-moon as food for his little ones—no! but as an ugly spectre-like fiend bringing trouble and misery and ruin, both temporal and everlasting, everywhere he appeared.

I was spellbound on the spot. At the risk of being discovered, and as I well enough knew, of being severely punished, I remained as I was, with my head thrust through the curtains listening. My father received Coppelius in a ceremonious manner.

"Come, to work!" cried the latter, in a hoarse snarling voice, throwing off his coat. Gloomily and silently my father took off his dressing gown, and both put on long black smock-frocks. Where they took them from I forgot to notice. Father opened the folding doors of a cupboard in the wall; but I saw that what I had so long taken to be a cupboard was really a dark recess, in which was a little hearth. Coppelius approached it, and a blue flame crackled upwards from it. Round about were all kinds of strange utensils.

Good God! as my father bent down over the fire how different he looked! His gentle features seemed to be drawn up by some dreadful convulsive pain into an ugly, repulsive Satanic mask. He looked like Coppelius. Coppelius plied the red-hot tongs and drew bright glowing masses out of the thick smoke and began assiduously to hammer them. I fancied that there were men's faces visible round about, but without eyes, having ghastly deep black holes where the eyes should have been.

"Eyes here! Eyes here!" cried Coppelius, in a hollow sepulchral voice. My blood ran cold with horror; I screamed and tumbled out of my hiding place onto the floor. Coppelius immediately seized me. "You little brute! You little brute!" he bleated, grinding his teeth. Then, snatching me up, he threw me on the hearth, so that the flames began to singe my hair. "Now we've got eyes—eyes—a beautiful pair of children's eyes," he whispered and, thrusting his hands into the flames he took out some red-hot grains and was about to throw them into my eyes.

Then my father clasped his hands and entreated him, saying, "Master, master, let my Nathanael keep his eyes—oh! let him keep them." Coppelius laughed shrilly and replied, "Well then, the boy may keep his eyes and whine and pule his way through the world; but we will at any rate examine the mechanism of the hand and the foot." And thereupon he roughly laid hold of me, so that my joints cracked, and twisted my hands and my feet, pulling them now this way, and now that, "That's not quite right altogether! It's better as it was!—the old fellow knew what he was about." Thus lisped and hissed Coppelius; but all around me grew black and dark; a sudden convulsive pain shot through all my nerves and bones; I knew nothing more.

I felt a soft warm breath fanning my cheek; I awakened as if out of the sleep of death; my mother was bending over me. "Is the Sandman still here?" I stammered. "No, my dear child; he's been gone a long, long time; he'll not hurt you." Thus spoke my mother, as she kissed her recovered darling and pressed him to her heart. But why should I tire you, my dear Lothair? why do I dwell at such length on these details, when there's so much remains to be said? Enough—I was detected in my eavesdropping, and roughly handled by Coppelius. Fear and terror brought on a violent fever, of which I lay ill several weeks. "Is the Sandman still there?" these were the first words I uttered on coming to myself again, the first sign of my recovery, of my safety. Thus, you see, I have only to relate to you the most terrible moment of my youth for you to thoroughly understand that it must not be ascribed to the weakness of my eyesight if all that I see is colourless, but to the fact that a mysterious destiny has hung a dark veil of clouds about my life, which I shall perhaps only break through when I die.

Coppelius did not show himself again; it was reported he had left the town.

It was about a year later when, in our old manner, we sat around the round table in the evening. Father was in very good spirits, and was telling us amusing tales about his youthful travels. As it was striking nine we all at once heard the street door creak on its hinges, and slow ponderous steps echoed across the passage and up the stairs. "That is Coppelius," said my mother, turning pale. "Yes, it is Coppelius," replied my father in a faint broken voice. The tears started from my mother's eyes. "But, father, father," she cried, "must it be so?" "This is the last time," he replied; "this is the last time he will come to me, I promise you. Go now, go and take the children. Go, go to bed—good-night."

As for me, I felt as if I were converted into cold, heavy stone; I could not get my breath. As I stood there immovable, my mother seized me by the arm. "Come, Nathanael! come along!" I suffered myself to be led away; I went into my room. "Be a good boy and keep quiet," mother called after me; "get into bed and go to sleep." But, tortured by indescribable fear and uneasiness, I could not close my eyes. It seemed that hateful, hideous Coppelius stood before me with his glittering eyes, smiling maliciously down upon me; in vain did I strive to banish the image. Somewhere about midnight there was a terrific explosion, as if a cannon were being fired off. The whole house shook; something went rustling and clattering past my door; the house door was pulled to with a bang.

"That is Coppelius," I cried, terror-stricken, and leaped out of bed. Then I heard a wild heart-rending scream; I rushed into my father's room; the door stood open, and clouds of suffocating smoke came rolling towards me. The servant maid shouted, "Oh! my master! my master!" On the floor in front of the smoking hearth lay my father, dead, his face burned black and fearfully distorted, my sisters weeping and moaning around him, and my mother lying near them in a swoon.

"Coppelius, you atrocious fiend, you've killed my father," I shouted. My senses left me. Two days later, when my father was placed in his coffin, his features were mild and gentle again as they had been when he was alive. I found great consolation in the thought that his association with the diabolical Coppelius could not have ended in his everlasting ruin.

Our neighbours had been awakened by the explosion; the affair got talked about, and came before the magisterial authorities, who wished to cite Coppelius to clear himself. But he had disappeared from the place, leaving no traces behind him.

Now when I tell you, my dear friend, that the peddler I spoke of was the villain Coppelius, you will not blame me for seeing impending mischief in his inauspicious reappearance. He was differently dressed; but Coppelius's figure and features are too deeply impressed upon my mind for me to be capable of making a mistake in the matter. Moreover, he has not even changed his name. He proclaims himself here, I learn, to be a Piedmontese mechanician, and styles himself Giuseppe Coppola.

I am resolved to enter the lists against him and avenge my father's death, let the consequences be what they may.

Don't say a word to mother about the reappearance of this odious monster. Give my love to my darling Clara; I will write to her when I am in a somewhat calmer frame of mind. Adieu, &c.

Clara to Nathanael

You are right, you have not written to me for a very long time, but nevertheless I believe that I still retain a place in your mind and thoughts. It is a proof that you were thinking a good deal about me when you were sending off your last letter to brother Lothair, for instead of directing it to him you directed it to me. With joy I tore open the envelope, and did not perceive the mistake until I read the words, "Oh! my dear, dear Lothair."

Now I know I ought not to have read any more of the letter, but ought to have given it to my brother. But as you have so often in innocent raillery made it a sort of reproach against me that I possessed such a calm and, for a woman, cool-headed temperament that I should be like the woman we read of—if the house was threatening to tumble down, I should stop before hastily fleeing, to smooth down a crumple in the window curtains—I need hardly tell you that the beginning of your letter quite upset me. I could scarcely breathe; there was a bright mist before my eyes.

Oh! my darling Nathanael! what could this terrible thing be that had happened? Separation from you—never to see you again, the thought was like a sharp knife in my heart. I read on and on. Your description of that horrid Coppelius made my flesh creep. I now learned for the first time what a terrible and violent death your good old father died. Brother Lothair, to whom I handed over his property, sought to comfort me, but with little success. That horrid peddler Giuseppe Coppola followed me everywhere; and I am almost ashamed to confess it, but he was able to disturb my sleep, which is usually sound and calm, with all sorts of wonderful dream shapes. But soon—the next day—I saw everything in a different light. Oh! do not be angry with me, my best beloved, if, despite your strange presentiment that Coppelius will do you some mischief, Lothair tells you I am in quite as good spirits, and just the same as ever.

I will frankly confess, it seems to me that all the horrors of which you speak existed only in your own self, and that the real true outer world had but little to do with it. I can quite admit that old Coppelius may have been highly obnoxious to you children, but your real detestation of him arose from the fact that he hated children.

Naturally enough, the gruesome Sandman of the old nurse's story was associated in your childish mind with old Coppelius, who even though you had not believed in the Sandman, would have been to you a ghostly bugbear, especially dangerous to children. His mysterious labours along with your father at nighttime were, I daresay, nothing more than secret experiments in alchemy, with which your mother could not be over-well pleased, owing to the large sums of money that most likely were thrown away upon them; and besides, your father, his mind full of the deceptive striving after higher knowledge, may probably have become rather indifferent to his family, as so often happens in the case of such experimentalists.

So also it is equally probable that your father brought about his death by his own imprudence, and that Coppelius is not to blame for it. I must tell you that yesterday I asked our experienced neighbour, the chemist, whether in experiments of this kind an explosion could take place which would have a momentarily fatal effect. He said, "Oh, certainly!" and described to me in his prolix and circumstantial way how it could be occasioned, mentioning at the same time so many strange and funny words that I could not remember them at all. Now I know you will be angry at your Clara, and will say, "Of the Mysterious which often clasps man in its invisible arms there's not a ray can find its way into her cold heart. She sees only the varied surface of the things of the world and, like the little child, is pleased with the golden glittering fruit, at the kernel of which lies the fatal poison."

Oh! my beloved Nathanael, do you believe then that the intuitive prescience of a dark power working within us to our own ruin cannot exist also in minds which are cheerful, natural, free from care? But please forgive me that I, a simple girl, presume in any way to indicate to you what I really think of such an inward strife. After all, I should not find the proper words, and you would only laugh at me, not because my thoughts were stupid, but because I was so foolish as to attempt to tell them to you.

If there is a dark and hostile power which traitorously fixes a thread in our hearts in order that, laying hold of it and drawing us by means of it along a dangerous road to ruin, which otherwise we should not have trod—if, I say, there is such a power, it must assume within us a form like ourselves, nay, it must be ourselves; for only in that way can we believe in it, and only so understood do we yield to it so far that it is able to accomplish its secret purpose. So long as we have sufficient firmness, fortified by cheerfulness, always to acknowledge foreign hostile influences for what they really are, while we quietly pursue the path pointed out to us by both inclination and calling, then this mysterious power perishes in its futile struggles to attain the form which is to be the reflected image of ourselves.

It is also certain, Lothair adds, that if we have once voluntarily given ourselves up to this dark physical power, it often reproduces within us the strange forms which the outer world throws in our way, so that thus it is we ourselves who engender within ourselves the spirit which by some remarkable delusion we imagine to speak in that outer form. It is the phantom of our own self whose intimate relationship with, and whose powerful influence upon our soul, either plunges us into hell or elevates us to heaven.

Thus you will see, my beloved Nathanael, that I and brother Lothair have talked over the subject of dark powers and forces well; and now, after I have written down the principal results of our discussion with some difficulty, they seem to me to contain many really profound thoughts. Lothair's last words, however, I don't quite understand; I only dimly guess what he means; and yet I cannot help thinking it is all very true.

I beg you, dear, strive to forget the ugly lawyer Coppelius as well as the peddler Giuseppe Coppola. Try and convince yourself that these foreign influences can have no power over you, that it is only belief in their hostile power which can in reality make them dangerous to you.

If every line of your letter did not betray the violent excitement of your mind, and if I did not sympathize with your condition from the bottom of my heart, I could in truth jest about the lawyer Sandman and peddler Coppelius. Pluck up your spirits! Be cheerful! I have resolved to appear to you as your guardian angel if that ugly man Coppola should dare take it into his head to bother you in your dreams, and drive him away with a good hearty laugh. I'm not afraid of him and his nasty hands, not the least little bit; I won't let him either as lawyer spoil any dainty tit-bit I've taken, or as Sandman rob me of my eyes.

My darling, darling Nathanael,
Eternally your, &c. &c.

Nathanael to Lothair

I am very sorry that Clara opened and read my last letter to you; of course the mistake is to be attributed to my own absence of mind. She has written me a very deep philosophical letter, proving conclusively that Coppelius and Coppola only exist in my own mind and are phantoms of my own self, which will at once be dissipated, as soon as I look upon them in that light. In very truth one can hardly believe that the mind which so often sparkles in those bright, beautifully smiling, childlike eyes of hers like a sweet lovely dream could draw such subtle and scholastic distinctions. She also mentions your name. You have been talking about me. I suppose you have been giving her lectures, since she sifts and refines everything so acutely. But enough of this! I must now tell you it is most certain that Giuseppe Coppola is not Coppelius. I am attending the lectures of our recently appointed Professor of Physics, who, like the distinguished naturalist, is called Spalanzani, and is of Italian origin. He has known Coppola for many years; and it is also easy to tell from Coppola's accent that he really is a Piedmontese. Coppelius was a German, though no honest German, I fancy.

Nevertheless I am not quite satisfied. You and Clara will perhaps take me for a gloomy dreamer, but in no way can I get rid of the impression which Coppelius's cursed face made upon me. I am glad to learn from Spalanzani that he has left town.

This Professor Spalanzani is a very queer fish. He is a little fat man, with prominent cheekbones, thin nose, projecting lips, and small piercing eyes. You cannot get a better picture of him than by turning over one of the Berlin pocket almanacs and looking at Cagliostro's portrait engraved by Chodowiecki; Spalanzani looks just like him.

Once lately, as I went up the steps to his house, I perceived that beside the curtain which generally covered a glass door there was a small chink. What it was that excited my curiosity I cannot explain; but I looked through. In the room I saw a female, tall, very slender, but of perfect proportions, and splendidly dressed, sitting at a little table, on which she had placed both her arms, her hands being folded together. She sat opposite the door, so that I could easily see her angelically beautiful face. She did not appear to notice me, and there was moreover a strangely fixed look about her eyes. I might almost say they appeared as if they had no power of vision; I thought she was sleeping with her eyes open. I felt quite uncomfortable, and so I slipped away quietly into the Professor's lecture-room, which was close at hand.

Afterwards I learned that the figure which I had seen was Spalanzani's daughter, Olimpia, whom he keeps locked up in a most wicked and unaccountable way. No man is ever allowed to come near her. Perhaps, however, there is something peculiar about her after all; perhaps she's an idiot or something of that sort.

But why am I telling you all this? I could tell you it all better and in more detail when I see you. For in a fortnight I shall be among you. I must see my dear sweet angel, my Clara, again. Then the little bit of ill-temper which, I must confess, took possession of me after her fearfully sensible letter, will be blown away. And that is the reason why I am not writing to her as well today.

With all best wishes, &c.

NOTHING MORE STRANGE and extraordinary can be imagined, gracious reader, than what happened to my poor friend, the young student Nathanael, and which I have undertaken to relate to you. Have you ever experienced anything that completely took possession of your heart and mind and thoughts to the utter exclusion of everything else? All was seething and boiling within you; your blood, heated to fever pitch, leaped through your veins and inflamed your cheeks. Your gaze was so peculiar, as if seeking to grasp in empty space forms not seen by any other eye, and all your words ended in sighs betokening some mystery.

Then your friends asked you, "What is the matter with you, my dear friend? What do you see?" And, wishing to describe the inner pictures in all their vivid colours, with their lights and their shades, you struggled in vain to find words with which to express yourself. But you felt as if you must gather up all the events that had happened, wonderful, splendid, terrible, jocose, and awful, in the very first word, so that the whole might be revealed by a single electric discharge, so to speak.

Yet every word and everything that partook of the nature of communication by intelligible sounds seemed to be colourless, cold, and dead. Then you try and try again, and stutter and stammer, while your friends' prosy questions strike like icy winds upon your heart's hot fire until they extinguish it. But if, like a bold painter, you had first sketched in a few audacious strokes the outline of the picture you had in your soul, you would then easily have been able to deepen and intensify the colours one after the other, until the varied throng of living figures carried your friends away and they, like you, saw themselves in the midst of the scene that had proceeded out of your own soul.

Strictly speaking, indulgent reader, I must indeed confess to you, nobody has asked me for the history of young Nathanael; but you are very well aware that I belong to that remarkable class of authors who, when they bear anything about in their minds in the manner I have just described, feel as if everybody who comes near them, and also the whole world to boot, were asking, "Oh! what is it? Oh! do tell us, my good sir?"

Hence I was most powerfully impelled to narrate to you Nathanael's ominous life. I was completely captivated by the elements of marvel and alienness in his life; but, for this very reason, and because it was necessary in the very beginning to dispose you, indulgent reader, to bear with what is fantastic—and that is not a small matter—I racked my brain to find a way of commencing the story in a significant and original manner, calculated to arrest your attention. To begin with "Once upon a time," the best beginning for a story, seemed to me too tame; with "In the small country town S—— lived," rather better, at any rate allowing plenty of room to work up to the climax; or to plunge at once *in medias res*, " 'Go to the devil!' cried the student Nathanael, his eyes blazing wildly with rage and fear, when the weather-glass peddler Giuseppe Coppola"—well, that is what I really had written, when I thought I detected something of the ridiculous in Nathanael's wild glance; and the history is anything but laughable. I could not find any words which seemed fitted to reflect in even the feeblest degree the brightness of the colours of my mental vision.

I determined not to begin at all. So I pray you, gracious reader, accept the three letters which my friend Lothair has been so kind as to communicate to me as the outline of the picture, into which I will endeavour to introduce more and more colour as I proceed with my narrative. Perhaps, like a good portrait painter, I may succeed in depicting Nathanael in such a way that you will recognize it as a good likeness without being acquainted with the original, and will feel as if you had very often seen him with your own bodily eyes. Perhaps, too, you will then believe that nothing is more wonderful, nothing more fantastic than real life, and that all that a writer can do is to present it as "in a glass, darkly."

In order to make the beginning more intelligible, it is necessary to add to the letters that, soon after the death of Nathanael's father, Clara and Lothair, the children of a distant relative, who had likewise died, leaving them orphans, were taken by Nathanael's mother into her own house. Clara and Nathanael conceived a warm affection for each other, to which there could be no objection. When therefore Nathanael left home to prosecute his studies in G——, they were engaged. It is from G—— that his last letter is written, where he is attending the lectures of Spalanzani, the distinguished Professor of Physics.

I might now proceed comfortably with my narration, if at this moment Clara's image did not rise up so vividly before my eyes that I cannot turn them away from it, just as I never could when she looked upon me and smiled so sweetly. Nowhere would she have passed for beautiful; that was the unanimous opinion of everyone who professed to have any technical knowledge of beauty. But while architects praised the pure proportions of her figure and form, painters averred that her neck, shoulders, and bosom were almost too chastely modelled, and yet, on the other hand, one and all were in love with her glorious Magdalene hair, and talked a good deal of nonsense about Battoni-like colouring. One of them, a veritable romanticist, strangely enough likened her eyes to a lake by Ruisdael, in which is reflected the pure azure of the cloudless sky, the beauty of woods and flowers, and all the bright and varied life of a living landscape. Poets and musicians went still further and said, "What's all this talk about seas and reflections? How can we look upon the girl without feeling that wonderful heavenly songs and melodies beam upon us from her eyes, penetrating deep down into our hearts, till everything becomes awake and throbbing with emotion? And if we cannot sing anything at all passable then, why, we are not worth much; and this we can also plainly read in the rare smile which flits around her lips when we have the hardihood to squeak out something in her presence which we pretend to call singing, in spite of the fact that it is nothing more than a few single notes confusedly linked together."

And it really was so. Clara had the powerful fancy of a bright, innocent, unaffected child, a woman's deep and sympathetic heart, and an understanding clear, sharp, and discriminating. Dreamers and visionaries had a bad time of it with her; for without saying very much—she was not by nature of a talkative disposition—she plainly asked, by her calm steady look and rare ironical smile, "How can you imagine, my dear friends, that I can take these fleeting shadowy images for true living and breathing forms?" For this reason many found fault with her as being cold, unimaginative, and devoid of feeling; others, however, who had reached a clearer and deeper conception of life, were extremely fond of the intelligent, childlike, large-hearted girl.

No one else had such an affection for her as Nathanael, who was a zealous and cheerful cultivator of the fields of science and art. Clara clung to her lover with all her heart; the first clouds she encountered in life were when he had to separate from her. With what delight did she fly into his arms when, as he had promised in his last letter to Lothair, he really came back to his native town and entered his mother's room! And as Nathanael had foreseen, the moment he saw Clara again he no longer thought about either the lawyer Coppelius or her sensible letter; his ill-humour had quite disappeared.

Nevertheless Nathanael was right when he told his friend Lothair that the repulsive vendor of weather glasses, Coppola, had exercised a fatal and disturbing influence upon his life. It was quite patent to all; for even during the first few days he showed that he was completely and entirely changed. He gave himself up to gloomy reveries, and moreover acted so strangely; they had never observed anything at all like it in him before. Everything, even his own life, was to him but dreams and presentiments. His constant theme was that every man who delusively imagined himself to be free was merely the plaything of the cruel sport of mysterious powers, and it was vain for man to resist them; he must humbly submit to whatever destiny had decreed for him. He went so far as to maintain that it was foolish to believe that a man could do anything in art or science of his own accord; for the inspiration in which alone any true artistic work could be done did not proceed from the spirit within outwards, but was the result of the operation directed inwards of some Higher Principle existing without and beyond ourselves.

This mystic extravagance was in the highest degree repugnant to Clara's clear intelligent mind, but it seemed vain to enter upon any attempt at refutation. Yet when Nathanael went on to prove that Coppelius was the Evil Principle which had entered into him and taken possession of him at the time he was listening behind the curtain, and that this hateful demon would in some terrible way ruin their happiness, then Clara grew grave and said, "Yes, Nathanael. You are right; Coppelius is an Evil Principle; he can do dreadful things, as bad as could a Satanic power which should assume a living physical form, but only—only if you do not banish him from your mind and thoughts. As long as you believe in him he exists and is at work; your belief in him is his only power."

Whereupon Nathanael, quite angry because Clara would only grant the existence of the demon in his own mind, began to dilate at large upon the whole mystic doctrine of devils and awful powers, but Clara abruptly broke off the theme by making, to Nathanael's very great disgust, some quite commonplace remark.

Such deep mysteries are sealed books to cold, unsusceptible characters, he thought, without its being clearly conscious to himself that he counted Clara among these inferior natures, and accordingly he did not remit his efforts to initiate her into these mysteries. In the morning, when she was helping to prepare breakfast, he would take his stand beside her, and read all sorts of mystic books to her, until she begged him—"But, my dear Nathanael, I shall have to scold you as the Evil Principle which exercises a fatal influence upon my coffee. For if I do as you wish, and let things go their own way, and look into your eyes while you read, the coffee will all boil over into the fire, and you will none of you get any breakfast." Then Nathanael hastily banged the book shut and ran away in great displeasure to his own room.

Formerly he had possessed a peculiar talent for writing pleasing, sparkling tales, which Clara took the greatest delight in hearing; but now his productions were gloomy, unintelligible, and wanting in form, so that, although Clara out of forbearance towards him did not say so, he nevertheless felt how very little interest she took in them. There was nothing that Clara disliked so much as what was tedious; at such times her intellectual sleepiness was not to be overcome; it was betrayed both in her glances and in her words. Nathanael's effusions were, in truth, exceedingly tedious.

His ill-humour at Clara's cold prosaic temperament continued to increase; Clara could not conceal her distaste for his dark, gloomy, wearying mysticism; and thus both began to be more and more estranged from each other without exactly being aware of it themselves. The image of the ugly Coppelius had, as Nathanael was obliged to confess to himself, faded considerably in his fancy, and it often cost him great pains to present him in vivid colours in his literary efforts, in which Coppelius played the part of the ghoul of Destiny.

At length it entered into his head to make his dismal presentiment that Coppelius would ruin his happiness the subject of a poem. He made himself and Clara, united by true love, the central figures, but represented a black hand as being from time to time thrust into their life, plucking out a joy that had blossomed for them. At length, as they were standing at the altar, the terrible Coppelius appeared and touched Clara's lovely eyes, which leaped into Nathanael's own bosom, burning and hissing like bloody sparks. Then Coppelius laid hold of him, and hurled him into a blazing circle of fire, which spun round with the speed of a whirlwind, and storming and blustering, dashed away with him. The fearful noise it made was like a furious hurricane lashing the foaming sea waves until they rise up like black, white-headed giants in the midst of the raging struggle. But through the midst of the savage fury of the tempest he heard Clara's voice calling, "Can you not see me, dear? Coppelius has deceived you; they were not my eyes which burned so in your bosom; they were fiery drops of your own heart's blood. Look at me, I have got my own eyes still." Nathanael thought, "Yes, that is Clara, and I am hers forever." Then this thought laid a powerful grasp upon the fiery circle so that it stood still, and the riotous turmoil died away, rumbling down into a dark abyss. Nathanael looked into Clara's eyes; but it was death whose gaze rested so kindly upon him.

While Nathanael was writing this work he was very quiet and sober-minded; he filed and polished every line, and as he had chosen to submit himself to the limitations of meter, he did not rest until all was pure and musical. When, however, he had at length finished it and read it aloud to himself he was seized with horror and awful dread, and he screamed, "Whose hideous voice is this?" But he soon came to see in it again nothing beyond a very successful poem, and he confidently believed it would enkindle Clara's cold temperament, though to what end she should be thus aroused was not quite clear to his own mind, nor yet what would be the real purpose served by tormenting her with these dreadful pictures, which prophesied a terrible and ruinous end to her affection.

Nathanael and Clara sat in his mother's little garden. Clara was bright and cheerful, since for three entire days her lover, who had been busy writing his poem, had not teased her with his dreams or forebodings. Nathanael, too, spoke in a gay and vivacious way of things of merry import, as he formerly used to do, so that Clara said, "Ah! now I have you again. We have driven away that ugly Coppelius, you see." Then it suddenly occurred to him that he had got the poem in his pocket which he wished to read to her. He at once took out the manuscript and began to read.

Clara, anticipating something tedious as usual, prepared to submit to the infliction, and calmly resumed her knitting. But as the sombre clouds rose up darker and darker she let her knitting fall on her lap and sat with her eyes fixed in a set stare upon Nathanael's face. He was quite carried away by his own work, the fire of enthusiasm coloured his cheeks a deep red, and tears started from his eyes. At length he concluded, groaning and showing great lassitude; grasping Clara's hand, he sighed as if he were being utterly melted in inconsolable grief, "Oh! Clara! Clara!" She drew him softly to her heart and said in a low but very grave and impressive tone, "Nathanael, my darling Nathanael, throw that foolish, senseless, stupid thing into the fire."

Then Nathanael leaped indignantly to his feet, crying, as he pushed Clara from him, "You damned lifeless automaton!" and rushed away. Clara was cut to the heart, and wept bitterly. "Oh! he has never loved me, for he does not understand me," she sobbed.

Lothair entered the arbour. Clara was obliged to tell him all that had taken place. He was passionately fond of his sister; and every word of her complaint fell like a spark upon his heart, so that the displeasure which he had long entertained against his dreamy friend Nathanael was kindled into furious anger. He hastened to find Nathanael, and upbraided him in harsh words for his irrational behaviour towards his beloved sister.

The fiery Nathanael answered him in the same style. "A fantastic, crack-brained fool," was retaliated with, "A miserable, common, everyday sort of fellow." A meeting was the inevitable consequence. They agreed to meet on the following morning behind the garden wall, and fight, according to the custom of the students of the place, with sharp rapiers. They went about silent and gloomy; Clara had both heard and seen the violent quarrel, and also observed the fencing master bring the rapiers in the dusk of the evening. She had a presentiment of what was to happen. They both appeared at the appointed place wrapped up in the same gloomy silence, and threw off their coats. Their eyes flaming with the bloodthirsty light of pugnacity, they were about to begin their contest when Clara burst through the garden door. Sobbing, she screamed, "You savage, terrible men! Cut me down before you attack each other; for how can I live when my lover has slain my brother, or my brother slain my lover?"

Lothair let his weapon fall and gazed silently at the ground, while Nathanael's heart was rent with sorrow, and all the affection which he had felt for his lovely Clara in the happiest days of her golden youth was reawakened within him. His murderous weapon, too, fell from his hand; he threw himself at Clara's feet. "Oh! can you ever forgive me, my only, my dearly loved Clara? Can you, my dear brother Lothair, also forgive me?" Lothair was touched by his friend's great distress; the three young people embraced each other amid endless tears, and swore never again to break their bond of love and fidelity.

Nathanael felt as if a heavy burden that had been weighing him down to the earth was now rolled from off him, nay, as if by offering resistance to the dark power which had possessed him, he had rescued his own self from the ruin which had threatened him. Three happy days he now spent amidst the loved ones, and then returned to G——, where he had still a year to stay before settling down in his native town for life.

Everything having reference to Coppelius had been concealed from Nathanael's mother, for they knew she could not think of Coppelius without horror, since she as well as Nathanael believed him to be guilty of causing her husband's death.

When Nathanael came to the house where he lived in G——, he was greatly astonished to find it burned down to the ground, so that nothing but the bare outer walls were left standing amid a heap of ruins. Although the fire had broken out in the laboratory of the chemist who lived on the ground floor, and had therefore spread upwards, some of Nathanael's bold, active friends had succeeded in time in forcing a way into his room in the upper story and saving his books and manuscripts and instruments. They had carried them all uninjured into another house, where they engaged a room for him; this he now at once took possession of.

That he lived opposite Professor Spalanzani did not strike him particularly, nor did it occur to him as anything more singular that he could, as he observed, by looking out of his window, see straight into the room where Olimpia often sat alone. Her figure he could plainly distinguish, although her features were uncertain and confused. It did at length occur to him, however, that she remained for hours together in the same position in which he had first discovered her through the glass door, sitting at a little table without any occupation whatever, and it was evident that she was constantly gazing across in his direction. He could not but confess to himself that he had never seen a finer figure. However, with Clara mistress of his heart, he remained perfectly unaffected by Olimpia's stiffness and apathy; and it was only occasionally that he sent a fugitive glance over his compendium across to her—that was all.

He was writing to Clara; a light tap came at the door. At his summons to "Come in," Coppola's repulsive face appeared peeping in. Nathanael felt his heart beat with trepidation; but, recollecting what Spalanzani had told him about his fellow countryman Coppola, and what he himself had so faithfully promised his beloved in respect to the Sandman Coppelius, he was ashamed at himself for this childish fear of specters. Accordingly, he controlled himself with an effort, and said, as quietly and as calmly as he possibly could, "I don't want to buy any weather glasses, my good friend; you had better go elsewhere."

Then Coppola came right into the room, and said in a hoarse voice, screwing up his wide mouth into a hideous smile, while his little eyes flashed keenly from beneath his long gray eyelashes, "Eh! No want weather glass? No weather glass? I got eyes-a too. Fine eyes-a." In some fright, Nathanael cried, "You idiot, how can you have eyes?—eyes—eyes?" But Coppola, laying aside his barometers, thrust his hands into his big coat pockets and brought out several spyglasses and spectacles, and put them on the table. "Looka! Looka! Spettacles for nose. Spettacles. Those my eyes-a." And he continued to produce more and more spectacles from his pockets until the table began to gleam and flash all over. Thousands of eyes were looking and blinking convulsively and staring up at Nathanael; he could not avert his gaze from the table. Coppola went on heaping up his spectacles, while wilder and ever wilder burning flashes crossed through and through each other and darted their blood-red rays into Nathanael's breast.

Quite overcome and frantic with terror, he shouted, "Stop! stop! you fiend!" and he seized Coppola by the arm, which Coppola had again thrust into his pocket in order to bring out still more spectacles, although the whole table was covered all over with them. With a harsh disagreeable laugh Coppola gently freed himself; and with the words "So! want none! Well, here fine glass!" he swept all his spectacles together, and put them back into his coat pockets, while from a breast pocket he produced a great number of larger and smaller perspectives. As soon as the spectacles were gone Nathanael recovered his equanimity again; and, bending his thoughts upon Clara, he clearly discerned that the gruesome incubus had proceeded only from himself, and that Coppola was an honest mechanician and optician, and far from being Coppelius's dreaded double and ghost. And then, besides, none of the glasses which Coppola now placed on the table had anything at all singular about them, at least nothing so weird as the spectacles; so, in order to square accounts with himself Nathanael now really determined to buy something of the man. He took up a small, very beautifully cut pocket perspective, and by way of proving it looked through the window.

Never before in his life had he had a glass in his hands that brought out things so clearly and sharply and distinctly. Involuntarily he directed the glass upon Spalanzani's room; Olimpia sat at the little table as usual, her arms laid upon it and her hands folded. Now he saw for the first time the regular and exquisite beauty of her features. The eyes, however, seemed to him to have a singular look of fixity and lifelessness. But as he continued to look closer and more carefully through the glass he fancied a light like humid moonbeams came into them. It seemed as if their power of vision was now being enkindled; their glances shone with ever-increasing vivacity.

Nathanael remained standing at the window as if glued to the spot by a wizard's spell, his gaze riveted unchangeably upon the divinely beautiful Olimpia. A coughing and shuffling of the feet awakened him out of his enchaining dream, as it were. Coppola stood behind him, "Tre zechini" (three ducats). Nathanael had completely forgotten the optician; he hastily paid the sum demanded. "Ain't 't? Fine-a glass? Fine-a glass?" asked Coppola in his harsh unpleasant voice, smiling sardonically. "Yes, yes, yes," rejoined Nathanael impatiently; "adieu, my good friend." But Coppola did not leave the room without casting many peculiar side glances upon Nathanael; and the young student heard him laughing loudly on the stairs. "Ah well!" thought he, "he's laughing at me because I've paid him too much for this little perspective—because I've given him too much money—that's it."

As he softly murmured these words he fancied he detected a gasping sigh as of a dying man stealing awfully through the room; his heart stopped beating with fear. But to be sure he had heaved a deep sigh himself; it was quite plain. "Clara is quite right," said he to himself, "in holding me to be an incurable ghost-seer; and yet it's very ridiculous—more ridiculous, that the stupid thought of having paid Coppola too much for his glass should cause me this strange anxiety; I can't see any reason for it."

Now he sat down to finish his letter to Clara; but a glance through the window showed him Olimpia still in her former posture. Urged by an irresistible impulse he jumped up and seized Coppola's perspective; nor could he tear himself away from the fascinating Olimpia until his friend Siegmund called for him to go to Professor Spalanzani's lecture. The curtains before the door of the all-important room were closely drawn, so that he could not see Olimpia. Nor could he even see her from his own room during the two following days, notwithstanding that he scarcely ever left his window, and maintained a scarce interrupted watch through Coppola's perspective upon her room.

On the third day curtains were drawn across the window. Plunged into the depths of despair,—goaded by longing and ardent desire, he hurried outside the walls of the town. Olimpia's image hovered about his path in the air and stepped forth out of the bushes, and peeped up at him with large and lustrous eyes from the bright surface of the brook. Clara's image was completely faded from his mind; he had no thoughts except for Olimpia. He uttered his love plaints aloud and in a lachrymose tone, "Oh! my glorious, noble star of love, have you only risen to vanish again, and leave me in the darkness and hopelessness of night?"

Returning home, he became aware that there was a good deal of noisy bustle going on in Spalanzani's house. All the doors stood wide open; men were taking in all kinds of gear and furniture; the windows of the first floor were all lifted off their hinges; busy maid-servants with immense hair-brooms were driving backwards and forwards dusting and sweeping, while from inside could be heard the knocking and hammering of carpenters and upholsterers. Utterly astonished, Nathanael stood still in the street; then Siegmund joined him, laughing, and said, "Well, what do you say to our old Spalanzani?" Nathanael assured him that he could not say anything, since he did not know what it all meant. To his great astonishment, he could hear, however, that they were turning the quiet gloomy house almost inside out with their dusting and cleaning and alterations. Then he learned from Siegmund that Spalanzani intended giving a great concert and ball on the following day, and that half the university was invited. It was generally reported that Spalanzani was going to let his daughter Olimpia, whom he had so long so jealously guarded from every eye, make her first appearance.

Nathanael received an invitation. At the appointed hour, when the carriages were rolling up and the lights were gleaming brightly in the decorated halls, he went across to the Professor's, his heart beating high with expectation. The company was both numerous and brilliant.

Olimpia was richly and tastefully dressed. One could not but admire her figure and the regular beauty of her features. Yet the striking inward curve of her back, as well as the wasplike smallness of her waist, appeared to be the result of too-tight lacing, and there was something stiff and measured in her gait and bearing that made an unfavourable impression upon many. It was ascribed to the constraint imposed upon her by the company.

The concert began. Olimpia played on the piano with great skill; and sang as skillfully an *aria di bravura*, in a voice which was, if anything, almost too brilliant, but clear as glass bells. Nathanael was transported with delight; he stood in the background farthest from her, and owing to the blinding lights could not quite distinguish her features. So, without being observed, he took Coppola's glass out of his pocket, and directed it upon the beautiful Olimpia. Oh! then he perceived how her yearning eyes sought him, how every note only reached its full purity in the loving glance which penetrated to and inflamed his heart. Her roulades seemed to him to be the exultant cry towards heaven of the soul refined by love; and when at last, after the cadenza, the long trill rang loudly through the hall, he felt as if he were suddenly grasped by burning arms and could no longer control himself—he could not help shouting aloud in his mingled pain and delight, "Olimpia!" All eyes were turned upon him; many people laughed.

The concert came to an end, and the ball began. Oh! to dance with her—with her—that was now the aim of all Nathanael's wishes, of all his desires. But how should he have courage to request her, the queen of the ball, to grant him the honour of a dance? And yet he couldn't tell how it came about, just as the dance began, he found himself standing close beside her, nobody having as yet asked her to be his partner. So, with some difficulty stammering out a few words, he grasped her hand. It was cold as ice; he shook with an awful, frosty shiver. But, fixing his eyes upon her face, he saw that her glance was beaming upon him with love and longing, and at the same moment he thought that the pulse began to beat in her cold hand, and the warm life-blood to course through her veins. And passion burned more intensely in his own heart also; he threw his arm round her beautiful waist and whirled her round the hall. He had always thought that he kept good and accurate time in dancing, but from the perfectly rhythmical evenness with which Olimpia danced, and which frequently put him quite out, he perceived how very faulty his own time really was. Notwithstanding, he would not dance with any other lady; and everybody else who approached Olimpia to call upon her for a dance, he would have liked to kill on the spot. This, however, only happened twice; to his astonishment Olimpia remained after this without a partner, and he did not fail on each occasion to take her out again.

If Nathanael had been able to see anything else except the beautiful Olimpia, there would inevitably have been a good deal of unpleasant quarrelling and strife; for it was evident that Olimpia was the object of the smothered laughter suppressed only with difficulty, which was heard in various corners amongst the young people; and they followed her with very curious looks.

Nathanael, excited by dancing and the plentiful supply of wine he had consumed, had laid aside the shyness which at other times characterized him. He sat beside Olimpia, her hand in his own, and declared his love enthusiastically and passionately in words which neither of them understood, neither he nor Olimpia. And yet perhaps she did, for she sat with her eyes fixed unchangeably upon his, sighing repeatedly, "Ah! Ah! Ah!" Upon this Nathanael would answer, "Oh, you glorious heavenly lady! You ray from the promised paradise of love! Oh! what a profound soul you have! my whole being is mirrored in it!" and a good deal more in the same strain. But Olimpia only continued to sigh "Ah! Ah!" again and again.

Professor Spalanzani passed by the two happy lovers once or twice, and smiled with a look of peculiar satisfaction. All at once it seemed to Nathanael, albeit he was far away in a different world, as if it were growing perceptibly darker down below at Professor Spalanzani's. He looked about him, and to his very great alarm became aware that there were only two lights left burning in the hall, and they were on the point of going out. The music and dancing had long ago ceased. "We must part—part!" he cried, wildly and despairingly; he kissed Olimpia's hand; he bent down to her mouth, but ice-cold lips met his burning ones. As he touched her cold hand, he felt his heart thrill with awe; the legend of "The Dead Bride" shot suddenly through his mind. But Olimpia had drawn him closer to her, and the kiss appeared to warm her lips into vitality.

Professor Spalanzani strode slowly through the empty apartment, his footsteps giving a hollow echo; and his figure had, as the flickering shadows played about him, a ghostly, awful appearance. "Do you love me? Do you love me, Olimpia? Only one little word—do you love me?" whispered Nathanael, but she only sighed, "Ah! Ah!" as she rose to her feet.

"Yes, you are my lovely, glorious star of love," said Nathanael, "and will shine for ever, purifying and ennobling my heart." "Ah! Ah!" replied Olimpia, as she moved along. Nathanael followed her; they stood before the Professor. "You have had an extraordinarily animated conversation with my daughter," said he, smiling. "Well, well, my dear Mr. Nathanael, if you find pleasure in talking to the stupid girl, I am sure I shall be glad for you to come and do so." Nathanael took his leave, his heart singing and leaping in a perfect delirium of happiness.

During the next few days Spalanzani's ball was the general topic of conversation. Although the Professor had done everything to make the thing a splendid success, yet certain gay spirits related more than one thing that had occurred which was quite irregular and out of order. They were especially keen in pulling Olimpia to pieces for her taciturnity and rigid stiffness; in spite of her beautiful form they alleged that she was hopelessly stupid, and in this fact they discerned the reason why Spalanzani had so long kept her concealed from publicity. Nathanael heard all this with inward wrath, but nevertheless he held his tongue; for, thought he, would it indeed be worth while to prove to these fellows that it is their own stupidity which prevents them from appreciating Olimpia's profound and brilliant parts?

One day Siegmund said to him, "Pray, brother, have the kindness to tell me how you, a clever fellow, came to lose your head over that Miss Wax-face—that wooden doll across there?" Nathanael was about to fly into a rage, but he recollected himself and replied, "Tell me, Siegmund, how came it that Olimpia's divine charms could escape your eye, so keenly alive as it always is to beauty, and your acute perception as well? But Heaven be thanked for it, otherwise I should have had you for a rival, and then the blood of one of us would have had to be spilled."

Siegmund, perceiving how matters stood with his friend, skillfully changed his tactics and said, after remarking that all argument with one in love about the object of his affections was out of place, "Yet it's very strange that several of us have formed pretty much the same opinion about Olimpia. We think she is—you won't take it ill, brother?—that she is singularly statuesque and soulless. Her figure is regular, and so are her features, that can't be gainsaid; and if her eyes were not so utterly devoid of life, I may say, of the power of vision, she might pass for a beauty. She is strangely measured in her movements, they all seem as if they were dependent upon some wound-up clockwork. Her playing and singing have the disagreeably perfect, but insensitive timing of a singing machine, and her dancing is the same. We felt quite afraid of this Olimpia, and did not like to have anything to do with her; she seemed to us to be only acting like a *living* creature, and as if there was some secret at the bottom of it all."

Nathanael did not give way to the bitter feelings which threatened to master him at these words of Siegmund's; he fought down and got the better of his displeasure, and merely said, very earnestly, "You cold prosaic fellows may very well be afraid of her. It is only to its like that the poetically organized spirit unfolds itself. Upon me alone did her loving glances fall, and through my mind and thoughts alone did they radiate; and only in her love can I find my own self again. Perhaps, however, she doesn't do quite right not to jabber a lot of nonsense and stupid talk like other shallow people. It is true, she speaks but few words; but the few words she does speak are genuine hieroglyphs of the inner world of Love and of the higher cognition of the intellectual life revealed in the intuition of the Eternal beyond the grave. But you have no understanding for all these things, and I am only wasting words."

"God be with you, brother," said Siegmund very gently, almost sadly, "but it seems to me that you are in a very bad way. You may rely upon me, if all—No, I can't say any more." It all at once dawned upon Nathanael that his cold prosaic friend Siegmund really and sincerely wished him well, and so he warmly shook his proffered hand.

Nathanael had completely forgotten that there was a Clara in the world, whom he had once loved—and his mother and Lothair. They had all vanished from his mind; he lived for Olimpia alone. He sat beside her every day for hours together, rhapsodizing about his love and sympathy enkindled into life, and about psychic elective affinity—all of which Olimpia listened to with great reverence.

He fished up from the very bottom of his desk all the things that he had ever written—poems, fancy sketches, visions, romances, tales, and the heap was increased daily with all kinds of aimless sonnets, stanzas, canzonets. All these he read to Olimpia hour after hour without growing tired; but then he had never had such an exemplary listener. She neither embroidered, nor knitted; she did not look out of the window, or feed a bird, or play with a little pet dog or a favourite cat, neither did she twist a piece of paper or anything of that kind round her finger; she did not forcibly convert a yawn into a low affected cough—in short, she sat hour after hour with her eyes bent unchangeably upon her lover's face, without moving or altering her position, and her gaze grew more ardent and more ardent still. And it was only when at last Nathanael rose and kissed her lips or her hand that she said, "Ah! Ah!" and then "Goodnight, dear."

Back in his own room, Nathanael would break out with, "Oh! what a brilliant—what a profound mind! Only you—you alone understand me." And his heart trembled with rapture when he reflected upon the wondrous harmony which daily revealed itself between his own and his Olimpia's character; for he fancied that she had expressed in respect to his works and his poetic genius the identical sentiments which he himself cherished deep down in his own heart, and even as if it was his own heart's voice speaking to him. And it must indeed have been so; for Olimpia never uttered any other words than those already mentioned. And when Nathanael himself in his clear and sober moments, as, for instance, directly after waking in a morning, thought about her utter passivity and taciturnity, he only said, "What are words—but words? The glance of her heavenly eyes says more than any tongue. And anyway, how can a child of heaven accustom herself to the narrow circle which the exigencies of a wretched mundane life demand?"

Professor Spalanzani appeared to be greatly pleased at the intimacy that had sprung up between his daughter Olimpia and Nathanael, and showed the young man many unmistakable proofs of his good feeling towards him. When Nathanael ventured at length to hint very delicately at an alliance with Olimpia, the Professor smiled all over his face at once, and said he should allow his daughter to make a perfectly free choice.

Encouraged by these words, and with the fire of desire burning in his heart, Nathanael resolved the very next day to implore Olimpia to tell him frankly, in plain words, what he had long read in her sweet loving glances—that she would be his for ever. He looked for the ring which his mother had given him at parting; he would present it to Olimpia as a symbol of his devotion, and of the happy life he was to lead with her from that time onwards.

While looking for it he came across his letters from Clara and Lothair; he threw them carelessly aside, found the ring, put it in his pocket, and ran across to Olimpia. While still on the stairs, in the entrance passage, he heard an extraordinary hubbub; the noise seemed to proceed from Spalanzani's study. There was a stamping—a rattling—pushing—knocking against the door, with curses and oaths intermingled. "Leave hold—leave hold—you monster—you rascal—put your life's work into it?—Ha! ha! ha! ha!—That was not our wager—I, I made the eyes—I the clockwork.—Go to the devil with your clockwork—you damned dog of a watchmaker—be off—Satan—stop—you paltry turner—you infernal beast—stop—begone—let me go." The voices which were thus making all this racket and rumpus were those of Spalanzani and the fearsome Coppelius.

Nathanael rushed in, impelled by some nameless dread. The Professor was grasping a female figure by the shoulders, the Italian Coppola held her by the feet; and they were pulling and dragging each other backwards and forwards, fighting furiously to get possession of her.

Nathanael recoiled with horror on recognizing that the figure was Olimpia. Boiling with rage, he was about to tear his beloved from the grasp of the madmen, when Coppola by an extraordinary exertion of strength twisted the figure out of the Professor's hands and gave him such a terrible blow with her, that Spalanzani reeled backwards and fell over the table among the phials and retorts, the bottles and glass cylinders, which covered it: all these things were smashed into a thousand pieces. But Coppola threw the figure across his shoulder, and, laughing shrilly and horribly, ran hastily down the stairs, the figure's ugly feet hanging down and banging and rattling like wood against the steps.

Nathanael was stupefied—he had seen only too distinctly that in Olimpia's pallid waxed face there were no eyes, merely black holes in their stead; she was an inanimate puppet. Spalanzani was rolling on the floor; the pieces of glass had cut his head and breast and arm; the blood was escaping from him in streams. But he gathered his strength together by an effort.

"After him—after him! What do you stand staring there for? Coppelius—Coppelius—he's stolen my best automaton—at which I've worked for twenty years—my life work—the clockwork—speech—movement—mine—your eyes—stolen your eyes—damn him—curse him—after him—fetch me back Olimpia—there are the eyes." And now Nathanael saw a pair of bloody eyes lying on the floor staring at him; Spalanzani seized them with his uninjured hand and threw them at him, so that they hit his breast.

Then madness dug her burning talons into Nathanael and swept down into his heart, rending his mind and thoughts to shreds. "Aha! aha! aha! Fire-wheel—fire-wheel! Spin round, fire-wheel! merrily, merrily! Aha! wooden doll! spin round, pretty wooden doll!" and he threw himself upon the Professor, clutching him fast by the throat.

He would certainly have strangled him had not several people, attracted by the noise, rushed in and torn away the madman; and so they saved the Professor, whose wounds were immediately dressed. Siegmund, with all his strength, was not able to subdue the frantic lunatic, who continued to scream in a dreadful way, "Spin round, wooden doll!" and to strike out right and left with his doubled fists. At length the united strength of several succeeded in overpowering him by throwing him on the floor and binding him. His cries passed into a brutish bellow that was awful to hear; and thus raging with the harrowing violence of madness, he was taken away to the madhouse.

Before continuing my narration of what happened further to the unfortunate Nathanael, I will tell you, indulgent reader, in case you take any interest in that skillful mechanician and fabricator of automata, Spalanzani, that he recovered completely from his wounds. He had, however, to leave the university, for Nathanael's fate had created a great sensation; and the opinion was pretty generally expressed that it was an imposture altogether unpardonable to have smuggled a wooden puppet instead of a living person into intelligent tea-circles—for Olimpia had been present at several with success. Lawyers called it a cunning piece of knavery, and all the harder to punish since it was directed against the public; and it had been so craftily contrived that it had escaped unobserved by all except a few preternaturally acute students, although everybody was very wise now and remembered to have thought of several facts which occurred to them as suspicious. But these latter could not succeed in making out any sort of a consistent tale. For was it, for instance, a thing likely to occur to anyone as suspicious that, according to the declaration of an elegant beau of these tea-parties, Olimpia had, contrary to all good manners, sneezed oftener than she had yawned? The former must have been, in the opinion of this elegant gentleman, the winding up of the concealed clockwork; it had always been accompanied by an observable creaking, and so on.

The Professor of Poetry and Eloquence took a pinch of snuff, and, slapping the lid to and clearing his throat, said solemnly, "My most honourable ladies and gentlemen, don't you see then where the rub is? The whole thing is an allegory, a continuous metaphor. You understand me? *Sapienti sat.*"

But several most honourable gentlemen did not rest satisfied with this explanation; the history of this automaton had sunk deeply into their souls, and an absurd mistrust of human figures began to prevail. Several lovers, in order to be fully convinced that they were not paying court to a wooden puppet, required that their mistress should sing and dance a little out of time, should embroider or knit or play with her little pug, &c., when being read to, but above all things else that she should do something more than merely listen—that she should frequently speak in such a way as to really show that her words presupposed as a condition some thinking and feeling. The bonds of love were in many cases drawn closer in consequence, and so of course became more engaging; in other instances they gradually relaxed and fell away. "I cannot really be made responsible for it," was the remark of more than one young gallant.

At the tea-gatherings everybody, in order to ward off suspicion, yawned to an incredible extent and never sneezed. Spalanzani was obliged, as has been said, to leave the place in order to escape a criminal charge of having fraudulently imposed an automaton upon human society. Coppola, too, had also disappeared.

When Nathanael awoke he felt as if he had been oppressed by a terrible nightmare; he opened his eyes and experienced an indescribable sensation of mental comfort, while a soft and most beautiful sensation of warmth pervaded his body. He lay on his own bed in his own room at home; Clara was bending over him, and at a little distance stood his mother and Lothair. "At last, at last, O my darling

Nathanael; now we have you again; now you are cured of your grievous illness, now you are mine again." And Clara's words came from the depths of her heart; and she clasped him in her arms. The bright scalding tears streamed from his eyes, he was so overcome with mingled feelings of sorrow and delight; and he gasped forth, "My Clara, my Clara!"

Siegmund, who had staunchly stood by his friend in his hour of need, now came into the room. Nathanael gave him his hand—"My faithful brother, you have not deserted me." Every trace of insanity had left him, and in the tender hands of his mother and his beloved, and his friends, he quickly recovered his strength again. Good fortune had in the meantime visited the house; a niggardly old uncle, from whom they had never expected to get anything, had died, and left Nathanael's mother not only a considerable fortune, but also a small estate, pleasantly situated not far from the town. There they resolved to go and live, Nathanael and his mother, and Clara, to whom he was now to be married, and Lothair. Nathanael had become gentler and more childlike than he had ever been before, and now began really to understand Clara's supremely pure and noble character. None of them ever reminded him, even in the remotest degree, of the past. But when Siegmund took leave of him, Nathanael said, "By heaven, brother! I was in a bad way, but an angel came just at the right moment and led me back upon the path of light. Yes, it was Clara." Siegmund would not let him speak further, fearing lest the painful recollections of the past might arise too vividly and too intensely in his mind.

The time came for the four happy people to move to their little property. At noon they were going through the streets. After making several purchases they found that the lofty tower of the town hall was throwing its giant shadows across the market place. "Come," said Clara, "let us go up to the top once more and have a look at the distant hills." No sooner said than done. Both of them, Nathanael and Clara, went up the tower; their mother, however, went on with the servant-girl to her new home, and Lothair, not feeling inclined to climb up all the many steps, waited below. There the two lovers stood arm in arm on the topmost gallery of the tower, and gazed out into the sweet-scented wooded landscape, beyond which the blue hills rose up like a giant's city.

"Oh! do look at that strange little gray bush, it looks as if it were actually walking towards us," said Clara. Mechanically he put his hand into his side pocket; he found Coppola's perspective and looked for the bush; Clara stood in front of the glass.

Then a convulsive thrill shot through his pulse and veins; pale as a corpse, he fixed his staring eyes upon her; but soon they began to roll, and a fiery current flashed and sparkled in them, and he yelled fearfully, like a hunted animal. Leaping up high in the air and laughing horribly at the same time, he began to shout in a piercing voice, "Spin round, wooden doll! Spin round, wooden doll!" With the strength of a giant he laid hold upon Clara and tried to hurl her over, but in an agony of despair she clutched fast hold of the railing that went round the gallery.

Lothair heard the madman raging and Clara's scream of terror: a fearful presentiment flashed across his mind. He ran up the steps; the door of the second flight was locked. Clara's scream for help rang out more loudly. Mad with rage and fear, he threw himself against the door, which at length gave way. Clara's cries were growing fainter and fainter—"Help! save me! save me!" and her voice died away in the air. "She is killed—murdered by that madman," shouted Lothair. The door to the gallery was also locked.

Despair gave him the strength of a giant; he burst the door off its hinges. Good God! there was Clara in the grasp of the madman Nathanael, hanging over the gallery in the air, holding on to the iron bar with only one hand. Quick as lightning, Lothair seized his sister and pulled her back, at the same time dealing the madman a blow in the face with his doubled fist, which sent him reeling backwards, forcing him to let go his victim.

Lothair ran down with his insensible sister in his arms. She was saved. But Nathanael ran round and round the gallery, leaping up in the air and shouting, "Spin round, fire-wheel! Spin round, fire-wheel!" The people heard the wild shouting, and a crowd began to gather. In the midst of them towered the lawyer Coppelius, like a giant; he had only just arrived in the town, and had gone straight to the market place.

Some were for going up to overpower and take the madman, but Coppelius laughed and said, "Ha! ha! wait a bit; he'll come down of his own accord"; and he stood gazing up along with the rest.

All at once Nathanael stopped as if spellbound; he bent down over the railing and perceived Coppelius. With a piercing scream, "Eh! Fine eyes-a, fine eyes-a!" he leaped over the railing.

When Nathanael lay on the stone pavement with a shattered head, Coppelius had disappeared in the crush and confusion.

Several years afterwards it was reported that, outside the door of a pretty country house in a remote district, Clara had been seen sitting hand in hand with a pleasant gentleman, while two bright boys were playing at her feet. From this it may be concluded that she eventually found that quiet domestic happiness which her cheerful, blithesome character required, and which Nathanael, with his tempest-tossed soul, could never have been able to give her.

SIR WALTER SCOTT

Wandering Willie's Tale

(1824)

In Walter Scott's historical tale about Scotland in the seventeenth century, the beyond is virtually identical to the kind of life the damned souls led in life. It is a feudal inferno where people eat, drink, and dance. But the living being who through an authorized intercession (the devil in the form of a gentleman) gains access to that world, must resist the temptations offered him there. Lord help him if he brings to his lips the Scottish flute he's asked to play! It is ablaze with the incandescent heat of the infernal fires. And if he accepts a taste of food or drink, he will never be able to return. The injunction against tasting the food in the land of the dead is an ancient belief, traces of which we find both in Homer (Ulysses in the land of the lotus eaters) and in Oriental religions.

Local legends and traditions constitute one of the inexhaustible sources of fantastic literature. Here the supernatural in religious legends mixes with the art of the historical novel, of which Walter Scott

(1771–1832) may be considered a precursor. To that is added the liveliness of a tale told in the first person, an antecedent of the detective story. Another unforeseeable element is the important role played by a monkey, an animal that since Bandello and the Renaissance serves the purposes of the fantastic genre.

YE MAUN have heard of Sir Robert Redgauntlet of that Ilk, who lived in these parts before the dear years. The country will lang mind him; and our fathers used to draw breath thick if ever they heard him named. He was out wi' the Hielandmen in Montrose's time; and again he was in the hills wi' Glencairn in the saxteen hundred and fifty-twa; and sae when King Charles the Second came in, wha was in sic favour as the Laird of Redgauntlet? He was knighted at Lonon court, wi' the King's ain sword; and being a red-hot prelatist, he came down here, rampauging like a lion, with commissions of lieutenancy, and of lunacy for what I ken, to put down a' the Whigs and Covenanters in the country. Wild wark they made of it; for the Whigs were as dour as the Cavaliers were fierce, and it was which should first tire the other. Redgauntlet was aye for the stronghand; and his name is kenn'd as wide in the country as Claverhouse's or Tam Dalyell's. Glen, nor dargle, nor mountain, nor cave, could hide the puir hill-folk when Redgauntlet was out with bugle and bloodhound after them, as if they had been sae mony deer. And troth when they fand them, they didna mak muckle mair ceremony than a Hielandman wi' a roe-buck—It was just, "Will ye tak the test?"—if not, "Make ready—present—fire!"—and there lay the recusant.

Far and wide was Sir Robert hated and feared. Men thought he had a direct compact with Satan—that he was proof against steel—and that bullets happed aff his buff-coat like hail-stanes from a hearth—that he had a mear that would turn a hare on the side of Carrifra-gawns—and muckle to the same purpose, of whilk mair anon. The best blessing they wared on him was, "De'il scowp wi' Redgauntlet!" He wasna a bad master to his ain folk though, and was weel aneugh liked by his tenants; and as for the lackies and troopers that raid out wi' him to the persecutions, as the Whigs ca'ad these killing times, they wad hae drunken themsels blind to his health at ony time.

Now ye are to ken that my gudesire lived on Redgauntlet's grund—they ca' the place Primrose-Knowe. We had lived on the grund, and under the Redgauntlets, since the riding days, and lang before. It was a pleasant bit; and I think the air is callerer and fresher there than onywhere else in the country. It's a' deserted now; and I sat on the broken doorcheck three days since, and was glad I couldna see the plight the place was in; but that's a' wide o' the mark. There dwelt my gudesire, Steenie Steenson, a rambling, rattling chiel' he had been in his young days, and could play weel on the pipes; he was famous at "Hoopers and Girders"—a' Cumberland couldna touch him at "Jockie Lattin"—and he had the finest finger for the back-lill between Berwick and Carlisle. The like o' Steenie wasna the sort that they made Whigs o'. And so he became a Tory, as they ca' it, which we now ca' Jacobites, just out of a kind of needcessity, that he might belang to some side or other. He had nae ill-will to the Whig bodies, and likedna to see the blude rin, though, being obliged to follow Sir Robert in hunting and hosting, watching and warding, he saw muckle mischief, and maybe did some, that he couldna avoid.

Now Steenie was a kind of favourite with his master, and kenn'd a' the folks about the castle, and was often sent for to play the pipes when they were at their merriment. Auld Dougal MacCallum, the butler, that had followed Sir Robert through gude and ill, thick and thin, pool and stream, was specially fond of the pipes, and aye gae my gudesire his gude word wi' the Laird; for Dougal could turn his master round his finger.

Weel, round came the Revolution, and it had like to have broken the hearts baith of Dougal and his master. But the change was not a'thegether sae great as they feared, and other folk thought for. The Whigs made an unca crawing what they wad do with their auld enemies, and in special wi' Sir Robert Redgauntlet. But there were ower mony great folks dipped in the same doings, to make a spick and span new warld. So Parliament passed it a' ower easy; and Sir Robert, bating that he was held to hunting foxes instead of Covenanters, remained just the man he was. His revel was as loud, and his hall as weel lighted, as ever it had been, though maybe he lacked the fines of the non-conformists, that used to come to stock larder and cellar; for it is certain he began to be keener about the rents than his tenants used to find him before, and they behoved to be prompt to the rent-day, or else the Laird wasna pleased. And he was sic an awsome body, that naebody cared to anger him; for the oaths he swore, and the rage that he used to get into, and the looks that he put on, made men sometimes think him a deevil incarnate.

Weel, my gudesire was nae manager—no that he was a very great misguider—but he hadna the saving gift, and he got twa terms rent in arrear. He got the first brash at Whitsunday put ower wi' fair words and piping; but when Martinmas came, there was a summons from the grund-officer to come wi' the rent on a day preceese, or else Steenie behoved to flitt. Sair wark he had to get the siller; but he was weel-freended, and at last he got the haill scraped thegether—a thousand merks—the maist of it was from a neighbour they ca'd Laurie Lapraik—a sly tod. Laurie had walth o' gear—could hunt wi' the hound and rin wi' the hare—and be Whig or Tory, saunt or sinner, as the wind stood. He was a professor in this Revolution warld, but he liked an orra sound and a tune on the pipes weel aneugh at a bye-time; and abune a', he thought he had gude security for the siller he lent my gudesire over the stocking at Primrose-Knowe.

Away trots my gudesire to Redgauntlet Castle wi' a heavy purse and a light heart, glad to be out of the Laird's danger. Weel, the first thing he learned at the Castle was, that Sir Robert had fretted himsell into a fit of the gout, because he did not appear before twelve o'clock. It wasna a'thegether for sake of the money, Dougal thought; but because he didna like to part wi' my gudesire aff the grund. Dougal was glad to see Steenie, and brought him into the great oak parlour, and there sat the Laird his leesome lane, excepting that he had beside him a great, ill-favoured jackanape, that was a special pet of his; a cankered beast it was, and mony an ill-natured trick it played—ill to please it was, and easily angered—ran about the haill castle, chattering and yowling, and pinching, and biting folk, specially before ill-weather, or disturbances in the state. Sir Robert ca'ad it Major Weir, after the warlock that was burned; and few folk liked either the name or the conditions of the creature—they thought there was something in it by ordinar—and my gudesire was not just easy in mind when the door shut on him, and he saw himself in the room wi' naebody but the Laird, Dougal MacAllum, and the Major, a thing that hadna chanced to him before.

Sir Robert sat, or, I should say, lay, in a great armed chair, wi' his grand velvet gown, and his feet on a cradle; for he had baith gout and gravel, and his face looked as gash and ghastly as Satan's. Major Weir sat opposite to him, in a red-laced coat, and the Laird's wig on his head; and aye as Sir Robert girned wi' pain, the jackanape girned too, like a sheep's-head between a pair of tangs—an ill-faur'd, fearsome couple they were. The Laird's buff-coat was hung on a pin behind him, and his broadsword and his pistols within reach; for he keepit up the auld fashion of having the weapons ready, and a horse saddled day and night, just as he used to do when he was able to loup on horseback, and away after ony of the hill-folk he could get speerings of. Some said it was for fear of the Whigs taking vengeance, but I judge it was just his auld custom—he wasna gien to fear onything. The rental-book, wi' its black cover and brass clasps, was lying beside him; and a book of sculduddry sangs was put betwixt the leaves, to keep it open at the place where it bore evidence against the Goodman of Primrose-Knowe, as behind the hand with his mails and duties. Sir Robert gave my gudesire a look, as if he would have withered his heart in his bosom. Ye maun ken he had a way of bending his brows, that men saw the visible mark of a horse-shoe in his forehead, deep-dinted, as if it had been stamped there.

"Are ye come light-handed, ye son of a toom whistle?" said Sir Robert. "Zounds! if you are. . . ."

My gudesire, with as gude a countenance as he could put on, made a leg, and placed the bag of money on the table wi' a dash, like a man that does something clever. The Laird drew it to him hastily—"Is it all here, Steenie, man?"

"Your honour will find it right," said my gudesire.

"Here, Dougal," said the Laird, "gie Steenie a tass of brandy down stairs, till I count the siller and write the receipt."

But they werena weel out of the room, when Sir Robert gied a yelloch that garr'd the castle rock. Back ran Dougal—in flew the liverymen—yell on yell gied the Laird, ilk ane mair awfu' than the ither. My gudesire knew not whether to stand or flee, but he ventured back into the parlour, where a' was gaun hirdy-girdie—naebody to say "come in" or "gae out." Terribly the Laird roared for cauld water to his feet, and wine to cool his throat; and, Hell, hell, hell, and its flames, was aye the word in his mouth. They brought him water, and when they plunged his swoln feet into the tub, he cried out it was burning; and folk say that it *did* bubble and sparkle like a seething cauldron. He flung the cup at Dougal's head, and said he had given him blood instead of burgundy; and, sure aneugh, the lass washed clottered blood aff the carpet the neist day. The jackanape they ca'd Major Weir, it jibbered and cried as if it was mocking its master; my gudesire's head was like to turn—he forgot baith siller and receipt, and down stairs he banged; but as he ran, the shrieks came faint and fainter; there was a deep-drawn shivering groan, and word gaed through the Castle, that the Laird was dead.

Weel, away came my gudesire, wi' his finger in his mouth, and his best hope was, that Dougal had seen the money-bag, and heard the Laird speak of writing the receipt. The young Laird, now Sir John, came from Edinburgh, to see things put to rights. Sir John and his father never gree'd weel—he had been bred an advocate, and afterwards sat in the last Scots Parliament and voted for the Union, having gotten, it was thought, a rug of the compensations—if his father could have come out of his grave, he would have brained him for it on his awn hearthstane. Some thought it was easier counting with the auld rough Knight than the fair-spoken young ane—but mair of that anon.

Dougal MacCallum, poor body, neither grat nor graned, but gaed about the house looking like a corpse, but directing, as was his duty, a' the order of the grand funeral. Now, Dougal looked aye waur and waur when night was coming, and was aye the last to gang to his bed, whilk was in a little round just opposite the chamber of dais, whilk his master occupied while he was living, and where he now lay in as they ca-ad it, well-a-day! The night before the funeral, Dougal could keep his awn counsel nae langer; he came doun with his proud spirit, and fairly asked auld Hutcheon to sit in his room with him for an hour. When they were in the round, Dougal took ae tass of brandy to himsel, and gave another to Hutcheon, and wished him all health and lang life, and said that, for himsel, he wasna lang for this world; for that, every night since Sir Robert's death, his silver call had sounded from the state chamber, just as it used to do at nights in his lifetime, to call Dougal to help to turn him in his bed. Dougal said, that being alone with the dead on that floor of the tower, (for nae-body cared to wake Sir Robert Redgauntlet like another corpse), he had never daured to answer the call, but that now his conscience checked him for neglecting his duty; for, "though death breaks service," said MacCallum, "it shall never break my service to Sir Robert; and I will answer his next whistle, so be you will stand by me, Hutcheon."

Hutcheon had nae will to the wark, but he had stood by Dougal in battle and broil, and he wad not fail him at this pinch; so down the carles sat over a stoup of brandy, and Hutcheon, who was something of a clerk, would have read a chapter of the Bible; but Dougal would hear naething but a blaud of Davie Lindsay, whilk was the waur preparation.

When midnight came, and the house was quiet as the grave, sure aneugh the silver whistle sounded as sharp and shrill as if Sir Robert was blowing it, and up got the twa auld serving-men, and tottered into the room where the dead man lay. Hutcheon saw aneugh at the first glance; for there were torches in the room, which shewed him the foul fiend, in his ain shape, sitting on the Laird's coffin! Over he cowped as if he had been dead. He could not tell how lang he lay in a trance at the door, but when he gathered himself, he cried on his neighbour, and getting no answer, raised the house, when Dougal was found lying dead within twa steps of the bed where his master's coffin was placed. As for the whistle, it was gaen anes and aye; but mony a time was it heard on the top of the house in the bartizan, and amang the auld chimnies and turrets, where the howlets have their nests. Sir John hushed the matter up, and the funeral passed over without mair bogle-wark.

But when a' was over, and the Laird was beginning to settle his affairs, every tenant was called up for his arrears, and my gudesire for the full sum that stood against him in the rental-book. Weel, away he trots to the Castle, to tell his story, and there he is introduced to Sir John, sitting in his father's chair, in deep mourning, with weepers and hanging cravat, and a small walking rapier by his side, instead of the auld broad-sword that had a hundred-weight of steel about it, what with blade, chape, and basket-hilt. I have heard their communing so often tauld ower, that I almost think I was there mysell, though I couldna be born at the time. (In fact, Alan, my companion mimicked, with a good deal of humour, the flattering, conciliating tone of the tenant's address, and the hypocritical melancholy of the Laird's reply. His grandfather, he said, had, while he spoke, his eye fixed on the rental-book, as if it were a mastiff-dog that he was afraid would spring up and bite him.)

"I wuss ye joy, sir, of the head-seat, and the white loaf, and the braid lairdship. Your father was a kind man to friends and followers; muckle grace to you, Sir John, to fill his shoon—his boots, I suld say, for he seldom wore shoon, unless it were muils when he had the gout."

"Ay, Steenie," quoth the Laird, sighing deeply, and putting his napkin to his een, "his was a sudden call, and he will be missed in the country; no time to set his house in order—weel prepared God-ward, no doubt, which is the root of the matter—but left us behind a tangled hesp to wind, Steenie. —Hem! hem! We maun go to business, Steenie; much to do, and little time to do it in."

Here he opened the fatal volume; I have heard of a thing they call Doomsday-book—I am clear it has been a rental of back-ganging tenants.

"Stephen," said Sir John, still in the same soft, sleekit tone of voice—"Stephen Stevenson, or Steenson, ye are down here for a year's rent behind the hand—due at last term."

Stephen. "Please your honour, Sir John, I paid it to your father."

Sir John. "Ye took a receipt then, doubtless, Stephen; and can produce it?"

Stephen. "Indeed I hadna time, an it like your honour; for nae sooner had I set doun the siller, and just as his honour, Sir Robert, that's gaen, drew it till him to count it, and write out the receipt, he was ta'en wi' the pains that removed him."

"That was unlucky," said Sir John, after a pause. "But ye maybe paid it in the presence of somebody. I wan but a *talis qualis* evidence, Stephen. I would go ower strictly to work with no poor man."

Stephen. "Troth, Sir John, there was naebody in the room but Dougal MacCallum the butler. But, as your honour kens, he has e'en followed his auld master."

"Very unlucky again, Stephen," said Sir John, without altering his voice a single note. "The man to whom ye paid the money is dead—and the man who witnessed the payment is dead too—and the siller, which should have been to the fore, is neither seen nor heard tell of in the repositories. How am I to believe a' this?"

Stephen. "I dinna ken, your honour; but there is a bit memorandum note of the very coins; for, God help me! I had to borrow out of twenty purses; and I am sure that ilk man there set down will take his grit oath for what purpose I borrowed the money."

Sir John. "I have little doubt ye *borrowed* the money, Steenie. It is the *payment* that I want to have some proof of."

Stephen. "The siller maun be about the house, Sir John. And since your honour never got it, and his honour that was canna have taen it wi' him, maybe some of the family may have seen it."

Sir John. "We will examine the servants, Stephen; that is but reasonable."

But lackey and lass, and page and groom, all denied stoutly that they had ever seen such a bag of money as my gudesire described. What was waur, he had unluckily not mentioned to any living soul of them his purpose of paying his rent. Ae quean had noticed something under his arm, but she took it for the pipes.

Sir John Redgauntlet ordered the servants out of the room, and then said to my gudesire, "Now, Steenie, ye see you have fair play; and, as I have little doubt ye ken better where to find the siller than ony other body, I beg, in fair terms, and for your own sake, that you will end this fasherie; for, Stephen, ye maun pay or flitt."

"The Lord forgie your opinion," said Stephen, driven almost to his wits' end—"I am an honest man."

"So am I, Stephen," said his honour; "and so are all the folks in the house, I hope. But if there be a knave amongst us, it must be he that tells the story he cannot prove." He paused, and then added, mair sternly, "If I understand your trick, sir, you want to take advantage of some malicious reports concerning things in this family, and particularly respecting my father's sudden death, thereby to cheat me out of the money, and perhaps take away my character, by insinuating that I have received the rent I am demanding. —Where do you suppose this money to be? —I insist upon knowing."

My gudesire saw everything look so muckle against him, that he grew nearly desperate—however, he shifted from one foot to another, looked to every corner of the room, and made no answer.

"Speak out, sirrah," said the Laird, assuming a look of his father's, a very particular ane, which he had when he was angry—it seemed as if the wrinkles of his frown made that self-same fearful shape of a horse's shoe in the middle of his brow; —"Speak out, sir! I *will* know your thoughts; do you suppose that I have this money?"

"Far be it frae me to say so," said Stephen.

"Do you charge any of my people with having taken it?"

"I wad be laith to charge them that may be innocent," said my gudesire; "and if there by any one that is guilty, I have nae proof."

"Somewhere the money must be, if there is a word of truth in your story," said Sir John; "I ask where you think it is—and demand a correct answer."

"In hell, if you will have my thoughts of it," said my gudesire, driven to extremity,—"in hell! with your father and his silver whistle."

Down the stairs he ran (for the parlour was nae place for him after such a word) and he heard the Laird swearing blood and wounds behind him, as fast as ever did Sir Robert, and roaring for the baillie and the baron-officer.

Away rode my gudesire to his chief creditor (him they ca'd Laurie Lapraik), to try if he could make onything out of him; but when he tauld his story, he got but the warst word in his wame—thief, beggar, and dyvour, were the safest terms; and to the boot of these hard terms, Laurie brought up the auld story of his dipping his hand in the blood of God's saints, just as if a tenant could have helped riding with the Laird, and that a laird like Sir Robert Redgauntlet. My gudesire was, by this time, far beyond the bounds of patience, and, while he and Laurie were at de'il speed the liars, he was wanchancie aneugh to abuse his doctrine was weel as the man, and said things that gar'd folks flesh grew that heard them; —he wasna just himsell, and he had lived wi' a wild set in his day.

At last they parted, and my gudesire was to ride hame through the wood of Pitmarkie, that is a' fou of black firs, as they say. —I ken the wood, but the firs may be black or white for what I can tell. —At the entry of the wood there is a wild common, and on the edge of the common, a little lonely change-house, that was keepit then by an ostler-wife, they suld hae ca'd her Tibbie Faw, and there puir Steenie cried for a mutchkin of brandy, for he had had no refreshment the hail day. Tibbie was earnest wi him to take a bite of meat, but he couldna think o't, nor would he take his foot out of the stirrup, and took off the brandy wholely at twa draughts, and named a toast at each: —the first was, the memory of Sir Robert Redgauntlet, and might he never lie quiet in his grave till he had righted his poor bond-tenant; and the second was, a health to Man's Enemy, if he would but get him back the pock of siller, or tell him what came o't, for he saw the hail world was like to regard him as a thief and a cheat, and he took that waur than even the ruin of his house and hauld.

On he rode, little caring where. It was a dark night turned, and the trees made it yet darker, and he let the beast take its ain road through the wood; when, all of a sudden, from tired and wearied that it was before, the nag began to spring, and flee, and stend, that my gudesire could hardly keep the saddle—Upon the whilk, a horseman, suddenly riding up beside him, said, "That's a mettle beast of yours, freend; will you sell him?"—So saying, he touched the horse's neck with his riding-wand, and it fell into its auld heigh-ho of a stumbling trot; "But his spunk's soon out of him, I think," continued the stranger, "and that is like mony a man's courage, that thinks he wad do great things till he come to the proof."

My gudesire scarce listened to this, but spurred his horse, with "Gude e'en to you, freend."

But it's like the stranger was ane that does na lightly yield his point; for, ride as Steenie liked, he was aye beside him at the self-same pace. At last my gudesire, Steenie Steenson, grew half angry; and, to say the truth, half feared.

"What is that ye want with me, freend?" he said. "If ye be a robber, I have nae money; if ye be a leal man, wanting company, I have nae heart to mirth or speaking; and if ye want to ken the road, I scarce ken it mysell."

"If you will tell me your grief," said the stranger, "I am one that, though I have been sair miscaad in the world, am the only hand for helping my friends."

So my gudesire, to ease his ain heart, mair than from any hope of help, told him the story from beginning to end.

"It's a hard pinch," said the stranger; "but I think I can help you."

"If you could lend the money, sir, and take a lang day—I ken nae other help on earth," said my gudesire.

"But there may be some under the earth," said the stranger. "Come, I'll be frank wi' you; I could lend you the money on bond, but you would maybe scruple my terms. Now, I can tell you, that your auld Laird is disturbed in his grave by your curses, and the wailing of your family, and—if ye daur venture to go to see him, he will give you the receipt."

My gudesire's hair stood on end at this proposal, but he thought his companion might be some humoursome chield that was trying to frighten him, and might end with lending him the money. Besides, he was bauld wi' brandy, and desperate wi' distress; and he said, he had courage to go to the gate of hell, and a step farther, for that receipt.—The stranger laughed.

Weel, they rode on through the thickest of the wood, when, all of a sudden, the horse stopped at the door of a great house; and, but that he knew the place was ten miles off, my father would have thought he was at Redgauntlet Castle. They rode into the outer-yard, through the muckle faulding yetts, and aneath the auld portcullis; and the whole front of the house was lighted, and there were pipes and fiddles, and as much dancing and deray within as used to be in Sir Robert's house at Pace and Yule, and such high seasons. They lap off, and my gudesire, as seemed to him, fastened his horse to the very ring he had tied him to that morning, when he gaed to wait on the young Sir John.

"God!" said my father, "if Sir Robert's death be but a dream!"

He knocked at the ha' door, just as he wont, and his auld acquaintance, Dougal MacCallum, just after his wont, too,—came to open the door, and said, "Piper Steenie, are ye there, lad? Sir Robert has been crying for you."

My gudesire was like a man in a dream—he looked for the stranger, but he was gaen for the time. At last, he just tried to say, "Ha! Dougal Driveower, are ye living? I thought ye had been dead."

"Never fash yoursell wi' me," said Dougal, "but look to yoursell; and see ye tak naething frae onybody here, neither meat, drink, or siller, except just the receipt that is your ain."

So saying, he led the way out through halls and trances that were weel kenn'd to my gudesire, and into the auld oak parlour; and there was as much singing of profane sangs, and birling of red wine, and speaking blasphemy and sculduddry, as had ever been in Redgauntlet Castle when it was at the blythest.

But, Lord take us in keeping! what a set of ghastly revellers they were that sat round that table!—My gudesire kenn'ed mony that had long before gane to their place. There was the fierce Middleton, and the dissolute Rothes, and the crafty Lauderdale; and Dalyell, with his bald head and a beard to his girdle; and Earlshall, with Cameron's blude on his hand; and wild Bonshaw, that tied blessed Mr. Cargill's limbs till the blude sprung; and Dumbarton Douglas, the twice-turned traitor baith to country and king. There was the Bluidy Advocate MacKenyie, who, for his wordly wit and wisdom, had been to the rest as a god. And there was Claverhouse, as beautiful as when he lived, with his long, dark, curled locks, streaming down to his laced buff-coat, and his left hand always on his right spule-blade, to hide the wound that the silver bullet had made. He sat apart from them all, and looked at them with a melancholy, haughty countenance; while the rest hallooed, and sung, and laughed, that the room rang. But their smiles were fearfully contorted from time to time; and their laughter passed into such wild sounds, as made my gudesire's very nails grow blue, and chilled the marrow in his banes.

They that waited at the table were just the wicked serving-men and troopers, that had done their work and wicked bidding on earth. There was the Lang Lad of the Nethertown, that helped to take Argyle; and the Bishop's summoner, that they called the De'il's Rattle-bag; and the wicked guardsmen, in their laced coats; and the savage Highland Amorites, that shed blood like water; and many a proud serving-man, haughty of heart and bloody of hand, cringing to the rich, and making them wickeder than they would be; grinding the poor to powder, when the rich had broken them to fragments. And mony, mony mair were coming and ganging, a' as busy in their vocation as if they had been alive.

Sir Robert Redgauntlet, in the midst of a' this fearful riot, cried, wi' a voice like thunder, on Steenie Piper, to come to the board-head where he was sitting; his legs stretched out before him, and swathed up with flannel, with his holster pistols aside him, and the great broad-sword rested against his chair, just as my gudesire had seen him the last time upon earth—the very cushion for the jackanape was close to him, but the creature itsell was not there—it wasna its hour, it's likely; for he heard them say as he came forward, "Is not the Major come yet?" And another answered, "The jackanape will be here betimes the morn." And when my gudesire came forward, Sir Robert, or his ghaist, or the deevil in his likeness, said, "Weel, piper, hae ye settled wi' my son for the year's rent?"

With much ado my father gat breath to say, that Sir John would not settle without his honour's receipt.

"Ye shall hae that for a tune of the pipes, Steenie," said the appearance of Sir Robert—"Play us up 'Weel hoddled, Luckie.' "

Now this was a tune my gudesire learned frae a warlock, that heard it when they were worshipping Satan at their meetings; and my gudesire had sometimes played it at the ranting suppers in Redgauntlet Castle, but never very willingly; and now he grew cauld at the very name of it, and said, for excuse, he hadna his pipes wi' him.

"MacCallum, ye limb of Beelzebub," said the fearfu' Sir Robert, "bring Steenie the pipes that I am keeping for him!"

MacCallum brought a pair of pipes might have served the piper of Donald of the Isles. But he gave my gudesire a nudge as he offered them; and looking secretly and closely, Steenie saw that the chanter was of steel, and heated to a white heat; so he had fair warning not to trust his fingers with it. So he excused himself again, and said, he was faint and frightened, and had not wind aneugh to fill the bag.

"Then ye maun eat and drink, Steenie," said the figure; "for we do little else here; and it's ill speaking between a fou man and a fasting."

Now these were the very words that the bloody Earl of Douglas said to keep the King's messenger in hand, while he cut the head off MacLellan of Bombie, at the Threave Castle; and that put Steenie mair and mair on his guard. So he spoke up like a man, and said he came neither to eat, or drink, or make minstrelsy; but simply for his ain—to ken what was come o' the money he had paid, and to get a discharge for it; and he was so stout-hearted by this time, that he charged Sir Robert for conscience-sake—(he had no power to say the holy name)—and as he hoped for peace and rest, to spread no snares for him, but just to give him his ain.

The appearance gnashed its teeth and laughed, but it took from a large pocket-book the receipt, and handed it to Steenie. "Here is your receipt, ye pitiful cur; and for the money, my dog-whelp of a son may go look for it in the Cat's Cradle."

My gudesire uttered mony thanks, and was about to retire, when Sir Robert roared aloud, "Stop though, thou sack-doudling son of a whore! I am not done with thee. HERE we do nothing for nothing; and you must return on this very day twelvemonth, to pay your master the homage that you owe me for my protection."

My father's tongue was loosed of a suddenty, and he said aloud, "I refer mysell to God's pleasure, and not to yours."

He had no sooner uttered the word than all was dark around him; and he sunk on the earth with such a sudden shock, that he lost both breath and sense.

How lang Steenie lay there, he could not tell; but when he came to himsell, he was lying in the auld kirkyard of Redgauntlet parishine, just at the door of the family aisle, and the scutcheon of the auld knight, Sir Robert, hanging over his head. There was a deep morning fog on grass and gravestone around him, and his horse was feeding quietly beside the minister's twa cows. Steenie would have thought the whole was a dream, but he had the receipt in his hand, fairly written and signed by the auld Laird; only the last letters of his name were a little disorderly, written like one seized with sudden pain.

Sorely troubled in his mind, he left that dreary place, rode through the mist to Redgauntlet Castle, and with much ado he got speech of the Laird. "Well, you dyvour bankrupt," was the first word, "have you brought me my rent?"

"No," answered my gudesire, "I have not; but I have brought your honour Sir Robert's receipt for it."

"How, sirrah?—Sir Robert's receipt!—You told me he had not given you one."

"Will your honour please to see if that bit line is right?"

Sir John looked at every line, and at every letter, with much attention; and at last, at the date, which my gudesire had not observed,—"*From my appointed place*," he read, "*this twenty-fifth of November*."—"What!—That is yesterday! Villain, thou must have gone to hell for this!"

"I got it from your honour's father—whether he be in heaven or hell, I know not," said Steenie.

"I will delate you for a warlock to the Privy Council!" said Sir John. "I will send you to your master, the devil, with the help of a tar-barrel and a torch!"

"I intend to delate mysell to the Presbytery," said Steenie, "and tell them all I have seen last night, whilk are things fitter for them to judge of than a borrel man like me."

Sir John paused, composed himsell, and desired to hear the full history; and my gudesire told it him from point to point, as I have told it you—word for word, neither more nor less.

Sir John was silent again for a long time, and at last he said, very composedly, "Steenie, this story of yours concerns the honour of many a noble family besides mine; and if it be a leasing-making, to keep yourself out of my danger, the least you can expect is to have a red-hot iron driven through your tongue, and that will be as bad as scauding your fingers wi' a red-hot chanter. But yet it may be true, Steenie; and if the money cast up, I will not know what to think of it.—But where shall we find the Cat's Cradle? There are cats enough about the old house, but I think they kitten without the ceremony of bed or cradle."

"We were best ask Hutcheon," said my gudesire; "he kens a' the odd corners about as weel as—another serving-man that is now gane, and that I wad not like to name."

Aweel, Hutcheon, when he was asked, told them, that a ruinous turret, lang disused, next to the clock-house, only accessible by a ladder, for the opening was on the outside, and far above the battlements, was called of old the Cat's Cradle.

"There will I go immediately," said Sir John; and he took (with what purpose, Heaven kens) one of his father's pistols from the hall-table, where they had lain since the night he died, and hastened to the battlements.

It was a dangerous place to climb, for the ladder was auld and frail, and wanted ane or twa rounds. However, up got Sir John, and entered at the turret door, where his body stopped the only little light that was in the bit turret. Something flees at him wi' a vengeance, maist dang him back ower—bang gaed the knight's pistol, and Hutcheon, that held the ladder, and my gudesire that stood beside him, hears a loud skelloch. A minute after, Sir John flings the body of the jackanape down to them, and cries that the siller is fund, and that they should come up and help him. And there was the bag of siller sure aneugh, and mony orra things besides, that had been missing for mony a day. And Sir John, when he had riped the turret weel, led my gudesire into the dining-parlour, and took him by the hand, and spoke kindly to him, and said he was sorry he should have doubted his word, and that he would hereafter be a good master to him, to make amends.

"And now, Steenie," said Sir John, "although this vision of yours tends, on the whole, to my father's credit, as an honest man, that he should, even after his death, desire to see justice done to a poor man like you, yet you are sensible that ill-dispositioned men might make bad constructions upon it, concerning his soul's health. So, I think, we had better lay the hail dirdum on that ill-deedie creature, Major Weir, and say naething about your dream in the wood of Pitmurkie. You had taken ower mickle brandy to be very certain about onything; and, Steenie, this receipt (his hand shook while he held it out)—it's but a queer kind of document, and we will do best, I think, to put it quietly in the fire."

"Od, but for as queer as it is, it's a' the voucher I have for my rent," said my gudesire, who was afraid, it may be, of losing the benefit of Sir Robert's discharge.

"I will bear the contents to your credit in the rental-book, and give you a discharge under my own hand," said Sir John, "and that on the spot. And, Steenie, if you can hold your tongue about this matter, you shall sit, from this term downward, at an easier rent."

"Mony thanks to your honour," said Steenie, who saw easily in what corner the wind sat; "doubtless I will be conformable to all your honour's commands; only I would willingly speak wi' some powerful minister on the subject, for I do not like the sort of soumons of appointment whilk your honour's father—"

"Do not call the phantom my father!" said Sir John, interrupting him.

"Weel, then, the thing that was so like him,"—said my gudesire; "he spoke of my coming back to him this time twelvemonth, and it's a weight on my conscience."

"Aweel, then," said Sir John, "if you be so much distressed in mind, you may speak to our minister of the parish; he is a douce man, regards the honour of our family, and the mair that he may look for some patronage from me."

Wi' that, my father readily agreed that the receipt should be burnt, and the Laird threw it into the chimney with his ain hand. Burn it would not for them, though; but away it flew up the lumm, wi'a lang train of sparks at its tail, and a hissing noise like a squib.

My gudesire gaed down to the Manse, and the minister, when he had heard the story, said, it was his real opinion, that though my gudesire had gaen very far in tampering with dangerous matters, yet, as he had refused the devil's arles, (for such was the offer of meat and drink), and had refused to do homage by piping at his bidding, he hoped, that if he held a circumspect walk hereafter, Satan could take little advantage by what was come and gane. And, indeed, my gudesire, of his ain accord, lang forswore baith the pipes and brandy—it was not even till the year was out, and the fatal day passed, that he would so much as take the fiddle, or drink usquebaugh or tippenny.

Sir John made up his story about the jackanape as he liked himsell; and some believe till this day there was no more in the matter than the filching nature of the brute. Indeed ye'll no hinder some to threap, that it was nane o' the Auld Enemy that Dougal and my gudesire saw in the Laird's room, but only that wanchancy creature, the Major, capering on the coffin; and that, as to the blawing on the Laird's whistle that was heard after he was dead, the filthy brute could do that as weel as the Laird himsell, if no better. But Heaven kens the truth, whilk first came out by the minister's wife, after Sir John and her ain gudeman were baith in the moulds. And then my gudesire, wha was failed in his limbs, but not in his judgement or memory—at least nothing to speak of—was obliged to tell the real narrative to his friends, for the credit of his gude name. He might else have been charged for a warlock.

HONORÉ DE BALZAC

*

The Elixir of Life

(L'élixir de longue vie, 1830)

If Balzac's glory rests on The Human Comedy, *the great fresco of French society during his time, it is no less true that fantastic works occupy a significant place within his production, especially his first period, when he was more influenced by Swedenborg's occultism. A fantastic novel,* Peau de chagrin (The wild ass's skin) *(1831), is one of his best books. But even in the novels usually considered "realist," there is a strong component of the fantastic transfiguration that constitutes an essential element of his art.*

When Balzac undertook the project of The Human Comedy, *he left at the margin of his production the fantastic writing of his youth. "L'élixir de longue vie," first published in a magazine in 1830, was printed again among his* Études Philosophiques, *preceded by a headnote that presented the story as a moral study of heirs who impatiently wait for the death of their parents. I have not included that clever addition and present the text in its primitive version.*

The satantic aspect of a learned nature is an ancient medieval and Renaissance theme (e.g., Faust, the legends of the alchemists) that the nineteenth century, first the Romantics and later the Symbolists, took full advantage of (just think of Mary Shelley's Frankenstein, *a work not included in this anthology because of its length) and then passed on to science fiction.*

We are in sixteenth-century Ferrara. A rich old man has acquired an oriental unguent that revives the dead. Balzac has many ideas, perhaps too many: Renaissance Italy, both papal and pagan; pious and penitential Spain, the alchemical challenge to the laws of nature; the damnation of Don Juan (with the curious variation that it is Don Juan who turns into the stone dinner guest); and a spectacular ending replete with great ecclesiastical pomp as well as blasphemous sarcasm. But the story is successful because of the macabre effect of the body parts that live on their own: an eye, an arm, and even a head that, separating itself from the dead body, bites the skull of a living person, like Count Ugolino in Dante's Inferno.

To the Reader

At the very outset of the writer's literary career, a friend, long since dead, gave him the subject of this Study. Later on he found the same story in a collection published about the beginning of the present century. To the best of his belief, it is some stray fancy of the brain of Hoffmann of Berlin; probably it appeared in some German almanac, and was omitted in the published editions of his collected works. The *Comédie Humaine* is sufficiently rich in original creations for the author to own to this innocent piece of plagiarism; when, like the worthy La Fontaine, he has told unwittingly, and after his own fashion, a tale already related by another. This is not one of the hoaxes in vogue in the year 1830, when every author wrote his "tale of horror" for the amusement of young ladies. When you have read the account of Don Juan's decorous parricide, try to picture to yourself the part which would be played under very similar circumstances by honest folk who, in this nineteenth century, will take a man's money and undertake to pay him a life annuity on the faith of a chill, or let a house to an ancient lady for the term of her natural life. Would they be for resuscitating their clients? I should dearly like a connoisseur in consciences to consider how far there is a resemblance between a Don Juan and fathers who marry their children to great expectations. Does humanity, which, according to certain philosophers, is making progress, look on the art of waiting for dead men's shoes as a step in the right direction? To this art we owe several honorable professions, which open up ways of living on death. There are people who rely entirely on an expected demise; who brood over it, crouching each morning upon a corpse, that serves again for their pillow at night. To this class belong bishops' coadjutors, cardinals' supernumeraries, *tontiniers*, and the like. Add to the list many delicately scrupulous persons eager to buy landed property beyond their means, who calculate with dry logic and in cold blood the probable duration of the life of a father or of a stepmother, some old man or woman of eighty or ninety, saying to themselves, "I shall be sure to come in for it in three years' time, and then—" A murderer is less loathsome to us than a spy. The murderer may have acted on a sudden mad impulse; he may be penitent and amend; but a spy is always a spy, night and day, in bed, at table, as he walks abroad; his vileness pervades every moment of his life. Then what must it be to live when every moment of your life is tainted with murder? And have we not just admitted that a host of human creatures in our midst are led by our laws, customs, and usages to dwell without ceasing on a fellow-creature's death? There are men who put the weight of a coffin into their deliberations as they bargain for Cashmere shawls for their wives, as they go up the staircase of a theatre, or think of going to the Bouffons, or of setting up a carriage; who are murderers in thought when dear ones, with the irresistible charm of innocence, hold up childish foreheads to be kissed with a "Good-night, father!" Hourly they meet the gaze of eyes that they would fain close for ever, eyes that still open each morning to the light, like Belvidero's in this Study. God alone knows the number of those who are parricides in thought. Picture to yourself the state of mind of a man who must pay a life annuity to some old woman whom he scarcely knows; both live in the country with a brook between them, both sides are free to hate cordially, without offending against the social conventions that require two brothers to wear a mask if the older will succeed to the entail, and the other to the fortune of a younger son. The whole civilization of Europe turns upon the principle of hereditary succession as upon a pivot; it would be madness to subvert the principle; but could we not, in an age that prides itself upon its mechanical inventions, perfect this essential portion of the social machinery?

If the author has preserved the old-fashioned style of address *To the Reader* before a work wherein he endeavors to represent all literary forms, it is for the purpose of making a remark that applies to several of the Studies, and very specially to this. Every one of his compositions has been based upon ideas more or less novel, which, as it seemed to him, needed literary expression; he can claim priority for certain forms and for certain ideas which have since passed into the domain of literature, and have there, in some instances, become common property; so that the date of the first publication of each Study cannot be a matter of indifference to those of his readers who would fain do him justice.

Reading brings us unknown friends, and what friend is like a reader? We have friends in our own circle who read nothing of ours. The author hopes to pay his debt, by dedicating this work *Diis ignotis*.

ONE WINTER EVENING, in a princely palace at Ferrara, Don Juan Belvidero was giving a banquet to a prince of the house of Este. A banquet in those times was a marvelous spectacle which only royal wealth or the power of a mightly lord could furnish forth. Seated about a table lit up with perfumed tapers, seven laughter-loving women were interchanging sweet talk. The white marble of the noble works of art about them stood out against the red stucco walls, and made strong contrasts with the rich Turkey carpets. Clad in satin, glittering with gold, and covered with gems less brilliant than their eyes, each told a tale of energetic passions as diverse as their styles of beauty. They differed neither in their ideas nor in their language; but the expression of their eyes, their glances, occasional gestures, or the tones of their voices supplied a commentary, dissolute, wanton, melancholy, or satirical, to their words.

One seemed to be saying—"The frozen heart of age might kindle at my beauty."

Another—"I love to lounge upon cushions, and think with rapture of my adorers."

A third, a neophyte at these banquets, was inclined to blush. "I feel remorse in the depths of my heart! I am a Catholic, and afraid of hell. But I love you, I love you so that I can sacrifice my hereafter to you."

The fourth drained a cup of Chian wine. "Give me a joyous life!" she cried; "I begin life afresh each day with the dawn. Forgetful of the past, with the intoxication of yesterday's rapture still upon me, I drink deep of life—a whole lifetime of pleasure and of love!"

The woman who sat next to Juan Belvidero looked at him with a feverish glitter in her eyes. She was silent. Then—"I should need no hired bravo to kill my lover if he forsook me!" she cried at last, and laughed, but the marvelously wrought gold comfit box in her fingers was crushed by her convulsive clutch.

"When are you to be Grand Duke?" asked the sixth. There was the frenzy of a Bacchante in her eyes, and her teeth gleamed between the lips parted with a smile of cruel glee.

"Yes, when is that father of yours going to die?" asked the seventh, throwing her bouquet at Don Juan with bewitching playfulness. It was a childish girl who spoke, and the speaker was wont to make sport of sacred things.

"Oh! don't talk about it," cried Don Juan, the young and handsome giver of the banquet. "There is but one eternal father, and, as ill luck will have it, he is mine."

The seven Ferrarese, Don Juan's friends, the Prince himself, gave a cry of horror. Two hundred years later, in the days of Louis XV, people of taste would have laughed at this witticism. Or was it, perhaps, that at the outset of an orgy there is a certain unwonted lucidity of mind? Despite the taper light, the clamor of the senses, the gleam of gold and silver, the fumes of wine, and the exquisite beauty of the women, there may perhaps have been in the depths of the revelers' hearts some struggling glimmer of reverence for things divine and human, until it was drowned in glowing floods of wine! Yet even then the flowers had been crushed, eyes were growing dull, and drunkenness, in Rabelais' phrase, had "taken possession of them down to their sandals."

During that brief pause a door opened; and as once the Divine presence was revealed at Belshazzar's feast, so now it seemed to be manifest in the apparition of an old white-haired servant, who tottered in, and looked sadly from under knitted brows at the revelers.

He gave a withering glance at the garlands, the golden cups, the pyramids of fruit, the dazzling lights of the banquet, the flushed scared faces, the hues of the cushions pressed by the white arms of the women.

"My lord, your father is dying!" he said; and at those solemn words, uttered in hollow tones, a veil of crape seemed to be drawn over the wild mirth.

Don Juan rose to his feet with a gesture to his guests that might be rendered by, "Excuse me; this kind of thing does not happen every day."

Does it so seldom happen that a father's death surprises youth in the full-blown splendour of life, in the midst of the mad riot of an orgy? Death is as unexpected in his caprice as a courtesan in her disdain; but death is truer—Death has never forsaken any man.

Don Juan closed the door of the banqueting-hall; and as he went down the long gallery, through the cold and darkness, he strove to assume an expression in keeping with the part he had to play; he had thrown off his mirthful mood, as he had thrown down his table napkin, at the first thought of this rôle. The night was dark. The mute servitor, his guide to the chamber where the dying man lay, lighted the way so dimly that Death, aided by cold, silence, and darkness, and it may be by a reaction of drunkenness, could send some sober thoughts through the spendthrift's soul. He examined his life, and became thoughtful, like a man involved in a lawsuit on his way to the Court.

Bartolommeo Belvidero, Don Juan's father, was an old man of ninety, who had devoted the greatest part of his life to business pursuits. He had acquired vast wealth in many a journey in magical Eastern lands, and knowledge, so it was said, more valuable than the gold and diamonds, which had almost ceased to have any value for him.

"I would give more to have a tooth in my head than for a ruby," he would say at times with a smile. The indulgent father loved to hear Don Juan's story of this and that wild freak of youth. "So long as these follies amuse you, dear boy—" he would say laughingly, as he lavished money on his son. Age never took such pleasure in the sight of youth; the fond father did not remember his own decaying powers while he looked on that brilliant young life.

Bartolommeo Belvidero, at the age of sixty, had fallen in love with an angel of peace and beauty. Don Juan had been the sole fruit of this late and short-lived love. For fifteen years the widower had mourned the loss of his beloved Juana; and to this sorrow of age, his son and his numerous household had attributed the strange habits that he had contracted. He had shut himself up in the least comfortable wing of his palace, and very seldom left his apartments; even Don Juan himself must first ask permission before seeing his father. If this hermit, unbound by vows, came or went in his palace or in the streets of Ferrara, he walked as if he were in a dream, wholly engrossed, like a man at strife with a memory, or a wrestler with some thought.

The young Don Juan might give princely banquets, the palace might echo with clamorous mirth, horses pawed the ground in the courtyards, pages quarreled and flung dice upon the stairs, but Bartolommeo ate his seven ounces of bread daily and drank water. A fowl was occasionally dressed for him, simply that the black poodle, his faithful companion, might have the bones. Bartolommeo never complained of the noise. If huntsmen's horns and baying dogs disturbed his sleep during his illness, he only said, "Ah! Don Juan has come back again." Never on earth has there been a father so little exacting and so indulgent; and, in consequence, young Belvidero, accustomed to treat his father unceremoniously, had all the faults of a spoiled child. He treated old Bartolommeo as a wilful courtesan treats an elderly adorer; buying indemnity for insolence with a smile, selling good-humor, submitting to be loved.

Don Juan, beholding scene after scene of his younger years, saw that it would be a difficult task to find his father's indulgence at fault. Some new-born remorse stirred the depths of his heart; he felt almost ready to forgive this father now about to die for having lived so long. He had an accession of filial piety, like a thief's return in thought to honesty at the prospect of a million adroitly stolen.

Before long Don Juan had crossed the lofty, chilly suite of rooms in which his father lived; the penetrating influences of the damp close air, the mustiness diffused by old tapestries and presses thickly covered with dust had passed into him, and now he stood in the old man's antiquated room, in the repulsive presence of the deathbed, beside a dying fire. A flickering lamp on a Gothic table sent broad uncertain shafts of light, fainter or brighter, across the bed, so that the dying man's face seemed to wear a different look at every moment. The bitter wind whistled through the crannies of the ill-fitting casements; there was a smothered sound of snow lashing the windows. The harsh contrast of these sights and sounds with the scenes which Don Juan had just quitted was so sudden that he could not help shuddering. He turned cold as he came towards the bed; the lamp flared in a sudden vehement gust of wind and lighted up his father's face; the features were wasted and distorted; the skin that cleaved to their bony outlines had taken wan livid hues, all the more ghastly by force of contrast with the white pillows on which he lay. The muscles about the toothless mouth had contracted with pain and drawn apart the lips; the moans that issued between them with appalling energy found an accompaniment in the howling of the storm without.

In spite of every sign of coming dissolution, the most striking thing about the dying face was its incredible power. It was no ordinary spirit that wrestled there with Death. The eyes glared with strange fixity of gaze from the cavernous sockets hollowed by disease. It seemed as if Bartolommeo sought to kill some enemy sitting at the foot of his bed by the intent gaze of dying eyes. That steady remorseless look was the more appalling because the head that lay upon the pillow was passive and motionless as a skull upon a doctor's table. The outlines of the body, revealed by the coverlet, were no less rigid and stiff; he lay there as one dead, save for those eyes. There was something automatic about the moaning sounds that came from the mouth. Don Juan felt something like shame that he must be brought thus to his father's bedside, wearing a courtesan's bouquet, redolent of the fragrance of the banqueting-chamber and the fumes of wine.

"You were enjoying yourself!" the old man cried as he saw his son.

Even as he spoke the pure high notes of a woman's voice, sustained by the sound of the viol on which she accompanied her song, rose above the rattle of the storm against the casements, and floated up to the chamber of death. Don Juan stopped his ears against the barbarous answer to his father's speech.

"I bear you no grudge, my child," Bartolommeo went on.

The words were full of kindness, but they hurt Don Juan; he could not pardon this heart-searching goodness on his father's part.

"What a remorseful memory for me!" he cried, hypocritically.

"Poor Juanino," the dying man went on, in a smothered voice, "I have always been so kind to you, that you could not surely desire my death?"

"Oh, if it were only possible to keep you here by giving up a part of my own life!" cried Don Juan.

("We can always *say* this sort of thing," the spendthrift thought; "it is as if I laid the whole world at my mistress' feet.")

The thought had scarcely crossed his mind when the old poodle barked. Don Juan shivered; the response was so intelligent that he fancied the dog must have understood him.

"I was sure that I could count upon you, my son!" cried the dying man. "I shall live. So be it; you shall be satisfied. I shall live, but without depriving you of a single day of your life."

"He is raving," thought Don Juan. Aloud he added, "Yes, dearest father, yes; you shall live, of course, as long as I live, for your image will be for ever in my heart."

"It is not that kind of life that I mean," said the old noble, summoning all his strength to sit up in bed; for a thrill of doubt ran through him, one of those suspicions that come into being under a dying man's pillow. "Listen, my son," he went on, in a voice grown weak with that last effort, "I have no more wish to give up life than you to give up wine and mistresses, horses and hounds, and hawks and gold—"

"I can well believe it," thought the son; and he knelt down by the bed and kissed Bartolommeo's cold hands. "But, father, my dear father," he added aloud, "we must submit to the will of God."

"I am God!" muttered the dying man.

"Do not blaspheme!" cried the other, as he saw the menacing expression on his father's face. "Beware what you say; you have received extreme unction, and I should be inconsolable if you were to die before my eyes in mortal sin."

"Will you listen to me?" cried Bartolommeo, and his mouth twitched.

Don Juan held his peace; an ugly silence prevailed. Yet above the muffled sound of the beating of the snow against the windows rose the sounds of the beautiful voice and the viol in unison, far off and faint as the dawn. The dying man smiled.

"Thank you," he said, "for bringing those singing voices and the music, a banquet, young and lovely women with fair faces and dark tresses, all the pleasure of life! Bid them wait for me; for I am about to begin life anew."

"The delirium is at its height," said Don Juan to himself.

"I have found out a way of coming to life again," the speaker went on. "There, just look in that table drawer, press the spring hidden by the griffin, and it will fly open."

"I have found it, father."

"Well, then, now take out a little phial of rock crystal."

"I have it."

"I have spent twenty years in—" but even as he spoke the old man felt how very near the end had come, and summoned all his dying strength to say, "As soon as the breath is out of me, rub me all over with that liquid, and I shall come to life again."

"There is very little of it," his son remarked.

Though Bartolommeo could no longer speak, he could still hear and see. When those words dropped from Don Juan, his head turned with appalling quickness, his neck was twisted like the throat of some marble statue which the sculptor had condemned to remain stretched out for ever, the wide eyes had come to have a ghastly fixity.

He was dead, and in death he lost his last and sole illusion.

He had sought a shelter in his son's heart, and it had proved to be a sepulchre, a pit deeper than men dig for their dead. The hair on his head had risen and stiffened with horror, his agonized glance still spoke. He was a father rising in just anger from his tomb, to demand vengeance at the throne of God.

"There! it is all over with the old man!" cried Don Juan.

He had been so interested in holding the mysterious phial to the lamp, as a drinker holds up the wine-bottle at the end of a meal, that he had not seen his father's eyes fade. The cowering poodle looked from his master to the elixir, just as Don Juan himself glanced again and again from his father to the flask. The lamplight flickered. There was a deep silence; the viol was mute. Juan Belvidero thought that he saw his father stir, and trembled. The changeless gaze of those accusing eyes frightened him; he closed them hastily, as he would have closed a loose shutter swayed by the wind of an autumn night. He stood there motionless, lost in a world of thought.

Suddenly the silence was broken by a shrill sound like the creaking of a rusty spring. It startled Don Juan; he all but dropped the phial. A sweat, colder than the blade of a dagger, issued through every pore. It was only a piece of clockwork, a wooden cock that sprang out and crowed three times, an ingenious contrivance by which the learned of that epoch were wont to be awakened at the appointed hour to begin the labors of the day. Through the windows there came already a flush of dawn. The thing, composed of wood, and cords, and wheels, and pulleys, was more faithful in its service than he in his duty to Bartolommeo—he, a man with that peculiar piece of human mechanism within him that we call a heart.

Don Juan the sceptic shut the flask again in the secret drawer in the Gothic table—he meant to run no more risks of losing the mysterious liquid.

Even at that solemn moment he heard the murmur of a crowd in the gallery, a confused sound of voices, of stifled laughter and light footfalls, and the rustling of silks—the sounds of a band of revelers struggling for gravity. The door opened, and in came the Prince and Don Juan's friends, the seven courtesans, and the singers, disheveled and wild like dancers surprised by the dawn, when the tapers that have burned through the night struggle with the sunlight.

They had come to offer the customary condolence to the young heir.

"Oho! is poor Don Juan really taking this seriously?" said the Prince in Brambilla's ear.

"Well, his father was very good," she returned.

But Don Juan's night-thoughts had left such unmistakable traces on his features, that the crew was awed into silence. The men stood motionless. The women, with wine-parched lips and cheeks marbled with kisses, knelt down and began a prayer. Don Juan could scarce help trembling when he saw splendour and mirth and laughter and song and youth and beauty and power bowed in reverence before Death. But in those times, in that adorable Italy of the sixteenth century, religion and revelry went hand in hand; and religious excess became a sort of debauch, and a debauch a religious rite!

The Prince grasped Don Juan's hand affectionately, then when all faces had simultaneously put on the same grimace—half-gloomy, half-indifferent—the whole masque disappeared, and left the chamber of death empty. It was like an allegory of life.

As they went down the staircase, the Prince spoke to Rivabarella: "Now, who would have taken Don Juan's impiety for a boast? He loves his father."

"Did you see that black dog?" asked La Brambilla.

"He is enormously rich now," sighed Bianca Cavatolino.

"What is that to me?" cried the proud Veronese (she who had crushed the comfit-box).

"What does it matter to you, forsooth?" cried the Duke. "With his money he is as much a prince as I am."

At first Don Juan was swayed hither and thither by countless thoughts, and wavered between two decisions. He took counsel with the gold heaped up by his father, and returned in the evening to the chamber of death, his whole soul brimming over with hideous selfishness. He found all his household busy there. "His lordship" was to lie in state to-morrow; all Ferrara would flock to behold the wonderful spectacle; and the servants were busy decking the room and the couch on which the dead man lay. At a sign from Don Juan all his people stopped, dumfounded and trembling.

"Leave me alone here," he said, and his voice was changed, "and do not return until I leave the room."

When the footsteps of the old servitor, who was the last to go, echoed but faintly along the paved gallery, Don Juan hastily locked the door, and, sure that he was quite alone, "Let us try," he said to himself.

Bartolommeo's body was stretched on a long table. The embalmers had laid a sheet over it, to hide from all eyes the dreadful spectacle of a corpse so wasted and shrunken that it seemed like a skeleton, and only the face was uncovered. This mummy-like figure lay in the middle of the room. The limp clinging linen lent itself to the outlines it shrouded—so sharp, bony, and thin. Large violet patches had already begun to spread over the face; the embalmers' work had not been finished too soon.

Don Juan, strong as he was in his scepticism, felt a tremor as he opened the magic crystal flask. When he stood over that face, he was trembling so violently that he was actually obliged to wait for a moment. But Don Juan had acquired an early familiarity with evil; his morals had been corrupted by a licentious court, a reflection worthy of the Duke of Urbino crossed his mind, and it was a keen sense of curiosity that goaded him into boldness. The devil himself might have whispered the words that were echoing through his brain, *Moisten one of the eyes with the liquid*! He took up a linen cloth, moistened it sparingly with the precious fluid, and passed it lightly over the right eyelid of the corpse. The eye unclosed. . . .

"Aha!" said Don Juan. He gripped the flask tightly, as we clutch in dreams the branch from which we hang suspended over a precipice.

For the eye was full of life. It was a young child's eye set in a death's head; the light quivered in the depths of its youthful liquid brightness. Shaded by the long dark lashes, it sparkled like the strange lights that travelers see in lonely places in winter nights. The eye seemed as if it would fain dart fire at Don Juan; he saw it thinking, upbraiding, condemning, uttering accusations, threatening doom;

it cried aloud, and gnashed upon him. All anguish that shakes human souls was gathered there; supplications the most tender, the wrath of kings, the love in a girl's heart pleading with the headsman; then, and after all these, the deeply searching glance a man turns on his fellows as he mounts the last step of the scaffold. Life so dilated in this fragment of life that Don Juan shrank back; he walked up and down the room, he dared not meet that gaze, but he saw nothing else. The ceiling and the hangings, the whole room was sown with living points of fire and intelligence. Everywhere those gleaming eyes haunted him.

"He might very likely have lived another hundred years!" he cried involuntarily. Some diabolical influence had drawn him to his father, and again he gazed at that luminous spark. The eyelid closed and opened again abruptly; it was like a woman's sign of assent. It was an intelligent movement. If a voice had cried "Yes!" Don Juan could not have been more startled.

"What is to be done?" he thought.

He nerved himself to try to close the white eyelid. In vain.

"Kill it? That would perhaps be parricide," he debated with himself.

"Yes," the eye said, with a strange sardonic quiver of the lid.

"Aha!" said Don Juan to himself, "here is witchcraft at work!" And he went closer to crush the thing. A great tear trickled over the hollow cheeks, and fell on Don Juan's hand.

"It is scalding!" he cried. He sat down. The struggle exhausted him; it was as if, like Jacob of old, he was wrestling with an angel.

At last he rose. "So long as there is no blood—" he muttered.

Then, summoning all the courage needed for a coward's crime, he extinguished the eye, pressing it with the linen cloth, turning his head away. A terrible groan startled him. It was the poor poodle, who died with a long-drawn howl.

"Could the brute have been in the secret?" thought Don Juan, looking down at the faithful creature.

Don Juan Belvidero was looked upon as a dutiful son. He reared a white marble monument on his father's tomb, and employed the greatest sculptors of the time upon it. He did not recover perfect ease of mind till the day when his father knelt in marble before Religion, and the heavy weight of the stone had sealed the mouth of the grave in which he had laid the one feeling of remorse that sometimes flitted through his soul in moments of physical weariness.

He had drawn up a list of the wealth heaped up by the old merchant in the East, and he became a miser: had he not to provide for a second lifetime? His views of life were the more profound and penetrating; he grasped its significance, as a whole, the better, because he saw it across a grave. All men, all things, he analyzed once and for all; he summed up the Past, represented by its records; the Present in the law, its crystallized form; the Future, revealed by religion. He took spirit and matter, and flung them into his crucible, and found—Nothing. Thenceforward he became DON JUAN.

At the outset of his life, in the prime of youth and the beauty of youth, he knew the illusions of life for what they were; he despised the world, and made the utmost of the world. His felicity could not have been of the bourgeois kind, rejoicing in periodically recurrent *bouilli*, in the comforts of a warming-pan, a lamp of a night, and a new pair of slippers once a quarter. Nay, rather he seized upon existence as a monkey snatches a nut, and after so long toying with it, proceeds deftly to strip off the mere husks to reach the savory kernel within.

Poetry and the sublime transports of passion scarcely reached ankle-depth with him now. He in nowise fell into the error of strong natures who flatter themselves now and again that little souls will believe in a great soul, and are willing to barter their own lofty thoughts of the future for the small change of our life-annuity ideas. He, even as they, had he chosen, might well have walked with his feet on the earth and his head in the skies; but he liked better to sit on earth, to wither the soft, fresh, fragrant lips of a woman with kisses, for, like Death, he devoured everything without scruple as he passed; he would have full fruition; he was an Oriental lover, seeking prolonged pleasures easily obtained. He sought nothing but a woman in women, and cultivated cynicism, until it became with him a habit of mind. When his mistress, from the couch on which she lay, soared and was lost in regions of ecstatic bliss, Don Juan followed suit, earnest, expansive, serious as any German student. But he said I, while she, in the transports of intoxication, said We. He understood to admiration the art of abandoning himself to the influence of a woman; he was always clever enough to make her believe that he trembled like some boy fresh from college before his first partner at a dance, when he asks her, "Do you like dancing?" But, no less, he could be terrible at need, could unsheathe a formidable sword and make short work of Commandants. Banter lurked beneath his simplicity, mocking laughter behind his tears—for he had tears at need, like any woman nowadays who says to her husband, "Give me a carriage, or I shall go into a consumption."

For the merchant the world is a bale of goods or a mass of circulating bills; for most young men it is a woman, and for a woman here and there it is a man; for a certain order of mind it is a salon, a coterie, a quarter of the town, or some single city; but Don Juan found his world in himself.

This model of grace and dignity, this captivating wit, moored his bark by every shore; but wherever he was led he was never carried away, and was only steered in a course of his own choosing. The more he saw, the more he doubted. He watched men narrowly, and saw how, beneath the surface, courage was often rashness; and prudence, cowardice; generosity, a clever piece of calculation; justice, a wrong; delicacy, pusillanimity; honesty, a *modus vivendi*; and by some strange dispensation of fate, he must see that those who at heart were really honest, scrupulous, just, generous, prudent, or brave were held cheaply by their fellow-men.

"What a cold-blooded jest!" said he to himself. "It was not devised by a God."

From that time forth he renounced a better world, and never uncovered himself when a Name was pronounced, and for him the carven saints in the churches became works of art. He understood the mechanism of society too well to clash wantonly with its prejudices; for, after all, he was not as powerful as the executioner, but he evaded social laws with the wit and grace so well rendered in the scene with M. Dimanche. He was, in fact, Molière's Don Juan, Goethe's Faust, Byron's Manfred, Mathurin's Melmoth—great allegorical figures drawn by the greatest men of genius in Europe, to which Mozart's harmonies, perhaps, do no more justice than Rossini's lyre. Terrible allegorical figures that shall endure as long as the principle of evil existing in the heart of man shall produce a few copies from century to century. Sometimes the type becomes half-human when incarnate as a Mirabeau, sometimes it is an inarticulate force in a Bonaparte, sometimes it overwhelms the universe with irony as a Rabelais; or, yet again, it appears when a Maréchal de Richelieu elects to laugh at human beings instead of scoffing at things, or when one of the most famous of our ambassadors goes a step further and scoffs at both men and things. But the profound genius of Juan Belvidero anticipated and resumed all these. All things were a jest to him. His was the life of a mocking spirit. All men, all institutions, all realities, all ideas were within its scope. As for eternity, after half an hour of familiar conversation with Pope Julius II, he had said, laughing:

"If it is absolutely necessary to make a choice, I would rather believe in God than in the Devil; power combined with goodness always offers more resources than the spirit of Evil can boast."

"Yes: still God requires repentance in this present world—"

"So you always think of your indulgences," returned Don Juan Belvidero. "Well, well, I have another life in reserve in which to repent of the sins of my previous existence."

"Oh, if you regard old age in that light," cried the Pope, "you are in danger of canonization——"

"After your elevation to the Papacy nothing is incredible." And they went to watch the workmen who were building the huge basilica dedicated to Saint Peter.

"Saint Peter, as the man of genius who laid the foundation of our double power," the Pope said to Don Juan, "deserves this monument. Sometimes, though, at night, I think that a deluge will wipe all this out as with a sponge, and it will be all to begin over again."

Don Juan and the Pope began to laugh; they understood each other. A fool would have gone on the morrow to amuse himself with

Julius II, in Raphael's studio or at the delicious Villa Madama; not so Belvidero. He went to see the Pope as pontiff, to be convinced of any doubts that he (Don Juan) entertained. Over his cups the Rovere would have been capable of denying his own infallibility and of commenting on the Apocalypse.

NEVERTHELESS, THIS LEGEND has not been undertaken to furnish materials for future biographies of Don Juan; it is intended to prove to honest folk that Belvidero did not die in a duel with stone, as some lithographers would have us believe.

When Don Juan Belvidero reached the age of sixty he settled in Spain, and there in his old age he married a young and charming Andalusian wife. But of set purpose he was neither a good husband nor a good father. He had observed that we are never so tenderly loved as by women to whom we scarcely give a thought. Doña Elvira had been devoutly brought up by an old aunt in a castle a few leagues from San-Lucar in a remote part of Andalusia. She was a model of devotion and grace. Don Juan foresaw that this would be a woman who would struggle long against a passion before yielding, and therefore hoped to keep her virtuous until his death. It was a jest undertaken in earnest, a game of chess which he meant to reserve till his old age. Don Juan had learned wisdom from the mistakes made by his father Bartolommeo; he determined that the least details of his life in old age should be subordinated to one object—the success of the drama which was to be played out upon his death-bed.

For the same reason the largest part of his wealth was buried in the cellars of his palace at Ferrara, whither he seldom went. As for the rest of his fortune, it was invested in a life annuity, with a view to give his wife and children an interest in keeping him alive; but this Machiavellian piece of foresight was scarcely necessary. His son, young Felipe Belvidero, grew up as a Spaniard as religiously conscientious as his father was irreligious, in virtue, perhaps, of the old rule, "A miser has a spendthrift son." The Abbot of San-Lucar was chosen by Don Juan to be the director of the consciences of the Duchess of Belvidero and her son Felipe. The ecclesiastic was a holy man, well shaped, and admirably well proportioned. He had fine dark eyes, a head like that of Tiberius, worn with fasting, bleached by an ascetic life, and, like all dwellers in the wilderness, was daily tempted. The noble lord had hopes, it may be, of despatching yet another monk before his term of life was out.

But whether because the Abbot was every whit as clever as Don Juan himself, or Doña Elvira possessed more discretion or more virtue than Spanish wives are usually credited with, Don Juan was compelled to spend his declining years beneath his own roof, with no more scandal under it than if he had been an ancient country parson. Occasionally he would take wife and son to task for negligence in the duties of religion, peremptorily insisting that they should carry out to the letter the obligations imposed upon the flock by the Court of Rome. Indeed, he was never so well pleased as when he had set the courtly Abbot discussing some case of conscience with Doña Elvira and Felipe.

At length, however, despite the prodigious care that the great magnifico, Don Juan Belvidero, took of himself, the days of decrepitude came upon him, and with those days the constant importunity of physical feebleness, an importunity all the more distressing by contrast with the wealth of memories of his impetuous youth and the sensual pleasures of middle age. The unbeliever who in the height of his cynical humor had been wont to persuade others to believe in laws and principles at which he scoffed must repose nightly upon a *perhaps.* The great Duke, the pattern of good breeding, the champion of many a carouse, the proud ornament of Courts, the man of genius, the graceful winner of hearts that he had wrung as carelessly as a peasant twists an osier withe, was now the victim of a cough, of a ruthless sciatica, of an unmannerly gout. His teeth gradually deserted him, as at the end of an evening the fairest and best-dressed women take their leave one by one till the room is left empty and desolate. The active hands became palsy-stricken, the shapely legs tottered as he walked. At last, one night, a stroke of apoplexy caught him by the throat in its icy clutch. After that fatal day he grew morose and stern.

He would reproach his wife and son with their devotion, casting it in their teeth that the affecting and thoughtful care that they lavished so tenderly upon him was bestowed because they knew that his money was invested in a life annuity. Then Elvira and Felipe would shed bitter tears and redouble their caresses, and the wicked old man's insinuating voice would take an affectionate tone—"Ah, you will forgive me, will you not, dear friends, dear wife? I am rather a nuisance. Alas, Lord in heaven, how canst Thou use me as the instrument by which Thou provest these two angelic creatures? I who should be the joy of their lives am become their scourge . . ."

In this manner he kept them tethered to his pillow, blotting out the memory of whole months of fretfulness and unkindness in one short hour when he chose to display for them the ever-new treasures of his pinchbeck tenderness and charm of manner—a system of paternity that yielded him an infinitely better return than his own father's indulgence had formerly gained. At length his bodily infirmities reached a point when the task of laying him in bed became as difficult as the navigation of a felucca in the perils of an intricate channel. Then came the day of his death; and this brilliant sceptic, whose mental faculties alone had survived the most dreadful of all destructions, found himself between his two special antipathies—the doctor and the confessor. But he was jovial with them. Did he not see a light gleaming in the future beyond the veil? The pall that is like lead for other men was thin and translucent for him; the light-footed, irresistible delights of youth danced beyond it like shadows.

It was on a beautiful summer evening that Don Juan felt the near approach of death. The sky of Spain was serene and cloudless; the air was full of the scent of orange-blossom; the stars shed clear, pure gleams of light; nature without seemed to give the dying man assurance of resurrection; a dutiful and obedient son sat there watching him with loving and respectful eyes. Towards eleven o'clock he desired to be left alone with this single-hearted being.

"Felipe," said the father, in tones so soft and affectionate that the young man trembled, and tears of gladness came to his eyes; never had that stern father spoken his name in such a tone. "Listen, my son," the dying man went on. "I am a great sinner. All my life long, however, I have thought of my death. I was once the friend of the great Pope Julius II; and that illustrious Pontiff, fearing lest the excessive excitability of my senses should entangle me in mortal sin between the moment of my death and the time of my anointing with the holy oil, gave me a flask that contains a little of the holy water that once issued from the rock in the wilderness. I have kept the secret of this squandering of a treasure belonging to Holy Church, but I am permitted to reveal the mystery *in articulo mortis* to my son. You will find the flask in a drawer in that Gothic table that always stands by the head of the bed. . . . The precious little crystal flask may be of use yet again for you, dearest Felipe. Will you swear to me, by your salvation, to carry out my instructions faithfully?"

Felipe looked at his father, and Don Juan was too deeply learned in the lore of the human countenance not to die in peace with that look as his warrant, as his own father had died in despair at meeting the expression in his son's eyes.

"You deserved to have a better father," Don Juan went on. "I dare to confess, my child, that while the reverend Abbot of San-Lucar was administering the Viaticum I was thinking of the incompatibility of the co-existence of two powers so infinite as God and the Devil—"

"Oh, father!"

"And I said to myself, when Satan makes his peace he ought surely to stipulate for the pardon of his followers, or he will be the veriest scoundrel. The thought haunted me; so I shall go to hell, my son, unless you carry out my wishes."

"Oh, quick; tell me quickly, father."

"As soon as I have closed my eyes," Don Juan went on, "and that may be in a few minutes, you must take my body before it grows cold and lay it on a table in this room. Then put out the lamp; the light of the stars should be sufficient. Take off my clothes, reciting *Aves* and *Paters* the while, raising your soul to God in prayer, and carefully anoint my lips and eyes with this holy water; begin with the face, and proceed successively to my limbs and the rest of my body; my dear son, the power of God is so great that you must be astonished at nothing."

Don Juan felt death so near, that he added in a terrible voice, "Be careful not to drop the flask."

Then he breathed his last gently in the arms of his son, and his son's tears fell fast over his sardonic, haggard features.

It was almost midnight when Don Felipe Belvidero laid his father's body upon the table. He kissed the sinister brow and the gray hair; then he put out the lamp.

By the soft moonlight that lit strange gleams across the country without, Felipe could dimly see his father's body, a vague white thing among the shadows. The dutiful son moistened a linen cloth with the liquid, and, absorbed in prayer, he anointed the revered face. A deep silence reigned. Felipe heard faint, indescribable rustlings; it was the breeze in the tree-tops, he thought. But when he had moistened the right arm, he felt himself caught by the throat, a young strong hand held him in a tight grip—it was his father's hand! He shrieked aloud; the flask dropped from his hand and broke in pieces. The liquid evaporated; the whole household hurried into the room, holding torches aloft. That shriek had startled them, and filled them with as much terror as if the Trumpet of the Angel sounding on the Last Day had rung through earth and sky. The room was full of people, and a horror-stricken crowd beheld the fainting Felipe upheld by the strong arm of his father, who clutched him by the throat. They saw another thing, an unearthly spectacle—Don Juan's face grown young and beautiful as Antinoüs, with its dark hair and brilliant eyes and red lips, a head that made horrible efforts, but could not move the dead, wasted body.

An old servitor cried, "A miracle! a miracle!" and all the Spaniards echoed, "A miracle! a miracle!"

Doña Elvira, too pious to attribute this to magic, sent for the Abbot of San-Lucar; and the Prior beholding the miracle with his own eyes, being a clever man, and withal an Abbot desirous of augmenting his revenues, determined to turn the occasion to profit. He immediately gave out that Don Juan would certainly be canonized; he appointed a day for the celebration of the apotheosis in his convent, which thenceforward, he said, should be called the convent of San Juan of Lucar. At these words a sufficiently facetious grimace passed over the features of the late Duke.

The taste of the Spanish people for ecclesiastical solemnities is so well known that it should not be difficult to imagine the religious pantomime by which the Convent of San-Lucar celebrated the translation of the *blessed Don Juan Belvidero* to the abbey-church. The tale of the partial resurrection had spread so quickly from village to village, that a day or two after the death of the illustrious nobleman the report had reached every place within fifty miles of San-Lucar, and it was as good as a play to see the roads covered already with crowds flocking in on all sides, their curiosity whetted still further by the prospect of a *Te Deum* sung by torchlight. The old abbey church of San-Lucar, a marvelous building erected by the Moors, a mosque of Allah, which for three centuries had heard the name of Christ, could not hold the throng that poured in to see the ceremony. Hidalgos in their velvet mantles, with their good swords at their sides, swarmed like ants, and were so tightly packed in among the pillars that they had not room to bend the knees, which never bent save to God. Charming peasant girls, in the basquina that defines the luxuriant outlines of their figures, lent an arm to white-haired old men. Young men, with eyes of fire, walked beside aged crones in holiday array. Then came couples tremulous with joy, young lovers led thither by curiosity, newly wedded folk; children timidly clasping each other by the hand. This throng, so rich in colouring, in vivid contrasts, laden with flowers, enameled like a meadow, sent up a soft murmur through the quiet night. Then the great doors of the church opened.

Late comers who remained without saw afar, through the three great open doorways, a scene of which the theatrical illusions of modern opera can give but a faint idea. The vast church was lighted up by thousands of candles, offered by saints and sinners alike eager to win the favor of this new candidate for canonization, and these self-commending illuminations turned the great building into an enchanted fairyland. The black archways, the shafts and capitals, the recessed chapels with gold and silver gleaming in their depths, the galleries, the Arab traceries, all the most delicate outlines of that delicate sculpture, burned in the excess of light like the fantastic figures in the red heart of a brazier. At the further end of the church, above that blazing sea, rose the high altar like a splendid dawn. All the glories of the golden lamps and silver candlesticks, of banners and tassels, of the shrines of the saints and votive offerings, paled before the gorgeous brightness of the reliquary in which Don Juan lay. The blasphemer's body sparkled with gems, and flowers, and crystal, with diamonds and gold, and plumes white as the wings of seraphim; they had set it up on the altar, where the pictures of Christ had stood. All about him blazed a host of tall candles; the air quivered in the radiant light. The worthy Abbot of San-Lucar, in pontifical robes, with his mitre set with precious stones, his rochet and golden crosier, sat enthroned in imperial state among his clergy in the choir. Rows of impassive aged faces, silver-haired old men clad in fine linen albs, were grouped about him, as the saints who confessed Christ on earth are set by painters, each in his place, about the throne of God in heaven. The precentor and the dignitaries of the chapter, adorned with the gorgeous insignia of ecclesiastical vanity, came and went through the clouds of incense, like stars upon their courses in the firmament.

When the hour of triumph arrived, the bells awoke the echoes far and wide, and the whole vast crowd raised to God the first cry of praise that begins the *Te Deum*. A sublime cry! High, pure notes, the voices of women in ecstasy, mingled in it with the sterner and deeper voices of men; thousands of voices sent up a volume of sound so mighty, that the straining, groaning organ-pipes could not dominate that harmony. But the shrill sound of children's singing among the choristers, the reverberation of deep bass notes, awakened gracious associations, visions of childhood, and of man in his strength, and rose above that entrancing harmony of human voices blended in one sentiment of love.

Te Deum laudamus!

The chant went up from the black masses of men and women kneeling in the cathedral, like a sudden breaking out of light in darkness, and the silence was shattered as by a peal of thunder. The voices floated up with the clouds of incense that had begun to cast thin bluish veils over the fanciful marvels of the architecture, and the aisles were filled with splendour and perfume and light and melody. Even at the moment when that music of love and thanksgiving soared up to the altar, Don Juan, too well bred not to express his acknowledgments, too witty not to understand how to take a jest, bridled up in his reliquary, and responded with an appalling burst of laughter. Then the Devil having put him in mind of the risk he was running of being taken for an ordinary man, a saint, a Boniface, a Pantaleone, he interrupted the melody of love by a yell, the thousand voices of hell joined in it. Earth blessed, Heaven banned. The church was shaken to its ancient foundations.

Te Deum laudamus! cried the many voices.

"Go to the devil, brute beasts that you are! *Dios! Dios! Garajos demonios*! Idiots! What fools you are with your dotard God!" and a torrent of imprecations poured forth like a stream of red-hot lava from the mouth of Vesuvius.

"*Deus Sabaoth! . . . Sabaoth*!" cried the believers.

"You are insulting the majesty of Hell," shouted Don Juan, gnashing his teeth. In another moment the living arm struggled out of the reliquary, and was brandished over the assembly in mockery and despair.

"The saint is blessing us," cried the old women, children, lovers, and the credulous among the crowd.

And note how often we are deceived in the homage we pay; the great man scoffs at those who praise him, and pays compliments now and again to those whom he laughs at in the depths of his heart.

Just as the Abbot, prostrate before the altar, was chanting "*Sancte Johannes, ora pro nobis*!" he heard a voice exclaim sufficiently distinctly: "*O coglione*!"

"What can be going on up there?" cried the Sub-prior, as he saw the reliquary move.

"The saint is playing the devil," replied the Abbot.

Even as he spoke the living head tore itself away from the lifeless body, and dropped upon the sallow cranium of the officiating priest.

"Remember Doña Elvira!" cried the thing, with its teeth set fast in the Abbot's head.

The Abbot's horror-stricken shriek disturbed the ceremony; all the ecclesiastics hurried up and crowded about their chief.

"Idiot, tell us now if there is a God!" the voice cried, as the Abbot, bitten through the brain, drew his last breath.

Paris, October 1830

PHILARÈTE CHASLES

✻

The Eye with No Lid

(L'oeil sans paupière, 1832)

Little-known authors of fantastic tales are no doubt more numerous than very well known authors. It is only proper that this anthology grant sanctuary to at least one. Philarète Chasles (1799–1873), the son of a member of the Convention who voted to condemn Louis XVI to death, had to flee France while still very young because of the Restoration. He lived in England and Germany before returning to France in 1823. Professor of foreign languages at the Collège de France and conservator at the Bibliothèque Mazarine, he is a member of a clan of librarian-writers, like Nodier before him, and Schwob and Borges after.

"L'oeil sans paupière," published in the anonymous collection Contes Bruns *(1832), in which Balzac also collaborated, is a story with a Scottish milieu. It is filled with folk beliefs in spirits and fairies, beliefs represented in adherence to their terror-producing, pagan spirit, but also taking into account Christian anathema, which assimilates them into devil worship. The tale dates from the era of the Romantic discovery of folklore as well as the fashion for Scottish things established by Walter Scott. But this story doesn't deserve to be remembered*

today only because of its folkloristic documentation. The dominant image is that of a perturbing psychological ghost: a wide-open eye that is always behind a man, never losing sight of him. Given that this man, because of his jealousy, had caused the death of his wife, the lidless eye that follows him around constitutes a kind of contrapasso, *or revenge.*

The ending takes us abroad, among the pioneers in Ohio and the Indians. But it's quite clear that geographic barriers mean nothing to Scottish spirits.

"HALLOWE'EN! HALLOWE'EN!" they were all shouting. "This is the holy night, the great night of the *skelpies** and the fairies! Carrick, and you, Colean, are you coming along? Everyone from Carrick-Border is already there, and our Meg and Jeannie are going to come too. We're bringing canteens full of good whiskey, frothy beer, and thick *parritch*. The weather's fine, and the moon will be out. Friends, the Cassilis ruins will not have known a jollier jamboree."

Thus spoke Jock Muirland, a widowed farmer, still a young man. Like the majority of the Scots peasantry, he was half theologian and half poet, a great drinker but nonetheless sober and hardworking.

Murdock, Will Lapraik, and Tom Duckat were bystanders to the conversation, which took place very near the village of Cassilis.

It's quite likely you don't know what Hallowe'en is: it's the night of spirits and takes place toward the middle of August. On that night, the village warlock is consulted and all the mischievous spirits dance across the heat and cross the fields astride tenuous moonbeams. It's a carnival for spirits and imps. There is no cave or peak that doesn't celebrate its festival and its ball; there is no flower that doesn't tremble under the breath of a nymph, no woman who doesn't carefully lock her door so the spunkies† don't steal her next day's food or with their pranks ruin the food meant for the children, who sleep embracing each other in the same cradle.

Thus was that solemn night, woven of capricious fantasy and a secret fear that crept up the Cassilis hills. Imagine a mountainous

* *skelpies:* water imps.

† spirits.

landscape, as wavy as the sea, and the many hills carpeted with brilliant green moss. In the distance, on a sheer peak, the crenelated battlements of a ruined castle whose chapel, roofless now, has remained almost whole and still raises to the ceiling slim pilasters, as fragile as tree branches in winter. In the surrounding area, the land is barren. The golden broom provides the hares a refuge, and the stone seems bare as far as the eye can see. Man, who sees the supreme power only in the face of desolation and fear, views these lands as marked by the seal of the Divinity. The immense and fecund benevolence of the Most High inspires little gratitude in us: we only recognize His severity and punishments.

The spunkies were already dancing over Cassilis green, and the moon was emerging, huge and red, through the broken glass in the chapel's entry door. It seemed suspended, like a scarlet rose window above which appeared the outline of a small clover leaf of mutilated stone. The spunkies were dancing.

The spunkie! A woman, white as snow, with long, glistening hair. Her beautiful wings, made of and fastened by thin, elastic fibers, do not spring from her shoulders but from her arms, whose outline they follow. The spunkie is a hermaphrodite; it has a feminine face and the delicate elegance of virile puberty. The spunkie's only clothing are its wings—a fine, light weave, soft and compact, impenetrable and airy, like the wings of a bat. A dark veil, shot through with purple and iridescent blue, shines over this natural garment that folds around the spunkie when it rests like the folds of a flag around the staff that holds it up. Long filaments, as shiny as burnished steel, support those ample veils in which the spunkie wraps itself. Its extremities are armed with iron claws. Woe to the woman who ventures at eventide through the swamps or forests where the spunkie hides!

The spunkies were already dancing on the banks of the Doon when the jolly company—women, children, young girls—drew near. The spirits instantly disappeared. Their huge wings, unfolded in unison, darkened the air, as if a flock of birds had suddenly taken flight from among the reeds. For a second, the moonlight was darkened. Muirland and his companions stopped.

"I'm afraid," a girl cried out.

"Don't be silly," answered the farmer. "Just wild ducks flying away."

"Muirland," said young Colean reproachfully, "you're going to end up badly. You believe in nothing."

"Let's roast the walnuts and crack the hazelnuts," Muirland went on, paying no attention to his comrade's reproach. "Let's sit down right here and open the baskets. There's good shelter here: the rock will cover us and the meadow offers us a soft bed. It would take Satan himself to upset my meditations in the heat of drink."

"But the *bogillies* and the *brownillies* might also find us," a young girl timidly pointed out.

"May the cranreuch carry them off!" answered Muirland. "Get a move on, Lapraik: light a fire with leaves and twigs next to the rock. We'll warm some whiskey, and if the girls want to know which husband the good God or the Devil has reserved for them, we have the means to satisfy them. Bome Lesley has brought mirrors and hazelnuts, linseed, plates, and butter. Lasses, that's all you need for your ceremonies, isn't that so?"

"Yes, yes," answered the girls.

"But before anything, let's drink," went on the farmer, who because of his authoritarian character, his patrimony, his well-stocked larder, his crammed-full barn, and his skill as a husbandman had acquired a certain authority in the neighborhood.

Friends, it's time you knew that of all the countries in the world, it's in Scotland that the lower classes have at the same time the greatest culture and the greatest number of superstitions. If you don't believe me, just consult Walter Scott, the illustrious Scotsman who owes his greatness to his God-given skill at symbolically representing the national character and humor. In Scotland, people believe in all manner of spirits, while in the cottages people argue philosophy.

Hallowe'en night is dedicated, above all, to superstition. People gather to discover the mysteries of the future. The rites practiced to that end are well known and inalterable: no system of worship is more rigorous in the observance of its rituals. And this ceremony, where each person is at the same time priest and witch, was the object of the excursion and the nocturnal festivity to which the inhabitants of Cassilis were going. This rustic magic has an indescribable charm. It lies, you might say, on the ambiguous border between poetry and reality. People communicate with the infernal powers without entirely abandoning God. The most ordinary objects become sacred and magic: an ear of wheat or a willow branch can create hopes and fears.

The Hallowe'en tradition requires that the rituals start when the bells toll midnight. It's at that hour that the air fills with supernatural beings, that not only the spunkies but all the magic host of Scotland are the principal actors in the drama, come to take possession of their domain.

Our peasants, gathered since nine o'clock, passed the time drinking, singing old and charming ballads, whose melancholy, ingenuous language blends harmoniously with the measured rhythm in a melody that descends capriciously by intervals of fourths through a singular use of chromaticism. The young girls with their multicolored plaids, their impeccable wool dresses; the smiling women; the children with the pretty red ribbon tied around their knee, serving as both garter and ornament; the young men, whose hearts beat faster and faster as the mysterious moment drew near when destiny would be interrogated; one or two old folks, to whom the tasty beer restored the joy of youth: they all formed a delightful group, which Wilkie would have painted with pleasure, and which would have gladdened the sensitive souls of Europe, immersed in so many tribulations and toils, with its true and deeply felt joviality.

Muirland, more than anyone else, was giving himself over to the noisy joy that frothed up like the dense spume on the beer and spread among the rest.

He was one of those creatures life never manages to tame, one of those men of energetic intelligence who fight on against all odds. A young lass from the county who had linked her destiny to Muirland's had died giving birth after two years of matrimony, and Muirland swore he'd never marry again. No one in the neighborhood was ignorant of the cause of Tuilzie's death: Muirland's jealousy. Tuilzie, fragile and still almost a girl, was barely sixteen when she married the farmer. She loved him but did not know his passionate nature, the violence that could animate him, the torment he could inflict daily on himself and others. Jock Muirland was jealous, and the sweet tenderness of his spouse did not manage to calm him. Once, in the harshest wintertime, he sent her to Edinburgh to take her away from the courting supposedly being paid her by a minor laird who insisted on spending the winter on his lands.

All his friends, even the pastor, had shown him their dismay and reproached him for his conduct. He would only respond that he loved Tuilzie passionately, that he was the one to judge what was best for the success of their marriage. Under Jock's rustic roof were heard frequent laments, shouts, and weeping, whose echoes reached outside the house. Tuilzie's brother visited his brother-in-law to tell him his behavior was unpardonable, but the only result of this intervention was a violent fight. Day by day, the young woman withered away. Finally, the pain that consumed her took her life.

Muirland sank into a deep despair that lasted many years. But, since everything passes in this life and because he swore to remain a widower, slowly but surely he forgot the woman whose involuntary executioner he'd been. Other women, who for years had viewed him with horror, ended up forgiving him. Hallowe'en night found him as he'd been a long time back: jolly, ironic, amusing, a good drinker and teller of magnificent tales, full of jokes, adept at making sparkling comments that kept everyone's good humor awake and prolonged the nocturnal gathering.

They'd already sung all the old epic romances when the twelve rings of the bell sounded midnight, and the echo spread in the distance. Everyone had drunk a great deal. The moment of the customary superstitious rites had come. Everyone got up, except Muirland.

"Let's look for the *kail*," they shouted, "let's look for the *kail*."

Boys and girls scattered over the fields and came back, one by one, carrying a root pulled from the earth: the *kail*. You must pull up by the roots the first plant that appears in your path; if the root is straight, your wife or husband will be elegant and tender; if the root is twisted, you will marry someone unpleasant-looking.* If soil sticks to the roots, your marriage will be happy and fertile; but if the root is thin and bare, your marriage will not last long. You can imagine the explosions of laughter, the merrymaking, and the jokes to which these conjugal indignities opened the way: the young men shoved one another, huddled together, compared results. Even the smallest children had their root.

"Poor Will Haverel!" exclaimed Muirland, studying the root one young man held in his hand. "Your wife will be ugly; the root you found looks like my pig's tail."

Then they sat down in a circle, and all tasted their roots. A bitter root presaged a bad husband; a sweet root, a foolish husband; if the root was aromatic, the husband would have an agreeable character.

This ceremony was followed by the *tap-pickle*. Blindfolded, the girls went out to pick three ears of wheat. If one of the three has no grain, no one doubts that the future husband will have to forgive her a premarital weakness. "Oh Nelly! Nelly! None of your ears has the *tap-pickle*, and you won't be able to escape the jokes. And the fact is that just yesterday, the *fause-house*, or granary, witnessed a long conversation between you and Robert Luath."

Muirland watched the games, without participating himself.

"The hazelnuts! The hazelnuts!" everyone shouted. Out of the basket they took a little bag of hazelnuts, and they all clustered around the fire they'd kept burning all this time. The moon shone brilliantly. Each one took a hazelnut. This is a celebrated and venerable rite. Couples form, and each hazelnut has on it the name of the person who chose it. Then all are tossed into the fire at the same time, both the nut with the sweetheart's name and the nut with the name of the suitor. If the two nuts burn calmly next to each other, there will be a long and pleasant union, but if they burst and separate while burning, there will be discord and disharmony in the marriage. Often it's the girl who deposits the image to which her soul is united in the

* This practice is still quite common in Scotland.

flames. And what must her pain be when a separation occurs, and the future husband leaps crackling far away from her.

The bells had already struck one o'clock, and the peasants were still not tired of consulting the mystical oracles. The fear and faith that went along with the rituals infused the incantations with an unknown enchantment. The spunkies began to move through the reeds again. The girls trembled. The moon, now high in the sky, hid behind a cloud. They carried out the ceremony of the cobblestones, the candle ceremony, and the apple rite, great incantations I will not reveal. Willie Maillie, one of the most beautiful of the young women, sank her arm three times into the waters of the Doon, shouting: "My future husband, my unknown husband, where are you? Here is my hand." Three times she repeated the incantation, and they heard her scream.

"Oh woe is me! The spunkie has caught my hand!" They all ran to her in fear. Only Muirland was unafraid. Maillie showed her bloody hand. The judges of both sexes, whose long experience made them skillful interpreters of magic signs, declared without hesitation that the scratches were not caused, as Muirland said, by the spiny points of the reeds, but that the young woman's arm bore the marks of the sharp claw of the spunkie. And all recognized that meant the shadow of a jealous husband was to hang over Maillie's future. The widowed farmer had drunk, perhaps, one too many.

"Jealous!" he exclaimed. "Jealous."

He seemed to detect in his comrades' declaration a malevolent allusion to his disgrace.

"I," he continued, gulping down a canteen that had been filled to the brim with whiskey, "would prefer—a hundred times over—to marry a spunkie than to remarry. I know what it is to live chained up. It's the same as living in a bottle with a monkey, a cat, or the hangman for a company. I was jealous of my poor Tuilzie. And perhaps I was wrong, but tell me, how could I not be jealous? What woman should not be watched over continuously? I didn't sleep at night; I never left her alone for a moment during the day; I never closed my eyes, not for a moment. The business of the farm was going badly; everything was falling apart. Tuilzie herself was fading before my eyes. The devil take marriage!"

Some laughed; others maintained a scandalized silence. There still remained the last and most fearful of the incantations: the ceremony of the mirror.

Holding a candle in one hand, a person must stand before a small mirror. You breathe three times on the glass and dry it three times, repeating: "Appear, my husband," or "Appear, my wife." Then, over the shoulder of the person who inquires of destiny there appears a figure that is clearly reflected in the little mirror.

No one, after what happened to Maillie, dared to challenge the supernatural powers again. The mirror and candle were already prepared, but no one seemed to have any intention of using them. The murmur of the Doon could be heard among the rushes. The long silver ribbon that trembled over the waters in the distance seemed, in the eyes of the villagers, the sparkling trace of the spunkies, or the water imps. Muirland's mare, a small Highland mare with black tail and white chest, whinnied with all her strength, in that way revealing the proximity of an evil spirit. The wind became ice cold, and the stalks of the reeds shook with a long and sad whisper. The women began to talk of going home, not omitting any good reason, including reproaches for husbands and brothers, alarms about the health of parents—in sum, the full domestic eloquence to which we, the kings of nature and the world, submit so easily.

"Well then! Which of you dares to try the mirror?" exclaimed Muirland.

No one answered.

"What little courage you have," the farmer went on. "You start trembling with the willows as soon as a bit of wind blows. I—as you well know—don't want to remarry, because I want to sleep, and my eyelids refuse to close when I'm married, so I can't begin the ceremony. You know it as well as I."

But finally, since no one wanted to pick up the mirror, Jock Muirland took charge of it. "I'll be an example to you," and without hesitating he seized hold of the mirror. A candle was lit, and Muirland bravely spoke the words of the incantation.

"Appear then, my wife."

Suddenly, a pale image with shining blond hair appeared over his shoulder. Muirland started with surprise and turned around, in case there might be a young girl behind him simulating the apparition. But no one had pretended to be the specter. The mirror slipped from his hands and smashed, but behind his shoulder there still appeared the white face with shining hair: Muirland shouted and fell facedown on the ground.

You should have seen how the villagers fled every which way, like leaves carried by the wind. In the place where, just a short time before everyone had given themselves to country amusements, there remained nothing except the remains of the festivity, the almost extinguished fire, empty jugs and canteens, and Muirland stretched out on the ground. Now the spunkies and their company returned en masse, and the storm, which was already in the air, joined their mysterious chants, the long howl to which the Scots give a picturesque name, Sugh. Muirland, getting to his feet, looked over his shoulder once again: that face was still there. It smiled at the farmer without saying a word, and Muirland could not tell if that head belonged to a body, since it only appeared when he turned around.

Muirland's mouth was dry, and he felt his frozen tongue stuck to his palate. Gathering all his courage, he tried to engage that infernal being in conversation, but in vain: just seeing those pale features, those flaming curls, made his whole body tremble. He tried to flee, hoping to free himself from the apparition. He jumped on the small white mare and already had his foot in the stirrup to try one last time; but fear overwhelmed him. The head was still next to him, his inseparable companion. It was attached to his shoulder like those heads without a body whose profiles Gothic sculptors would sometimes place on top of a pillar or at the end of a cornice. Poor Meg, the little mare, whinnied with all her strength and kicked against the air, showing the same panic as her owner. Whenever Muirland turned around, the spunkie (it was doubtless one of those inhabitants of the marshes that was persecuting him) fixed on him its brilliant eyes of a deep blue, without brows to darken them or eyelids to veil their intolerable glow.

Muirland spurred the mare, always tormented by the anxiety of wanting to know if his pursuer was still there. But she did not abandon him; in vain, he made Meg gallop; in vain the moors and peaks fled behind him. Muirland no longer knew which road he was taking or where he was driving poor Meg. A single idea obsessed him: the spunkie, his companion; or rather his lady-friend, since she had all the malice and the charm of an eighteen-year-old girl. The vault of heaven became covered with thick clouds that seemed to devour him bit by bit. No poor devil ever found himself more alone out in the open fields, in a darkness so infernal. The wind blew as if to awaken the dead, and the rain fell obliquely from the violence of the tempest. The flashes of lightning faded, consumed by the clouds from which came an awe-inspiring roar. Poor Muirland! Your blue and red Scottish cap blew off, and you didn't dare go back to retrieve it. The storm redoubled its fury; the Doon overflowed its banks, and Muirland, having galloped for an hour, discovered to his grief that he'd come right back to the spot where his ride had begun. There, under his eyes, was the ruined Cassilis church, and it looked as if a fire were blazing among the remains of the old pilasters; the flames shot out of the broken apertures, and the carvings stood out against that lugubrious background. Meg refused to go on, but the farmer, who'd lost his reason and thought he could feel the horrible head leaning against his shoulder, dug his spurs so hard into poor Meg's flanks that she flew forward in spite of herself, in the face of the violence that had befallen her.

"Jock," said a sweet voice, "marry me and you'll never be afraid again."

Imagine the profound horror of the wretched Muirland.

"Marry me," repeated the spunkie.

Meanwhile, they were fleeing toward the cathedral that was in flames. Muirland, stopped in his tracks by the mutilated pillars and fallen statues, got off his horse; he'd drunk so much wine that night, so much beer, and spirits, had galloped so much and lived so many emotions that he'd finally grown accustomed to that state of mysterious excitation. Our farmer strode bravely into the roofless nave from which emerged an infernal fire.

The scene that then appeared before his eyes was new to him. A figure squatting at the center of the nave was holding on its bowed back an octagonal vessel in which a green and red flame was burning. The altar was arranged with the ancient ornaments of the Catholic rite. Demons with red hair standing on end had taken over the place meant for candles and were standing on the altar. All the grotesque and infernal forms that the fantasy of the painter or poet could ever imagine were crowding in, running around, and mixing together in multiple and strange forms. The seats meant for the chorus were taken by grave personages who were still wearing the clothing appropriate for their rank. But under their mozzettas skeletal hands could be seen, and from their empty eye sockets came no light. I will not say—because no human language could go that far—what incense they burned in that church, or what abominable parody of holy mysteries the demons were representing there.

Forty devils perched on the ancient gallery which long ago housed the cathedral organ, held Scottish bagpipes of different sizes. Twelve of them formed a throne for an enormous black cat that beat the time with a prolonged meow. The diabolical symphony made the half-ruined vault tremble, and from time to time, chunks of stone fell from above. Amid that tumult, some svelte *skelpies*, who resembled charming girls except for their tails, which showed beneath their white habits, were kneeling; and more than fifty *skelpies*, with their wings either extended or withdrawn, were dancing or resting. In the niches reserved for saints, arranged symmetrically around the central nave, desecrated tombs were opening. Out of them came death, in his white shroud, holding in his hands the funerary candle. With regard to the relics that hung from the walls: I will not stop to describe them. All the crimes committed in Scotland for twenty years were there, decorating the walls of the church abandoned to the demons.

There was the hangman's noose, the murderer's knife, the horrifying remnants of abortion, and the traces of incest. There were the hearts of the pitiless, blackened by vice, and the white hairs of a paternal head still stuck to the blade that committed parricide. Muirland stopped and turned around. The head of his traveling companion had not left its place. One of the monsters in charge of the infernal service took Muirland by the hand; he offered no resistance. He led Muirland to the altar, and Muirland followed his guide. He was overwhelmed, with no strength left. They all kneeled, and Muirland kneeled; they intoned some strange chants, but Muirland heard nothing. He remained immobile, in shock, as if petrified, awaiting his fate.

Meanwhile the diabolical hymns became more audible. The spunkies assigned to the corps of dancers spun around more and more frenetically in their infernal ring. The bagpipes screamed, bellowed, howled, and whistled with greater vehemence. Muirland turned around to see his ill-fated shoulder, which an undesirable guest had chosen as her residence.

"Ah!" he shouted with a long sigh of satisfaction.

The head had disappeared.

But when his hallucinated and astonished eyes returned to the objects that surrounded him, he was shocked to see, beside him, kneeling on a coffin, a young girl whose face was that of the ghost who'd chased him. A gray linen dress covered her only to midthigh, and he could see the charming décolleté, her shoulders, hidden by her blond hair, her virginal bosom, whose beauty shone through the light dress. Muirland was touched. Those graceful and delicate forms contrasted with the horrible apparitions that appeared around her. The skeleton that parodied the mass took Muirland's hand in his twisted fingers and joined it to that of the young girl. When his strange fiancée squeezed his hand, Muirland felt the cold pain the common people attribute to the spunkie's claws. It was too much for him. He closed his eyes and felt he was fainting. Partially overcome by a swoon he fought against, he thought he could guess whose infernal hands were putting him back up on his mare, which seemed to be waiting at the church doors. But his perceptions were confused, his sensations vague.

As you might imagine, a night like that left its traces on Muirland; he awoke as if he were coming out of a stupor and was surprised to find out he'd been married for some days. After Hallowe'en night he'd traveled to the mountains and brought back with him a young wife, who was now lying next to him in the old bed at the farm.

He rubbed his eyes and thought he was dreaming. Then he wanted to take a good look at the woman he'd chosen without knowing it and who was now Mrs. Muirland. The sun was already up. How charming his wife was! How sweet the light was in her ample gaze! What splendor in those eyes! And yet Muirland felt trapped by the strange light that emanated from those eyes. He came close to her; to his surprise, his wife—or at least so it seemed to him—had no eyelids. Large blue pupils of a deep blue appeared under the dark arch of her eyebrows, whose line was admirably subtle. Muirland sighed; the vague memory of the spunkie, of the nocturnal chase and the horrifying marriage in the cathedral, suddenly returned to his mind.

Observing his new wife more closely, he seemed to detect in her the traits of that mysterious being, but modified, somewhat softened. The young woman's fingers were long and thin, her nails white and sharp; her hair reached to the floor. He remained as if abstracted in a fantasy; nevertheless, the neighbors told him the young woman's family lived in the Highlands, that at the end of the wedding he'd suffered an extremely high fever, and that he shouldn't be surprised that the memory of the ceremony had been erased from his mind, which was still convalescing, and that very soon he would behave better with the young woman, since she was charming, sweet, and a very good housewife.

"But she has no eyelids!" exclaimed Muirland.

The neighbors laughed at him and said he wasn't over the fever yet. No one except the farmer noticed that strange characteristic.

Night fell. For Muirland, it was his wedding night, since until that moment he'd been married in name only. His wife's beauty had softened him, even if he did see her without eyelids. So he vowed again and again to overcome his fear and enjoy the singular gift heaven or hell had sent him.

Now we ask the reader to allow us the advantages and tricks of the novel and the fable and permit us to omit the details of the first events of the evening. We will not tell how beautifully lovely Spellie (such was the bride's name) was dressed for that night.

Muirland woke up dreaming that the light of the sun was illuminating the room that held the nuptial bed. Dazzled by the burning rays, he jumped to his feet and saw the eyes of his wife fixed tenderly on him.

"The Devil!" he thought. "Sleeping now is a real offense against her beauty."

So he put aside sleep and whispered tender phrases of love to Spellie, to which the young Highland girl responded the best she could.

Spellie still hadn't fallen asleep when morning came.

"And how would she sleep," Muirland asked himself, "when she has no eyelids?"

And his poor mind again fell into an abyss of doubts and fears.

The sun rose. Muirland was pale and dejected. Mrs. Muirland's eyes were resplendent—as never before. They spent the morning strolling along the banks of the Doon. The young wife was so charming that the husband, despite the wonder of it all and the fever he still had, could not contemplate her without admiration.

"Jock," she said, "I love you just as you loved Tuilzie. All the girls round about envy me, so you'd better be on guard, my love, because I'll be jealous and keep close watch on you."

Muirland's kisses closed her mouth, but the nights passed, and in the deepest part of each one, Spellie's radiant eyes pulled the farmer up out of his sleep: Muirland's strength was declining.

"But my love," Jock asked his wife, "don't you ever sleep?"

"Sleep? Me?"

"Yes, sleep. Ever since our wedding day, I don't think you've slept a single instant."

"In my family, no one ever sleeps."

And her blue pupils seemed to shine even more.

"She doesn't sleep!" exclaimed Muirland in despair. "She doesn't sleep!"

And again he fell back on the pillow, exhausted and horrified.

Poor Muirland! His wife's beautiful eyes gave him no rest. They were, as the poet puts it, stars eternally burning to dazzle him. More than thirty ballads were written in the county to celebrate Spellie's eyes. As for Muirland: one day he disappeared. Three months had passed; the torture he suffered had ruined his life and thinned his blood. He felt that Spellie's gaze of fire would consume him. Whenever he came back from the fields, whenever he stayed at home, whenever he went to church, he was always at the mercy of that terrible, radiant beam of light that penetrated to the deepest part of his being and overwhelmed him with terror. Ultimately, he came to hate the sun and flee the day.

The torture that had destroyed poor Tuilzie was now his own: the spiritual disquiet that had turned him into the executioner of his first young wife—what men call jealousy—had been transformed into the scrutinizing, inescapable eye that pursued him constantly. Always jealousy, but metamorphosed into that palpable image, into the prototype of suspicion.

Muirland abandoned the farm and his land, crossed the sea, and immersed himself in the forests of America, where many of his compatriots had founded towns and built welcoming homes. He was sure the prairies of Ohio would provide him with a safe asylum. He preferred poverty, the settler's life, the snakes hidden in the thick underbrush, simple and uncertain food, to his Scottish domicile, where the jealous, perpetually open eye shone only for the sake of tormenting him. After spending a year in that solitude, he finally blessed his luck: at least he'd found rest in the bosom of that fertile nature. He had no correspondence with anyone in Great Britain out of fear of hearing news about his wife. Sometimes, in dreams, he still saw those eyes without eyelids and would wake up with a start. He would carefully make sure those terribly vigilant eyes were nowhere near him, that they weren't piercing him and devouring him with their unbearable light. Then he would fall back to sleep, happy.

The Narragansetts, a tribe that lived in the area, had chosen for their sachem, or chief, one Massasoit, a sickly old man of a peaceful character. Early on, Muirland had won his affection by making him a present of some whiskey, which he knew how to distill. Massasoit fell sick one day, and his friend Muirland paid him a visit in his tent.

Imagine an Indian wigwam, a kind of conical structure with an opening at the top to let the smoke out. At the center of this humble palace, a fire was burning; on some buffalo skins, stretched out on the floor, lay the sick old chief. Around him, the men of the tribe whooped, shouted, and wept, making such a din that not only did they not cure the sick man but they would have made a healthy man ill. A *powam*, or medicine man, led the lugubrious chorus and dance. The echo reverberated with the noise of that strange ceremony: it was public prayer offered to the local divinity.

Six young women were massaging the naked and cold members of the old man's body: one of them, barely sixteen years old, was weeping. Muirland's common sense made him understand that the only result of all that medical hocus-pocus would be the death of Massasoit. Because he was a white European, everyone thought he was a born doctor. So, taking advantage of the authority that title conferred on him, he ordered all the men who were shouting out of the tent. Then he approached the sachem:

"Who is that coming to me?" asked the old man.

"Jock the White Man."

"Oh!" answered the sachem, extending his rough hand, "we won't be seeing each other any more, Jock."

Jock, though he knew precious little about medicine, quickly came to the conclusion that the sachem was simply suffering from indigestion. Muirland took personal care of him and prepared an excellent Scottish soup for him which the old man wolfed down as if it were medicine. In three days, Massasoit had come back to life: now the whoops of our savages expressed gratitude and joy. Massasoit had Jock seated next to him, gave him his calumet to smoke, and introduced him to his daughter Anauket, the youngest and most beautiful girl of all those Muirland had seen in the tent.

"You have no squaw," said the old warrior. "Take my daughter and honor my gray hair."

Jock trembled. He remembered Tuilzie and Spellie: matrimony had never brought him happiness. But on the other hand, the young squaw was sweet, naive, and obedient. Moreover, a marriage in those solitary lands involves very little solemnity and has no great value to a European. Jock accepted, and the beautiful Anauket never gave him any reason to repent his decision.

One day, the eighth since their union, they were paddling along the Ohio River on a beautiful fall morning. Jock carried his hunting rifle. Anauket, used to these expeditions typical of life in the forests, helped and served her husband. The weather was magnificent. The shores of the river presented delightful landscapes to the lovers. Jock had a good day's hunting, but suddenly a pheasant with splendid wings caught his eye. He aimed, wounded it, and the bird, mortally wounded, fell to earth screeching in the underbrush. Muirland did not want to lose such a magnificent object. He anchored the canoe and ran in search of the wounded bird. He beat his way through thicket after thicket—in vain, but his Scottish obstinacy constantly pushed him toward the heart of the forest. Very soon, he found himself in one of those natural green clearings that are to be found in the forests of America, all surrounded by trees of great height. Suddenly, a flash traversed the foliage and reached him. Muirland's heart sank: the ray was burning him. That unbearable light forced him to lower his eyes.

The eye without an eyelid was there, eternally vigilant.

Spellie had crossed the ocean, had found her husband's trail, and had dogged his footsteps. She'd kept her word, and her terrible jealousy was crushing Muirland with its just reproaches. The man ran toward the river followed by the gaze of the eye with no lid. He saw the clear, pure waters of the Ohio and dove in, impelled by terror.

That was the end of Jock Muirland, just as it's told in a Scottish legend the old women tell in their way. It's an allegory, so they say, and the *eye with no lid* is the ever-vigilant eye of the jealous woman, the most horrifying torture of all.

GÉRARD DE NERVAL

*

The Enchanted Hand

(La main enchantée, 1832)

Gérard de Nerval (1808–1855) created a new genre within Romantic fantastic narrative: the lyrical-amorous evocation suspended between dream and memory. His most characteristic texts of this kind, Aurélia *and* Sylvie, *are difficult to anthologize, but Nerval is also the author of a classic in the more familiar fantastic: "The Enchanted Hand," a story based on an effective and heavily exploited theme—the hand that lives its own life separate from the body.*

In addition to the moral symbolism that the enchanted hand assumes with persuasive clarity—the aggressive violence each of us carries within—we find here also a minute reconstruction of seventeenth-century Paris. A tailor, obliged to fight a duel with a soldier, resorts to the aid of a gypsy alchemist who puts a charm on his right hand. The tailor kills the swordsman in the duel. Hunted by the police, he seeks the protection of a magistrate, but his enchanted hand, contrary to his own will, attacks the jurist. While the tailor is in prison, condemned to hang, the gypsy comes to see him: the hand of a hanged man is an extraordinary talisman for thieves because it will open any door. The gypsy demands the hand, and when the executioner, on the gallows, cuts it off the dead man, we see it move, flee, and open a path through the crowd to make its way to the gypsy.

I. La Place Dauphine

There is nothing more beautiful than the seventeenth-century houses majestically grouped in the Place Royale. When we contemplate their brick façades, interrupted and framed by moldings and stone corners, and their tall windows ablaze with the splendid rays of the afternoon sun, we feel the same awe we would feel standing before a tribunal of magistrates dressed in red, ermine-lined robes. And, if the comparison weren't puerile, one might say that the long, green table around which those fearsome magistrates sit, forming a square, in some ways resembles the chain of linden trees that lines the four sides of Place Royale, completing its grave harmony.

There is another plaza in Paris that is no less agreeable, for its regularity and style, than the Place Royale, though triangular in form while the other is square. It was constructed during the reign of Henri le Grand, who named it Place Dauphine. At the time, people were surprised at how little time it took for buildings to cover the Ile Gourdaine. The invasion of that area was a cruel shock to the clerics who would go there to amuse themselves noisily, as well as for the lawyers who used to meditate there on their pleadings—a green and flower-filled place to promenade after leaving the tainted Palace law courts . . . !

No sooner had those three rows of houses arisen over their heavy porticos, themselves burdened and pierced by salients and partitions, no sooner were they faced with brick, their windows opened with balusters and their roofs covered with heavy slates, than that same lineage of men of law invaded the entire plaza, each one occupying a floor whose elevation betrayed, in inverse proportion, the status and means of its occupant. The entire place turned into a kind of multi-level court of beggars, an underworld of privileged thieves, a den of pettifogging lawyers built of brick and stone where others were made of mud and timber.

During the last years of the reign of Henri le Grand, there lived in one of those houses that made up the Place Dauphine a rather important personage by the name of Godinot Chevassut, magistrate of the provost of Paris, an office both laborious and lucrative in an age when thieves were much more numerous than they are nowadays—how honesty has declined in our France since those days!—and when the number of women of easy virtue was much more considerable—so far have our customs declined! Since humanity changes not a whit, we can say, along with an ancient author, that no matter how many rogues are serving in the galleys, there are many more who are not.

We would also have to say that the thieves of that era were less ignoble than those of today, and that this miserable profession was in those days a kind of art, such that sons of good family did not disdain to practice it. Many fine abilities that would have been wasted in a society of barriers and privileges developed to a considerable extent in that way—enemies rather more dangerous to ordinary citizens than to the state, whose machinery would perhaps have exploded without this safety valve. Also, most certainly, justice in those times treated distinguished thieves with much more respect, and no one exercised that tolerance with more pleasure than our magistrate from the Place Dauphine, and for reasons that will soon be made known to you. By the same token, no one was more severe with the clumsy: they paid for the others and "crowded the gallows that cast their shadow over the Paris of that age," to borrow an expression from d'Aubigné, to the great delight of the bourgeoisie, who in those days were merely robbed better, and with the perfection of the art of fraud.

Godinot Chevassut was a plump little man whose hair was beginning to turn gray. And he was delighted about it, the opposite of what normally occurs with old people, because when his hair finally turned white it would lose the fiery color it had since his birth and which won him the disagreeable nickname "Rousseau," which those who knew him freely employed as it was easier to pronounce and remember than his own name. Also, his eyes were crossed and very shrewd, though they were generally half closed beneath his thick brows. His mouth was wrinkled, like the mouths of people who laugh a lot. Nevertheless, even though his features almost always had an air of malice to them, he was never heard to laugh out loud, or, as some say, to show his back teeth. But when he said something amusing would he accentuate it at the end with an *Ah!* or an *Oh!* that came from the depths of his lungs, and with a singular effect. And this occurred quite often, because our magistrate loved to pepper his conversation with witty remarks, double entendres, and roguish remarks, even in the tribunal. In any case, that was the custom among the jurists of that age, one that today survives almost nowhere but in the provinces.

To finish his portrait, we would have to hang in its usual place a rather long nose, squared off at the tip. Then his ears, quite small and smooth, and a sense of hearing so sharp that he could pick out the jingle of a quarter-escudo a quarter-league away, and the sound of a doubloon from still further off. Which is why when on one occasion a certain litigant sought to know if the magistrate had some friend whose influence might aid his case, he was told that, yes, Rousseau did have some friends to whom he paid close attention, and that they were, among others, Monsieur Doubloon, Maestro Ducat, and even Don Escudo, and that, moreover, it was necessary to set several of them to work at the same time, and in this way the gentleman could be sure he would be fervently attended.

II. A Fixed Idea

There are people who feel more strongly about one quality or another, or about one virtue or another.

Some hold the grandeur and valor of the warrior in the highest esteem and are satisfied only with tales of heroic martial deeds; others put above all things the genius and inventions of the arts, letters, and sciences. Others feel moved by generosity and virtuous deeds aimed at helping our fellow man and dedicate themselves to his salvation with no prompting. But the personal inclination of Godinot Chevassut was the same as that of the wise Charles IX, namely, that no virtue exists superior to that of wit and skill, and that those who possess those qualities are the only ones worthy of admiration and honor in this world. In no other place did our magistrate find those qualities shining more brightly, or developed more highly, than in the great society of thieves, confidence men, scoundrels, and vagrants, whose noble life and singular tricks appeared daily before his eyes, and with inexhaustible variety.

His favorite hero was Master François Villon, a Parisian as celebrated in the art of poetry as he was in those of fraud and theft. He most certainly would have traded the *Iliad* and the *Aeneid*, as well as the no less admirable novel *Huon de Bordeaux*, for the poem of the gluttonous housewives, and even for the *Légende de maître Faifeu*, that rhymed epic of the underworld! Du Bellay's *Illustrations*, the *Aristotle Peripoliticon*, and the *Cymbalum Mundi* seemed very weak to him next to the *Jargon, Followed by the States General of the Kingdom of Argot and of the Dialogues of the Rogue and the Scamp Written by a Simpleton and Printed in Tours by Authorization of the King of Thunes, Fiacre the Packer*, Tours, 1603.

Naturally, those in possession of a virtue profoundly disdain the contrary defect, so for Godinot there was nothing more odious than simple souls, people of torpid intelligence and uncomplicated minds. This reached such an extreme in him that he wanted to change the distribution of justice completely, such that when some serious theft were discovered, it would not be the robber who was hanged but the victim. It was an idea; it was his idea. He thought he saw in it the only way to accelerate intellectual emancipation and to make the men of his age attain a supreme progress in wit, skill, and inventiveness, which, as he was in the habit of saying, were the true crown of humanity and the perfection that most pleased God.

This with regard to morality. With respect to politics, he was convinced that theft organized on a grand scale favored, more than anything else, the division of great fortunes and the circulation of the smaller ones, which would result in the well-being and liberation of the lower classes.

As you shall see, only high-quality fraud filled him with joy, the subtleties and adulation of the true clerics of Saint Nicholas, the old tricks of Master Gonin, which had retained their charm and ingenious quality for two hundred years. That man Villon was his true compatriot, and not highwaymen like Guilleris or Captain Crossroads. Most certainly, the bandit stationed on the highway who brutally despoils a traveler seemed as horrible to him as he would to any sound mind; nor did he feel any differently about those who, with no effort of imagination, enter an isolated house, sack it, and, perhaps, murder the owners. But if he had learned of some distinguished thief who had opened a hole in the wall to get inside a mansion, he would have adorned the opening with a Gothic trefoil, so that the next day, when the theft was discovered, people would see that it had been done by a man of good taste. Certainly Godinot Chevassut would have held such a thief in greater esteem than he would Bertrand de Clasquin, or Caesar himself, to say the least.

III. The Magistrate's Wide Breeches

Having said all this, I think it high time to raise the curtain and, following the custom of the ancient comedians, to give a good kick in the backside to Monsieur Prologue, who has been so annoyingly prolix that it's been necessary to trim the candle wicks three times since his exordium. May he finish quickly, as Bruscambille did, by begging the spectators to "clean up the imperfections of his speech with the brush of humanity and to receive an enema of excuses in the intestine of their impatience." That's that, and now the action will begin.

We are in a great hall, dark and furnished. The old magistrate, seated in a wide, carved chair with twisted feet, the chair back upholstered in fringed damask, was trying on a new pair of starched breeches just brought to him by Eustache Bouteroue, apprentice to Master Goubard, tailor and hosier. Master Chevassut, tying the laces, stands up and sits down again, from time to time addressing the apprentice, who, as rigid as a stone saint and staring at Chevassut timidly, is sitting on the edge of a low stool, having acceded to the magistrate's invitation.

"Huh! These have already done their job!" he said, pushing away with his foot the old breeches he'd just taken off. "They were as worn out as a prohibitive ordinance of the provostship, and all the pieces were saying adieu—a ripping farewell!"

Nevertheless, the jocular magistrate picked up his old necessary suit to get his wallet, from which he extracted a few coins, which he held out in his hand. "It's clear," he went on, "that we men of law get a lot of wear out of our clothes thanks to the toga under which we wear them, as long as the weave holds and the seams stay closed. For that reason, and because all of us have to make a living—including thieves, and, therefore, tailor-hosiers—I will not bargain about the six escudos Master Goubard is charging me and to which I generously add besides one counterfeit escudo for the apprentice, on condition that he not change it at a loss but pass it off as good to some knavish bourgeois, using all the resources of his wit to do so. If that idea doesn't please you, I'll keep the aforementioned escudo for Sunday collection tomorrow at Notre-Dame."

Eustache Bouteroue took the six escudos as well as the counterfeit escudo, thanking the magistrate in a low voice.

"All right, my son!" said the magistrate. "Have you begun dying the cloth yet? And can you cut and measure it by eye? Can you exchange the old for the new, and make the customer believe that what is black is really white? In other words, are you maintaining the grand reputation of the merchants of the Les Halles market?"

Eustache raised his eyes toward the magistrate with a certain fear, and, supposing he was joking, began to laugh; but the magistrate wasn't joking. "I most certainly do not like the style of robbery carried out by merchants," he added. "The thief steals and doesn't trick you. The merchant robs and tricks. A comrade of mine with the gift of the gab, and who knows Latin as well, buys a pair of breeches. He argues over the price and ends up paying six escudos for them. A good Christian turns up, one of those whom some call pariahs and the merchants call customers, and it can happen that he takes a pair of breeches just like the other's, and believing in the clothier, who invokes the Virgin and the saints as witnesses of his honesty, pays eight escudos for them. In that instance, I'm not sorry for him because he's an idiot. But if, as the merchant is counting the sums he's just charged—satisfied with himself and jingling in his hand the two extra escudos from the second sale—there passes a poor devil condemned to the galleys for having stolen from some pocket a dirty, torn handkerchief, the merchant exclaims, 'Look at this great criminal! If justice were just, this villain would be quartered alive, and I would go to see him!' And he says that with the two escudos in his hand, Eustache. What do you think would happen if, following the merchant's desire, justice were really just?"

Eustache Bouteroue was no longer laughing. The paradox was too extreme for him to dare to answer, and the mouth from which it issued made it even more disturbing. Master Chevassut, seeing that the boy was as flustered as a wolf caught in a trap, began to laugh with his special laugh. Then he patted the apprentice on the cheek and sent him away. Now quite pensive, Eustache walked down the staircase with its stone bannister, and although he heard in the distance, in the patio of the palace, the trumpet of Galinette la Galine, the clown of the celebrated quack healer Jerome, who was calling the curious to hear his jokes and to buy his master's concoctions, this time he pretended to be deaf and prepared to cross the Pont-Neuf to get into the neighborhood of the Les Halles market.

IV. The Pont-Neuf

The Pont-Neuf, finished while Henri IV was king, is the most important monument of his reign. There is nothing comparable to the enthusiasm it produced when, after huge labors, its twelve arches completely crossed the Seine and linked the three ancient cities of the capital even more tightly.

Soon it also became the meeting place of all idle Parisians, whose number is considerable, and, for that reason, of troubadours, unguent sellers, and swindlers, whose abilities keep the masses moving just as the flowing waters move the mill.

When Eustache emerged from the triangle of Place Dauphine, the sun was pouring its dusty rays onto the bridge, which was very crowded despite the fact that in general the most popular walkways were the paved ones that stood in the shadow of the houses and city walls and were adorned with shop windows.

With considerable difficulty, Eustache made his way into the river of people that crossed that other river and ran slowly along from one end of the bridge to the other, stopping here and there for the slightest obstacle, like the ice floes the water drags along, turning, spinning around some sleight-of-hand artist, or a singer, or a merchant crying out his merchandise. Many stopped along the railing to watch the rafts pass under the arches or to see the boats sailing by, or to contemplate the magnificent panorama the Seine offered downstream as it wound its way around the Louvre on the right and the Pré-aux-Clercs on the left, divided by the beautiful avenues of linden trees and surrounded by gray, disorderly willows, or green willows weeping over the water. Beyond, and on both shores, the Nesle tower and the Bois tower looked like sentinels at the gates of Paris, like the giants of the old novels.

Suddenly a great noise of fireworks called the eyes of the passersby and gawkers toward one spot and announced a spectacle worthy of notice. It was in the center of one of those half-moon-shaped platforms that were covered in other times by stone stores and which now formed empty spaces on top of each of the bridge's pillars outside the walkway. A magician had set himself up there. He'd arranged a table on top of which strolled a handsome monkey dressed in black and red like a perfect devil, tail and all, and which, without the slightest timidity, tossed a huge number of firecrackers and skyrockets, to the bitter disgust of the other vendors who had not attracted nearly as much attention so quickly.

The monkey's owner was one of those gypsies who were so common a century ago, though already scarce then, and today sunk and lost in ugliness, in the insignificance of our bourgeois heads: an axe-blade profile; high but straight forehead; a long nose with a bump in it, curved, though not in the style of a Roman nose, no, to the contrary, snubbed and barely more extended than the mouth; thin, prominent lips; a sunken chin; then, slanted eyes under brows that formed a V; and long black hair completed the picture. A certain air, let's say, of ease and agility in his comportment denoted a skillful rogue, busy from an early age in all kinds of endeavors.

He was dressed in an old clown costume that he wore with great dignity and on his head a great black hat made of felt with a wide brim, very wrinkled and old. Everyone called him Master Gonin, perhaps because of his skill at prestidigitation, or perhaps because in effect he was a descendant of that famous troubadour who under Charles VI founded the theater of the Enfants-sans-Souci and was the first to bear the title of Prince of Fools, inherited by Monsieur Chotacabras, who maintained his sovereign prerogatives, even in parliament.

V. Good Fortune

The prestidigitator, seeing he'd gathered a good number of spectators, ran through a series of tricks that produced a noisy admiration. The fact is that the fellow had chosen his spot in the half-moon quite deliberately, and not, as it seemed, merely so he wouldn't block traffic. This way, he kept all of the spectators in front of him. The art of the magician was not then what it has become today, when the sleight-of-hand artist works surrounded by his audience.

Once the tricks were over, the monkey made his way through the crowd, collecting a large number of coins, for which he thanked people in a most charming way, accompanying his little salutes with a cry rather like that of a cricket. The hand tricks, it seemed, were but a prelude to something else, something quite different, and in a very well executed prologue the new Master Gonin announced he possessed the gift of telling the future through cartomancy, chiromancy, and pythagorean numbers. This was something that could not be paid for, but which he did for just a sou, to please the public. And on saying that, he shuffled the cards and had the monkey, whose name was Pacolet, distribute them among those who held out a hand to receive them.

When the monkey had satisfied all requests, his master began calling, by the names of their cards, all the curious so that they would approach the half-moon. He then predicted for each one his good or bad fortune while Pacolet, to whom he'd given an onion as a reward for his labor, amused the others with the contortions the treat provoked in him, simultaneously delighted and sobbing, a smile on his mouth and tears in his eyes, and emitting with each bite a grunt of satisfaction while making a horrible face.

Eustache Bouteroue, who had also taken a card, was the last called. Master Gonin stared attentively into his naïve, long face and spoke to him in emphatic terms. "Here is your past: you have neither father nor mother, and for six years you've been an apprentice breeches-maker in the plaza of Les Halles. Here is your present: your master has promised you his only daughter and is planning to retire and leave you his business. For the future, show me your hand."

Eustache, quite astonished, held out his hand. The prestidigitator carefully examined the lines, wrinkled his brow with an expression of doubt, and called over his monkey as if to consult with him. The monkey took Eustache's hand, observed it, and, climbing up on Master Gonin's shoulder, seemed to speak in his ear. But he only moved his lips very quickly, which is what animals do when they are uneasy.

Finally, Master Gonin exclaimed, "What a strange thing! How an existence at first so simple and bourgeois can transform itself into something so uncommon and toward an end that is so elevated! . . . Ah, my little chick! You will break out of your shell. You will reach a high place, very high . . . You will die a great man!"

"Of course!" said Eustache to himself. "These are the things these people always promise . . . But how could he have known the things he told me first? That was astonishing! . . . Unless he knows me from somewhere."

Nevertheless, he took the magistrate's counterfeit escudo out of his pocket, asking Master Gonin for the change. Now, perhaps he was speaking in a very low voice. And perhaps the magician didn't hear him, for he took the escudo, and, rolling it between his fingers, went on to say: "Well now. I see you know how to live, and for that reason I'll add some details to the prediction I just made for you, which, though true, was a bit ambiguous. Yes, my dear friend, you were right not to pay me with a sou as the others did—even if your escudo loses a fourth part of its value. It doesn't matter, because this bright coin will be for you a shining mirror in which the pure truth will be reflected."

"But what you just said to me, about my rising up, is that not the truth?" asked Eustache.

"You asked me for your forture, and I told it to you. But what's missing is the gloss, the commentary. This elevated end to your life which I've predicted—how do you understand it?"

"I think I could become a syndic for the tailor-hosiers, the superintendent of a parish, an alderman . . ."

"That's certainly hitting the nail on the head! Why not Grand Sultan of Turkey while you're at it? No, my dear friend! You'll have to understand it in a different sense. And since you desire an explanation of this sibylline oracle, I will tell you that for us, 'reaching a high place' is said of those sent to tend sheep on the moon, just as we say 'he'll go far' about those who are sent to write their story in the ocean with fifteen-foot quills . . ."

"Oh, certainly! . . . Now, if you will please explain your explanation to me, I'm sure I'll understand it."

"They are two honest phrases that stand in for two words: 'gallows' and 'galleys.' You will reach a high place, and I will go far. I can see it very clearly in this central line, cut into right angles by these other, less pronounced lines. In your case, by one line that cuts the one in between without going very far, and another that cuts obliquely through both of them."

"The gallows!" exclaimed Eustache.

"What? Do you have some special fondness for horizontal death?" quipped Gonin. "It would be puerile. In any case, in this way you'll be spared from falling into the other kinds of ends to which every mortal is exposed. Besides, it's possible that when Madame Gallows raises you up by the neck and your arms hang down you'll be nothing more than a poor old man disgusted with the world and everything in it. . . . But the bell says it's twelve o'clock, and at this hour the order from the Paris provost is to throw us off the bridge until afternoon. However, if sometime you need advice, a charm, a spell, or a philtre to use in the event of danger, or for love, or revenge, I live over there, at the end of the bridge in Château-Gaillard. Can you see the pointy little tower from here?"

"Only one more thing," said Eustache, trembling. "Will I be happy in my marriage?"

"Bring your wife to see me, and I'll tell you. . . . Pacolet, bow to the gentleman and kiss his hand."

The prestidigitator folded his table, put it under his arm, loaded the monkey on his shoulder, and made his way toward Château-Gaillard, humming an old song between his teeth.

VI. Crosses and Miseries

It's true that Eustache Bouteroue was going to marry the daughter of the master breeches-maker quite soon. He was a formal young man, serious about business, who did not spend his free time playing skittles or ball as the other apprentices did but instead examined the bills or read the *Bocage des six corporations* or learned a bit of Spanish, very sensible at that time for a merchant, as English is today, because of the large number of people from that nation who live in Paris.

Master Goubard, convinced after six years of the apprentice's perfect honesty and excellent character, and having noticed as well between his daughter and the boy a certain inclination—completely virtuous and severely restrained on both sides—had decided to join them on Saint John the Baptist's Day and then to retire to Laon, in Picardy, where he had some family property.

Eustache did not possess a fortune, but in those days it was not the custom to marry one sack of escudos with another. Parents would take into account the tastes and sympathies of the future husband and wife and set about carefully studying the character, conduct, and ability of the persons who were going to wed. Very different from today's parents, who demand greater moral guarantees from a servant than from a future son-in-law.

Meanwhile, the troubadour's prediction had reduced the already rather stagnant thoughts of the clothier to such an extent that he remained standing in the center of the half-moon, completely dazed, not hearing the crystalline voices chattering in the bell towers of the Samaritaine, repeating: "Midday! Midday!" But in Paris, striking twelve takes an hour, and the clock at the Louvre soon took over the speaker's podium with more solemnity; then that of the Augustinians; and afterward, that of the Châtelet. Eustache, terrified because it had become so late, began to run as quickly as he could, leaving behind in a matter of minutes the streets of la Monnaie, Borrel, and Tirechappe. Then he slowed down, and, once he'd turned the corner of the Boucherie-de-Beauvais, joy covered his face when he spied the red canvases of Les Halles, the stands of the Enfants-sans-Souci, the scale, the cross, and the handsome lantern of the spire with its small, lead-covered roof.

It was in that square, and under one of those canvases, that Javotte Goubard, Eustache's betrothed, was awaiting his return. Most of the merchants had a stand in the plaza of the Les Halles market, a branch of their dark stores that was overseen by a family member. Javotte took her place every morning in her father's stand, and there, actually sitting on the merchandise, she tried to draw customers in. Sometimes she would get up to call them or grab them by the arm, not releasing them until they bought something. All of which, at the same time, did not keep her from being the most timid of all the young ladies who, not having married, had reached the age when a girl is considered an old maid. Full of charm, pretty, blond, tall, and slightly slumped, as were the majority of the girls dedicated to commerce, with a slim, delicate figure. She also blushed easily at any word spoken out of turn, although she was better than anyone at the game of "fast and loose" (the business style of the period).

Eustache usually came to take her place at midday under the red canvas so that she could eat with her father at the store. And it was his intention of doing just that which made Eustache move along, fearing his lateness might make Javotte impatient. However, from a distance he could see that she seemed quite calm, with her elbow leaning on a roll of fabric and paying close attention to the animated, noisy chatter of a handsome soldier who was leaning on the same roll and who seemed to be a customer rather than anything one might imagine.

"It's my fiancé!" said Javotte, smiling at the stranger, who turned his head without changing position to take the measure of the apprentice with that disdain soldiers have for ordinary townspeople.

"He looks like a bugler," he observed gravely, "except that a bugler has a little more *purpose* in his gait. But you know, Javotte, the bugler in a company is something less than a horse and something more than a dog . . ."

"This is my nephew," said Javotte to Eustache, looking at him with her big blue eyes and smiling in satisfaction. "He managed to get a leave to attend our wedding. Isn't that wonderful? He's a harquebusier in the cavalry. Oh! What a wonderful uniform! If you were dressed that way, Eustache!—but, you aren't as tall, or as strong . . ."

"And for how long," said the young Eustache timidly, "will you be doing us the honor of staying with us in Paris?"

"That depends," said the soldier, standing up after delaying his answer. "They've sent us to Berri to exterminate the peasants, and if they keep quiet for a while, I can give you a month. But in any case, come Saint Martin's Day we're to be sent to Paris to replace the Humières regiment, and then I'll see you every day, indefinitely."

Eustache examined the harquebusier when he managed to evade his gaze, and found him to be physically not what he would expect in a nephew.

"Well, I said every day, and that's not the case," the nephew went on, "because Thursdays we take part in the grand parade. But since we have our nights free, I'll always be able to dine that evening at your house."

"How does he count on eating the other days?" thought Eustache.

"But, Mademoiselle Goubard, you never told me your nephew was so . . ."

"So *spruce*? Oh yes! How he's grown! Well, it's been seven years since we've seen poor Joseph, and a lot of water has passed under the bridge since then."

"And a lot of wine under his nose," thought the apprentice, put off by the ruddy face of his future nephew. "No one's face get's that fiery from drinking watered-down wine. Master Goubard's bottles are going to dance the dance of the dead before the wedding . . . and perhaps afterward as well."

"Let's eat. Papa must be getting impatient," said Javotte, walking out of the stand. "Joseph, give me your arm! And to think that once upon a time, when I was twelve and you ten, I was the bigger one, and you called me Mama. . . . How proud I'll be to be walking on the arm of a harquebusier! You'll take me out walking, won't you? I go out so little! And since I may not go out alone . . . Sunday evenings, I have to attend religion classes, because I'm in the Sisterhood of the Virgin of the Holy Innocents. I wear a ribbon of the standard."

The young woman's chatter, rhythmically marked by the military gait of the soldier—that light and graceful form leaping along, entwined with the heavy and rigid form of the other—faded quickly in the dull shadow of the pillars that lined rue Tonnellerie, leaving nothing in Eustache's eyes but a shadow, and in his ears a buzz.

VII. Miseries and Crosses

Up until now, we've been closely following this bourgeois tale without taking more time to tell it than it needed to take place. And now, despite our respect, or, better yet, despite our profound esteem for maintaining the three unities in the novel, we find ourselves forced to have one of them leap some days ahead. Eustache's tribulations with regard to his future nephew might be sufficiently interesting to tell, but they were, in the event, less bitter than what one might have expected after all we've said. Eustache soon felt more at ease with regard to his fiancée. Javotte really had done nothing more than retain a too-intense impression of her childhood memories, which in an uneventful life like hers must acquire a disproportionate importance.

At first, all she'd seen in the cavalry harquebusier was the happy, noisy boy, her playmate of former times, but it did not take her long to realize that the boy had grown up, that he'd taken other paths in life, and she soon became more reserved with him.

As far as the soldier was concerned: aside from the customary familiarities, he did not seem to harbor any dishonorable intentions toward his young aunt. It might even be said that he was one of those men—there are many—whose desire is not aroused by respectable women. For the moment he, like Tabarin, could say "that the bottle was his lover." The first three days he was in Paris, he never left Javotte for a moment, and even brought her at night to the Cours de la Reine, the two of them accompanied only by an old servant woman, all to Eustache's disgust. But that did not last long, because he soon tired of her company and got into the habit of going out alone all day—politely, let it be said, returning at dinnertime.

The only thing bothering the future husband was seeing this relative so comfortably established in the house that was going to be his after the wedding, a guest, so it seemed, who would be difficult to dislodge because with each passing day he appeared more firmly ensconced. And he was only a nephew once removed of Javotte, being the child of Master Goubard's deceased wife's first marriage. But how was Eustache going to make her understand that she was exaggerating the importance of family ties, and that she had ideas that were too strict about the rights and principles of relatives—even, to put it bluntly, too antiquated and patriarchal?

Even so, it was possible that the soldier himself would realize his indiscretion, so Eustache was obliged to be patient—"like the ladies of Fontainebleau when the court is in Paris," as the proverb goes.

However, the wedding did not change the habits of the harquebusier, who thought that thanks to the peacefulness of the peasants he would be granted permission to remain in Paris until his regiment arrived. Eustache made a few epigrammatic allusions to people who take a store for an inn, or to those who were not welcome and who seemed weak. By the same token, he did not dare to speak frankly to his wife and father-in-law lest he appear too selfish at the outset of his married life, when he really owed them everything he was.

Besides, the soldier's company was in no way amusing. His mouth was the eternal bell ringing out his own glory: of his triumphs in individual combat which had made him the terror of the army, and of his prodigious deeds carried out against the peasants, miserable French villagers whom the soldiers of King Henri fought because they couldn't pay their taxes, and who did not exactly seem to be enjoying their famous chicken *paysanne* . . .

This swaggering was quite common in those days, as is obvious in literary characters like Taillebras and Captain Matamoros, constantly reproduced in the comedies of the period. And this is due, in my own opinion, to the victorious irruption of the Gascon, followed by the Navarese, into Paris. But this vainglorious character grew weaker over time, and, a few years later, the figure Foeneste was merely a weak caricature, though a perfect comic type; and in the comedy *Le Menteur*, in 1662, it had already shrunk to almost ordinary proportions.

But what our good Eustache took most careful note of in the soldier's habits was his constant mania to treat him, Eustache, as if he were a little boy, to emphasize his less attractive features, and, whenever he could, to make him look ridiculous in front of Javotte, something that was quite damaging in the first days, when a newly married groom must establish his respect with regard to the future. Besides, it was very easy to wound the honor of a man who only recently had been set up in business, licensed, and sworn in.

A new tribulation came swiftly along to push things over the limit. Since Eustache was going to be made a member of the guild guards, and since he did not want, like the honorable Master Goubard, to carry out that office wearing civilian clothes and with a borrowed halberd, he bought a basket-handled sword (though lacking the basket handle), a helmet, and a cuirass—all made of a red copper that looked more appropriate for pots. After spending three days cleaning and polishing the pieces, he managed to give them a shine they'd never had. But when he put it all on and marched proudly through the store asking if he had "the grace to wear armor," the harquebusier laughed his head off and swore he seemed to be decked out in kitchenwear.

VIII. The Tweak

With things standing in this fashion, it happened that one afternoon—it was the twelfth or thirteenth of the month, of course a Thursday—Eustache closed the store early, a liberty he would never have taken if Master Goubard hadn't departed the previous day to visit his property in Picardy, where he intended to move three months later, once his successor was solidly established and fully merited the confidence of the other merchants.

It happened that the harquebusier, when he returned home as usual, found the door locked and the lights out. That shocked him a great deal, as the evening watch had not passed through Châtelet; and since he always returned a bit fired-up with wine, his contrary nature translated itself into a curse that made Eustache, who had still not gone to bed, apprehensive about the boldness of his action, tremble.

"Hello there! Hey!" shouted the soldier, kicking the door. "What, is there some holiday this afternoon? Is today Saint Michael's Day, the holiday of clothiers, thieves, and pickpockets . . . ?"

And he pounded his fist against the shopwindow, which had no more effect than grinding water in a mortar.

"Hey! Uncle! Aunt! Do you want me to sleep out of doors, on the paving stones, at the mercy of dogs and other beasts . . . ? Hey, hey! Come down right away, you bourgeois, I'm bringing you money! May the plague take you, churl!"

The poor nephew's harangue did not move even slightly the wooden face of the door. His words were not heard, as when the Venerable Bede preached to a mountain of stones.

But while doors may be deaf, windows are not blind, and there is a very simple method for making them see. The soldier quickly reached that very conclusion, walked out from the somber gallery of porticos, retreated to the center of rue Tonnellerie, picked up a stone, and aimed so well that he smashed one of the small windows on the mezzanine. Eustache had not foreseen that eventuality, a formidable question mark that summarized the soldier's monologue: "Why won't you open the door for me?"

Eustache quickly made a decision: a coward who loses his head is like a peasant who starts to squander his money, and besides, he had decided to face up to the soldier once and for all in the presence of his wife, whose respect for her husband may have declined somewhat after seeing him play the fool for the harquebusier—the difference being that even a fool occasionally hits back. He slipped his mantle over his head, and before Javotte could stop him, ran down the narrow staircase to the street floor. He took his sword off the wall as he passed through the rear of the store, and only when he felt the cold of the copper haft in his hot hand did he stop an instant to walk with leaden feet toward the door, the key to which he was carrying in his other hand. But then a second window broke with a huge racket, and the footsteps of his wife, which he heard behind his own, restored all his energy. He quickly opened the heavy door and stood on the threshold with his sword bared, like an archangel at the gates of the earthly paradise.

"Now what does this night owl want? This worthless drunk? This lunatic looking for fights . . . ?" he shouted in a tone of voice that would have sounded tremulous if he'd done it two notes lower. "Is this the way to behave around honorable people . . . ? Go on, get out of here and go sleep under the tents with the other thugs, or I'll rouse the neighbors and the night watch will come and take you away!"

"Well, well, well! Just look at how our simpleton sings! What's gotten into you tonight? This is something new! I like seeing you speak like a character from tragedy, like Tranchemontagne. The brave are my friends! Come, let Picrochole embrace you!"

"Get out of here, you cur! Can't you see that you're waking the neighbors with all the noise you're making and that they're going to have you arrested for a swindler or a thief? Go on, then, go your way quietly, and never come back!"

But instead of leaving, the soldier came toward the door, which weakened somewhat the end of Eustache's response.

"Very well spoken!" said the harquebusier. "The warning you've just given me is honest and deserves to be paid for."

And in the twinkling of an eye, he was standing right before Eustache and tweaked his nose so hard that it turned scarlet.

"There! And you can keep the change. Farewell to you, Uncle!"

Eustache could not stand patiently by and tolerate an insult like that in the presence of his wife—something even more humiliating than a slap—and despite Javotte's efforts to hold him back, he fell upon his adversary, who was leaving, and gave him a slash that would have honored the arm of the Roger the Crusader—if his sword had had something resembling an edge on it. But Eustache's sword hadn't cut anything since the religious wars, so it didn't even cut through the soldier's leather straps. The harquebusier caught Eustache's hands in his own and smartly disarmed him. Eustache then began to shout as loudly as he could and kicked the boots of his persecutor. Luckily,

Javotte got between them, because even though the neighbors could see the fight from their windows, they hadn't the slightest intention of stopping it. Eustache finally managed to extract his bluish fingers from the human vise that held them and had to rub them for a long time to make them lose the square shape they'd acquired.

"I'm not afraid of you!" he exclaimed. "And we'll meet again! If you've got any dignity, you'll be at Pré-aux-Clercs tomorrow morning! At six, you rogue, you braggart, And we'll fight to the death!"

"A very well-chosen site, my little champion, and we'll comport ourselves like gentlemen! Until tomorrow, then, and by Saint George, may the night seem short to you!"

The soldier pronounced those words in a considerate tone he'd never used until then. Eustache proudly returned to his wife: his challenge had caused him to increase six palms in height. He picked up his sword and noisily slammed the door.

IX. Château-Gaillard

When the young clothier awoke, he felt completely bereft of his valor of the previous evening. It was not difficult for him to recognize that he'd made a fool of himself in challenging the harquebusier to a duel, he who could manage no other weapon than the willow wand, with which he'd often played as an apprentice in the field of the Carthusians with his friends. It took him no time at all to resolve that he would stay at home and leave his adversary strolling, showing himself off, wandering back and forth like a goose on a lead.

When the hour set for the duel had passed, he got up, opened the store, and said not a word to his wife about what had happened the previous night. For her part, she also made no references to it. They had breakfast in silence, and then Javotte, as always, went to take her place under the red tent, leaving her husband occupied in examining, with the help of a maid, a bolt of cloth in order to find its defects. It must be said that he frequently looked toward the door, each time fearing that his terrible relative was coming to reproach him for his cowardice and for not keeping his word. And at around eight-thirty he saw the harquebusier's uniform appear under the gallery of the porticos, like one of Rembrandt's German soldiers, shining from the triple glow of his helmet, his cuirass, and his nose—an ill-fated apparition that rapidly became larger and clearer, and whose metallic footsteps seemed to mark each minute of the clothier's last hour.

But the same uniform was not covering the same body, or, to say it more simply, it was a fellow soldier, a friend of the other's, who stopped outside Eustache's store. To Eustache, who had barely recovered from his shock, he spoke in a calm and very civilized tone.

He informed him that, in the first place, his adversary, after having waited for him for two hours in the designated place and not seeing him, had imagined that some unforeseen accident had kept Eustache from attending, and, for that reason, would return the next day at the same time and would remain there the same amount of time, and if this meeting were also not to take place, he would come instantly to the store, cut off Eustache's ears, and put them in his pocket, as, in 1605, the celebrated Brusquet had done to a squire of the Duke de Chevreuse for the same reason. He had obtained the applause of the court, which found his action to be in very good taste.

Eustache answered that his adversary offended his valor with such a threat, that it doubled the motive for the duel. He added that the obstacle was nothing more than his not having found someone to be his second.

The other appeared satisfied with the explanation and even informed the merchant that he would find excellent seconds at the Pont-Neuf, opposite the Samaritaine. That was where people who had no other profession strolled about, always ready to embrace, for an escudo, whatever cause might come along, and could even supply swords. After those observations, he made a deep bow and departed.

When Eustache was alone, he began to think and remained immersed in confusion for a long time, as his mind was entangled in three different resolutions: first, he thought of informing the judge of the soldier's annoyances and threats, and of asking permission to bear arms to defend himself. But that would expose him to the risk of combat. Or he could decide to go to the site of the duel having advised the sergeants so that they would arrive just at the moment when the duel was to begin. But what guarantee did he have that they wouldn't arrive after it was all over? Finally, he thought of consulting the gypsy from the Pont-Neuf. And that is what he decided to do.

At midday, the maid replaced Javotte under the red tent, and she went home to dine with her husband. Eustache said nothing about the visit he'd had that morning, but later he asked her to take charge of the store while he went to pay a business call at the house of a gentleman who had just come to Paris and wanted to have clothing made. He took up his samples and went off to the Pont-Neuf.

Château-Gaillard, located on the bank of the river, at the southern end of the bridge, and crowned by a round tower which in other times served as a prison, was now beginning to fall into ruins and collapse, being inhabited only by those who had no other refuge. Eustache, after pacing out his vacillation for some time on the rocky soil, found a small door in the center of which a bat was nailed. He knocked softly, and Master Gonin's monkey instantly opened, lifting a latch, a service for which he was trained, as are at times house cats.

The prestidigitator was sitting at a table, reading. He turned gravely and signaled to the young man to sit down on a footstool. When Eustache had told him of his adventure, he replied that he had just the thing for him, and that he'd been wise to come.

"What you desire is a charm," he added, "a magic charm to overcome your adversary. Is that not what you want?"

"Yes, if it's possible."

"Although everyone makes them, you will find none as efficacious as mine. Besides, it is not like the others, which are derived from diabolical arts, but is the result of a deep knowledge of white magic and will in no way compromise the salvation of your soul."

"That's good, because if it were any other way, I would certainly refrain from using it. But, how much does your magic product cost? I'm not sure that I can pay it."

"Consider now that it's your life you are buying, and glory besides.

That being the case, do you think that these two excellent things could be acquired for less than a hundred escudos?"

"A hundred devils take you!" grumbled Eustache, whose countenance darkened. "That's more than I have! And what's life worth without bread to eat, what's glory worth without clothes to wear? And anyway, how do I know these aren't the false promises of a charlatan who gulls credulous folks?"

"Pay me afterward."

"That puts a different light on things. What would you like as security?"

"Only your hand."

"Come now, do you take me for a fool listening to your boasting? Didn't you tell me I'd end up on the gallows?"

"No question about it, and I won't withdraw the statement."

"Then, if that's so, why should I be afraid of the duel?"

"No reason, except a few stabs and scratches that will open the greatest doors to your soul. . . . After that, you will be taken up, dead or alive, and raised to the high but short half-cross, as the sentence reads. And there you will carry out your destiny. Do you understand?"

The clothier understood so well that he hastened to offer his hand to the prestidigitator as a proof of his acceptance, asking him for ten days in which to find the money. The other agreed, after marking the final day for payment on the wall. Then he took up the book of Albertus Magnus—containing also the commentaries of Cornelius Agrippa and the Abbot Trithemius—and opened it to the chapter "Individual Combat." And to convince Eustache even more that his operation had nothing diabolical to it, he told him he could go on saying his prayers without fear that they would be an obstacle.

Then he raised the lid of a coffer and took out an unglazed clay jar in which he mixed several ingredients, following, it appeared, the book's instructions while quietly reciting some sort of incantation. When he was finished, he took Eustache's right hand (Eustache was crossing himself with the other) and daubed it with the mixture he'd just made, right up to the wrist. Immediately after that, he removed a very old, greasy jar from another coffer and, tipping it very carefully, he poured a few drops over the back of the hand, pronouncing a few words in Latin that resembled the formula priests use at baptisms.

At that, Eustache felt a kind of electric thrill that ran though his entire arm, and this frightened him a great deal. It seemed to him his hand was swelling, and yet—strange to tell—it clenched and stretched several times, cracking its joints, as when an animal awakens. Then he felt nothing more, his circulation seemed to return to normal, and Master Gonin said it was all over, that he could challenge the most celebrated swordsmen in the court and army and cut them buttonholes for all the useless buttons fashion loaded onto their uniforms.

X. At Pré-aux-Clercs

The next morning, four men were crossing the green avenues of Pré-aux-Clercs looking for a spot that would serve their purpose and be sufficiently hidden. When they reached the bottom of a small hill that bordered the southern part, they stopped at the place where people played skittles, which seemed to them a satisfactory place to fight. Then Eustache and his adversary removed their doublets, and their seconds, in accordance with the rules, searched under their shirts and breeches. The clothier was excited because he had faith in the gypsy's charm, and it is well known that magical business—charms, philtres, spells—never were believed so much as in that period, when they were the cause of so many legal trials, filling the registers of the tribunals because the judges shared in the general credulity.

Eustache's second, whom he'd found at the Pont-Neuf and paid one escudo, greeted the harquebusier's friend and asked him if he too intended to fight. Since the friend answered that he didn't, the hired second crossed his arms indifferently and stepped back to contemplate the combatants.

The clothier could not avoid feeling some anxiety when his adversary saluted him with his sword, a salute he did not return. He stood stock-still, holding his sword as if it were a candle, so awkwardly assuming the *en garde* position that the soldier, out of decency, promised himself he would no more than scratch him. But no sooner had their weapons touched than Eustache noticed that his hand was dragging his arm forward, violently resisting any attempt to control it.

More exactly, Eustache felt in his hand the powerful force it exercised over the muscles in his arm, whose movements had a prodigious strength and elasticity, comparable to that of a steel spring. Thus the soldier almost dislocated his wrist parrying a third-position thrust, but a fourth-position cut sent his sword flying ten paces, while Eustache's, without pausing to gain new impetus, and in the same initial movement, pierced the harquebusier's body so violently that the basket handle was embedded in the soldier's chest. Eustache, who had not thrown himself forward completely but was dragged by an unforeseen shake of his right hand, would have broken his head in falling if he hadn't landed on his adversary's stomach.

"My God, what a wrist!" exclaimed the soldier's second. "This man could give a lesson to the knight Oaktwister! He doesn't have his grace or his physique, but as far as the strength of his arm is concerned, it's worse than that of a Welsh archer."

Meanwhile, Eustache had gotten to his feet with the help of his second and stood there, transfixed by what had just happened. But when he could clearly make out the harquebusier at his feet, nailed to the ground like a frog in a magic circle, he ran away so quickly that he left behind him on the grass, forgotten, his Sunday doublet, the one with the silk trim.

Since the soldier was beyond question dead, the two seconds had no reason to remain and rapidly departed. They'd gone about a hundred paces when Eustache's man exclaimed, slapping himself on the forehead, "I forgot the sword I lent him!" He let the other go his way and, back at the scene of the duel, began to search the dead man's pockets, finding only some dice, a piece of string, and a dirty, old tarot deck.

"A cardsharp, and what a cardsharp! Another thug who doesn't even have a miserable watch! Let the devil take you, fuse-blower!"

The encyclopedic education of our age frees us from the obligation of explaining everything in his remarks except the last term, which refers to the deceased's profession as a harquebusier, whose weapon was fired with a burning fuse.

Not daring to take anything from the man's uniform, the sale of which might have gotten him into trouble, he limited himself to stealing his boots, which he rolled up under his cape together with Eustache's doublet and went off grumbling.

XI. Obsession

The clothier was several days locked up in his house, his heart heavy because of that tragic death which he had caused over such insignificant offenses—and the means he'd used, as reprehensible and blameworthy in this world as in the next. There were moments when he thought it was all a dream, and if it hadn't been for the doublet he'd left on the grass, evidence that shone by its very absence, he would have doubted his own memory.

Finally, one afternoon, he tried to open his eyes to the evidence and went to the Pré-aux-Clercs, as if he were taking a walk. His eyes clouded over when he recognized the skittles field where the duel had taken place and he had to sit down. Some lawyers were playing there, as they often did before dining. Eustache, when the mist clouding his eyes had lifted, thought he saw on the ground between the spread legs of one of the players a huge bloodstain.

He convulsively got up and hastened to leave the field, bearing in his eyes the bloodstain, which retained its form and settled onto all the objects on which his gaze rested. It was like those livid stains that jump around in front of our eyes when we look into the sun.

When he returned home, he discovered he'd been followed. Only then did he think that someone from the Hôtel de la Reine Margarite, before which he'd passed the other morning and this afternoon, might have recognized him. And even though the laws about dueling were not rigorously enforced in that era, he feared the authorities might find it convenient to hang a poor merchant as a warning to the courtiers, whom at that time the law did not dare to attack as it would later on.

These thoughts and many others caused him to spend a very agitated night. He could not close his eyes without there appearing to him a thousand gallows, from each one hanging a rope, and from each rope a dead man who twisted around laughing in a horrible way, or a skeleton whose ribs shone bright white in the light of the full moon.

But a happy idea came to erase all those twisted visions: Eustache remembered the magistrate, the old customer of his father-in-law who had welcomed him in such a friendly way. He proposed to visit him the next morning and tell him everything, persuaded that he would protect him, even if it were only for the sake of Javotte, whom he'd seen and caressed since she was a little girl, and for Master Goubard, whom he held in great esteem. The poor tailor finally calmed down and slept until the morning, resting in the pillow of his sound resolution.

The next day, at around nine, he knocked at the magistrate's door. The magistrate's secretary, thinking he'd come to take measurements for some suit or to propose a sale, immediately led him to his master, who, half-reclined in an armchair covered with cushions, was reading a jolly book. He had in his hand the ancient poem of Merlinus Coccaius and was taking special pleasure in his narration of the deeds of Baldus, the valiant precursor of Pantagruel, and even more in the incomparable subtleties and thefts of Cingar, that grotesque model who happily gave form to our Panurge.

Master Chevassut was reading the story of the sheep Cingar tosses overboard—he tosses into the sea the one sheep he'd bought which is instantly followed by all the others—when he noticed his visitor. Leaving the book on a table, he turned to the clothier in a very good mood.

He asked Eustache about his wife's health, about his father-in-law, and badgered him with all manner of banal jokes, alluding to his condition as a newlywed. The young man took advantage of that moment to tell him of his adventure, of his dispute with the harquebusier, and, encouraged by the magistrate's calm, paternal air, he also confessed the tragic outcome.

Master Chevassut stared at him with the same astonishment with which he would have stared at the giant Fracasse in his book, or the faithful Falquet, who resembled a greyhound. But Master Eustache Bouteroue, a merchant from the porticos? Even though he had heard that a certain Eustache was presently a suspect, he'd not given the least credence to such reports, nor to the deed itself, attributed to a dwarf who was servant to the clothier, no taller than Gribouille or Triboulet, and which had left a soldier of the king nailed to the ground.

But when he was no longer in any doubt about the facts, he promised the poor clothier he would use his influence to silence the matter and throw the agents of justice off his trail. He assured him, as well, that so long as no witnesses came forward to accuse him, he need not worry.

Master Chevassut was accompanying him to the door, reiterating his promises, when, at the instant he was humbly saying good-bye to him, Eustache gave the magistrate a slap that turned his head around, a stunning blow that turned the magistrate's face half red and half blue, like the shield of Paris, and left him mute in astonishment, his mouth open wide and as silent as a fish.

Poor Eustache was so horrified by his action that he threw himself at the magistrate's feet, begging his pardon in the most supplicating and pious terms, swearing that it had been a convulsive, unforeseen movement in which his own will had no part and for which he hoped for mercy, from him and from God. The old man got up, more astounded than angry. But no sooner was he on his feet than Eustache slapped him on the other cheek so it was even with the first. The blow was so hard that his five fingers left an imprint from which it would have been possible to make a mold.

This was now intolerable, and Master Chevassut ran to the bell to summon his people. But the tailor followed him, continuing his dance, which constituted a singular scene, because with each blow he gave to thank his protector, the unhappy man dissolved in tears, excuses, and choked supplications that contrasted with the action in the most comic way. But it was useless to try to stop the impulses governing his hand. He was like a boy holding on to a huge bird by a string. The bird drags the frightened child all around the room, and the boy neither dares to let it go free nor has the strength to stop it. Thus was the unfortunate Eustache dragged along by his hand in the pursuit of the magistrate, who ran around tables and chairs, ringing the bell and shouting furiously in pain and anger. Finally, the servants came in and subdued Eustache, who was out of breath and fainting. Master Chevassut, who of course did not believe in white magic, could only think that he'd been made a fool of and mistreated by that young man for some reason he could not imagine. He summoned the police and handed over his man under the double accusation of homicide committed during a duel and assault on a magistrate in his own home. Eustache only recovered consciousness when he heard the locks of the cell to which he was destined. "I'm innocent!" he shouted to the jailer who led him. "For God's sake!" replied the jailer gravely, "where do you think you are? All of you here are innocent!"

XII. Concerning Albertus Magnus and Death

Eustache was locked in one of those cells in the Châtelet of which Cyrano said that when people saw him there they took him for a candle under a cupping glass. "If they're giving me," Eustache thought after examining all the corners in a pirouette turn—"if they're giving me this stone suit as clothing, it's too large; if they're giving it to me as a tomb, it's too small. The teeth of the fleas are longer than their bodies, and you suffer from gallstones here, which is no less painful for being external."

Here our hero could reflect at his leisure on his bad luck and curse the fatal help he'd received from the gypsy, who had distracted one of his limbs from the natural authority of his head, with disastrous consequences. But his surprise was enormous when he saw him appear one day in his cell, calmly asking him how he was. "May the devil hang you by your guts, you damned charlatan and fortune-teller! Your cursed charms are to blame for all this!"

"What?" answered the other. "Is it my fault you didn't come on the tenth day to have me remove the charm by bringing me the sum we'd agreed on?"

"What? Did I know you needed the money so badly?" said Eustache, lowering his voice. "You who can make gold whenever you want it, like the writer Flamel!"

"That's not so!" answered the other. "It's the other way around! Some day I will accomplish that great hermetic task, because I am on the way to discovering it. But until now I've only managed to transform fine gold into a very good and pure iron, a secret that the great Ramon Llull possessed at the end of his life."

"An extraordinary knowledge!" said the tailor. "Now, you have finally come to get me out of here! For heaven's sake! It's high time! I'd given up hope."

"This is the key to the situation, my friend. This is, in effect, what I am going to try to bring about, to open the doors without keys, in order to be able to enter and leave, and you will see through which operation that is obtained."

Saying that, the gypsy took his volume of Albertus Magnus out of his pocket and, by the light of a lantern he'd brought with him, he read the following paragraph:

Heroic Means Used by Thieves to Enter Houses

> You take the severed hand of a hanged man, which must be purchased before his death; you submerge it meticulously, taking care to have it almost enclosed in a copper receptacle that contains cyma and saltpeter with *spondillis* grease. You place the receptacle in a fire made of ferns and completely dry verbena until the hand, after a quarter of an hour, is completely dry and ready to be preserved. Later you make a candle with seal grease and Lapland

sesame and you cause the hand to take hold of the candle as if it were a candlestick. Wherever you go, carrying it before you, all barriers will fall, all locks will open, and the people who come before you will remain motionless.

The hand prepared in this manner receives the name *hand of glory*.

"What an invention!" exclaimed Eustache Bouteroue.

"Wait a minute! Although you haven't formally sold me your hand, it belongs to me because you didn't redeem it on the appointed day. And the proof of it is that after the agreed-on time limit passed, it has behaved itself—owing to the spirit that possesses it—in such a way that I could enjoy it in the shortest possible time. Tomorrow, Parliament will sentence you to the gallows; the day after tomorrow, the sentence will be carried out, and that same day will I harvest this so very desired fruit and prepare it in the proper way."

"Oh no you won't!" exclaimed Eustache. "Tomorrow, I will reveal the entire mystery to those *gentlemen*!"

"Ah, very well! Do it . . . and you will be burned alive for having made use of magic. That will get you accustomed to the Devil's grill. . . . But that will never happen, because your horoscope says the gallows, and nothing can free you from it."

Then the unfortunate Eustache began to shout so desperately and to weep so bitterly that it was heartrending.

"Come, come, dear friend!" said Master Gonin tenderly. "Why rebel against destiny?"

"Heavens above! It's easy for you to talk that way," said Eustache between sobs. "But when death is so near . . ."

"But what is so strange about death? Death doesn't matter a fig to me! 'No one dies before his time,' said the tragedian Seneca. Are you perhaps the only vassal of that Lady, my friend? I am as well, and so is he, and he, and he, and Martin, and Philippe. . . . Death respects no one. It's so bold that it condemns, kills, and carries away with no discrimination whatsoever popes, emperors, and kings, as well as provosts, sergeants, and other scum. Which is why you ought not be so afflicted in doing now what others will do later. Their luck is more deplorable than yours, for if death is an evil, it's only an evil for those who are going to die. Only one day remains to you to suffer this evil, but the majority of people have twenty or thirty years, or even more.

"An ancient author said: 'The hour life has given you, you are already letting slip away.' We are in death even in the midst of life, because when we are no longer in life, we are beyond death. Or, to put it better, death doesn't concern you dead or alive—alive because you exist, and dead because you no longer exist.

"These arguments, my friend, should be sufficient to give you courage when you drink the absinthe of death. Until then, meditate on this beautiful verse by Lucretius, the gist of which is: 'Live as long as you can, for it will take nothing away from the eternity of your death.' "

After delivering these maxims, the quintessence of classic and modern authors, chosen for their subtlety and sophistication in the taste of the age, Master Gonin put away his lantern and knocked at the cell door, which the jailer opened. And the darkness again fell on the prisoner like a lead plate.

XIII. Wherein the Author Speaks His Mind

Those who wish to know all the details of Eustache Bouteroue's trial will find the documents in the *Arrêts memorables du Parlement de Paris*, which are in the manuscript library. You will find them with the aid of Monsieur Paris, with his accustomed solicitude. This trial—they are arranged in alphabetical order—comes right before the trial of the Baron de Boutteville, also quite curious for the singularity of his duel with the Marquis de Bussi, in which, to challenge the law, he came expressly from Lorrain to Paris and fought right in the Place Royale at three o'clock in the afternoon on Easter Sunday (1627). But this does not interest us now. In the trial of Eustache Bouteroue, only the duel and the outrages perpetrated on the person of the magistrate are dealt with, not the magic spell that caused the disorder. But an early note remits the reader to the *Recueil d'histoires tragiques de Belleforest* (in the edition published at The Hague, the Rouen edition being incomplete). It is there you will find the details we need with regard to the adventure Belleforest quite properly entitles: *The Possessed Hand.*

XIV. Conclusion

The day of his execution, Eustache, who was then lodged in a cell less dark than the first, received a visit from a confessor who mumbled some spiritual advice to him in the same style as that of the gypsy, and produced no better effect. He was an ordained priest from one of those good families that have an abbot son in order to glorify their name. He wore an embroidered collar, had his beard trimmed in the shape of a spindle, and a curled and twisted mustache. His hair was curled tightly and he spoke in a mellow voice and with an affected style. Eustache, seeing how superficial and pleased with himself he was, did not have the courage to confess all his sins and relied on his own prayers to be forgiven.

The priest absolved him and to pass the time, since he had to remain with the condemned man until two, shared with him a book entitled *The Tears of the Penitent Soul, or the Return of the Sinner Toward His God*. Eustache opened the book to the first page, where the king's permission to publish it was recorded, and began to read, quite remorsefully, where it said: "Henri, King of France and Navarre, to our subjects and vassals" etc., up to the phrase "considering these causes and desiring to treat the aforementioned favorably . . ." Here he could not hold back his tears and returned the book to the priest, telling him it was too moving and that he was afraid he would be overcome if he went on reading. Then the confessor took a deck of cards out of his pocket and suggested to the penitent they play a few hands. The priest won some money Javotte had sent Eustache to procure him some consolation. The poor Eustache was not able to pay much attention to the game and didn't really notice the loss.

At two, Eustache left the Châtelet, his voice trembling when he said the routine Our Fathers and was led to the square of the Augustinians, located between the two arches that form the entrance to rue Dauphine and the Pont-Neuf, where he was honored with a stone gallows. He showed quite a bit of resolve as he climbed the ladder. After all, since the location of this execution was one of the most frequented of places, there were many people watching him. Of course, since we take as much time as possible to make that leap into the void, in the instant when the executioner prepared to put the noose around his neck with the same ceremony as he would in bestowing the Golden Fleece—this kind of person, when they exercise their profession before the public, carry things out with ability and even with a certain grace—Eustache begged him to stop for an instant so he could say just two prayers, one to Saint Ignatius and the other to Saint Aloysius Gonzaga, saints he'd reserved for last because they'd been beatified that same year of 1609. But the executioner replied that the public also had its business to take care of and that it was in bad taste to make them wait for a spectacle as simple as a mere execution. The noose, which he tightened as he pushed him off the stepladder, cut off Eustache's reply.

It is stated as fact that when everything seemed over and the executioner was on his way home, Master Gonin appeared at one of the pathways to the Château-Gaillard that overlooked the square. Instantly, even though the tailor's body was hanging completely lax and inanimate, his arm rose, and his hand began to wave in a merry way, like the tail of a dog that sees its master. That drew a surprised gasp from the crowd and caused those who were leaving to return in haste, like people who think the show is over when another act remains.

The executioner put the stepladder back and touched the dead man's ankles: there was no pulse. He cut an artery: no blood flowed. But even so, the arm continued in its disordered movements.

The executioner was not a man who was easily frightened. He climbed up onto the back of his victim, accompanied by the shouts of those present, but the hand showed the same irreverence to him as it had to Magistrate Chevassut. The executioner, cursing, took out the huge knife he always carried with him and with two strokes cut off the possessed hand.

The hand made a prodigious leap and fell, bloody, amid the crowd, which scattered in shock. Then, making several leaps, thanks to the elasticity of its fingers, and since everyone got out of its path, it quickly made its way to the foot of the little tower of the Château-Gaillard. Then, scrambling with its fingers like a crab along the salients and the rough spots in the wall, it climbed to the little window where the gypsy was waiting for it.

Belleforest ends his singular history here, closing with these words:

> This adventure, annotated, commented, and illustrated, constituted for a long time the principal subject of conversation in polite society as well as among the lower classes, always eager for strange and supernatural tales. But even today it is a good story for amusing children by the fireside, although it should not be taken lightly by serious persons of good judgment.

NATHANIEL HAWTHORNE

*

Young Goodman Brown

(1835)

New England's Puritan fantastic is born from an obsession with universal damnation, which triumphs in the witches' Sabbath of this story. Every one of the inhabitants of the villages—even the most devout—is a witch! Not in vain was Nathaniel Hawthorne (1804–1864) a descendant of one of the judges who passed sentence on the witches of Salem. In this story, which displays Hawthorne's desperate religiosity, the witches' Sabbath is depicted the way the Puritans imagined it to be (with the interesting syncretic addition of the Indians' magic rites), but involving here an entire Puritan society that was in need of salvation.

Before Poe and sometimes better than Poe, Hawthorne was the great narrator in the fantastic genre in the United States.

Young Goodman Brown came forth at sunset into the street at Salem village; but put his head back, after crossing the threshold, to exchange a parting kiss with his young wife. And Faith, as the wife was aptly named, thrust her own pretty head into the street, letting the wind play with the pink ribbons of her cap while she called to Goodman Brown.

"Dearest heart," whispered she, softly and rather sadly, when her lips were close to his ear, "prithee put off your journey until sunrise and sleep in your own bed to-night. A lone woman is troubled with such dreams and such thoughts that she's afeard of herself sometimes. Pray tarry with me this night, dear husband, of all nights in the year."

"My love and my Faith," replied young Goodman Brown, "of all nights in the year, this one night must I tarry away from thee. My journey, as thou callest it, forth and back again, must needs be done 'twixt now and sunrise. What, my sweet, pretty wife, dost thou doubt me already, and we but three months married?"

"Then God bless you!" said Faith, with the pink ribbons; "and may you find all well when you come back."

"Amen!" cried Goodman Brown. "Say thy prayers, dear Faith, and go to bed at dusk, and no harm will come to thee."

So they parted; and the young man pursued his way until, being about to turn the corner by the meeting-house, he looked back and saw the head of Faith still peeping after him with a melancholy air, in spite of her pink ribbons.

"Poor little Faith!" thought he, for his heart smote him. "What a wretch am I to leave her on such an errand! She talks of dreams, too. Methought as she spoke there was trouble in her face, as if a dream had warned her what work is to be done to-night. But no, no; 't would kill her to think it. Well, she's a blessed angel on earth; and after this one night I'll cling to her skirts and follow her to heaven."

With this excellent resolve for the future, Goodman Brown felt himself justified in making more haste on his present evil purpose. He had taken a dreary road, darkened by all the gloomiest trees of the forest, which barely stood aside to let the narrow path creep through, and closed immediately behind. It was all as lonely as could be; and there is this peculiarity in such a solitude, that the traveller knows not who may be concealed by the innumerable trunks and the thick boughs overhead; so that with lonely footsteps he may yet be passing through an unseen multitude.

"There may be a devilish Indian behind every tree," said Goodman Brown to himself; and he glanced fearfully behind him as he added, "What if the devil himself should be at my very elbow!"

His head being turned back, he passed a crook of the road, and, looking forward again, beheld the figure of a man, in grave and decent attire, seated at the foot of an old tree. He arose at Goodman Brown's approach and walked onward side by side with him.

"You are late, Goodman Brown," said he. "The clock of the Old South was striking as I came through Boston, and that is full fifteen minutes agone."

"Faith kept me back a while," replied the young man, with a tremor in his voice, caused by the sudden appearance of his companion, though not wholly unexpected.

It was now deep dusk in the forest, and deepest in that part of it where these two were journeying. As nearly as could be discerned, the second traveller was about fifty years old, apparently in the same rank of life as Goodman Brown, and bearing a considerable resemblance to him, though perhaps more in expression than features. Still they might have been taken for father and son. And yet, though the elder person was as simply clad as the younger, and as simple in manner too, he had an indescribable air of one who knew the world, and who would not have felt abashed at the governor's dinner table or in

King William's court, were it possible that his affairs should call him thither. But the only thing about him that could be fixed upon as remarkable was his staff, which bore the likeness of a great black snake, so curiously wrought that it might almost be seen to twist and wriggle itself like a living serpent. This, of course, must have been an ocular deception, assisted by the uncertain light.

"Come, Goodman Brown," cried his fellow-traveller, "this is a dull pace for the beginning of a journey. Take my staff, if you are so soon weary."

"Friend," said the other, exchanging his slow pace for a full stop, "having kept covenant by meeting thee here, it is my purpose now to return whence I came. I have scruples touching the matter thou wot'st of."

"Sayest thou so?" replied he of the serpent, smiling apart. "Let us walk on, nevertheless, reasoning as we go; and if I convince thee not thou shalt turn back. We are but a little way in the forest yet."

"Too far! too far!" exclaimed the Goodman, unconsciously resuming his walk. "My father never went into the woods on such an errand, nor his father before him. We have been a race of honest men and good Christians since the days of the martyrs; and shall I be the first of the name of Brown that ever took this path and kept—"

"Such company, thou wouldst say," observed the elder person, interpreting his pause. "Well said, Goodman Brown! I have been as well acquainted with your family as with ever a one among the Puritans; and that's no trifle to say. I helped your grandfather, the constable, when he lashed the Quaker woman so smartly through the streets of Salem; and it was I that brought your father a pitch-pine knot, kindled at my own hearth, to set fire to an Indian village, in King Philip's war. They were my good friends, both; and many a pleasant walk have we had along this path, and returned merrily after midnight. I would fain be friends with you for their sake."

"If it be as thou sayest," replied Goodman Brown, "I marvel they never spoke of these matters; or, verily, I marvel not, seeing that the least rumour of the sort would have driven them from New England.

We are a people of prayer, and good works to boot, and abide no such wickedness."

"Wickedness or not," said the traveller with the twisted staff, "I have a very general acquaintance here in New England. The deacons of many a church have drunk the communion wine with me; the selectmen of divers towns make me their chairman; and a majority of the Great and General Court are firm supporters of my interest. The governor and I, too—But these are state secrets."

"Can this be so?" cried Goodman Brown, with a stare of amazement at his undisturbed companion. "Howbeit, I have nothing to do with the governor and council; they have their own ways, and are no rule for a simple husbandman like me. But, were I to go on with thee, how should I meet the eye of that good old man, our minister, at Salem village? Oh, his voice would make me tremble both Sabbath day and lecture day."

Thus far the elder traveller had listened with due gravity; but now burst into a fit of irrepressible mirth, shaking himself so violently that his snake-like staff actually seemed to wriggle in sympathy.

"Ha! ha! ha!" shouted he again and again; then composing himself, "Well, go on, Goodman Brown, go on; but, prithee, don't kill me with laughing."

"Well, then, to end the matter at once," said Goodman Brown, considerably nettled, "there is my wife, Faith. It would break her dear little heart; and I'd rather break my own."

"Nay, if that be the case," answered the other, "e'en go thy ways, Goodman Brown. I would not for twenty old women like the one hobbling before us that Faith should come to any harm."

As he spoke he pointed his staff at a female figure on the path, in whom Goodman Brown recognized a very pious and exemplary dame, who had taught him his catechism in youth, and was still his moral and spiritual adviser, jointly with the minister and Deacon Gookin.

"A marvel, truly, that Goody Cloyse should be so far in the wilderness at nightfall," said he. "But with your leave, friend, I shall take a cut through the woods until we have left this Christian woman behind. Being a stranger to you, she might ask whom I was consorting with and whither I was going."

"Be it so," said his fellow-traveller. "Betake you the woods, and let me keep the path."

Accordingly the young man turned aside, but took care to watch his companion, who advanced softly along the road until he had come within a staff's length of the old dame. She, meanwhile, was making the best of her way, with singular speed for so aged a woman, and mumbling some indistinct words—a prayer, doubtless—as she went. The traveller put forth his staff and touched her withered neck with what seemed the serpent's tail.

"The devil!" screamed the pious old lady.

"Then Goody Cloyse knows her old friend?" observed the traveller, confronting her and leaning on his writhing stick.

"Ah, forsooth, and is it your worship indeed?" cried the good dame. "Yea, truly is it, and in the very image of my old gossip, Goodman Brown, the grandfather of the silly fellow that now is. But—would your worship believe it?—my broomstick hath strangely disappeared, stolen, as I suspect, by that unhanged witch, Goody Cory, and that, too, when I was all anointed with the juice of smallage, and cinquefoil, and wolf's bane—"

"Mingled with fine wheat and the fat of a new-born babe," said the shape of old Goodman Brown.

"Ah, your worship knows the recipe," cried the old lady, cackling aloud. "So, as I was saying, being all ready for the meeting, and no horse to ride on, I made up my mind to foot it; for they tell me there is a nice young man to be taken into communion to-night. But now your good worship will lend me your arm, and we shall be there in a twinkling."

"That can hardly be," answered her friend. "I may not spare you my arm, Goody Cloyse; but here is my staff, if you will."

So saying, he threw it down at her feet, where, perhaps, it assumed life, being one of the rods which its owner had formerly lent to the Egyptian magi. Of this fact, however, Goodman Brown could not take cognizance. He had cast up his eyes in astonishment, and, looking down again, beheld neither Goody Cloyse nor the serpentine staff, but this fellow-traveller alone, who waited for him as calmly as if nothing had happened.

"That old woman taught me my catechism," said the young man; and there was a world of meaning in this simple comment.

They continued to walk onward, while the elder traveller exhorted his companion to make good speed and persevere in the path, discoursing so aptly that his arguments seemed rather to spring up in the bosom of his auditor than to be suggested by himself. As they went, he plucked a branch of maple to serve for a walking stick, and began to strip it of the twigs and little boughs, which were wet with evening dew. The moment his fingers touched them they became strangely withered and dried up as with a week's sunshine. Thus the pair proceeded, at a good free pace, until suddenly, in a gloomy hollow of the road, Goodman Brown sat himself down on the stump of a tree and refused to go any farther.

"Friend," said he, stubbornly, "my mind is made up. Not another step will I budge on this errand. What if a wretched old woman do choose to go to the devil when I thought she was going to heaven: is that any reason why I should quit my dear Faith and go after her?"

"You will think better of this by and by," said his acquaintance, composedly. "Sit here and rest yourself a while; and when you feel like moving again, there is my staff to help you along."

Without more words, he threw his companion the maple stick, and was as speedily out of sight as if he had vanished into the deepening gloom. The young man sat a few moments by the roadside, applauding himself greatly, and thinking with how clear a conscience he should meet the minister in his morning walk, nor shrink from the eye of good old Deacon Gookin. And what calm sleep would be his that very night, which was to have been spent so wickedly, but so purely and sweetly now, in the arms of Faith! Amidst these pleasant and praiseworthy meditations, Goodman Brown heard the tramp of horses along the road, and deemed it advisable to conceal himself within the verge of the forest, conscious of the guilty purpose that had brought him thither, though now so happily turned from it.

On came the hoof tramps and the voices of the riders, two grave old voices, conversing soberly as they drew near. These mingled sounds appeared to pass along the road, within a few yards of the young man's hiding-place; but, owing doubtless to the depth of the gloom at that particular spot, neither the travellers nor their steeds were visible. Though their figures brushed the small boughs by the wayside, it could not be seen that they intercepted, even for a moment, the faint gleam from the strip of bright sky athwart which they must have passed. Goodman Brown alternately crouched and stood on tiptoe, pulling aside the branches and thrusting forth his head as far as he durst without discerning so much as a shadow. It vexed him the more, because he could have sworn, were such a thing possible, that he recognized the voices of the minister and Deacon Gookin, jogging along quietly, as they were wont to do, when bound to some ordination or ecclesiastical council. While yet within hearing, one of the riders stopped to pluck a switch.

"Of the two, reverend sir," said the voice like the deacon's, "I had rather miss an ordination dinner than to-night's meeting. They tell me that some of our community are to be here from Falmouth and beyond, and others from Connecticut and Rhode Island, besides several of the Indian powwows, who, after their fashion, know almost as much deviltry as the best of us. Moreover, there is a goodly young woman to be taken into communion."

"Mighty well, Deacon Gookin!" replied the solemn old tones of the minister. "Spur up, or we shall be late. Nothing can be done, you know, until I get on the ground."

The hoofs clattered again; and the voices, talking so strangely in the empty air, passed on through the forest, where no church had ever been gathered or solitary Christian prayed. Whither, then, could these holy men be journeying so deep into the heathen wilderness? Young Goodman Brown caught hold of a tree for support, being ready to sink down on the ground, faint and overburdened with the heavy sickness of his heart. He looked up to the sky, doubting whether there really was a heaven above him. Yet there was the blue arch, and the stars brightening in it.

"With heaven above and Faith below, I will yet stand firm against the devil!" cried Goodman Brown.

While he still gazed upward into the deep arch of the firmament and had lifted his hands to pray, a cloud, though no wind was stirring, hurried across the zenith and hid the brightening stars. The blue sky was still visible, except directly overhead, where this black mass of cloud was sweeping swiftly northward. Aloft in the air, as if from the depths of the cloud, came a confused and doubtful sound of voices. Once the listener fancied that he could distinguish the accents of towns-people of his own, men and women, both pious and ungodly, many of whom he had met at the communion table, and had seen others rioting at the tavern. The next moment, so indistinct were the sounds, he doubted whether he had heard aught but the murmur of the old forest, whispering without a wind. Then came a stronger swell of those familiar tones, heard daily in the sunshine at Salem village, but never until now from a cloud of night. There was one voice, of a young woman, uttering lamentations, yet with an uncertain sorrow, and entreating for some favor, which, perhaps, it would grieve her to obtain; and all the unseen multitude, both saints and sinners, seemed to encourage her onward.

"Faith!" shouted Goodman Brown, in a voice of agony and desperation; and the echoes of the forest mocked him, crying, "Faith! Faith!" as if bewildered wretches were seeking her all through the wilderness.

The cry of grief, rage, and terror was yet piercing the night, when the unhappy husband held his breath for a response. There was a scream, drowned immediately in a louder murmur of voices, fading into far-off laughter, as the dark cloud swept away, leaving the clear and silent sky above Goodman Brown. But something fluttered lightly down through the air and caught on the branch of a tree. The young man seized it, and beheld a pink ribbon.

"My Faith is gone!" cried he, after one stupefied moment. "There is no good on earth; and sin is but a name. Come, devil; for to thee is this world given."

And, maddened with despair, so that he laughed loud and long, did Goodman Brown grasp his staff and set forth again, at such a rate that he seemed to fly along the forest path rather than to walk or run. The road grew wilder and drearier and more faintly traced, and vanished at length, leaving him in the heart of the dark wilderness, still rushing onward with the instinct that guides mortal man to evil. The whole forest was peopled with frightful sounds—the creaking of the trees, the howling of wild beasts, and the yell of Indians; while sometimes the wind tolled like a distant church bell, and sometimes gave a broad roar around the traveller, as if all Nature were laughing him to scorn. But he was himself the chief horror of the scene, and shrank not from its other horrors.

"Ha! ha! ha!" roared Goodman Brown when the wind laughed at him. "Let us hear which will laugh loudest. Think not to frighten me with your deviltry. Come witch, come wizard, come Indian powwow, come devil himself, and here comes Goodman Brown. You may as well fear him as he fear you."

In truth, all through the haunted forest there could be nothing more frightful than the figure of Goodman Brown. On he flew among the black pines, brandishing his staff with frenzied gestures, now giving vent to an inspiration of horrid blasphemy, and now shouting forth such laughter as set all the echoes of the forest laughing like demons around him. The fiend in his own shape is less hideous than when he rages in the breast of man. Thus sped the demoniac on his course, until, quivering among the trees, he saw a red light before him, as when the felled trunks and branches of a clearing have been set on fire, and throw up their lurid blaze against the sky, at the hour of midnight. He paused, in a lull of the tempest that had driven him onward, and heard the swell of what seemed a hymn, rolling solemnly from a distance with the weight of many voices. He knew the tune; it was a familiar one in the choir of the village meeting-house. The verse died heavily away, and was lengthened by a chorus, not of human voices, but of all the sounds of the benighted wilderness pealing in awful harmony together. Goodman Brown cried out, and his cry was lost to his own ear by its unison with the cry of the desert.

In the interval of silence he stole forward until the light glared full upon his eyes. At one extremity of an open space, hemmed in by the dark wall of the forest, arose a rock, bearing some rude, natural resemblance either to an altar or a pulpit, and surrounded by four blazing pines, their tops aflame, their stems untouched, like candles at an evening meeting. The mass of foliage that had overgrown the summit of the rock was all on fire, blazing high into the night and fitfully illuminating the whole field. Each pendent twig and leafy festoon was in a blaze. As the red light arose and fell, a numerous congregation alternately shone forth, then disappeared in shadow, and again grew, as it were, out of the darkness, peopling the heart of the solitary woods at once.

"A grave and dark-clad company," quoth Goodman Brown.

In truth they were such. Among them, quivering to and fro between gloom and splendour, appeared faces that would be seen next day at the council board of the province, and others which, Sabbath after Sabbath, looked devoutly heavenward, and benignantly over the crowded pews, from the holiest pulpits in the land. Some affirm that the lady of the governor was there. At least there were high dames well known to her, and wives of honored husbands, and widows, a great multitude, and ancient maidens, all of excellent repute, and fair young girls, who trembled lest their mothers should espy them. Either the sudden gleams of light flashing over the obscure field bedazzled Goodman Brown, or he recognized a score of the church members of Salem village famous for their especial sanctity. Good old Deacon Gookin had arrived, and waited at the skirts of that venerable saint, his revered pastor. But, irreverently consorting with these grave, reputable, and pious people, these elders of the church, these chaste dames and dewy virgins, there were men of dissolute lives and women of spotted fame, wretches given over to all mean and filthy vice, and suspected even of horrid crimes. It was strange to see that the good shrank not from the wicked, nor were the sinners abashed by the saints. Scattered also among their pale-faced enemies were the Indian priests, or powwows, who had often scared their native forest with more hideous incantations than any known to English witchcraft.

"But where is Faith?" thought Goodman Brown; and as hope came into his heart, he trembled.

Another verse of the hymn arose, a slow and mournful strain, such as the pious love, but joined to words which expressed all that our nature can conceive of sin, and darkly hinted at far more. Unfathomable to mere mortals is the lore of fiends. Verse after verse was sung; and still the chorus of the desert swelled between like the deepest tone of a mighty organ; and with the final peal of that dreadful anthem there came a sound, as if the roaring wind, the rushing streams, the howling beasts, and every other voice of the unconcerted wilderness were mingling and according with the voice of guilty man in homage to the prince of all. The four blazing pines threw up a loftier flame, and obscurely discovered shapes and visages of horror on the smoke wreaths above the impious assembly. At the same moment the fire on the rock shot redly forth and formed a glowing arch above its base, where now appeared a figure. With reverence be it spoken, the figure bore no slight similitude, both in garb and manner, to some grave divine of the New England churches.

"Bring forth the converts!" cried a voice that echoed through the field and rolled into the forest.

At the word, Goodman Brown stepped forth from the shadow of the trees and approached the congregation, with whom he felt a loathful brotherhood by the sympathy of all that was wicked in his heart. He could have well-nigh sworn that the shape of his own dead father beckoned him to advance, looking downward from a smoke wreath, while a woman, with dim features of despair, threw out her hand to warn him back. Was it his mother? But he had no power to retreat one step, nor to resist, even in thought, when the minister and good old Deacon Gookin seized his arms and led him to the blazing rock. Thither came also the slender form of a veiled female, led between Goody Cloyse, that pious teacher of the catechism, and Martha Carrier, who had received the devil's promise to be queen of hell. A rampant hag was she. And there stood the proselytes beneath the canopy of fire.

"Welcome, my children," said the dark figure, "to the communion of your race. Ye have found thus young your nature and your destiny. My children, look behind you!"

They turned; and flashing forth, as it were, in a sheet of flame, the fiend worshippers were seen; the smile of welcome gleamed darkly on every visage.

"There," resumed the sable form, "are all whom ye have reverenced from youth. Ye deemed them holier than yourselves, and shrank from your own sin, contrasting it with their lives of righteousness and prayerful aspirations heavenward. Yet here are they all in my worshipping assembly. This night it shall be granted you to know their secret deeds: how hoary-bearded elders of the church have whispered wanton words to the young maids of their households; how many a woman, eager for widows' weeds, has given her husband a drink at bedtime and let him sleep his last sleep in her bosom; how beardless youths have made haste to inherit their fathers' wealth; and how fair damsels—blush not, sweet ones—have dug little graves in the garden, and bidden me, the sole guest, to an infant's funeral. By the sympathy of your human hearts for sin ye shall scent out all the places—whether in church, bed-chamber, street, field, or forest—where crime has been committed, and shall exult to behold the whole earth one stain of guilt, one mighty blood spot. Far more than this. It shall be yours to penetrate, in every bosom, the deep mystery of sin, the fountain of all wicked arts, and which inexhaustibly supplies more evil impulses than human power—than my power at its utmost—can make manifest in deeds. And now, my children, look upon each other."

They did so; and, by the blaze of the hell-kindled torches, the wretched man beheld his Faith, and the wife her husband, trembling before that unhallowed altar.

"Lo, there ye stand, my children," said the figure, in a deep and solemn tone, almost sad with its despairing awfulness, as if his once angelic nature could yet mourn for our miserable race. "Depending upon one another's hearts, ye had still hoped that virtue were not all a dream. Now are ye undeceived. Evil is the nature of mankind. Evil must be your only happiness. Welcome again, my children, to the communion of your race."

"Welcome," repeated the fiend worshippers, in one cry of despair and triumph.

And there they stood, the only pair, as it seemed, who were yet hesitating on the verge of wickedness in this dark world. A basin was hollowed, naturally, in the rock. Did it contain water, reddened by the lurid light? or was it blood? or, perchance, a liquid flame? Herein did the shape of evil dip his hand and prepare to lay the mark of baptism upon their foreheads, that they might be partakers of the mystery of sin, more conscious of the secret guilt of others, both in deed and thought, than they could now be of their own. The husband cast one look at his pale wife, and Faith at him. What polluted wretches would the next glance show them to each other, shuddering alike at what they disclosed and what they saw?

"Faith! Faith!" cried the husband, "look up to heaven, and resist the wicked one."

Whether Faith obeyed he knew not. Hardly had he spoken when he found himself amid calm night and solitude, listening to a roar of the wind which died heavily away through the forest. He staggered against the rock, and felt it chill and damp; while a hanging twig, that had been all on fire, besprinkled his cheek with the coldest dew.

The next morning young Goodman Brown came slowly into the street of Salem village, staring around him like a bewildered man. The good old minister was taking a walk along the graveyard to get an appetite for breakfast and meditate his sermon, and bestowed a blessing, as he passed, on Goodman Brown. He shrank from the venerable saint as if to avoid an anathema. Old Deacon Gookin was at domestic worship, and the holy words of his prayer were heard through the open window. "What God doth the wizard pray to?" quoth Goodman Brown. Goody Cloyse, that excellent old Christian, stood in the early sunshine at her own lattice, catechizing a little girl who had brought her a pint of morning's milk. Goodman Brown snatched away the child as from the grasp of the fiend himself. Turning the corner by the meeting-house, he spied the head of Faith, with the pink ribbons, gazing anxiously forth, and bursting into such joy at sight of him that she skipped along the street and almost kissed her husband before the whole village. But Goodman Brown looked sternly and sadly into her face, and passed on without a greeting.

Had Goodman Brown fallen asleep in the forest and only dreamed a wild dream of a witch-meeting?

Be it so if you will; but, alas! it was a dream of evil omen for young Goodman Brown. A stern, a sad, a darkly meditative, a distrustful, if not a desperate man did he become from the night of that fearful dream. On the Sabbath day, when the congregation were singing a holy psalm, he could not listen because an anthem of sin rushed loudly upon his ear and drowned all the blessed strain. When the minister spoke from the pulpit with power and fervid eloquence, and, with his hand on the open Bible, of the sacred truths of our religion, and of saint-like lives and triumphant deaths, and of future bliss or misery unutterable, then did Goodman Brown turn pale, dreading lest the roof should thunder down upon the gray blasphemer and his hearers. Often, awaking suddenly at midnight, he shrank from the bosom of Faith; and at morning or eventide, when the family knelt down at prayer, he scowled and muttered to himself, and gazed sternly at his wife, and turned away. And when he had lived long, and was borne to his grave a hoary corpse, followed by Faith, an aged woman, and children and grandchildren, a goodly procession, besides neighbors not a few, they carved no hopeful verse upon his tombstone, for his dying hour was gloom.

NIKOLAI VASILYEVICH GOGOL

⁕

The Nose

(Nos, 1835)

Up to this point, I have focused on sinister, macabre, and horrifying themes. To change the atmosphere and represent visionary humor, I present this marvelous tale by Gogol (1809–1852), which develops one of the preeminent themes of fantastic literature: a body part that separates and acts independently from the rest of the body. But that discovery is not what makes "The Nose" a masterpiece; it is set apart by virtue of its power, its inventiveness, and what is unforeseeable about it sentence by sentence. Gogol's laughter, as we know, is always subtly bitter: as, for instance, in the attempts to reattach the relocated nose to the face.

In one way, this text is separate from the genre. Fantastic stories usually have an irreproachable internal logic, but Gogol happily mocks all logic, even more than Hoffmann, who is the direct inspiration for this vein of his. If we enter into the symbolic elements in the tale, we see that this nose—like the shadow in Chamisso—does not allow itself to be enclosed within a single interpretation. The story is, no doubt, a satire of the functionary decorum of the Russian bureaucracy, but to say that is really to say nothing.

Gogol's entire fantastic production should be included in this anthology, from the early peasant tales about fear (like "Vij," the marvelous story of the seminary student seduced by the witch) to an example more closely related to the typology of the Romantic fantastic, such as "The Portrait," notable because it exists in two versions (1835 and 1836), and its intent is decidedly moral.

CHAPTER 1

AN INCREDIBLE THING happened in Petersburg on March 25th. Ivan Yakovlevich, the barber on Voznesensky Avenue (his last name has been lost and does not even figure on the signboard bearing a picture of a gentleman with a soapy cheek and the inscription WE ALSO LET BLOOD HERE), woke up rather early and detected a smell of newly baked bread. He raised himself a little and saw that his wife, a quite respectable woman and one extremely fond of coffee, was taking fresh rolls out of the oven.

"Praskovia Osipovna," he said to his wife, "no coffee for me this morning. I'll have a hot roll with onions instead."

Actually Ivan Yakovlevich would have liked both but he knew his wife frowned on such whims. And, sure enough, she thought:

"It's fine with me if the fool wants bread. That'll leave me another cup of coffee."

And she tossed a roll onto the table.

Mindful of his manners, Ivan Yakovlevich put his frock coat on over his nightshirt, seated himself at the table, poured some salt, got a couple of onions, took a knife and, assuming a dignified expression, proceeded to cut the roll in two.

Suddenly he stopped, surprised. There was something whitish in the middle of the roll. He poked at it with his knife, then felt it with his finger.

"It's quite compact . . ." he muttered under his breath. "Whatever can it be? . . ."

He thrust in two fingers this time and pulled it out. It was a nose.

He almost fell off his chair. Then he rubbed his eyes and felt the thing again. It was a nose all right, no doubt about it. And, what's more, a nose that had something familiar about it. His features expressed intense horror.

But the intensity of the barber's horror was nothing compared with the intensity of his wife's indignation.

"Where," she screamed, "did you lop off that nose, you beast? You crook," she shouted, "you drunkard! I'll report you to the police myself, you thug! Three customers have complained to me before this about the way you keep pulling their noses when you shave them, so that it's a wonder they manage to stay on at all."

But Ivan Yakovlevich, at that moment more dead than alive, was immune to her attack. He had remembered where he had seen the nose before and it was on none other than Collegiate Assessor Kovalev, whom he shaved regularly each Wednesday and Sunday.

"Wait, my dear, I'll wrap it in a rag and put it away somewhere in a corner. Let it stay there for a while, then I'll take it away."

"I won't even listen to you! Do you really imagine that I'll allow a cut-off nose to remain in my place, you old crumb! All you can do is strop your damn razor and when it comes to your duties, you're no good. You stupid, lousy, skirt-chasing scum! So you want me to get into trouble with the police for your sake? Is that it, you dirty mug? You're a stupid log, you know. Get it out of here. Do what you like with it, you hear me, but don't let me ever see it here again."

The barber stood there dumfounded. He thought and thought but couldn't think of anything.

"I'll be damned if I know how it happened," he said in the end, scratching behind his ear. "Was I drunk last night when I came home? I'm not sure. Anyway, it all sounds quite mad: bread is a baked product while a nose is something else again. Makes no sense to me. . . ."

So he fell silent. The thought that the police would find the nose on him and accuse him drove him to despair. He could already see the beautiful silver-braided, scarlet collars of the police and started trembling all over.

Still, in the end he stirred and went to get his trousers and his boots. He pulled on these sorry garments, wrapped the nose in a rag, and left under Praskovia Osipovna's unendearing barrage of recriminations.

He wanted to get rid of the nose, to leave it under a seat, stick it in a doorway, or just drop it as if by accident and then rush down a side street. But he kept meeting acquaintances who immediately proceeded to inquire where he was going or whom he was planning to shave so early in the morning, and he missed every opportunity. At one point he actually dropped the nose, but a watchman pointed to it with his halberd and informed him that he'd lost something. And Ivan Yakovlevich had to pick up the nose and stuff it back into his pocket. Things began to look completely hopeless for him when the stores began opening and the streets became more and more crowded.

Then he decided to try throwing the nose into the Neva from the Isakievsky Bridge. . . .

But, at this point, we should say a few words about Ivan Yakovlevich, a man who had a number of good points.

Like every self-respecting Russian tradesman, Ivan Yakovlevich was a terrible drunkard. And although he shaved other people's chins every day, his own looked permanently unshaven. His frock coat (he never wore an ordinary coat) was piebald. That is to say, it had been black originally but now it was studded with yellowish brown and gray spots. His collar was shiny and three threads dangling from his coat indicated where the missing buttons should have been. Ivan Yakovlevich was a terrible cynic.

While being shaved the collegiate assessor often complained:

"Your hands always stink, Ivan Yakovlevich!"

He would answer: "How can they stink?"

"I don't know how, man, but they stink!" the other would say.

In answer Ivan Yakovlevich would take a pinch of snuff and proceed to soap Kovalev's cheeks and under his nose and behind his ears and under his chin, in fact, anywhere he felt like.

By and by, this worthy citizen reached the Isakievsky Bridge. He glanced around and then, leaning over the parapet, peered under the bridge as if to ascertain the whereabouts of some fish. But actually he discreetly dropped the rag containing the nose. He felt as if a three-hundred-pound weight had been taken off his back. He let out a little laugh and, instead of going back to shave the chins of government employees, he decided he had to recuperate. He was setting out for an establishment which operated under the sign MEALS AND TEA, to treat himself to a glass of punch, when all of a sudden he saw a police inspector of most imposing appearance—handlebar mustache, three-cornered hat, saber and all. He froze in his tracks. The policeman beckoned to him and said:

"Just step over here, fellow!"

Having great respect for this particular uniform, Ivan Yakovlevich pulled off his cap while he was still a good distance away, trotted toward the policeman and said:

"Good morning, officer."

"Instead of good morning, you'd better tell me what you were doing in the middle of the bridge over there."

"I was on my way to shave people, officer, and I wanted to see whether the current was fast—"

"You're lying, man. You won't get away with it. You'd better answer my question."

"Officer, I'll give you two . . . no, three free shaves every week . . . what do you say, officer?" said Ivan Yakovlevich.

"Not a chance. I have three barbers to shave me as it is. And they consider it a great honor, too. So you get on with it and explain what you were doing."

Ivan Yakovlevich turned ashen. . . . But here the incident becomes befogged and it is completely unknown what happened after this point.

CHAPTER 2

That morning Collegiate Assessor Kovalev had awakened rather early. He went brrr . . . brrr with his lips as he always did upon waking, although he himself could not explain why. He stretched himself and asked his man for the small mirror that stood on his dressing table. He needed it to examine a pimple that had broken out on his nose the day before. But he was bewildered to find that instead of his nose there was nothing but a bare smooth surface. Horrified, he asked for water and rubbed his eyes with a towel. There was no doubt about it: his nose was not there. He felt himself all over to make sure he was not asleep. It seemed he wasn't. Collegiate Assessor Kovalev jumped up then and shook himself. Still no nose. He called for his clothes and rushed directly to the police inspector.

But, in the meantime, a few things should be said about Kovalev to show what sort of collegiate assessor he was. Collegiate assessors who reach their positions by obtaining academic degrees cannot be compared with the collegiate assessors that used to be appointed in the Caucasus. They are two completely unrelated species. The collegiate assessors equipped with learning . . .

But Russia is a strange place and if we say something about one collegiate assessor, all of them, from Riga to Kamchatka, will take it personally. The same is true of all vocations and ranks.

Kovalev was a Caucasus-made collegiate assessor. Moreover, he had been a collegiate assessor for only two years. In order to feel distinguished and important he never referred to himself as a collegiate assessor but employed the equivalent military rank of major.

"Look here, my good woman," he used to say when he met a woman selling shirt fronts in the street, "I want you to deliver them to my place. I live on Sadovaya Street. Just ask for Major Kovalev's, anybody'll show you."

And if he met someone pretty, he would whisper to her discreetly: "You just ask for Major Kovalev's apartment, deary."

As a rule, Major Kovalev went out for a daily walk along Nevsky Avenue. The collar of his shirt was always clean and well starched. He had whiskers such as are still to be found on provincial surveyors, and architects if they happen to be Russian, among persons performing various police functions, and, in general, on men who have full faces, ruddy cheeks, and play a strong hand at certain games of chance. Whiskers of this type flow straight across the middle of the cheek up to the very nostrils.

Major Kovalev always carried with him a great quantity of seals, both seals engraved with coats of arms and others on which were carved WEDNESDAY, THURSDAY, MONDAY, and that sort of thing. He had come to Petersburg on business, namely, to find a position commensurate with his rank. He hoped, if lucky, to get a Vice-Governorship; otherwise, he would consider a post as executive in some administration. Nor was Major Kovalev averse to matrimony, as long as the bride happened to have a capital of about two hundred thousand rubles.

And now that all this has been said about the major, it can be imagined how he felt when, instead of a quite acceptable-looking, medium-sized nose, he found an absurd, smooth flatness.

And, to make things worse, there was not a cab to be seen in the street and he was forced to walk all the way wrapped in his cloak, his face covered with a handkerchief, pretending he was bleeding, and repeating to himself:

"Maybe it's just imagination. How could I possibly have lost my nose so stupidly? . . ."

He entered a tearoom simply to have a look in a mirror. Fortunately the place was empty except for waiters sweeping the floor and moving chairs around and some others who, with sleepy eyes, were carrying trays with hot buns somewhere. Yesterday's newspapers spotted with coffee were strewn around on tables and chairs.

"Well, thank heaven there's no one here," he said. "I'll be able to have a look."

Gingerly he approached the mirror and looked.

"Filth," he said, spitting, "goddammit. If only there was something to take the nose's place! But it's completely blank!"

He bit his lip in anger and, leaving the tearoom, decided that, contrary to his usual custom, he wouldn't look at the people he met or smile at anyone. Suddenly he stopped dead near the entrance door of a house. An incredible sequence of events unrolled before his eyes. A carriage stopped at the house entrance. Its door opened. A uniformed gentleman appeared. Stooping, he jumped out of the carriage, ran up the steps and entered the house. A combination of horror and amazement swept over Kovalev when he recognized the stranger as his own nose. At this eerie sight, everything swayed before his eyes. But although he could hardly stand on his feet, he felt compelled to wait until the nose returned to the carriage. He waited, shaking as though he had malaria.

After two minutes or so, the nose emerged from the house. He wore a gold-braided, brightly colored uniform, buckskin breeches, a three-cornered hat, and a saber. The plumes on his hat indicated the rank of state councilor. From everything else it could be inferred that he was setting off on some sort of official visit. He looked left, then right, called out to the coachman to bring the carriage up to the very door, got in and was off.

This almost drove poor Kovalev insane. He could no longer think coherently about the whole affair. No, really, how was it possible that the nose, until yesterday on his face, utterly incapable of walking or driving around, should show up like this today and, what's more, wearing a uniform! And Kovalev ran after the carriage, which, luckily for him, did not have far to go. It stopped before Kazan Cathedral.

Kovalev reached the spot and, rushing after the nose, had to elbow his way through a throng of old beggar-women who used to make him laugh because of the way they kept their faces completely wrapped in rags, leaving only slits for their eyes. He entered the cathedral. There were a few worshippers around, all standing near the entrance. Kovalev was in such a depressed state that he could not possibly muster the strength to pray and instead his eyes scrutinized every recess in search of the gentleman. Finally he discovered him standing in a corner. The nose's face was completely concealed by his high, stand-up collar and he was praying with an expression of the utmost piety.

"How shall I address him?" Kovalev wondered. "From his uniform, his hat, everything about him, he must be a state councilor. Damned if I know what to do. . . ."

He approached and cleared his throat. But the nose never even changed his pious posture and remained absorbed in his worship.

"Excuse me, sir . . ." Kovalev said, scraping up all his courage.

"Yes?" the nose said, turning around.

"I don't know how to put it, sir . . . I would say . . . it seems . . . it seems you ought to know where you belong, and where do I find you? Of all places, in church. You must surely agree—"

"Pardon me, but I can make neither head nor tail of what you're saying. Just what do you want?"

Kovalev tried to think how he could explain to the nose what he had in mind and, taking a deep breath, said:

"Of course, sir, for my part . . . but, after all, I am a major, you know, and it's most improper, in my position, to walk around without a nose. Some old woman selling peeled oranges by the Voskresensky Bridge might be able to get along without a nose. But for someone who is almost certain of a high administrative appointment . . . you can judge for yourself, sir. I really fail to understand . . ." At this point Kovalev shrugged. "You'll excuse me, but if this affair were handled according to the code of honor and duty . . . You can see for yourself—"

"I don't see anything," the nose said. "Kindly come to the point."

"Sir," Kovalev said with dignity, "I don't know how to interpret your words. The matter is quite clear, I believe. Unless you are trying . . . Don't you realize that you are my nose?"

The nose looked at the major and frowned slightly.

"You're mistaken, sir. I'm all on my own. Moreover, there couldn't possibly have been close relations between us. Judging by your dress, you must be employed by the Senate, or possibly by the Ministry of Justice, whereas my field is science."

And having said this, the nose turned away and resumed his prayers.

Kovalev was now completely at a loss. Then he heard the pleasant rustle of a feminine dress. He saw a middle-aged lady covered with lace and, with her, a pretty, slender thing in a white dress which set off a very moving waistline, and with a straw hat as light as whipped cream. Behind them walked a tall man with side whiskers and a very complicated collar.

Kovalev worked his way toward them, pulled up the spotless collar of his shirt front to make sure it showed, straightened the seals that hung on a golden chain, and concentrated his attention on the young lady who, like a spring blossom, raised her white hand with its half-transparent fingers to her forehead. And Kovalev's smile spread twice as wide when, under the hat, he made out a chin of a tender whiteness and a cheek touched by the early spring coloring of a rose. But then he jumped back as though burned. He had remembered that instead of a nose he had absolutely nothing, and the tears sprang to his eyes.

He turned to the gentleman dressed as a state councilor to tell him that he was nothing but a fraud and a crook, nothing but his, Kovalev's, personally owned nose.

But the nose was nowhere to be seen. He must have driven off on another official visit.

Kovalev was in despair. He retraced his steps, stopped for a while under the colonnade, and looked intently around him in the hope of catching sight of the nose. He remembered that the nose had had a plumed hat and a gold-braided uniform, but he hadn't noticed his greatcoat, or the color of his carriage, or his horses, or even whether he had had a footman up behind him and, if so, what livery he wore. And then there were so many carriages rushing back and forth, all going so fast that he would have had difficulty in picking one out and no way of stopping it anyway. It was a lovely sunny day. Nevsky Avenue was thronged with people; from the central police station to Anichkin Bridge, ladies poured over the sidewalks in a colorful cascade. There went an acquaintance of his, a court councilor, whom he addressed as Lieutenant-Colonel, especially in the presence of outsiders. Then Kovalev saw Yaryzhkin, head clerk in the Senate, a good friend who always lost whenever they played cards together. And there was another major, another Caucasus-made collegiate assessor, beckoning . . .

"Goddammit," Kovalev said, "what the hell does he want from me? Cabbie! To the police commissioner's!"

He got into the cab and kept exhorting the cabbie again and again: "Come on, let's go! Quick! Now turn into Ivanovskaya Street."

"Is the Commissioner in?" he called out, as soon as he entered the house.

"No, sir," the doorman answered. "He left only a minute ago."

"That's really too much. . . ."

"Yes, sir," the doorman said. "If you'd come a minute earlier, you'd have caught him."

Kovalev, still holding his handkerchief to his face, got back into the cab and shouted in a desperate voice:

"Get going."

"Where to?"

"Straight ahead."

"Straight ahead? But this is a dead end. Shall I go right or left?"

Kovalev was caught off balance and forced to give the matter some thought. In his position, he ought first to go to the National Security Administration, not because it was directly connected with the police, but because its orders would be acted on more rapidly than those of others.

Certainly it was no use taking his grievance to the scientific department where the nose claimed to have a post. At best, it would be unwise, since, judging by his statement that he had never seen Kovalev before, it was obvious that he held nothing sacred and he might lie whenever he found it convenient. So Kovalev was about to tell the cabman to drive him to the National Security Administration when it occurred to him that the crook and impostor, who had just behaved so unscrupulously toward him, might very well try to slip out of town, in which case finding him would be quite hopeless or would take, God forbid, a whole month perhaps. Finally, he had what seemed like a divine inspiration. He decided to go straight to the

Press Building to have an advertisement put in the papers with a detailed description of the nose in all his aspects, so that anyone who met him could turn him over to Kovalev, or at least inform him of the nose's whereabouts. So, having decided this, he told the cabman to take him to the Press Building and, during the entire ride, he kept pommeling him on the back with his fist and shouting:

"Faster, damn you! Faster!"

"Really, sir!" the cabman said, shaking his head and flicking the reins at his horse, which had hair as long as a lap dog's.

At last the cab came to a stop, and Kovalev, panting, burst into the small outer office where a gray-haired, bespectacled employee in an ancient frock coat was seated at a table, his pen clenched between his teeth, counting out the change someone had paid in.

"Who handles advertisements here?" shouted Kovalev. "Ah," he said, "good morning!"

"Good morning, sir," the gray-haired employee said, raising his eyes for a moment and lowering them again to the little piles of coins before him.

"I want to insert—"

"Excuse me. Would you mind waiting just a moment, please," the employee said, writing down a figure with his right hand while his left hand moved two beads on his abacus.

A footman, whose gold-braided livery and whole appearance testified to his service in an aristocratic house, stood by the old employee holding a piece of paper in his hand and, to prove his worldliness, started chattering away:

"Believe me, I'm quite sure the mutt isn't worth eighty kopeks. In fact, I wouldn't give eight kopeks, if you ask me. But the Countess loves that cur—she has to if she's willing to give a hundred rubles to the person who finds it. Since we are among people who understand, I'll tell you one thing: it's all a matter of taste. I can understand a dog lover. But then, go and get a deerhound or maybe a poodle. Then, if you want to spend five hundred or a thousand on it, it's only natural. But, in my opinion, when you pay you are entitled to a *real* dog. . . ."

The elderly employee was listening to this speech with an important expression and was counting the number of letters in the text of the advertisement the manservant had handed him. The room was full of old women, shopkeepers, and doormen, all holding pieces of paper on which advertisements had been written out. In one a coachman, sober and dependable, was for hire; another announced that a carriage with very little mileage, brought from Paris in 1814, was for sale; a nineteen-year-old girl, a washer-woman's assistant, but suitable for other work too, wanted employment; also for sale were an excellent hansom cab (one spring missing) and a young, seventeen-year-old dappled-gray horse, as well as a consignment of turnip and radish seeds straight from London, a summer house with a two-carriage coach house, and a piece of land very suitable for planting a lovely birch wood. Another advertisement invited persons desirous of buying secondhand shoe soles to present themselves in a certain salesroom between 8 A.M. and 3 P.M.

The reception room in which all these people waited was quite small and the air was getting stuffy. But the smell didn't bother Collegiate Assessor Kovalev because he kept his face covered with a handkerchief and also because his nose happened to be God knew where.

"Excuse me, sir . . . I don't want to bother you, but this is an emergency," he said impatiently at last.

"Wait, wait . . . two rubles, forty-three kopeks, please. One minute, please! . . . One ruble, sixty-four, over there . . ." the old employee said, shoving sheets of paper under the noses of porters and old women. "Now, what can I do for you?" he said finally, turning to Kovalev.

"I wanted," Kovalev said, "to ask you to . . . a fraud, or perhaps a theft, has been committed. I'm still not clear. I want you to run an advertisement simply saying that whoever delivers that robber to me will get a handsome reward."

"Your name, please."

"My name? What for? I can't tell you my name. I have too many acquaintances, such as Mrs. Chekhtareva, the wife of a civil servant, and Palageya Grigorievna Podtochina, who's married to Captain Podtochin, an officer on the Army General Staff. . . . Suppose they found out, God forbid. Write simply 'a collegiate assessor' or, better still, 'a major.' "

"And the runaway, was he a household serf?"

"A household serf. That wouldn't be half so vicious a crime. The runaway is my nose . . . yes, my own nose. . . ."

"Hm . . . odd name. And now may I inquire the sum, the amount, of which this Mr. Nose has defrauded you?"

"No, no, you don't understand. I said nose. My own nose, which has disappeared God knows where. I am the victim of some foul joke. . . ."

"But how could it disappear? I still don't understand, sir."

"Well, I can't explain how, but the main thing is that he mustn't go all over town impersonating a state councilor. That's why I want you to advertise that anyone who catches him should contact me as quickly as possible. Besides, imagine how I feel with such a conspicuous part of my body missing. It's not just a matter of, say, a toe. You could simply stick your foot into your shoe and no one would be the wiser. On Thursdays, I usually visit Mrs. Chekhtareva, the wife of a state councilor. . . . And Mrs. Podtochina, the wife of the staff officer, has an extremely pretty daughter. They are close friends of mine, you see, and now tell me, what am I to do? . . . How can I show myself to them?"

The employee was thinking hard, as could be seen from his tightly pressed lips.

"I am sorry, sir, but I cannot accept your advertisement," he said, after a long silence.

"What's that! Why?"

"I just can't. A newspaper could lose its good name if everybody started advertising vagrant noses. . . . No, sir, as it is, too many absurdities and unfounded rumors manage to slip into print."

"Why is it absurd? I don't see anything so unusual about it."

"It may look that way to you. But just let me tell you . . . Last week, for instance, a government employee came to see me just as you have now. I even remember that his advertisement came to two rubles, seventy-three kopeks. But what it all boiled down to was that a black poodle had run away. You'd think there was nothing to it, wouldn't you? But wait. Turned out to be deliberate libel because the poodle in question happened to be the treasurer of I can't recall exactly what."

"But listen, I'm not advertising about a poodle but about my own nose which is the same as myself."

"Sorry, I can't accept the advertisement."

"But I have lost my nose!"

"If you have, it is a matter for a doctor. I've heard that there are specialists who can fit you with any sort of nose you want. But I'm beginning to think that you are one of these cheerful people who likes to have his little joke."

"But I swear to you by all that's holy! And if it comes to that, I'll show you."

"Why take the trouble," the employee said, taking a pinch of snuff. "But then, after all, if you really don't mind," he added, making a slight movement indicating curiosity, "why, I wouldn't mind having a look."

Kovalev removed the handkerchief from his face.

"My! It *is* strange!" the employee said. "Why, it's as flat as a fresh-cooked pancake, incredibly smooth!"

"Well, now you won't refuse to run my advertisement, will you? It simply must be published. I will be very much obliged to you, and I'm very happy that this accident has given me a chance to make your acquaintance. . . ."

The major, it can be seen, had decided that he'd better make up to him a bit.

"Certainly, running it is no great problem," the employee said, "but I don't see that it would do you any good. However, if you absolutely want to see it in print, why not entrust it to someone who can really write and ask him to present it as a rare natural phenomenon and have it published in the *Northern Bee*"—here he took another pinch of snuff—"for the edification of the young"—here he wiped his nose—"or just as a matter of general interest."

The collegiate assessor was taken aback. He lowered his eyes and his glance happened to fall on the theatrical announcements at the bottom of the page of a newspaper. His face was just about to break into a smile at the sight of the name of a very pretty actress and his hand had already plunged into his pocket to see whether he had a five-ruble bill on him, since, in his opinion, an officer of his rank should sit in the stalls, when he remembered the nose and everything was ruined.

The employee, too, seemed touched by Kovalev's awkward position. To alleviate his distress, he thought it would be appropriate to express his sympathy in a few words:

"I'm very sorry that such a painful thing should have happened to you. Perhaps you'd feel better if you took a pinch of snuff. It eases people's headaches and cheers them up. It's even good for hemorrhoids."

As he said this, the employee offered Kovalev his snuff-box, rather deftly folding back the lid which had a picture on it of some lady in a hat.

At this unintentional provocation, Kovalev's patience snapped.

"I simply don't understand how you can make a joke of it," he said angrily. "Can't you see that I am missing just what I would need to take a pinch of snuff with? You know what you can do with your snuff! I can't even look at it now, especially not at your cheap Berezinsky brand. You might at least have offered me something better. . . ."

Incensed, he rushed out of the Press Building. He decided to take his case to the borough Police Commissioner.

At the moment when Kovalev entered the office of the Commissioner, the latter had just finished stretching himself and reflecting:

"I might as well treat myself to a nap. A couple of hours or so."

Thus it would have been easy to predict that the major's visit was rather poorly timed. Incidentally, the Commissioner, though a great lover of the arts and of commerce, still preferred a bill put in circulation by the Imperial Russian Bank over anything else. His opinion on the matter was as follows:

"It has everything: it doesn't have to be fed, it doesn't take up much room, and, in any case, can always be fitted into a pocket. If you drop it, it doesn't break."

The Commissioner was rather cold with Kovalev. Right after a meal, he said, was not the proper time for investigations. Nature itself, he said, dictated rest when one's belly was full. From this, the collegiate assessor was able to gather that the Commissioner was rather familiar with the maxims of the wise men of antiquity.

"Moreover," the Commissioner said, "they don't tear noses off decent citizens' faces."

Bull's-eye! We must note here that Kovalev was quick to take offense. He could forgive anything that was said about himself personally, but he couldn't stand anything that he considered a slur on his rank and position. He even held the view that, in dramatic works, while a disparaging reference to subaltern ranks was permissible, it became intolerable when applied to officers above the rank of captain. He was so disconcerted by the reception given him by the Commissioner that he shook his head slightly, shrugged, and, on his way out, said in a dignified tone:

"Well, I must say . . . after your offensive remarks I have nothing further to add."

He reached home hardly able to feel his feet beneath him. It was getting dark. After his futile search, his place looked sad and repulsive. As he walked in, he saw Ivan, his manservant, lying on his back on the old leather divan in the entrance hall spitting at the ceiling—very successfully it must be said. Ivan was hitting the same spot again and again. But such indifference enraged Kovalev. He hit him on the head with his hat and said bitterly:

"Swine! You think of nothing but trivialities."

Ivan jumped up and started anxiously to help Kovalev off with his coat.

The major went into his room and let himself fall into an armchair, sad and exhausted. He let out a few sighs, after which he said:

"Good heavens! Why is all this happening to *me*? What have *I* done wrong? It would have been better to have lost an arm or a leg. It would have been bad enough without ears, yet still bearable. But without a nose a man is not a man but God knows what—neither fish nor fowl. He can't even be a proper citizen any more. If only I had had it lopped off during a war or in a duel or if *I* had been responsible for the loss. But I lost it for no reason and for nothing; I haven't even got a kopek out of it! No, it's impossible," he added after a pause, "it is impossible that the nose could have disappeared. Incredible! It is probably a dream or just a hallucination . . . maybe, by mistake, I drank a glassful of the vodka with which I rub my face after shaving? That fool Ivan must have forgotten to put it away and I must have swallowed it inadvertently."

To prove to himself that he was really drunk, the major pinched himself so hard that he let out a moan. The pain convinced him that he was quite sober. Then, slowly, as though stalking something, he approached the mirror, his eyes half closed, in the vague hope that, who knows, perhaps the nose would be in its proper place. But immediately he jumped away.

"What a slanderous sight!"

It was really quite bewildering. Many things get lost: a button, a silver spoon, a watch, or some such object. But to disappear just like that. . . . And what's more, in his own apartment! Having weighed the matter, Major Kovalev came to what seemed to be the most likely explanation: the culprit behind it all was Mrs. Podtochina, who wanted him to marry her daughter. He rather enjoyed the girl's company himself but he was just not ready for a final decision. And when Mrs. Podtochina had told him plainly that she wanted him to marry her daughter, he had quietly beaten a polite retreat, saying that he was still very young and that he ought to devote another five years or so to his career, after which he would be at least forty-two. So, probably, that was when Mrs. Podtochina had decided to maim him and had hired witches or something for the purpose, because by no stretch of the imagination could it be assumed that the nose had been cut off; no one had entered his bedroom; Ivan Yakovlevich, the barber, hadn't shaved him since Wednesday and during the rest of that day and even on Thursday, his nose, all in one piece, had been on his face. He was absolutely certain of it. Moreover, had the nose been cut off he would have felt pain and the wound could never have healed so fast and become as smooth as a pancake. . . .

All sorts of plans clashed in his head: should he take the lady to court or would it be better to go directly to her and denounce her to her face? But his thoughts were interrupted by light seeping in through the cracks in the door, indicating that Ivan had lit a candle in the entrance hall. Soon Ivan appeared carrying the candle high above his head, lighting up the entire room. Kovalev's first thought was to grab the handkerchief and cover the place where, only yesterday, the nose had sat, so that this stupid man should not stand there gaping, noticing the peculiar state of his master's face.

But no sooner had Ivan left than he heard an unknown voice coming from the apartment door ask:

"Does Collegiate Assessor Kovalev live here?"

"Come in. Major Kovalev is in," Kovalev shouted, jumping up and rushing into the hall.

It was a police officer, a quite handsome man with whiskers neither too light nor too dark and with rather full cheeks. In fact it was the same one who, at the beginning of this story, had been standing by the Isakievsky Bridge.

"Did you happen to lose your nose, sir?"

"Yes, I did."

"It has been found."

"Is it possible?"

Joy paralyzed the major's tongue. He stared at the police officer standing in front of him, the reflection of the candlelight shining on his damp, full lips.

"How did it happen?" he managed to say at last.

"By sheer coincidence. Your nose was caught as he was getting on the stagecoach for Riga. He had a passport made out in the name of a government official and the strange thing is that, at first, I myself took him for a gentleman. But luckily I had my glasses with me, so I put them on and recognized immediately that he was a nose. The thing is, I am very shortsighted, sir, and with you standing right in front of me there, I can make out your face but I can't discern your beard, or your nose, or anything else. My mother-in-law, that's the mother of my wife, can't see a thing either."

Kovalev was beside himself with excitement.

"Where is he? Where? I'll run over there now. . . ."

"Don't trouble, sir. I thought you might need it, so I brought it along. But you know, the funny part about it is that the main suspect in the affair is the barber from Voznesensky Avenue, a crook who's now being held at the police station. I've had my eye on him for some time because I suspected him of being a thief and a drunkard. As a matter of fact, he lifted a box of buttons in a store the other day. By the way, your nose is exactly as before, sir."

Saying this, the police officer put his hand in his pocket and extracted the nose wrapped in a piece of paper.

"That's it! That's it!" Kovalev shouted. "No doubt about it! Do come in and have some tea with me, won't you?"

"It would be a great honour, sir, but I am afraid I can't. I must stop over at the house of correction—prices are going up, sir. . . . My mother-in-law, I mean the wife's mother, is living with me . . . we have children too. The eldest son is particularly promising, a very clever boy, but we have no money for his education. . . ."

When the police officer had left, the collegiate assessor remained for some minutes in an indeterminate state, just barely able to see and feel. It was his immense joy that had plunged him into his half-consciousness. Very carefully he held his just-recovered nose in his cupped hands and once again looked it over.

"Yes, that's it, that's it all right. And here, on the left side, is the pimple that sprang up the other day."

The major almost shouted with pleasure.

But there is nothing long-lived in this world and one's joy in the minute that follows the first is no longer as vivid. It further weakens during the third and finally dissolves into one's everyday state just as the circles produced on the surface of a pond by the fall of a pebble dissolve into the smooth surface. Kovalev began to ponder and realized that his troubles were not quite over: the nose had been found. That was fine; but it still had to be put back, fixed in its old place.

"And what if it doesn't stick?"

As he asked himself this question, the major turned white.

With inexpressible anxiety he leapt toward his dressing table and pulled the mirror closer, fearing that he would stick the nose on crooked. His hands trembled. Finally, with infinite hesitations and precautions he pressed the nose into place. Oh, horror! It wouldn't stick! He brought it close to his mouth and warmed it slightly with his breath. Then he placed it again on top of the smooth area between his two cheeks. But the nose would not stay on.

"Come on! Come on now! Stick—you fool!" Kovalev told the nose again and again. But the nose felt as if it were made of wood and kept falling off. And as it hit the dressing table it produced a queer light sound, like a cork. The major's face twisted spasmodically. Panic pervaded him.

"Can it possibly *not* stick?"

He repeatedly pressed the nose against the approximate spot, but his efforts were futile. Then he decided to send Ivan to fetch the doctor who occupied the best apartment in the house where the major lived.

The doctor was a fine figure of a man. He had pitch-black whiskers and a quite fresh and healthy wife. Furthermore, he ate fresh apples in the morning and kept his mouth in a state of incredible cleanliness, rinsing it for about three-quarters of an hour at a time and then brushing his teeth with five different kinds of toothbrush.

The doctor arrived within the minute. Having asked the major how long ago the misfortune had struck, he grabbed him by the chin and tweaked him so hard on the former site of his nose that Kovalev recoiled violently and banged the back of his head against the wall. The doctor said that it was quite all right and, advising him to move a bit further away from the wall, ordered him to bend his head to the right, felt the spot vacated by the nose with his fingers and said, "Hmmm . . ." Then he asked him to bend his head to the left, touched the spot again and said, "Hmmm. . . ." Finally the doctor delivered another tweak with his thumb and forefinger, making Kovalev toss up his head like a horse whose teeth are being inspected.

Having thus completed his examination, the doctor shook his head and declared:

"No. Can't be done. You'd better stay as you are or your condition might deteriorate even further. Of course, it is possible to stick it on. I could have stuck it on now. But, take my advice, that would make it worse for you."

"That's fine! And how can I stay without a nose? And how could I be worse off than I am? It is absolutely disgusting! And where can I show myself in this obscene condition? I have an active social life. Why, even today I was invited to two important parties. And I have many connections . . . Mrs. Chekhtareva, the wife of a state councilor, Mrs. Podtochina, the wife of a senior army officer . . . although after this business I don't want to have anything to do with her, except through the police. . . ."

And Kovalev added imploringly:

"Do me a great favor, Doctor, can't you think of a way? Make it stick somehow. It doesn't matter if it doesn't hold too well—just as long as it stays on somehow. I could even support it with my hand in case of emergency. I don't even dance, you know, and so couldn't jeopardize it by some inadvertent jerk. As to my appreciation of your services, please rest assured that in the measure of my resources—"

"Believe it or not," the doctor said neither too loudly nor too softly but with persuasiveness and magnetic force, "I never dispense my services out of material considerations. It would be contrary to my principles and to professional ethics. True, I do charge for my visits but only in order not to offend people by refusing to accept a fee. Of course I could stick your nose back on, but I assure you, on my honor, if you won't take my simple word for it, that it will be much worse. You're better off letting things take their natural course. Wash often with cold water and I assure you that you'll feel just as healthy without a nose as you felt with one. As to the nose, you can put it in a jar of alcohol or, better still, add two soupspoonfuls of vodka and warmed-up vinegar to it. I'll bet you could make money out of it. In fact, I'd purchase it myself if it weren't too expensive."

"No, no! I'll never sell it," shouted the desolate major, "I'd rather it disappeared again!"

"Forgive me," the doctor said, "I was simply trying to help. Well, I can do no more. At least you see that I tried."

The doctor departed with dignity. Kovalev had not even looked at his face; dazed as he was, he was only aware of the spotless white cuffs sticking out of the black sleeves of the doctor's frock coat.

THE NEXT DAY Kovalev decided to write to Mrs. Podtochina asking her to restore to him voluntarily what was rightfully his and saying that otherwise he would be forced to lodge a complaint. The letter he composed read as follows:

> Dear Madam,
>
> I am at a loss to understand your strange action. Rest assured that you will achieve nothing by acting this way, and you certainly won't force me to marry your daughter. Please believe me, Madam, that I am fully aware of exactly what happened to my nose as well as of the fact that you, and nobody else, are the prime instigator of this affair. Its sudden detachment from its assigned place, its desertion, and its masquerading first as a state councilor and then in its natural shape is nothing but the result of witchcraft practiced by you or by those specialized in such pursuits. For my part, I deem it my duty to warn you that if the above-mentioned nose is not back in its proper place this very day, I shall be forced to avail myself of my rights and ask for the protection of the law.
>
> I remain,
> Faithfully yours,
> Platon Kovalev.

To which the lady sent an immediate reply:

> My dear Platon,
>
> I was very surprised by your letter. To be perfectly frank, I never expected anything of this kind from you, especially your unfair

reproaches. For your information, I have never received the state councilor you mention at my house, either in disguise or in his natural shape. However, I did receive Philip Ivanovich, but, despite the fact that he asked me for my daughter's hand and was a man of irreproachable character, sober habits, and great learning, I never held out any hopes for him. You also mention your nose. If you mean it symbolically, that I wanted you to stop nosing around my daughter, i.e., that I had decided to refuse you her hand, I am surprised at your saying such things when you are fully aware of my feelings on the subject, namely that, if you asked for her hand formally tomorrow, I would be prepared to grant your request forthwith, since it has always been in agreement with my wishes and in hope of which,

I remain,

Always at your service,

Alexandra Podtochina.

"She," Kovalev said, after he had read the letter, "is certainly not involved. Someone guilty of a crime couldn't write such a letter."

And the collegiate assessor knew what he was talking about because he had taken part in several judicial investigations back in the Caucasus.

"But then, how the devil did it happen, after all? How'll I ever get it straight?" he said, dropping his arms to his sides.

In the meantime, rumours about the extraordinary occurrence spread all over the capital and, as was to be expected, not without all sorts of embellishments. At that time people were prone to fall for supernatural things: only a short time before, experiments with magnetism had caused a sensation. Also, the story about the dancing chairs of Stables Street was still fresh, and people soon began to repeat that Collegiate Assessor Kovalev's nose was to be seen taking a daily walk on Nevsky Avenue at 3:00 P.M. sharp. And every day a multitude of the curious gathered there. Then someone said that the nose was in Junker's Department Store, and, as a result, such a melee developed there that the police had to interfere. A shady character with side whiskers, who nevertheless looked very respectable, and who sold all sorts of dry cakes at the entrance to the theatre, got hold of some special wooden benches, perfectly safe to stand on, and invited the curious to do so for a fee of eighty kopeks per person. A highly respected colonel, who had left his home especially early for this purpose, managed to make his way through the dense throng with great difficulty only to see in the display window not a nose but an ordinary woollen sweater and a lithograph of a girl pulling up her stocking with a well-dressed gentleman wearing a waist-coat with lapels and a small beard, a lithograph that had rested there, in the identical spot, for more than ten years. As the colonel left, he declared:

"It shouldn't be allowed—befuddling people with such stupid and improbable rumours!"

Then a rumour spread that Major Kovalev's nose was taking promenades, not on Nevsky Avenue, but in the Tavrichesky Gardens, and that it had been doing so for some time now. In fact, even when Khosrov Mirza lived there he used to marvel at this freak of nature. Students from the School of Surgeons went there. One socially prominent lady wrote a special letter to the director of the park suggesting that he show this rare object to children, if possible with explanations and instructions that would edify the younger generation.

All this was quite welcome to those who never miss a party and like to display their wit before the ladies; without it topics of conversation would have been exhausted. But there was also a dissatisfied and displeased minority among respectable people. One gentleman said he could not understand how it was possible in our enlightened age for such preposterous lies to be believed and that he was flabbergasted at the passivity of the authorities. Apparently this gentleman was one of those who desire the government to interfere in everything, including his daily fights with his wife.

Following these events . . . but here again, things become beclouded and what followed these events has remained completely unknown.

CHAPTER 3

The world is full of absolute nonsense. Sometimes it is really unbelievable. Suddenly, the very nose that used to go around as a state councilor and caused such a stir all over the city turned up, as though nothing had happened, in its proper place, namely between the cheeks of Major Kovalev. This happened on April 7. Waking up and chancing to glance in the mirror, what did he see but his nose! He grabbed it with his hand—no doubt about it—it was his nose, all right!

"Aha!" Kovalev said.

And in his infinite joy he would have performed a jig, barefoot as he was, had not Ivan come in at that moment. He ordered Ivan to bring him some water to wash with and, while washing, looked again into the mirror: he had his nose. Drying himself with his towel, he looked again—the nose was still there!

"Here, Ivan, look, I think I have a pimple on my nose," he said, all the while thinking anxiously: "Wouldn't it be terrible if Ivan came out with something like, 'No, sir, not only is there no pimple on your nose, there is no nose on your face.' "

But Ivan simply said:

"Nothing, sir, I see no pimple, the nose is clear."

"Feels good, dammit!" the major said to himself and snapped his fingers gaily.

At that moment, through the partly opened door, there appeared the head of Ivan Yakovlevich, the barber, wearing the expression of a cat that had just been smacked for the theft of a piece of suet.

"Your hands clean?" Kovalev shouted out to him.

"They're clean, sir."

"Liar!"

"I swear they're clean."

"You know, they'd better be."

Kovalev sat down. The barber wrapped a towel around his neck and in one instant transformed the major's whiskers and a part of his cheek into whipped cream of the kind that is likely to be served at a birthday party in the house of a rich merchant.

"Well, I'll be damned!" Ivan Yakovlevich muttered under his breath, looking at the nose. Then he turned the major's head and looked at the nose from the other side and muttered. "Well, well, well . . . who would have thought . . ." and he stared at the nose for a moment.

Then, with a daintiness that can only be imagined, he lifted two fingers to catch the nose by its tip. Such was Ivan Yakovlevich's shaving style.

"Look out, look out, careful!" Kovalev shouted and Ivan Yakovlevich dropped his hand and stood there frozen and embarrassed as never before. Finally he snapped out of it and started carefully tickling the major under his chin with the razor. And although it felt quite awkward and unusual for him to shave someone without holding him by the olfactory organ of the human body, he managed, somehow, by resting his rough thumb on Kovalev's cheek, then on his lower gum, to overcome all the obstacles and complete the shaving operation.

When he was through being shaved, Kovalev hurried to get dressed, rushed out, took a cab and drove to the tearoom. Before even sitting down, he shouted: "Waiter, a cup of chocolate!" then rushed over to the mirror: the nose was there. Happy, he glanced around the room and twisted his face into a sarcastic expression by slightly screwing up his eyes, when he saw two army officers, one of whom had a nose about the size of a waistcoat button. Then he left for the department through which he was trying to get the vice-gubernatorial post or, failing that, a position in the administration. Walking through the reception room, he glanced in the mirror: the nose was in its place.

Then he drove to see another collegiate assessor, that is, a major like himself. This major was a biting wit, and, parrying his digs, Kovalev would often say to him:

"Oh, I see through you clearly, you needler!"

On his way there, Kovalev thought: "Now, if the major does not split his sides with laughter when he sees me, that will be a sure sign that whatever I may have is sitting in its proper place."

And when the other collegiate assessor showed no signs of hilarity, Kovalev thought:

"Fine! It feels good, it feels good, dammit!"

In the street he met Mrs. Podtochina and her daughter and was greeted with joyful exclamations which went to show that they did not find he was missing anything. He had a very long talk with them and, on purpose, took out his snuff-box and filled his nose with great deliberation, through both orifices, muttering under his breath:

"Here, look and admire, you hens! But still, I won't marry the daughter, just *par amour* as they say, but nothing more. . . ."

And from then on, Major Kovalev could be seen on Nevsky Avenue, in theatres, everywhere. And the nose was there, sitting on his face, as though nothing had happened. And after that, Major Kovalev was always in good spirits, smiling, pursuing absolutely every pretty lady without exception and even stopping one day in front of a small shop and purchasing some sort of ribbon for his lapel, although his reason for doing so remained a mystery because he had never been made a knight of any order.

So that's what happened in the northern capital of our vast country. Only now, on further thought, do we see that there is much that is improbable in it. Without even mentioning the strangeness of such a supernatural severance of the nose and its appearance in various places in the form of a state councilor, how could Kovalev have failed to understand that he could not go and advertise about a nose in the press? I don't mean that I think that an advertisement would have cost too much, that would be nonsense and I'm not stingy; but it's not decent, it's not clever, and it's not proper! And then too, how could the nose have got into the roll of bread, and how could Ivan Yakovlevich himself? . . . Now, that I cannot understand. It's absolutely beyond me. But strangest of all, the most incomprehensible thing, is that there are authors who can choose such subjects to write about. This, I confess, is completely inexplicable, it's like . . . no, no, I can't understand it at all. In the first place, there is absolutely no advantage in it for our mother country. Secondly . . . well, what advantage is there in it at all? I simply cannot understand what it is. . . .

However, when all is said and done, and although, of course, we conceive the possibility, one and the other, and maybe even . . . Well, but then what exists without inconsistencies? And still, if you give it a thought, there *is* something to it. Whatever you may say, such things *do* happen—seldom, but they do.

THÉOPHILE GAUTIER

The Beautiful Vampire

(*La morte amoureuse*, 1836)

Aside from being the celebrated master of high Romanticism and the first phase of Parnassianism, Théophile Gautier (1811–1872) was Hoffmann's first follower in France. Among his numerous fantastic stories, "La morte amoureuse" is the most famous and most perfect (too perfect perhaps, as is Gautier's habit), a work conceived and carried out following all the rules. The theme of the living dead and vampires (a female vampire in this case) is found here in a realization of the highest quality, one that deserved Baudelaire's praises.

The temptation of Romuald, the newly ordained priest who meets the beautiful Clarimonde; the vision of the city from the towers above, with the palace of the courtesans illuminated by the sun; the life of penitence in the distant parish until a servant on horseback summons Romuald to give Clarimonde the last rites; love with the dead woman; the uncertainty as to whether the dream is his days as a poor priest or his nights in Renaissance orgies; the discovery that Clarimonde is a vampire who drinks her lover's blood: there are so many great passages that create a tradition. A tradition as well in second-class literature and film: for instance, the exhumation of Clarimonde's cadaver, intact in its coffin and with blood on its lips, that suddenly turns into a skeleton.

You ask me, brother, if I have loved; yes. It is a strange and terrible story, and although I am sixty-six years old, I scarcely dare to stir the ashes of that memory. I am reluctant to refuse any request of yours, but I would not tell such a story to any soul less tempered by experience.

The events are so strange that I cannot believe that they ever happened to me. For more than three years I was the victim of an extraordinary, diabolical obsession. I, a poor country priest, led every night in a dream (pray God it was a dream!) the life of a lost soul, a voluptuary, a Sardanapalus. One single glance thrown at a woman nearly cost me the loss of my soul; but in the end, with the help of God and my patron saint, I was able to drive out the malignant spirit that possessed me. My life was complicated with a nocturnal existence of quite a different nature. During the day I was a priest of the Lord, chaste, occupied in prayer and holy works; at night, from the moment I closed my eyes, I became a young nobleman, a connoisseur of women, dogs and horses, dicing, drinking, blaspheming; and when I awoke at daybreak, it seemed as if I fell asleep and dreamed I was a priest.

Of that nocturnal life I have preserved memories of things and of words which I cannot banish from my mind; and although I have never left the walls of my presbytery, one would say, to hear me talk, that I was a man who had tasted every experience and turned his back on the world, one who had sought refuge in religion and desired to end his troubled days in the bosom of the Church, rather than a humble priest grown old in an obscure parish in the depths of a wood, wholly cut off from the life of the day.

Yes, I have loved as no one in the world has loved, with a mad furious passion, so violent that I wonder it did not burst my heart. Ah! what nights! what nights!

From my earliest childhood I felt that the priesthood was my vocation; all my studies were therefore directed to that end, and my life up to the age of twenty-four was nothing but a long novitiate. Having finished my theological training, I took all the minor orders in turn, and my superiors thought me fit, despite my youth, to receive the last and most serious degree. The day of my ordination was appointed for Easter-week.

I had never gone into society; for me the world was bounded by the limits of college and seminary. I knew vaguely that there was something which was called woman, but I gave no thought to it; I was perfectly innocent. I saw my old and infirm mother twice a year only. That was the only link I had with the outside world.

I felt no regret, not the slightest hesitation, in face of this irrevocable pledge; I was full of joy and impatience. Never did a young bridegroom count the hours with more feverish eagerness; I could not sleep for thinking of it; I dreamt that I was saying mass. To be a priest seemed to me to be the most wonderful thing in the world; I would have refused to be a king or a poet. My ambition knew no higher flight.

I am telling you this to show you that I was the last person in the world to whom such a thing should have happened, and of what inexplicable fascination I was the victim.

When the great day came, I walked to the church with so light a step that I seemed to tread on air or to have wings on my shoulders. I felt as if I were an angel, and I was astonished at the serious and preoccupied faces of my companions; for there were several of us. I had passed the night in prayer and was in a frame of mind that bordered on ecstasy. The bishop, a venerable old man, seemed to be God the Father contemplating His eternity, and I saw heaven through the vaulted roof of the sacred building.

You know the details of the ceremony: the benediction, the communion, the anointing of the palms of the hands with the oil of the catechumens, and lastly the holy sacrifice offered together with the bishop. I will not dwell upon this. Oh! how right Job is when he says that the man is imprudent who does not close a bargain with his eyes!

I chanced to raise my head, which till then I had held bowed down, and saw before me—so near that I could have touched her, although in reality she was some distance away and on the other side of the railing—I saw, I say, a young woman of rare beauty and dressed with regal splendour. It was as though scales had fallen from my eyes. I experienced the sensation of a blind man who suddenly recovers his sight. The bishop, so radiant a moment before, faded out all of a sudden; the tapers grew pale in their gold sconces like the stars at daybreak, and the whole church became quite dark. The lovely creature stood out against the background of shadow like an angelic vision; she seemed to be illuminated of herself, to create rather than to receive light.

I lowered my eye-lids, firmly resolved not to lift them again, so as to be free from the influence of external objects; for my thoughts wandered more and more, and I hardly knew what I was doing.

A minute later I opened my eyes again, for through my lashes I saw her, glittering with all the colours of the prism, and in a roseate twilight, as when one looks at the sun.

Oh! how beautiful she was! The greatest painters, searching for ideal beauty in heaven and bringing down to earth the divine portrait of the Madonna, do not approach this fabulous reality. Neither poet's verse nor painter's palette can give an idea of it.

She was fairly tall, with the figure and carriage of a goddess. Her soft fair hair was parted and flowed over her temples like two waves of gold; a queen with her diadem, one might fancy; her forehead of a bluish, transparent whiteness, spread broad and serene over almost brown eyebrows, a peculiarity which still further enhanced the effect of sea-green eyes that shone with a sparkle and brilliance that were unbearable. What eyes! With one flash they decided the fate of a man; they had a life, a limpidity, a liquid brightness, which I have never seen in a human eye; rays like arrows darted from them straight to the heart. I know not whether the flame that illuminated them came from heaven or hell, but of a surety it came from one or the other. This woman was an angel or a demon, perhaps both: certainly she did not spring from the womb of Eve, the common mother. Teeth of purest Orient pearl gleamed through the red of her smiling lips, and at each movement of her mouth little dimples showed in the roseate softness of her adorable cheeks. The nose was well cut and of truly royal pride, and betokened the most noble descent. Bright agates wantoned on the smooth, shining skin of her half-revealed shoulders, and rows of large pearls, nearly as white as her neck, fell on her breast. From time to time she raised her head with the undulating motion of a snake or of a bridling peacock, which sent a movement through the high open-work ruff that encircled her throat like a silver trellis.

She wore a dress of red velvet, and from the broad ermine-trimmed sleeves emerged patrician hands of infinite delicacy, with long rounded fingers, so translucent that the light shone through them, like those of Aurora.

All these details are still as present to my eyes as if they dated from yesterday, for though my mind was extremely troubled, nothing escaped me: the minutest details, the tiny black spot on the side of the chin, the scarcely perceptible down at the corners of the lips, the velvet softness of the brow, the quivering shadow of the eyelashes on the cheeks—I took everything in with an astonishing clearness.

As I looked at her, I felt doors which hitherto had been closed open within me: it was as if little windows were unshuttered in every direction to open up unknown vistas; life appeared to me in a wholly new aspect. I had just been born into another world of thought and feeling. A frightful anguish gripped my heart; each minute that passed seemed a second and an age.

Meanwhile, the ceremony proceeded, and carried me far away from the world the entrance to which my growing desires were furiously besieging. I said yes when I wanted to say no, while everything in me revolted and protested against the wrong my tongue was doing to my soul: in spite of myself, some mysterious power tore the words from my throat. Thus it is, perhaps, that so many young women go to the altar with the fixed intention of refusing emphatically the husbands forced upon them, and not one carries out her project. It is thus, doubtless, that poor novices take the veil, for all their determination to tear it in shreds at the moment of uttering their vows. One dares not cause such a scandal in public, or disappoint the expectations of so many people; the wishes of all, the looks of all, seem to weigh on one like a casque of lead; and then the procedure has been so well arranged, everything so completely regulated in advance, in a manner so manifestly irrevocable, that thought yields to the weight of facts and becomes completely impotent.

The gaze of the beautiful stranger changed its expression as the ceremony proceeded. Tender and caressing at first, it took the air of disdain and dissatisfaction of one misunderstood.

I made an effort, violent enough to uproot a mountain, to cry out that I did not wish to be a priest; but I could not do it; my tongue clove to the roof of my mouth, and I could not translate my desire into the faintest movement of refusal. Wide awake, I was in a condition like that of nightmare, when you want to utter the word upon which your life depends, and cannot do it.

She seemed to be aware of the torture I was suffering, and, as if to give me courage, cast upon me a look full of divine promise. Her eyes were a poem, of which each look was a verse. They said:

"If you will be mine, I will make you happier than God Himself in His paradise; the angels will envy you. Tear off that funeral winding-sheet in which you are about to wrap yourself. I am Beauty, I am Youth, I am Life; come to me, and we will be Love. What could Jehovah offer you in exchange for that? Our life will glide by like a dream, and be but a kiss prolonged to eternity.

"Dash that cup from your lips, and you are free. I will transport you to unknown isles; you shall sleep upon my breast in a bed of pure gold under a canopy of silver. For I love you, and would take you from your God, before Whom so many noble hearts melt into floods of love that reach Him not."

I seemed to hear these words in a rhythm of infinite sweetness; for her look all but had sound, and the sentences her eyes sent to me echoed in the depths of my heart as if invisible lips had breathed them into my soul. I felt myself ready to renounce God, yet my lips went mechanically through the formalities of the ceremony. The beautiful one flung me a second glance so beseeching, so despairing, that steel blades went through my heart, and I felt more darts in my breast than the Mother of Sorrows.

It was done; I was a priest.

Never did human countenance portray such poignant anguish. The girl who sees her betrothed die suddenly at her side, the mother beside the empty cradle of her child, Eve sitting on the threshold of Paradise, the miser who finds a stone in the place of his treasure, the poet who has dropped into the fire the only manuscript of his finest work—none of these could seem more prostrated by grief, more inconsolable. The blood fled from her lovely cheek and she became as white as marble; her beautiful arms fell beside her body, as though the muscles had lost their power, and she leaned against a pillar as if her legs were weakening and slipping from under her.

As for me—livid, my forehead bathed in a bloodier sweat than that of Calvary, I tottered to the door of the church; I was suffocated; it seemed as if the vaulted roof above was falling upon my shoulders and that my head alone was supporting the whole weight of the dome.

As I was about to cross the threshold a hand suddenly grasped mine—a woman's hand! I had never touched one. It was cold as a snake's skin, and its impress remained, burning into my flesh like the brand of a red-hot iron. It was she. "Unhappy man! unhappy man! what have you done?" she said to me in a low voice; then she disappeared in the crowd.

The old bishop passed by; he looked at me with a severe expression. My demeanour must have been strange; I paled, I flushed, my vision was clouded. One of my companions took compassion on me and led me away; alone, I could not have found my way back to the seminary. At a turn of a street, while the young priest's head was turned another way, a Negro page, fantastically dressed, came towards me and handed me, without stopping, a little pocket-book with gilt-edged corners, signing to me to hide it.

I slipped it into my sleeve and kept it there until I was alone in my cell. I undid the clasp. There were but two leaves with the words: "Clarimonde, Concini Palace." I was then so little conversant with life that I had never heard of Clarimonde, in spite of her celebrity, and had no idea where the Concini Palace was. I made a thousand conjectures, each one more extravagant than the last, but to tell the truth, provided I could see her again, I cared little what she might be, great lady or courtesan.

This love, just born, had taken root imperishably; I did not even think of attempting to eradicate it, I felt so strongly that it was impossible. This woman had taken complete possession of me; one look had sufficed to work the change in me; she had breathed her will into me; my life was no more my own, but hers, drawing its breath from her. I committed a thousand extravagances; I kissed the place on my hand which she had touched, and repeated her name for hours together. I had only to close my eyes to see her as clearly as if she had really been present, and I kept repeating the words she had spoken at the church door: "Unhappy man! unhappy man! what have you done?"

I realized all the horror of the situation, and the funereal and dreadful aspects of the state into which I had just been initiated were clearly revealed to me. To be a priest! That is to say, to be chaste, not to love, to make no distinction of sex or age, to turn aside from all beauty, to cower beneath the icy shadow of a monastery or a church, to see only the dying, to keep watch beside unknown corpses, to wear your own mourning in the shape of your black cassock, until at last your priest's robe shall be your own coffin-cloth!

And I felt life rising within me like an underground lake that fills and overflows; my blood throbbed violently in my arteries; my youth, so long repressed, burst out all at once like the aloe that takes a hundred years to flower and blossoms with a clap of thunder.

What should I do to see Clarimonde again? I had no pretext for leaving the seminary, knowing no one in the town; I was not even to remain there, was only waiting until the parish which was to be under my charge should be allotted to me. I tried to loosen the bars of the window; but it was a fearful height, and descent without a ladder was not to be dreamed of. Besides, it could only be made at night; and how find my way in the intricate maze of the streets? All these difficulties, which would have been nothing to others, were immense to me, a poor seminarist, a lover without experience, without money, without clothes.

If I had not been a priest I might have seen her every day; I should have been her lover, her husband, I told myself in my infatuation. Instead of being wrapped in my dismal shroud, I should have clothes of silk and velvet, gold chains, a sword at my side and a feather in my cap, like handsome young cavaliers. My hair, instead of being spoilt by a large tonsure, would play about my neck in wavy curls. I should have a beautiful waxed moustache and be a gallant. But an hour passed before an altar, a few scarcely articulated words, had cut me off for ever from the number of the living; I had myself sealed the stone of my tomb, pushed with my own hand the bolt of my prison!

I went to the window. The sky was beautifully blue, the trees were clad in their spring dress; Nature seemed to make parade of an ironic gaiety. The square was full of people; they came and went; young sparks and young beauties, couple by couple, made their way towards gardens and arbours. Boon companions passed by arm-in-arm singing drinking-songs. There was movement, life, bustle; liveliness that contrasted sadly with my mourning and my loneliness. A young mother on the doorstep played with her child, kissed the rosy little mouth still beaded with drops of milk, teased it with a thousand of those divine childishnesses which mothers alone can invent. The father, who stood at a little distance, smiled quietly on the charming group, and with folded arms hugged his happiness to his heart. I could not bear the sight; I closed the window and threw myself on my bed, my heart filled with hatred and fearful jealousy, gnawing my fingers and my blanket like a tiger that has hungered for three days.

I do not know how long I remained thus; but, turning with a convulsive movement, I saw the Abbé Sérapion standing in the middle of the room and watching me with fixed attention. I was overcome with shame, and letting my head fall on my breast, I covered my eyes with my hands.

"Romuald, my friend, something extraordinary is taking place in you," said Sérapion, after a few minutes' silence; "your behaviour is truly unaccountable! You, so pious, so calm, so gentle, you rage in your cell like a wild beast. Be on your guard, my brother, and do not listen to the promptings of the devil; the evil spirit, incensed because you are for ever consecrated to the Lord, is prowling round you like a ravenous wolf and making a last effort to draw you to him. Instead of letting yourself be downcast, my dear Romuald, make yourself a breastplate of prayers, a buckler of mortifications, and valiantly do battle with the enemy; you will conquer him. Virtue must be put to the test; gold comes out of the cupel finer than before. Do not be afraid or discouraged; the most watchful and steadfast souls have had moments such as these. Pray, fast, meditate, and the evil spirit will leave you."

The words of the Abbé Sérapion recalled me to myself, and I regained something of my composure.

"I came," he continued, "to announce to you your nomination to the living of C——. The priest who had it has just died, and Monseigneur the Bishop has directed me to instal you there; be ready to start to-morrow."

I replied with a movement of the head that I would be ready, and the Abbé withdrew. I opened my missal and began to read prayers; but the lines soon became confused; the sequence of thoughts in my brain became tangled, and the book dropped from my hand without my noticing it.

I must leave to-morrow without seeing her again! Add another obstacle to all those that already lay between us! Lose for ever the hope of meeting her except by a miracle! Should I write to her? By whom could I send a letter? Considering the sacred character with which I was invested, to whom should I unbosom myself, in whom could I confide? I was distracted with doubts and fears. Then, what the Abbé Sérapion had said about the wiles of the devil came back to my mind. The strangeness of the adventure, the unearthly beauty of Clarimonde, the phosphorescent brilliance of her eyes, the burning impress of her hand, the trouble of mind into which she had thrown me, the sudden change which had taken place in me, my pious aspirations dispelled in a moment—all this proved clearly the presence of the devil, and that soft hand was perhaps only the glove with which he had sheathed his claw.

These ideas threw me into a great terror; I picked up the missal which had fallen from my knees and betook myself again to prayer.

The next day Sérapion came to fetch me. Two mules awaited us before the door, laden with our scanty baggage; he mounted one and I the other. As we traversed the streets of the town I glanced at all the windows and balconies in the hope of seeing Clarimonde; but it was too early, and the town was not yet awake. My eyes tried to penetrate the blinds and curtains of all the mansions before which we passed. Sérapion, doubtless, attributed this curiosity to the admiration which the beauty of the architecture excited in me, for he slackened his mount's pace in order to give me time to look. At length we reached the town-gate and began to climb the hill. When I was at the top, I turned to take a last look at the place where Clarimonde lived. The shadow of a cloud completely covered the town; its blue and red roofs were merged in a general half-tone over which the morning smoke floated here and there, like white wisps of foam. By a curious optical effect, one edifice stood out shining and golden under a single ray of light, a house higher than the buildings near it, which were completely lost in the mist; although more than a league distant, it seemed quite near. The smallest details could be distinguished—turrets, leads, windows, even its swallow-tailed weather-cocks.

"What is that palace I see down there lit up by a sunbeam?" I asked Sérapion.

He shaded his eyes with his hand, and, looking towards it, answered:

"It is the ancient palace which the Prince Concini has given to the courtesan Clarimonde; fearful things take place there."

At that moment—I do not know even now whether it was reality or an illusion—I thought I saw a slim white figure glide on to the terrace; it sparkled there for a moment and faded out. It was Clarimonde!

Oh! did she know that at that very moment, from the top of the steep road that was leading me away from her, and which I was never more to descend, I was gazing, ardent and troubled, on the palace where she lived, and which a mocking play of light seemed to bring close to me, as if to bid me enter it as master? Without doubt she knew it, for her soul was linked to mine in too intimate a sympathy not to feel its faintest vibrations; and it was this consciousness that had impelled her, still arrayed in her night-robe, to ascend the terrace in the shining dews of morning.

The shadow enveloped the palace, and there was now only a motionless sea of roofs and summits, in which nothing could be distinguished but an undulating expanse. Sérapion urged his mule forward, my own immediately fell into pace, and a bend in the road placed the town of S—— for ever beyond my view, for I was never to return to it. After three days of travel through rather dreary country, we saw peeping out from among the trees the weather-cock of the church at which I was to officiate; and after passing along a few crooked roads between thatched cottages and crofts, we found ourselves before its front, which was not magnificent. A porch adorned with a few flutings and two or three roughly-sculptured columns of sandstone, a tiled roof and buttresses of the same sandstone as the pillars; to the left the church-yard, overgrown with rank herbage, with a large iron cross in the middle; to the right, over-shadowed by the church, the presbytery. It was a dwelling of extreme simplicity and severe cleanliness.

We went in. Some fowls were pecking the ground in search of

scantily strewn grains of oats; apparently accustomed to the black robes of priests, they were not at all disconcerted at our intrusion, and barely disturbed themselves to allow us to pass. A cracked and husky barking reached our ears, and we saw an old dog come running towards us.

It was my predecessor's dog. He had the dimmed eye, gray jowl, and all the signs of the most advanced age a dog can live to. I patted him gently, and he at once began to walk by my side with an air of inexpressible satisfaction. An oldish woman, who had been housekeeper to the old curé, also came out to meet us, and after showing us into a low-ceilinged room, asked me if it was my intention to keep her. I said that I would keep her, the dog, the fowls, and all the furniture that her master had left her at his death, which threw her into transports of joy; the Abbé Sérapion paid her on the spot the price she asked.

My installation complete, the Abbé Sérapion returned to the seminary. I was left alone with no one but myself to rely on. The thought of Clarimonde began again to obsess me, and, strive to banish it as I might, I did not always succeed. One evening, as I strolled along the box-bordered walks of my little garden, I fancied I saw through the trimmed hedge the figure of a woman, who was following all my movements, her two sea-green eyes shining through the leaves; but it was only an illusion, for on reaching the further end of the walk, I found nothing but a foot-print on the sand, so small that one would have pronounced it the foot-mark of a child. The garden was surrounded by very high walls; I searched every nook and corner of it, but no one was there. I have never been able to explain this occurrence, which indeed was nothing compared with the strange things which were to happen to me.

I lived thus for a year, fulfilling punctually all the duties of my state, praying, fasting, exhorting, ministering to the sick, giving so much in alms as to be deprived of the most indispensable necessities. But I felt that all was barren within me, and that the fountains of grace had dried up. I did not enjoy the happiness that the fulfilment of a holy mission gives; my thoughts were elsewhere; and Clarimonde's words often returned to my lips like a kind of involuntary refrain. Brother, meditate well on this! For having once raised my eyes to a woman, for a fault apparently so trifling, I have suffered for years the most grievous torment; my whole life has been troubled, always and for ever.

I will not detain you longer with these secret defeats, the victories always followed by a deeper relapse, but will pass at once to a decisive event. One night the door-bell rang violently. The old housekeeper went to open it, and a man of swarthy appearance, richly but outlandishly dressed and wearing a long sword, stood revealed in the light of Barbara's lantern. Her first feeling was one of fear, but the man reassured her and told her that he must see me immediately on a matter that concerned me as a priest. Barbara brought him upstairs to me. I was just going to bed. The man informed me that his mistress, a very great lady, was at the point of death and wished to see a priest. I replied that I was ready to accompany him; I took with me the requisites for extreme unction, and went down as quickly as I could.

Before the door, two horses, black as night, their chests streaked with two long waves of foam, were impatiently pawing the ground. The man held the stirrup for me and helped me to mount one of them; then, resting his hand upon the pommel of the saddle, vaulted on to the other. He gripped his horse with his knees, gave it free rein, and it shot forward like an arrow. Mine, the bridle of which he held, set off at a gallop also, and kept exactly abreast of the other. We tore over the ground; the earth swept beneath us gray and streaked, and the dark outline of the trees fled past like a routed army. We passed through a forest of such dense and chilly darkness that I felt my flesh creep with a thrill of superstitious terror. The showers of sparks that our horses' hoofs beat from the stones left a trail of fire in our wake; and if anyone had seen my guide and me at that hour of the night, he would have taken us for two phantom horsemen careering through a nightmare. Will-o'-the-wisps crossed our path from time to time, and jackdaws squawked piteously in the depths of the wood, where the phosphorescent eyes of wild cats gleamed now and then. The manes of our horses streamed more and more wildly, the sweat poured down their sides, the breath came from their nostrils panting and laboured. But when he saw them failing, the groom, to rally them, uttered a guttural cry such as human lips never uttered, and the furious pace was resumed.

At last the whirlwind subsided; a black mass, dotted with a few points of light, rose suddenly before us; our horses' hoofs rang more sharply on an iron causeway, and we passed under a vaulted passage which opened its dark jaws between two gigantic towers. Great excitement prevailed in the castle; servants with torches in their hands were hurrying through the courtyard in all directions, and lights were going up and down from landing to landing. I had a confused view of a vast structure, columns, arcades, and stairways, an architectural splendour altogether regal and fantastic. A Negro page, the same who had brought me Clarimonde's pocket-book, whom I recognized immediately, came to help me dismount, and a major-domo dressed in black velvet, with a gold chain about his neck and an ivory staff in his hand, advanced to meet me. Tears flowed from his eyes, and trickled down his cheeks on to his white beard.

"Too late!" he said, shaking his head. "Too late, sir Priest! But if you have not been able to save the soul, come and watch by the poor body."

He took my arm and led me to the chamber of death. I wept as bitterly as he, for I knew now that the dead woman was no other than Clarimonde, loved so much and so madly.

A *prie-Dieu* was placed at the bedside; a bluish flame flickering over a bronze cup threw a feeble and uncertain light through the room and brought into twinkling prominence here and there some projecting angle of furniture or moulding. On the table, in a vase of chased silver, was a faded white rose, whose petals, save one which still clung to its stem, had fallen at the foot of the vase like fragrant tears. A broken black mask, a fan, fancy dresses of every kind lay about on the chairs, and showed that Death had come into this sumptuous dwelling unexpected and unannounced. I knelt down without daring to look towards the bed, and began to recite psalms with fervour, thanking God for having placed the tomb between the thought of this woman and myself, so that I might add to my prayers her name, henceforth sanctified.

But little by little my enthusiasm abated, and my thoughts wandered. There was nothing of the death-chamber about this room. Instead of the fetid, corpse-infected atmosphere which I was accustomed to breathe in these funereal vigils, a languishing vapour of Eastern perfumes, an indefinable, feminine, love-inspiring scent floated gently on the warm air. The pale light suggested rather a twilight arranged for voluptuous pleasure than the yellow rays of the night-light that flickers beside a corpse. I reflected on the strange chance by which I had found Clarimonde again at the moment when I was losing her for ever, and a sigh of regret escaped my breast. It seemed as if someone sighed behind me also, and I turned involuntarily. It was an echo. As I turned, my eyes fell upon the death-bed they had till then avoided. The red damask curtains, embroidered with large flowers and relieved by spiral fringes of gold, showed the dead woman lying at full length, her hands joined on her breast. It was covered with linen drapery of dazzling whiteness, a whiteness accentuated by the dark purple of the tapestry, and so fine in texture that it in no way concealed the exquisite form of the body, and permitted the eye to follow the beautiful outlines, undulous as a swan's neck, which death itself had not been able to stiffen. One would have said it was an alabaster statue, wrought by a clever sculptor for the tomb of a queen, or, still better, a young girl asleep with snow fallen on her.

I could contain myself no longer: the atmosphere intoxicated me, the feverish scent of half-faded roses went to my brain; and I strode up and down the room, pausing each time before the bed to look upon the beauty that lay dead under its transparent burial robe. Strange thoughts passed through my mind; I pictured to myself that she was not really dead at all, that it was only a stratagem which she had employed to draw me to her castle and tell me of her love. For a moment I even imagined that I saw her foot move under the whiteness of her coverings, and the straight folds of the shroud change their outline.

And then I said to myself: "Is this really Clarimonde? What proof of it have I? May not that black page have entered the service of another woman? I must be mad so to distress and agitate myself." But my beating heart replied: "It is she, it is she!" I approached the bed again, and gazed with redoubled attention at the object of my uncertainty. Shall I confess it? That perfection of form, although purified and sanctified by the shadow of death, affected me more pleasurably than it should have done, and that repose was so like sleep as to deceive the onlooker.

I forgot that I had come to discharge a funeral rite, and imagined myself a young bridegroom entering the chamber of his bride, who hides her face in modesty and will not let her charms be seen. Torn with grief, mad with joy, shivering with fear and delight, I bent towards her and took hold of the corner of the sheet; I raised it gently, holding my breath for fear of waking her. My heart beat so wildly that I felt a rushing noise in my temples, and my forehead streamed with sweat as though I had moved a slab of marble.

It was indeed Clarimonde, as I had seen her in the church on the day of my ordination; she was just as charming, and death, with her, seemed but one form of coquetry the more. The pallor of her cheeks, the fuller rose of her lips, the long drooping lashes that made a brown fringe on the whiteness of the face, gave her an expression of melancholy chastity and pensive suffering that was inexpressibly seductive; her long loosened hair, in which a few little blue flowers were still mingled, made a pillow for her head and covered her bare shoulders with its curls; her beautiful hands, purer, more transparent than the sacrificial wafer, were crossed in an attitude of pious repose and mute prayer—an attitude that counter-balanced the too great seduction, it might have been, even in death, of the exquisite moulding and ivory whiteness of her bare arms, from which the bracelets of pearls had not been taken.

I remained for a long time absorbed in silent contemplation, and the longer I looked, the less could I believe that life had for ever deserted that beautiful body. I do not know if it was an illusion or a reflection from the lamp, but it seemed that the blood began to flow again under that dull pallor. I touched her arm lightly; it was cold, but no colder than was her hand on the day that it had touched mine under the portal of the church. I resumed my former position, bending my face over hers, and letting the warm dew of my tears rain upon her cheeks. Ah! what a bitter sensation of despair and impotence I felt! What an agony that vigil was! I should have liked to be able to gather together all my life that I might give it to her and breathe into those icy relics the fire that consumed me. The night was advancing; and feeling that the moment of eternal separation was at hand, I could not deny myself the last and supreme pleasure of leaving a kiss upon the dead lips of her who had all my love.

Oh, miracle! light breath mingled with my breath, and Clarimonde's mouth replied to the pressure of mine: her eyes opened and regained a little brilliance: she sighed, and uncrossing her arms, put them round my neck with a look of inexpressible bliss.

"Ah! it is you, Romuald," she said, in a voice as languishing and sweet as the last vibration of a harp; "what have you been doing? I have waited for you so long that I have died; but now that we are betrothed, I shall be able to see you and come to you. Farewell, Romuald, farewell! I love you; that is all I wished to tell you, and I give you back the life which you recalled in me for a minute by your kiss. Farewell, for a little while!"

Her head fell back, but she still held me in her arms as if to keep me with her. A furious gust of wind blew through the window and swept into the room; the last petal of the white rose quivered for a moment like a wing at the end of its stalk, then it broke away and flew out through the open window, bearing with it the soul of Clarimonde. The light went out, and I fell senseless on the bosom of the beautiful corpse.

When I came to myself I was lying on my bed in my little room at the presbytery, and the former curé's old dog was licking my hand, which lay outside the blanket. Barbara was busying herself about the room with the trembling movements of old age, opening and shutting drawers or stirring powders in glasses. On seeing me open my eyes, the old woman uttered a cry of joy, and the dog barked and wagged his tail; but I was so weak that I could not speak a word or make the least movement.

I learned afterwards that I had been in this condition for three days, giving no sign of life except an almost imperceptible breathing. Those three days were a blank in my life, and I do not know whither my spirit had gone during the whole of that time; I remember nothing at all about it. Barbara told me that the same man of swarthy aspect, who had come to fetch me in the night, had brought me back the next morning in a closed litter, and had immediately taken his departure. As soon as I could collect my thoughts, I went over in my mind all the events of that fatal night. At first I believed that I had been the plaything of a magical illusion; but actual and tangible circumstances soon demolished that supposition. I could not think that I had been dreaming, since Barbara as well as myself had seen the man with the two black horses and accurately described their trappings and appearance. At the same time, no one in the neighbourhood had any knowledge of a castle answering the description of the castle where I had found Clarimonde.

One morning the Abbé Sérapion entered my room. Barbara had sent to tell him that I was ill, and he had lost no time in coming to me. Although this promptitude was a proof of his affection and concern for me, his visit did not give me the pleasure that it ought to have given me. There was something searching and inquisitorial in the Abbé Sérapion's look that made me uncomfortable. I felt embarrassed and guilt-stricken in his presence. He had been the first to discover that something was preying on my mind, and I was angry with him for his perception.

Even while he was inquiring about my health in hypocritically honeyed tones, he fixed his two yellow lion's eyes on mine and plunged his gaze into my soul like a plummet. Then he asked me a few questions about the way I managed my parish, asked whether I took pleasure in my work, how I passed the time my duties left free, if I had made any acquaintances among the inhabitants of the place, what were my favourite books, and a thousand other details of the kind. I replied to all this as briefly as possible, and he, without waiting till I had finished speaking, passed on to something else. This conversation had evidently nothing to do with what he wished to say. Then, without the least preface, and as if he were giving me a piece of news which he had just remembered and was afraid of forgetting, he said, in a clear and ringing voice that sounded in my ears like the trumpets of the Last Judgement:

"The famous courtesan Clarimonde died lately, after an orgy that lasted eight days and eight nights. It was something hellishly splendid. The abominations of Balthazar's and Cleopatra's feasts were revived. Good God! in what an age we live! The guests were served by copper-complexioned slaves who spoke an unknown language, and who, I believe, were real demons; the livery of the lowest among them might have served as the gala dress of an emperor. There have always been very strange stories about this Clarimonde; and all her lovers have come to a miserable and violent end. The tale went that she was a ghoul, a female vampire; but I believe she was Beelzebub in person."

He ceased speaking, and watched me more narrowly than ever to see the effect of his words upon me. I could not prevent myself from starting on hearing the name of Clarimonde, and this news of her death, besides the grief it caused me, by its strange coincidence with the night scene I had witnessed, threw me into a state of agitation and fear which was reflected in my face, do what I would to control it. Sérapion cast an anxious and severe glance on me; then he said:

"My son, I must do my duty and warn you that you are on the brink of a precipice; beware lest you fall. Satan has long claws, and tombs are not always secure. The stone that covers Clarimonde should be sealed with a triple seal; for according to what men say, this is not the first time she had died. May God watch over you, Romuald!"

When he had uttered these words, Sérapion went slowly to the door, and I did not see him again; for he set out for S——immediately.

I had now entirely recovered and had resumed my accustomed

duties. The memory of Clarimonde and the old Abbé's words were always in my mind; however, no extraordinary event had occurred to confirm Sérapion's gloomy forebodings, and I began to think that his fears and my own terrors had been exaggerated; but one night I had a dream. I had hardly fallen asleep when I heard the rings of my bed-curtains slide along the rods with a loud clatter; I raised myself sharply upon my elbow and saw the shadowy form of a woman standing before me.

At once I recognized Clarimonde.

She held in her hand a small lamp like those which are placed in tombs, and its rays gave her slender fingers a rosy transparence which spread upward, fading by insensible degrees into the dull, milky white of her bare arm. She had no other garment than the linen shroud that covered her on her death-bed, the folds of which she held to her breast as if ashamed of being so scantily clothed, but her little hand was too small for the task; she was so pale that the colour of the drapery, under the faint rays of the lamp, was confused with that of her flesh. Wrapped in this fine tissue which revealed all the outlines of her body, she looked like a marble statue of an antique bather rather than a woman endowed with life. Dead or living, statue or woman, shade or body, her beauty was always the same; only the green sparkle of her eyes was a little dulled, and her mouth, before so vermilion, was now only tinged with a soft faint rose almost as pale as that of her cheeks. The little blue flowers I had noticed in her hair were quite withered and had lost nearly all their petals; but nonetheless she was charming, so charming that, despite the strangeness of the adventure and the mysterious manner in which she had entered my room, I was not for one moment afraid.

She placed the lamp on the table and seated herself on the foot of my bed; then, leaning towards me, she spoke in that voice, at once silvery and soft as velvet, which I have never heard from any lips but hers:

"I have kept you waiting a long time, dear Romuald, and you must have thought that I had forgotten you. But I have come a very long way, from a place from which no one has ever yet returned; there is neither sun nor moon in the country I come from; nothing but space and shadow; neither road nor pathway; no earth for the foot, no air for the wings; and yet I am here, for love is stronger than death and will conquer it in the end. Ah! what gloomy faces, what terrible things I have seen on my journey! How difficult it has been for my soul, come back to this world by the power of my will, to find its body and take up its abode there! What efforts I had to make before I could lift the stone with which they had covered me! See! the inside of my poor hands is all bruised. Kiss them and heal them, dear love!"

She pressed the cold palms of her hands, in turn, to my lips; I did indeed kiss them again and again, and she watched me do so with a smile of inexpressible content.

I confess to my shame that I had wholly forgotten the Abbé Sérapion's advice and the sacred character I had assumed. I had fallen without resistance and at the first assault. I had not even made an effort to repel the tempter; the coolness of Clarimonde's hand penetrated mine, and I felt voluptuous shivers run over my body. Poor child! In spite of all that I have seen of her, I can still hardly believe that she was a demon; at least she had not the appearance of one, and never has Satan better hidden his claws and hoofs. She had tucked her heels under her and sat on the edge of my couch in an attitude full of unstudied coquetry. Now and again she passed her little hand through my hair and rolled it into curls, as if to try how new ways of arranging it would suit me. I submitted to this with a most guilty satisfaction, and she kept up an accompaniment of the most charming prattle.

It is remarkable that I felt no astonishment at such an extraordinary adventure, and with that faculty which one has in dreams of accepting the most bizarre events as quite ordinary, I saw in it nothing that was not perfectly natural.

"I loved you long before I saw you, dear Romuald, and sought you everywhere. You were my ideal, and when I saw you in the church at the fatal moment, I said at once 'It is he!' I gave you a look into which

I put all the love that I had, and that I was to have for you; a look to damn a cardinal, to bring a king to his knees at my feet before all his court. You remained obdurate and preferred your God to me.

"Ah! how jealous I am of God, Whom you loved and still love better than me!

"How unhappy I am! I shall never have your heart for my very own; I, whom you recalled to life with a kiss; I, the dead Clarimonde, who, for your sake, has broken the doors of the tomb, and has come to devote to you the life which she has only resumed to make you happy!"

These words were broken by intoxicating caresses which benumbed my senses and my reason to such a point that I did not fear, in order to console her, to utter a frightful blasphemy and tell her that I loved her as much as God.

New life came into her eyes; they shone like chrysoprases.

"Truly? truly? as much as God!" she said, clasping me in her beautiful arms. "If it is so, you will come with me, you will follow me where I wish. You will leave your ugly black robes. You will be the proudest, the most envied of cavaliers; you will be my lover. To be the acknowledged lover of Clarimonde, who has refused a Pope, think of it! Ah! the happy life, the golden existence that we shall lead! When shall we start, my gallant?"

"To-morrow! To-morrow!" I cried, in my delirium.

"To-morrow, then!" she replied. "I shall have time to change my clothes, for these are a little scanty and not suited for travelling. I must also tell my servants, who believe me to be dead in good earnest and are broken-hearted. Money, clothes, carriages, everything will be ready. I will come and fetch you at this time to-morrow. Farewell, dear heart."

She touched my forehead with her lips. The lamp went out, the curtains closed again, and I saw no more; a leaden, dreamless sleep weighed me down and held me torpid until next morning. I woke later than usual, and the recollection of that strange vision disturbed my mind throughout the day; I persuaded myself at last that it was a mere product of a heated imagination. Yet the sensations had been so vivid that it was difficult to believe that they were not real, and it was not without fear of what was going to happen that I went to bed, after praying God to banish evil thoughts from my mind and to watch over my sleep.

I was soon fast asleep, and my dream continued. The curtains were drawn apart, and I saw Clarimonde, not, as the first time, pale in her white shroud and with the hues of death upon her cheeks, but gay, lively and elegant, in a magnificent travelling-dress of green velvet edged with gold and looped up on one side to show a satin skirt. Her fair hair escaped in large curls under a large black felt hat trimmed with white feathers fancifully twisted; she held in her hand a little riding-whip, the handle of which ended in a golden whistle. She touched me lightly with it and said:

"Well, fair sleeper, is this how you make your preparations? I counted on finding you waiting. Get up quickly; we have no time to lose."

I jumped out of bed.

"Come, dress and let us be off," she said, pointing to a small parcel she had brought; "the horses are impatient and are champing their bits at the door. We ought to be ten leagues from here already."

I dressed myself in haste, and she herself handed me the articles of clothing, going into fits of laughter at my awkwardness and showing me how to put them on when I made mistakes. She dressed my hair with a light touch and, when this was done, put into my hand a little pocket mirror of Venetian crystal framed in silver filigree, saying:

"What do you think of yourself? Would you take me into your service as valet?"

I was no longer the same person. I did not recognize myself. I was no more like my old self than a finished statue is like a block of stone. The face I knew seemed but a coarse sketch of the face the mirror reflected. I was handsome; and my vanity was roused by the transformation. The fine clothes, the rich embroidered waist-coat, made quite another man of me; and I marvelled at the power of a few ells of cloth cut in a certain fashion. The spirit of my costume found its way under my skin, and in ten minutes I was a passable coxcomb.

I walked round the room several times to give myself an easy bearing. Clarimonde watched me with an air of motherly pride, and seemed well pleased with her work.

"Come, we have been childish long enough; we must be off, dear Romuald! We have far to go and we shall not get there in time."

She took me by the hand and led me away. All the doors opened to her immediately she touched them, and we passed the dog without waking him.

At the door we found Margheritone, the groom who had already been my guide; he held by their bridles three horses, black like the first, one for me, one for himself, and one for Clarimonde. Those horses must have been Spanish jennets out of mares by Zephyr; for they went as fast as the wind, and the moon, which had risen at our departure to light us on our way, rolled through the sky like a wheel broken loose from its chariot; we saw it on our right leaping from tree to tree as if it lost breath in pursuit of us. Soon we came to a plain where, by a clump of trees, a carriage drawn by four powerful beasts was waiting for us; we got into it, and the postillions set off at a furious gallop. I had one arm round Clarimonde and I held one of her hands clasped in mine; she laid her head on my shoulder, and I felt her half-uncovered bosom against my arm. I had never known such perfect happiness. In that moment I forgot everything, and I no more remembered having been a priest than I remembered what I had done in my mother's womb, so great was the fascination the malignant spirit exercised over me.

From that night onward my nature was in some way doubled; there were within me two men, neither of whom knew the other. Sometimes I thought I was a priest who dreamed every night that he was a nobleman, sometimes that I was a nobleman who dreamed that he was a priest. I could no longer distinguish dreams from real life; I did not know where reality began and illusion ended. The dissolute, supercilious young lord jeered at the priest, and the priest abhorred the dissipations of the young lord. Two spirals, entwined and confused, yet never actually touching, would give a good idea of this two-headed existence of mine. Despite the strangeness of the situation, I do not believe that I was ever insane. I always retained quite clearly the perception of my two existences. Only, there was one absurd fact that I could never explain to myself; this was that the feeling of the same identity should exist in two such different men. It was an anomaly I could not account for, whether I believed myself to be the curé of the little parish of C—— or Signor Romualdo, the acknowledged lover of Clarimonde.

I was always, or at least imagined myself to be, in Venice; even now I cannot properly disentangle illusion from reality in this bizarre adventure. We lived in a great marble palace on the Canaleio, full of frescoes and statues, with two Titians of the best period in Clarimonde's bedroom, a palace fit for a king. We had each our own gondola with gondoliers in our livery, our own music-room and our own poet.

Clarimonde understood life in the grand style; she had a little of Cleopatra in her nature. As for me, I adopted the airs of a prince's son, and was as arrogant as if I had been descended from one of the twelve apostles or the four evangelists of the Most Serene Republic; I would not have turned aside to make way for the Doges, and I do not believe that there has been anyone more insolent since Satan fell from heaven. I went to the Ridotto and played the devil's own game. I frequented the best society, sons of ruined noble houses, actresses, swindlers, parasites, and cut-throats.

Yet, in spite of the dissipated life I led, I remained faithful to Clarimonde. I loved her to distraction. She would have awakened satiety itself from its slumbers, and kept inconstancy constant. To possess Clarimonde was to possess twenty mistresses, it was to possess all the women in the world, so versatile was she, so changeable, so unlike herself; a veritable chameleon! An infidelity you would have committed with someone else, she made you commit with her by completely assuming the character, the style and the type of beauty of the woman you seemed to admire.

She returned my love a hundredfold; and it was in vain that young nobles and even elders of the Council of Ten made her the most magnificent offers. A Foscari even went so far as to propose to marry her.

She refused everything. She had money enough; she wanted nothing but love, a young love, a pure love, a love awakened by her, a love that must be the first and the last. I should have been perfectly happy but for an accursed nightmare that returned every night, in which I fancied myself a village curé mortifying the flesh and doing penance for my excesses of the day. Reassured by being with her, I hardly thought any more of the strange manner in which I had made her acquaintance. But the Abbé Sérapion's words still returned to my mind at times, and did not cease to make me uneasy.

For some time Clarimonde's health had not been so good; her colour faded day by day. The doctors who were sent for did not understand what her illness was or what treatment to give. They prescribed a few medicines that could do neither good nor harm, and did not come again. Meanwhile she grew visibly paler and became colder and colder. She was almost as white and as dead as on the memorable night in the mysterious castle. I was heart-broken to see her thus slowly fading away. Touched by my grief, she smiled upon me softly and sadly, with the resigned smile of those who know they are going to die.

One morning I was sitting at her bedside, eating my breakfast at a little table, so as not to leave her for a minute. As I was cutting some fruit, I happened to make a rather deep gash in my finger. The blood spurted out immediately in crimson jets, and some of the drops were sprinkled upon Clarimonde. Her eyes lit up, her features assumed an expression of fierce, wild joy that I had never seen in them before. She leapt out of bed with the agility of an animal, a monkey or a cat, flew at my wound, and began to suck it with an air of unspeakable delight. She swallowed the blood in small draughts, slowly and grudgingly, like an epicure tasting Xeres or Syracuse wine; she half closed her eyes, and the pupils of her green eyes became elongated instead of round. Now and again she stopped to kiss my hand, then she began again to press the wound with her lips, to coax out a few more red drops. When she saw that no more blood was coming, she stood up with moist and shining eyes, rosier than a May dawn, her face full, her hand warm and soft, lovelier than ever and in perfect health.

"I shall not die! I shall not die!" she cried, half mad with joy, and hanging on my neck; "I shall be able to love you for a long time still. My life is in yours, and all that is me comes from you. A few drops of your rich and noble blood, more precious and more potent than all the elixirs in the world, have given me back my life."

This scene made a deep impression upon me and filled me with strange doubts concerning Clarimonde; and that very evening, when sleep had taken me back to my presbytery, I saw the Abbé Sérapion, graver and more anxious than ever. He observed me attentively, and said: "Not content with destroying your soul, you wish to destroy your body also. Unhappy young man, into what a snare you are fallen!" The tone in which he uttered these words struck me sharply, but in spite of its vividness, the impression was soon dispelled, and a thousand other cares effaced it from my mind.

One evening, however, looking in my mirror, the treacherous position of which she had not taken count of, I saw Clarimonde drop a powder into the cup of spiced wine which she used to prepare after the meal. I took the cup and pretended to sip from it; then I put it down on a table as if to finish it later at my leisure, and taking advantage of a moment when her back was turned, I threw the contents under the table; after which I retired to my room and went to bed, resolved to keep awake and see what would happen. I had not long to wait; Clarimonde came in and, having taken off her wrap, lay down in bed by my side. When she felt quite sure that I was asleep, she bared my arm and drew a golden pin from her hair; then she began to murmur in a low voice:

"One drop, just one little red drop, a ruby on the point of my needle! . . . Since you love me still, I must not die . . . Ah! poor love! his beautiful blood, so red, I am going to drink it! Sleep, my only treasure; sleep, my god, my child; I will not hurt you, I will only take from your life what I need to keep mine from going out. If I did not love you so much, I could bring myself to have other lovers, whose veins I would drain dry; but since I have known you, I have held all other men in abhorrence. . . . Ah! what a lovely arm! how round it is! how white it is! I shall never dare to prick that pretty blue vein."

And as she said this she wept, and I felt her tears rain upon my arm as she held it. At length she decided to act; she made a little prick in my arm with her needle, and began to sip the blood that flowed from it. Before she had taken more than a few drops she was seized with the fear of exhausting me; she carefully bound my arm with a little bandage, after smearing the wound with an ointment that closed it at once.

I could no longer be in doubt, the Abbé Sérapion was right. But in spite of this conviction, I could not suppress my love for Clarimonde, and I would willingly have given her all the blood she needed to maintain her artificial existence. Besides, I was not really frightened; to me, the woman made up for the vampire, and what I had heard and seen reassured me; I had then rich veins that would not quickly be exhausted, and I was not bargaining away my life drop by drop. I would have opened my arm myself and said to her: "Drink! let my love enter your body with my blood!" I avoided making the least allusion to the powder she had poured out for me, or to the scene with the needle, and we went on living in the most perfect harmony.

Nevertheless, my priest's scruples tormented me more than ever, and I was always seeking new penances to tame and mortify my flesh. Although all this visionary existence was involuntary, and my other self took no part in it, I dared not touch the Christ with hands so contaminated and a soul polluted by such debaucheries, real or imagined. To avoid falling into these fatiguing hallucinations, I tried to prevent myself from sleeping; I held my eye-lids open with my fingers and stood upright against the wall, struggling against sleep with all my strength; but my eyes were soon full of drowsiness, and finding that the struggle was in vain, I let my arms fall in discouragement and weariness, and the tide swept me back towards the treacherous shores.

Sérapion remonstrated with me with the greatest vehemence, and reproached me bitterly for my supineness and lack of fervour. One day, when I had been more agitated than usual, he said to me:

"There is only one way to rid you of this obsession, and although it is an extreme measure, it must be taken; for desperate ills, desperate remedies. I know where Clarimonde was buried; we must dig up her body, and let you see in what a wretched state the object of your love now is; you will not be tempted to lose your soul for a filthy corpse, devoured by worms and ready to fall to dust; it will surely bring you to your right mind."

For my own part, I was so worn out with this double life that I agreed, wishing to learn, once for all, whether the priest or the nobleman was the victim of an illusion; I was prepared to kill one of these two men who were in me for the benefit of the other, whichever it might be, or to kill them both, for such a life could not last. The Abbé Sérapion provided himself with a mattock, crow-bar, and lantern, and at midnight we set out for the cemetery of ——, the arrangement of which, below and above ground, he knew perfectly.

After turning the light of the dark lantern on the inscriptions on several tombstones, we came at last to a stone half buried in long grass and covered with moss and parasitic plants, on which we deciphered the beginning of an epitaph:

Here lies Clarimonde
Beautiful beyond
All that earth could...

"This is it," said Sérapion, and placing the lantern on the ground, he slipped the crow-bar into the interstice of the stone and began to lift it. The stone gave way, and he set to work with the mattock. I watched him, gloomier and more silent than the night itself; he himself, bent over his dismal work, dripped sweat and panted; his laboured breath sounded like a death-rattle.

It was a strange sight, and anyone who had seen us from outside would have taken us for sacrilegious shroud-stealers rather than for priests of God. There was something hard and savage in Sérapion's zeal that gave him the look more of a demon than that of an apostle or angel, and his face, with its large austere features accentuated by the rays of the lantern, was not reassuring. I felt an icy sweat gathering in beads on my limbs, and my hair stood up on my head with a tingling sensation; in my heart I looked upon the action of the pitiless Sérapion as an abominable desecration, and would have been glad if, from the flank of the dark clouds that rolled heavily over us, a triangle of flame had shot out and reduced him to ashes. The owls perched in the cypresses, disturbed by the light of the lantern, came flapping heavily against the glass with their dusty wings and uttering plaintive cries; foxes yelped in the distance; and a thousand sinister sounds broke the silence.

At length Sérapion's mattock struck against the coffin, the boards of which echoed with a hollow, sonorous sound, that awful sound which nothingness gives when touched; he lifted the lid, and I saw Clarimonde, pale as marble, with clasped hands; her white shroud made only one single fold from head to feet. A little red drop gleamed like a rose at the corner of her discoloured mouth.

Sérapion, on seeing this, burst into a fury:

"Ah! there you are, demon, shameless harlot, drinker of blood and gold!" and he sprinkled with holy water the corpse and the coffin also, tracing upon it the figure of a cross.

No sooner had poor Clarimonde been touched by the sacred dew than her lovely body crumbled into dust; nothing remained but a horrible, shapeless heap of ashes, flesh, and half-calcined bones.

"Behold your mistress, my lord Romuald!" said the pitiless priest, pointing to the miserable relics. "Will you ever again be tempted to go walking with your beautiful lady at Lido and Fusine?"

I bowed my head; a great change had taken place in me. I returned to my presbytery, and the lord Romuald, lover of Clarimonde, took leave of the poor priest with whom he had so long and so strangely kept company. I only saw Clarimonde once more; the following night she appeared and said to me, as at our first meeting under the portal of the church:

"Unhappy man! unhappy man! what have you done? Why did you listen to that idiot priest? Were you not happy? And what had I done to you, that you should violate my poor grave and strip bare the horror of my annihilation? All communication between our souls and our bodies is broken. Farewell, you will regret me."

She vanished into the air like smoke, and I never saw her again.

Alas, she spoke the truth! I have regretted her more than once, and I still regret her. My soul's peace has been very dearly bought; the love of God was not too great a thing to replace hers.

There, brother, is the story of my youth. Never look on a woman, but go with your eyes fixed on the ground, for chaste and steadfast as you may be, one minute may make you lose Eternity.

PROSPER MÉRIMÉE

The Venus of Ille

(La Vénus d'Ille, 1837)

Yet another great theme of nineteenth-century fantastic literature is the survival of classical antiquity, the nullification of the historical discontinuity that separates us from the Greco-Roman world.

I could also have chosen Gautier's "Arria Marcella" (1852) to represent this theme, a story set in Pompeii possessing notes of great sexual delicacy. The trace of a girl's breast in lava allows us to enter the world of the past. Another example is Henry James's "The Last of the Valerii" (1874). There have been many variations on the theme, but I prefer this story because it is very representative of Mérimée (1803–1870) and his consummate skill in the presentation of local color, climates, and human atmosphere.

Mérimée wrote few fantastic stories, but they constitute an essential part of his narrative production: "Lokis" (1868), a story of Lithuanian superstitions, contains an unforgettable vision of the animal world of the forests.

The Venus of Ille, a bronze statue—Greek or Roman—is looked upon most unfavorably by the inhabitants of the town in Roussillon, where it has recently been discovered. They consider it an "idol." The fiancé of the archeologist's daughter, teasing her, takes off her ring and slips it onto the statue's finger. He can't get it off. Has he become engaged to the statue? The gigantic Venus, dream of serenity and Olympian beauty, is transformed on the wedding night into a terrifying nightmare.

I WAS GOING DOWN the last slope of the Canigou, and, although the sun had already set, I could distinguish on the plain the houses of the little town of Ille, towards which I was making.

"You know, no doubt," I said to the Catalan who had been my guide since the previous day, "where Monsieur de Peyrehorade lives?"

"Do I know where?" he exclaimed. "I know his house as well as I know my own; and if it wasn't so dark I would point it out to you. It is the prettiest in Ille. Monsieur de Peyrehorade is a rich man; and he is marrying his son to a lady even richer than himself."

"Is the marriage to take place soon?" I asked.

"Very soon; indeed, the fiddlers may already have been ordered for the wedding. Perhaps it will be tonight, or tomorrow, or the day after, for all I know. It'll be at Puygarrig; for the son is to marry Mademoiselle de Puygarrig. Oh, it'll be a very grand affair!"

I had been recommended to call on Monsieur de Peyrehorade by my friend Monsieur de P., who told me he was a very learned antiquarian and extremely good-natured. He would be delighted to show me all the ruins for miles around. So I had been looking forward to visiting with him the district surrounding Ille, which I knew to be rich in monuments both of ancient times and the Middle Ages. This wedding, of which I now heard for the first time, would upset all my plans. I said to myself that I was going to be a killjoy; but I was expected, and as Monsieur de P. had written to say I was coming, I should have to present myself.

"I'll bet you, Monsieur," said my guide, when we were already in the plain—"I'll bet you a cigar that I can guess why you're going to Monsieur de Peyrehorade's."

"But that is not a difficult thing to guess," I replied, offering him a cigar. "At this hour, after travelling six leagues on the Canigou hills, the main thing is to have supper."

"Yes, but tomorrow? . . . I'll bet that you have come to Ille to see the idol. I guessed that when I saw you drawing pictures of the Saints at Serrabona."

"The idol! What idol?" The word had aroused my curiosity.

"What! Did nobody tell you at Perpignan that Monsieur de Peyrehorade had found an idol in the earth?"

"Do you mean a statue in terracotta, in clay?"

"No, I don't. It's made of copper, and there's enough of it to make hundreds of coins. It weighs as much as a church bell. It was a good way down, at the foot of an olive tree, that we dug it up."

"So you were present at the find?"

"Yes, sir. Monsieur de Peyrehorade told Jean Coll and me, a fortnight ago, to uproot an old olive tree which had been killed by the frost last year, for there was a very hard frost, you'll remember. Well, then, while he was working at it with all his might, Jean Coll gave a blow with his pickaxe, and I heard a ting, just as if he had hit a bell. 'What's that?' I said. We went on picking away, and a black hand appeared, which looked like the hand of a dead man coming out of the ground. I felt frightened; I went up to Monsieur and I said to him: 'There's dead folk, master, under the olive tree; you'll have to send for the priest.' 'What dead folk?' he asked. He came along, and he'd no sooner seen the hand than he cried out: 'An antique statue! An antique statue!' You might have thought he'd found buried treasure. And then he set to with a pickaxe and hands, as if his life depended on it, and did almost as much work as the two of us together."

"And what did you find in the end?"

"A huge black woman, more than half naked, saving your presence, sir, all in copper, and Monsieur de Peyrehorade told us it was an idol of pagan times . . . you know, when Charlemagne was alive."

"I see what it is . . . a statue of the Virgin in bronze which belonged to a convent that has been destroyed."

"The Blessed Virgin? Not on your life! . . . I'd have known straight away if it had been the Blessed Virgin. I tell you it's an idol; you can see from her appearance. She looks straight at you with her great white eyes. . . . Anybody'd think she was trying to stare you out, because you daren't look her in the eyes."

"White eyes, were they? No doubt they are inlaid in the bronze; it might be a Roman statue."

"Roman! That's it! Monsieur de Peyrehorade said that it was Roman. Ah! I can see that you're a learned man like him."

"Is it whole and in good condition?"

"Oh, it's all there, Monsieur. It's much more beautiful and better finished than the painted plaster bust of Louis-Philippe in the town hall. But for all that, I don't fancy the idol's face. She looks wicked . . . and she is wicked, too."

"Wicked! What harm has she done you?"

"None to me exactly; but you can judge for yourself. We had gone down on all fours to raise her up on end, and Monsieur de Peyrehorade, too, was tugging at the rope, although he's no stronger than a chicken, the dear man! After a lot of trouble we got her upright. I was picking up a tile to prop her up, when—bang!—she fell slap on her back. 'Look out!' I yelled, but I wasn't quick enough, for Jean Coll didn't have time to pull his leg away."

"And was he injured?"

"His poor leg was broken as clean as a whistle. By heavens, when I saw it I was furious. I wanted to break up the idol with my pickaxe, but Monsieur de Peyrehorade wouldn't let me. He gave some money to Jean Coll, but all the same, he's been in bed the whole fortnight since it happened, and the doctor says he'll never walk with that leg again as well as with the other. It's a crying shame; he was our best runner and, after Monsieur de Peyrehorade's son, our best tennis player too. Monsieur Alphonse de Peyrehorade was terribly upset, for he always played against Coll. It was a treat to see them sending the balls back and forth. Biff! Biff! They never touched the ground."

Chatting like this, we reached Ille, and I soon found myself in the presence of Monsieur de Peyrehorade. He was a little old man, still spry and active; he had powdered hair, a red nose, and a jovial, bantering manner. Before opening Monsieur de P.'s letter he had installed me at a well-appointed table and presented me to his wife and son as a famous archaeologist, who was going to raise the province of Roussillon from the obscurity in which it had been left by the neglect of the learned.

While I was eating with a good appetite—for nothing makes one so hungry as mountain air—I examined my hosts. I have said a word or two about Monsieur de Peyrehorade; I should add that he was vivacity itself. He talked and ate, got up, ran to his library, brought me books, showed me engravings, and poured out drinks for me; he was never still for two minutes at a time. His wife was rather too stout, like most Catalan women over forty, and she seemed to me an out-and-out provincial, completely taken up with the cares of her household. Although the supper was ample for six people at least, she ran to the kitchen, had scores of pigeons killed and fried, and opened heaven knows how many pots of preserves. In a trice the table was littered with dishes and bottles, and I should undoubtedly have died of indigestion if I had so much as tasted all that was offered me. However, at each dish that I refused there were fresh apologies. They were afraid I would be very badly off at Ille—they had so few resources in the provinces, and Parisians were so hard to please!

Monsieur Alphonse de Peyrehorade stirred no more than a statue in the midst of his parents' comings and goings. He was a tall young man of twenty-six, with handsome, regular features, but which were lacking in expression. His figure and his athletic build fully justified the reputation he had enjoyed in the region as an indefatigable tennis player. That evening he was exquisitely dressed, just like the latest fashion plate. But he seemed to me to be ill at ease in his garments; he was as stiff as a post in his velvet collar, and did not turn round unless all of a piece. His large sunburnt hands, with their short nails, contrasted strangely with his costume. They were the hands of a ploughman poking out of the sleeves of a dandy. For the rest, although he studied me from head to foot very inquisitively in my capacity as a

Parisian, he only spoke to me once in the whole evening, and that was to ask me where I had bought my watchchain.

"Ah, now, my honoured guest," Monsieur de Peyrehorade said to me when supper was drawing to its conclusion, "you belong to me. You are in my house and I shall not give you any peace until you have seen everything of any interest among our mountains. You must learn to know our Roussillon and to do it justice. You have no idea what we can show you—Phoenician, Celtic, Roman, Arab, and Byzantine monuments. You shall see them all—lock, stock, and barrel. I shall take you everywhere, and I shan't spare you a single stone."

A fit of coughing compelled him to stop. I took advantage of it to tell him I should be greatly distressed if I disturbed him during the important event about to take place in his family. If he would be so kind as to give me the benefit of his valuable advice about the outings I ought to go on, then without putting him to the inconvenience of accompanying me, I would be able to . . .

"Ah, you're referring to this young fellow's marriage!" he exclaimed, interrupting me. "That's nothing. It takes place the day after tomorrow. You shall celebrate the wedding with us; it will be a quiet affair, for the bride is in mourning for an aunt, whose heiress she is. So there won't be any festivities, and there won't be a ball. . . . That's a pity. . . . You would have seen our Catalan women dance. . . . They're very pretty, and you might have been tempted to follow Alphonse's example. One marriage, they say, leads to others. . . . On Saturday, after the young people are married, I shall be at liberty, and we'll set out. I must apologize for boring you with a provincial wedding. To a Parisian who has had his fill of festivities . . . And a wedding without a ball too! However, you will see a bride . . . a bride . . . who will take your breath away. . . . But you are a serious man, and you are no longer interested in women. I have better things to show you. I'm going to give you something to feast your eyes on! I've a fine surprise in store for you tomorrow."

"Ah," I replied, "it isn't easy to have a treasure in your house without the public knowing about it. I think I can guess the surprise you have in store for me. If it's your statue you're talking about, I'm quite prepared to admire it, for my guide's description of it has whetted my curiosity."

"Ah, so he's told you about the idol, for that is what they call my beautiful Venus Tur—but I refuse to say another word. Tomorrow, as soon as it is daylight, you shall see her, and you shall tell me if I am not right in considering her a masterpiece. Upon my word, you couldn't have arrived at a better time! There are inscriptions which I in my ignorance explain as best I can . . . but a scholar from Paris! . . . You'll probably laugh at my interpretation, for I have written a treatise on it. . . . I—an old provincial antiquarian—I've been so bold . . . I want to set the press groaning. If you would be so good as to read and correct it, I might hope . . . For example, I would very much like to know how you would translate this inscription on the pedestal: 'CAVE. . . .' But I don't want to ask you anything yet! Tomorrow, tomorrow! Not a word about the Venus today."

"You're quite right, Peyrehorade," said his wife, "to stop talking about your idol. You ought to see that you're preventing our guest from eating. Why, he has seen far more beautiful statues in Paris than yours. There are dozens of them in the Tuileries, and in bronze too."

"Now there's ignorance for you—the blessed ignorance of the provinces!" interrupted Monsieur de Peyrehorade. "Fancy comparing a splendid antique statute to the mediocre figures of Coustou!

How irreverently of the gods
My wife is pleased to talk!

"Do you know my wife wanted me to have my statue melted down to make a bell for our church? She would have been its godmother. A masterpiece of Myron's, Monsieur!"

"A masterpiece! A masterpiece! A fine masterpiece it is to break a man's leg!"

"Look here, wife," said Monsieur de Peyrehorade in a determined voice, as he stretched his right leg out towards her, clad in a shadowed silk stocking, "if my Venus had broken this leg I wouldn't have complained."

"Good gracious! Peyrehorade, how can you say a thing like that? Fortunately, the man is getting better. . . . All the same, I can't bring myself to look at a statue which did a dreadful thing like that. Poor Jean Coll!"

"Wounded by Venus, Monsieur," said Monsieur de Peyrehorade, laughing loudly. "The rascal complains of being wounded by Venus!

Veneris nec praemia nôris.

Who hasn't been wounded by Venus in his time?"

Monsieur Alphonse, who understood French better than Latin, gave a knowing wink, and looked at me as if to say: "Do you understand that, you Parisian?"

Supper came to an end. For an hour I had not been able to eat any more. I was tired, and I could not manage to hide my frequent yawns. Madame de Peyrehorade was the first to notice and said that it was time to retire. Then began fresh apologies for the poor bed I was going to have. I would not be as comfortable as I was in Paris; in the country things were so inferior. I must make allowances for the people of Roussillon. It was in vain I protested that after a journey among the mountains a bundle of straw would seem a wonderful bed: they still begged me to pardon poor country folk if they did not treat me as well as they would have wished. At last, accompanied by Monsieur de Peyrehorade, I reached the room prepared for me. The staircase, the top steps of which were of wood, led to the centre of a corridor, off which several rooms opened.

"To the right," said my host, "is the set of rooms I intend for the future Madame Alphonse. Your room is at the other end of the corridor. You will understand," he added, with a look which he meant to be sly, "you will readily understand that newly married people have to be isolated. You are at one end of the house and they at the other."

We entered a handsomely furnished room, where the first object which met my eye was a bed seven feet long, six feet wide, and so high that one needed a stool to get into it. My host pointed out the position of the bell, and after making sure that the sugar-bowl was full, and the bottles of eau-de-Cologne in their proper places on the dressing-table, and asking me several times if I had all I wanted, wished me good night and left me alone.

The windows were shut. Before undressing, I opened one to breathe the cool night air, which was delicious after such a lengthy supper. In front was the Canigou, which is always a wonderful sight, but which that night struck me as the most beautiful mountain in the world, lighted up as it was by a splendid moon. I stood for a few minutes contemplating its marvellous outline, and I was just going to close my window when, lowering my gaze, I saw the statue on a pedestal about forty yards from the house. It had been placed at a corner of the quickset hedge which separated a little garden from a large, perfectly level, square plot which, I learnt later, was the town tennis court. This ground had been Monsieur de Peyrehorade's property, but he had given it to the public at his son's urgent request.

From where I was, it was difficult for me to make out the posture of the statue; I could only judge its height, which I guessed was about six feet. At that moment two town rowdies passed along the tennis court, close to the hedge, whistling the pretty Roussillon tune, *Montagnes régalades*. They stopped to look at the statue, and one of them even apostrophized her in a loud voice. He spoke the Catalan dialect, but I had been long enough in the province of Roussillon to be able to understand nearly all that he said.

"So there you are, you hussy!" (The Catalan expression was more forcible than that.) "There you are," he said. "So it was you as broke Jean Coll's leg! If you belonged to me I'd break your neck."

"Bah! What with?" asked the other. "She's made of copper, and so hard that Étienne broke his file on her, trying to cut into her. It's copper from pagan times, and harder than anything I can think of."

"If I had my cold chisel" (apparently he was a locksmith's apprentice), "I'd soon knock out her big white eyes; it would be like getting a couple of almonds out of their shells. There's over five francs' worth of silver in them."

They moved a few paces farther off.

"I must wish the idol good night," said the taller of the apprentices, stopping suddenly.

He stooped, and probably picked up a stone. I saw him stretch out his arm and throw something, and immediately after, I heard a loud noise come from the bronze. At the same moment the apprentice raised his hand to his head and cried out in pain.

"She's thrown it back at me!" he exclaimed.

And the two scamps took to their heels as fast as they could. The stone had obviously rebounded from the metal, and had punished the rascal for the outrage done to the goddess.

I shut the window, laughing heartily.

"Yet another vandal punished by Venus! Would that all destroyers of our ancient monuments could have their heads broken like that!"

And with this charitable wish I fell asleep.

It was broad daylight when I awoke. On one side of the bed stood Monsieur de Peyrehorade in a dressing-gown; on the other, a servant sent by his wife with a cup of chocolate in his hand.

"Come now, Parisian, get up! How lazy you people from the capital are!" said my host, while I hurriedly dressed. "It's eight o'clock and here you are, still in bed. I've been up since six o'clock. I've been upstairs three times; I've tiptoed up to your door; but there was no sign of life at all. It is bad for you to sleep too much at your age. And my Venus waiting to be seen! Come along, drink this cup of Barcelona chocolate as fast as you can. . . . It's real contraband. You can't get chocolate like this in Paris. Take in all the nourishment you can, for when you see my Venus, no one will be able to tear you away."

I was ready in five minutes, that is to say, I was only half shaved, carelessly buttoned, and scalded by the chocolate which I had swallowed boiling hot. I went down into the garden and soon found myself in front of an admirable statue.

It was indeed a Venus, and one of extraordinary beauty. The upper part of her body was bare, just as the ancients usually depicted their great deities; her right hand, raised to the level of her breast, was turned palm inwards, the thumb and two first fingers extended, while the other two were slightly curved. The other hand was near the hips, and held up the drapery which covered the lower part of the body. The attitude of this statue reminded me of that of the Morra player, which, for some reason or other, goes by the name of Germanicus. Perhaps the sculptor wished to depict the goddess playing the game of Morra.

However that might be, it is impossible to imagine anything more perfect than the body of that Venus; nothing could be more harmonious or more voluptuous than her outlines, nothing more graceful or dignified than her drapery. I had expected some work of the Later Empire, and I was confronted with a masterpiece of the most perfect period of sculpture. What struck me most of all was the exquisite truth of form, which might have led one to suppose that it had been moulded by nature herself, if nature ever produced such perfect specimens.

The hair, which was raised off the forehead, looked as if it had been gilded at some time. The head was small, like those of nearly all Greek statues, and bent slightly forward. As for the face, I should never be able to express its strange character; it was of quite a different type from that of any other antique statue I could remember. It was not at all the calm and austere beauty of the Greek sculptors, whose rule was to give a majestic immobility to every feature. Here, on the contrary, I noticed with astonishment that the artist had deliberately set out to express ill-nature raised to the level of wickedness. Every feature was slightly contracted: the eyes were rather slanted, the mouth turned up at the corners, and the nostrils somewhat distended. Disdain, irony, cruelty, could be distinguished in that face which was, notwithstanding, of incredible beauty. Indeed, the longer one looked at that wonderful statue, the more distress one felt at the thought that such a marvellous beauty could be united with an utter absence of goodness.

"If the model ever existed," I said to Monsieur de Peyrehorade, "and I doubt if Heaven ever produced such a woman, how I pity her lovers! She must have delighted in making them die of despair. There is something ferocious in her expression, and yet I have never seen anything so beautiful."

> *"Venus with all her might has fastened*
> *on her prey,"*

exclaimed Monsieur de Peyrehorade, pleased with my enthusiasm.

That expression of fiendish scorn was perhaps enhanced by the contrast offered by her eyes, which were encrusted with silver and shone brightly, with the greenish black patina which time had given to the whole statue. Those bright eyes produced a kind of illusion which recalled real life. I remembered what my guide had said, that she made those who looked at her lower their eyes. That was almost true, and I could hardly restrain an impulse of anger with myself for feeling rather ill at ease before that bronze face.

"Now that you have admired it in detail, my dear colleague in antiquarian research," said my host, "let us, by your leave, open a scientific conference. What do you think about this inscription, which you haven't noticed yet?"

He showed me the pedestal of the statue, and I read on it these words:

CAVE AMANTEM

"*Quid dicis, doctissime*?" he asked me, rubbing his hands together. "Let us see if we agree on the meaning of this *cave amantem.*"

"But," I answered, "it has two meanings. It can be translated: 'Beware of him who loves thee; mistrust thy lovers.' But in that sense I don't know whether *cave amantem* would be good Latin. Looking at the lady's diabolical expression, I would rather think that the artist intended to put the spectator on his guard against her terrible beauty; I would therefore translate it: 'Beware if she loves thee.' "

"Humph!" said Monsieur de Peyrehorade; "yes, that is an admissible interpretation; but, with all respect, I prefer the first translation, and I will tell you why. You know who Venus's lover was?"

"There were several."

"Yes, but the chief one was Vulcan. Didn't the sculptor mean: 'In spite of all thy beauty and thy scornful expression, thou shalt have for thy lover a blacksmith, an ugly cripple'? What a profound lesson, Monsieur, for flirts!"

I could hardly help smiling at this far-fetched explanation.

"Latin is a difficult tongue, because of its conciseness," I remarked, to avoid contradicting my antiquarian friend outright; and I stepped back a few paces to see the statue better.

"One moment, colleague," said Monsieur de Peyrehorade, seizing me by the arm, "you haven't seen everything. There is another inscription. Climb up on the pedestal and look at the right arm." And saying this, he helped me up.

I held on rather unceremoniously to the Venus's neck, and began to make myself better acquainted with her. I even looked at her right in the face for a moment, and found her even more spiteful and beautiful at close quarters. Then I discovered that there were some written characters, in what seemed to me an ancient, running hand, engraved on the arm. With the help of my spectacles I spelt out the following, while Monsieur de Peyrehorade repeated every word as soon as I uttered it, with approving gestures and voice. It read thus:

VENERI TVRBVL . . .
EVTYCHES MYRO
IMPERIO FECIT.

After the word *TVRBVL* in the first line, I thought that there were some letters which had been effaced; but *TVRBVL* was perfectly legible.

"What does that mean?" asked my gleeful host, mischievously smiling, for he knew very well that I would not find it easy to make much of this *TVRBVL*.

"There is one thing which I cannot explain yet," I said to him; "all the rest is easy. Eutyches Myron made this offering to Venus by her order."

"Good. But what do you make of *TVRBVL*? What is *TVRBVL*?"

"*TVRBVL* puzzles me greatly; I cannot think of any epithet normally applied to Venus which might assist me. Let us see: what would you say to *TVRBVLENTA*? Venus who troubles and disturbs. . . . You notice I am still preoccupied with her spiteful expression. *TVRBVLENTA* is not at all a bad epithet for Venus," I added modestly, for I myself was not quite satisfied with my explanation.

"Venus the turbulent! Venus the disturber! Ah! So you think that my Venus is a Venus of the pot-house? Nothing of the sort, Monsieur. She is a Venus of good society. And now I will explain this *TVRBVL* to you. You will at least promise not to divulge my discovery before my treatise is published. I am rather proud, you see, of this find. . . . You really must leave us poor provincial devils a few ears to glean. You Parisian savants are rich enough."

From the top of the pedestal, where I was still perched, I solemnly promised that I would never be so dishonourable as to steal his discovery.

"For *TVRBVL*, Monsieur," he said, coming nearer and lowering his voice for fear that anyone else but myself might hear, "read *TVRBVLNERAE*."

"I don't understand any better."

"Listen carefully. A league from here, at the foot of the mountain, there is a village called Boulternère. That is a corruption of the Latin word *TVRBVLNERA*. Nothing is commoner than such an inversion. Boulternère, Monsieur, was a Roman town. I had always thought so, but I had never had any proof of it. The proof lies here. This Venus was the local goddess of the city of Boulternère; and this word Boulternère, which I have just shown to be of ancient origin, proves a still more curious thing, namely, that Boulternère, after being a Roman town, became a Phoenician one!"

He stopped a minute to take breath, and to enjoy my surprise. I had to repress a strong inclination to laugh.

"Indeed," he went on, "*TVRBVLNERA* is pure Phoenician. *TVR* can be pronounced *TOUR*. . . . *TOUR* and *SOUR* are the same word, are they not? *SOUR* is the Phoenician name for Tyre. I need not remind you of its meaning. *BVL* is Baal, Bâl, Bel, Bul, slight differences in pronunciation. As for *NERA*, that gives me some trouble. I am tempted to think, for want of a Phoenician word, that it comes from the Greek νηρος—damp, marshy. That would make it a hybrid word. To justify νηρος I will show you at Boulternère how the mountain streams there form foul pools. On the other hand, the ending *NERA* might have been added much later, in honour of Nera Pivesuvia, the wife of Tetricus, who may have rendered some service to the city of Turbul. But, on account of the pools, I prefer the derivation from νηρος."

He took a pinch of snuff with a satisfied air.

"But let us leave the Phoenicians and return to the inscription. I translate, then: 'To the Venus of Boulternère Myron dedicates at her command this statue, the work of his hand.' "

I took good care not to criticize his etymology, but I wanted, in my turn, to give some proof of perspicacity, so I said to him:

"Wait a bit, Monsieur. Myron dedicated something, but I don't in the least see that it was this statue."

"What!" he exclaimed. "Wasn't Myron a famous Greek sculptor? The talent would pass on to his descendants; and one of them made this statue. Nothing can be clearer."

"But," I replied, "I see a little hole in the arm. I fancy it has been used to fasten something, perhaps a bracelet, which this Myron gave to Venus as an expiatory offering, for Myron was an unlucky lover. Venus was angry with him, and he appeased her by consecrating a golden bracelet. You must remember that *fecit* is often used for *consecravit*. The terms are synonymous. I could show you more than one instance if I had access to Gruter or, better still, Orelli. It is natural that a lover should see Venus in his dreams, and that he should imagine that she ordered him to give her statue a golden bracelet. Myron consecrated a bracelet to her. . . . Then the barbarians, or perhaps some sacrilegious thief. . . ."

"Ah, it's easy to see that you have written some novels," exclaimed my host, helping me down. "No, Monsieur, it is a work of Myron's school. Just look at the workmanship, and you'll agree."

Having made it a rule never to contradict pig-headed antiquarians outright, I bowed my head as if convinced, and said: "It's a splendid piece of work."

"Good gracious!" exclaimed Monsieur de Peyrehorade, "here's another piece of vandalism! Someone has thrown a stone at my statue!"

He had just noticed a white mark a little above the breast of the Venus. I saw a similar mark on the fingers of the right hand, which I then supposed had been touched by the stone in passing, or else a fragment of it might have been broken off by the shock and hit the hand. I told my host about the insult I had witnessed and the prompt punishment which had followed. He laughed heartily, and compared the apprentice to Diomedes, expressing the hope that he would see all his comrades changed into white birds, as the Greek hero did.

The breakfast bell interrupted this classical conversation; and, as on the previous evening, I was forced to eat as much as four people. Then Monsieur de Peyrehorade's tenants came to see him, and, while he was giving them audience, his son took me to see a carriage which he had bought for his fiancée at Toulouse, and which I naturally admired. After that I went with him to the stables, where he kept me for half an hour praising his horses, telling me their pedigrees, and listing the prizes he had won at the country races. At last he spoke of his future bride, in connexion with a gray mare which he intended to give her.

"We shall see her today. I don't know if you will think her pretty. You are so hard to please in Paris; but everybody here and at Perpignan thinks her lovely. The best of it is she's very rich. Her aunt, who lived at Prades, left her all her money. Oh, I'm going to be ever so happy!"

I was deeply shocked to see a young man appear more affected by the dowry than by the beauty of his bride-to-be.

"Do you know anything about jewellery?" continued Monsieur Alphonse. "What do you think of this ring which I'm going to give her tomorrow?"

As he said this, he drew from the first joint of his little finger a large ring blazing with diamonds, and formed with two clasped hands: a most poetic conceit, I thought. It was of ancient workmanship, but I guessed that it had been retouched when the diamonds were set. Inside the ring was engraved in gothic letters: "*Sempr' ab ti*" ("Ever thine").

"It is a pretty ring," I said, but added: "The diamonds have detracted slightly from its original character."

"Oh, it's much prettier as it is now," he replied with a smile. "There are one thousand two hundred francs' worth of diamonds in it. My mother gave it to me. It was an old family ring . . . from the days of chivalry. It was worn by my grandmother, who had it from her grandmother. Goodness knows when it was made!"

"The custom in Paris," I said, "is to give a perfectly plain ring, usually made of two different metals, such as gold and platinum. For instance, the other ring which you have on that finger would be most suitable. This one is so large, with its diamonds and its hands in relief, that no glove would go over it."

"Oh, Madame Alphonse can do as she likes. I think that she will be glad to have it in any case. Twelve hundred francs on one's finger is very pleasing. That little ring," he added, looking with a satisfied expression at the plain ring which he was holding, "was given me one Shrove Tuesday by a woman in Paris. Ah, what a time I had when I was staying there two years ago. That's the place to enjoy oneself, and no mistake! . . ." And he sighed regretfully.

We were to dine at Puygarrig that day, at the house of the bride's parents; we drove over to the château, which was about a league and a half from Ille. I was introduced and received as a friend of the family. I will not talk of the dinner, nor of the conversation which followed, and in which I took little part. Monsieur Alphonse, who was seated next to his future bride, whispered in her ear every quarter of an hour. As for her, she hardly raised her eyes, and blushed modestly every time her intended spoke to her, though she replied without embarrassment.

Mademoiselle de Puygarrig was eighteen years old, and her lithe, delicate figure was a great contrast to the bony frame of her sturdy fiancé. She was not just beautiful: she was enchanting. I admired the perfect naturalness of all her replies. Her expression was kindly, but nevertheless was not devoid of a slight touch of maliciousness which reminded me, in spite of myself, of my host's Venus. While making this comparison to myself, I wondered if the superior beauty which the statue undoubtedly possessed was not largely due to her tigerish expression, for strength, even in the evil passions, always arouses wonder and a sort of involuntary admiration.

What a pity, I reflected, as we left Puygarrig, that such a charming person should be so rich, and that her dowry should be the cause of her being courted by a man unworthy of her!

On the way back to Ille, not knowing what to talk about to Madame de Peyrehorade, but thinking I ought to speak to her, I said:

"You are very sceptical folk here in Roussillon, to have a wedding on a Friday. In Paris, we are more superstitious; nobody would dare to get married on that day."

"Oh, please don't talk about it," she said; "if it had depended only on me, I would certainly have chosen another day. But Peyrehorade wanted it, and I had to give in to him. It worries me, though. Suppose some misfortune should happen? There must be something in it, or else why should everybody be afraid of a Friday?"

"Friday," her husband exclaimed, "is the day dedicated to Venus. An excellent day for a wedding. You will notice, my dear colleague, that I think of nothing but my Venus. Naturally, it was on her account that I chose a Friday. Tomorrow, if you are willing, we will offer her a small sacrifice before the ceremony—two ring-doves and, if I can find any, some incense. . . ."

"For shame, Peyrehorade!" interrupted his wife, who was deeply shocked. "Offer incense to an idol! It would be an outrage! What would people say about you round here?"

"At all events," said Monsieur de Peyrehorade, "you will let me put a wreath of roses and lilies on her head.

Manibus date lilia plenis.

"You see, Monsieur, the Charter is a vain thing. We have no religious freedom."

The arrangements for the next day were made in the following manner. Everyone had to be ready and dressed for the wedding at ten o'clock sharp. After taking chocolate we were to drive over to Puygarrig. The civil marriage was to take place at the village registry, and the religious ceremony in the château chapel. After that there would be a luncheon. Then we would be able to spend the time as we liked until seven o'clock, when we were all to return to Monsieur de Peyrehorade's house, where the two families would have supper together. The rest followed naturally. Since there could be no dancing, it had been decided to have as much eating as possible.

As early as eight o'clock, I was sitting in front of the Venus, pencil in hand, beginning again for the twentieth time the statue's head, without being able to seize the expression. Monsieur de Peyrehorade bustled about, giving me advice and repeating his Phoenician derivations. Then he placed some Bengal roses on the pedestal of the statue and addressed to it, in a tragi-comical voice, supplications for the couple who were going to live under his roof. He went in to change about nine o'clock, and at the same time Monsieur Alphonse appeared, wearing a close-fitting suit, white gloves, patent-leather shoes, chased buttons, and a rose in his buttonhole.

"You must do my wife's portrait," he said, leaning over my drawing; "she is pretty, too."

Just then, on the tennis court which I have already mentioned, a game started that at once attracted Monsieur Alphonse's attention. I was tired and, despairing of being able to reproduce that diabolical face, I soon left my drawing to watch the players. There were among them a few Spanish muleteers who had arrived the night before. They were men from Aragon and from Navarre, almost all remarkable players. Although the local players were encouraged by the presence and advice of Monsieur Alphonse, they were very soon beaten by these new champions. The patriotic onlookers were aghast. Monsieur

Alphonse looked at his watch. It was still only half past nine. His mother was not ready yet. He hesitated no longer, threw off his coat, asked for a jacket, and challenged the Spaniards. I looked at him with amusement and in some surprise.

"The honour of our country must be upheld," he said.

At that moment I admired him. His blood was up. His clothes, which a little earlier had filled his thoughts to the exclusion of everything else, were completely forgotten. A few minutes before he would not have dared turn his head, for fear of disturbing his cravat. Now he no longer gave a thought to his curled hair or his beautifully pleated jabot. As for his fiancée, I do believe that, if necessary, he would have postponed the wedding. I saw him hastily put on a pair of sandals, roll up his sleeves, and with a confident air put himself at the head of the defeated side, like Caesar when he rallied his soldiers at Dyrrachium. I jumped over the hedge and took up a convenient position in the shade of a nettle tree in such a way as to be able to see both sides.

Contrary to general expectation, Monsieur Alphonse missed the first ball; true, it grazed the ground, hit with astonishing force by one of the players from Aragon, who seemed to be the leader of the Spaniards.

He was a man of about forty, six feet tall, slim and wiry; and his olive skin was almost as dark as the bronze of the Venus.

Monsieur Alphonse threw his racquet on the ground in a rage.

"It's this damned ring," he exclaimed, "which is too tight on my finger and made me miss a sure thing."

With some difficulty he took off his diamond ring, and I went over to him to take it, but he forestalled me, ran to the Venus, slipped the ring on her third finger, and resumed his position at the head of his fellow villagers.

He was pale, but calm and determined. From then on he made no more mistakes, and the Spaniards were soundly beaten. The enthusiasm of the spectators was a fine sight: some uttered shrieks of joy and threw their caps in the air; others shook hands with him and called him the pride of the region. If he had repulsed an invasion I doubt if he would have received heartier or more sincere congratulations. The disappointment of the vanquished added still more to the splendour of his victory.

"We must have another match, my good fellow," he said to the muleteer from Aragon in a condescending tone; "but I must give you points."

I would have preferred Monsieur Alphonse to be more modest, and I was almost sorry for his rival's humiliation.

The Spanish giant felt the insult keenly. I saw him go pale under his tanned skin. He looked miserably at his racquet and ground his teeth; then in a choking voice he muttered: "Me lo pagarás."[1]

The voice of Monsieur de Peyrehorade interrupted his son's triumph; my host was astonished not to find him superintending the preparation of the new carriage, and even more astonished to see him holding a racquet and dripping with sweat.

Monsieur Alphonse ran to the house, washed his face and hands, put on his new coat again and his patent-leather shoes, and five minutes later we were in full trot on the road to Puygarrig. All the tennis players of the town and a large crowd of spectators followed us with shouts of joy. The stout horses which drew us could only just keep ahead of those dauntless Catalans.

We had reached Puygarrig, and the procession was about to set off for the village hall when Monsieur Alphonse suddenly slapped his forehead, and whispered to me:

"What a blunder! I've forgotten the ring! It's on the Venus's finger, damn her! Don't tell my mother, whatever happens. Perhaps she won't notice anything."

"You could send someone for it," I said.

"No. My servant has stayed behind at Ille, and I can't trust these fellows here. There's more than one of them who might be tempted by twelve hundred francs' worth of diamonds. Besides, what would the people here think of my absent-mindedness? They'd make fun of

[1] "You'll pay for this."

me and call me the statue's husband. . . . If only nobody steals it! Fortunately, the idol frightens the young rascals. They daren't go within arm's length of her. Well, it doesn't matter. I have another ring."

The two ceremonies, civil and religious, were performed with suitable pomp. Mademoiselle de Puygarrig received the ring of a Paris milliner, little thinking that her fiancé had sacrificed a love-token to her. Then we sat down and drank, ate, and sang for long enough. I felt sorry for the bride, who had to put up with the coarse jollity which was going on all around her; however, she took it better than I would have thought possible, and her embarrassment was neither awkward nor affected. Perhaps courage comes to people in difficult situations.

The luncheon eventually came to an end, and at four o'clock the men went for a walk in the park, which was a magnificent one, or watched the peasant girls of Puygarrig dance on the château lawn, dressed in their best clothes. We spent a few hours like this. In the meantime the women crowded round the bride, who showed them her wedding presents. Then she changed, and I noticed that she covered up her beautiful hair with a cap and a hat with feathers in it, for women are always in a hurry to don as quickly as possible those adornments which custom forbids them to wear while they are still unmarried.

It was nearly eight o'clock when we made ready to go back to Ille. But first a pathetic scene took place. Mademoiselle de Puygarrig's aunt, who had been a mother to her, a lady of advanced age and very religious, was not due to come to Ille with us. On our departure she gave her niece a touching sermon on her wifely duties, which resulted in a flood of tears and endless embraces. Monsieur de Peyrehorade compared this parting to the Rape of the Sabines. However, we set off at last, and during the journey everyone did their utmost to cheer up the bride and make her laugh, but in vain.

At Ille supper was waiting for us; and what a supper! If the morning's coarse jollity had shocked me, I was even more disgusted by the quips and jokes of which bride and bridegroom were the chief butts.

The bridegroom, who had disappeared for a moment before sitting down to supper, was as pale and chilly as an iceberg. He kept drinking the old wine of Collioure, which is almost as strong as brandy. I was sitting beside him, and felt I ought to warn him:

"Have a care. They say that wine . . ."

I don't know what nonsense I said to him to put myself in unison with the other guests.

He nudged my knee and whispered:

"When we get up from the table I have something to say to you."

His solemn tone surprised me. I looked at him more closely, and noticed a strange alteration in his features.

"Do you feel ill?" I asked.

"No."

And he started drinking again.

In the meantime, in the midst of all the shouting and clapping of hands, a child of eleven, who had slipped under the table, showed the company a pretty white and pink ribbon which he had just taken from the bride's ankle. They called it her garter. It was promptly cut and distributed among the young people, who decorated their buttonholes with it, in accordance with a very old custom which is still observed in a few patriarchal families. This made the bride blush to the whites of her eyes. But her confusion reached its height when Monsieur de Peyrehorade, after calling for silence, sang some Catalan verses to her, which he said were impromptu. This is the meaning, so far as I understand it.

"What is the matter with me, my friends? Has the wine I have drunk made me see double? There are two Venuses here. . . ."

The bridegroom turned round suddenly with a frightened expression, which set everybody laughing.

"Yes," continued Monsieur de Peyrehorade, "there are two Venuses under my roof. One I found in the earth, like a truffle; the other came down to us from the heavens to share her girdle with us."

He meant, of course, her garter.

"My son chose between the Roman and the Catalan Venus. The rascal chooses the Catalan, the better part, for the Roman is black and the Catalan is white; the Roman is cold, and the Catalan sets on fire all who come near her."

This conclusion aroused such an uproar of noisy applause and loud laughter that I thought the roof would fall on our heads. There were only three grave faces at the table—those of the bridal couple and mine. I had a splitting headache; besides, I don't know why, a wedding always makes me feel melancholy. This one disgusted me slightly too.

The last couplets were sung by the deputy mayor, and, I must say, they were very broad; then we went into the drawing-room to witness the departure of the bride, who was soon to be conducted to her bedroom, as it was nearly midnight.

Monsieur Alphonse drew me aside into the recess of a window, and, turning his eyes away, said to me:

"You will laugh at me . . . but I don't know what is the matter with me . . . I am bewitched, dammit!"

My first thought was that he fancied he was threatened with some misfortune of the sort referred to by Montaigne and Madame de Sévigné: "The whole realm of love is full of tragic stories."

"I thought that this kind of mishap only happened to men of genius," I said to myself.

"You have drunk too much Collioure wine, my dear Monsieur Alphonse," I said. "I did warn you."

"That may be. But this is something much worse."

His voice was broken, and I thought he was quite drunk.

"You know my ring?" he continued, after a pause.

"Yes. Has it been taken?"

"No."

"In that case you have it?"

"No—I—I could not get it off the finger of that confounded Venus."

"Nonsense! You didn't pull hard enough."

"Yes, I did. . . . But the Venus . . . has clenched her finger."

He looked at me fixedly with a haggard expression, leaning against the window-latch to keep himself from falling.

"What a ridiculous tale!" I said. "You pushed the ring too far. Tomorrow you must use pincers, only be careful not to injure the statue."

"No, I tell you. The Venus's finger has contracted and bent up; she has closed her hand, do you hear? . . . She's my wife, apparently, because I gave her my ring. . . . She won't give it back."

I shivered suddenly, and for a moment my blood ran cold. Then a deep sigh he gave sent a breath of wine into my face and all my emotion disappeared.

"The wretch is completely drunk," I thought.

"You are an antiquarian, Monsieur," the bridegroom added in dismal tones; "you know all about such statues. . . . There may be some spring, some devilish trick, I don't know about. If you would go and see. . . ."

"Willingly," I said. "Come with me."

"No, I would rather you went by yourself."

I left the drawing-room.

The weather had changed during supper, and rain was beginning to fall heavily. I was going to ask for an umbrella, when I stopped short and reflected. "I should be a fool," I said to myself, "to go and verify the tale of a man who is drunk. Besides, perhaps he intended to play some stupid trick on me to amuse these country people; and the least that could happen to me would be that I should get wet through and catch a bad cold."

I cast a glance at the dripping statue from the door, and went up to my room without returning to the drawing-room. I went to bed, but sleep was a long time coming. All the scenes that had occurred during the day returned to my mind. I thought of that beautiful, innocent young girl given up to a drunken brute. "What an odious thing," I said to myself, "is a marriage of convenience! A mayor puts on a tricolour sash, and a priest a stole, and the most innocent of girls may be handed over to the Minotaur. What can two beings who do not love each other say at such a moment, a moment which lovers would buy at the price of life itself? Can a woman ever love a man whom she has once seen behaving in a vulgar way? First impressions can never be obliterated, and I am certain Monsieur Alphonse will deserve to be hated."

During my monologue, which I have considerably abridged, I had heard much coming and going about the house, doors opening and shutting and carriages driving away; then I thought I could hear the light steps of several women on the stairs going towards the end of the passage opposite my room. It was probably the procession leading the bride to bed. Then they went downstairs again, and Madame de Peyrehorade's door shut. "How unhappy and ill at ease that poor girl must feel!" I said to myself. I tossed about in my bed in a bad temper. A bachelor cuts a poor figure in a house where there is a wedding going on.

Silence had reigned for some time when it was interrupted by heavy steps coming up the stairs. The wooden stairs creaked loudly.

"What a clumsy lout!" I cried. "I bet he'll fall downstairs."

Then all became quiet again. I took a book to change the course of my thoughts. It was a statistical report on the Department, embellished with a memoir by Monsieur de Peyrehorade on the druidical monuments in the *Arrondissement* of Prades. I dozed off at the third page.

I slept badly and awoke several times. It must have been five in the morning, and I had been awake for over twenty minutes when the cock began to crow. Dawn was about to break. Then I distinctly heard the same heavy steps and the same creaking of the stairs that I had heard before I went to sleep. This struck me as very strange. I tried in the midst of my yawning to guess why Monsieur Alphonse should rise so early; I could not think of any likely reason. I was going to close my eyes again when my attention was aroused once more by a strange stamping noise which was soon mingled with the ringing of bells and the banging of doors, after which I distinguished some confused cries.

"That drunkard must have set fire to the house!" I thought, jumping out of bed.

I dressed rapidly and went into the corridor. Cries and wails were coming from the opposite end, and one piercing cry sounded above all the others: "My son! My son!" Obviously some accident had happened to Monsieur Alphonse. I ran to the bridal-chamber; it was full of people. The first sight which met my eyes was the young man, half dressed, stretched across the bed, the wood of which was broken. He was livid and motionless, and his mother was weeping and crying by his side. Monsieur de Peyrehorade was busy rubbing his son's temples with eau-de-Cologne and holding smelling salts under his nose. Alas, his son had been dead a long time. On a couch at the other end of the room, the bride was in the grip of terrible convulsions. She was uttering inarticulate cries, and two strapping servants were having the greatest difficulty in holding her down.

"Good God!" I exclaimed. "What has happened?"

I went to the bedside and raised the body of the unfortunate young man; he was already cold and stiff. His clenched teeth and blackened face denoted the most frightful pain. It was obvious that his death had been violent and his agony terrible. There was, however, no trace of blood on his clothes. I opened his shirt and found a livid mark on his breast which extended down his sides and over his back. It was as if he had been crushed in a band of iron. My foot stepped on something hard which was lying on the rug; I bent down and saw the diamond ring.

I led Monsieur de Peyrehorade and his wife away into their room; then I had the bride carried there.

"You have a daughter left," I said to them; "you must give all your care to her." Then I left them to themselves.

There seemed to me to be no doubt that Monsieur Alphonse had been the victim of a murder, and that the murderers had found some means of entering the bride's room during the night. Those bruises, however, on the chest and their circular direction puzzled me greatly, for neither a stick nor an iron bar could have produced them. Suddenly I remembered having heard that in Valence hired assassins used long leather bags full of fine sand to crush the people whom they had been paid to kill. I immediately recalled the muleteer from Aragon and his threat, though I found it hard to believe that he could have taken such a terrible revenge for a light jest.

I went round the house, looking everywhere for traces of someone having broken in, but I found none whatever. I went down into the garden to see if the murderers had got in from there, but I could not find any definite clue. The previous night's rain had, moreover, so soaked the ground that it could not have retained a clear imprint. But I noticed several deep footmarks in the earth; they were in two contrary directions, but in the same line, beginning at the corner of the hedge next to the tennis court and ending at the front door of the house. These might have been the footmarks made by Monsieur Alphonse when he had gone to get his ring from the statue's finger. Moreover, the hedge at that spot was not as thick as it was elsewhere, and it must have been there that the murderers had got through it. Passing to and fro in front of the statue, I stopped for a moment to look at it. I must admit that I could not look at its expression of ironical malice without fear, and my head was so full of the ghastly scenes I had just witnessed that I felt as if I were looking at an infernal divinity gloating over the misfortune which had befallen the house.

I went back to my room and remained there until noon. Then I went down and asked for news of my host and hostess. They were a little calmer. Mademoiselle de Puygarrig—or rather Monsieur Alphonse's widow—had regained consciousness; she had even spoken to the public attorney of Perpignan, then at Ille on an official visit, and this magistrate had taken down her statement. He asked me for mine. I told him what I knew, and did not conceal my suspicions regarding the muleteer from Aragon. He gave orders for him to be arrested immediately.

"Have you learnt anything from Madame Alphonse?" I asked the magistrate, when my statement had been taken down and signed.

"That unfortunate young lady has gone mad," he said, with a sad smile. "Mad, completely mad. This is what she told me:

"She had been in bed, she said, for a few minutes with the curtains drawn, when the bedroom door opened and someone came in. Madame Alphonse was lying on the inside of the bed, with her face turned to the wall. She did not stir, convinced that it was her husband. A moment later the bed creaked as though it were burdened with an enormous weight. She was terribly frightened, but did not dare to turn round. Five minutes, or perhaps ten—she could not tell how long—passed. Then she made an involuntary movement, or else the other person in the bed made one, and she felt the touch of something as cold as ice—those are her very words. She pressed herself to the wall, trembling in every limb. Shortly after, the door opened again, and someone entered, who said: 'Good evening, my little wife,' and a little later the curtains were drawn. She heard a stifled cry. The person who was in bed beside her sat up, and seemed to stretch out both arms in front. Then she turned her head . . . and saw, so she says, her husband on his knees by the bed, with his head on a level with the pillow, in the arms of a sort of greenish giant who was embracing him with all its might. She said—and she repeated it to me over and over again, poor woman!—she said that she recognized . . . can you guess? The bronze Venus, Monsieur de Peyrehorade's statue. . . . Since it was found here, everybody has been dreaming about it. But to go on with the story of the poor mad girl, she lost consciousness at this sight, and probably she had lost her reason a little earlier. She cannot say how long she remained in a faint. When she came to, she saw the phantom again—or the statue, as she persists in calling it—motionless, its legs and the lower half of its body on the bed, the bust and arms stretched out before it, and in its arms her lifeless husband. A cock crew, and then the statue got out of the bed, dropped the dead body, and went out. Madame Alphonse tugged at the bell, and you know the rest."

They brought in the Spaniard; he was calm, and defended himself with great coolness and presence of mind. He did not attempt to deny the remark I had heard; he explained it by maintaining that he meant nothing by it, but that on the following day, when he had had a rest, he would have won a game of tennis against his victor. I remember that he added:

"A native of Aragon, when he is insulted, does not wait for the next day to take his revenge. If I had thought that Monsieur Alphonse meant to insult me, I would have immediately stabbed him with my knife."

His shoes were compared with the marks in the garden; but they were much larger than the footprints.

Finally, the innkeeper with whom the man was staying asserted that he had spent the whole night rubbing and doctoring one of his sick mules.

Moreover, this man from Aragon was highly respected and well known in the district, to which he came annually to do business. He was therefore released with many apologies.

I had nearly forgotten the deposition of a servant who had been the last person to see Monsieur Alphonse alive. It had been just as he was going upstairs to his wife, and he had called the man and asked him in an anxious manner if he knew where I was. The servant had replied that he had not seen me. Then Monsieur Alphonse had heaved a sigh, and stood there for a moment in silence. Then he had said:

"Well, the devil must have carried him off too!"

I asked this man if Monsieur Alphonse had had his diamond ring on when he had spoken to him. The servant hesitated before he replied; then he said that he thought not, that at all events he had not paid any attention.

"If he had been wearing that ring," he added, correcting himself, "I should certainly have noticed it, because I thought that he had given it to Madame Alphonse."

While I was questioning this man I felt a little of the superstitious terror that Madame Alphonse's deposition had spread throughout the house. The magistrate looked at me and smiled, and I refrained from pressing the point.

A few hours after Monsieur Alphonse's funeral, I prepared to leave Ille. Monsieur de Peyrehorade's carriage was to take me to Perpignan. In spite of his feeble condition the poor old man insisted on accompanying me to the gate of his garden. We crossed the garden in silence, with him hardly able to drag himself along even with the help of my arm. Just as we were parting, I cast a last glance at the Venus. I could see that my host, although he did not share the terror and hatred which it inspired in the rest of his family, would want to get rid of an object which would otherwise be a constant reminder of a frightful misfortune. I intended to try and persuade him to give it to a museum. I was wondering how to broach the subject when Monsieur de Peyrehorade automatically turned his head in the direction in which he saw me gazing. He saw the statue, and immediately burst into tears. I embraced him and, without daring to say a single word, I got into the carriage.

Since my departure I have not heard of any fresh discovery being made to throw light on that mysterious catastrophe.

Monsieur de Peyrehorade died a few months after his son. In his will he bequeathed me his manuscripts, which some day I may publish. But I have not been able to find among them the treatise relating to the inscription on the Venus.

P.S. MY FRIEND Monsieur de P. has just written to me from Perpignan to tell me that the statue no longer exists. After her husband's death, the first thing Madame de Peyrehorade did was to have it melted down and made into a bell, and in this new form it is used in the church at Ille. But, adds Monsieur de P., it would seem that an evil fate pursues those who possess that piece of bronze. Since that bell began to ring in Ille, the vines have twice been frost-bitten.

JOSEPH SHERIDAN LE FANU

*

The Ghost and the Bonesetter

(1838)

Written by the most famous author of ghost stories in Victorian English fiction, Joseph Sheridan Le Fanu (Dublin, 1814–1873), an Irish Protestant descended from French Huguenots, this is an early tale, probably the first he ever published. "The Ghost and the Bonesetter" is halfway between the fantastic story of the Gothic school and the transcription of a legend from local folklore. The man "without fear" who spends the night in a castle dominated by a ghost is an old theme in folk literature from every land. In Le Fanu's narrative, an Irish tradition is added to the theme: the most recently buried person in a cemetery must fetch water for the older dead, who suffer from thirst because of the flames in purgatory. As a result of this belief, if two funerals take place at the same time, there is a race between the two deceased and the loser must take on the laborious task. (Guido Almansi, using this episode as an example, recalls the high-speed funeral in René Clair's film Entr'acte.*)*

The language of the original imitates Anglo-Irish pronunciation, so its spirit has the tone of oral narrative. It is one of the few stories by Le Fanu where irony predominates.

In looking over the papers of my late valued and respected friend, Francis Purcell, who for nearly fifty years discharged the arduous duties of a parish priest in the south of Ireland, I met with the following document. It is one of many such, for he was a curious and industrious collector of old local traditions—a commodity in which the quarter where he resided mightily abounded. The collection and arrangement of such legends was, as long as I can remember him, his *hobby*; but I had never learned that his love of the marvellous and whimsical had carried him so far as to prompt him to commit the results of his enquiries to writing, until, in the character of *residuary legatee*, his will put me in possession of all his manuscript papers. To such as may think the composing of such productions as these inconsistent with the character and habits of a country priest, it is necessary to observe, that there did exist a race of priests—those of the old school, a race now nearly extinct—whose habits were from many causes more refined, and whose tastes more literary than are those of the alumni of Maynooth.

It is perhaps necessary to add that the superstition illustrated by the following story, namely, that the corpse last buried is obliged, during his juniority of interment, to supply his brother tenants of the churchyard in which he lies, with fresh water to allay the burning thirst of purgatory, is prevalent throughout the south of Ireland. The writer can vouch for a case in which a respectable and wealthy farmer, on the borders of Tipperary, in tenderness to the corns of his departed helpmate, enclosed in her coffin two pair of brogues, a light and a heavy, the one for dry, the other for sloppy weather; seeking thus to mitigate the fatigues of her inevitable perambulations in procuring water, and administering it to the thirsty souls of purgatory.

Fierce and desperate conflicts have ensued in the case of two funeral parties approaching the same churchyard together, each endeavouring to secure to his own dead priority of sepulture, and a consequent immunity from the tax levied upon the pedestrian powers of the last comer. An instance not long since occurred, in which one of two such parties, through fear of losing to their deceased friend this inestimable advantage, made their way to the churchyard by a *short cut*, and in violation of one of their strongest prejudices, actually threw the coffin over the wall, lest time should be lost in making their entrance through the gate. Innumerable instances of the same kind might be quoted, all tending to shew how strongly, among the peasantry of the south, this superstition is entertained. However, I shall not detain the reader further, by any prefatory remarks, but shall proceed to lay before him the following:

Extract from the Ms. Papers of the Late Rev. Francis Purcell, of Drumcoolagh

I tell the following particulars, as nearly as I can recollect them, in the words of the narrator. It may be necessary to observe that he was what is termed a *well-spoken* man, having for a considerable time instructed the ingenious youth of his native parish in such of the liberal arts and sciences as he found it convenient to profess—a circumstance which may account for the occurrence of several big words, in the course of this narrative, more distinguished for euphonious effect, than for correctness of application. I proceed then, without further preface, to lay before you the wonderful adventures of Terry Neil.

"Why, thin, 'tis a quare story, an' as thrue as you're sittin' there; and I'd make bould to say there isn't a boy in the seven parishes could tell it better nor crickther than myself, for 'twas my father himself it happened to, an' many's the time I heerd it out iv his own mouth; an' I can say, an' I'm proud av that same, my father's word was as incredible as any squire's oath in the counthry; and so signs an' if a poor man got into any unlucky throuble, he was the boy id go into the court an' prove; but that doesn't signify—he was as honest and as sober a man, barrin' he was a little bit too partial to the glass, as you'd find in a day's walk; an' there wasn't the likes of him in the counthry round for nate labourin' an' *baan* diggin'; and he was mighty handy entirely for carpenther's work, and mendin' ould spudethrees, an' the likes i' that. An' so he tuck up with bone-setting, as was most nathural, for none of them could come up to him in mendin' the leg iv a stool or a table; an' sure, there never was a bonesetter got so much custom—man an' child, young an' ould—there never was such breakin' and mendin' of bones known in the memory of man. Well, Terry Neil, for that was my father's name, began to feel his heart growin' light and his purse heavy; an' he took a bit iv a farm in Squire Phalim's ground, just undher the ould castle, an' a pleasant little spot it was; an' day an' mornin', poor crathurs not able to put a foot to the ground, with broken arms and broken legs, id be comin' ramblin' in from all quarters to have their bones spliced up. Well, yer honour, all this was as well as well could be; but it was customary when Sir Phalim id go any where out iv the country, for some iv the tinants to sit up to watch in the ould castle, just for a kind of a compliment to the ould family—an' a mighty unpleasant compliment it was for the tinants, for there wasn't a man of them but knew there was some thing quare about the ould castle. The neighbours had it, that the squire's ould grandfather, as good a gintleman, God be with him, as I heer'd as ever stood in shoe leather, used to keep walkin' about in the middle iv the night, ever sinst he bursted a blood vessel pullin' out a cork out iv a bottle, as you or I might be doin', and will too, plase God; but that doesn't signify. So, as I was sayin', the ould squire used to come down out of the frame, where his picthur was hung up, and to brake the bottles and glasses, God be marciful to us all, an' dhrink all he could come at—an' small blame to him for that same; and then if any of the family id be comin' in, he id be up again in his place, looking as quite an' innocent as if he didn't know any thing about it—the mischievous ould chap.

"Well, your honour, as I was sayin', one time the family up at the castle was stayin' in Dublin for a week or two; and so as usual, some of the tenants had to sit up in the castle, and the third night it kem to my father's turn. 'Oh, tare an ouns,' says he unto himself, 'an' must I sit up all night, and that ould vagabond of a sperit, glory be to God,' says he, 'serenading through the house, an' doin' all sorts iv mischief.' However, there was no gettin' aff, and so he put a bould face on it, an' he went up at night-fall with a bottle of pottieen, and another of holy wather.

"It was rainin' smart enough, an' the evenin' was darksome and gloomy, when my father got in, and the holy wather he sprinkled on himself, it wasn't long till he had to swallee a cup iv the pottieen, to keep the cowld out iv his heart. It was the ould steward, Lawrence Connor, that opened the door—and he an' my father wor always very great. So when he seen who it was, an' my father tould him how it was his turn to watch in the castle, he offered to sit up along with him; and you may be sure my father wasn't sorry for that same. So says Larry,

" 'We'll have a bit iv fire in the parlour,' says he.

" 'An' why not in the hall?' says my father, for he knew that the squire's picthur was hung in the parlour.

" 'No fire can be lit in the hall,' says Lawrence, 'for there's an ould jackdaw's nest in the chimney.'

" 'Oh thin,' says my father, 'let us stop in the kitchen, for it's very umproper for the likes iv me to be sittin' in the parlour,' says he.

" 'Oh, Terry, that can't be,' says Lawrence; 'if we keep up the ould custom at all, we may as well keep it up properly,' says he.

" 'Divil sweep the ould custom,' says my father—to himself, do ye mind, for he didn't like to let Lawrence see that he was more afeard himself.

" 'Oh, very well,' says he. 'I'm agreeable, Lawrence,' says he; and so down they both went to the kitchen, until the fire id be lit in the parlour—an' that same wasn't long doin'.

"Well, your honour, they soon wint up again, an' sat down mighty comfortable by the parlour fire, and they beginn'd to talk, an' to smoke, an' to dhrink a small taste iv the pottieen; and, moreover, they had a good rousing fire of bogwood and turf, to warm their shins over.

"Well, sir, as I was sayin' they kep convarsin' and smokin' together most agreeable, until Lawrence beginn'd to get sleepy, as was but nathural for him, for he was an ould sarvint man, and was used to a great dale iv sleep.

" 'Sure it's impossible,' says my father, 'it's gettin' sleepy you are?'

" 'Oh, divil a taste,' says Larry, 'I'm only shuttin' my eyes,' says he, 'to keep out the parfume of the tibacky smoke, that's makin' them wather,' says he. 'So don't you mind other people's business,' says he stiff enough (for he had a mighty high stomach av his own, rest his sowl), 'and go on,' says he, 'with your story, for I'm listenin',' says he, shuttin' down his eyes.

"Well, when my father seen spakin' was no use, he went on with his story. —By the same token, it was the story of Jim Soolivan and his ould goat he was tellin'—an' a pleasant story it is—an' there was so much divarsion in it, that it was enough to waken a dormouse, let alone to pervint a Christian goin' asleep. But, faix, the way my father tould it, I believe there never was the likes heerd sinst nor before for he bawled out every word av it, as if the life was fairly leavin' him thrying to keep ould Larry awake; but, faix, it was no use, for the hoorsness came an him, an' before he kem to the end of his story, Larry O'Connor beginned to snore like a bagpipes.

" 'Oh, blur an' agres,' says my father, 'isn't this a hard case,' says he, 'that ould villain, lettin' on to be my friend, and to go asleep this way, an' us both in the very room with a sperit,' says he. 'The crass o' Christ about us,' says he; and with that he was goin' to shake Lawrence to waken him, but he just remimbered if he roused him, that he'd surely go off to his bed, an lave him completely alone, an' that id be by far worse.

" 'Oh thin,' says my father, 'I'll not disturb the poor boy. It id be neither friendly nor good-nathured,' says he, 'to tormint him while he is asleep,' says he; 'only I wish I was the same way myself,' says he.

"An' with that he beginned to walk up an' down, an' sayin' his prayers, until he worked himself into a sweat, savin' your presence. But it was all no good; so he dhrunk about a pint of sperits, to compose his mind.

" 'Oh,' says he, 'I wish to the Lord I was as asy in my mind as Larry there. Maybe,' says he, 'if I thried I could go asleep'; an' with that he pulled a big arm-chair close beside Lawrence, an' settled himself in it as well as he could.

"But there was one quare thing I forgot to tell you. He couldn't help, in spite av himself, lookin' now an' thin at the picthur, an' he immediately observed that the eyes av it was follyin' him about, an' starin' at him, an' winkin' at him, wherever he wint. 'Oh,' says he, when he seen that, 'it's a poor chance I have,' says he; 'an' bad luck was with me the day I kem into this unforthunate place,' says he; 'but any way there's no use in bein' freckened now,' says he; 'for if I am to die, I may as well parspire undaunted,' says he.

"Well, your honour, he thried to keep himself quite an' asy, an' he thought two or three times he might have wint asleep, but for the way the storm was groanin' and creekin' through the great heavy branches outside, an' whistlin' through the ould chimnies iv the castle. Well, afther one great roarin' blast iv the wind, you'd think the walls iv the castle was just goin' to fall, quite an' clane, with the shakin' iv it. All av a suddint the storm stopt, as silent an' as quite as if it was a July evenin'. Well, your honour, it wasn't stopped blowin' for three minnites, before he thought he hard a sort iv a noise over the chimney-piece; an' with that my father just opened his eyes the smallest taste in life, an' sure enough he seen the ould squire gettin' out iv the picthur, for all the world as if he was throwin' aff his ridin' coat, until he stept out clane an' complate, out av the chimly-piece, an' thrun himself down an the floor. Well, the slieveen ould chap—an' my father thought it was the dirtiest turn iv all—before he beginned to do anything out iv the way, he stopped, for a while, to listen wor they both asleep; an' as soon as he thought all was quite, he put out his hand, and tuck hould iv the whiskey bottle, an' dhrank at laste a pint iv it. Well, your honour, when he tuck his turn out iv it, he settled it back mighty cute intirely, in the very same spot it was in before. An' he beginn'd to walk up an' down the room, lookin' as sober an' as solid as if he never done the likes at all. An' whinever he went apast my father, he thought he felt a great scent of brimstone, an' it was that that freckened him entirely; for he knew it was brimstone that was burned in hell, savin' your presence. At any rate, he often heer'd it from Father Murphy, an' he had a right to know what belonged to it—he's dead since, God rest him. Well, your honour, my father was asy enough until the sperit kem past him; so close, God be marciful to us all, that the smell iv the sulphur tuck the breath clane out iv him; an' with that he tuck such a fit iv coughin', that it al-a-most shuck him out iv the chair he was sittin' in.

" 'Ho, ho!' says the squire, stoppin' short about two steps aff, and turnin' round facin' my father, 'is it you that's in it?—an' how's all with you, Terry Neil?'

" 'At your honour's sarvice,' says my father (as well as the fright id let him, for he was more dead than alive), 'an' it's proud I am to see your honour to-night,' says he.

" 'Terence,' says the squire, 'you're a respectable man (an' it was thrue for him), an industhrious, sober man, an' an example of inebriety to the whole parish,' says he.

" 'Thank your honour,' says my father, gettin' courage, 'you were always a civil spoken gintleman, God rest your honour.'

" 'Rest my honour,' says the sperit (fairly gettin' red in the face with the madness), 'Rest my honour?' says he. 'Why, you ignorant spalpeen,' says he, 'you mane, niggarly ignoramush,' says he, 'where did you lave your manners?' says he. 'If I *am* dead, it's no fault iv mine,' says he; 'an' it's not to be thrun in my teeth at every hand's turn, by the likes iv you,' says he, stampin' his foot an the flure, that you'd think the boords id smash undher him.

" 'Oh,' says my father, 'I'm only a foolish, ignorant, poor man,' says he.

" 'You're nothing else,' says the squire; 'but any way,' says he, 'it's not to be listenin' to your gosther, nor convarsin' with the likes iv you, that I came *up*—down I mane,' says he—(an' as little as the mistake was, my father tuck notice iv it). 'Listen to me now, Terence Neil,' says he, 'I was always a good masther to Pathrick Neil, your grandfather,' says he.

" 'Tis thrue for your honour,' says my father.

" 'And, moreover, I think I was always a sober, riglar gintleman,' says the squire.

" 'That's your name, sure enough,' says my father (though it was a big lie for him, but he could not help it).

" 'Well,' says the sperit, 'although I was as sober as most men—at laste as most gintlemen'—says he; 'an' though I was at different pariods a most extempory Christian, and most charitable and inhuman to the poor,' says he; 'for all that I'm not as asy where I am now,' says he, 'as I had a right to expect,' says he.

" 'An' more's the pity,' says my father; 'maybe your honour id wish to have a word with Father Murphy?'

" 'Hould your tongue, you misherable bliggard,' says the squire; 'it's not iv my sowl I'm thinkin'—an' I wondher you'd have the impitence to talk to a gintleman consarnin' his sowl; —and when I want *that* fixed,' says he, slappin' his thigh, 'I'll go to them that knows what belongs to the likes,' says he. 'It's not my sowl,' says he, sittin' down opposite my father; 'it's not my sowl that's annoyin' me most—I'm unasy on my right leg,' says he, 'that I bruck at Glenvarloch cover the day I killed black Barney.'

"(My father found out afther, it was a favourite horse that fell undher him, afther leapin' the big fince that runs along by the glen.)

" 'I hope,' says my father, 'your honour's not unasy about the killin' iv him?'

" 'Hould your tongue, ye fool,' said the squire, 'an' I'll tell you why I'm anasy an my leg,' says he. 'In the place, where I spend most iv my time,' says he, 'except the little leisure I have for lookin' about me here,' says he, 'I have to walk a great dale more than I was ever used to,' says he, 'and by far more than is good for me either,' says he; 'for I must tell you,' says he, 'the people where I am is ancommonly fond iv could wather, for there is nothin' betther to be had; an', moreover, the weather is hotter than is altogether plisint,' says he; 'and I'm appinted,' says he, 'to assist in carryin' the wather, an' gets a mighty poor share iv it myself,' says he, 'an' a mighty throublesome, warin' job it is, I can tell you,' says he; 'for they're all iv them surprisingly dhry, an' dhrinks it as fast as my legs can carry it,' says he; 'but what kills me intirely,' says he, 'is the wakeness in my leg,' says he, 'an' I want you to give it a pull or two to bring it to shape,' says he, 'and that's the long an' the short iv it,' says he.

" 'Oh, plase your honour,' says my father (for he didn't like to handle the sperit at all), 'I wouldn't have the impitence to do the likes to your honour,' says he; 'it's only to poor crathurs like myself I'd do it to,' says he.

" 'None iv your blarney,' says the squire, 'here's my leg,' says he, cockin' it up to him, 'pull it for the bare life,' says he; 'an' if you don't, by the immortial powers I'll not lave a bone in your carcish I'll not powdher,' says he.

" 'When my father heerd that, he seen there was no use in purtendin', so he tuck hould iv the leg, an' he kept pullin' an' pullin', till the sweat, God bless us, beginned to pour down his face."

" 'Pull, you divil,' says the squire.

" 'At your sarvice, your honour,' says my father.

" 'Pull harder,' says the squire.

"My father pulled like the divil.

" 'I'll take a little sup,' says the squire, rachin' over his hand to the bottle, 'to keep up my courage,' says he, lettin' an to be very wake in himself intirely. But, as cute as he was, he was out here, for he tuck the wrong one. 'Here's to your good health, Terence,' says he, 'an' now pull like the very divil,' 'an' with that he lifted the bottle of holy wather, but it was hardly to his mouth, whin he let a screech out, you'd think the room id fairly split with it, an' made one chuck that sent the leg clane aff his body in my father's hands; down wint the squire over the table, an' bang wint my father half way across the room on his back, upon the flure. Whin he kem to himself the cheerful mornin' sun was shinin' through the windy shutthers, an' he was lying flat an his back, with the leg iv one of the great ould chairs pulled clane out iv the socket an' tight in his hand, pintin' up to the ceilin', an' ould Larry fast asleep, an' snorin' as loud as ever. My father wint that mornin' to Father Murphy, an' from that to the day of his death, he never neglected confission nor mass, an' what he tould was betther believed that he spake av it but seldom. An', as for the squire, that is the sperit, whether it was that he did not like his liquor, or by rason iv the loss iv his leg, he was never known to walk again."

II

*

The Everyday Fantastic of the Nineteenth Century

EDGAR ALLAN POE

The Tell-Tale Heart

(1843)

What would be the best way to represent an author like Poe (1809–1849), who, within the fantastic narrative of the nineteenth century, is the central, the most famous, and the defining figure? The obvious choice would be The Fall of the House of Usher *(1839), which includes all of Poe's idiosyncratic traits: the crumbling house that exudes an aura of dissolution, the lifeless woman, the man absorbed in esoteric studies, premature burial, the dead woman who leaves her grave. Afterward, all the literature of decadentism was able to feed on those motifs; the film industry, since its very beginnings, has propagated them to the point of saturation.*

However, I wanted a different Poe to open this second part, the Poe who inaugurates a new kind of fantastic tale, one obtained using the very limited means that will dominate the second half of the century: the completely mental and psychological fantastic story.

In my opinion, "The Tell-Tale Heart," a murderer's interior monologue, is Poe's masterpiece. The killer is in his victim's room, hidden in the darkness. The victim is a frightened old man who keeps one eye open. The existence of the old man reveals itself only through that eye ("the vulture eye") and the beating of his heart, or at least what the murderer thinks is the beating of the old man's heart, which will continue to obsess him even after the crime.

TRUE!—NERVOUS—VERY, very dreadfully nervous I had been and am; but why *will* you say that I am mad? The disease had sharpened my senses—not destroyed—not dulled them. Above all was the sense of hearing acute. I heard all things in the heaven and in the earth. I heard many things in hell. How, then, am I mad? Hearken! and observe how healthily—how calmly I can tell you the whole story.

It is impossible to say how first the idea entered my brain; but once conceived, it haunted me day and night. Object there was none. Passion there was none. I loved the old man. He had never wronged me. He had never given me insult. For his gold I had no desire. I think it was his eye! yes, it was this! He had the eye of a vulture—a pale blue eye, with a film over it. Whenever it fell upon me, my blood ran cold; and so by degrees—very gradually—I made up my mind to take the life of the old man, and thus rid myself of the eye forever.

Now this is the point. You fancy me mad. Madmen know nothing. But you should have seen *me*. You should have seen how wisely I proceeded—with what caution—with what foresight—with what dissimulation I went to work! I was never kinder to the old man than during the whole week before I killed him. And every night, about midnight, I turned the latch of his door and opened it—oh so gently! And then, when I had made an opening sufficient for my head, I put in a dark lantern, all closed, closed, so that no light shone out, and then I thrust in my head. Oh, you would have laughed to see how cunningly I thrust it in! I moved it slowly—very, very slowly, so that I might not disturb the old man's sleep. It took me an hour to place my whole head within the opening so far that I could see him as he lay upon his bed. Ha!—would a madman have been so wise as this? And then, when my head was well in the room, I undid the lantern cautiously—oh, so cautiously—cautiously (for the hinges creaked)—I undid it just so much that a single thin ray fell upon the vulture eye. And this I did for seven long nights—every night just at midnight—but I found the eye always closed; and so it was impossible to do the work; for it was not the old man who vexed me, but his Evil Eye. And every morning, when the day broke, I went boldly into the chamber, and spoke courageously to him, calling him by name in a hearty tone, and inquiring how he had passed the night. So you see he would have been a very profound old man, indeed, to suspect that every night, just at twelve, I looked in upon him while he slept.

Upon the eighth night I was more than usually cautious in opening the door. A watch's minute hand moves more quickly than did mine. Never before that night, had I *felt* the extent of my own powers—of my sagacity. I could scarcely contain my feelings of triumph. To think that there I was, opening the door, little by little, and he not even to dream of my secret deeds or thoughts. I fairly chuckled at the idea; and perhaps he heard me: for he moved on the bed suddenly, as if startled. Now you may think that I drew back—but no. His room was as black as pitch with the thick darkness, (for the shutters were close fastened, through fear of robbers,) and so I knew that he could not see the opening of the door, and I kept pushing it on steadily, steadily.

I had my head in, and was about to open the lantern, when my thumb slipped upon the tin fastening, and the old man sprang up in the bed, crying out—"Who's there?"

I kept quite still and said nothing. For a whole hour I did not move a muscle, and in the meantime I did not hear him lie down. He was still sitting up in the bed listening;—just as I have done, night after night, hearkening to the death watches in the wall.

Presently I heard a slight groan, and I knew it was the groan of mortal terror. It was not a groan of pain or of grief—oh, no!—it was the low stifled sound that arises from the bottom of the soul when overcharged with awe. I knew the sound well. Many a night, just at midnight, when all the world slept, it has welled up from my own bosom, deepening, with its dreadful echo, the terrors that distracted me. I say I knew it well. I knew what the old man felt, and pitied him, although I chuckled at heart. I knew that he had been lying awake ever since the first slight noise, when he had turned in the bed. His fears had been ever since growing upon him. He had been trying to fancy them causeless, but could not. He had been saying to himself—"It is nothing but the wind in the chimney—it is only a mouse crossing the floor," or "it is merely a cricket which has made a single chirp." Yes, he had been trying to comfort himself with these suppositions: but he had found all in vain. *All in vain;* because Death, in approaching him, had stalked with his black shadow before him, and enveloped the victim. And it was the mournful influence of the unperceived shadow that caused him to feel—although he neither saw nor heard—to *feel* the presence of my head within the room.

When I had waited a long time, very patiently, without hearing him lie down, I resolved to open a little—a very, very little crevice in the lantern. So I opened it—you cannot imagine how stealthily, stealthily—until, at length a single dim ray, like the thread of the spider, shot from out the crevice and fell full upon the vulture eye.

It was open—wide, wide open—and I grew furious as I gazed upon it. I saw it with perfect distinctness—all a dull blue, with a hideous veil over it that chilled the very marrow in my bones; but I could see nothing else of the old man's face or person: for I had directed the ray as if by instinct, precisely upon the damned spot.

And have I not told you that what you mistake for madness is but over acuteness of the senses?—now, I say, there came to my ears a low, dull, quick sound, such as a watch makes when enveloped in cotton. I knew *that* sound well, too. It was the beating of the old man's heart. It increased my fury, as the beating of a drum stimulates the soldier into courage.

But even yet I refrained and kept still. I scarcely breathed. I held the lantern motionless. I tried how steadily I could maintain the ray upon the eye. Meantime the hellish tattoo of the heart increased. It grew quicker and quicker, and louder and louder every instant. The old man's terror *must* have been extreme! It grew louder, I say, louder every moment!—do you mark me well? I have told you that I am nervous: so I am. And now at the dead hour of the night, amid the dreadful silence of that old house, so strange a noise as this excited me to uncontrollable terror. Yet, for some minutes longer I refrained and stood still. But the beating grew louder, louder! I thought the heart must burst. And now a new anxiety seized me—the sound would be heard by a neighbour! The old man's hour had come! With a loud yell, I threw open the lantern and leaped into the room. He shrieked once—once only. In an instant I dragged him to the floor, and pulled the heavy bed over him. I then smiled gaily, to find the deed so far done. But, for many minutes, the heart beat on with a muffled sound. This, however, did not vex me; it would not be heard through the wall. At length it ceased. The old man was dead. I removed the bed and examined the corpse. Yes, he was stone, stone dead. I placed my hand upon the heart and held it there many minutes. There was no pulsation. He was stone dead. His eye would trouble me no more.

If still you think me mad, you will think so no longer when I describe the wise precautions I took for the concealment of the body. The night waned, and I worked hastily, but in silence. First of all I dismembered the corpse. I cut off the head and the arms and the legs.

I then took up three planks from the flooring of the chamber, and deposited all between the scantlings. I then replaced the boards so cleverly, so cunningly, that no human eye—not even *his*—could have detected any thing wrong. There was nothing to wash out—no stain of any kind—no blood-spot whatever. I had been too wary for that. A tub had caught all—ha! ha!

When I had made an end of these labors, it was four o'clock—still dark as midnight. As the bell sounded the hour, there came a knocking at the street door. I went down to open it with a light heart,—for what had I *now* to fear? There entered three men, who introduced themselves, with perfect suavity, as officers of the police. A shriek had been heard by a neighbour during the night; suspicion of foul play had been aroused; information had been lodged at the police office, and they (the officers) had been deputed to search the premises.

I smiled—for *what* had I to fear? I bade the gentlemen welcome. The shriek, I said, was my own in a dream. The old man, I mentioned, was absent in the country. I took my visitors all over the house. I bade them search—search *well.* I led them, at length, to *his* chamber. I showed them his treasures, secure, undisturbed. In the enthusiasm of my confidence, I brought chairs into the room, and desired them *here* to rest from their fatigues, while I myself, in the wild audacity of my perfect triumph, placed my own seat upon the very spot beneath which reposed the corpse of the victim.

The officers were satisfied. My *manner* had convinced them. I was singularly at ease. They sat, and while I answered cheerily, they chatted of familiar things. But, ere long, I felt myself getting pale and wished them gone. My head ached, and I fancied a ringing in my ears: but still they sat and still chatted. The ringing became more distinct:—it continued and became more distinct: I talked more freely to get rid of the feeling: but it continued and gained definitiveness—until, at length, I found that the noise was *not* within my ears.

No doubt I now grew *very* pale—but I talked more fluently, and with a heightened voice. Yet the sound increased—and what could I do? It was *a low, dull, quick sound—much such a sound as a watch makes when enveloped in cotton.* I gasped for breath—and yet the officers heard it not. I talked more quickly—more vehemently; but the noise steadily increased. I arose and argued about trifles, in a high key and with violent gesticulations; but the noise steadily increased. Why *would* they not be gone? I paced the floor to and fro with heavy strides, as if excited to fury by the observations of the men—but the noise steadily increased. Oh God! what *could* I do? I foamed—I raved—I swore! I swung the chair upon which I had been sitting, and grated it upon the boards, but the noise arose over all and continually increased. It grew louder—louder—*louder!* And still the men chatted pleasantly, and smiled. Was it possible they heard not? Almighty God!—no, no! They heard!—they suspected!—they *knew!*—they were making a mockery of my horror!—this I thought, and this I think. But anything was better than this agony! Anything was more tolerable than this derision! I could bear those hypocritical smiles no longer! I felt that I must scream or die!—and now—again!—hark! louder! louder! louder! *louder!*

"Villains!" I shrieked, "dissemble no more! I admit the deed!—tear up the planks!—here, here!—it is the beating of his hideous heart!"

HANS CHRISTIAN ANDERSEN

*

The Shadow

(1847)

Aside from his reputation as a writer of children's literature, Hans Christian Andersen (1805–1875) is one of the great nineteenth-century authors of marvelous tales, proof of which is this story, constructed with extraordinary inventiveness and delicacy. The idea comes to him in Naples, on a very sunny day: the shadow that separates from the body is one of the great themes of the fantastic imagination, and here it is linked to an essential aspect of Andersen's psychology, his pessimistic bitterness with regard to himself.

Adalbert von Chamisso, in "Peter Schlemihls" (1813), created the first, unsurpassable story of losing a shadow. In the context of Goethe's Faust, *the loss of one's shadow was interpreted as the loss of one's soul, but the symbol is more undefinable and complex. The shadow is an essence that flees from the person, a double that we all bear with us. E. T. A. Hoffmann, who was always obsessed with the idea of the double, admired Chamisso's story so much he introduced Peter Schlemihls in his* New Year's Eve Adventures *(1817), causing him to meet a man who casts no reflection in the mirror.*

Hoffmann's character abandons his image in a mirror inside the house of a woman, a diabolical sorceress, so his love of her can continue. Andersen's shadow also slips away from a man as an emanation of his desire to be near the girl he loves. But the shadow carries on its own independent life, accumulates a fortune, frequents high society, and when it again finds the man from whom it has separated, it forces him *to serve* it, *to be* its *shadow. The situation is therefore inverted: the shadow is a pitiless master and enemy. Finding the shadow again is a kind of condemnation.*

The symbol of the lost shadow is present in the literature of our century, as we see in Hugo von Hofmannsthal's "Woman Without a Shadow."

IN THE HOT countries the sun can burn properly. People become as brown as mahogany all over; in the very hottest countries they are even burnt into negroes—but it was only to the hot countries that a learned man from the cold ones had come. He imagined he would be able to run about as he did at home, but he soon got out of the habit of doing that. He and all sensible people had to stop indoors. The window-shutters and the doors were kept shut all day, and it looked as if the whole house were asleep or else nobody was at home. The narrow street with the tall houses, where he lived, was so built that from morning to night the sunshine lay on it; really it was unbearable. This learned man from the cold countries—he was a young man and a clever one—he felt as if he was living in a fiery furnace. It exhausted him, and he grew quite thin, and even his shadow contracted and got much smaller than it was at home; the sun exhausted it, too. Not until evening, when the sun was down, did they begin to revive.

That, now, was really a pleasure to see. As soon as lights were brought into the room the Shadow stretched itself all up the wall—yes, up to the ceiling, too, so long did it make itself, for it had to stretch itself to get its strength back. The learned man went out on the balcony, to stretch himself there, and as the stars came out in the lovely clear sky he seemed to himself to be coming to life again.

On all the balconies in the street—and in the hot countries every window has a balcony—people came out, for air one must have, even if one's accustomed to be the colour of mahogany. Very lively it became—upstairs and downstairs. Shoemakers and tailors and everybody else moved out into the street; tables and chairs were brought out and lamps lit—thousands of them—and some talked and others sang; and the people took walks, and the carriages drove out, and the donkeys with bells on them went by—"Kling-a-ling-a-ling!" There were funerals, with singing of psalms; the street-boys fired off throw-downs; the church bells rang out, and altogether it was very lively down in the street. Only in one house, straight opposite to that in which the foreign learned man lived, was there complete stillness. And yet somebody lived in it, for there were flowers on the balcony, that grew splendidly in the hot sun, which they couldn't have done without being watered, and there must be somebody to water them; so there must be people there. The door of it, too, was opened at night, but inside it was quite dark; at any rate in the front room. But from further in there was a sound of music. To the foreign scholar it seemed incomparably beautiful, but it might easily be that he fancied it so, for in the hot countries everything seemed to him matchless, but for the heat. The landlord said he didn't know who had taken the house opposite, for you couldn't see any people, and as for the music, he thought it horribly tiresome. "It's like someone sitting practising a piece he can't get on with—always the same piece. No doubt he's saying, 'I shall get it right in time,' but he won't get it right, however long he goes on playing."

One night the foreign scholar woke up. The door to the balcony stood open where he slept and the curtain before it was lifted by the breeze, and he thought tnere was a marvellous light coming from the balcony opposite. All the flowers were shining like flames of the most lovely colours, and among the flowers stood a slender, graceful maiden; herself, too, shining, as it seemed. It positively dazzled his eyes, and he shut them as tight as ever he could, and woke up completely. With a single jump he was on the floor, and very quietly he stole behind the curtain, but the maiden was gone, the light was gone, the flowers shone no longer, though they stood there as fair as ever. The door was ajar, and from far within the music was sounding, soft and beautiful; such as would entrance one into delicious thought. It really was like magic—and who was it that lived there? Where was the proper entrance? The whole ground floor was a succession of shops, and people couldn't always be passing through them.

One evening the foreign scholar was sitting out on his balcony, and a lamp was hung in the room behind him, and so it very naturally happened that his shadow passed across to the wall opposite, and there it stayed, right opposite among the flowers on the balcony, and when the learned man moved the shadow moved, too—it always does.

"I think my Shadow is the only living thing to be seen over there," said the learned man. "Look how snug it's sitting among the flowers, and the door's standing ajar. Now if only the Shadow was sharp enough to go in and look about and then come and tell me what it saw! Yes, you'd be some use then," he said in joke. "Do, please, go in there! Do! Are you going?" With that he nodded to the Shadow, and the Shadow nodded back. "Well, go then, but don't stay away!" The learned man got up and his Shadow, on the balcony opposite, got up too. The learned man turned, and the Shadow turned too, and if anyone had been observing carefully, they would have seen, quite plain, that the Shadow went in by the half-open door of the balcony over the way, at the moment when the learned man went into his own room and let fall the long curtain behind him.

Next morning the learned man went out to take his coffee and read the papers. "What's this?" he said, when he came out into the sunshine. "I haven't got any shadow! Why, then it really did go away last night and has not come back; that's rather tiresome, that is."

It did annoy him, but not so much because his shadow was gone, as because he knew that there was a story about a man without a shadow which everyone at home in the cold countries knew; and if the learned man went there and told them his own story they would say he was merely imitating the other, and that he had no business to do. So he determined to say nothing at all about it, which was very sensible of him.

In the evening he went out on to his balcony again; he had put the lamp behind him, very properly, for he knew that a shadow always needs its master for a screen, but he couldn't entice it back. He made himself little and he made himself big, but no shadow came, nobody came. He coughed loudly, but it was no good.

It was amazing, to be sure; but in those hot countries everything grows very fast, and after a week had passed he saw, to his great delight, that a new shadow was growing out of his feet when he went into the sunlight: the root must have been left behind. In three weeks' time he had a very tolerable shadow, which, when he betook himself home to the northern country, grew more and more on the way, so that at last it was so long and so big that he would have been contented with half as much.

So the learned man came home and wrote books about what there was of truth and goodness and beauty in the world; and days passed by, and years—many years.

He was sitting in his room one evening, and there came a very gentle knock at the door. "Come in!" said he; but nobody came in, so he opened the door, and there standing before him was an extraordinarily thin man, so thin as to be quite remarkable. This person was, for the rest, extremely well dressed, and evidently a man of distinction.

"Whom have I the honour of addressing?" asked the learned man.

"Ah, I thought very likely you wouldn't recognize me," said the well-dressed man. "I've become so much of a body that I've actually got flesh and clothes; you never expected to see me in such fine condition. Don't you recognize your old shadow? To be sure, you certainly never thought I should ever come back. Things have gone wonderfully well with me since I was with you last, and I have become very well-to-do in every respect. If I wish to buy myself out of service, I have the means." And he rattled a large bunch of valuable seals that hung to his watch, and put his hand to the heavy gold chain that was round his neck: and how his fingers did glitter with diamond rings, and all real too!

"Well, well! I can't get over it," said the learned man. "What does it all mean?"

"I admit, it's by no means an ordinary affair," said the Shadow. "But, then, you yourself are not an ordinary man; and I, as you very well know, have trod in your footsteps from a child. As soon as you found that I was ripe to go out into the world by myself, I went my own way. I am now in the most brilliant circumstances, but there came a sort of longing over me to see you once more before you die, as die you must. I wanted, too, to see this part of the world again, for one has always a fondness for one's Fatherland. I am aware that you have got another shadow in my place; if I have anything to pay, either to it or to you, I hope you will be so good as to let me know."

"Well, and is it really you?" said the scholar. "It is indeed most remarkable! I could never have believed that my old shadow could come back to me as a man."

"Do tell me what I have to pay," said the Shadow; "I don't at all like to be in debt of any kind."

"How can you talk so?" said the learned man. "What debt is there to talk of? Be as free as the next man; I am extraordinarily pleased at your good fortune. Do sit down, old friend, and just tell me a little about how it all came about, and what you saw at the house over the way, out there in the hot country."

"I will tell you," said the Shadow, seating himself; "but you must promise me that you won't tell anyone here in the town, wherever you may meet me, that I was once your Shadow. I have some thoughts of becoming engaged. I could support more families than one."

"Be quite easy," said the scholar; "I won't tell anyone who you really are. Here's my hand on it. I promise it, and one man, one word, you know." "One word, one shadow," said the Shadow; he was obliged to phrase it so.

It was indeed most remarkable to see how much of a man the Shadow was: all dressed out in the finest possible black broadcloth, with varnished boots and a hat that would shut up so that it was only crown and brim, not to speak of what we know already, the seals, the gold chain, and the diamond rings. The Shadow was, in fact, extraordinarily well dressed, and this was just what made him a complete man.

"Now I'll tell you my story," said the Shadow, planting his feet, in the varnished boots, as firmly as he could on the arm of the learned man's new shadow, which lay at his feet like a poodle dog: and this was either out of pride or perhaps in hopes of getting it to stick to him; while the prostrate shadow kept very quiet in order to listen, for it wanted to know how a shadow could get free as this one had done, and work up to be its own master.

"Do you know who it was that lived in the house over the way?" said the Shadow. "It was the most beautiful thing there is: it was Poetry. I was there for three weeks, and the effect was the same as if one had spent three thousand years in reading everything that has been sung and written. I say it, and it is the truth. I have seen everything, and I know everything."

"Poetry!" cried the learned man. "Yes! Yes! She often dwells, a hermit, in great cities. Poetry! I saw her for one single brief moment, but my eyes were full of sleep. She was standing on the balcony and shining as the Northern Lights shine. Tell me, tell me of her. Thou wast on the balcony, thou wentest through the door, then—" "Then I was in the ante-room," said the Shadow. "You were always sitting looking across at the ante-room. There was no light there at all; there was a sort of twilight, but one door stood open, leading straight to a second, and into a long row of rooms and halls. There was light there. I should have been killed outright by the light, had I gone in to where the maiden was, but I was careful, I gave myself time—as indeed one must."

"And what sawest thou then?" asked the scholar.

"I saw everything, and I will tell you about it. But—it isn't that I'm in the least proud—but considering I'm a free man, and what accomplishments I possess, not to mention my good position and my very easy circumstances—I should very much prefer you to address me as 'you.' "

"I beg your pardon," said the scholar; "it's merely old habit which sticks by me. You're perfectly right, and I shall keep it in mind. But now, do tell me everything you saw."

"Everything!" said the Shadow. "For I saw everything and I know everything."

"What was it like in the innermost hall?" asked the scholar. "Was it like being in the green wood? Was it like a solemn temple? Were the halls like the starlit sky seen from the top of the high mountains?" "Everything was there," said the Shadow; "I didn't go absolutely in, I stayed in the room next to it in the twilight, but I was admirably placed, and saw everything and know everything. I have been in the court of Poetry, in the ante-chamber."

"But what did you see? Did all the gods of ancient days pass through the vast halls? Did the heroes of old times fight their battles there? Were there lovely children playing and telling of their dreams?"

"I tell you I was there, and you may imagine I saw everything there was to be seen. Had you been over there you would not have turned into a man, but I did; and, moreover, I learned to know my innermost nature, all that was inborn in me, the kinship I had with Poetry. When I was with you I never thought about it, but, as you know, every time the sun rose or set I used to become amazingly large. In the moonlight, indeed, I was almost plainer to be seen than you yourself. At that time I did not comprehend my own nature, but in that ante-room it became clear to me; I became a man. When I came out I was matured, but you were no longer in the hot countries. I was ashamed, as a man, to go about as I was. I needed boots and clothes and all the human paraphernalia that make a man recognizable. I made my way (I tell you this, you won't put it in a book), I made my way to the cake-woman's skirt, and hid myself under it. Little did the woman think how great a thing she had in hiding, and not till the evening did I come out. I ran along the street in the moonlight. I stretched myself right up the wall (it tickles one in the back deliciously). I ran up, I ran down; I peeped through the topmost windows, into the rooms, on to the roof. I peeped where no one else could, and saw what nobody else saw, and what nobody was meant to see. Take it all round, the world's a mean place. I wouldn't have become a man if it hadn't been generally assumed that it's a good thing to be one. I saw the most incredible things, among wives, among husbands, among parents and among those darling admirable children. I saw," said the Shadow, "what no human being was allowed to know, but what everybody very much wants to know, that is their neighbours' wrongdoings. If I'd written a newspaper it would have been read, I tell you! But I wrote direct to the people concerned, and there was a panic in every town I visited. They were terribly afraid of me, and they became amazingly fond of me. The professors made me a professor, the tailors gave me new clothes. I'm admirably fitted out. The master of the mint coined money for me, and the women said I was very good-looking. In this way I became the man I am. And now I must bid you good-bye. Here's my card; I live on the sunny side, and I'm always at home when it rains." And off went the Shadow.

"That is a most remarkable affair," said the learned man.

A year and a day passed, and the Shadow came again. "How goes it?" he asked.

"Alas!" said the learned man. "I write about the true and the good and the beautiful. But nobody cares to hear about such things, and I'm quite in despair. I feel it very keenly."

"But I don't," said the Shadow; "I'm getting fat and that's what everybody ought to try to be. You don't understand the way of the world, you know; you'll get quite ill like this, you ought to travel. I'm going to travel this summer; will you come with me? I should like to have a companion; will you go with me as my shadow? It'll be a real pleasure to have you with me, and I'll pay expenses."

"That's going a bit too far," said the learned man.

"Why, that's as you take it," said the Shadow. "It'll do you all the good in the world to travel. If you'll be my shadow you shan't have a penny to pay for the trip."

"That's absolute madness!" said the learned man.

"But after all, the world's like that," said the Shadow, "and so it always will be." And off he went.

The learned man was in a bad way: sorrow and trouble were on him, and as for his talk about the true and the beautiful and the good, most people appreciated it as a cow does roses. At last he became quite ill. "You really look like a shadow," people said to him; and the learned man shivered, for it was exactly what he was thinking.

"You ought to take some baths," said the Shadow, who paid him a visit. "There's nothing else for it. I'll take you with me for old acquaintance sake. I'll pay expenses, and you shall write a description and amuse me with it on the journey. I'm going to the baths, for my beard won't grow as it should, and that is an ailment; one must have a beard. Now do be reasonable and accept my invitation; we'll travel as friends."

So they set off. The Shadow was the master and the master was the shadow. They drove together, they rode and walked together side by side or in front or behind, according as the sun shone. The Shadow was always careful to keep in the master's place, and the learned man didn't really think much about that; he was a very good soul, extremely kind and friendly. And so one day said he to the Shadow: "As we've become travelling companions (as we are) and as we've grown up together from childhood, wouldn't it be nice to drink brotherhood, and call each other 'thou'. It's more sociable, isn't it?"

"Now you're talking," said the Shadow (who was in fact the master). "What you say is very frank and very well meant. I'll be equally frank and well meaning. You as a scholar know very well what an odd thing Nature is. Some people can't bear to touch brown paper, it makes them sick; others feel it all over their body when someone scratches a pane of glass with a nail. Now I get just that sensation when I hear you say 'thou' to me. I feel absolutely as if I were crushed down on the ground, as I was in my first situation with you. You understand, it's merely a sensation, not pride at all. I can't bear you saying 'thou' to me, but I'll gladly say 'thou' to you; and that's meeting you halfway."

So the Shadow addressed his former master as "thou."

"Upon my word, it's rather much," thought the learned man, "that I should have to say 'you' and he should say 'thou'." But he had to put up with it.

Eventually they came to a watering-place where there were a number of visitors, and among them a beautiful Princess, who was suffering from the complaint of seeing too well; which is, of course, very distressing.

She noticed at once that the newcomer was a very different sort of person from all the rest. "People say he has come here to get his beard to grow, but I can see the real reason. He can't cast a shadow."

Her curiosity was roused, and very soon she got into conversation with the strange gentleman, on the promenade. Being a Princess, she did not need to beat about the bush, so she said: "What's the matter with you is that you can't cast a shadow."

"Your Royal Highness must be considerably better," said the Shadow. "I am aware that your complaint is that you see too well; but it has yielded, and you are cured. I have, in fact, a quite unusual shadow. Do you see the person who always goes about with me? Other people have an ordinary shadow, but I don't care about what is ordinary. You give your servant finer clothes for his livery than you wear yourself, and just so I have had my shadow smartened up into a man. What's more, you can see that I have even given him a shadow. It costs money, but I do like to have something peculiar to myself."

"What!" thought the Princess. "Can I really have recovered? These baths are the best that exist! Waters certainly have an amazing power in these days. Still, I shan't go away; it's becoming lively here. I have an extraordinary liking for that stranger. I only hope his beard won't grow, for he'll go away if it does."

In the evening the Princess and the Shadow danced together in the great ball-room. She was light, but he was lighter, and such a partner she had never had. She told him what country she came from, and he knew it; he had been there, but at a time when she was not at home. He had peeped in at windows, upstairs and downstairs, and seen one thing and another, and so he could answer the Princess's questions and give her information that quite astounded her. He must be the wisest man on earth, she thought, and she conceived the greatest respect for his knowledge; and when they danced together a second time she fell in love with him. Of this the Shadow was well aware, for she gazed at him as if she would see through him. Yet once again they danced together, and she was on the point of speaking out. But she was careful. She thought of her country and realm and the many people she had to govern. "Wise he is," she thought to herself; "and that is a good point. He dances beautifully, and that's another. But is his knowledge thorough? That's equally important; that must be sifted." So she began very gradually to put to him some of the very most difficult questions, things she couldn't have answered herself, and the Shadow pulled a very odd face.

"Can't you answer me that?" asked the Princess.

"That was part of my nursery lessons," said the Shadow. "I really believe my shadow there behind the door can answer that."

"Your shadow?" said the Princess. "That would be most remarkable."

"Well, I don't say for certain that he can," said the Shadow, "but I think it, seeing he has been following me and listening to me all these years—I do think it. But your Royal Highness will permit me to call your attention to the fact that he takes such pride in passing for a man, that if he's to be in the right temper (as he must be to answer properly), he must be treated exactly like a man." "I'm perfectly agreeable to that," said the Princess. So she went across to the learned man at the door and talked to him about the sun and the moon, and about human nature, both outward and inward, and he answered her most wisely and well.

"What a man must he be who has so wise a shadow!" thought she. "It would be a real blessing for my people and my realm if I chose him for my consort. I will!"

And very soon they were agreed, the Princess and the Shadow, but no one was to know of it till she got back to her own kingdom.

"No one, not even my shadow," said the Shadow, who had his own thoughts about the matter.

And now they were in the country over which the Princess ruled when she was at home.

"Listen, my good friend," said the Shadow to the learned man. "I am now become as fortunate and as powerful as anyone can be, and now I will do something special for you. You shall always live with me in the palace, and drive out with me in my royal coach, and you shall have a hundred thousand rix-dollars a year. But you must allow yourself to be called a shadow by everyone, you must never say that you were at one time a man, and once a year, when I sit on the balcony in the sunshine and allow myself to be looked at, you must lie at my feet as a shadow ought to do. I may as well tell you that I am going to marry the Princess. The wedding is to take place this evening."

"No, no! That is really too much," said the learned man. "I won't allow it. I won't do it! It's deceiving the whole country and the Princess too. I shall tell the whole story—that I am the man and you are the shadow; you're only dressed up."

"Nobody will believe it," said the Shadow. "Do be reasonable, or I shall call the guard."

"I shall go straight to the Princess," said the learned man. "But I shall go first," said the Shadow, "and you'll go to prison." And there he had to go, for the sentries obeyed the one whom they knew the Princess was to marry.

"You are all in a tremble," said the Princess, when the Shadow came into her room. "Has anything happened? You mustn't be ill tonight; we're going to be married."

"I have had the most terrible experience that can occur to anyone," said the Shadow. "Only think of it—to be sure, a poor shadow's brain isn't equal to the strain—only think, my shadow has gone mad! He believes that he is the man and that I—just think of it—am his shadow!"

"That is awful," said the Princess; "I hope he is shut up?"

"Indeed he is. I'm afraid he'll never get the better of it."

"Poor shadow," said the Princess; "it's most unfortunate for him. It would really be a kindness to rid him of his little bit of life: indeed, when I come to think of it, I do believe it is essential that he should be quite quietly put out of the way."

"It's really very hard!" said the Shadow. "He was a faithful servant to me," and with that he seemed to sigh.

"You are a noble character," said the Princess.

That evening the whole town was illuminated, and the cannons went off "Boom!" And the soldiers presented arms. It *was* a wedding, to be sure! The Princess and the Shadow went out on the balcony to show themselves and receive one last "Hurrah!"

The learned man heard nothing of all this, for he had already been executed.

CHARLES DICKENS

✳

The Signal-Man

(1866)

Charles Dickens (1812–1870) published his fantastic tales in small magazines (for which he was often both editor and primary contributor) that printed serialized novels and short stories. His best story in the genre, "The Signal-Man," appeared in 1866 in All the Year Round. *It is an extremely dense and compact tale; the action takes place amid rails and train noises, with sunsets over the desolate landscape of railheads and figures glimpsed just beyond the embankments. The industrial world as the setting now enters literature: we find ourselves far away from the visions of the first half of the century. The fantastic becomes a professional nightmare.*

"HALLOA! Below there!"

When he heard a voice thus calling to him, he was standing at the door of his box, with a flag in his hand, furled around its short pole. One would have thought, considering the nature of the ground, that he could not have doubted from what quarter the voice came; but, instead of looking up to where I stood on the top of the steep cutting nearly over his head, he turned himself about, and looked down the Line. There was something remarkable in his manner of doing so, though I could not have said for my life what. But I know it was remarkable enough to attract my notice, even though his figure was foreshortened and shadowed, down in the deep trench, and mine was high above him, so steeped in the glow of an angry sunset, that I had shaded my eyes with my hand before I saw him at all.

"Halloa! Below!"

From looking down the Line, he turned himself about again, and, raising his eyes, saw my figure high above him.

"Is there any path by which I can come down and speak to you?"

He looked up at me without replying, and I looked down at him without pressing him too soon with a repetition of my idle question. Just then there came a vague vibration in the earth and air, quickly changing into a violent pulsation, and an oncoming rush that caused me to start back, as though it had force to draw me down. When such vapor as rose to my height from this rapid train had passed me, and was skimming away over the landscape, I looked down again, and saw him refurling the flag he had shown while the train went by.

I repeated my inquiry. After a pause, during which he seemed to regard me with fixed attention, he motioned with his rolled-up flag towards a point on my level, some two or three hundred yards distant. I called down to him, "All right!" and made for that point. There, by dint of looking closely about me, I found a rough zigzag descending path notched out, which I followed.

The cutting was extremely deep, and unusually precipitate. It was made through a clammy stone that became oozier and wetter as I went down. For these reasons, I found the way long enough to recall a singular air of reluctance or compulsion with which he had pointed out the path.

When I came down low enough upon the zigzag descent to see him again, I saw that he was standing between the rails on the way by which the train had lately passed, in an attitude as if he were waiting for me to appear. He had his left hand at his chin, and that left elbow rested on his right hand, crossed over his breast. His attitude was one of such expectation and watchfulness, that I stopped a moment, wondering at it.

I resumed my downward way, and stepping out upon the level of the railroad, and drawing nearer to him, saw that he was a dark, sallow man, with a dark beard and rather heavy eyebrows. His post was in as solitary and dismal a place as ever I saw. On either side a dripping-wet wall of jagged stone, excluding all view but a strip of sky: the perspective one way only a crooked prolongation of this great dungeon; the shorter perspective in the other direction terminating in a gloomy red light, and the gloomier entrance to a black tunnel, in whose massive architecture there was a barbarous, depressing, and forbidding air. So little sunlight ever found its way to this spot, that it had an earthy, deadly smell; and so much cold wind rushed through it, that it struck chill to me, as if I had left the natural world.

Before he stirred, I was near enough to him to have touched him. Not even then removing his eyes from mine, he stepped back one step, and lifted his hand.

This was a lonesome post to occupy (I said), and it had riveted my attention when I looked down from up yonder. A visitor was a rarity,

I should suppose; not an unwelcome rarity, I hoped? In me, he merely saw a man who had been shut up within narrow limits all his life, and who, being at last set free, had a newly awakened interest in these great works. To such purpose I spoke to him; but I am far from sure of the terms I used; for, besides that I am not happy in opening any conversation, there was something in the man that daunted me.

He directed a most curious look towards the red light near the tunnel's mouth, and looked all about it, as if something were missing from it, and then looked at me.

That light was part of his charge—was it not?

He answered in a low voice, "Don't you know it is?"

The monstrous thought came into my mind, as I perused the fixed eyes and the saturnine face, that this was a spirit, not a man. I have speculated, since, whether there may have been infection in his mind.

In my turn I stepped back. But, in making the action, I detected in his eyes some latent fear of me. This put the monstrous thought to flight.

"You look at me," I said, forcing a smile, "as if you had a dread of me."

"I was doubtful," he returned, "whether I had seen you before."

"Where?"

He pointed to the red light he had looked at.

"There?" I said.

Intently watchful of me, he replied (but without sound), "Yes."

"My good fellow, what should I do there? However, be that as it may, I never was there, you may swear."

"I think I may," he rejoined. "Yes. I am sure I may."

His manner cleared, like my own. He replied to my remarks with readiness, and in well-chosen words. Had he much to do there? Yes; that was to say, he had enough responsibility to bear; but exactness and watchfulness were what was required of him, and of actual work—manual labor—he had next to none. To change that signal, to trim those lights, and to turn this iron handle now and then, was all he had to do under that head. Regarding those many long and lonely hours of which I seemed to make so much, he could only say that the routine of his life had shaped itself into that form, and he had grown used to it. He had taught himself a language down here, if only to know it by sight, and to have formed his own crude ideas of its pronunciation, could be called learning it. He had also worked at fractions and decimals, and tried a little algebra; but he was, and had been as a boy, a poor hand at figures. Was it necessary for him when on duty always to remain in that channel of damp air, and could he never rise into the sunshine from between those high stone walls? Why, that depended upon times and circumstances. Under some conditions there would be less upon the Line than under others, and the same held good as to certain hours of the day and night. In bright weather, he did choose occasions for getting a little above these lower shadows; but, being at all times liable to be called by his electric bell, and at such times listening for it with redoubled anxiety, the relief was less than I would suppose.

He took me into his box, where there was a fire, a desk for an official book in which he had to make certain entries, a telegraphic instrument with its dial, face, and needles, and the little bell of which he had spoken. On my trusting that he would excuse the remark that he had been well educated, and (I hoped I might say without offence) perhaps educated above that station, he observed that instances of slight incongruity in such wise would rarely be found wanting among large bodies of men; that he had heard it was so in workhouses, in the police force, even in that last desperate resource, the army; and that he knew it was so, more or less, in any great railway staff. He had been, when young (if I could believe it, sitting in that hut, he scarcely could), a student of natural philosophy, and had attended lectures; but he had run wild, misused his opportunities, gone down, and never risen again. He had no complaint to offer about that. He had made his bed, and he lay upon it. It was far too late to make another.

All that I have here condensed he said in a quiet manner, with his grave dark regards divided between me and the fire. He threw in the word, "Sir," from time to time, and especially when he referred to his youth, as though to request me to understand that he claimed to be nothing but what I found him. He was several times interrupted by the little bell, and had to read off messages, and send replies. Once he had to stand without the door, and display a flag as a train passed, and make some verbal communication to the driver. In the discharge of his duties, I observed him to be remarkably exact and vigilant, breaking off his discourse at a syllable, and remaining silent until what he had to do was done.

In a word, I should have set this man down as one of the safest of men to be employed in that capacity, but for the circumstance that while he was speaking to me he twice broke off with a fallen color, turned his face towards the little bell when it did NOT ring, opened the door of the hut (which was kept shut to exclude the unhealthy damp), and looked out towards the red light near the mouth of the tunnel. On both of those occasions he came back to the fire with the inexplicable air upon him which I had remarked, without being able to define, when we were so far asunder.

Said I, when I rose to leave him, "You almost make me think that I have met with a contented man."

(I am afraid I must acknowledge that I said it to lead him on.)

"I believe I used to be so," he rejoined, in the low voice in which he had first spoken; "but I am troubled, sir, I am troubled."

He would have recalled the words if he could. He had said them, however, and I took them up quickly.

"With what? What is your trouble?"

"It is very difficult to impart, sir. It is very, very difficult to speak of. If ever you make me another visit, I will try to tell you."

"But I expressly intend to make you another visit. Say, when shall it be?"

"I go off early in the morning, and I shall be on again at ten to-morrow night, sir."

"I will come at eleven."

He thanked me, and went out at the door with me. "I'll show my white light, sir," he said, in his peculiar low voice, "till you have found the way up. When you have found it, don't call out! And when you are at the top, don't call out!"

His manner seemed to make the place strike colder to me, but I said no more than, "Very well."

"And when you come down to-morrow night, don't call out! Let me ask you a parting question. What made you cry, 'Halloa! Below there!' to-night?"

"Heaven knows," said I. "I cried something to that effect—"

"Not to that effect, sir. Those were the very words. I know them well."

"Admit those were the very words. I said them, no doubt, because I saw you below."

"For no other reason?"

"What other reason could I possibly have?"

"You had no feeling that they were conveyed to you in any supernatural way?"

"No."

He wished me good-night, and held up his light. I walked by the side of the down Line of rails (with a very disagreeable sensation of a train coming behind me) until I found the path. It was easier to mount than to descend, and I got back to my inn without any adventure.

Punctual to my appointment, I placed my foot on the first notch of the zigzag next night as the distant clocks were striking eleven. He was waiting for me at the bottom, with his white light on. "I have not called out," I said, when we came close together; "may I speak now?" "By all means, sir." "Good-night, then, and here's my hand." "Good-night, sir, and here's mine." With that we walked side by side to his box, entered it, closed the door, and sat down by the fire.

"I have made up my mind, sir," he began, bending forward as soon as we were seated, and speaking in a tone but a little above a whisper, "that you shall not have to ask me twice what troubles me. I took you for some one else yesterday evening. That troubles me."

"That mistake?"

"No. That some one else."

"Who is it?"

"I don't know."

"Like me?"

"I don't know. I never saw the face. The left arm is across the face, and the right arm is waved, violently waved. This way."

I followed his action with my eyes, and it was the action of an arm gesticulating with the utmost passion and vehemence, "For God's sake clear the way!"

"One moonlight night," said the man, "I was sitting here, when I heard a voice cry, 'Halloa! Below there!' I started up, looked from that door, and saw this Some one else standing by the red light near the tunnel, waving as I just now showed you. The voice seemed hoarse with shouting, and it cried, 'Look out! Look out!' And then again, 'Halloa! Below there! Look out!' I caught up my lamp, turned it on red, and ran towards the figure, calling, 'What's wrong? What has happened? Where?' It stood just outside the blackness of the tunnel. I advanced so close upon it that I wondered at its keeping the sleeve across its eyes. I ran right up at it, and had my hand stretched out to pull the sleeve away, when it was gone."

"Into the tunnel," said I.

"No. I ran on into the tunnel, five hundred yards. I stopped, and held my lamp above my head, and saw the figures of the measured distance, and saw the wet stains stealing down the walls and trickling through the arch. I ran out again faster than I had run in (for I had a mortal abhorrence of the place upon me), and I looked all round the red light, with my own red light, and I went up the iron ladder to the gallery atop of it, and I came down again, and ran back here. I telegraphed both ways, 'An alarm has been given. Is anything wrong?' The answer came back, both ways, 'All well.' "

Resisting the slow touch of a frozen finger tracing out my spine, I showed him how that this figure must be a deception of his sense of sight; and how that figures, originating in disease of the delicate nerves that minister to the functions of the eye, were known to have often troubled patients, some of whom had become conscious of the nature of their affliction, and had even proved it by experiments upon themselves. "As to an imaginary cry," said I, "do but listen for a moment to the wind in this unnatural valley while we speak so low, and to the wild harp it makes of the telegraph wires!"

That was all very well, he returned, after we had sat listening for a while, and he ought to know something of the wind and wires,—he who so often passed long winter nights there, alone and watching. But he would beg to remark that he had not finished.

I asked his pardon, and he slowly added these words, touching my arm:

"Within six hours after the Appearance, the memorable accident on this Line happened, and within ten hours the dead and wounded were brought along through the tunnel over the spot where the figure had stood."

A disagreeable shudder crept over me, but I did my best against it. It was not to be denied, I rejoined, that this was a remarkable coincidence, calculated deeply to impress his mind. But it was unquestionable that remarkable coincidences did continually occur, and they must be taken into account in dealing with such a subject. Though to be sure I must admit, I added (for I thought I saw that he was going to bring the objection to bear upon me), men of common sense did not allow much for coincidence in making the ordinary calculations of life.

He again begged to remark that he had not finished.

I again begged his pardon for being betrayed into interruptions.

"This," he said, again laying his hand upon my arm, and glancing over his shoulder with hollow eyes, "was just a year ago. Six or seven months passed, and I had recovered from the surprise and shock, when one morning, as the day was breaking, I, standing at that door, looked towards the red light, and saw the spectre again." He stopped, with a fixed look at me.

"Did it cry out?"

"No. It was silent."

"Did it wave its arm?"

"No. It leaned against the shaft of the light, with both hands before the face. Like this."

Once more I followed his action with my eyes. It was an action of mourning; I have seen such an attitude in stone figures on tombs.

"Did you go up to it?"

"I came in and sat down, partly to collect my thoughts, partly because it had turned me faint. When I went to the door again, daylight was above me, and the ghost was gone."

"But nothing followed? Nothing came of this?"

He touched me on the arm with his forefinger twice or thrice, giving a ghastly nod each time.

"That very day, as the train came out of the tunnel, I noticed, at a carriage window on my side, what looked like a confusion of hands and heads, and something waved. I saw it just in time to signal the driver, stop! He shut off, and put his brake on, but the train drifted past here a hundred and fifty yards or more. I ran after it, and, as I went along, heard terrible screams and cries. A beautiful young lady had died instantaneously in one of the compartments, and was brought in here, and laid down on this floor between us."

Involuntarily I pushed my chair back, as I looked from the boards at which he pointed to himself.

"True, sir. True. Precisely as it happened, so I tell it you."

I could think of nothing to say, to any purpose, and my mouth was very dry. The wind and the wires took up the story with a long lamenting wail.

He resumed. "Now, sir, mark this, and judge how my mind is troubled. The spectre came back a week ago. Ever since it has been there, now and again, by fits and starts."

"At the light?"

"At the Danger-light."

"What does it seem to do?"

He repeated, if possible with increased passion and vehemence, that former gesticulation of, "For God's sake, clear the way!"

Then he went on. "I have no peace or rest for it. It calls to me, for many minutes together, in an agonized manner, 'Below there! Look out! Look out!' It stands waving to me. It rings my little bell—"

I caught at that. "Did it ring your bell yesterday evening when I was here, and you went to the door?"

"Twice."

"Why, see," said I, "how your imagination misleads you. My eyes were on the bell, and my ears were open to the bell, and if I am a living man, it did NOT ring at those times. No, nor at any other time, except when it was rung in the natural course of physical things by the station communicating with you."

He shook his head. "I have never made a mistake as to that yet, sir. I have never confused the spectre's ring with the man's. The ghost's ring is a strange vibration in the bell that it derives from nothing else, and I have not asserted that the bell stirs to the eye. I don't wonder that you failed to hear it. But *I* heard it."

"And did the spectre seem to be there, when you looked out?"

"It WAS there."

"Both times?"

He repeated firmly: "Both times."

"Will you come to the door with me and look for it now?"

He bit his under lip as though he were somewhat unwilling, but arose. I opened the door, and stood on the step, while he stood in the doorway. There was the Danger-light. There was the dismal mouth of the tunnel. There were the high, wet stone walls of the cutting. There were the stars above them.

"Do you see it?" I asked him, taking particular note of his face. His eyes were prominent and strained, but not very much more so, perhaps, than my own had been when I had directed them earnestly towards the same spot.

"No," he answered. "It is not there."

"Agreed," said I.

We went in again, shut the door, and resumed our seats. I was thinking how best to improve this advantage, if it might be called one, when he took up the conversation in such a matter-of-course way, so assuming that there could be no serious question of fact between us, that I felt myself placed in the weakest of positions.

"By this time, you will fully understand, sir," he said, "that what troubles me so dreadfully is the question, What does the sceptre mean?"

I was not sure, I told him, that I did fully understand.

"What is its warning against?" he said, ruminating, with his eyes on the fire, and only by times turning them on me. "What is the danger? Where is the danger? There is danger overhanging somewhere on the Line. Some dreadful calamity will happen. It is not to be doubted this third time, after what has gone before. But surely this is a cruel haunting of *me*. What can *I* do?"

He pulled out his handkerchief, and wiped the drops from his heated forehead.

"If I telegraph Danger, on either side of me, or on both, I can give no reason for it," he went on, wiping the palms of his hands. I should get into trouble, and do no good. They would think I was mad. This is the way it would work, Message: 'Danger! Take care!' Answered: 'What Danger? Where?' Message: 'Don't know. But for God's sake, take care!' They would displace me. What else could they do?"

His pain of mind was most pitiable to see. It was the mental torture of a conscientious man, oppressed beyond endurance by an unintelligible responsibility involving life.

"When it first stood under the Danger-light," he went on, putting his dark hair back from his head, and drawing his hands outward across and across his temples in an extremity of feverish distress, "why not tell me where that accident was to happen, if it must happen? Why not tell me how it could be averted, if it could have been averted? When on its second coming it hid its face, why not tell me, instead, 'She is going to die. Let them keep her at home'? If it came, on those two occasions, only to show me that its warnings were true, and so to prepare me for the third, why not warn me plainly now? And I, Lord help me! A mere poor signal-man on this solitary station! Why not go to somebody with credit to be believed, and power to act?"

When I saw him in this state, I saw that for the poor man's sake, as well as for the public safety, what I had to do for the time was to compose his mind. Therefore, setting aside all question of reality or unreality between us, I represented to him that whoever thoroughly discharged his duty must do well, and that at least it was his comfort that he understood his duty, though he did not understand these confounding Appearances. In this effort I succeeded far better than in the attempt to reason him out of his conviction. He became calm; the occupations incidental to his post as the night advanced began to make larger demands on his attention; and I left him at two in the morning. I had offered to stay through the night, but he would not hear of it.

That I more than once looked back at the red light as I ascended the pathway; that I did not like the red light, and that I should have slept but poorly if my bed had been under it, I see no reason to conceal. Nor did I like the two sequences of the accident and the dead girl. I see no reason to conceal that, either.

But what ran most in my thoughts was the consideration, how ought I to act, having become the recipient of this disclosure? I had proved the man to be intelligent, vigilant, painstaking, and exact; but how long might he remain so, in his state of mind? Though in a subordinate position, still he held a most important trust, and would I (for instance) like to stake my own life on the chances of his continuing to execute it with precision?

Unable to overcome a feeling that there would be something treacherous in my communicating what he had told me to his superiors in the Company, without first being plain with himself and proposing a middle course to him, I ultimately resolved to offer to accompany him (otherwise keeping his secret for the present) to the wisest medical practitioner we could hear of in those parts, and to take his opinion. A change in his time of duty would come round next night, he had apprised me, and he would be off an hour or two after sunrise, and on again soon after sunset. I had appointed to return accordingly.

Next evening was a lovely evening, and I walked out early to enjoy it. The sun was not yet quite down when I traversed the field-path near the top of the deep cutting. I would extend my walk for an hour, I said to myself, half an hour on and half an hour back, and it would then be time to go to my signal-man's box.

Before pursuing my stroll, I stepped to the brink, and mechanically looked down, from the point from which I had first seen him. I cannot describe the thrill that seized upon me, when, close at the mouth of the tunnel, I saw the appearance of a man, with his left sleeve across his eyes, passionately waving his right arm.

The nameless horror that oppressed me passed in a moment, for in a moment I saw that this appearance of a man was a man indeed, and that there was a little group of other men, standing at a short distance, to whom he seemed to be rehearsing the gesture he made. The Danger-light was not yet lighted. Against its shaft, a little low hut, entirely new to me, had been made of some wooden supports and tarpaulin. It looked no bigger than a bed.

With an irresistible sense that something was wrong—with a flashing self-reproachful fear that fatal mischief had come of my leaving the man there, and causing no one to be sent to overlook or correct what he did—I descended the notched path with all the speed I could make.

"What is the matter?" I asked the men.

"Signal-man killed this morning, sir."

"Not the man belonging to that box?"

"Yes, sir."

"Not the man I know?"

"You will recognize him, sir, if you knew him," said the man who spoke for the others, solemnly uncovering his own head and raising an end of the tarpaulin, "for his face is quite composed."

"O, how did this happen, how did this happen?" I asked, turning from one to another as the hut closed in again.

"He was cut down by an engine, sir. No man in England knew his work better, but somehow he was not clear of the outer rail. It was just at broad day. He had struck the light, and had the lamp in his hand. As the engine came out of the tunnel, his back was towards her, and she cut him down. That man drove her, and was showing how it happened. Show the gentleman, Tom."

The man, who wore a rough dark dress, stepped back to his former place at the mouth of the tunnel:

"Coming round the curve in the tunnel, sir," he said, "I saw him at the end, like as if I saw him down a perspective-glass. There was no time to check speed, and I knew him to be very careful. As he didn't seem to take heed of the whistle, I shut it off when we were running down upon him, and called to him as loud as I could call."

"What did you say?"

"I said, 'Below there! Look out! Look out! For God's sake, clear the way!' "

I started.

"Ah! it was a dreadful time, sir. I never left off calling to him. I put this arm before my eyes not to see, and I waved this arm to the last; but it was no use."

WITHOUT PROLONGING THE narrative to dwell on any one of its curious circumstances more than any other, I may, in closing it, point out the coincidence that the warning of the Engine-Driver included not only the words which the unfortunate Signal-man had repeated to me as haunting him, but also the words which I myself—not he—had attached, and that only in my own mind, to the gesticulation he had imitated.

IVAN SERGEYEVICH TURGENEV

❋

The Dream

(Son, 1876)

Turgenev (1818–1883) cannot be called a writer of fantastic literature, because the number of stories he wrote in the genre can be counted with the fingers of one hand. "The Dream" is a tale whose ambiguity is perfect. It maintains the uncertainty whether the mysterious character is dead or alive, an uncertainty that continues in the extremely beautiful final scene involving the body on the algae-covered beach.

Aside from being an example of psychological modernity, uncommon in its time and announcing themes psychoanalysis would render canonical, this story presents us with one of the rare cases of a written dream that resembles the dreams we really have.

I

I WAS LIVING at that time with my mother in a small seaside town. I had turned seventeen, while my mother was not yet thirty-five; she had married very young. When my father died I was just six, but I remembered him well. My mother was a small, fair-haired woman, with a delightful face which was, however, perpetually sad. She had a quiet, languid voice, and was timid in her movements. In her youth she had been renowned for her beauty and to the end she remained attractive and lovely. I have never seen deeper, sadder or more tender eyes, nor have I seen more graceful hands. I adored her, and she loved me. . . . But the life we led was not a merry one. Some secret, incurable and undeserved sorrow seemed to be constantly gnawing away at the very root of her existence. This sorrow was not to be explained as mere sadness about my father, however great that sadness was, however passionately my mother had loved him, however sacred the memory she kept of him. . . . No! There was something else hidden there, something I did not understand, but which I felt, felt confusedly and strongly, as soon as I looked at those quiet eyes which did not move, at those beautiful lips which did not move either, and which were not set tight in bitterness but were seemingly frozen still forever.

I have said that my mother loved me. Yet there were moments when she pushed me away, when my presence was burdensome to her, unbearable. At such times she felt, as it were, an involuntary disgust for me—and later she would feel horrified, blame herself tearfully, and press me to her heart. I put these momentary outbursts of hostility down to the breakdown in her health, to her misfortune. . . . It is true that these hostile feelings may have been prompted to some extent by certain strange fits of evil and criminal feelings which surged up in me from time to time and which I myself did not comprehend. . . . But these fits did not coincide with those moments of disgust. My mother always wore black, as if in mourning. We lived quite grandly, although we were on close terms with almost nobody.

II

All my mother's plans and cares were concentrated on me. Her life had merged with mine. That kind of relationship between parents and children is not always healthy for the children . . . rather is it harmful. Apart from that, I was all my mother had, and almost all only children grow up badly. As they bring them up, the parents worry as much about themselves as about the child. This was not the case here. I was not spoilt and I did not become hard (both occur in such children), but my nerves gave out prematurely; in addition I had a fairly weak constitution—in this I took after my mother, and I looked very like her as well. I avoided the company of children my own age; indeed, I shunned people in general. I even talked little with my mother. More than anything I loved to read, to take walks alone—and to dream, to dream! It is difficult to say exactly what I dreamed of: sometimes, it's true, I seemed to see myself standing in front of a half-closed door behind which unknown mysteries were hidden, I would stand, and wait, and fall into a trance—and not cross the threshold—and keep imagining what was ahead—and I would keep waiting with sinking heart . . . or go to sleep. If I had had a poetic streak in me, I would no doubt have taken to writing verse; if I had felt any inclination towards the religious life, I might have become a monk; but there was none of this in me, and I continued to dream—and wait.

III

I have just mentioned how I would fall asleep sometimes under the influence of vague thoughts and reveries. I always slept a lot, and dreams played an important part in my life. I dreamt almost every night. I did not forget my dreams, I attributed some significance to them, I considered them predictions, trying to unravel their mysterious meaning; from time to time I would have the same dream over again, which always seemed surprising and odd to me. There was one dream in particular which disturbed me. I seemed to be walking along a narrow, badly paved street in an old city, between stone houses several storeys high with pointed roofs. I was searching for my father, who had not died, but was for some reason hiding from us and living in one of these houses. I now stepped into a low, dark gateway, crossed a long courtyard covered in piles of logs and boards, and finally entered a small room with two round windows. In the middle of the room stood my father in a dressing-gown, smoking a pipe. He was not at all like my real father: he was tall, drawn, black-haired, and had a hooked nose, and sullen and penetrating eyes; he appeared to be about forty. He was not pleased that I had found him; nor was I at all happy at our meeting—I stood baffled. He would turn away slightly, begin to mumble something and walk backwards and forwards with small steps. Then he would move away a little, mumbling all the while and now and then looking round over his shoulder; the room expanded and disappeared in a fog. . . . Suddenly I would become fearful at the thought that I was losing my father again, I would rush after him—but I could no longer see him—and I could only hear his muttering, angry like a bear's. . . . My heart would sink—I would awake and not be able to go to sleep again for a long time. . . . All the following day I would think about the dream and, naturally, not arrive at any conclusions.

IV

June arrived. At about this time of the year the town my mother and I lived in livened up enormously. A multitude of ships docked at the wharf, a multitude of new faces appeared on the streets. It was then that I loved to wander along the quay, past the coffee-houses and hotels, contemplating the multifarious figures of the sailors and other people sitting under the canvas awnings at small white tables with tin mugs in front of them, brim-full of beer.

Once, when passing a certain coffee-house, I caught sight of a man who immediately riveted my whole attention. Dressed in a long, black, loose garment, with a straw hat pulled down over his eyes, he was sitting quite still, his arms crossed on his chest. Thin curling strands of black hair fell almost down to his nose; his thin lips clenched the mouthpiece of a short pipe. This man seemed so familiar to me, every line of his dark, sallow face, his whole figure was so stamped beyond doubt in my memory, that I couldn't help coming to a halt in front of him, couldn't help asking myself the question: who is this man? where have I seen him? Probably feeling my stare, he lifted his black, sharp eyes. . . . I gave an involuntary cry. . . .

This man was the father I had been seeking and seen in my dream!

There was no possibility of a mistake—the likeness was too striking. Even the long-skirted garment draping his thin limbs was reminiscent in its colour and the way it hung of the gown my father had appeared to me in.

"I must be asleep," I thought. . . . No. . . . It was broad daylight; I was surrounded by the noisy crowd, the sun was shining brightly in the blue sky, and in front of me was, not a ghost, but a live man.

I went up to a table, ordered a mug of beer and a newspaper—and sat down a short distance from the enigmatic being.

V

Raising the newspaper level with my face I continued avidly to take in everything about the stranger. He made almost no movement, only occasionally lifting his downcast head. He was obviously waiting for somebody. I kept watching, watching. . . . It sometimes seemed to me that I had dreamt it all up, that there wasn't really any likeness at all, that I had given in to a half-involuntary deception of the imagination . . . but the man would suddenly turn a little on his chair or lift his hands slightly—and again I would almost let out a cry and again see before me my "nocturnal" father! Finally he noticed my persistent attention, and at first in bafflement, and then with annoyance he glanced in my direction, made to get up—and knocked over a small cane he had leant against the table. I instantly leapt up, picked it up and gave it to him. My heart was beating hard.

He gave me a strained smile, thanked me and, bringing his face up close to mine, raised his eyebrows and parted his lips a little, as if struck by something.

"That's very courteous of you, young man," he said suddenly in a dry, sharp, and nasal voice. "Nowadays that's rare. Let me congratulate you on being so well brought up."

I don't remember exactly how I replied; but we soon struck up a conversation. I discovered that he was a countryman of mine and that he had recently come back from America, where he had lived for many years and would soon set out for again. He called himself baron . . . but I didn't catch the name properly. Just like my "nocturnal" father he finished every statement by muttering indistinctly to himself. He asked if he might know my name. When he heard it, he again appeared astounded; then he asked me if I had lived in the town for a long time and with whom. I replied that I lived with my mother.

—And what about your father?

—My father died a long time ago.

He inquired about my mother's Christian name and immediately broke into awkward laughter—and then excused himself, saying that it was an American habit of his and that he was on the whole quite an eccentric. Then he showed some interest in knowing where our apartment was. I told him.

VI

The excitement which had gripped me at the beginning of our conversation had gradually abated. I was finding our rapprochement somewhat strange, but that was all. I did not like the little smile with which the baron questioned me; nor did I like the expression in his eyes which I felt to be stabbing into me. There was something predatory and supercilious . . . something horrible in them. I had not seen these eyes in my dream. The baron had a strange face! It was drained of colour, tired, and at the same time youngish, unpleasantly youngish! Neither had my "nocturnal" father had the deep scar which cut across the forehead of my new acquaintance at an angle and which I hadn't noticed until I moved up closer to him.

I had not had time to finish telling the baron the name of the street and the number of the house where we lived, when a tall negro, wrapped in a cloak right up to his eyes, came up to him from behind and tapped him on the shoulder. The baron turned around and said: "Aha! About time!" and, giving me a slight nod, went off with the negro into the coffee-house. I stayed outside under the awning. I wanted to wait for the baron to come back out, not so much for the purpose of starting up a conversation with him again (I didn't actually know what I could converse with him about) as for the purpose of checking again my first impression. However, half an hour went by, and then an hour. . . . There was no sign of the baron. I went into the coffee-house and quickly went around all the rooms—but couldn't see the baron or the negro anywhere. They must both have left through a back door.

My head had begun to ache a little, and so, to get some fresh air, I set off along the seafront towards the spacious park outside the town, laid out some two hundred years earlier. After walking for two hours or so in the shade of the huge oaks and plane trees, I returned home.

VII

Our maid rushed to meet me, greatly alarmed, as soon as I appeared in the entrance-hall. I immediately guessed by the expression on her face that while I had been away something bad had happened in our house. And it proved to be so: I learnt that an hour earlier there had suddenly been a terrible cry from my mother's bedroom; the maid, on rushing in, had found her on the floor unconscious. She had remained unconscious for several minutes. Eventually my mother had regained her senses, but she had been forced to take to her bed and had looked frightened and queer; she had not said a word or answered questions, she had just kept looking around her and quivering. The maid had sent the gardener for the doctor. The doctor had come and prescribed a sedative; but my mother had refused to say anything even to him. The gardener affirmed that several moments after the cry had rung out in my mother's room, he had caught sight of an unfamiliar figure running in haste across the garden beds towards the gate into the street. (We lived in a single-storey house whose windows opened onto a fairly large garden.) The gardener had not had time to get a good look at the man's face; but he had appeared thin, and had been wearing a low straw hat and a long overcoat. . . . "The baron's clothes!" I thought in a flash. The gardener had not been able to catch up with him; besides, he had soon been called into the house and sent for the doctor. I went into my mother's room; she was lying on her bed, paler than the pillow on which her head was resting. Recognizing me, she gave a weak smile and stretched out her hand to me. I sat down beside her and began asking her questions. At first she would not answer; however, she finally admitted that she had seen something which had very much frightened her. "Did someone come in here?" I asked. "No," she answered hurriedly, "no one came, but I seemed to see . . . there appeared to me . . ." She fell silent and covered her eyes with her hand. I was on the point of telling her what I had learnt from the gardener, and at the same time tell her of my meeting with the baron, but for some reason the words died away on my lips. However, I did venture to remark that visions don't appear by day. . . . "Leave me be," she whispered, "I beg of you. Don't torture me now. One day you'll know. . . ." She fell silent again. Her hands were cold, and her pulse was beating quickly and unevenly. I gave her some medicine to drink and moved away from her a little so as not to disturb her. She remained in bed the whole day. She lay motionless and quiet, only giving an occasional deep sigh and opening her eyes fearfully. The whole household was baffled.

VIII

By nightfall Mother had become slightly feverish, and she sent me away. However, I didn't go away to my own room, but lay down on a sofa in the room next to hers. Every quarter of an hour I would get up, tiptoe to her door and listen. . . . Everything remained silent—but my mother hardly went to sleep at all that night. When I went in to her early the next morning, her face appeared inflamed and her eyes had an unnatural gleam. In the course of the day she found some relief, but towards evening her temperature went up again. Until that time she had remained stubbornly silent, but now she suddenly began talking in a hurried, jerky voice. She was not delirious, there was sense in what she said—but she spoke disjointedly. Suddenly, not long before midnight, she sat up in bed with a convulsive movement (I was sitting beside her) and in the same hurried voice, all the time taking gulps of water from a glass, waving her arms around feebly and without once looking at me, she began to tell a story. . . . She would stop, make an effort and continue again. . . . It was all so strange, just as if she were acting it all out in her sleep, as if she herself were not there and someone else were speaking with her lips or forcing her to speak.

IX

"Listen to what I'm going to tell you," she began, "you're no longer a young boy, it's time you knew everything. I had a good friend. . . . She married a man she loved with all her heart—and she was very happy with her husband. During the first year of their marriage, they went together to the capital to spend a few weeks there and enjoy themselves. They put up in a good hotel and went out a lot to theatres and gatherings. My friend was very good-looking—everyone noticed her and young men courted her favour—but amongst them there was a certain . . . officer. He was inseparable from her, following her everywhere, and wherever she was, she saw his black, evil eyes. He didn't introduce himself to her and never once spoke to her—just kept looking at her—so insolently and strangely. All the pleasures of the capital were poisoned by his presence—she began to urge her husband to leave as soon as they could—and they were already preparing to leave. On one occasion her husband went off to the club: he had been invited by some officers—from the same regiment as the other officer—for a game of cards. . . . For the first time she was left alone. Her husband was away for a long time—she dismissed the maid and went to bed. . . . And suddenly she was gripped by such terror, that she actually went quite cold and began shaking. She thought she heard a light knocking on the other side of the wall—it sounded like a dog scratching—and began looking at the wall. In the corner a lamp was burning; the walls were all covered in silk damask. . . . Suddenly something over there moved, rose up, opened up. . . . And from right out of the wall, tall, all in black, came that terrible man with the evil eyes! She wanted to cry out but couldn't. She froze from fright. He came up to her quickly, like a predatory animal, threw something over her head, something smothering, heavy, white. . . . What happened next I don't remember. . . . I don't remember! It was like death, like murder. . . . When the terrible fog finally cleared—when I . . . when my friend came to her senses, there was no one in the room. For a long time she didn't have the strength to cry out, then at last she gave a cry. . . . Then once more everything became confused.

"Then she saw beside her her husband, who had been detained at the club until two o'clock in the morning. He was in a terrible state. He started to ask her questions, but she told him nothing. Then she became quite ill. However, I recall that once she was alone in the room she examined the place in the wall. . . . Under the damask wall-covering there turned out to be a concealed door. And from her own hand her engagement ring had disappeared. This ring had an unusual shape: there were seven gold stars on it alternating with seven silver ones; it was one of the old family valuables. Her husband asked her what had become of the ring: she could not give him an answer. Her husband thought that she had somehow dropped it, searched everywhere, but couldn't find it anywhere. He found himself in a state of anguish, he determined to leave for home as soon as possible, and as soon as the doctor gave his permission—they left the capital. . . . But imagine! On the very day they left they suddenly came upon a stretcher in the street. On the stretcher lay a man who had just been killed, with his head split open—and imagine!—this man was the selfsame terrible night visitor with the evil eyes! They had killed him while they were playing cards. . . .

"Then my friend went away to the country . . . she became a mother for the first time . . . and lived there with her husband for several years. He never found out anything, and anyway what could she have told him? She herself knew nothing.

"But their former happiness had gone. Their life became dark and the darkness was now quite unbroken. . . . There were no other children, either before or after . . . and this son . . ."

My mother began trembling and covered her face with her hands. . . .

"But I ask you," she went on with renewed strength, "my friend wasn't in any way to blame, was she? What could she have reproached herself with? She was punished, but does she not have the right to declare before God Himself that the punishment which befell her was unjust? Why should the past be able to come to her after so many years in such a terrible light, as to a criminal tortured by the pangs of conscience? Macbeth killed Banquo, so it's not surprising that he should imagine he saw . . . but I . . ."

But at this point my mother's speech became so confused and mixed up that I could no longer understand her. . . . I was no longer in any doubt that she was delirious.

X

Anyone can readily understand what a staggering impression my mother's story made on me! From the very first word she spoke I surmised that she was speaking about herself and not about some friend of hers; her slip of the tongue only confirmed my surmise. Thus it really was the father I had searched for in my dream I had seen in real life! He had not been killed, as my mother had supposed, but only wounded. . . . And he had come to her and then run off, alarmed by her alarm. Suddenly everything became clear to me: the feeling of involuntary revulsion towards me which was sometimes awakened in my mother, and her constant sadness, and our isolated life. . . . I remember how my head was going around in circles—and I grasped it in both hands as if wanting to hold it in place. But there was one thought which became firmly fixed in my mind: I determined to find that man again, without fail, cost what it may. Why? What was my purpose?—I didn't go into that, but to find him, to find him—for me that became a matter of life and death! The next morning my mother finally became calmer . . . the fever went . . . she fell asleep. Entrusting her to the charge of our hosts and servants, I embarked on the search.

XI

First of all, naturally, I set out for the coffee-house, where I had met the baron, but in the coffee-house no one either knew or had even noticed him; he had been a casual customer there. The owners had noticed the negro—he was such a conspicuous figure; but who he was or where he was staying no one was aware, either. Leaving my address at the coffee-house just in case, I started walking about the streets and quays of the city, around the wharf, along the boulevards, looking in at all the places frequented by the public and nowhere found anyone like either the baron or his companion! Not having caught the baron's name I was not in a position to go to the police for help; however, I quietly let two or three guardians of public order I happened to come across know (it's true, they regarded me with astonishment and didn't wholly trust me) that I would generously reward their diligence should they succeed in coming on the tracks of the two persons whose appearance I tried to describe as exactly as possible. Having spent the morning scouring the town in this way, I returned home exhausted. My mother rose from her bed; but her customary melancholy was now mixed with something new, a sort of pensive puzzlement, which cut into my heart like a knife. I spent the evening sitting with her. We almost didn't speak at all: she laid out her patience and I watched her game in silence. She made not the slightest reference to her story nor to what had happened the previous day. It was as if we had a secret agreement not to touch on these fearful and strange happenings. . . . It was as if she were annoyed with herself and felt ashamed of what she had unintentionally blurted out; or perhaps she didn't remember very well what she had said in her half-feverish ravings—and hoped that I would spare her. . . . And I did indeed spare her, and she was conscious of this; she avoided my eyes as she had the day before. All that night I could not go to sleep. Outside a terrible storm suddenly arose. The tearing wind howled furiously, the window-panes rang and rattled, there were shrieks and groans of despair carried on the air as if something were being torn apart on high and were flying over the quaking houses. Just before dawn I sank into a drowsy oblivion . . . suddenly it seemed to me that someone had come into my room and called me, pronouncing my name in a soft but firm voice. I lifted up my head and could see nobody; but strange to relate, I not only didn't take fright—I was glad; all of a sudden I felt within myself the conviction that now I would unfailingly achieve my goal. I hastily dressed and left the house.

XII

The storm died down . . . but its final stirrings could still be felt. The hour was still early—there were no people to be met on the streets, in many places were lying pieces of chimneys, tiles, palings from fences blown about, broken boughs from trees. . . . "What must it have been like at sea last night!" I couldn't help thinking as I saw the traces left by the storm. I was on the point of going to the wharf, but my legs, as if they were obeying an irresistible pull, carried me in the other direction. Not ten minutes later I was already in a part of town I had never visited before. I did not walk quickly, but at an even pace, step after step, with a strange feeling in my heart; I was anticipating something extraordinary, impossible, and at the same time I was certain that this extraordinary thing would come true.

XIII

And eventuate it did, this extraordinary thing I anticipated. Suddenly, some twenty paces in front of me, I caught sight of the same negro who had spoken to the baron in my presence in the coffee-house! Wrapped up in the same cloak I had already noticed him wearing on that occasion, he seemed to spring up out of the ground, and, turning his back to me, walked with a light step along the narrow pavement of the crooked street! I immediately rushed after him, but he also doubled his pace, although he didn't look behind him, and suddenly he turned sharply around the corner of a house which stuck out. I ran up to the corner and rounded it no less quickly than the negro. . . . How amazing! Before me stretched a long, narrow and perfectly empty street; it was flooded with the dull lead colour of the morning fog—but peering I could see to the very end of it, I could account for every single building in it . . . and there was not one living object moving in it anywhere. The tall negro in the cloak had disappeared as suddenly as he had appeared! I was astounded . . . but only for an instant. Another feeling immediately seized me: this street which stretched out before my eyes, utterly soundless as if dead—I recognized it! It was the street from my dream. I gave a start and hunched myself—the morning was so fresh—then straight away, without the slightest hesitation, and somewhat startled at my assuredness, I went forward!

I began to look carefully. . . . And there it was, there on the right, with a corner facing the footpath, there was the house from my dream, there was the old gate with the stonework scrolls on both sides. The windows of the house were certainly not round, but square . . . but that wasn't important. I knocked at the gate, knocked twice, three times, louder and louder. . . . The gate opened slowly, with a heavy creak, as if it were yawning. In front of me stood a young serving-girl, sleepy-eyed and with tousled hair. She had obviously just woken up.

"Does the baron live here?" I asked, while casting an eye quickly around the deep, narrow courtyard. . . . Exactly. Everything was exactly right . . . there were the boards and logs I had seen in my dream.

"No," answered the maid, "the baron doesn't live here."

"What do you mean? He must!"

"He's not here any more. He left yesterday."

"Where did he go?"

"To America."

"To America!" I repeated without meaning to. "He's coming back, isn't he?"

The girl gave me a suspicious look. "We don't know. He may not come back at all."

"And did he stay here long?"

"Not long, a week or so. He's not here now."

"And what was this baron's name?"

The girl looked at me intently.

"Don't you know his name? We called him simply 'the baron.' Hey! Peter!" she called out, seeing me push forward. "Come over here; there's a stranger here asking all sorts of questions."

The ungainly figure of a hefty workman appeared from inside the house.

"What is it? What do you want?" he asked in a hoarse voice, and after listening to me sullenly, he repeated what the girl had told me.

"So who lives here, then?" I said.

"Our master."

"And who is he?"

"A carpenter. On this street everyone is a carpenter."

"May I see him?"

"Not now, he's asleep."

"Can't I come into the house?"

"No, you can't. You'd better be off."

"Well, will I be able to see your master later?"

"Yes, why not? You can see him any time. He's a tradesman, isn't he? But you'd better clear off now. Don't you know how early it is?"

"And what about the negro?" I suddenly asked.

The workman looked in a puzzled way first at me, then at the maid.

"What negro are you talking about?" he said finally. "You'd better be going, sir. You can come again later. You can have a talk with the master."

I went out onto the street. The gates at once banged shut behind me, heavily and abruptly, this time without creaking.

I took good note of the street and the house, and set off, but not home. I had a feeling akin to disenchantment. Everything that had happened to me had been so strange, so extraordinary—and yet how stupidly it had ended! I had been sure, I had been convinced, that in that house I would see the room that was familiar to me—and in the middle of the room my father, the baron, in a dressing-gown smoking a pipe. . . . And instead of that the master of the house was a carpenter, and he could be visited as often as you wished—and he would even probably take an order for furniture. . . .

And my father had gone away to America! So what did it remain for me to do now? Tell my mother everything—or bury forever the very memory of this meeting? I was decidedly not in the frame of mind to come to terms with the notion that such a supernatural and mysterious beginning could have such a senseless, such an ordinary ending!

I didn't want to go back home—and just followed my nose, right out of town.

XIV

I walked, with my head down, not thinking about anything, not even feeling anything very much, but completely absorbed in myself. I was dragged from my torpor by an even, muffled, angry beat. I looked up: it was the sea making a noise and droning, only about fifty paces from me. I saw that I was walking across a sand-dune. Stirred up by the night storm, the sea was white with sea-horses right up to the horizon, and the steep-walled ridges of the long waves rolled in one after the other and smashed on the flat shore. I went closer to them—and walked along the very line left by their ebbing and flowing on the yellow, ribbed sand, littered with torn pieces of rubbery sea-weed, fragments of seashells, and snake-like ribbons of sedge. Sharp-winged seagulls, flying in on the wind with a pitiful cry from some far airy abyss, soared, white as snow against the grey cloudy sky, then fell steeply, and, almost skipping from crest to crest, flew off again and were swallowed up, sparks of silver in the strips of swirling foam. A few of them, I noticed, were persistently wheeling above a large rock which was sticking out alone in the middle of the monotonous sheet of the sandy shore. On one side of the rock grew coarse sedge in uneven piles; and where its tangled stems grew out of the yellow salty soil, I could see something black, something quite long, rounded, and not very big. . . . I started to look closely. . . . There was some dark object lying there, lying motionless beside the rock. . . . The closer I approached, the clearer the object became, the more defined. . . .

I was only some thirty paces from the rock. . . .

Why, it was the outline of a human body! It was a corpse; somebody drowned and thrown up by the sea! I went right up to the rock.

It was the corpse of the baron, my father! I stood rooted to the spot. Only now did I realize that from early morning I had been led by some unknown forces—that I was in their power—and for several instants my mind was empty of everything except the incessant splashing of the sea—and numb fear at the fate which had taken possession of me. . . .

XV

He was lying on his back, tilting a little to one side, his left arm thrown back behind his head . . . his right arm was twisted under his body, which was doubled up. His feet, in high sailor's boots, had been sucked into the boggy slime; his short dark-blue jacket, saturated with salt, had not come undone; a red scarf was still tightly knotted around his neck. His swarthy face, turned to the sky, seemed to be laughing quietly; his upper lip was turned back and I could see his fine, close-set teeth; the dull pupils of his half-closed eyes could scarcely be distinguished from the darkened whites; his hair, clotted and covered in tiny foam bubbles, was strewn on the ground, baring his smooth forehead with the lilac-coloured line of the scar; his narrow nose stuck up in a steep, whitish line between his sunken cheeks. The storm of the previous night had done its work. . . . He hadn't seen America! The man who had so wounded my mother, who had so disfigured her life—my father—yes! my father—I could have no doubt about this—was now lying, spread out helplessly in the mud at my feet. I had a feeling of vengeance gained, and pity, and repulsion, and, more than anything, horror—double horror: at what I saw and at what had happened. What was evil and criminal in me, about which I've already spoken, those mysterious urges were rising up in me . . . were suffocating me. Aha! I thought: that's why I am as I am. . . . This is when blood makes itself felt! I stood beside the corpse, and looked, and waited: would those dead pupils flicker? Would those frozen lips twitch? No, he was completely motionless; even the sedge, onto which the breakers had cast him, seemed to have died; even the seagulls had flown off—and there was not a single piece of debris anywhere, not a single board, nor piece of smashed rigging. The whole beach was empty—there was just he, and I, and the sea roaring in the distance. I looked back: the same emptiness there too—a chain of lifeless hills on the horizon—and that was all! I felt terrified at leaving this wretched man so utterly alone, in the slime of the seashore, for fish and birds to eat; an inner voice told me that I should find some people, call them, if not to help—how could they!—then at least to gather him up and take him to some shelter . . . but I was suddenly gripped by an indescribable fear. It seemed to me that the dead man knew that I had come there, that he himself had arranged this last meeting—I even thought I heard the familiar, muffled muttering. . . . I ran to one side . . . looked around again. . . . Something glinting on the body caught my eye: it brought me to a halt. It was the rim of something gold on the hand which was thrown back. . . . I recognized my mother's engagement ring. I remember how I made myself turn back, go up to the body, bend over it. . . . I remember the sticky touch of the cold fingers, I remember how I choked, screwed up my eyes, and ground my teeth, trying to pull off the stubborn ring. . . .

At last it was off—and I ran off at breakneck speed—and something was borne along behind me, overtaking me, trying to catch me.

XVI

Everything I had experienced and felt was no doubt written all over my face when I got home. As soon as I entered my mother's room, she suddenly straightened up and gave me such an insistently questioning look that, after trying in vain to give some explanation, I ended up wordlessly holding out to her the ring. She became terribly pale, her eyes widened extraordinarily and became lifeless like *his*—

she gave a feeble cry, seized the ring, staggered, fell on my breast and became utterly still, her head thrown back and her wide, crazed eyes devouring me. I held her in both arms and without moving from that spot, without hurrying, I quietly told her everything, not concealing the smallest detail. She listened to my story to the end without saying a single word, although her breast heaved more and more heavily—and her eyes suddenly came to life and she lowered her eyelids. Then she put the ring on her third finger, and, stepping aside a little, began getting her mantilla and hat. I asked her where she meant to go: she raised her eyes with an astounded expression and tried to reply but her voice failed her. She shuddered several times, rubbed her hands as if trying to warm herself and finally said: "Let's go there."

"Where, Mother?"

"Where he's lying. . . . I want to see. . . . I want to find out. . . . I shall find out. . . ."

I tried to talk her out of going; but she almost had an attack of nerves. I realized that it was impossible to oppose her wish—and we set off.

XVII

And so now I was again walking across the sand of the dune—but this time not alone. I was leading my mother by the arm. The sea had receded, moved even further off; it was quietening down, but its weakened sound was still threatening and malevolent. Here at last appeared in front of us the lonely rock—and the sedge. I looked carefully, trying to make out the rounded object lying on the ground—but I couldn't see anything. We drew closer; I unintentionally slowed my steps. But where was that black, motionless thing? There were only the stems of the sedge showing dark above the sand, which had already dried out. We went right up to the rock. . . . There was no corpse anywhere—there was only an imprint left in the place where it had been lying and you could tell where the arms and legs had been. . . . Around about the sedge seemed to be trampled—and a man's footsteps were noticeable; they went across the dune, then disappeared on reaching a stony ridge.

Mother and I exchanged glances and were ourselves frightened at what we read on our faces. . . .

Had he risen and walked away himself?

"But he was dead when you saw him, wasn't he?" she asked in a whisper.

I could only nod my head. It wasn't three hours since I had stumbled on the baron's body. . . . Someone had discovered it and carried it away. We had to seek out who had done this and what had become of him.

XVIII

As she was on her way to the fateful place, she had been racked by fever, but she had kept her self-control. The disappearance of the body struck her as the final misfortune. She was stunned. I feared for her reason. It was with great difficulty that I got her home again. I put her back to bed, and put her under the doctor's care again; but as soon as my mother came to her senses again somewhat, she immediately demanded that I go off and search for "that man" without delay. I obeyed. But, despite all possible measures, I found nothing. I went to the police several times, visited all the surrounding villages, had several advertisements printed in the newspapers, sought information everywhere—and all in vain! I did actually hear that a drowned man was brought to one of the small seaside villages. . . . I rode off there immediately, but he had already been buried, and anyway his description was not at all like the baron's. I found out what ship he had sailed on for America; at first, everyone was sure that that ship had been lost during the storm; but several months later rumours began to circulate to the effect that the ship had been seen at anchor in New York harbour. Not knowing what action to take, I started looking for the negro I had seen, offering him through the newspapers quite a significant sum of money if he would present himself at our house.

Some tall negro in a cloak did indeed come to our house while I was away. . . . However, after asking the maid a lot of questions, he suddenly went away and did not return again.

Thus it was that all trace of my . . . my father was lost; thus it was that he sank without return into soundless darkness. My mother and I never spoke of him; only once, I remember, she expressed surprise at my not having mentioned my uncanny dream earlier; and she at once added "so it was really . . ." but didn't finish her idea. My mother was ill for a long time, and even after she was recovered our earlier relationship was not reestablished. She felt awkward with me—right up to her death. . . . Yes, awkward. This is a sorrow nothing can be done about. Everything is eventually smoothed over, memories of the most tragic events in the family gradually lose their strength and painfulness; but if a feeling of awkwardness has taken root between two people who have been close—this is impossible to eradicate. I did not have again the dream which used to trouble me so; I am no longer "searching" for my father; but sometimes in a dream I would seem to hear—and still do—certain far-away cries, incessant, mournful plaining; these sounds are carried from behind a high wall somewhere which it is impossible to climb over, they strain my heart—and I cry with closed eyes—and I am in no way able to understand whether it's a live man moaning or whether it's the drawn-out, wild howl of the turbulent sea I can hear. And then it again turns into that animal muttering—and I awaken with anguish and horror in my heart.

NIKOLAI SEMYONOVICH LESKOV

❋

A Shameless Rascal

(Chertogón, 1879)

Among the stories of this great Russian writer, there are some that qualify better as "fantastic" than this one. But there are many reasons why I chose this tale: the rhythm of an infernal dance that animates it, the transfiguration of an evening's events that takes place before the eyes of a young man (the result of the powerful vitality of a rich sinner), and the lightness with which a story that seems to be about damnation turns into a tale of repentance and salvation, even though both courses are impelled by the same impulse.

As always in Leskov (1831–1895), it is the narrator's "voice" that makes the story, and this is one instance in which this "voice" manages to reach us even through a translation.

We had weathered a squall at sea in a horribly flimsy little tub, though what was wrong with it, incidentally, I didn't understand. When we dropped anchor, the crew set everything to rights in a matter of half an hour; we too shook ourselves into shape, ate a makeshift dinner and found ourselves in quite a celebratory mood.

We were a small company: the skipper, two naval officers, the navigator, together with myself and the old sailor Porfiry Nikitich. We two had been taken on board for friendship's sake, just to get a breath of sea air.

The sense of euphoria we shared at having narrowly escaped disaster loosened our tongues: the foul weather we had been through served as a natural topic of conversation. A variety of even more perilous moments at sea were recalled, and imperceptibly the conversation shifted to the way a man's character is affected by a life at sea. Needless to say, in a company of seafaring men the sea had champions aplenty: to hear us talk, you would have thought the sea to be a panacea for practically all ills, including that shallowness of feeling, thought and character which was the mark of contemporary man.

"Hm!" said old Porfiry Nikitich. "I see. That's all right then. There's a simple cure for everything. All you have to do is take all those petty-minded landlubbers, put them aboard ships and send them off to sea."

"Hang on a minute, that's an odd conclusion to draw!"

"What's so odd about it?"

"Well, that isn't what we were saying at all. We were saying that a man's character is formed by a life spent at sea, not that you can produce an instant change in a fellow by simply taking him and shoving him into a sailor's jacket. The idea is obviously ridiculous."

"Hold on, hold on," Porfiry Nikitich interrupted. "Firstly, this isn't an idea I thought up at all. These are the words of a sage, an actual historical person."

"Oh, to hell with all those Greeks and Romans!"

"Well, for a start, my actual historical sage wasn't a Greek or a Roman at all, but a Russian, and he worked in the government victualling service; moreover, everything he said on this subject was publicly acknowledged at the time by a sizeable and honourable company of men to be a certain and unquestionable truth. Now I, being a good patriot, would like to defend the idea, because it all touches upon the versatility and virtuosity of the Russian character."

"Couldn't you tell us the story behind this actual historical declaration?"

"If you wish."

HAVING RETURNED TO Petersburg after the Crimean War, I turned up one day at the house of Stepan Aleksandrovich Khrulyov and encountered there a large and motley company: there were military men from all the services, amongst them a few of our lads from the Black Sea Fleet, who'd got to know Stepan Aleksandrovich in the trenches at Sebastopol. I needn't tell you how delighted I was to meet these mates of mine, and we sailors settled ourselves down at a separate table: we were having a yarn and taking a glass of sherry or two. Now what went on at these parties of Khrulyov's was that people mostly played cards, and, what's more, for pretty high stakes—"chalked wins and losses on the slate, and never let the game abate," as the poet has it. The gallant Khrulyov—may God rest his soul and his sins not be remembered!—was a man who liked strong sensations: indeed, at that time he couldn't do without them. Well now, we sailors did without cards and got down to a round-the-table debate; I can remember what started the conversation off—it was a book that had just come out called *The Dirty Side of the Crimean War*. It caused quite a sensation at the time; we had all read every last word of it and were pretty hot under the collar as a result. Well, you can understand it. The book dealt with the abuses that lay at the root of most of our recent suffering—suffering that was still very fresh in the memory of all those who had taken part in the defence of Sebastopol; it all touched us on a very raw nerve. Above all else the book exposed the thieving and embezzlement by people in the commissariat and victualling service, thanks to which all of us had time and again tasted the pleasures of hunger and thirst, cold and damp.

Now as you can imagine, the exposure in print of all these dirty goings-on sparked off individual memories in every one of us, and brought to the boil a good deal of simmering resentment: so, naturally enough, we started blowing off steam. It was a very companionable activity: there we sat, vying to think up ever ruder names for those good friends of ours, the commissaries. At this point, the chap sitting alongside me, another of our Black Sea lads, Captain Yevgraf Ivanovich, a graduate of the Nakhimov Naval Academy, an extraordinarily kindly fellow and a bit of a stutterer, grabs me by the knee under the table and goes suddenly all coy. . . .

"What on earth can he want?" I think to myself.

"Excuse me, my dear chap," I say, "but if you need something a bit private, call a waiter, will you? I'm a visitor here myself, and I don't know where it is."

But he just stammered something or other and started doing the same thing again. Now I'm the sort of silly fellow who gets all worked up for no reason at all; what's more, I was already fairly steamed up by all these reminiscences, and on top of that I'm terribly ticklish, and there was this Yevgraf Ivanovich, as bold as brass, tickling my knee with his fingers, just like the soft lips of a nuzzling calf.

"Hey, Yevgraf Ivanovich, turn it in, will you?" I say. "What do you think you're up to? I'm not a woman, you know, for you to play kneesy-kneesy with under the table. You can tell me your feelings out loud."

At which poor old Yevgraf Ivanovich—what a priceless fellow!—gets even more flustered, and says in a whisper: "What a sh-sh-shameless fellow you are, Porfiry Nikitich."

"I don't know about me," I say, "it's you that looks more like the shameless one to me. The way you go on, anyone could suspect us of belonging to some pernicious sect or other."

"How c-c-can you . . . I m-m-mean, really, one sh-sh-shouldn't speak of c-c-commissaries and supply officers like that."

"And why should you," I ask, "why should you want to speak up for them?"

"I'm not s-s-speaking up for them," whispers Yevgraf Ivanovich in an even more hushed voice, "but can't you see who's sitting two paces away behind your back?"

"Who's sitting behind my back? How should I know? I haven't got eyes in the back of my head."

Thereupon I turned round and looked: at the table behind me sat this great lump of a man in the uniform jacket of the victualling service, the very image, as Gogol put it, of "a pig in a skull-cap." There he sits, the swine, stacking huge amounts of money on the cards, in the sort of nonchalant manner that was guaranteed to outrage downtrodden beggars like me: it was as if he were saying: "Win or lose, I don't care. I do this strictly for the fun of it, because my granary is full. Eat, drink and be merry, that's my motto!" In a word, it was enough to make any poor beggar's gorge rise!

"Well, how do you like that?" I said. "A prize specimen, and no mistake! How didn't I notice him before?" And, do you know, seeing the enemy at close range like that, I don't know what devil got into me, and instead of keeping my mouth shut, I started off on the same tack, even louder than before, and, what's more, laying it on as thick as I knew how.

"Brigands!" I say, "leeches, that's what they are, these greedy-guts of commissaries! While the blood of us poor officers and soldiers was, as you might say, dripping into the Crimean dirt like beetroot kvass through a leaky bung, what were they doing? Robbing us, they were, lining their rascally pockets, building themselves houses and buying themselves country estates!"

Yevgraf Ivanovich nearly choked as he whispered:

"G-G-Give it a rest!"

But I go on:

"Why should I? Isn't it the truth that we were perishing of hunger: that thanks to their good offices what we got for grub was mouldy salt beef and cabbage; that we bound our wounds with straw instead of lint, while they were swigging their sherry and dry madeira?"

I really went to town at their expense, I can tell you. The chaps I'd been talking to, seeing that I was getting up a good head of steam, let me get on with it, though now and again the ones who'd had a drop more to drink would laugh and start tapping their sherry glasses with their fingernails. As for dear old Yevgraf Ivanovich, poor timid chap, he was absolutely covered in confusion on my behalf: he picked up a handful of deuces from the table, spread them with both hands into a fan and hid his face behind them, whispering:

"Ooh, Porfiry Nikitich, ooh, the sh-sh-shameless fellow, what is he going on about? Have a bit of m-m-mercy. . . ."

This coyness of his made me even more furious.

"That's just the way it always is with us Russians," I thought, "the man who's right, the one with a clean conscience, sits and blushes, while the double-dyed rogue, just like Vaska, the cat who's stolen the cream, stuffs his belly with what he's pinched and doesn't twitch a whisker."

And with that I took a look behind me at the table where the commissary who had irritated me so much was sitting, and I could see that indeed he hadn't twitched a whisker. It just wasn't possible that he hadn't heard all my pronouncements to the world at large about his esteemed fraternity: yet he was sitting quite unmoved, smoking a large fragrant cigar and playing a trump. And since everything about a man depends a good deal on the mood he's in, it seemed to me that he played his trump, or, for that matter, all his cards, in a somehow similarly revolting manner. You know what I mean—it was as though he tossed them down without so much as a flick of the fingers, as if to say: "There, you scum, take that, and see if I care." I hated him all the more because he had, you might say, scored a point off me by remaining so unruffled. There's me, splitting my seams, hurling abuse, snapping at him like a mongrel at an elephant, and he doesn't even bat an eyelid. So I come on even stronger.

"You're having us on," I thought to myself, "and may the wolves devour you! I'll stir you into action, you see if I don't. I, my lad, am a Russian and I shan't stand on ceremony. Whether my host likes it or not, I'm going to hit you where it hurts." And hit him I did. I let fly everything I knew about him personally, in light allegorical disguise.

"We decent Russian folk," I said, "whom nobody would dare accuse of thieving, we, who were wounded and maimed in the war, still can't get a job for ourselves anywhere; we haven't even got enough to feed our wives. But these arch-swindlers, once they've made a name for themselves as first-rate locusts, they never look back; they've got a job in the service even in peacetime, their wives go around in silk and velvet, and their floozies are even better turned out. . . ."

On I went, ranting and raving, till I finally gave up, exhausted. . . . I was running out of words and my throat was getting sore, but still he didn't turn a hair. The fact was, he was holding all the trumps: even Yevgraf Ivanovich noticed as much, and started chaffing me:

"W-W-Well," he whispers, "well, old f-f-fellow, and where's all your eff-ff-ffrontery got you, eh?"

"You keep your 'old f-f-fellow' to yourself," I answered, "and sit quiet."

But to be honest, you know, I really did feel crushed. What's more, all I'd seen so far was the blossom; the berries were still to come.

SHORTLY BEFORE SUPPER the card game broke up; the players started settling their accounts. Our victualler had won a fortune; he pulled from his pocket a monstrous great wallet stuffed with hundred-ruble notes and added his winnings to them—another twenty or so of the same. He then tucked the whole lot back in his pocket with the same unperturbed, but very perturbing, nonchalance.

Well, at this point everyone got to their feet and took a stroll to stretch their legs. Just then our host came up to our table and said:

"So, my good fellows, what have you been up to? Loafing about and scandal-mongering, it would appear."

"Could you hear us too?" I said.

"I should think I could," he says. "Your worship was bawling as though he were on the deck of a ship."

"Stepan Aleksandrovich," I said, "I beg you, please forgive me."

"What do I have to forgive you for? It's God that'll forgive you."

"I lost my temper," I said, "I just couldn't restrain myself."

"And why should you have?"

"When I saw him," I said, "I just boiled up inside, and even though I felt that I was putting you in an awkward position . . ."

"What on earth did you do that affects me?"

"Well, he *is* your guest. . . ."

"Oh that. . . . Listen, old man, that's nothing to me. All sorts of types turn up here. I've set up the ark, and all sorts of creatures come in two by two: the riff-raff come in dozens. This Anempodist Petrovich, by the way, is a very clever type; he won't take umbrage at trifles like that."

"He won't?" I asked in surprise.

"Of course he won't."

"You mean he's so thick-skinned?"

"Thick-skinned? Good heavens, no. On the contrary, he's a sensitive man; but he's canny, and takes a broad view of things. What's more, he's no raw apprentice in these matters; he's taken a beating or two in his time, I don't doubt. As for your rude names, people call his type rude names wherever they go."

"And yet they still do go everywhere—to people's houses?"

"Why shouldn't they, if people let them in, or even invite them?"

Host or no host, that angered me.

"That's just the problem with us, your honour," I say. "We curse worthless types like that, then welcome them into our homes. Griboyedov commented upon that fact in his time, and nothing has changed since."

"Nor will it, because there's no other way it can be."

"Don't go on," I said, genuinely dismayed. "Why is it, for instance, that in England . . ." (At that time, owing to the influence of Katkov's journal *The Russian Messenger*, England was all the rage.)

But I had hardly got the word "England" out before Stepan Aleksandrovich measured me with his sombre eye and interrupted: "What are you trying to do, foist Katkov's mumbo-jumbo on us? It's no good our trying to ape the English."

"Why not? Are you trying to say the English are angels, not ordinary people like us?"

"Oh, they're people all right; it's just that they have different ways."

"I'm not talking about politics," I said.

"Nor am I. We, thank God, are Russian gentry, not English lords; we don't have to stuff our noble heads full of politics. That there are perhaps more honest or, at least, decent folk in England than here in Russia—that's the truth as you see it. But then what's so surprising about that? In England it makes sense to be an honest man, whereas there's no profit in being a rogue: in those circumstances, the honest have bred and multiplied. Over there, everyone is brought up that way from earliest childhood, told to 'be a gentleman'; and they explain to the child what that means. But we instill a different maxim: 'Righteous men do not live in fine houses.' Now a child is no fool: he knows which side his bread is buttered on. So he follows the path that he has been shown. You've got to look at all this in a sensible way, from the point of view of personal advantage, and not like you sailors do, with your silly idealism. That's why you're such a useless lot."

"What do you mean by that?" I said.

"Exactly what I say: you're about as useful as a fifth leg on a donkey. Let's imagine, for instance, that you're looking for a job and I put in a good word for you along the following lines: 'This chap is an officer in the Black Sea Fleet, as honest as the day is long, never puts his hand in the till or lets anyone else do the same, and will go to the wall in the cause of justice.' Well, I won't get you the job, and I won't do myself any good either. They'll call me a fool for taking your part. They'll say: 'He's a fine enough fellow, that friend of yours, but we don't need a man like that, we need someone who's not quite so perfect.' So the fact is, I shan't go and put in a word for you, whereas for him, for that fine gentleman over there"—our host nodded in the direction of the commissary, who was standing at the buffet table—"I'd put my oar in anywhere, because in our sort of society types like that are always in demand, and guarantee success to whoever takes them on."

"Are you trying to tell me," I said, "that that's how it has to be?"

"Yes, of course. You see, he's a very smart, adaptable sort of fellow; anyone can see how best to make use of him; whereas you—what good are you to anyone? With your fine sense of truth and justice, you'll just squabble with everybody. The only thing to do with your sort is pick them up by the tail and toss them back on to a ship, because here on shore you'll just sit and gather dust."

WELL NOW, take note, gentlemen—said Porfiry Nikitich emphatically—I'm not spinning a yarn. This is no tale made up to amuse you. I'm reporting the actual words of a real person, which must have some historical significance, if not in history textbooks, then at least in the oral traditions of our seafaring brotherhood. That's how people saw us in those days, gentlemen—not just as men of honour among ourselves, but as impeccably moral types in general. But that's all beside the point. Let me tell you more of what happened over supper at Khrulyov's.

"SO YOU SEE, my good honest fellow," said Stepan Aleksandrovich in conclusion, giving me a friendly slap on the back, "the age of ideals is past. Nowadays even a man who doesn't know a word of Latin will tell you 'suum cuique'—'to each his own.' Why don't we go and have a bite to eat instead, or else your Anempodist Petrovich, regular pig that he is, will as likely as not scoff all the salmon single-handed—which would be a pity, for it's a good one. I got it as a sample from Smurov's on Morskaya Street. Incidentally, while we're eating, I'll introduce you to him."

"Introduce me? To whom?"

"To Anempodist Petrovich."

"No, thanks very much."

"What? You mean you'd rather not?"

"Absolutely."

"A shame: he's a very shrewd man—statesmanlike, you might almost say—and yet at the same time he's a Russian through and through. He's a man who sees to the very heart of things, a man who'll go far."

"Well, good luck to him, that's what I say."

"Yes, quite. But you know, he's an amiable fellow and one you could learn a good deal from."

"Good grief!" I thought. "What virtues will he find in him next! The sort you can learn from, indeed! Pah!"

We went over to the buffet and mingled with the throng. Anempodist Petrovich, who had established himself at its centre, was delivering an edifying address. I concentrated on trying to catch a few of the prophecies emanating from this oracle.

The only thing he talked about at first, however, was the salmon. His comments were indeed substantial and founded on a considerable expertise. All of which seemed to me quite enough to make any decent man sick.

He sucked and chewed and smacked his lips, voluptuously testing each morsel on his tongue and palate; this procedure ensured a more precise sampling, a finer evaluation of the salmon. He delicately savoured it, then, just like Gogol's Petukh, pronounced through closed lips:

"Mm . . . mm . . . yes . . . not bad . . . not at all bad . . . in fact, pretty good . . . you might say."

"Very good salmon indeed," someone remarked.

"Mm . . . mm . . . yes . . . possibly . . . mm . . . pretty fair . . . it *is* tender. . . ."

"Why, it's as soft as butter."

"Mm . . . mm . . . yes . . . you could say it has . . . mm . . . a certain buttery quality. . . ."

"Well, I must say, you're sparing in your praise." This intervention came from a colonel with a scar running the width of his forehead and across the bridge of his nose. "After the muck we got in the Crimea, anything seems good. You couldn't get hold of stuff like this down there."

"Mm . . . mm . . . well . . . is that really so? . . . We . . . mm . . . managed to get it all right, even there."

"But at a price, I'll warrant."

"Mm . . . true, yes, of course, one had to pay . . . but we got plenty of it . . . for ourselves . . . through Kiev . . . we ordered it from the merchant Pokrovsky . . . good salmon it was, too . . . they actually called it 'commissariat salmon.' Yes . . . this Pokrovsky, incidentally, also supplied salmon for the royal table—only that, of course, wasn't quite the same quality; you see, they didn't dare charge His Majesty what they charged us. But we . . . it didn't matter to us—we had the money."

The colonel with the scar heaved a sigh.

"You certainly weren't short of money," he said, "in fact you had so much you didn't know what to do with it."

"That's perfectly true; indeed, some of our chaps were not used to it and didn't know where to stop . . . mm . . . one of them, I remember, heard about 'jeroboam pockets,' and ordered his tailor to make him some. Well, it was a farce; the tailor thought it must mean some sort of fine material, and so made the pockets out of damask. That really caused some amusement."

"What *did* it mean then?"

"Well, big enough to hold a jeroboam of wine . . . mm . . . mm . . . you see, our wallets were . . . mm . . . so fat. . . ."

"Why, you unholy swine!" I thought. "And he hasn't even the decency to keep his mouth shut!"

Meanwhile he was going on with a tale about some fellow of theirs in victualling or the commissariat, who at that terrible time, in the midst of universal suffering and the hardships of war, went even more berserk.

"This chap," says he, "all of a sudden lost whatever sense of taste he ever had, and started guzzling God knows what crazy stuff."

"Aha," I thought, "that's splendid. I wish the whole lot of you would do the same and poison yourselves." But the "crazy stuff" in question turned out to be something quite unexpected.

"This chap had always liked kvass," Anempodist Petrovich went on, and kvass was his regular tipple. He came from a good solid background—he'd been educated at a seminary. His father was an archpriest and a well-known preacher; in his last testament he enjoined his son, if he had the means to buy wine, to drink beer; if he had the means to buy beer, to drink kvass; and if he had the means to buy kvass, to drink water. But in fact he touched nothing but kvass, and wanted nothing but kvass—but then during the campaign he began to add champagne to it. . . ."

"How do you mean?"

"Just like I say . . . mm . . . he mixed them in equal portions: he'd pour half a glass of kvass and half a glass of champagne, stir and drink."

"What a pig!" I muttered, but so indiscreetly that Anempodist Petrovich heard me and, casting a glance in my direction, observed:

"Yes, pretty loutish behaviour, I grant you. Mind you, I should just say that champagne and kvass is not such a bad mixture as you might think. . . . Indeed, during the war, it became quite a fashion among our chaps in the victualling service . . . mm . . . quite a few of the lads still drink it . . . they've acquired the taste. Now foreigners, they can't drink it . . . we did try giving them some just for the fun of it . . . and they . . . er . . . spat it out . . . just didn't have the stomach for it."

Now I may not be a foreigner, but I myself felt like spitting and leaving—when suddenly this splendid specimen of an Anempodist Petrovich turns to me in the most casual fashion and says:

"By the way, forgive me, I beg you, but, if you'll allow me, I'd like to raise one tiny objection to what you were saying about the Russian character."

I really can't say why, but instead of cutting him dead with some insult or other, I answered:

"Oh, do be so kind, tell me."

"Well," says he, "in a nutshell, I'll say only this: what you had to say about us Russians was hurtful and unfair."

That brought me to my feet, I can tell you.

"What! I? Hurtful!"

"Yes. While I was sitting playing cards, I kept picking up snatches of what you were saying to your comrades, and I rather took offence on behalf of all my compatriots. Believe me, you've really no right to defame the Russian nation in that way."

"Who—I?" I said. "You say *I* defame the Russian nation?"

"Why yes, of course you do. What was it you were saying? . . . I listened to you for some time . . . you divided the Russian people into two halves, your suggestion being that one half consisted of entirely honourable folk, heroes as it were, while the other half were nothing but thieves and scoundrels."

"Aha!" I said, "so that's what you find hurtful, is it?"

"No, sir. Absolutely nothing offends me personally, because I also inherited a precept from my father, a nobleman—namely, that one should never take anything unpleasant that one hears as referring to oneself. But I do take offence on behalf of all other Russians at your unwarranted slur. I believe that we Russians are all, without exception, capable of every possible human virtue. You stated, sir, that when you—that is to say, fighting soldiers—were shedding your blood in the mud of the Crimea, at that same time we in the victualling service were robbing and stealing—and that is perfectly true."

"Yes," I replied heatedly, "I can assure you it is true. And now, having heard your disgraceful story about the kvass and the champagne, I'm even more convinced that I was right to say what I did."

"Well, let's leave aside the kvass and the champagne: that's just a matter of taste—some like one thing, some like another. King Friedrich added asafoetida to his food, but I don't see anything particularly disgraceful even in that. But as concerns your division of us Russians into two widely differing categories—with that I cannot agree. The way I see it, you know, one shouldn't go giving a bad name to no less than half a nation. We're all created from the same rib and anointed with the same oil."

"Now wait a minute," I said. "All anointed with the same oil we may be, but that doesn't mean we're all thieves."

He tried to give the impression he hadn't quite caught what I had said, and asked:

"What was that?"

I repeated, straight to his face:

"*We* are not thieves."

"That I know, sir. How could you be expected to be thieves? Why, you haven't had the chance yet to learn the art of stealing. The late Admiral Lazarev instilled in you a sense of honesty, to which, for the time being anyway, you still cling. But what lies in the future—that God alone knows. . . ."

"No, that will never change!"

"And why not?"

"Because those who serve with me are honourable men."

"Honourable men! For goodness' sake, I'm not disputing that. They are very honourable men, but that's no reason to assert that only your chaps are honourable, whereas others are dishonourable. Fiddlesticks! I insist on speaking out in their defence, and in defence of all Russians, for that matter! Yes, sir! Take my word for it, you are not the only ones who can quietly suffer hunger, fight, and die like heroes; but to hear you talk, the only thing we have been capable of doing, since the day we were baptised, is thieving. Fiddlesticks, sir! Not true, sir! We Russians—it's the fate of every one of us, it's part of that breadth of character with which we are all endowed—we have the capacity for anything. We're like cats: throw us where you will, we'll never land face-down in the dirt; no, we'll land foursquare on our feet; whatever fits the bill, we'll show we've got it in full measure: if it's a question of dying, we'll die, if it's stealing, we'll steal. You were asked to fight, and you did it as well as it could be done—you fought and died like heroes and earned fame throughout Europe for it. But we found ourselves in a business where a man could steal: and we too made a name for ourselves; we thieved so well that our fame also spread far and wide. But if, let's say, an order had come through for us all to swap places, with us ending up in the trenches and you in army supply, then we thieves would have fought and died, and you . . . would have thieved. . . ."

That's what he said, as bold as brass!

I was just on the point of snapping back: "Why, you dirty dog!" But everybody else was absolutely delighted by the man's candour, and they started shouting:

"Bravo, bravo, Anempodist Petrovich! Shameless—but how neatly put!" And they all burst into jolly laughter, as though he'd just told them some marvellous good news or other about themselves. Even Yevgraf Ivanovich couldn't restrain himself and stuttered:

"It's the t-t-truth!"

Meanwhile, he, the thick-skinned devil, had stuffed his mouth full of salmon again, and started reading me another homily.

"Of course," he says, "if all that rubbish you were talking earlier can be put down to your inexperience, then God will forgive you: but in future, just you watch what you have to say about your own people. Why praise some and find fault with others? We are all, every single one of us, capable of absolutely everything, and, God willing, by the time you die, you will have come to see that for yourself."

So that's the way it ended. I was left the guilty party, and got a ticking off into the bargain from this paragon of practical wisdom, to the approval of all present. Well, as you will appreciate, after that little lesson, I pulled my horns in a bit and . . . to be perfectly honest, nowadays I quite often recall the brazen cheek of the man, and I get to thinking that, for all I know, the shameless rascal may have been right.

AUGUSTE VILLIERS DE L'ISLE-ADAM

The Very Image

(A S'y Méprende!, 1883)

This brief text from Villiers de l'Isle-Adam's Cruel Tales *is nothing more than a double description of Parisian locales that establishes an extremely simple equation between the world of business (a café near the stock exchange) and the world of the dead (a room in a funeral hall). In both cases, the vision is repeated, described in the same words, a method that is perhaps used here intentionally for the first time and that would be used by contemporary writers such as Alain Robbe-Grillet.*

Villiers de l'Isle-Adam (1838–1889) puts his ironic taste for intellectual cruelty and his proclivity to resolve tales using effects attained through rapid, sharp means at the service of fantastic invention.

FOR MONSIEUR HENRY DE BORNIER

Darting their dark eyes everywhere.
—C. Baudelaire

One grey November morning I was hurrying along the embankments. The air was damp with a cold drizzle. Black-clad passers-by, sheltering under shapeless umbrellas, came and went.

The yellow Seine swept its merchant vessels along as if they were outsize cockchafers. On the bridges, the wind kept snatching at hats whose owners fought with space to save them, with those convulsive gestures which are always such a painful sight for artists' eyes.

My ideas were pale and misty; the thought of a business appointment, arranged the day before, was nagging at my mind. Time was pressing; and I decided to shelter under the porch of a doorway, from where it would be easier for me to signal a cab.

At that very moment I noticed, right beside me, the entrance of a square, solid-looking building.

It had reared up in the mist like a stone apparition, and, despite its rigid architecture, despite the dismal, eerie vapour in which it was enveloped, I recognized a certain cordial air of hospitality about it which reassured me.

"The people who live here," I said to myself, "must surely be sedentary folk. This threshold has an inviting look: isn't the door open?"

So, in the politest possible way, with a contented air, hat in hand,

and even planning a complimentary speech to make to the mistress of the house, I went smilingly in, and promptly found myself before a room with a glass roof through which a ghastly light was falling.

There were pillars on which clothes, mufflers, and hats had been hung.

Marble tables were installed on all sides.

Some people were there with legs outstretched, heads raised, staring eyes, and matter-of-fact expressions, who appeared to be meditating.

And their gaze was devoid of thought, their faces the colour of the weather.

There were portfolios lying open and papers spread out beside each one of them.

And then I realized that the mistress of the house, on whose courteous welcome I had been counting, was none other than Death.

I looked at my hosts.

It was obvious that, in order to escape from the worries of a harassing life, most of them had murdered their bodies, hoping in that way to obtain a little more comfort.

As I was listening to the noise of the brass taps fastened to the wall and intended for the daily refreshment of those mortal remains, I heard the rumbling of a cab. It was stopping outside the establishment. I reflected that my businessmen were waiting, and turned round to take advantage of my good luck.

The cab had, in fact, just disgorged, on the threshold of the building, some students on the spree who needed to see death to believe in it.

I looked at the empty carriage and said to the driver:

"The Passage de l'Opéra!"

A little later, on the boulevards, the weather struck me as duller than ever, on account of the absence of any horizon. The skeletal trees looked as if, with the tips of their black branches, they were vaguely pointing out pedestrians to the sleepy policemen.

The carriage sped along.

The passers-by, seen through the window, gave me the impression of flowing water.

On arriving at my destination, I jumped out on to the pavement and plunged into the arcade, which was full of care-worn faces.

At the end I noticed, right in front of me, the entrance to a café—since burnt down in a famous fire (for life is a dream). It was tucked away at the back of a sort of shed, under a square, sinister archway.

"It is there," I thought, "that my businessmen are waiting for me, glass in hand, their shining eyes defying Fate."

I accordingly turned the handle of the door and promptly found myself in a room into which a ghastly light was filtering through the windows.

There were pillars on which clothes, mufflers, and hats had been hung.

Marble tables were installed on all sides.

Some people were there with legs outstretched, heads raised, staring eyes, and matter-of-fact expressions, who appeared to be meditating.

And their faces were the colour of the weather, their gaze devoid of thought.

There were portfolios lying open and papers spread out beside each one of them.

I looked at those men.

It was obvious that, in order to escape from the obsessions of an unbearable conscience, most of them had long ago murdered their "souls," hoping in that way to obtain a little more comfort.

As I was listening to the noise of the brass taps fastened to the wall and intended for the daily refreshment of those mortal remains, the memory of the rumbling of the cab came back to my mind.

"That driver," I said to myself, "must have been afflicted in the course of time by a sort of coma, to have brought me back, after so many circumconvolutions, to my starting-point. All the same, I must admit (if there has been a mistake) that *the second glimpse is more sinister than the first!*"

I therefore silently shut the glass door and went home, firmly resolved—despite the force of example and whatever might become of me—never to do any business.

GUY DE MAUPASSANT

❋

Night: A Nightmare

(La Nuit, 1887)

An example of the fantastic achieved through minimal means, this narrative is nothing more than a stroll through Paris, a careful account of the sensations Maupassant felt every evening during his nightly walks. But here an oppressive, nightmarish sensation fills the picture from start to finish, growing more and more intense with each step. The city is always the same, street by street, palace by palace, but then the people disappear, and afterward the lights. The familiar scene seems to contain only a fear of the absurd and of death.

Maupassant (1850–1893) also has a place in fantastic literature because of a series of stories written during the years that precede his plunge into madness: quotidian images unleash a feeling of terror.

I LOVE NIGHT PASSIONATELY. I love it as one loves one's country or one's mistress. I love it with all my senses, with my eyes, which see it; with my sense of smell, which inhales it; with my ears, which listen to its silence; with my whole body, which is caressed by its shadows. The larks sing in the sunlight, in the blue heavens, in the warm air, in the light air of clear mornings. The owl flies at night; a somber patch passing through black space, and, rejoicing in the black immensity that intoxicates him, he utters a vibrant and sinister cry.

In the daytime I am tired and bored. The day is brutal and noisy. I rarely get up, I dress myself languidly, and I go out regretfully. Every movement, every gesture, every word, every thought, tires me as though I were raising a crushing load.

But when the sun goes down a confused joy invades my whole being. I awaken and become animated. As the shadows lengthen I feel quite different, younger, stronger, more lively, happier. I watch the great soft shadows falling from the sky and growing deeper. They envelop the city like an impenetrable and impalpable wave; they hide, efface and destroy colors and forms; they embrace houses, people and buildings in their imperceptible grasp. Then I would like to cry out with joy like the screech owls, to run upon the roofs like the cats, and an impetuous, invincible desire to love burns in my veins. I go, I walk, sometimes in the darkened outskirts of Paris, sometimes in the neighboring woods, where I hear my sisters, the beasts, and my brothers, the poachers, prowling.

One is finally killed by what one violently loves. But how shall I explain what happens to me? How can I ever make people understand that I am able to tell it? I do not know, I cannot tell. I only know that this is—that is all.

Well, yesterday—was it yesterday?—yes, no doubt, unless it was earlier, a day, a month, a year earlier. . . . I do not know, but it must have been yesterday, because since then no day has risen, no sun has dawned. But how long has it been night? How long? Who can tell? Who will ever know?

Yesterday, then, I went out after dinner, as I do every evening. It was very fine, very mild, very warm. As I went down towards the boulevards I looked above my head at the black streams full of stars, outlined in the sky between the roofs of the houses, which were turning round and causing this rolling stream of stars to undulate like a real river.

Everything was distinct in the clear air, from the planets to the gaslight. So many lights were burning above, in the city, that the shadows seemed luminous. Bright nights are more joyful than days of bright sunshine. The cafés on the boulevard were flaring; people were laughing, passing up and down, drinking. I went into a theater for a few moments. Into what theater, I cannot tell. There was so much light in there that I was depressed, and I came out again with my heart saddened by the clash of brutal light on the gold of the balcony, by the factitious glitter of the great crystal chandelier, by the glaring footlights, by the melancholy of this artificial and crude light. I arrived at the Champs-Elysées, where the open-air concerts look like conflagrations in the branches. The chestnut trees, touched with yellow light, look as if they were painted, like phosphorescent trees. The electric bulbs, like pale dazzling moons, like eggs from the moon, fallen from heaven, like monstrous, living pearls, caused the streaks of gaslight, filthy, ugly gaslight and the garlands of colored, lighted glasses to grow pale beneath their pearly, mysterious and regal light.

I stopped beneath the Arc de Triomphe to look at the avenue, the long and wonderful, starry avenue, leading to Paris between two rows of fire and the stars! The stars above, the unknown stars, thrown haphazard through infinity, where they form those strange shapes which make us dream and think so much.

I entered the Bois de Boulogne, where I remained for a long, long time. I was seized by a strange thrill, a powerful and unforeseen emotion, and exaltation of mind which bordered on frenzy. I walked on and on, and then I returned. What time was it when I passed again beneath the Arc de Triomphe? I do not know. The city was sleeping, and clouds, great black clouds, were slowly spreading over the sky.

For the first time I felt that something strange was going to happen, something new.

It seemed to be getting cold, that the air was becoming thicker, that night, my beloved night, was weighing heavily upon my heart. The avenue was deserted now. Two solitary policemen were walking near the cabstand, and a string of vegetable carts was going to the Halles along the roadway, scarcely lit by the gas jets, which seemed to be dying out. They moved along slowly, laden with carrots, turnips, and cabbages. The invisible drivers were asleep, the horses were walking with an even step, following the carts in front of them and making no noise on the wooden pavement. As they passed each lamp on the footpath, the carrots showed up red in the light, the turnips white, the cabbages green, and they passed one after another, these carts which were as red as fire, as white as silver, and as green as emeralds. I followed them, then I turned into the Rue Royale and returned to the boulevards. There was nobody to be seen; none of the cafés was open and only a few belated pedestrians in a hurry. I had never seen Paris so dead and so deserted. I looked at my watch. It was two o'clock.

Some force was driving me, the desire to walk. So I went as far as the Bastille. There I became aware that I had never seen so dark a night, for I could not even see the Colonne de Juillet, whose Genius in gold was lost in the impenetrable obscurity. A curtain of clouds as dense as the ether had buried the stars and seemed to be descending upon the world to blot it out.

I retraced my steps. There was nobody about me. However, at the

Place de Château d'Eau, a drunken man almost bumped into me, then disappeared. For some time I could hear his sonorous and uneven steps. I went on. At the top of the Faubourg Montmartre a cab passed, going in the direction of the Seine. I hailed it but the driver did not reply. Near the Rue Drouot a woman was loitering: "Listen, dearie—" I hastened my steps to avoid her outstretched hand. Then there was nothing more. In front of the Vaudeville Theater a rag picker was searching in the gutter. His little lantern was moving just above the ground. I said to him: "What time is it, my good man?"

"How do I know?" he grumbled. "I have no watch."

Then I suddenly perceived that the lamps had all been extinguished. I know that at this time of year they are put out early, before dawn, for the sake of economy. But daylight was still far off, very far off indeed!

"Let us go to the Halles," I said to myself; "there at least I shall find life."

I set off, but it was too dark even to see the way. I advanced slowly, as one does in a forest, recognizing the streets by counting them. In front of the Crédit Lyonnais a dog growled. I turned up the Rue de Grammont and lost my way. I wandered about, and then I recognized the Bourse by the iron railings around it. The whole of Paris was sleeping, a deep, terrifying sleep. In the distance a cab rumbled, one solitary cab, perhaps it was the one which had passed me a while back. I tried to reach it, going in the direction of the noise, through streets that were lonely and dark, dark and somber as death. Again I lost my way. Where was I? What nonsense to put out the lights so soon! Not one person passing by. Not one late reveler, not one thief, not even the mewing of an amorous cat? Nothing.

Where on earth were the police? I said to myself: "I will shout and they will come." I shouted. There was no answer. I called more loudly. My voice vanished without an echo, weak, muffled, stifled by the night, the impenetrable night. I yelled: "Help! Help! Help!" My desperate cry remained unanswered. What time was it? I pulled out my watch, but I had no matches. I listened to the gentle ticktick of the little mechanism with a strange and unfamiliar pleasure. It seemed to be a living thing. I felt less lonely. What a mystery! I resumed my walk like a blind man, feeling my way along the wall with my stick, and every moment I raised my eyes to the heavens, hoping that day would dawn at last. But the sky was dark, all dark, more profoundly dark than the city.

What could the time be? It seemed to me I had been walking an infinite length of time, for my legs were giving way beneath me, my breast was heaving and I was suffering horribly from hunger. I decided to ring at the first street door. I pulled the copper bell and it rang sonorously through the house. It sounded strangely, as if that vibrating noise were alone in the house. I waited. There was no answer. The door did not open. I rang again. I waited again—nothing! I got frightened! I ran to the next house, and, twenty times in succession, I rang the bells in the dark corridors where the concierge was supposed to sleep, but he did not awake. I went on further, pulling the bells and the knockers with all my strength, kicking and knocking with my hand and stick on the doors, which remained obstinately closed.

Suddenly I perceived that I had reached the Halles. The market was deserted, not a sound, not a movement, not a cart, not a man, not a bundle of flowers or vegetables—it was empty, motionless, abandoned, dead. I was seized with a horrible terror. What was happening? Oh, my God, what was happening?

I set off again. But the time? The time? Who would tell me the time? Not a clock struck in the churches or the public buildings. I thought: "I will open the glass of my watch and feel the hands with my fingers." I pulled out my watch. . . . It was not going. . . . It had stopped. Nothing more, nothing more, not a ripple in the city, not a light, not the slightest suspicion of a sound in the air. Nothing! Nothing more! not even the distant rumbling of a cab! Nothing more. I had reached the quays, and a cold chill rose from the river. Was the Seine still flowing? I wanted to know, I found the steps and went down. I could not hear the current rushing under the bridge. . . . A few more steps. . . . Then sand. . . . Mud . . . then water. I dipped my hand into it. It was flowing . . . flowing . . . cold . . . cold . . . cold . . . almost frozen . . . almost dried up . . . almost dead.

I fully realized that I should never have the strength to come up, and that I was going to die there . . . in my turn, of hunger, fatigue and cold.

VERNON LEE

A Lasting Love

(Amour Dure, 1890)

The literary and art critic Mario Praz, in Il patto col serpente *[Pact with the serpent] (Mondadori, 1972) and* Voce dietro la scena *[Voice behind the scene] (Adelphi, 1980), has left us a good portrait of Vernon Lee. Her real name was Violetta Lee (1856–1935), an Englishwoman who lived in Florence and dedicated herself to history and art. This story, in which a Polish scholar falls in love with a terrible lady of the Renaissance, the "Cinquecento marchigiano," facilitates the flowering of an evocation of a pitiless era (much as Stendhal's* Italian Chronicles *did) in the daily scene of the insignificant provincial life in one of our "cities of silence" during the nineteenth century. The magic of ancient objects unleashes a visionary hallucination. A century ago, foreigners could still view Italy as the country where the past eternally returns, where it is kept as immobile as the silver idol inside the equestrian statue of Duke Roberto.*

PART I

URBANIA, AUGUST *20th, 1885.* I had longed, these years and years, to be in Italy, to come face to face with the Past; and was this Italy, was this the Past? I could have cried, yes cried, for disappointment when I first wandered about Rome, with an invitation to dine at the German Embassy in my pocket, and three or four Berlin and Munich Vandals at my heels, telling me where the best beer and sauerkraut could be had, and what the last article by Grimm or Mommsen was about.

Is this folly? Is it falsehood? Am I not myself a product of modern, northern civilisation; is not my coming to Italy due to this very modern scientific vandalism, which has given me a travelling scholarship because I have written a book like all those other atrocious books of erudition and art-criticism? Nay, am I not here at Urbania on the express understanding that, in a certain number of months, I shall produce just another such book? Dost thou imagine, thou miserable Spiridion, thou Pole grown into the semblance of a German pedant, doctor of philosophy, professor even, author of a prize essay on the despots of the fifteenth century, dost thou imagine that thou, with thy ministerial letters and proof-sheets in thy black professorial coat-pocket, canst ever come in spirit into the presence of the Past?

Too true, alas! But let me forget it, at least, every now and then; as I forgot it this afternoon, while the white bullocks dragged my gig slowly winding along interminable valleys, crawling along interminable hill-sides, with the invisible droning torrent far below, and only the bare grey and reddish peaks all around, up to this town of Urbania, forgotten of mankind, towered and battlemented on the high Apennine ridge. Sigillo, Penna, Fossombrone, Mercatello, Montemurlo—each single village name, as the driver pointed it out, brought to my mind the recollection of some battle or some great act of treachery of former days. And as the huge mountains shut out the setting sun, and the valleys filled with bluish shadow and mist, only a band of threatening smoke-red remaining behind the towers and cupolas of the city on its mountain-top, and the sound of church bells floated across the precipice from Urbania, I almost expected, at every turning of the road, that a troop of horsemen, with beaked helmets and clawed shoes, would emerge, with armour glittering and pennons waving in the sunset. And then, not two hours ago, entering the town at dusk, passing along the deserted streets, with only a smoky light here and there under a shrine or in front of a fruit-stall, or a fire reddening the blackness of a smithy; passing beneath the battlements and turrets of the palace. . . . Ah, that was Italy, it was the Past!

August 21st. And this is the Present! Four letters of introduction to deliver, and an hour's polite conversation to endure with the Vice-Prefect, the Syndic, the Director of the Archives, and the good man to whom my friend Max had sent me for lodgings. . . .

August 22nd–27th. Spent the greater part of the day in the Archives, and the greater part of my time there in being bored to extinction by the Director thereof, who to-day spouted Æneas Sylvius' Commentaries for three-quarters of an hour without taking breath. From this sort of martyrdom (what are the sensations of a former racehorse being driven in a cab? If you can conceive them, they are those of a Pole turned Prussian professor) I take refuge in long rambles through the town. This town is a handful of tall black houses huddled on to the top of an Alp, long narrow lanes trickling down its sides, like the slides we made on hillocks in our boyhood, and in the middle the superb red brick structure, turreted and battlemented, of Duke Ottobuono's palace, from whose windows you look down upon a sea, a kind of whirlpool, of melancholy grey mountains. Then there are the people, dark, bushy-bearded men, riding about like brigands, wrapped in green-lined cloaks upon their shaggy pack-mules; or loitering about, great, brawny, low-headed youngsters, like the particoloured bravos in Signorelli's frescoes; the beautiful boys, like so many young Raphaels, with eyes like the eyes of bullocks, and the huge women, Madonnas or St. Elizabeths, as the case may be, with their clogs firmly poised on their toes and their brass pitchers on their heads, as they go up and down the steep black alleys. I do not talk much to these people; I fear my illusions being dispelled. At the corner of a street, opposite Francesco di Giorgio's beautiful little portico, is a great blue and red advertisement, representing an angel descending to crown Elias Howe, on account of his sewing-machines; and the clerks of the Vice-Prefecture, who dine at the place where I get my dinner, yell politics, Minghetti, Cairoli, Tunis, ironclads, &c., at each other, and sing snatches of *La Fille de Mme. Angot*, which I imagine they have been performing here recently.

No; talking to the natives is evidently a dangerous experiment. Except indeed, perhaps, to my good landlord, Signor Notaro Porri, who is just as learned, and takes considerably less snuff (or rather brushes it off his coat more often) than the Director of the Archives. I forgot to jot down (and I feel I must jot down, in the vain belief that some day these scraps will help, like a withered twig of olive or a three-wicked Tuscan lamp on my table, to bring to my mind, in that hateful Babylon of Berlin, these happy Italian days)—I forgot to record that I am lodging in the house of a dealer in antiquities. My window looks up the principal street to where the little column with Mercury on the top rises in the midst of the awnings and porticoes of the market-place. Bending over the chipped ewers and tubs full of sweet basil, clove pinks, and marigolds, I can just see a corner of the palace turret, and the vague ultramarine of the hills beyond. The house, whose back goes sharp down into the ravine, is a queer up-and-down black place, whitewashed rooms, hung with the Raphaels and Francias and Peruginos, whom mine host regularly carries to the chief inn whenever a stranger is expected; and surrounded by old carved chairs, sofas of the Empire, embossed and gilded wedding-chests, and the cupboards which contain bits of old damask and embroidered altar-cloths scenting the place with the smell of old incense and mustiness; all of which are presided over by Signor Porri's three maiden sisters—Sora Serafina, Sora Lodovica, and Sora Adalgisa—the three Fates in person, even to the distaffs and their black cats.

Sor Asdrubale, as they call my landlord, is also a notary. He regrets the Pontifical Government, having had a cousin who was a Cardinal's train-bearer, and believes that if only you lay a table for two, light four candles made of dead men's fat, and perform certain rites about which he is not very precise, you can, on Christmas Eve and similar nights, summon up San Pasquale Baylon, who will write you the winning numbers of the lottery upon the smoked back of a plate, if you have previously slapped him on both cheeks and repeated three Ave Marias. The difficulty consists in obtaining the dead men's fat for the candles, and also in slapping the saint before he has time to vanish.

"If it were not for that," says Sor Asdrubale, "the Government would have had to suppress the lottery ages ago—eh!"

Sept. 9th. This history of Urbania is not without its romance, although that romance (as usual) has been overlooked by our Dryasdusts. Even before coming here I felt attracted by the strange figure of a woman, which appeared from out of the dry pages of Gualterio's and Padre de Sanctis' histories of this place. This woman is Medea, daughter of Galeazzo IV Malatesta, Lord of Carpi, wife first of Pierluigi Orsini, Duke of Stimigliano, and subsequently of Guidalfonso II., Duke of Urbania, predecessor of the great Duke Robert II.

This woman's history and character remind one of that of Bianca Cappello, and at the same time of Lucrezia Borgia. Born in 1556, she was affianced at the age of twelve to a cousin, a Malatesta of the Rimini family. This family having greatly gone down in the world, her engagement was broken, and she was betrothed a year later to a member of the Pico family, and married to him by proxy at the age of fourteen. But this match not satisfying her own or her father's ambition, the marriage by proxy was, upon some pretext, declared null, and the suit encouraged of the Duke of Stimigliano, a great Umbrian feudatory of the Orsini family. But the bridegroom, Giovanfrancesco

Pico, refused to submit, pleaded his case before the Pope, and tried to carry off by force his bride, with whom he was madly in love, as the lady was most lovely and of most cheerful and amiable manner, says an old anonymous chronicle. Pico waylaid her litter as she was going to a villa of her father's, and carried her to his castle near Mirandola, where he respectfully pressed his suit; insisting that he had a right to consider her as his wife. But the lady escaped by letting herself into the moat by a rope of sheets, and Giovanfrancesco Pico was discovered stabbed in the chest, by the hand of Madonna Medea da Carpi. He was a handsome youth only eighteen years old.

The Pico having been settled, and the marriage with him declared null by the Pope, Medea da Carpi was solemnly married to the Duke of Stimigliano, and went to live upon his domains near Rome.

Two years later, Pierluigi Orsini was stabbed by one of his grooms at his castle of Stimigliano, near Orvieto; and suspicion fell upon his widow, more especially as, immediately after the event, she caused the murderer to be cut down by two servants in her own chamber; but not before he had declared that she had induced him to assassinate his master by a promise of her love. Things became so hot for Medea da Carpi that she fled to Urbania and threw herself at the feet of Duke Guidalfonso II., declaring that she had caused the groom to be killed merely to avenge her good fame, which he had slandered, and that she was absolutely guiltless of the death of her husband. The marvellous beauty of the widowed Duchess of Stimigliano, who was only nineteen, entirely turned the head of the Duke of Urbania. He affected implicit belief in her innocence, refused to give her up to the Orsinis, kinsmen of her late husband, and assigned to her magnificent apartments in the left wing of the palace, among which the room containing the famous fireplace ornamented with marble Cupids on a blue ground. Guidalfonso fell madly in love with his beautiful guest. Hitherto timid and domestic in character, he began publicly to neglect his wife, Maddalena Varano of Camerino, with whom, although childless, he had hitherto lived on excellent terms; he not only treated with contempt the admonitions of his advisers and of his suzerain the Pope, but went so far as to take measures to repudiate his wife, on the score of quite imaginary ill-conduct. The Duchess Maddalena, unable to bear this treatment, fled to the convent of the barefooted sisters at Pesaro, where she pined away, while Medea da Carpi reigned in her place at Urbania, embroiling Duke Guidalfonso in quarrels both with the powerful Orsinis, who continued to accuse her of Stimigliano's murder, and with the Varanos, kinsmen of the injured Duchess Maddalena; until at length, in the year 1576, the Duke of Urbania, having become suddenly, and not without suspicious circumstances, a widower, publicly married Medea da Carpi two days after the decease of his unhappy wife. No child was born of this marriage; but such was the infatuation of Duke Guidalfonso, that the new Duchess induced him to settle the inheritance of the Duchy (having, with great difficulty, obtained the consent of the Pope) on the boy Bartolommeo, her son by Stimigliano, but whom the Orsinis refused to acknowledge as such, declaring him to be the child of that Giovanfrancesco Pico to whom Medea had been married by proxy, and whom, in defence, as she had said, of her honour, she had assassinated; and this investiture of the Duchy of Urbania on to a stranger and a bastard was at the expense of the obvious rights of the Cardinal Robert, Guidalfonso's younger brother.

In May 1579 Duke Guidalfonso died suddenly and mysteriously, Medea having forbidden all access to his chamber, lest, on his deathbed, he might repent and reinstate his brother in his rights. The Duchess immediately caused her son, Bartolommeo Orsini, to be proclaimed Duke of Urbania, and herself regent; and, with the help of two or three unscrupulous young men, particularly a certain Captain Oliverotto da Narni, who was rumoured to be her lover, seized the reins of government with extraordinary and terrible vigour, marching an army against the Varanos and Orsinis, who were defeated at Sigillo, and ruthlessly exterminating every person who dared question the lawfulness of the succession; while, all the time, Cardinal Robert, who had flung aside his priest's garb and vows, went about in Rome, Tuscany, Venice—nay, even to the Emperor and the King of Spain, imploring help against the usurper. In a few months he had turned the tide of sympathy against the Duchess-Regent; the Pope solemnly declared the investiture of Bartolommeo Orsini worthless, and published the accession of Robert II., Duke of Urbania and Count of Montemurlo; the Grand Duke of Tuscany and the Venetians secretly promised assistance, but only if Robert were able to assert his rights by main force. Little by little, one town after the other of the Duchy went over to Robert, and Medea da Carpi found herself surrounded in the mountain citadel of Urbania like a scorpion surrounded by flames. (This simile is not mine, but belongs to Raffaello Gualterio, historiographer to Robert II.) But, unlike the scorpion, Medea refused to commit suicide. It is perfectly marvellous how, without money or allies, she could so long keep her enemies at bay; and Gualterio attributes this to those fatal fascinations which had brought Pico and Stimigliano to their deaths, which had turned the once honest Guidalfonso into a villain, and which were such that, of all her lovers, not one but preferred dying for her, even after he had been treated with ingratitude and ousted by a rival; a faculty which Messer Raffaello Gualterio clearly attributed to hellish connivance.

At last the ex-Cardinal Robert succeeded, and triumphantly entered Urbania in November 1579. His accession was marked by moderation and clemency. Not a man was put to death, save Oliverotto da Narni, who threw himself on the new Duke, tried to stab him as he alighted at the palace, and who was cut down by the Duke's men, crying, "Orsini, Orsini! Medea, Medea! Long live Duke Bartolommeo!" with his dying breath, although it is said that the Duchess had treated him with ignominy. The little Bartolommeo was sent to Rome to the Orsinis; the Duchess, respectfully confined in the left wing of the palace.

It is said that she haughtily requested to see the new Duke, but that he shook his head, and, in his priest's fashion, quoted a verse about Ulysses and the Sirens; and it is remarkable that he persistently refused to see her, abruptly leaving his chamber one day that she had entered it by stealth. After a few months a conspiracy was discovered to murder Duke Robert, which had obviously been set on foot by Medea. But the young man, one Marcantonio Frangipani of Rome, denied, even under the severest torture, any complicity of hers; so that Duke Robert, who wished to do nothing violent, merely transferred the Duchess from his villa at Sant' Elmo to the convent of the Clarisse in town, where she was guarded and watched in the closest manner. It seemed impossible that Medea should intrigue any further, for she certainly saw and could be seen by no one. Yet she contrived to send a letter and her portrait to one Prinzivalle degli Ordelaffi, a youth, only nineteen years old, of noble Romagnole family, and who was betrothed to one of the most beautiful girls of Urbania. He immediately broke off his engagement, and, shortly afterwards, attempted to shoot Duke Robert with a holster-pistol as he knelt at mass on the festival of Easter Day. This time Duke Robert was determined to obtain proofs against Medea. Prinzivalle degli Ordelaffi was kept some days without food, then submitted to the most violent tortures, and finally condemned. When he was going to be flayed with red-hot pincers and quartered by horses, he was told that he might obtain the grace of immediate death by confessing the complicity of the Duchess; and the confessor and nuns of the convent, which stood in the place of execution outside Porta San Romano, pressed Medea to save the wretch, whose screams reached her, by confessing her own guilt. Medea asked permission to go to a balcony, where she could see Prinzivalle and be seen by him. She looked on coldly, then threw down her embroidered kerchief to the poor mangled creature. He asked the executioner to wipe his mouth with it, kissed it, and cried out that Medea was innocent. Then, after several hours of torments, he died. This was too much for the patience even of Duke Robert. Seeing that as long as Medea lived his life would be in perpetual danger, but unwilling to cause a scandal (somewhat of the priest-nature remaining), he had Medea strangled in the convent, and, what is remarkable, insisted that only women—two infanticides to whom he remitted their sentence—should be employed for the deed.

"This clement prince," writes Don Arcangelo Zappi in his life of him, published in 1725, "can be blamed only for one act of cruelty, the more odious as he had himself, until released from his vows by the Pope, been in holy orders. It is said that when he caused the death of the infamous Medea da Carpi, his fear lest her extraordinary charms should seduce any man was such, that he not only employed women as executioners, but refused to permit her a priest or monk, thus forcing her to die unshriven, and refusing her the benefit of any penitence that may have lurked in her adamantine heart."

Such is the story of Medea da Carpi, Duchess of Stimigliano Orsini, and then wife of Duke Guidalfonso II. of Urbania. She was put to death just two hundred and ninety-seven years ago, December 1582, at the age of barely seven-and-twenty, and having, in the course of her short life, brought to a violent end five of her lovers, from Giovanfrancesco Pico to Prinzivalle degli Ordelaffi.

Sept. 20th. A grand illumination of the town in honour of the taking of Rome fifteen years ago. Except Sor Asdrubale, my landlord, who shakes his head at the Piedmontese, as he calls them, the people here are all Italianissimi. The Popes kept them very much down since Urbania lapsed to the Holy See in 1645.

Sept. 28th. I have for some time been hunting for portraits of the Duchess Medea. Most of them, I imagine, must have been destroyed, perhaps by Duke Robert II.'s fear lest even after her death this terrible beauty should play him a trick. Three or four I have, however, been able to find—one a miniature in the Archives, said to be that which she sent to poor Prinzivalle degli Ordelaffi in order to turn his head; one a marble bust in the palace lumber-room; one in a large composition, possibly by Baroccio, representing Cleopatra at the feet of Augustus. Augustus is the idealised portrait of Robert II., round cropped head, nose a little awry, clipped beard and scar as usual, but in Roman dress. Cleopatra seems to me, for all her Oriental dress, and although she wears a black wig, to be meant for Medea da Carpi; she is kneeling, baring her breast for the victor to strike, but in reality to captivate him, and he turns away with an awkward gesture of loathing. None of these portraits seem very good, save the miniature, but that is an exquisite work, and with it, and the suggestions of the bust, it is easy to reconstruct the beauty of this terrible being. The type is that most admired by the late Renaissance, and, in some measure, immortalised by Jean Goujon and the French. The face is a perfect oval, the forehead somewhat over-round, with minute curls, like a fleece, of bright auburn hair; the nose a trifle over-aquiline, and the cheek-bones a trifle too low; the eyes grey, large, prominent, beneath exquisitely curved brows and lids just a little too tight at the corners; the mouth also, brilliantly red and most delicately designed, is a little too tight, the lips strained a trifle over the teeth. Tight eyelids and tight lips give a strange refinement, and, at the same time, an air of mystery, a somewhat sinister seductiveness; they seem to take, but not to give. The mouth, with a kind of childish pout, looks as if it could bite or suck like a leech. The complexion is dazzlingly fair, the perfect transparent roset lily of a red-haired beauty; the head, with hair elaborately curled and plaited close to it, and adorned with pearls, sits like that of the antique Arethusa on a long, supple, swan-like neck. A curious, at first rather conventional, artificial-looking sort of beauty, voluptuous yet cold, which, the more it is contemplated, the more it troubles and haunts the mind. Round the lady's neck is a gold chain with little gold lozenges at intervals, on which is engraved the posy or pun (the fashion of French devices is common in those days), "Amour Dure—Dure Amour." The same posy is inscribed in the hollow of the bust, and, thanks to it, I have been able to identify the latter as Medea's portrait. I often examine these tragic portraits, wondering what this face, which led so many men to their death, may have been like when it spoke or smiled, what at the moment when Medea da Carpi fascinated her victims into love unto death—"Amour Dure—Dure Amour," as runs her device—love that lasts, cruel love—yes indeed, when one thinks of the fidelity and fate of her lovers.

Oct. 13th. I have literally not had time to write a line of my diary all these days. My whole mornings have gone in those Archives, my afternoons taking long walks in this lovely autumn weather (the highest hills are just tipped with snow). My evenings go in writing that confounded account of the Palace of Urbania which Government requires, merely to keep me at work at something useless. Of my history I have not yet been able to write a word. . . . By the way, I must note down a curious circumstance mentioned in an anonymous MS. life of Duke Robert, which I fell upon to-day. When this prince had the equestrian statue of himself by Antonio Tassi, Gianbologna's pupil, erected in the square of the *Corte*, he secretly caused to be made, says my anonymous MS., a silver statuette of his familiar genius or angel—"familiaris ejus angelus seu genius, quod a vulgo dicitur *idolino*"—which statuette or idol, after having been consecrated by the astrologers—"ab astrologis quibusdam ritibus sacrato"—was placed in the cavity of the chest of the effigy by Tassi, in order, says the MS., that his soul might rest until the general Resurrection. This passage is curious, and to me somewhat puzzling; how could the soul of Duke Robert await the general Resurrection, when, as a Catholic, he ought to have believed that it must, as soon as separated from his body, go to Purgatory? Or is there some semipagan superstition of the Renaissance (most strange, certainly, in a man who had been a Cardinal) connecting the soul with a guardian genius, who could be compelled, by magic rites ("ab astrologis sacrato," the MS. says of the little idol), to remain fixed to earth, so that the soul should sleep in the body until the Day of Judgment? I confess this story baffles me. I wonder whether such an idol ever existed, or exists nowadays, in the body of Tassi's bronze effigy?

Oct. 20th. I have been seeing a good deal of late of the Vice-Prefect's son: an amiable young man with a love-sick face and a languid interest in Urbanian history and archæology, of which he is profoundly ignorant. This young man, who has lived at Siena and Lucca before his father was promoted here, wears extremely long and tight trousers, which almost preclude his bending his knees, a stick-up collar and an eyeglass, and a pair of fresh kid gloves stuck in the breast of his coat, speaks of Urbania as Ovid might have spoken of Pontus, and complains (as well he may) of the barbarism of the young men, the officials who dine at my inn and howl and sing like madmen, and the nobles who drive gigs, showing almost as much throat as a lady at a ball. This person frequently entertains me with his *amori*, past, present, and future; he evidently thinks me very odd for having none to entertain him with in return; he points out to me the pretty (or ugly) servant-girls and dressmakers as we walk in the street, sighs deeply or sings in falsetto behind every tolerably young-looking woman, and has finally taken me to the house of the lady of his heart, a great black-moustachioed countess, with a voice like a fish-crier; here, he says, I shall meet all the best company in Urbania and some beautiful women—ah, too beautiful, alas! I find three huge half-furnished rooms, with bare brick floors, petroleum lamps, and horribly bad pictures on bright wash-ball-blue and gamboge walls, and in the midst of it all, every evening, a dozen ladies and gentlemen seated in a circle, vociferating at each other the same news a year old; the younger ladies in bright yellows and greens, fanning themselves while my teeth chatter, and having sweet things whispered behind their fans by officers with hair brushed up like a hedgehog. And these are the women my friend expects me to fall in love with! I vainly wait for tea or supper which does not come, and rush home, determined to leave alone the Urbanian *beau monde*.

It is quite true that I have no *amori*, although my friend does not believe it. When I came to Italy first, I looked out for romance; I sighed, like Goethe in Rome, for a window to open and a wondrous creature to appear, "welch mich versengend erquickt." Perhaps it is because Goethe was a German, accustomed to German *Fraus*, and I am, after all, a Pole, accustomed to something very different from *Fraus*; but anyhow, for all my efforts, in Rome, Florence, and Siena, I never could find a woman to go mad about, either among the ladies, chattering bad French, or among the lower classes, as 'cute and cold as money-lenders; so I steer clear of Italian womankind, its shrill voice and gaudy toilettes. I am wedded to history, to the Past, to women like Lucrezia Borgia, Vittoria Accoramboni, or that Medea da Carpi, for the present; some day I shall perhaps find a grand passion, a woman to play the Don Quixote about, like the Pole that I am; a woman out of whose slipper to drink, and for whose pleasure to die; but not here! Few things strike me so much as the degeneracy of Italian women. What has become of the race of Faustinas, Marozias, Bianca Cappellos? Where discover nowadays (I confess she haunts me) another Medea da Carpi? Were it only possible to meet a woman of that extreme distinction of beauty, of that terribleness of nature, even if only potential, I do believe I could love her, even to the Day of Judgment, like any Oliverotto da Narni, or Frangipani or Prinzivalle.

Oct. 27th. Fine sentiments the above are for a professor, a learned man! I thought the young artists of Rome childish because they played practical jokes and yelled at night in the streets, returning from the Caffè Greco or the cellar in the Via Palombella; but am I not as childish to the full—I, melancholy wretch, whom they called Hamlet and the Knight of the Doleful Countenance?

Nov. 5th. I can't free myself from the thought of this Medea da Carpi. In my walks, my mornings in the Archives, my solitary evenings, I catch myself thinking over the woman. Am I turning novelist instead of historian? And still it seems to me that I understand her so well; so much better than my facts warrant. First, we must put aside all pedantic modern ideas of right and wrong. Right and wrong in a century of violence and treachery does not exist, least of all for creatures like Medea. Go preach right and wrong to a tigress, my dear sir! Yet is there in the world anything nobler than the huge creature, steel when she springs, velvet when she treads, as she stretches her supple body, or smooths her beautiful skin, or fastens her strong claws into her victim?

Yes; I can understand Medea. Fancy a woman of superlative beauty, of the highest courage and calmness, a woman of many resources, of genius, brought up by a petty princelet of a father, upon Tacitus and Sallust, and the tales of the great Malatestas, of Cæsar Borgia and such-like!—a woman whose one passion is conquest and empire—fancy her, on the eve of being wedded to a man of the power of the Duke of Stimigliano, claimed, carried off by a small fry of a Pico, locked up in his hereditary brigand's castle, and having to receive the young fool's red-hot love as an honour and a necessity! The mere thought of any violence to such a nature is an abominable outrage; and if Pico chooses to embrace such a woman at the risk of meeting a sharp piece of steel in her arms, why, it is a fair bargain. Young hound—or, if you prefer, young hero—to think to treat a woman like this as if she were any village wench! Medea marries her Orsini. A marriage, let it be noted, between an old soldier of fifty and a girl of sixteen. Reflect what that means: it means that this imperious woman is soon treated like a chattel, made roughly to understand that her business is to give the Duke an heir, not advice; that she must never ask "wherefore this or that?" that she must courtesy before the Duke's counsellors, his captains, his mistresses; that, at the least suspicion of rebelliousness, she is subject to his foul words and blows; at the least suspicion of infidelity, to be strangled or starved to death, or thrown down an oubliette. Suppose that she know that her husband has taken it into his head that she has looked too hard at this man or that, that one of his lieutenants or one of his women have whispered that, after all, the boy Bartolommeo might as soon be a Pico as an Orsini. Suppose she know that she must strike or be struck? Why, she strikes, or gets some one to strike for her. At what price? A promise of love, of love to a groom, the son of a serf! Why, the dog must be mad or drunk to believe such a thing possible; his very belief in anything so monstrous makes him worthy of death. And then he dares to blab! This is much worse than Pico. Medea is bound to defend her honour a second time; if she could stab Pico, she can certainly stab this fellow, or have him stabbed.

Hounded by her husband's kinsmen, she takes refuge at Urbania. The Duke, like every other man, falls wildly in love with Medea, and neglects his wife; let us even go so far as to say, breaks his wife's heart. Is this Medea's fault? Is it her fault that every stone that comes beneath her chariot-wheels is crushed? Certainly not. Do you suppose that a woman like Medea feels the smallest ill-will against a poor, craven Duchess Maddalena? Why, she ignores her very existence. To suppose Medea a cruel woman is as grotesque as to call her an immoral woman. Her fate is, sooner or later, to triumph over her enemies, at all events to make their victory almost a defeat; her magic faculty is to enslave all the men who come across her path; all those who see her, love her, become her slaves; and it is the destiny of all her slaves to perish. Her lovers, with the exception of Duke Guidalfonso, all come to an untimely end; and in this there is nothing unjust. The possession of a woman like Medea is a happiness too great for a mortal man; it would turn his head, make him forget even what he owed her; no man must survive long who conceives himself to have a right over her; it is a kind of sacrilege. And only death, the willingness to pay for such happiness by death, can at all make a man worthy of being her lover; he must be willing to love and suffer and die. This is the meaning of her device—"Amour Dure—Dure Amour." The love of Medea da Carpi cannot fade, but the lover can die; it is a constant and a cruel love.

Nov. 11th. I was right, quite right in my idea. I have found—Oh, joy! I treated the Vice-Prefect's son to a dinner of five courses at the Trattoria La Stella d'Italia out of sheer jubilation—I have found in the Archives, unknown, of course, to the Director, a heap of letters—letters of Duke Robert about Medea da Carpi, letters of Medea herself! Yes, Medea's own handwriting—a round, scholarly character, full of abbreviations, with a Greek look about it, as befits a learned princess who could read Plato as well as Petrarch. The letters are of little importance, mere drafts of business letters for her secretary to copy, during the time that she governed the poor weak Guidalfonso. But they are her letters, and I can imagine almost that there hangs about these mouldering pieces of paper a scent as of a woman's hair.

The few letters of Duke Robert show him in a new light. A cunning, cold, but craven priest. He trembles at the bare thought of Medea—"la pessima Medea"—worse than her namesake of Colchis, as he calls her. His long clemency is a result of mere fear of laying violent hands upon her. He fears her as something almost supernatural; he would have enjoyed having had her burnt as a witch. After letter on letter, telling his crony, Cardinal Sanseverino, at Rome his various precautions during her lifetime—how he wears a jacket of mail under his coat; how he drinks only milk from a cow which has been milked in his presence; how he tries his dog with morsels of his food, lest it be poisoned; how he suspects the wax-candles because of their peculiar smell; how he fears riding out lest some one should frighten his horse and cause him to break his neck—after all this, and when Medea has been in her grave two years, he tells his correspondent of his fear of meeting the soul of Medea after his own death, and chuckles over the ingenious device (concocted by his astrologer and a certain Fra Gaudenzio, a Capuchin) by which he shall secure the absolute peace of his soul until that of the wicked Medea be finally "chained up in hell among the lakes of boiling pitch and the ice of Caina described by the immortal bard"—old pedant! Here, then, is the explanation of that silver image—*quod vulgo dicitur* idolino—which he caused to be soldered into his effigy by Tassi. As long as the image of his soul was attached to the image of his body, he should sleep awaiting the Day of Judgment, fully convinced that Medea's soul will then be properly tarred and feathered, while his—honest man!—will fly straight to Paradise. And to think that, two weeks ago, I believed this man to be a hero! Aha! my good Duke Robert, you shall be shown up in my history; and no amount of silver *idolinos* shall save you from being heartily laughed at!

Nov. 15th. Strange! That idiot of a Prefect's son, who has heard me talk a hundred times of Medea da Carpi, suddenly recollects that, when he was a child at Urbania, his nurse used to threaten him with a visit from Madonna Medea, who rode in the sky on a black he-goat. My Duchess Medea turned into a bogey for naughty little boys!

Nov. 20th. I have been going about with a Bavarian Professor of mediæval history, showing him all over the country. Among other places we went to Rocca Sant' Elmo, to see the former villa of the Dukes of Urbania, the villa where Medea was confined between the accession of Duke Robert and the conspiracy of Marcantonio Frangipani, which caused her removal to the nunnery immediately outside the town. A long ride up the desolate Apennine valleys, bleak beyond words just now with their thin fringe of oak scrub turned russet, thin patches of grass sered by the frost, the last few yellow leaves of the poplars by the torrents shaking and fluttering about in the chill Tramontana; the mountain-tops are wrapped in thick grey cloud; to-morrow, if the wind continues, we shall see them round masses of snow against the cold blue sky. Sant' Elmo is a wretched hamlet high on the Apennine ridge, where the Italian vegetation is already replaced by that of the North. You ride for miles through leafless chestnut woods, the scent of the soaking brown leaves filling the air, the roar of the torrent, turbid with autumn rains, rising from the precipice below; then suddenly the leafless chestnut woods are replaced, as at Vallombrosa, by a belt of black, dense fir plantations. Emerging from these, you come to an open space, frozen blasted meadows, the rocks of snow clad peak, the newly fallen snow, close above you; and in the midst, on a knoll, with a gnarled larch on either side, the ducal villa of Sant' Elmo, a big black stone box with a stone escutcheon, grated windows, and a double flight of steps in front. It is now let out to the proprietor of the neighbouring woods, who uses it for the storage of chestnuts, faggots, and charcoal from the neighbouring ovens. We tied our horses to the iron rings and entered: an old woman, with dishevelled hair, was alone in the house. The villa is a mere hunting-lodge, built by Ottobuono IV., the father of Dukes Guidalfonso and Robert, about 1530. Some of the rooms have at one time been frescoed and panelled with oak carvings, but all this has disappeared. Only, in one of the big rooms, there remains a large marble fireplace, similar to those in the palace at Urbania, beautifully carved with Cupids on a blue ground; a charming naked boy sustains a jar on either side, one containing clove pinks, the other roses. The room was filled with stacks of faggots.

We returned home late, my companion in excessively bad humour at the fruitlessness of the expedition. We were caught in the skirt of a snowstorm as we got into the chestnut woods. The sight of the snow falling gently, of the earth and bushes whitened all round, made me feel back at Posen, once more a child. I sang and shouted, to my companion's horror. This will be a bad point against me if reported at Berlin. A historian of twenty-four who shouts and sings, and that when another historian is cursing at the snow and the bad roads! All night I lay awake watching the embers of my wood fire, and thinking of Medea da Carpi mewed up, in winter, in that solitude of Sant' Elmo, the firs groaning, the torrent roaring, the snow falling all round; miles and miles away from human creatures. I fancied I saw it all, and that I, somehow, was Marcantonio Frangipani come to liberate her—or was it Prinzivalle degli Ordelaffi? I suppose it was because of the long ride, the unaccustomed pricking feeling of the snow in the air; or perhaps the punch which my professor insisted on drinking after dinner.

Nov. 23rd. Thank goodness, that Bavarian professor has finally departed! Those days he spent here drove me nearly crazy. Talking over my work, I told him one day my views on Medea da Carpi; whereupon he condescended to answer that those were the usual tales due to the mythopœic (old idiot!) tendency of the Renaissance; that research would disprove the greater part of them, as it had disproved the stories current about the Borgias, &c.; that, moreover, such a woman as I made out was psychologically and physiologically impossible. Would that one could say as much of such professors as he and his fellows!

Nov. 24th. I cannot get over my pleasure in being rid of that imbecile; I felt as if I could have throttled him every time he spoke of the Lady of my thoughts—for such she has become—*Metea*, as the animal called her!

Nov. 30th. I feel quite shaken at what has just happened; I am beginning to fear that that old pedant was right in saying that it was bad for me to live all alone in a strange country, that it would make me morbid. It is ridiculous that I should be put into such a state of excitement merely by the chance discovery of a portrait of a woman dead these three hundred years. With the case of my uncle Ladislas, and other suspicions of insanity in my family, I ought really to guard against such foolish excitement.

Yet the incident was really dramatic, uncanny. I could have sworn that I knew every picture in the palace here; and particularly every picture of Her. Anyhow, this morning, as I was leaving the Archives, I passed through one of the many small rooms—irregular-shaped closets—which fill up the ins and outs of this curious palace, turreted like a French château. I must have passed through that closet before, for the view was so familiar out of its window; just the particular bit of round tower in front, the cypress on the other side of the ravine, the belfry beyond, and the piece of the line of Monte Sant' Agata and the Leonessa, covered with snow, against the sky. I suppose there must be twin rooms, and that I had got into the wrong one; or rather, perhaps some shutter had been opened or curtain withdrawn. As I was passing, my eye was caught by a very beautiful old mirror-frame let into the brown and yellow inlaid wall. I approached, and looking at the frame, looked also, mechanically, into the glass. I gave a great start, and almost shrieked, I do believe (it's lucky the Munich professor is safe out of Urbania!). Behind my own image stood another, a figure close to my shoulder, a face close to mine; and that figure, that face, hers! Medea da Carpi's! I turned sharp round, as white, I think, as the ghost I expected to see. On the wall opposite the mirror, just a pace or two behind where I had been standing, hung a portrait. And such a portrait!—Bronzino never painted a grander one. Against a background of harsh, dark blue, there stands out the figure of the Duchess (for it is Medea, the real Medea, a thousand times more real, individual, and powerful than in the other portraits), seated stiffly in a high-backed chair, sustained, as it were, almost rigid, by the stiff brocade of skirts and stomacher, stiffer for plaques of embroidered silver flowers and rows of seed pearl. The dress is, with its mixture of silver and pearl, of a strange dull red, a wicked poppy-juice colour, against which the flesh of the long, narrow hands with fringe-like fingers; of the long slender neck, and the face with bared forehead, looks white and hard, like alabaster. The face is the same as in the other portraits: the same rounded forehead, with the short fleece-like, yellowish-red curls; the same beautifully curved eyebrows, just barely marked; the same eyelids, a little tight across the eyes; the same lips, a little tight across the mouth; but with a purity of line, a dazzling splendour of skin, and intensity of look immeasurably superior to all the other portraits.

She looks out of the frame with a cold, level glance; yet the lips smile. One hand holds a dull-red rose; the other, long, narrow, tapering, plays with a thick rope of silk and gold and jewels hanging from the waist; round the throat, white as marble, partially confined in the tight dull-red bodice, hangs a gold collar, with the device on alternate enamelled medallions, "AMOUR DURE—DURE AMOUR."

On reflection, I see that I simply could never have been in that room or closet before; I must have mistaken the door. But, although the explanation is so simple, I still, after several hours, feel terribly shaken in all my being. If I grow so excitable I shall have to go to Rome at Christmas for a holiday. I feel as if some danger pursued me here (can it be fever?); and yet, and yet, I don't see how I shall ever tear myself away.

Dec. 10th. I have made an effort, and accepted the Vice-Prefect's son's invitation to see the oil-making at a villa of theirs near the coast. The villa, or farm, is an old fortified, towered place, standing on a hillside among olive-trees and little osier-bushes, which look like a bright orange flame. The olives are squeezed in a tremendous black cellar, like a prison: you see, by the faint white daylight, and the smoky yellow flare of resin burning in pans, great white bullocks moving round a huge millstone; vague figures working at pulleys and handles: it looks, to my fancy, like some scene of the Inquisition. The Cavaliere regaled me with his best wine and rusks. I took some long walks by the seaside; I had left Urbania wrapped in snow-clouds; down on the coast there was a bright sun; the sunshine, the sea, the bustle of the little port on the Adriatic seemed to do me good. I came back to Urbania another man. Sor Asdrubale, my landlord, poking about in slippers among the gilded chests, the Empire sofas, the old cups and saucers and pictures which no one will buy, congratulated me upon the improvement in my looks. "You work too much," he says; "youth requires amusement, theatres, promenades, *amori*—it is time enough to be serious when one is bald"—and he took off his greasy red cap. Yes, I am better! and, as a result, I take to my work with delight again. I will cut them out still, those wiseacres at Berlin!

Dec. 14th. I don't think I have ever felt so happy about my work. I see it all so well—that crafty, cowardly Duke Robert; that melancholy Duchess Maddalena; that weak, showy, would-be chivalrous Duke Guidalfonso; and above all, the splendid figure of Medea. I feel as if I were the greatest historian of the age; and, at the same time, as if I were a boy of twelve. It snowed yesterday for the first time in the city, for two good hours. When it had done, I actually went into the square and taught the ragamuffins to make a snow-man; no, a snow-woman; and I had the fancy to call her Medea. "La pessima Medea!" cried one of the boys, "the one who used to ride through the air on a goat?" "No, no," I said, "she was a beautiful lady, the Duchess of Urbania, the most beautiful woman that ever lived." I made her a crown of tinsel, and taught the boys to cry "Evviva, Medea!" But one of them said, "She is a witch! She must be burnt!" At which they all rushed to fetch burning faggots and tow; in a minute the yelling demons had melted her down.

Dec. 15th. What a goose I am, and to think I am twenty-four, and known in literature! In my long walks I have composed to a tune (I don't know what it is) which all the people are singing and whistling in the street at present, a poem in frightful Italian, beginning "Medea, mia dea," calling on her in the name of her various lovers. I go about humming between my teeth, "Why am I not Marcantonio? or Prinzivalle? or he of Narni? or the good Duke Alfonso? that I might be beloved by thee, Medea, mia dea," &c. &c. Awful rubbish! My landlord, I think, suspects that Medea must be some lady I met while I was staying by the seaside. I am sure Sora Serafina, Sora Lodovica, and Sora Adalgisa—the three Parcæ or *Norns*, as I call them—have some such notion. This afternoon, at dusk, while tidying my room, Sora Lodovica said to me, "How beautifully the Signorino has taken to singing!" I was scarcely aware that I had been vociferating, "Vieni, Medea, mia dea," while the old lady bobbed about making up my fire. I stopped; a nice reputation I shall get! I thought, and all this will somehow get to Rome, and thence to Berlin. Sora Lodovica was leaning out of the window, pulling in the iron hook of the shrine-lamp which marks Sor Asdrubale's house. As she was trimming the lamp previous to swinging it out again, she said in her odd, prudish little way, "You are wrong to stop singing, my son" (she varies between calling me Signor Professore and such terms of affection as "Nino," "Viscere mie," &c.); "you are wrong to stop singing, for there is a young lady there in the street who has actually stopped to listen to you."

I ran to the window. A woman, wrapped in a black shawl, was standing in an archway, looking up to the window.

"Eh, eh! the Signor Professore has admirers," said Sora Lodovica.

"Medea, mia dea!" I burst out as loud as I could, with a boy's pleasure in disconcerting the inquisitive passer-by. She turned suddenly round to go away, waving her hand at me; at that moment Sora Lodovica swung the shrine-lamp back into its place. A stream of light fell across the street. I felt myself grow quite cold; the face of the woman outside was that of Medea da Carpi!

What a fool I am to be sure!

PART II

Dec. 17th. I fear that my craze about Medea da Carpi has become well known, thanks to my silly talk and idiotic songs. That Vice-Prefect's son—or the assistant at the Archives, or perhaps some of the company at the Contessa's, is trying to play me a trick! But take care, my good ladies and gentlemen, I shall pay you out in your own coin! Imagine my feelings when, this morning, I found on my desk a folded letter addressed to me in a curious handwriting which seemed strangely familiar to me, and which, after a moment, I recognised as that of the letters of Medea da Carpi at the Archives. It gave me a horrible shock. My next idea was that it must be a present from some one who knew my interest in Medea—a genuine letter of hers on which some idiot had written my address instead of putting it into an envelope. But it was addressed to me, written to me, no old letter; merely four lines, which ran as follows:

> TO SPIRIDION. A person who knows the interest you bear her will be at the Church of San Giovanni Decollato this evening at nine. Look out, in the left aisle, for a lady wearing a black mantle, and holding a rose.

By this time I understood that I was the object of a conspiracy, the victim of a hoax. I turned the letter round and round. It was written on paper such as was made in the sixteenth century, and in an extraordinarily precise imitation of Medea da Carpi's characters. Who had written it? I thought over all the possible people. On the whole, it must be the Vice-Prefect's son, perhaps in combination with his lady-love, the Countess. They must have torn a blank page off some old letter; but that either of them should have had the ingenuity of inventing such a hoax, or the power of committing such a forgery, astounds me beyond measure. There is more in these people than I should have guessed. How pay them off? By taking no notice of the letter? Dignified, but dull. No, I will go; perhaps some one will be there, and I will mystify them in their turn. Or, if no one is there, how I shall crow over them for their imperfectly carried out plot! Perhaps this is some folly of the Cavalier Muzio's to bring me into the presence of some lady whom he destines to be the flame of my future *amori*. That is likely enough. And it would be too idiotic and professorial to refuse such an invitation; the lady must be worth knowing who can forge sixteenth-century letters like this, for I am sure that languid swell Muzio never could. I will go! By Heaven! I'll pay them back in their own coin! It is now five—how long these days are!

Dec. 18th. Am I mad? Or are there really ghosts? That adventure of last night has shaken me to the very depth of my soul.

I went at nine, as the mysterious letter had bid me. It was bitterly cold, and the air full of fog and sleet; not a shop open, not a window unshuttered, not a creature visible; the narrow black streets, precipitous between their high walls and under their lofty archways, were only the blacker for the dull light of an oil-lamp here and there, with its flickering yellow reflection on the wet flags. San Giovanni Decollato is a little church, or rather oratory, which I have always hitherto seen shut up (as so many churches here are shut up except on great festivals); and situate behind the ducal palace, on a sharp ascent, and forming the bifurcation of two steep paved lanes. I have passed by the place a hundred times, and scarcely noticed the little church, except for the marble high relief over the door, showing the grizzly head of the Baptist in the charger, and for the iron cage close by, in which were formerly exposed the heads of criminals; the decapitated, or, as they call him here, decollated, John the Baptist, being apparently the patron of axe and block.

A few strides took me from my lodgings to San Giovanni Decollato. I confess I was excited; one is not twenty-four and a Pole for nothing. On getting to the kind of little platform at the bifurcation of the two precipitous streets, I found, to my surprise, that the windows of the church or oratory were not lighted, and that the door was locked! So this was the precious joke that had been played upon me; to send me on a bitter cold, sleety night, to a church which was shut up and had perhaps been shut up for years! I don't know what I couldn't have done in that moment of rage; I felt inclined to break open the church door, or to go and pull the Vice-Prefect's son out of bed (for I felt sure that the joke was his). I determined upon the latter course; and was walking towards his door, along the black alley to the left of the church, when I was suddenly stopped by the sound as of an organ close by; an organ, yes, quite plainly, and the voice of choristers and the drone of a litany. So the church was not shut, after all! I retraced my steps to the top of the lane. All was dark and in complete silence. Suddenly there came again a faint gust of organ and voices. I listened; it clearly came from the other lane, the one on the right-hand side. Was there, perhaps, another door there? I passed beneath the archway, and descended a little way in the direction whence the sounds seemed to come. But no door, no light, only the black walls, the black wet flags, with their faint yellow reflections of flickering oil-lamps; moreover, complete silence. I stopped a minute, and then the chant rose again; this time it seemed to me most certainly from the lane I had just left. I went back—nothing. Thus backwards and forwards, the sounds always beckoning, as it were, one way, only to beckon me back, vainly, to the other.

At last I lost patience; and I felt a sort of creeping terror, which only a violent action could dispel. If the mysterious sounds came neither from the street to the right, nor from the street to the left, they could come only from the church. Half-maddened, I rushed up the two or three steps, and prepared to wrench the door open with a tremendous effort. To my amazement, it opened with the greatest ease. I entered, and the sounds of the litany met me louder than before, as I paused a moment between the outer door and the heavy leathern curtain. I raised the latter and crept in. The altar was brilliantly illuminated with tapers and garlands of chandeliers; this was evidently some evening service connected with Christmas. The nave and aisles were comparatively dark, and about half-full. I elbowed my way along the right aisle towards the altar. When my eyes had got accustomed to the unexpected light, I began to look round me, and with a beating heart. The idea that all this was a hoax, that I should meet merely some acquaintance of my friend the Cavaliere's, had somehow departed: I looked about. The people were all wrapped up, the men in big cloaks, the women in woollen veils and mantles. The body of the church was comparatively dark, and I could not make out anything very clearly, but it seemed to me, somehow, as if, under the cloaks and veils, these people were dressed in a rather extraordinary fashion. The man in front of me, I remarked, showed yellow stockings beneath his cloak; a woman, hard by, a red bodice, laced behind with gold tags. Could these be peasants from some remote part come for the Christmas festivities, or did the inhabitants of Urbania don some old-fashioned garb in honour of Christmas?

As I was wondering, my eye suddenly caught that of a woman standing in the opposite aisle, close to the altar, and in the full blaze of its lights. She was wrapped in black, but held, in a very conspicuous way, a red rose, an unknown luxury at this time of the year in a place like Urbania. She evidently saw me, and turning even more fully into the light, she loosened her heavy black cloak, displaying a dress of deep red, with gleams of silver and gold embroideries; she turned her face towards me; the full blaze of the chandeliers and tapers fell upon it. It was the face of Medea da Carpi! I dashed across the nave, pushing people roughly aside, or rather, it seemed to me, passing through impalpable bodies. But the lady turned and walked rapidly down the aisle towards the door. I followed close upon her, but somehow I could not get up with her. Once, at the curtain, she turned round again. She was within a few paces of me. Yes, it was Medea. Medea herself, no mistake, no delusion, no sham; the oval face, the lips tightened over the mouth, the eyelids tight over the corner of the eyes, the exquisite alabaster complexion! She raised the curtain and glided out. I followed; the curtain alone separated me from her. I saw the wooden door swing to behind her. One step ahead of me! I tore open the door; she must be on the steps, within reach of my arm!

I stood outside the church. All was empty, merely the wet pavement and the yellow reflections in the pools: a sudden cold seized me; I could not go on. I tried to re-enter the church; it was shut. I rushed home, my hair standing on end, and trembling in all my limbs, and remained for an hour like a maniac. Is it a delusion? Am I too going mad? O God, God! am I going mad?

Dec. 19th. A brilliant, sunny day; all the black snow-slush has disappeared out of the town, off the bushes and trees. The snow-clad mountains sparkle against the bright blue sky. A Sunday, and Sunday weather; all the bells are ringing for the approach of Christmas. They are preparing for a kind of fair in the square with the colonnade, putting up booths filled with coloured cotton and woollen ware, bright shawls and kerchiefs, mirrors, ribbons, brilliant pewter lamps; the whole turnout of the pedlar in "Winter's Tale." The porkshops are all garlanded with green and with paper flowers, the hams and cheeses stuck full of little flags and green twigs. I strolled out to see the cattle-fair outside the gate; a forest of interlacing horns, an ocean of lowing and stamping: hundreds of immense white bullocks, with horns a yard long and red tassels, packed close together on the little piazza d'armi under the city walls. Bah! why do I write this trash? What's the use of it all? While I am forcing myself to write about bells, and Christmas festivities, and cattle-fairs, one idea goes on like a bell within me: Medea, Medea! Have I really seen her, or am I mad?

Two hours later. That Church of San Giovanni Decollato—so my landlord informs me—has not been made use of within the memory of man. Could it have been all a hallucination or a dream—perhaps a dream dreamed that night? I have been out again to look at that church. There it is, at the bifurcation of the two steep lanes, with its bas-relief of the Baptist's head over the door. The door does look as if it had not been opened for years. I can see the cobwebs in the window-panes; it does look as if, as Sor Asdrubale says, only rats and spiders congregated within it. And yet—and yet; I have so clear a remembrance, so distinct a consciousness of it all. There was a picture of the daughter of Herodias dancing, upon the altar; I remember her white turban with a scarlet tuft of feathers, and Herod's blue caftan; I remember the shape of the central chandelier; it swung round slowly, and one of the wax lights had got bent almost in two by the heat and draught.

Things, all these, which I may have seen elsewhere, stored unawares in my brain, and which may have come out, somehow, in a dream; I have heard physiologists allude to such things. I will go again: if the church be shut, why then it must have been a dream, a vision, the result of over-excitement. I must leave at once for Rome and see doctors, for I am afraid of going mad. If, on the other hand—pshaw! there *is no other hand* in such a case. Yet if there were—why then, I should really have seen Medea; I might see her again; speak to her. The mere thought sets my blood in a whirl, not with horror, but with . . . I know not what to call it. The feeling terrifies me, but it is delicious. Idiot! There is some little coil of my brain, the twentieth of a hair's-breadth out of order—that's all!

Dec. 20th. I have been again; I have heard the music; I have been inside the church; I have seen Her! I can no longer doubt my senses. Why should I? Those pedants say that the dead are dead, the past is past. For them, yes; but why for me?—why for a man who loves, who is consumed with the love of a woman?—a woman who, indeed—yes, let me finish the sentence. Why should there not be ghosts to such as can see them? Why should she not return to the earth, if she knows that it contains a man who thinks of, desires, only her?

A hallucination? Why, I saw her, as I see this paper that I write upon; standing there, in the full blaze of the altar. Why, I heard the rustle of her skirts, I smelt the scent of her hair, I raised the curtain which was shaking from her touch. Again I missed her. But this time, as I rushed out into the empty moonlit street, I found upon the church steps a rose—the rose which I had seen in her hand the moment before—I felt it, smelt it; a rose, a real, living rose, dark red and only just plucked. I put it into water when I returned, after having kissed it, who knows how many times? I placed it on the top of the cupboard; I determined not to look at it for twenty-four hours lest it should be a delusion. But I must see it again; I must. . . . Good Heavens! this is horrible, horrible; if I had found a skeleton it could not have been worse! The rose, which last night seemed freshly plucked, full of colour and perfume, is brown, dry—a thing kept for centuries between the leaves of a book—it has crumbled into dust between my fingers. Horrible, horrible! But why so, pray? Did I not know that I was in love with a woman dead three hundred years? If I wanted fresh roses which bloomed yesterday, the Countess Fiammetta or any little sempstress in Urbania might have given them me. What if the rose has fallen to dust? If only I could hold Medea in my arms as I held it in my fingers, kiss her lips as I kissed its petals, should I not be satisfied if she too were to fall to dust the next moment, if I were to fall to dust myself?

Dec. 22nd, Eleven at night. I have seen her once more!—almost spoken to her. I have been promised her love! Ah, Spiridion! you were right when you felt that you were not made for any earthly *amori.* At the usual hour I betook myself this evening to San Giovanni Decollato. A bright winter night; the high houses and belfries standing out against a deep blue heaven luminous, shimmering like steel with myriads of stars; the moon has not yet risen. There was no light in the windows; but, after a little effort, the door opened and I entered the church, the altar, as usual, brilliantly illuminated. It struck me suddenly that all this crowd of men and women standing all round, these priests chanting and moving about the altar, were dead—that they did not exist for any man save me. I touched, as if by accident, the hand of my neighbour; it was cold, like wet clay. He turned round, but did not seem to see me: his face was ashy, and his eyes staring, fixed, like those of a blind man or a corpse. I felt as if I must rush out. But at that moment my eye fell upon Her, standing as usual by the altar steps, wrapped in a black mantle, in the full blaze of the lights. She turned round; the light fell straight upon her face, the face with the delicate features, the eyelids and lips a little tight, the alabaster skin faintly tinged with pale pink. Our eyes met.

I pushed my way across the nave towards where she stood by the altar steps; she turned quickly down the aisle, and I after her. Once or twice she lingered, and I thought I should overtake her; but again, when, not a second after the door had closed upon her, I stepped out into the street, she had vanished. On the church step lay something white. It was not a flower this time, but a letter. I rushed back to the church to read it; but the church was fast shut, as if it had not been opened for years. I could not see by the flickering shrine-lamps—I rushed home, lit my lamp, pulled the letter from my breast. I have it before me. The handwriting is hers; the same as in the Archives, the same as in that first letter:

> To Spiridion. Let thy courage be equal to thy love, and thy love shall be rewarded. On the night preceding Christmas, take a hatchet and saw; cut boldly into the body of the bronze rider who stands in the Corte, on the left side, near the waist. Saw open the body, and within it thou wilt find the silver effigy of a winged genius. Take it out, hack it into a hundred pieces, and fling them in all directions, so that the winds may sweep them away. That night she whom thou lovest will come to reward thy fidelity.

On the brownish wax is the device

AMOUR DURE—DURE AMOUR

Dec. 23rd. So it is true! I was reserved for something wonderful in this world. I have at last found that after which my soul has been straining. Ambition, love of art, love of Italy, these things which have occupied my spirit, and have yet left me continually unsatisfied, these were none of them my real destiny. I have sought for life, thirsting for it as a man in the desert thirsts for a well; but the life of the senses of other youths, the life of the intellect of other men, have never slaked that thirst. Shall life for me mean the love of a dead woman? We smile at what we choose to call the superstition of the past, forgetting that all our vaunted science of to-day may seem just such another superstition to the men of the future; but why should the present be right and the past wrong? The men who painted the pictures and built the palaces of three hundred years ago were certainly of as delicate fibre, of as keen reason, as ourselves, who merely print calico and build locomotives. What makes me think this, is that I have been calculating my nativity by help of an old book belonging to Sor Asdrubale—and see, my horoscope tallies almost exactly with that of Medea da Carpi, as given by a chronicler. May this explain? No, no; all is explained by the fact that the first time I read of this woman's career, the first time I saw her portrait, I loved her, though I hid my love to myself in the garb of historical interest. Historical interest indeed!

I have got the hatchet and the saw. I bought the saw of a poor joiner, in a village some miles off; he did not understand at first what I meant, and I think he thought me mad; perhaps I am. But if madness means the happiness of one's life, what of it? The hatchet I saw lying in a timber-yard, where they prepare the great trunks of the fir-trees which grow high on the Apennines of Sant' Elmo. There was no one in the yard, and I could not resist the temptation; I handled the thing, tried its edge, and stole it. This is the first time in my life that I have been a thief; why did I not go into a shop and buy a hatchet? I don't know; I seemed unable to resist the sight of the shining blade. What I am going to do is, I suppose, an act of vandalism; and certainly I have no right to spoil the property of this city of Urbania. But I wish no harm either to the statue or the city; if I could plaster up the bronze, I would do so willingly. But I must obey Her; I must avenge Her; I must get at that silver image which Robert of Montemurlo had made and consecrated in order that his cowardly soul might sleep in peace, and not encounter that of the being whom he dreaded most in the world. Aha! Duke Robert, you forced her to die unshriven, and you stuck the image of your soul into the image of your body, thinking thereby that, while she suffered the tortures of Hell, you would rest in peace, until your well-scoured little soul might fly straight up to

Paradise;—you were afraid of Her when both of you should be dead, and thought yourself very clever to have prepared for all emergencies! Not so, Serene Highness. You too shall taste what it is to wander after death, and to meet the dead whom one has injured.

What an interminable day! But I shall see her again to-night.

Eleven o'clock. No; the church was fast closed; the spell had ceased. Until to-morrow I shall not see her. But to-morrow! Ah, Medea! did any of thy lovers love thee as I do?

Twenty-four hours more till the moment of happiness—the moment for which I seem to have been waiting all my life. And after that, what next? Yes, I see it plainer every minute; after that, nothing more. All those who loved Medea da Carpi, who loved and who served her, died: Giovanfrancesco Pico, her first husband, whom she left stabbed in the castle from which she fled; Stimigliano, who died of poison; the groom who gave him the poison, cut down by her orders; Oliverotto da Narni, Marcantonio Frangipani, and that poor boy of the Ordelaffi, who had never even looked upon her face, and whose only reward was that handkerchief with which the hangman wiped the sweat off his face, when he was one mass of broken limbs and torn flesh: all had to die, and I shall die also.

The love of such a woman is enough, and is fatal—"Amour Dure," as her device says. I shall die also. But why not? Would it be possible to live in order to love another woman? Nay, would it be possible to drag on a life like this one after the happiness of to-morrow? Impossible; the others died, and I must die. I always felt that I should not live long; a gypsy in Poland told me once that I had in my hand the cut-line which signifies a violent death. I might have ended in a duel with some brother-student, or in a railway accident. No, no; my death will not be of that sort! Death—and is not she also dead? What strange vistas does such a thought not open! Then the others—Pico, the Groom, Stimigliano, Oliverotto, Frangipani, Prinzivalle degli Ordelaffi—will they all be *there*? But she shall love me best—me by whom she has been loved after she has been three hundred years in the grave!

Dec. 24th. I have made all my arrangements. To-night at eleven I slip out; Sor Asdrubale and his sisters will be sound asleep. I have questioned them; their fear of rheumatism prevents their attending midnight mass. Luckily there are no churches between this and the Corte; whatever movement Christmas night may entail will be a good way off. The Vice-Prefect's rooms are on the other side of the palace; the rest of the square is taken up with state-rooms, archives, and empty stables and coach-houses of the palace. Besides, I shall be quick at my work.

I have tried my saw on a stout bronze vase I bought of Sor Asdrubale; and the bronze of the statue, hollow and worn away by rust (I have even noticed holes), cannot resist very much, especially after a blow with the sharp hatchet. I have put my papers in order, for the benefit of the Government which has sent me hither. I am sorry to have defrauded them of their "History of Urbania." To pass the endless day and calm the fever of impatience, I have just taken a long walk. This is the coldest day we have had. The bright sun does not warm in the least, but seems only to increase the impression of cold, to make the snow on the mountains glitter, the blue air to sparkle like steel. The few people who are out are muffled to the nose, and carry earthenware braziers beneath their cloaks; long icicles hang from the fountain with the figure of Mercury upon it; one can imagine the wolves trooping down through the dry scrub and beleaguering this town. Somehow this cold makes me feel wonderfully calm—it seems to bring back to me my boyhood.

As I walked up the rough, steep, paved alleys, slippery with frost, and with their vista of snow mountains against the sky, and passed by the church steps strewn with box and laurel, with the faint smell of incense coming out, there returned to me—I know not why—the recollection, almost the sensation, of those Christmas Eves long ago at Posen and Breslau, when I walked as a child along the wide streets, peeping into the windows where they were beginning to light the tapers of the Christmas-trees, and wondering whether I too, on returning home, should be let into a wonderful room all blazing with lights and gilded nuts and glass beads. They are hanging the last strings of those blue and red metallic beads, fastening on the last gilded and silvered walnuts on the trees out there at home in the North; they are lighting the blue and red tapers; the wax is beginning to run on to the beautiful spruce green branches; the children are waiting with beating hearts behind the door, to be told that the Christ-Child has been. And I, for what am I waiting? I don't know; all seems a dream; everything vague and unsubstantial about me, as if time had ceased, nothing could happen, my own desires and hopes were all dead, myself absorbed into I know not what passive dreamland. Do I long for to-night? Do I dread it? Will to-night ever come? Do I feel anything, does anything exist all round me? I sit and seem to see that street at Posen, the wide street with the windows illuminated by the Christmas lights, the green fir-branches grazing the window-panes.

Christmas Eve, Midnight. I have done it. I slipped out noiselessly. Sor Asdrubale and his sisters were fast asleep. I feared I had waked them, for my hatchet fell as I was passing through the principal room where my landlord keeps his curiosities for sale; it struck against some old armour which he has been piecing. I heard him exclaim, half in his sleep; and blew out my light and hid in the stairs. He came out in his dressing-gown, but finding no one, went back to bed again. "Some cat, no doubt!" he said. I closed the house door softly behind me. The sky had become stormy since the afternoon, luminous with the full moon, but strewn with grey and buff-coloured vapours; every now and then the moon disappeared entirely. Not a creature abroad; the tall gaunt houses staring in the moonlight.

I know not why, I took a roundabout way to the Corte, past one or two church doors, whence issued the faint flicker of midnight mass. For a moment I felt a temptation to enter one of them; but something seemed to restrain me. I caught snatches of the Christmas hymn. I felt myself beginning to be unnerved, and hastened towards the Corte. As I passed under the portico at San Francesco I heard steps behind me; it seemed to me that I was followed. I stopped to let the other pass. As he approached his pace flagged; he passed close by me and murmured, "Do not go: I am Giovanfrancesco Pico." I turned round; he was gone. A coldness numbed me; but I hastened on.

Behind the cathedral apse, in a narrow lane, I saw a man leaning against a wall. The moonlight was full upon him; it seemed to me that his face, with a thin pointed beard, was streaming with blood. I quickened my pace; but as I grazed by him he whispered, "Do not obey her; return home: I am Marcantonio Frangipani." My teeth chattered, but I hurried along the narrow lane, with the moonlight blue upon the white walls.

At last I saw the Corte before me: the square was flooded with moonlight, the windows of the palace seemed brightly illuminated, and the statue of Duke Robert, shimmering green, seemed advancing towards me on its horse. I came into the shadow. I had to pass beneath an archway. There started a figure as if out of the wall, and barred my passage with his outstretched cloaked arm. I tried to pass. He seized me by the arm, and his grasp was like a weight of ice. "You shall not pass!" he cried, and, as the moon came out once more, I saw his face, ghastly white and bound with an embroidered kerchief; he seemed almost a child. "You shall not pass!" he cried; "you shall not have her! She is mine, and mine alone! I am Prinzivalle degli Ordelaffi." I felt his ice-cold clutch, but with my other arm I laid about me wildly with the hatchet which I carried beneath my cloak. The hatchet struck the wall and rang upon the stone. He had vanished.

I hurried on. I did it. I cut open the bronze; I sawed it into a wider gash. I tore out the silver image, and hacked it into innumerable pieces. As I scattered the last fragments about, the moon was suddenly veiled; a great wind arose, howling down the square; it seemed to me that the earth shook. I threw down the hatchet and the saw, and fled home. I felt pursued, as if by the tramp of hundreds of invisible horsemen.

Now I am calm. It is midnight; another moment and she will be here! Patience, my heart! I hear it beating loud. I trust that no one will accuse poor Sor Asdrubale. I will write a letter to the authorities to declare his innocence should anything happen. . . . One! the clock in the palace tower has just struck. . . . "I hereby certify that, should anything happen this night to me, Spiridion Trepka, no one but myself is to be held . . ." A step on the staircase! It is she! it is she! At last, Medea, Medea! Ah! AMOUR DURE—DURE AMOUR!

NOTE.—Here ends the diary of the late Spiridion Trepka. The chief newspapers of the province of Umbria informed the public that, on Christmas morning of the year 1885, the bronze equestrian statue of Robert II. had been found grievously mutilated; and that Professor Spiridion Trepka of Posen, in the German Empire, had been discovered dead of a stab in the region of the heart, given by an unknown hand.

AMBROSE BIERCE

⁕

Chickamauga

(1891)

Macabre effects are the specialty of the American Ambrose Bierce (1842–1913) when he comes to depict the horrors of the Civil War (Tales of Soldiers and Civilians). *This, perhaps, is not a fantastic story: it is the documentary description of a battlefield after a bloody fight, but the distancing in the gaze that contemplates it confers a visionary transfiguration on the images. The fantastic atmosphere is born from the silence that envelops everything the story makes us see, although because of the silence there is also an explanation for it.*

ONE SUNNY AUTUMN afternoon a child strayed away from its rude home in a small field and entered a forest unobserved. It was happy in a new sense of freedom from control, happy in the opportunity of exploration and adventure; for this child's spirit, in bodies of its ancestors, had for thousands of years been trained to memorable feats of discovery and conquest—victories in battles whose critical moments were centuries, whose victors' camps were cities of hewn stone. From the cradle of its race it had conquered its way through two continents and passing a great sea had penetrated a third, there to be born to war and dominion as a heritage.

The child was a boy aged about six years, the son of a poor planter. In his younger manhood the father had been a soldier, had fought against naked savages and followed the flag of his country into the capital of a civilized race to the far South. In the peaceful life of a planter the warrior-fire survived; once kindled, it is never extinguished. The man loved military books and pictures and the boy had understood enough to make himself a wooden sword, though even the eye of his father would hardly have known it for what it was. This weapon he now bore bravely, as became the son of an heroic race, and pausing now and again in the sunny space of the forest assumed, with some exaggeration, the postures of aggression and defense that he had been taught by the engraver's art. Made reckless by the ease with which he overcame invisible foes attempting to stay his advance, he committed the common enough military error of pushing the pursuit to a dangerous extreme, until he found himself upon the margin of a wide but shallow brook, whose rapid waters barred his direct advance against the flying foe that had crossed with illogical ease. But the intrepid victor was not to be baffled; the spirit of the race which had passed the great sea burned unconquerable in that small breast and would not be denied. Finding a place where some bowlders in the bed of the stream lay but a step or a leap apart, he made his way across and fell again upon the rear-guard of his imaginary foe, putting all to the sword.

Now that the battle had been won, prudence required that he withdraw to his base of operations. Alas; like many a mightier conqueror, and like one, the mightiest, he could not

curb the lust for war,
Nor learn that tempted Fate will leave the loftiest star.

Advancing from the bank of the creek he suddenly found himself confronted with a new and more formidable enemy: in the path that he was following, sat, bolt upright, with ears erect and paws suspended before it, a rabbit! With a startled cry the child turned and fled, he knew not in what direction, calling with inarticulate cries for his mother, weeping, stumbling, his tender skin cruelly torn by brambles, his little heart beating hard with terror—breathless, blind with tears—lost in the forest! Then, for more than an hour, he wandered with erring feet through the tangled undergrowth, till at last, overcome by fatigue, he lay down in a narrow space between two rocks, within a few yards of the stream and still grasping his toy sword, no longer a weapon but a companion, sobbed himself to sleep. The wood birds sang merrily above his head; the squirrels, whisking their bravery of tail, ran barking from tree to tree, unconscious of the pity of it, and somewhere far away was a strange, muffled thunder, as if the partridges were drumming in celebration of nature's victory over the son of her immemorial enslavers. And back at the little plantation, where white men and black were hastily searching the fields and hedges in alarm, a mother's heart was breaking for her missing child.

Hours passed, and then the little sleeper rose to his feet. The chill of the evening was in his limbs, the fear of the gloom in his heart. But he had rested, and he no longer wept. With some blind instinct which impelled to action he struggled through the undergrowth about him and came to a more open ground—on his right the brook, to the left a gentle acclivity studded with infrequent trees; over all, the gathering gloom of twilight. A thin, ghostly mist rose along the water. It frightened and repelled him; instead of recrossing, in the direction whence he had come, he turned his back upon it, and went forward toward the dark inclosing wood. Suddenly he saw before him a strange moving object which he took to be some large animal—a dog, a pig—he could not name it; perhaps it was a bear. He had seen pictures of bears, but knew of nothing to their discredit and had vaguely wished to meet one. But something in form or movement of this object—something in the awkwardness of its approach—told him that it was not a bear, and curiosity was stayed by fear. He stood still and as it came slowly on gained courage every moment, for he saw that at least it had not the long, menacing ears of the rabbit. Possibly his impressionable mind was half conscious of something familiar in its shambling, awkward gait. Before it had approached near enough to resolve his doubts he saw that it was followed by another and another. To right and to left were many more; the whole open space about him was alive with them—all moving toward the brook.

They were men. They crept upon their hands and knees. They used their hands only, dragging their legs. They used their knees only, their arms hanging idle at their sides. They strove to rise to their feet, but fell prone in the attempt. They did nothing naturally, and nothing alike, save only to advance foot by foot in the same direction. Singly, in pairs and in little groups, they came on through the gloom, some halting now and again while others crept slowly past them, then resuming their movement. They came by dozens and by hundreds; as far on either hand as one could see in the deepening gloom they extended and the black wood behind them appeared to be inexhaustible. The very ground seemed in motion toward the creek. Occasionally one who had paused did not again go on, but lay motionless. He was dead. Some, pausing, made strange gestures with their hands, erected their arms and lowered them again, clasped their heads; spread their palms upward, as men are sometimes seen to do in public prayer.

Not all of this did the child note; it is what would have been noted by an elder observer; he saw little but that these were men, yet crept like babes. Being men, they were not terrible, though unfamiliarly clad. He moved among them freely, going from one to another and peering into their faces with childish curiosity. All their faces were singularly white and many were streaked and gouted with red. Something in this—something too, perhaps, in their grotesque attitudes and movements—reminded him of the painted clown whom he had seen last summer in the circus, and he laughed as he watched them. But on and ever on they crept, these maimed and bleeding men, as heedless as he of the dramatic contrast between his laughter and their own ghastly gravity. To him it was a merry spectacle. He had seen his father's Negroes creep upon their hands and knees for his amusement—had ridden them so, "making believe" they were his horses. He now approached one of these crawling figures from behind and with an agile movement mounted it astride. The man sank upon his breast, recovered, flung the small boy fiercely to the ground as an unbroken colt might have done, then turned upon him a face that lacked a lower jaw—from the upper teeth to the throat was a great red gap fringed with hanging shreds of flesh and splinters of bone. The unnatural prominence of nose, the absence of chin, the fierce eyes, gave this man the appearance of a great bird of prey crimsoned in throat and breast by the blood of its quarry. The man rose to his knees, the child to his feet. The man shook his fist at the child; the child, terrified at last, ran to a tree near by, got upon the farther side of it and took a more serious view of the situation. And so the clumsy multitude dragged itself slowly and painfully along in hideous pantomime—moved forward down the slope like a swarm of great black beetles, with never a sound of going—in silence profound, absolute.

Instead of darkening, the haunted landscape began to brighten. Through the belt of trees beyond the brook shone a strange red light, the trunks and branches of the trees making a black lacework against it. It struck the creeping figures and gave them monstrous shadows, which caricatured their movements on the lit grass. It fell upon their faces, touching their whiteness with a ruddy tinge, accentuating the stains with which so many of them were freaked and maculated. It sparkled on buttons and bits of metal in their clothing. Instinctively the child turned toward the growing splendor and moved down the slope with his horrible companions; in a few moments had passed the foremost of the throng—not much of a feat, considering his advantages. He placed himself in the lead, his wooden sword still in hand, and solemnly directed the march, conforming his pace to theirs and occasionally turning as if to see that his forces did not straggle. Surely such a leader never before had such a following.

Scattered about upon the ground now slowly narrowing by the encroachment of this awful march to water, were certain articles to which, in the leader's mind, were coupled no significant associations: an occasional blanket, tightly rolled lengthwise, doubled and the ends bound together with a string; a heavy knapsack here, and there a broken rifle—such things, in short, as are found in the rear of retreating troops, the "spoor" of men flying from their hunters. Everywhere near the creek, which here had a margin of lowland, the earth was trodden into mud by the feet of men and horses. An observer of better experience in the use of his eyes would have noticed that these footprints pointed in both directions; the ground had been twice passed over—in advance and in retreat. A few hours before, these desperate, stricken men, with their more fortunate and now distant comrades, had penetrated the forest in thousands. Their successive battalions, breaking into swarms and reforming in lines, had passed the child on every side—had almost trodden on him as he slept. The rustle and murmur of their march had not awakened him. Almost within a stone's throw of where he lay they had fought a battle; but all unheard by him were the roar of the musketry, the shock of the cannon, "the thunder of the captains and the shouting." He had slept through it all, grasping his little wooden sword with perhaps a tighter clutch in unconscious sympathy with his martial environment, but as heedless of the grandeur of the struggle as the dead who had died to make the glory.

The fire beyond the belt of woods on the farther side of the creek, reflected to earth from the canopy of its own smoke, was now suffusing the whole landscape. It transformed the sinuous line of mist to the vapor of gold. The water gleamed with dashes of red, and red, too, were many of the stones protruding above the surface. But that was blood; the less desperately wounded had stained them in crossing. On them, too, the child now crossed with eager steps; he was going to the fire. As he stood upon the farther bank he turned about to look at the companions of his march. The advance was arriving at the creek. The stronger had already drawn themselves to the brink and plunged their faces into the flood. Three or four who lay without motion appeared to have no heads. At this the child's eyes expanded with wonder; even his hospitable understanding could not accept a phenomenon implying such vitality as that. After slaking their thirst these men had not had the strength to back away from the water, nor to keep their heads above it. They were drowned. In rear of these, the open spaces of the forest showed the leader as many formless figures of his grim command as at first; but not nearly so many were in motion. He waved his cap for their encouragement and smilingly pointed with his weapon in the direction of the guiding light—a pillar of fire to this strange exodus.

Confident of the fidelity of his forces, he now entered the belt of woods, passed through it easily in the red illumination, climbed a fence, ran across a field, turning now and again to coquet with his responsive shadow, and so approached the blazing ruin of a dwelling. Desolation everywhere! In all the wide glare not a living thing was visible. He cared nothing for that; the spectacle pleased, and he danced with glee in imitation of the wavering flames. He ran about, collecting fuel, but every object that he found was too heavy for him to cast in from the distance to which the heat limited his approach. In despair he flung in his sword—a surrender to the superior forces of nature. His military career was at an end.

Shifting his position, his eyes fell upon some outbuildings which had an oddly familiar appearance, as if he had dreamed of them. He stood considering them with wonder, when suddenly the entire plantation, with its inclosing forest, seemed to turn as if upon a pivot. His little world swung half around; the points of the compass were reversed. He recognized the blazing building as his own home!

For a moment he stood stupefied by the power of the revelation, then ran with stumbling feet, making a half-circuit of the ruin. There, conspicuous in the light of the conflagration, lay the dead body of a woman—the white face turned upward, the hands thrown out and clutched full of grass, the clothing deranged, the long dark hair in tangles and full of clotted blood. The greater part of the forehead was torn away, and from the jagged hole the brain protruded, overflowing the temple, a frothy mass of gray, crowned with clusters of crimson bubbles—the work of a shell.

The child moved his little hands, making wild, uncertain gestures. He uttered a series of inarticulate and indescribable cries—something between the chattering of an ape and the gobbling of a turkey—a startling, soulless, unholy sound, the language of a devil. The child was a deaf mute.

Then he stood motionless, with quivering lips, looking down upon the wreck.

JEAN LORRAIN

*

The Holes in the Mask

(Les Trous du Masque)

A fin-de-siècle Parisian maudit *(he was a homosexual and an ether addict when the open display of these habits was much more scandalous than it would be today), Jean Lorrain (1855–1906) is the author of this tale about masks and nothingness. It possesses a rare nightmare power, especially because the narrator contemplates his own demise.*

The charm of horror only tempts the strong.

FOR MARCEL SCHOWB

I

"YOU DO WANT to see it," my friend De Jacquels said to me. "Well then, get yourself a domino costume and a mask, an elegant domino cloak made of black satin, put on some dancing pumps, and for this occasion, silk stockings as well. And wait for me at your house on Tuesday at around ten-thirty. I'll come for you then."

The following Tuesday, wrapped in the rustling folds of a long cloak, wearing a velvet mask with a satin beard fastened behind my ears, I waited for my friend De Jacquels in my bachelor flat on Taibout Street, warming my feet, which were stiff with cold and irritated from the unfamiliar touch of silk, at the fireplace. Outside, a jumble of horns and exasperating shrieks of a carnival night rose from the boulevard.

It was turning out odd, that solitary evening, consisting of a masked man reclining in an armchair in the chiaroscuro of a ground-floor apartment crammed with objects, insulated by rugs, with the high flame of an oil lamp and the flickering of two long, white, slender, almost funerary candles reflected in the mirrors hanging on the wall—even, in retrospect, little by little, disturbing. And still De Jacquels hadn't arrived! The shrieks of the masqueraders that broke out in the distance made the hostility of the silence seem even heavier. The two candles were burning so straight that, suddenly and impatiently, upset by those three lights, I got up to put one of them out.

At that moment one of the curtains parted, and De Jacquels entered.

De Jacquels? I'd heard no knocking, no opening of the door. How had he gotten into my apartment? I've often thought about it since then. In any case, there before me was De Jacquels. De Jacquels? Well, a long domino cloak, a large, somber form, veiled and masked, as I was.

"Are you ready?" asked his voice, which I did not recognize, so changed was it. "My carriage is here, let's go."

His carriage: I hadn't heard it arrive or stop outside my windows. Into what nightmare, shadow, and mystery had I begun to descend?

"It's your hood that's blocking your ears. You aren't used to the costume," De Jacquels reflected aloud, having penetrated my silence. So that night he had the power of divination; and, lifting my cloak, he checked on the quality of my silk stockings and my light footwear.

That gesture calmed me: it was De Jacquels and none other who was speaking from beneath the costume. No one else would have been aware of the admonition De Jacquels had made to me a week before.

"Well then, let's go," ordered his voice, and, in a whisper of silk and satin rubbing together, we sank into the carriage entrance like, it seems to me, two enormous bats, with the flutter of our two capes suddenly wafted above our domino cloaks.

Where had that strong wind come from, that strange gust? The weather of that carnival night was at once so damp and so mild!

II

Where were we traveling now, sunk into the darkness of the extraordinarily silent horse-drawn carriage, whose wheels made no noise beyond that of the horses' hooves on the wooden pavement of the streets and the macadam on the deserted avenues?

Where were we going along wharves and unfamiliar shores, barely illuminated here and there by the blurred light of an old lantern? We'd long since lost sight of Notre-Dame's fantastic silhouette, outlined on the other side of the river against a leaden sky. The Quai Saint-Michel, the Quai de la Tournelle, even the Quai de Bercy; we were far from the Opéra, from Drouot, Le Peletier streets, and the center of town. We weren't even going to Bullier, where shameful vices have their rendezvous and, escaping beneath their masks, whirl around almost like demons cynically confessed on carnival night. And my companion remained silent.

Alongside that taciturn and pale Seine, under those increasingly infrequent bridges, along those wharves planted with tall, thin trees with branches separated under the livid sky like the fingers of a dead man, I was overcome by an irrational fear, a fear aggravated by De Jacquels' implacable silence. I began to doubt he was there, to think I was next to a stranger. My companion's hand had seized my own, and even though his was soft and weak, he held mine in a vise that was crushing my fingers. . . . That hand of power and will nailed my words to my throat, and I felt any inclination to rebel melt and dissolve within me under its oppression. We were now driving beyond the fortifications and along highways lined by beech trees and the lugubrious stands of wine merchants, food stands on the outskirts of town closed long before. We made our way under the moon, which at last finished outlining a floating mass of clouds and seemed to shower down a coat of salt over that ambiguous suburban landscape. At that instant, it seemed to me that the horses' hooves were echoing on the embankment of the highway, and that the coach's wheels, ceasing to be ghosts, were grating on the gravel and the cobblestones.

"This is the place," my companion murmured. "We've arrived, we can get out." And to my stammered-out, timid "Where are we?" "At the tollhouse for the Italy road, outside the fortifications. We took the long way, but the safest. We'll return by another tomorrow morning." The horses stopped. De Jacquels let go of me to open the door, and then reached his hand out to me.

III

A large hall with high ceilings, its walls whitewashed, interior shutters hermetically sealed, and throughout the entire room, tables to which white tin cups were chained. To the rear, raised three steps on a dais, the zinc bar, crowded with liquors and bottles bearing the brightly colored labels of legendary wines. Inside that place the gas hissed, loud and clear. The hall, in sum, no more spacious or clean than a popular suburban tavern doing a brisk business.

"Above all, not a word to anyone at all. Don't speak to a soul; don't even answer. They would see we don't belong, and we could have a rough time. Me, they know." De Jacquels pushed me into the hall.

Some masked people, scattered about the hall, were drinking. When we entered, the owner of the establishment stood up and, dragging his feet, made his way heavily toward us as if to block our way. Without a word, De Jacquels raised the hem of our cloaks and showed him our feet shod in fine slippers. That, doubtless, was the "open sesame" for this strange establishment. The owner returned heavily to the bar, and I realized, strange to say, that he too was wearing a mask, but one made of rough cardboard, painted in a burlesque style, imitating a human face.

The two waiters, two giants with their shirtsleeves rolled up over their boxer's biceps, made their way in silence, they too invisible under the same frightful mask.

The few costumed people seated at the tables and drinking wore masks made of velvet and satin. Except for an enormous, uniformed cuirassier, a brutish type with a heavy jaw and reddish beard, seated next to two elegant dominoes wearing mauve silk, and drinking with his face exposed, his blue eyes already vague, none of the beings there had a human face.

In one corner, two huge figures wearing blouses and velvet caps, masked in black satin, were intriguing because of their suspicious elegance—their blouses were made of pale blue silk, and from beneath their too-new trousers peeked fine women's feet wrapped in silk and encased in slippers. As if hypnotized, I would have gone on contemplating that spectacle if De Jacquels hadn't dragged me to the back of the hall, toward a windowless door closed off by a red curtain. *Entrance to the Dance* was written above the door in the fancy lettering of an apprentice painter. A municipal policeman stood guard next to it. It was, at least, some sort of security, but when I passed and touched his hand, I realized it was made of wax, as was his pink face bristling with false whiskers. I had the horrible certitude that the only being whose presence had reassured me in that place of mystery was a mere manikin. . . .

IV

For how many hours was I wandering alone among silent masks in that hangar vaulted like a church. And in effect, it was a church: an abandoned, secularized church, that large hall with ogival windows, most of them half walled-up, between its ornate columns whitewashed with a thick yellowish coating into which the sculpted flowers on the capitals sank.

A strange ball, at which no one danced and at which there was no orchestra! De Jacquels had disappeared, and I was alone, abandoned amid that unknown crowd. An old wrought-iron chandelier burned bright and clear suspended in the dome, illuminating the dusty paving stones, some of which, blackened with inscriptions, perhaps covered tombs. In the rear, where the altar should have reigned, there were, hung at mid-height on the wall, cribs and eating-troughs, and in the corners were piled forgotten harnesses and halters. The ballroom was a stable. Here and there, huge barbershop mirrors framed with gold paper reflected, from one to the next, the silent passage of the masqueraders. That is to say, they no longer reflected it, since they'd all sat down, lined up, immobile, on both sides of the old church, entombed up to their shoulders in the old choir seats.

There they remained, mute, motionless, as if withdrawn into mystery under long monk's cowls made of silvery cloth, but a matte silver without reflection. Now there were no more dominoes, no silk blouses, no Columbines, no Pierrots, no grotesque disguises. But all those masked people were alike, swathed in the same green suit, a discolored green rather like gold sulfite, with capacious black sleeves, and all in dark green hoods with two holes for their eyes in their silver cowls in the hollow of the cape.

One might have said they were the limy faces of the lepers from the ancient lazaretto. And their black-gloved hands held erect a long stem of a black lily with pale leaves, and their hoods, like Dante's, were crowned with black fleurs-de-lis.

And all those cowls kept silent with the fixedness of ghosts, and above their funeral crowns, the orb of the windows, clearly outlined above the white sky of the moon, covered them with a transparent miter.

I felt my reason sinking away in horror. The supernatural was enveloping me! The rigidity, the silence of all those masked beings! What were they? Another moment of doubt would be madness. I couldn't stand it anymore, so, with my hand clenched in anguish, I advanced toward one of the masked figures and roughly raised his cowl.

Horror! There was nothing, nothing! My terrified eyes found only the hollow of the hood. The suit, the cloak were empty. That being who once lived was only shadow and nothingness.

Crazed with terror, I pulled off the cowl of the masked figure sitting in the next chair: the green velvet cowl was empty, as empty as the cowls of the other masked figures seated along the wall. They all had shadow faces; they were all nothing.

And the gas blazed higher, almost whistling in the high-ceilinged room. Through the broken glass of the ogives, the moonlight glowed, almost blinding. Then a horror seized me amid all those hollow beings with the empty appearance of ghosts, a horrible doubt oppressed my heart before all those vacant masks.

What if I were like them, what if I too had ceased to exist, and what if beneath my mask there was nothing, only nothingness! I ran to one of the mirrors. A dream figure rose before me, covered in dark green, crowned with black fleurs-de-lis, wearing a silver mask.

I was that masked figure, because I could recognize my gesture in the hand that raised the cowl, and, openmouthed with terror, I let loose an enormous shriek, because there was nothing under the mask of silvered fabric, nothing under the oval of the hood, only the hole of rounded cloth over the empty space. I was dead, and I . . .

"You've been drinking ether again," grumbled De Jacquels' voice in my ear. "A curious way to while away your boredom as you waited for me!"

I found myself down on the floor in the center of my room, my body on the rug, my head leaning against the armchair, and De Jacquels, dressed to the nines under a monk's tunic, was giving orders to my bewildered valet while the two candles, having burned all the way down, burst their sockets and awakened me . . . at last!

ROBERT LOUIS STEVENSON

*

The Bottle Imp

(1893)

The famous story of the bottle that contains a devil able to make any wish a reality was told by Stevenson to the indigenous people of Samoa and appears as such in the volume Island Nights Entertainments. *But all Stevenson did was set an old Scottish legend in the South Seas—at least insofar as the story's thematic origin is concerned. With regard to the literary result, "The Bottle Imp" is a masterpiece of narrative art. The plot develops with a mathematical, abstract precision. Here the supernatural too is reduced to a minimum: the anguish is completely a matter of conscience and materializes in a simple bottle inside which is a barely perceivable whitish form.*

There is no consensus about the authentic value of Robert Louis Stevenson (1850–1894). There are those who think him a minor writer and those who recognize greatness in him. I agree with the latter: because of the clean, light clarity of his style, but also because of the moral nucleus of all his narratives. In this story, the morality of human limitations receives a rich, modulated fantastic enactment.

Note. Any student of that very unliterary product, the English drama of the early part of the century, will here recognise the name and the root idea of a piece once rendered popular by the redoubtable B. Smith. The root idea is there and identical, and yet I believe I have made it a new thing. And the fact that the tale has been designed and written for a Polynesian audience may lend it some extraneous interest nearer home.—R. L. S.

THERE WAS A man of the island of Hawaii, whom I shall call Keawe; for the truth is, he still lives, and his name must be kept secret; but the place of his birth was not far from Honaunau, where the bones of Keawe the Great lie hidden in a cave. This man was poor, brave, and active; he could read and write like a schoolmaster; he was a first-rate mariner besides, sailed for some time in the island steamers, and steered a whaleboat on the Hamakua coast. At length it came in Keawe's mind to have a sight of the great world and foreign cities, and he shipped on a vessel bound to San Francisco.

This is a fine town, with a fine harbour, and rich people uncountable; and, in particular, there is one hill which is covered with palaces. Upon this hill Keawe was one day taking a walk, with his pocket full of money, viewing the great houses upon either hand with pleasure. "What fine houses there are!" he was thinking, "and how happy must these people be who dwell in them, and take no care for the morrow!" The thought was in his mind when he came abreast of a house that was smaller than some others, but all finished and beautified like a toy; the steps of that house shone like silver, and the borders of the garden bloomed like garlands, and the windows were bright like diamonds; and Keawe stopped and wondered at the excellence of all he saw. So stopping, he was aware of a man that looked forth upon him through a window, so clear, that Keawe could see him as you see a fish in a pool upon the reef. The man was elderly, with a bald head and a black beard; and his face was heavy with sorrow, and he bitterly sighed. And the truth of it is, that as Keawe looked in upon the man, and the man looked out upon Keawe, each envied the other.

All of a sudden the man smiled and nodded, and beckoned Keawe to enter, and met him at the door of the house.

"This is a fine house of mine," said the man, and bitterly sighed. "Would you not care to view the chambers?"

So he led Keawe all over it, from the cellar to the roof, and there was nothing there that was not perfect of its kind, and Keawe was astonished.

"Truly," said Keawe, "this is a beautiful house; if I lived in the like of it, I should be laughing all day long. How comes it, then, that you should be sighing?"

"There is no reason," said the man, "why you should not have a house in all points similar to this, and finer, if you wish. You have some money, I suppose?"

"I have fifty dollars," said Keawe; "but a house like this will cost more than fifty dollars."

The man made a computation. "I am sorry you have no more," said he, "for it may raise you trouble in the future; but it shall be yours at fifty dollars."

"The house?" asked Keawe.

"No, not the house," replied the man; "but the bottle. For, I must tell you, although I appear to you so rich and fortunate, all my fortune, and this house itself and its garden, came out of a bottle not much bigger than a pint. This is it."

And he opened a lockfast place, and took out a round-bellied bottle with a long neck; the glass of it was white like milk, with changing rainbow colours in the grain. Withinsides something obscurely moved, like a shadow and a fire.

"This is the bottle," said the man; and, when Keawe laughed, "You do not believe me?" he added. "Try, then, for yourself. See if you can break it."

So Keawe took the bottle up and dashed it on the floor till he was weary; but it jumped on the floor like a child's ball, and was not injured.

"This is a strange thing," said Keawe. "For by the touch of it, as well as by the look, the bottle should be of glass."

"Of glass it is," replied the man, sighing more heavily than ever; "but the glass of it was tempered in the flames of hell. An imp lives in it, and that is the shadow we behold there moving; or, so I suppose. If any man buy this bottle the imp is at his command; all that he desires—love, fame, money, houses like this house, ay, or a city like this city—all are his at the word uttered. Napoleon had this bottle, and by it he grew to be the king of the world; but he sold it at the last and fell. Captain Cook had this bottle, and by it he found his way to so many islands; but he, too, sold it, and was slain upon Hawaii. For, once it is sold, the power goes and the protection; and unless a man remain content with what he has, ill will befall him."

"And yet you talk of selling it yourself?" Keawe said.

"I have all I wish, and I am growing elderly," replied the man. "There is one thing the imp cannot do—he cannot prolong life; and, it would not be fair to conceal from you there is a drawback to the bottle; for if a man die before he sells it, he must burn in hell forever."

"To be sure, that is a drawback and no mistake," cried Keawe. "I would not meddle with the thing. I can do without a house, thank God; but there is one thing I could not be doing with one particle, and that is to be damned."

"Dear me, you must not run away with things," returned the man. "All you have to do is to use the power of the imp in moderation, and then sell it to someone else, as I do to you, and finish your life in comfort."

"Well, I observe two things," said Keawe. "All the time you keep sighing like a maid in love, that is one; and, for the other, you sell this bottle very cheap."

"I have told you already why I sigh," said the man. "It is because I fear my health is breaking up; and, as you said yourself, to die and go to the devil is a pity for anyone. As for why I sell so cheap, I must explain to you there is a peculiarity about the bottle. Long ago, when the devil brought it first upon earth, it was extremely expensive, and was sold first of all to Prester John for many millions of dollars; but it cannot be sold at all, unless sold at a loss. If you sell it for as much as you paid for it, back it comes to you again like a homing pigeon. It follows that the price has kept falling in these centuries, and the bottle is now remarkably cheap. I bought it myself from one of my great neighbours on this hill, and the price I paid was only ninety dollars. I could sell it for as high as eighty-nine dollars and ninety-nine cents, but not a penny dearer, or back the thing must come to me. Now, about this there are two bothers. First, when you offer a bottle so singular for eighty odd dollars, people suppose you to be jesting. And second—but there is no hurry about that—and I need not go into it. Only remember it must be coined money that you sell it for."

"How am I to know that this is all true?" asked Keawe.

"Some of it you can try at once," replied the man. "Give me your fifty dollars, take the bottle, and wish your fifty dollars back into your pocket. If that does not happen, I pledge you my honour I will cry off the bargain and restore your money."

"You are not deceiving me?" said Keawe.

The man bound himself with a great oath.

"Well, I will risk that much," said Keawe, "for that can do no harm," and he paid over his money to the man, and the man handed him the bottle.

"Imp of the bottle," said Keawe, "I want my fifty dollars back." And sure enough, he had scarce said the word before his pocket was as heavy as ever.

"To be sure this is a wonderful bottle," said Keawe.

"And now good-morning to you, my fine fellow, and the devil go with you for me," said the man.

"Hold on," said Keawe, "I don't want any more of this fun. Here, take your bottle back."

"You have bought it for less than I paid for it," replied the man, rubbing his hands. "It is yours now; and, for my part, I am only concerned to see the back of you." And with that he rang for his Chinese servant, and had Keawe shown out of the house.

Now, when Keawe was in the street, with the bottle under his arm, he began to think. "If all is true about this bottle, I may have made a losing bargain," thinks he. "But, perhaps the man was only fooling me." The first thing he did was to count his money; the sum was exact—forty-nine dollars American money, and one Chili piece. "That looks like the truth," said Keawe. "Now I will try another part."

The streets in that part of the city were as clean as a ship's decks, and though it was noon, there were no passengers. Keawe set the bottle in the gutter and walked away. Twice he looked back, and there was the milky, round-bellied bottle where he left it. A third time he looked back, and turned a corner; but he had scarce done so, when something knocked upon his elbow, and behold! It was the long neck sticking up; and, as for the round belly, it was jammed into the pocket of his pilot-coat.

"And that looks like the truth," said Keawe.

The next thing he did was to buy a corkscrew in a shop, and go apart into a secret place in the fields. And there he tried to draw the cork, but as often as he put the screw in, out it came again, and the cork as whole as ever.

"This is some new sort of cork," said Keawe, and all at once he began to shake and sweat, for he was afraid of that bottle.

On his way back to the port-side he saw a shop where a man sold shells and clubs from the wild islands, old heathen deities, old coined money, pictures from China and Japan, and all manner of things that sailors bring in their sea-chests. And here he had an idea. So he went in and offered the bottle for a hundred dollars. The man of the shop laughed at him at first, and offered him five; but, indeed, it was a curious bottle, such glass was never blown in any human glassworks, so prettily the colors shone under the milky white, and so strangely the shadow hovered in the midst; so, after he had disputed awhile after the manner of his kind, the shopman gave Keawe sixty silver dollars for the thing and set it on a shelf in the midst of his window.

"Now," said Keawe, "I have sold that for sixty which I bought for fifty—or, to say truth, a little less, because one of my dollars was from Chili. Now I shall know the truth upon another point."

So he went back on board his ship, and when he opened his chest, there was the bottle, and had come more quickly than himself. Now Keawe had a mate on board whose name was Lopaka.

"What ails you?" said Lopaka, "that you stare in your chest?"

They were alone in the ship's forecastle, and Keawe bound him to secrecy, and told all.

"This is a very strange affair," said Lopaka; "and I fear you will be in trouble about this bottle. But there is one point very clear—that you are sure of the trouble, and you had better have the profit in the bargain. Make up your mind what you want with it; give the order, and if it is done as you desire, I will buy the bottle myself; for I have an idea of my own to get a schooner, and go trading through the islands."

"That is not my idea," said Keawe; "but to have a beautiful house and garden on the Kona Coast, where I was born, the sun shining in at the door, flowers in the garden, glass in the windows, pictures on the walls, and toys and fine carpets on the tables, for all the world like the house I was in this day—only a story higher, and with balconies all about like the King's palace; and to live there without care and make merry with my friends and relatives."

"Well," said Lopaka, "let us carry it back with us to Hawaii; and if all comes true, as you suppose, I will buy the bottle, as I said, and ask a schooner."

Upon that they were agreed, and it was not long before the ship returned to Honolulu, carrying Keawe and Lopaka, and the bottle. They were scarce come ashore when they met a friend upon the beach, who began at once to condole with Keawe.

"I do not know what I am to be condoled about," said Keawe.

"Is it possible you have not heard," said the friend, "your uncle—

that good old man—is dead, and your cousin—that beautiful boy—was drowned at sea?"

Keawe was filled with sorrow, and, beginning to weep and to lament, he forgot about the bottle. But Lopaka was thinking to himself, and presently, when Keawe's grief was a little abated, "I have been thinking," said Lopaka, "had not your uncle lands in Hawaii, in the district of Kau?"

"No," said Keawe, "not in Kau: they are on the mountain-side—a little be south Hookena."

"These lands will now be yours?" asked Lopaka.

"And so they will," says Keawe, and began again to lament for his relatives.

"No," said Lopaka, "do not lament at present. I have a thought in my mind. How if this should be the doing of the bottle? For here is the place ready for your house."

"If this be so," cried Keawe, "it is a very ill way to serve me by killing my relatives. But it may be, indeed; for it was in just such a station that I saw the house with my mind's eye."

"The house, however, is not yet built," said Lopaka.

"No, nor like to be!" said Keawe; "for though my uncle has some coffee and ava and bananas, it will not be more than will keep me in comfort; and the rest of that land is the black lava."

"Let us go to the lawyer," said Lopaka; "I have still this idea in my mind."

Now, when they came to the lawyer's, it appeared Keawe's uncle had grown monstrous rich in the last days, and there was a fund of money.

"And here is the money for the house!" cried Lopaka.

"If you are thinking of a new house," said the lawyer, "here is the card of a new architect, of whom they tell me great things."

"Better and better!" cried Lopaka. "Here is all made plain for us. Let us continue to obey orders."

So they went to the architect, and he had drawings of houses on his table.

"You want something out of the way," said the architect. "How do you like this?" and he handed a drawing to Keawe.

Now, when Keawe set eyes on the drawing, he cried out aloud, for it was the picture of his thought exactly drawn.

"I am in for this house," thought he. "Little as I like the way it comes to me, I am in for it now, and I may as well take the good along with the evil."

So he told the architect all that he wished, and how he would have that house furnished, and about the pictures on the wall and the knick-knacks on the tables; and he asked the man plainly for how much he would undertake the whole affair.

The architect put many questions, and took his pen and made a computation; and when he had done he named the very sum that Keawe had inherited.

Lopaka and Keawe looked at one another and nodded.

"It is quite clear," thought Keawe, "that I am to have this house, whether or no. It comes from the devil, and I fear I will get little good by that; and of one thing I am sure, I will make no more wishes as long as I have this bottle. But with the house I am saddled, and I may as well take the good along with the evil."

So he made his terms with the architect, and they signed a paper; and Keawe and Lopaka took ship again and sailed to Australia; for it was concluded between them they should not interfere at all, but leave the architect and the bottle-imp to build and to adorn that house at their own pleasure.

The voyage was a good voyage, only all the time Keawe was holding in his breath, for he had sworn he would utter no more wishes, and take no more favours, from the devil. The time was up when they got back. The architect told them that the house was ready, and Keawe and Lopaka took a passage in the Hall, and went down Kona way to view the house, and see if all had been done fitly according to the thought that was in Keawe's mind.

Now, the house stood on the mountain-side, visible to ships. Above, the forest ran up into the clouds of rain; below, the black lava fell in cliffs, where the kings of old lay buried. A garden bloomed about that house with every hue of flowers; and there was an orchard of papaia on the one hand and an orchard of herdprint on the other, and right in front, toward the sea, a ship's mast had been rigged up and bore a flag. As for the house, it was three stories high, with great chambers and broad balconies on each. The windows were of glass, so excellent that it was as clear as water and as bright as day. All manner of furniture adorned the chambers. Pictures hung upon the wall in golden frames—pictures of ships, and men fighting, and of the most beautiful women, and of singular places; nowhere in the world are there pictures of so bright a colour as those Keawe found hanging in his house. As for the knick-knacks, they were extraordinarily fine: chiming clocks and musical boxes, little men with nodding heads, books filled with pictures, weapons of price from all quarters of the world, and the most elegant puzzles to entertain the leisure of a solitary man. And as no one would care to live in such chambers, only to walk through and view them, the balconies were made so broad that a whole town might have lived upon them in delight; and Keawe knew not which to prefer, whether the back porch, where you get the land breeze, and looked upon the orchards and the flowers, or the front balcony, where you could drink the wind of the sea, and look down the steep wall of the mountain and see the Hall going by once a week or so between Hookena and the hills of Pele, or the schooners plying up the coast for wood and ava and bananas.

When they had viewed all, Keawe and Lopaka sat on the porch.

"Well," asked Lopaka, "is it all as you designed?"

"Words cannot utter it," said Keawe. "It is better than I dreamed, and I am sick with satisfaction."

"There is but one thing to consider," said Lopaka, "all this may be quite natural, and the bottle-imp have nothing whatever to say to it. If I were to buy the bottle, and got no schooner after all, I should have put my hand in the fire for nothing. I gave you my word, I know; but yet I think you would not grudge me one more proof."

"I have sworn I would take no more favours," said Keawe. "I have gone already deep enough."

"This is no favour I am thinking of," replied Lopaka. "It is only to see the imp himself. There is nothing to be gained by that, and so nothing to be ashamed of, and yet, if I once saw him, I should be sure of the whole matter. So indulge me so far, and let me see the imp; and, after that, here is the money in my hand, and I will buy it."

"There is only one thing I am afraid of," said Keawe. "The imp may be very ugly to view, and if you once set eyes upon him you might be very undesirous of the bottle."

"I am a man of my word," said Lopaka. "And here is the money betwixt us."

"Very well," replied Keawe, "I have a curiosity myself. So come, let us have one look at you, Mr. Imp."

Now as soon as that was said, the imp looked out of the bottle, and in again, swift as a lizard; and there sat Keawe and Lopaka turned to stone. The night had quite come, before either found a thought to say or voice to say it with; and then Lopaka pushed the money over and took the bottle.

"I am a man of my word," said he, "and had need to be so, or I would not touch this bottle with my foot. Well, I shall get my schooner and a dollar or two for my pocket; and then I will be rid of this devil as fast as I can. For to tell you the plain truth, the look of him has cast me down."

"Lopaka," said Keawe, "do not you think any worse of me than you can help; I know it is night, and the roads bad, and the pass by the tombs an ill place to go by so late, but I declare since I have seen that little face, I cannot eat or sleep or pray till it is gone from me. I will give you a lantern, and a basket to put the bottle in, and any picture or fine thing in all my house that takes your fancy; and be gone at once, and go sleep at Hookena with Nahinu."

"Keawe," said Lopaka, "many a man would take this ill; above all, when I am doing you a turn so friendly, as to keep my word and buy the bottle; and for that matter, the night and the dark, and the way by the tombs, must be all tenfold more dangerous to a man with such a sin upon his conscience, and such a bottle under his arm. But for my part, I am so extremely terrified myself, I have not the heart to blame you. Here I go, then; and I pray God you may be happy in your house, and I fortunate with my schooner, and both get to heaven in the end in spite of the devil and his bottle."

So Lopaka went down the mountain; and Keawe stood in his front balcony, and listened to the clink of the horse's shoes, and watched the lantern go shining down the path, and along the cliff of caves where the old dead are buried; and all the time he trembled and clasped his hands, and prayed for his friend, and gave glory to God that he himself was escaped out of that trouble.

But the next day came very brightly, and that new house of his was so delightful to behold that he forgot his terrors. One day followed another, and Keawe dwelt there in perpetual joy. He had his place on the back porch; it was there he ate and lived, and read the stories in the Honolulu newspapers; but when anyone came by they would go in and view the chambers and the pictures. And the fame of the house went far and wide; it was called *Ka-Hale Nui*—the Great House—in all Kona; and sometimes the Bright House, for Keawe kept a Chinaman, who was all day dusting and furbishing; and the glass, and the gilt, and the fine stuffs, and the pictures, shone as bright as the morning. As for Keawe himself, he could not walk in the chambers without singing, his heart was so enlarged; and when ships sailed by upon the sea, he would fly his colours on the mast.

So time went by, until one day Keawe went upon a visit as far as Kailua to certain of his friends. There he was well feasted; and left as soon as he could the next morning, and rode hard, for he was impatient to behold his beautiful house; and, besides, the night then coming on was the night in which the dead of old days go abroad in the sides of Kona; and having already meddled with the devil, he was the more chary of meeting with the dead. A little beyond Honaunau, looking far ahead, he was aware of a woman bathing in the edge of the sea; and she seemed a well-grown girl, but he thought no more of it. Then he saw her white shift flutter as she put it on, and then her red holoku; and by the time he came abreast of her she was done with her toilet, and had come up from the sea, and stood by the track-side in her red holoku, and she was all freshened with the bath, and her eyes shone and were kind. Now Keawe no sooner beheld her than he drew rein.

"I thought I knew everyone in this country," said he. "How comes it that I do not know you?"

"I am Kokua, daughter of Kiano," said the girl, "and I have just returned from Oahu. Who are you?"

"I will tell you who I am in a little," said Keawe, dismounting from his horse, "but not now. For I have a thought in my mind, and if you knew who I was, you might have heard of me, and would not give me a true answer. But tell me, first of all, one thing: are you married?"

At this Kokua laughed out aloud. "It is you who ask questions," she said. "Are you married yourself?"

"Indeed, Kokua, I am not," replied Keawe, "and never thought to be until this hour. But here is the plain truth. I have met you here at the road-side, and I saw your eyes, which are like the stars, and my heart went to you as swift as a bird. And so now, if you want none of me, say so, and I will go on to my own place; but if you think me no worse than any other young man, say so, too, and I will turn aside to your father's for the night, and to-morrow I will talk with the good man."

Kokua said never a word, but she looked at the sea and laughed.

"Kokua," said Keawe, "if you say nothing, I will take that for the good answer; so let us be stepping to your father's door."

She went on ahead of him, still without speech; only sometimes she glanced back and glanced away again, and she kept the strings of her hat in her mouth.

Now, when they had come to the door, Kiano came out on his veranda, and cried out and welcomed Keawe by name. At that the girl looked over, for the fame of the great house had come to her ears; and, to be sure, it was a great temptation. All that evening they were very merry together; and the girl was as bold as brass under the eyes of her parents, and made a mark of Keawe, for she had a quick wit. The next day he had a word with Kiano, and found the girl alone.

"Kokua," said he, "you made a mark of me all the evening; and it is still time to bid me go. I would not tell you who I was, because I have so fine a house, and I feared you would think too much of that house and too little of the man that loves you. Now you know all, and if you wish to have seen the last of me, say so at once."

"No," said Kokua, but this time she did not laugh, nor did Keawe ask for more.

This was the wooing of Keawe; things had gone quickly; but so an arrow goes, and the ball of a rifle swifter still, and yet both may strike the target. Things had gone fast, but they had gone far also, and the thought of Keawe rang in the maiden's head; she heard his voice in the breach of the surf upon the lava, and for this young man that she had seen but twice she would have left father and mother and her native islands. As for Keawe himself, his horse flew up the path of the mountain under the cliff of tombs, and the sound of the hoofs, and the sound of Keawe singing to himself for pleasure, echoed in the caverns of the dead. He came to the Bright House, and still he was singing. He sat and ate in the broad balcony, and the Chinaman wondered at his master, to hear how he sang between the mouthfuls. The sun went down into the sea, and the night came; and Keawe walked the balconies by lamplight, high on the mountains, and the voice of his singing startled men on ships.

"Here am I now upon my high place," he said to himself. "Life may be no better; this is the mountain top; and all shelves about me toward the worse. For the first time I will light up the chambers, and bathe in my fine bath with the hot water and the cold, and sleep above in the bed of my bridal chamber."

So the Chinaman had word, and he must rise from sleep and light the furnaces; and as he walked below, beside the boilers, he heard his master singing and rejoicing above him in the lighted chambers. When the water began to be hot the Chinaman cried to his master: and Keawe went into the bath-room; and the Chinaman heard him sing as he filled the marble basin; and heard him sing, and the singing broken, as he undressed; until of a sudden, the song ceased. The Chinaman listened, and listened; he called up the house to Keawe to ask if all were well, and Keawe answered him "Yes," and bade him go to bed; but there was no more singing in the Bright House; and all night long the Chinaman heard his master's feet go round and round the balconies without repose.

Now, the truth of it was this: as Keawe undressed for his bath, he spied upon his flesh a patch like a patch of lichen on a rock, and it was then that he stopped singing. For he knew the likeness of that patch, and knew that he was fallen in the Chinese Evil.

Now, it is a sad thing for any man to fall into this sickness. And it would be a sad thing for anyone to leave a house so beautiful and so commodious, and depart from all his friends to the north coast of Molokai, between the mighty cliff and the sea-breakers. But what was that to the case of the man Keawe, he who had met his love but yesterday, and won her but that morning, and now saw all his hopes break, in a moment, like a piece of glass?

Awhile he sat upon the edge of the bath, then sprang, with a cry, and ran outside; and to and fro, to and fro, along the balcony, like one despairing.

"Very willingly could I leave Hawaii, the home of my fathers," Keawe was thinking. "Very lightly could I leave my house, the high-placed, the many-windowed, here upon the mountains. Very bravely could I go to Molokai, to Kalaupapa by the cliffs, to live with the smitten and to sleep there, far from my fathers. But what wrong have I done, what sin lies upon my soul, that I should have encountered Kokua coming cool from the sea-water in the evening? Kokua, the soul ensnarer! Kokua, the light of my life! Her may I never wed, her may I look upon no longer, her may I no more handle with my loving hand; and it is for this, it is for you, O Kokua! that I pour my lamentations!"

Now you are to observe what sort of a man Keawe was, for he might have dwelt there in the Bright House for years, and no one been the wiser of his sickness; but he reckoned nothing of that, if he must lose Kokua. And again he might have wed Kokua even as he was; and so many would have done, because they have the souls of pigs; but Keawe loved the maid manfully, and he would do her no hurt and bring her in no danger.

A little beyond the midst of the night, there came in his mind the recollection of that bottle. He went round to the back porch, and called to memory the day when the devil had looked forth; and at the thought ice ran in his veins.

"A dreadful thing is the bottle," thought Keawe, "and dreadful is the imp, and it is a dreadful thing to risk the flames of hell. But what other hope have I to cure my sickness or to wed Kokua? What!" he thought, "would I beard the devil once, only to get me a house, and not face him again to win Kokua?"

Thereupon he called to mind it was the next day the Hall went by on her return to Honolulu. "There must I go first," he thought, "and see Lopaka. For the best hope that I have now is to find that same bottle I was so pleased to be rid of."

Never a wink could he sleep; the food stuck in his throat; but he sent a letter to Kiano, and about the time when the steamer would be coming, rode down beside the cliff of the tombs. It rained; his horse went heavily; he looked up at the black mouths of the caves, and he envied the dead that slept there and were done with trouble; and called to mind how he had galloped by the day before, and was astonished. So he came down to Hookena, and there was all the country gathered for the steamer as usual. In the shed before the store they sat and jested and passed the news; but there was no matter of speech in Keawe's bosom, and he sat in their midst and looked without on the rain falling on the houses, and the surf beating among the rocks, and the sighs arose in his throat.

"Keawe of the Bright House is out of spirits," said one to another. Indeed, and so he was, and little wonder.

Then the Hall came, and the whaleboat carried him on board. The after-part of the ship was full of Haoles—whites—who had been to visit the volcano, as their custom is; and the midst was crowded with Kanakas, and the fore-part with wild bulls from Hilo and horses from Kau; but Keawe sat apart from all in his sorrow, and watched for the house of Kiano. There it sat low upon the shore in the black rocks, and shaded by the coron palms, and there by the door was a red holoku, no greater than a fly, and going to and fro with a fly's busyness. "Ah, queen of my heart," he cried, "I'll venture my dear soul to win you!"

Soon after darkness fell and the cabins were lit up, and the Haoles sat and played at the cards and drank whiskey as their custom is; but Keawe walked the deck all night; and all the next day, as they steamed under the lea of Maui or of Molokai, he was still pacing to and fro like a wild animal in a menagerie.

Toward evening they passed Diamond Head, and came to the pier of Honolulu. Keawe stepped out among the crowd and began to ask for Lopaka. It seemed he had become the owner of a schooner—none better in the islands—and was gone upon an adventure as far as Pola-Pola or Kahiki; so there was no help to be looked for from Lopaka. Keawe called to mind a friend of his, a lawyer in the town (I must not tell his name), and inquired of him. They said he was grown suddenly rich, and had a fine new house upon Waikiki shore; and this put a thought in Keawe's head, and he called a hack and drove to the lawyer's house.

The house was all brand new, and the trees in the garden no greater than walking-sticks, and the lawyer, when he came, had the air of a man well pleased.

"What can I do to serve you?" said the lawyer.

"You are a friend of Lopaka's," replied Keawe, "and Lopaka purchased from me a certain piece of goods that I thought you might enable me to trace."

The lawyer's face became very dark. "I do not profess to misunderstand you, Mr. Keawe," said he, "though this is an ugly business to be stirring in. You may be sure I know nothing, but yet I have a guess, and if you would apply in a certain quarter I think you might have news."

And he named the name of a man, which, again, I had better not repeat. So it was for days, and Keawe went from one to another, finding everywhere new clothes and carriages, and fine new houses and men everywhere in great contentment, although, to be sure, when he hinted at his business their faces would cloud over.

"No doubt I am upon the track," thought Keawe. "These new clothes and carriages are all the gifts of the little imp, and these glad faces are the faces of men who have taken their profit and got rid of the accursed thing in safety. When I see pale cheeks and hear sighing, I shall know that I am near the bottle."

So it befell at last that he was recommended to a Haole in Beritania Street. When he came to the door, about the hour of the evening meal, there were the usual marks of the new house, and the young garden, and the electric light shining in the windows; but when the owner came, a shock of hope and fear ran through Keawe; for here was a young man, white as a corpse, and black about the eyes, the hair shedding from his head, and such a look in his countenance as a man may have when he is waiting for the gallows.

"Here it is, to be sure," thought Keawe, and so with this man he noways veiled his errand. "I am come to buy the bottle," said he.

At the word, the young Haole of Beritania Street reeled against the wall.

"The bottle!" he gasped. "Buy the bottle!" Then he seemed to choke, and seizing Keawe by the arm, carried him into a room and poured out wine in two glasses.

"Here is my respects," said Keawe, who had been much about with Haoles in his time. "Yes," he added, "I am come to buy the bottle. What is the price by now?"

At that word the young man let his glass slip through his fingers, and looked upon Keawe like a ghost.

"The price," says he; "the price! You do not know the price?"

"It is for that I am asking you," returned Keawe. "But why are you so much concerned? Is there anything wrong about the price?"

"It has dropped a great deal in value since your time, Mr. Keawe," said the young man, stammering.

"Well, well, I shall have the less to pay for it," says Keawe. "How much did it cost you?"

The young man was as white as a sheet. "Two cents," said he.

"What?" cried Keawe, "two cents? Why, then, you can only sell it for one. And he who buys it—" The words died upon Keawe's tongue; he who bought it could never sell it again, the bottle and the bottle imp must abide with him until he died, and when he died must carry him to the red end of hell.

The young man of Beritania Street fell upon his knees. "For God's sake, buy it!" he cried. "You can have all my fortune in the bargain. I was mad when I bought it at that price. I had embezzled money at my store; I was lost else; I must have gone to jail."

"Poor creature," said Keawe, "you would risk your soul upon so desperate an adventure, and to avoid the proper punishment of your own disgrace; and you think I could hesitate with love in front of me. Give me the bottle, and the change which I make sure you have all ready. Here is a five-cent piece."

It was as Keawe supposed; the young man had the change ready in a drawer; the bottle changed hands, and Keawe's fingers were no sooner clasped upon the stalk than he had breathed his wish to be a clean man. And, sure enough, when he got home to his room, and stripped himself before a glass, his flesh was whole like an infant's. And here was the strange thing: he had no sooner seen this miracle than his mind was changed within him, and he cared naught for the Chinese Evil, and little enough for Kokua; and had but the one thought, that here he was bound to the bottle imp for time and for eternity, and had no better hope but to be a cinder forever in the flames of hell. Away ahead of him he saw them blaze with his mind's eye, and his soul shrank, and darkness fell upon the light.

When Keawe came to himself a little, he was aware it was the night when the band played at the hotel. Thither he went, because he feared to be alone; and there, among happy faces, walked to and fro, and heard the tunes go up and down, and saw Berger beat the measure, and all the while he heard the flames crackle, and saw the red fire burning in the bottomless pit. Of a sudden the band played *Hiki-ao-ao*; that was a song that he had sung with Kokua, and at the strain courage returned to him.

"It is done now," he thought, "and once more let me take the good along with the evil."

So it befell that he returned to Hawaii by the first steamer, and as soon as it could be managed he was wedded to Kokua, and carried her up the mountain-side to the Bright House.

Now it was so with these two, that when they were together Keawe's heart was stilled; but as soon as he was alone he fell into a brooding horror, and heard the flames crackle, and saw the red fire burn in the bottomless pit. The girl, indeed, had come to him wholly; her heart leaped in her side at sight of him, her hand clung to his; and she was so fashioned, from the hair upon her head to the nails upon her toes, that none could see her without joy. She was pleasant in her nature. She had the good word always. Full of song she was, and went to and fro in the Bright House, the brightest thing in its three stories, carolling like the birds. And Keawe beheld and heard her with delight, and then must shrink upon one side, and weep and groan to think upon the price that he had paid for her; and then he must dry his eyes, and wash his face, and go and sit with her on the broad balconies, joining in her songs, and, with a sick spirit, answering her smiles.

There came a day when her feet began to be heavy and her songs more rare; and now it was not Keawe only that would weep apart, but each would sunder from the other and sit in opposite balconies with the whole width of the Bright House betwixt. Keawe was so sunk in his despair, he scarce observed the change, and was only glad he had more hours to sit alone and brood upon his destiny, and was not so frequently condemned to pull a smiling face on a sick heart. But one day, coming softly through the house, he heard the sound of a child sobbing, and there was Kokua rolling her face upon the balcony floor, and weeping like the lost.

"You do well to weep in this house, Kokua," he said. "And yet I would give the head off my body that you (at least) might have been happy."

"Happy!" she cried. "Keawe, when you lived alone in your Bright House you were the word of the island for a happy man; laughter and song were in your mouth, and your face was as bright as the sunrise. Then you wedded poor Kokua; and the good God knows what is amiss in her—but from that day you have not smiled. Oh!" she cried, "what ails me? I thought I was pretty, and I knew I loved him. What ails me, that I throw this cloud upon my husband?"

"Poor Kokua," said Keawe. He sat down by her side, and sought to take her hand; but that she plucked away. "Poor Kokua," he said, again. "My poor child—my pretty. And I had thought all this while to spare you! Well, you shall know all. Then, at least, you will pity poor Keawe; then you will understand how much he loved you in the past—that he dared hell for your possession—and how much he loves you still (the poor condemned one), that he can yet call up a smile when he beholds you."

With that, he told her all, even from the beginning.

"You have done this for me?" she cried. "Ah, well, then what do I care!" and she clasped and wept upon him.

"Ah, child!" said Keawe, "and yet, when I consider of the fire of hell, I care a good deal!"

"Never tell me," said she, "no man can be lost because he loved Kokua, and no other fault. I tell you, Keawe, I shall save you with these hands, or perish in your company. What! you loved me and gave your soul, and you think I will not die to save you in return?"

"Ah, my dear, you might die a hundred times, and what difference would that make?" he cried, "except to leave me lonely till the time comes of my damnation?"

"You know nothing," said she. "I was educated in a school in Honolulu; I am no common girl. And I tell you I shall save my lover. What is this you say about a cent? But all the world is not American. In England they have a piece they call a farthing, which is about half a cent. Ah! sorrow!" she cried, "that makes it scarcely better, for the buyer must be lost, and we shall find none so brave as my Keawe! But, then, there is France; they have a small coin there which they call a centime, and these go five to the cent or thereabout. We could not do better. Come, Keawe, let us go to the French islands; let us go to Tahiti, as fast as ships can bear us. There we have four centimes, three centimes, two centimes, one centime; four possible sales to come and go on; and two of us to push the bargain. Come, my Keawe! kiss me, and banish care. Kokua will defend you."

"Gift of God!" he cried. "I cannot think that God will punish me for desiring aught so good! Be it as you will, then, take me where you please: I put my life and my salvation in your hands."

Early the next day Kokua was about her preparations. She took Keawe's chest that he went with sailoring; and first she put the bottle in a corner, and then packed it with the richest of their clothes and the bravest of the knick-knacks in the house. "For," said she, "we must seem to be rich folks, or who will believe in the bottle?" All the time of her preparation she was as gay as a bird; only when she looked upon Keawe the tears would spring in her eye, and she must run and kiss him. As for Keawe, a weight was off his soul; now that he had his secret shared, and some hope in front of him, he seemed like a new man, his feet went lightly on the earth, and his breath was good to him again. Yet was terror still at his elbow; and ever and again, as the wind blows out a taper, hope died in him, and he saw the flames toss and the red fire burn in hell.

It was given out in the country they were gone pleasuring to the States, which was thought a strange thing, and yet not so strange as the truth, if any could have guessed it. So they went to Honolulu in the Hall, and thence in the Umatilla to San Francisco with a crowd of Haoles, and at San Francisco took their passage by the mail brigantine, the Tropic Bird, for Papeete, the chief place of the French in the south islands. Thither they came, after a pleasant voyage, on a fair day of the Trade wind, and saw the reef with the surf breaking and Motuiti with its palms, and the schooner riding withinside, and the white houses of the town low down along the shore among green trees, and overhead the mountains and the clouds of Tahiti, the wise island.

It was judged the most wise to hire a house, which they did accordingly, opposite the British Consul's, to make a great parade of money, and themselves conspicuous with carriages and horses. This it was very easy to do, so long as they had the bottle in their possession; for Kokua was more bold than Keawe, and, whenever she had a mind, called on the imp for twenty or a hundred dollars. At this rate they soon grew to be remarked in the town; and the strangers from Hawaii, their riding and their driving, the fine holokus, and the rich lace of Kokua, became the matter of much talk.

They got on well after the first with the Tahitian language, which is indeed like to the Hawaiian, with a change of certain letters; and as soon as they had any freedom of speech, began to push the bottle. You are to consider it was not an easy subject to introduce; it was not easy to persuade people you are in earnest, when you offer to sell them for four centimes the spring of health and riches inexhaustible. It was necessary besides to explain the dangers of the bottle; and either people disbelieved the whole thing and laughed, or they thought the more of the darker part, became overcast as from persons who had dealings with the devil. So far from gaining ground, these two began to find they were avoided in the town; the children ran away from them screaming, a thing intolerable to Kokua; Catholics crossed themselves as they went by; and all persons began with one accord to disengage themselves from their advances.

Depression fell upon their spirits. They would sit at night in their new house, after a day's weariness, and not exchange one word, or the silence would be broken by Kokua bursting suddenly into sobs. Sometimes they would pray together; sometimes they would have the bottle out upon the floor, and sit all evening watching how the shadow hovered in the midst. At such times they would be afraid to go to rest. It was long ere slumber came to them, and, if either dozed off, it would be to wake and find the other silently weeping in the dark, or, perhaps, to wake alone, the other having fled from the house and the neighbourhood of that bottle, to pace under the bananas in the little garden, or to wander on the beach by moonlight.

One night it was so when Kokua awoke. Keawe was gone. She felt in the bed and his place was cold. Then fear fell upon her, and she sat up in bed. A little moonshine filtered through the shutters. The room was bright, and she could spy the bottle on the floor. Outside it blew high, the great trees of the avenue cried aloud, and the fallen leaves rattled in the veranda. In the midst of this Kokua was aware of another sound; whether of a beast or of a man she could scarce tell, but it was as sad as death, and cut her to the soul. Softly she arose, set the door ajar, and looked forth into the moonlit yard. There, under the bananas, lay Keawe, his mouth in the dust, and as he lay he moaned.

It was Kokua's first thought to run forward and console him; her second potently withheld her. Keawe had borne himself before his wife like a brave man; it became her little in the hour of weakness to intrude upon his shame. With the thought she drew back into the house.

"Heaven," she thought, "how careless have I been—how weak! It is he, not I, that stands in this eternal peril; it was he, not I, that took the curse upon his soul. It is for my sake, and for the love of a creature of so little worth and such poor help, that he now beholds so close to him the flames of hell—ay, and smells the smoke of it, lying without there in the wind and moonlight. Am I so dull of spirit that never till now I have surmised my duty, or have I seen it before and turned aside? But now, at least, I take up my soul in both the hands of my affection; now I say farewell to the white steps of heaven and the waiting faces of my friends. A love for a love, and let mine be equalled with Keawe's! A soul for a soul, and be it mine to perish!"

She was a deft woman with her hands, and was soon apparelled. She took in her hands the change—the precious centimes they kept ever at their side; for this coin is little used, and they had made provision at a government office. When she was forth in the avenue clouds came on the wind, and the moon was blackened. The town slept, and she knew not whither to turn till she heard one coughing in the shadow of the trees.

"Old man," said Kokua, "what do you here abroad in the cold night?"

The old man could scarce express himself for coughing, but she made out that he was old and poor, and a stranger in the island.

"Will you do me a service?" said Kokua. "As one stranger to another, and as an old man to a young woman, will you help a daughter of Hawaii?"

"Ah," said the old man. "So you are the witch from the eight islands, and even my old soul you seek to entangle. But I have heard of you, and defy your wickedness."

"Sit down here," said Kokua, "and let me tell you a tale." And she told him the story of Keawe from the beginning to the end.

"And now," said she, "I am his wife, whom he bought with his soul's welfare. And what should I do? If I went to him myself and offered to buy it, he will refuse. But if you go, he will sell it eagerly; I will await you here; you will buy it for four centimes, and I will buy it again for three. And the Lord strengthen a poor girl!"

"If you meant falsely," said the old man, "I think God would strike you dead."

"He would!" cried Kokua. "Be sure he would. I could not be so treacherous, God would not suffer it."

"Give me the four centimes and await me here," said the old man.

Now, when Kokua stood alone in the street, her spirit died. The wind roared in the trees, and it seemed to her the rushing of the flames of hell; the shadows towered in the light of the street lamp, and they seemed to her the snatching hands of evil ones. If she had had the strength, she must have run away, and if she had had the breath she must have screamed aloud; but, in truth, she could do neither, and stood and trembled in the avenue, like an affrighted child.

Then she saw the old man returning, and he had the bottle in his hand.

"I have done your bidding," said he, "I left your husband weeping like a child; to-night he will sleep easy." And he held the bottle forth.

"Before you give it me," Kokua panted, "take the good with the evil—ask to be delivered from your cough."

"I am an old man," replied the other, "and too near the gate of the grave to take a favour from the devil. But what is this? Why do you not take the bottle? Do you hesitate?"

"Not hesitate!" cried Kokua. "I am only weak. Give me a moment. It is my hand resists, my flesh shrinks back from the accursed thing. One moment only!"

The old man looked upon Kokua kindly. "Poor child!" said he, "you fear: your soul misgives you. Well, let me keep it. I am old, and can never more be happy in this world, and as for the next—"

"Give it me!" gasped Kokua. "There is your money. Do you think I am so base as that? Give me the bottle."

"God bless you, child," said the old man.

Kokua concealed the bottle under her holoku, said farewell to the old man, and walked off along the avenue, she cared not whither. For all roads were now the same to her, and led equally to hell. Sometimes she walked, and sometimes ran; sometimes she screamed out loud in the night, and sometimes lay by the wayside in the dust and wept. All that she had heard of hell came back to her; she saw the flames blaze, and she smelled the smoke, and her flesh withered on the coals.

Near day she came to her mind again, and returned to the house. It was even as the old man said—Keawe slumbered like a child. Kokua stood and gazed upon his face.

"Now, my husband," said she, "it is your turn to sleep. When you wake it will be your turn to sing and laugh. But for poor Kokua, alas! that meant no evil—for poor Kokua no more sleep, no more singing, no more delight, whether in earth or Heaven."

With that she lay down in the bed by his side, and her misery was so extreme that she fell in a deep slumber instantly.

Late in the morning her husband woke her and gave her the good news. It seemed he was silly with delight, for he paid no heed to her distress, ill though she dissembled it. The words stuck in her mouth, it mattered not; Keawe did the speaking. She ate not a bite, but who was to observe it? For Keawe cleared the dish. Kokua saw and heard him, like some strange thing in a dream; there were times when she forgot or doubted, and put her hands to her brow; to know herself doomed and hear her husband babble, seemed so monstrous.

All the while Keawe was eating and talking, and planning the time of their return, and thanking her for saving him, and fondling her, and calling her the true helper after all. He laughed at the old man that was fool enough to buy that bottle.

"A worthy old man he seemed," Keawe said. "But no one can judge by appearances. For why did the old reprobate require the bottle?"

"My husband," said Kokua, humbly, "his purpose may have been good."

Keawe laughed like an angry man.

"Fiddle-de-dee!" cried Keawe. "An old rogue, I tell you; and an old ass to boot. For the bottle was hard enough to sell at four centimes; and at three it will be quite impossible. The margin is not broad enough, the thing begins to smell of scorching—brr!" said he, and shuddered. "It is true I bought it myself at a cent, when I knew not there were smaller coins. I was a fool for my pains; there will never be found another, and whoever has that bottle now will carry it to the pit."

"O my husband!" said Kokua. "Is it not a terrible thing to save oneself by the eternal ruin of another? It seems to me I could not laugh. I would be humbled. I would be filled with melancholy. I would pray for the poor holder."

Then Keawe, because he felt the truth of what she said, grew the more angry. "Heighty-teighty!" cried he. "You may be filled with melancholy if you please. It is not the mind of a good wife. If you thought at all of me, you would sit shamed."

Thereupon he went out, and Kokua was alone.

What chance had she to sell that bottle at two centimes? None, she perceived. And if she had any, here was her husband hurrying her away to a country where there was nothing lower than a cent. And here—on the morrow of her sacrifice—was her husband leaving her and blaming her.

She would not even try to profit by what time she had, but sat in the house, and now had the bottle out and viewed it with unutterable fear, and now, with loathing, hid it out of sight.

By and by, Keawe came back, and would have her take a drive.

"My husband, I am ill," she said. "I am out of heart. Excuse me, I can take no pleasure."

Then was Keawe more wroth than ever. With her, because he thought she was brooding over the case of the old man; and with himself, because he thought she was right, and was ashamed to be so happy.

"This is your truth," cried he, "and this your affection! Your husband is just saved from eternal ruin, which he encountered for the love of you—and you can take no pleasure! Kokua, you have a disloyal heart."

He went forth again furious, and wandered in the town all day. He met friends, and drank with them; they hired a carriage and drove into the country, and there drank again. All the time Keawe was ill at ease, because he was taking this pastime while his wife was sad, and because he knew in his heart that she was more right than he; and the knowledge made him drink the deeper.

Now, there was an old brutal Haole drinking with him, one that had been a boatswain of a whaler—a runaway, a digger in gold mines, a convict in prisons. He had a low mind and a foul mouth; he loved to drink and to see others drunken; and he pressed the glass upon Keawe. Soon there was no more money in the company.

"Here, you!" says the boatswain, "you are rich, you have been always saying. You have a bottle or some foolishness."

"Yes," says Keawe, "I am rich; I will go back and get some money from my wife, who keeps it."

"That's a bad idea, mate," said the boatswain. "Never you trust a petticoat with dollars. They're all as false as water; you keep an eye on her."

Now, this word struck in Keawe's mind; for he was muddled with what he had been drinking.

"I should not wonder but she was false, indeed," thought he. "Why else should she be so cast down at my release? But I will show her I am not the man to be fooled. I will catch her in the act."

Accordingly, when they were back in town, Keawe bade the boatswain wait for him at the corner, by the old calaboose, and went forward up the avenue alone to the door of his house. The night had come again; there was a light within, but never a sound; and Keawe crept about the corner, opened the back door softly, and looked in.

There was Kokua on the floor, the lamp at her side; before her was a milk-white bottle, with a round belly and a long neck; and as she viewed it, Kokua wrung her hands.

A long time Keawe stood and looked in the doorway. At first he was struck stupid; and then fear fell upon him that the bargain had been made amiss, and the bottle had come back to him as it came at San Francisco; and at that his knees were loosened, and the fumes of the wine departed from his head like mists off a river in the morning. And then he had another thought; and it was a strange one, that made his cheeks to burn.

"I must make sure of this," thought he.

So he closed the door, and went softly round the corner again, and then came noisily in, as though he were but now returned. And, lo! by the time he opened the front door no bottle was to be seen; and Kokua sat in a chair and started up like one awakened out of sleep.

"I have been drinking all day and making merry," said Keawe. "I have been with good companions, and now I only come back for money, and return to drink and carouse with them again."

Both his face and voice were as stern as judgment, but Kokua was too troubled to observe.

"You do well to use your own, my husband," said she, and her words trembled.

"Oh, I do well in all things," said Keawe, and he went straight to the chest and took out money. But he looked besides in the corner where they kept the bottle, and there was no bottle there.

At that the chest heaved upon the floor like a sea-billow, and the house span about him like a wreath of smoke, for he saw she was lost now, and there was no escape. "It is what I feared," he thought. "It is she who has bought it."

And then he came to himself a little and rose up; but the sweat streamed on his face as thick as the rain and as cold as the well-water.

"Kokua," said he, "I said to you to-day what ill became me. Now I return to house with my jolly companions," and at that he laughed a little quietly. "I will take more pleasure in the cup if you forgive me."

She clasped his knees in a moment; she kissed his knees with flowing tears.

"Oh," she cried, "I asked but a kind word!"

"Let us never one think hardly of the other," said Keawe, and was gone out of the house.

Now, the money that Keawe had taken was only some of that store of centime pieces they had laid in at their arrival. It was very sure he had no mind to be drinking. His wife had given her soul for him, now he must give his for hers; no other thought was in the world with him.

At the corner, by the old calaboose, there was the boatswain waiting.

"My wife has the bottle," said Keawe, "and, unless you help me to recover it, there can be no more money and no more liquor to-night."

"You do not mean to say you are serious about that bottle?" cried the boatswain.

"There is the lamp," said Keawe. "Do I look as if I was jesting?"

"That is so," said the boatswain. "You look as serious as a ghost."

"Well, then," said Keawe, "here are two centimes; you must go to my wife in the house, and offer her these for the bottle, which (if I am not much mistaken) she will give you instantly. Bring it to me here, and I will buy it back from you for one; for that is the law with this bottle, that it still must be sold for a less sum. But whatever you do, never breathe a word to her that you have come from me."

"Mate, I wonder are you making a fool of me?" asked the boatswain.

"It will do you no harm if I am," returned Keawe.

"That is so, mate," said the boatswain.

"And if you doubt me," added Keawe, "you can try. As soon as you are clear of the house, wish to have your pocket full of money, or a bottle of the best rum, or what you please, and you will see the virtue of the thing."

"Very well, Kanaka," says the boatswain. "I will try; but if you are having your fun out of me, I will take my fun out of you with a belaying-pin."

So the whaler-man went off up the avenue; and Keawe stood and waited. It was near the same spot where Kokua had waited the night before; but Keawe was more resolved, and never faltered in his purpose; only his soul was bitter with despair.

It seemed a long time he had to wait before he heard a voice singing in the darkness of the avenue. He knew the voice to be the boatswain's; but it was strange how drunken it appeared upon a sudden.

Next the man himself came stumbling into the light of the lamp. He had the devil's bottle buttoned in his coat; another bottle was in his hand; and even as he came in view he raised it to his mouth and drank.

"You have it," said Keawe. "I see that."

"Hands off!" cried the boatswain, jumping back. "Take a step near me, and I'll smash your mouth. You thought you could make a cat's paw of me, did you?"

"What do you mean?" cried Keawe.

"Mean?" cried the boatswain. "This is a pretty good bottle, this is; that's what I mean. How I got it for two centimes I can't make out; but I am sure you sha'n't have it for one."

"You mean you won't sell?" gasped Keawe.

"No, sir," cried the boatswain. "But I'll give you a drink of the rum, if you like."

"I tell you," said Keawe, "the man who has that bottle goes to hell."

"I reckon I'm going anyway," returned the sailor; "and this bottle's the best thing to go with I've struck yet. No, sir!" he cried again, "this is my bottle now, and you can go and fish for another."

"Can this be true?" Keawe cried. "For your own sake, I beseech you, sell it me!"

"I don't value any of your talk," replied the boatswain. "You thought I was a flat, now you see I'm not; and there's an end. If you won't have a swallow of the rum, I'll have one myself. Here's your health, and good-night to you!"

So off he went down the avenue toward town, and there goes the bottle out of the story.

But Keawe ran to Kokua light as the wind; and great was their joy that night; and great, since then, has been the peace of all their days in the Bright House.

HENRY JAMES

*

The Friends of the Friends

(1896)

In the ghost stories of Henry James (1843–1916), the supernatural is invisible (the presence of the evil beyond all imagination, as in his famous The Turn of the Screw*) or almost invisible (the imperceptible doubling that takes place in "The Jolly Corner"). In any case, it is not the visible image of the ghost that matters but the knot of human relationships because of which the ghost is evoked or which the specter helps to establish. A story of impalpable, mundane relationships, as in "The Friends of the Friends" (or perhaps better put: "The Friends of Friends"), is charged with vibrations: all living beings project phantoms; the border between the persons of flesh and blood and the psychic emanations is porous. The "parapsychological" point of departure duplicates itself and multiplies. As often happens in James, the neutral-seeming character who stands behind the "voice of the narrator" has a decisive role precisely because of what he does not say: here, as in* The Turn of the Screw*, it is the voice of a woman who this time does not hide her dominant passion—jealousy—and her proclivity for intrigue.*

I FIND, AS you prophesied, much that's interesting, but little that helps the delicate question—the possibility of publication. Her diaries are less systematic than I hoped; she only had a blessed habit of noting and narrating. She summarised, she saved; she appears seldom indeed to have let a good story pass without catching it on the wing. I allude of course not so much to things she heard as to things she saw and felt. She writes sometimes of herself, sometimes of others, sometimes of the combination. It's under this last rubric that she's usually most vivid. But it's not, you will understand, when she's most vivid that she's always most publishable. To tell the truth she's fearfully indiscreet, or has at least all the material for making *me* so. Take as an instance the fragment I send you, after dividing it for your convenience into several small chapters. It is the contents of a thin blank-book which I have had copied out and which has the merit of being nearly enough a rounded thing, an intelligible whole. These pages evidently date from years ago. I've read with the liveliest wonder the statement they so circumstantially make and done my best to swallow the prodigy they leave to be inferred. These things would be striking, wouldn't they? to any reader; but can you imagine for a moment my placing such a document before the world, even though, as if she herself had desired the world should have the benefit of it, she has given her friends neither name nor initials? Have you any sort of clue to their identity? I leave her the floor.

I

I know perfectly of course that I brought it upon myself; but that doesn't make it any better. I was the first to speak of her to him—he had never even heard her mentioned. Even if I had happened not to speak some one else would have made up for it: I tried afterwards to find comfort in that reflection. But the comfort of reflections is thin: the only comfort that counts in life is not to have been a fool. That's a beatitude I shall doubtless never enjoy. "Why, you ought to meet her and talk it over," is what I immediately said. "Birds of a feather flock together." I told him who she was and that they were birds of a feather because if he had had in youth a strange adventure she had had about the same time just such another. It was well known to her friends—an incident she was constantly called on to describe. She was charming, clever, pretty, unhappy; but it was none the less the thing to which she had originally owed her reputation.

Being at the age of eighteen somewhere abroad with an aunt she had had a vision of one of her parents at the moment of death. The parent was in England, hundreds of miles away and so far as she knew neither dying nor dead. It was by day, in the museum of some great foreign town. She had passed alone, in advance of her companions, into a small room containing some famous work of art and occupied at that moment by two other persons. One of these was an old custodian; the second, before observing him, she took for a stranger, a tourist. She was merely conscious that he was bareheaded and seated on a bench. The instant her eyes rested on him however she beheld to her amazement her father, who, as if he had long waited for her, looked at her in singular distress, with an impatience that was akin to reproach. She rushed to him with a bewildered cry, "Papa, what *is* it?" but this was followed by an exhibition of still livelier feeling when on her movement he simply vanished, leaving the custodian and her relations, who were at her heels, to gather round her in dismay. These persons, the official, the aunt, the cousins were therefore in a manner witnesses of the fact—the fact at least of the impression made on her; and there was the further testimony of a doctor who was attending one of the party and to whom it was immediately afterwards communicated. He gave her a remedy for hysterics but said to the aunt privately: "Wait and see if something doesn't happen at home." Something *had* happened—the poor father, suddenly and violently seized, had died that morning. The aunt, the mother's sister, received before the day was out a telegram announcing the event and requesting her to prepare her niece for it. Her niece was already prepared, and the girl's sense of this visitation remained of course indelible. We had all as her friends had it conveyed to us and had conveyed it creepily to each other. Twelve years had elapsed and as a woman who had made an unhappy marriage and lived apart from her husband she had become interesting from other sources; but since the name she now bore was a name frequently borne, and since moreover her judicial separation, as things were going, could hardly count as a distinction, it was usual to qualify her as "the one, you know, who saw her father's ghost."

As for him, dear man, he had seen his mother's. I had never heard of that till this occasion on which our closer, our pleasanter acquaintance led him, through some turn of the subject of our talk, to mention it and to inspire me in so doing with the impulse to let him know that he had a rival in the field—a person with whom he could compare notes. Later on his story became for him, perhaps because of my unduly repeating it, likewise a convenient worldly label; but it had not a year before been the ground on which he was introduced to me. He had other merits, just as she, poor thing! had others. I can honestly say that I was quite aware of them from the first—I discovered them sooner than he discovered mine. I remember how it struck me even at the time that his sense of mine was quickened by my having been able to match, though not indeed straight from my own experience, his curious anecdote. It dated, this anecdote, as hers did, from some dozen years before—a year in which, at Oxford, he had for some reason of his own been staying on into the "Long." He had been in the August afternoon on the river. Coming back into his room while it was still distinct daylight he found his mother standing there as if her eyes had been fixed on the door. He had had a letter from her that morning out of Wales, where she was staying with her father. At the sight of him she smiled with extraordinary radiance and extended her arms to him, and then as he sprang forward and joyfully opened his own she vanished from the place. He wrote to her that night, telling her what had happened; the letter had been carefully preserved. The next morning he heard of her death. He was through this chance of our talk extremely struck with the little prodigy I was able to produce for him. He had never encountered another case. Certainly they ought to meet, my friend and he; certainly they would have something in common. I would arrange this, wouldn't I?—if *she* didn't mind; for himself he didn't mind in the least. I had promised to speak to her of the matter as soon as possible, and within the week I was able to do so. She "minded" as little as he; she was perfectly willing to see him. And yet no meeting was to occur—as meetings are commonly understood.

II

That's just half my tale—the extraordinary way it was hindered. This was the fault of a series of accidents; but the accidents continued for years and became, for me and for others, a subject of hilarity with either party. They were droll enough at first; then they grew rather a bore. The odd thing was that both parties were amenable: it wasn't a case of their being indifferent, much less of their being indisposed. It was one of the caprices of chance, aided I suppose by some opposition of their interests and habits. His were centred in his office, his eternal inspectorship, which left him small leisure, constantly calling him away and making him break engagements. He liked society, but he found it everywhere and took it at a run. I never knew at a given moment where he was, and there were times when for months together I never saw him. She was on her side practically suburban: she lived at Richmond and never went "out." She was a woman of distinction, but not of fashion, and felt, as people said, her situation.

Decidedly proud and rather whimsical she lived her life as she had planned it. There were things one could do with her, but one couldn't make her come to one's parties. One went indeed a little more than seemed quite convenient to hers, which consisted of her cousin, a cup of tea and the view. The tea was good; but the view was familiar, though perhaps not, like the cousin—a disagreeable old maid who had been of the group at the museum and with whom she now lived—offensively so. This connection with an inferior relative, which had partly an economical motive—she proclaimed her companion a marvellous manager—was one of the little perversities we had to forgive her. Another was her estimate of the proprieties created by her rupture with her husband. That was extreme—many persons called it even morbid. She made no advances; she cultivated scruples; she suspected, or I should perhaps rather say she remembered slights: she was one of the few women I have known whom that particular predicament had rendered modest rather than bold. Dear thing! she had some delicacy. Especially marked were the limits she had set to possible attentions from men: it was always her thought that her husband was waiting to pounce on her. She discouraged if she didn't forbid the visits of male persons not senile: she said she could never be too careful.

When I first mentioned to her that I had a friend whom fate had distinguished in the same weird way as herself I put her quite at liberty to say "Oh, bring him out to see me!" I should probably have been able to bring him, and a situation perfectly innocent or at any rate comparatively simple would have been created. But she uttered no such word; she only said: "I must meet him certainly; yes, I shall look out for him!" That caused the first delay, and meanwhile various things happened. One of them was that as time went on she made, charming as she was, more and more friends, and that it regularly befell that these friends were sufficiently also friends of his to bring him up in conversation. It was odd that without belonging, as it were, to the same world or, according to the horrid term, the same set, my baffled pair should have happened in so many cases to fall in with the same people and make them join in the funny chorus. She had friends who didn't know each other but who inevitably and punctually recommended *him*. She had also the sort of originality, the intrinsic interest that led her to be kept by each of us as a kind of private resource, cultivated jealously, more or less in secret, as a person whom one didn't meet in society, whom it was not for every one—whom it was not for the vulgar—to approach, and with whom therefore acquaintance was particularly difficult and particularly precious. We saw her separately, with appointments and conditions, and found it made on the whole for harmony not to tell each other. Somebody had always had a note from her still later than somebody else. There was some silly woman who for a long time, among the unprivileged, owed to three simple visits to Richmond a reputation for being intimate with "lots of awfully clever out-of-the-way people."

Every one has had friends it has seemed a happy thought to bring together, and every one remembers that his happiest thoughts have not been his greatest successes; but I doubt if there was ever a case in which the failure was in such direct proportion to the quantity of influence set in motion. It is really perhaps here the quantity of influence that was most remarkable. My lady and gentleman each declared to me and others that it was like the subject of a roaring farce. The reason first given had with time dropped out of sight and fifty better ones flourished on top of it. They were so awfully alike: they had the same ideas and tricks and tastes, the same prejudices and superstitions and heresies; they said the same things and sometimes did them; they liked and disliked the same persons and places, the same books, authors and styles; any one could see a certain identity even in their looks and their features. It established much of a propriety that they were in common parlance equally "nice" and almost equally handsome. But the great sameness, for wonder and chatter, was their rare perversity in regard to being photographed. They were the only persons ever heard of who had never been "taken" and who had a passionate objection to it. They just *wouldn't* be, for anything any one could say. I had loudly complained of this; him in particular I had so vainly desired to be able to show on my drawing-room chimney-piece in a Bond Street frame. It was at any rate the very liveliest of all the reasons why they ought to know each other—all the lively reasons reduced to naught by the strange law that had made them bang so many doors in each other's face, made them the buckets in the well, the two ends of the see-saw, the two parties in the state, so that when one was up the other was down, when one was out the other was in; neither by any possibility entering a house till the other had left it, or leaving it, all unawares, till the other was at hand. They only arrived when they had been given up, which was precisely also when they departed. They were in a word alternate and incompatible; they missed each other with an inveteracy that could be explained only by its being preconcerted. It was however so far from preconcerted that it had ended—literally after several years—by disappointing and annoying them. I don't think their curiosity was lively till it had been proved utterly vain. A great deal was of course done to help them, but it merely laid wires for them to trip. To give examples I should have to have taken notes; but I happen to remember that neither had ever been able to dine on the right occasion. The right occasion for each was the occasion that would be wrong for the other. On the wrong one they were most punctual, and there were never any but wrong ones. The very elements conspired and the constitution of man reinforced them. A cold, a headache, a bereavement, a storm, a fog, an earthquake, a cataclysm infallibly intervened. The whole business was beyond a joke.

Yet as a joke it had still to be taken, though one couldn't help feeling that the joke had made the situation serious, had produced on the part of each a consciousness, an awkwardness, a positive dread of the last accident of all, the only one with any freshness left, the accident that would bring them face to face. The final effect of its predecessors had been to kindle this instinct. They were quite ashamed—perhaps even a little of each other. So much preparation, so much frustration: what indeed could be good enough for it all to lead up to? A mere meeting would be mere flatness. Did I see them at the end of years, they often asked, just stupidly confronted? If they were bored by the joke they might be worse bored by something else. They made exactly the same reflections, and each in some manner was sure to hear of the other's. I really think it was this peculiar diffidence that finally controlled the situation. I mean that if they had failed for the first year or two because they couldn't help it they kept up the habit because they had—what shall I call it?—grown nervous. It really took some lurking volition to account for anything so absurd.

III

When to crown our long acquaintance I accepted his renewed offer of marriage it was humorously said, I know, that I had made the gift of his photograph a condition. This was so far true that I had refused to give him mine without it. At any rate I had him at last, in his high distinction, on the chimney-piece, where the day she called to congratulate me she came nearer than she had ever done to seeing him. He had set her in being taken an example which I invited her to follow; he had sacrificed his perversity—wouldn't she sacrifice hers? She too must give me something on my engagement—wouldn't she give me the companion-piece? She laughed and shook her head; she had headshakes whose impulse seemed to come from as far away as the breeze that stirs a flower. The companion-piece to the portrait of my future husband was the portrait of his future wife. She had taken her stand—she could depart from it as little as she could explain it. It was a prejudice, an *entêtement*, a vow—she would live and die unphotographed. Now too she was alone in that state: this was what she liked; it made her so much more original. She rejoiced in the fall of her late associate and looked a long time at his picture, about which she made no memorable remark, though she even turned it over to see the back. About our engagement she was charming—full of cordiality and sympathy. "You've known him even longer than I've *not*," she said, "and that seems a very long time." She understood how we had jogged together over hill and dale and how inevitable it was that we should now rest together. I'm definite about all this because what followed is so strange that it's a kind of relief to me to mark the point up to which our relations were as natural as ever. It was I myself who in a sudden madness altered and destroyed them. I see now that she gave me no pretext and that I only found one in the way she looked at the fine face in the Bond Street frame. How then would I have had her look at it? What I had wanted from the first was to make her care for him. Well, that was what I still wanted—up to the moment of her having promised me that he would on this occasion really aid me to break the silly spell that had kept them asunder. I had arranged with him to do his part if she would as triumphantly do hers. I was on a different footing now—I was on a footing to answer for him. I would positively engage that at five on the following Saturday he would be on that spot. He was out of town on pressing business; but pledged to keep his promise to the letter he would return on purpose and in abundant time. "Are you perfectly sure?" I remember she asked, looking grave and considering: I thought she had turned a little pale. She was tired, she was indisposed: it was a pity he was to see her after all at so poor a moment. If he only *could* have seen her five years before! However, I replied that this time I was sure and that success therefore depended simply on herself. At five o'clock on the Saturday she would find him in a particular chair I pointed out, the one in which he usually sat and in which—though this I didn't mention—he had been sitting when, the week before, he put the question of our future to me in the way that had brought me round. She looked at it in silence, just as she had looked at the photograph, while I repeated for the twentieth time that it was too preposterous it shouldn't somehow be feasible to introduce to one's dearest friend one's second self. "*Am* I your dearest friend?" she asked with a smile that for a moment brought back her beauty. I replied by pressing her to my bosom; after which she said: "Well, I'll come. I'm extraordinarily afraid, but you may count on me."

When she had left me I began to wonder what she was afraid of, for she had spoken as if she fully meant it. The next day, late in the afternoon, I had three lines from her: she had found on getting home the announcement of her husband's death. She had not seen him for seven years, but she wished me to know it in this way before I should hear of it in another. It made however in her life, strange and sad to say, so little difference that she would scrupulously keep her appointment. I rejoiced for her—I supposed it would make at least the difference of her having more money; but even in this diversion, far from forgetting that she had said she was afraid, I seemed to catch sight of a reason for her being so. Her fear as the evening went on became contagious, and the contagion took in my breast the form of a sudden panic. It wasn't jealousy—it was the dread of jealousy. I called myself a fool for not having been quiet till we were man and wife. After that I should somehow feel secure. It was only a question of waiting another month—a trifle surely for people who had waited so long. It had been plain enough she was nervous, and now that she was free she naturally wouldn't be less so. What was her nervousness therefore but a presentiment? She had been hitherto the victim of interference, but it was quite possible she would henceforth be the source of it. The victim in that case would be my simple self. What had the interference been but the finger of providence pointing out a danger? The danger was of course for poor *me*. It had been kept at bay by a series of accidents unexampled in their frequency; but the reign of accident was now visibly at an end. I had an intimate conviction that both parties would keep the tryst. It was more and more impressed upon me that they were approaching, converging. We had talked about breaking the spell; well, it would be effectually broken—unless indeed it should merely take another form and overdo their encounters as it had overdone their escapes. This was something I couldn't sit still for thinking of; it kept me awake—at midnight I was full of unrest. At last I felt there was only one way of laying the ghost. If the reign of accident was over I must just take up the succession. I sat down and wrote a hurried note which would meet him on his return and which as the servants had gone to bed I sallied forth bareheaded into the empty, gusty street to drop into the nearest pillar-box. It was to tell him that I shouldn't be able to be at home in the afternoon as I had hoped and that he must postpone his visit till dinner-time. This was an implication that he would find me alone.

IV

When accordingly at five she presented herself I naturally felt false and base. My act had been a momentary madness, but I had at least to be consistent. She remained an hour; he of course never came; and I could only persist in my perfidy. I had thought it best to let her come; singular as this now seems to me I thought it diminished my guilt. Yet as she sat there so visibly white and weary, stricken with a sense of everything her husband's death had opened up, I felt an almost intolerable pang of pity and remorse. If I didn't tell her on the spot what I had done it was because I was too ashamed. I feigned astonishment—I feigned it to the end; I protested that if ever I had had confidence I had had it that day. I blush as I tell my story—I take it as my penance. There was nothing indignant I didn't say about him; I invented suppositions, attenuations; I admitted in stupefaction, as the hands of the clock travelled, that their luck hadn't turned. She smiled at this vision of their "luck," but she looked anxious—she looked unusual: the only thing that kept me up was the fact that, oddly enough, she wore mourning—no great depths of crape, but simple and scrupulous black. She had in her bonnet three small black feathers. She carried a little muff of astrachan. This put me by the aid of some acute reflection a little in the right. She had written to me that the sudden event made no difference for her, but apparently it made as much difference as that. If she was inclined to the usual forms why didn't she observe that of not going the first day or two out to tea? There was some one she wanted so much to see that she couldn't wait till her husband was buried. Such a betrayal of eagerness made me hard and cruel enough to practise my odious deceit, though at the same time, as the hour waxed and waned, I suspected in her something deeper still than disappointment and somewhat less successfully concealed. I mean a strange underlying relief, the soft, low emission of the breath that comes when a danger is past. What happened as she spent her barren hour with me was that at last she gave him up. She let him go for ever. She made the most graceful joke of it that I've ever seen made of anything; but it was for all that a great date in her life. She spoke with her mild gaiety of all the other vain times, the long game of hide-and-seek, the unprecedented queerness of such a relation. For it *was*, or had been, a relation, wasn't it, hadn't it? That was just the absurd part of it. When she got up to go I said to her that it was more a relation than ever, but that I hadn't the face after what had occurred to propose to her for the present another opportunity. It was plain that the only valid opportunity would be my accomplished marriage. Of course she would be at my wedding? It was even to be hoped that *he* would.

"If *I* am, he won't be!" she declared with a laugh. I admitted there might be something in that. The thing was therefore to get us safely married first. "That won't help us. Nothing will help us!" she said as she kissed me farewell. "I shall never, never see him!" It was with those words she left me.

I could bear her disappointment as I've called it; but when a couple of hours later I received him at dinner I found that I couldn't bear his. The way my manœuvre might have affected him had not been particularly present to me; but the result of it was the first word of reproach that had ever yet dropped from him. I say "reproach" because that expression is scarcely too strong for the terms in which he conveyed to me his surprise that under the extraordinary circumstances I should not have found some means not to deprive him of such an occasion. I might really have managed either not to be obliged to go out or to let their meeting take place all the same. They would probably have got on in my drawing-room without me. At this I quite broke down—I confessed my iniquity and the miserable reason of it. I had not put her off and I had not gone out; she had been there and after waiting for him an hour had departed in the belief that he had been absent by his own fault.

"She must think me a precious brute!" he exclaimed. "Did she say of me—what she had a right to say?"

"I assure you she said nothing that showed the least feeling. She looked at your photograph, she even turned round the back of it, on which your address happens to be inscribed. Yet it provoked her to no demonstration. She doesn't care so much as all that."

"Then why are you afraid of her?"

"It was not of her I was afraid. It was of you."

"Did you think I would fall in love with her? You never alluded to such a possibility before," he went on as I remained silent. "Admirable person as you pronounced her, that wasn't the light in which you showed her to me."

"Do you mean that if it *had* been you would have managed by this time to catch a glimpse of her? I didn't fear things then," I added. "I hadn't the same reason."

He kissed me at this, and when I remembered that she had done so an hour or two before I felt for an instant as if he were taking from my lips the very pressure of hers. In spite of kisses the incident had shed a certain chill, and I suffered horribly from the sense that he had seen me guilty of a fraud. He had seen it only through my frank avowal, but I was as unhappy as if I had a stain to efface. I couldn't get over the manner of his looking at me when I spoke of her apparent indifference to his not having come. For the first time since I had known him he seemed to have expressed a doubt of my word. Before we parted I told him that I would undeceive her, start the first thing in the morning for Richmond and there let her know that he had been blameless. At this he kissed me again. I would expiate my sin, I said; I would humble myself in the dust; I would confess and ask to be forgiven. At this he kissed me once more.

V

In the train the next day this struck me as a good deal for him to have consented to; but my purpose was firm enough to carry me on. I mounted the long hill to where the view begins, and then I knocked at her door. I was a trifle mystified by the fact that her blinds were still drawn, reflecting that if in the stress of my compunction I had come early I had certainly yet allowed people time to get up.

"At home, mum? She has left home for ever."

I was extraordinarily startled by this announcement of the elderly parlour-maid. "She has gone away?"

"She's dead, mum, please." Then as I gasped at the horrible word: "She died last night."

The loud cry that escaped me sounded even in my own ears like some harsh violation of the hour. I felt for the moment as if I had killed her; I turned faint and saw through a vagueness the woman hold out her arms to me. Of what next happened I have no recollection, nor of anything but my friend's poor stupid cousin, in a darkened room, after an interval that I suppose very brief, sobbing at me in a smothered accusatory way. I can't say how long it took me to understand, to believe and then to press back with an immense effort that pang of responsibility which, superstitiously, insanely, had been at first almost all I was conscious of. The doctor, after the fact, had been superlatively wise and clear: he was satisfied of a long-latent weakness of the heart, determined probably years before by the agitations and terrors to which her marriage had introduced her. She had had in those days cruel scenes with her husband, she had been in fear of her life. All emotion, everything in the nature of anxiety and suspense had been after that to be strongly deprecated, as in her marked cultivation of a quiet life she was evidently well aware; but who could say that any one, especially a "real lady," could be successfully protected from every little rub? She had had one a day or two before in the news of her husband's death; for there were shocks of all kinds, not only those of grief and surprise. For that matter she had never dreamed of so near a release: it had looked uncommonly as if he would live as long as herself. Then in the evening, in town, she had manifestly had another: something must have happened there which it would be indispensable to clear up. She had come back very late—it was past eleven o'clock, and on being met in the hall by her cousin, who was extremely anxious, had said that she was tired and must rest a moment before mounting the stairs. They had passed together into the dining-room, her companion proposing a glass of wine and bustling to the sideboard to pour it out. This took but a moment, and when my informant turned round our poor friend had not had time to seat herself. Suddenly, with a little moan that was barely audible, she dropped upon the sofa. She was dead. What unknown "little rub" had dealt her the blow? What shock, in the name of wonder, *had* she had in town? I mentioned immediately the only one I could imagine—her having failed to meet at my house, to which by invitation for the purpose she had come at five o'clock, the gentleman I was to be married to, who had been accidentally kept away and with whom she had no acquaintance whatever. This obviously counted for little; but something else might easily have occurred: nothing in the London streets was more possible than an accident, especially an accident in those desperate cabs. What had she done, where had she gone on leaving my house? I had taken for granted she had gone straight home. We both presently remembered that in her excursions to town she sometimes, for convenience, for refreshment, spent an hour or two at the "Gentlewomen," the quiet little ladies' club, and I promised that it should be my first care to make at that establishment thorough inquiry. Then we entered the dim and dreadful chamber where she lay locked up in death and where, asking after a little to be left alone with her, I remained for half an hour. Death had made her, had kept her beautiful; but I felt above all, as I kneeled at her bed, that it had made her, had kept her silent. It had turned the key on something I was concerned to know.

On my return from Richmond and after another duty had been performed I drove to his chambers. It was the first time, but I had often wanted to see them. On the staircase, which, as the house contained twenty sets of rooms, was unrestrictedly public, I met his servant, who went back with me and ushered me in. At the sound of my entrance he appeared in the doorway of a further room, and the instant we were alone I produced my news: "She's dead!"

"Dead?"

He was tremendously struck, and I observed that he had no need to ask whom, in this abruptness, I meant.

"She died last evening—just after leaving me."

He stared with the strangest expression, his eyes searching mine as if they were looking for a trap. "Last evening—after leaving you?" He repeated my words in stupefaction. Then he brought out so that it was in stupefaction I heard: "Impossible! I saw her."

"You 'saw' her?"

"On that spot—where you stand."

This called back to me after an instant, as if to help me to take it in, the great wonder of the warning of his youth. "In the hour of death—I understand: as you so beautifully saw your mother."

"Ah! *not* as I saw my mother—not that way, not that way!" He was deeply moved by my news—far more moved, I perceived, than he would have been the day before: it gave me a vivid sense that, as I had then said to myself, there was indeed a relation between them and that he had actually been face to face with her. Such an idea, by its reassertion of his extraordinary privilege, would have suddenly presented him as painfully abnormal had he not so vehemently insisted on the difference. "I saw her living—I saw her to speak to her—I saw her as I see you now!"

It is remarkable that for a moment, though only for a moment, I found relief in the more personal, as it were, but also the more natural of the two odd facts. The next, as I embraced this image of her having come to him on leaving me and of just what it accounted for in the disposal of her time, I demanded with a shade of harshness of which I was aware—

"What on earth did she come for?"

He had now had a minute to think—to recover himself and judge of effects, so that if it was still with excited eyes he spoke he showed a conscious redness and made an inconsequent attempt to smile away the gravity of his words.

"She came just to see me. She came—after what had passed at your house—so that we *should*, after all, at last meet. The impulse seemed to me exquisite, and that was the way I took it."

I looked round the room where she had been—where she had been and I never had been.

"And was the way you took it the way she expressed it?"

"She only expressed it by being here and by letting me look at her. That was enough!" he exclaimed with a singular laugh.

I wondered more and more. "You mean she didn't speak to you?"

"She said nothing. She only looked at me as I looked at her."

"And you didn't speak either?"

He gave me again his painful smile. "I thought of *you*. The situation was every way delicate. I used the finest tact. But she saw she had pleased me." He even repeated his dissonant laugh.

"She evidently pleased you!" Then I thought a moment. "How long did she stay?"

"How can I say? It seemed twenty minutes, but it was probably a good deal less."

"Twenty minutes of silence!" I began to have my definite view and now in fact quite to clutch at it. "Do you know you're telling me a story positively monstrous?"

He had been standing with his back to the fire; at this, with a pleading look, he came to me. "I beseech you, dearest, to take it kindly."

I could take it kindly, and I signified as much; but I couldn't somehow, as he rather awkwardly opened his arms, let him draw me to him. So there fell between us for an appreciable time the discomfort of a great silence.

VI

He broke it presently by saying: "There's absolutely no doubt of her death?"

"Unfortunately none. I've just risen from my knees by the bed where they've laid her out."

He fixed his eyes hard on the floor; then he raised them to mine. "How does she look?"

"She looks—at peace."

He turned away again, while I watched him; but after a moment he began: "At what hour, then—?"

"It must have been near midnight. She dropped as she reached her house—from an affection of the heart which she knew herself and her physician knew her to have, but of which, patiently, bravely she had never spoken to me."

He listened intently and for a minute he was unable to speak. At last he broke out with an accent of which the almost boyish confidence, the really sublime simplicity rings in my ears as I write: "Wasn't she *wonderful*!" Even at the time I was able to do it justice enough to remark in reply that I had always told him so; but the next minute, as if after speaking he had caught a glimpse of what he might have made me feel, he went on quickly: "You see that if she didn't get home till midnight—"

I instantly took him up. "There was plenty of time for you to have seen her? How so," I inquired, "when you didn't leave my house till late? I don't remember the very moment—I was preoccupied. But you know that though you said you had lots to do you sat for some time after dinner. She, on her side, was all the evening at the 'Gentlewomen.' I've just come from there—I've ascertained. She had tea there; she remained a long, long time."

"What was she doing all the long, long time?"

I saw that he was eager to challenge at every step my account of the matter; and the more he showed this the more I found myself disposed to insist on that account, to prefer with apparent perversity an explanation which only deepened the marvel and the mystery, but which, of the two prodigies it had to choose from, my reviving jealousy found easiest to accept. He stood there pleading with a candour that now seems to me beautiful for the privilege of having in spite of supreme defeat known the living woman; while I, with a passion I wonder at to-day, though it still smoulders in a manner in its ashes, could only reply that, through a strange gift shared by her with his mother and on her own side likewise hereditary, the miracle of his youth had been renewed for him, the miracle of hers for her. She had been to him—yes, and by an impulse as charming as he liked; but oh! she had not been in the body. It was a simple question of evidence. I had had, I assured him, a definite statement of what she had done—most of the time—at the little club. The place was almost empty, but the servants had noticed her. She had sat motionless in a deep chair by the drawing-room fire; she had leaned back her head, she had closed her eyes, she had seemed softly to sleep.

"I see. But till what o'clock?"

"There," I was obliged to answer, "the servants fail me a little. The portress in particular is unfortunately a fool, though even she too is supposed to be a Gentlewoman. She was evidently at that period of the evening, without a substitute and against regulations, absent for some little time from the cage in which it's her business to watch the comings and goings. She's muddled, she palpably prevaricates; so I can't positively, from her observation, give you an hour. But it was remarked toward half-past ten that our poor friend was no longer in the club."

"She came straight here; and from here she went straight to the train."

"She couldn't have run it so close," I declared. "That was a thing she particularly never did."

"There was no need of running it close, my dear—she had plenty of time. Your memory is at fault about my having left you late: I left you, as it happens, unusually early. I'm sorry my stay with you seemed long; for I was back here by ten."

"To put yourself into your slippers," I rejoined, "and fall asleep in your chair. You slept till morning—you saw her in a dream!" He looked at me in silence and with sombre eyes—eyes that showed me he had some irritation to repress. Presently I went on: "You had a visit, at an extraordinary hour, from a lady—*soit*: nothing in the world is more probable. But there are ladies and ladies. How in the name of goodness, if she was unannounced and dumb and you had into the bargain never seen the least portrait of her—how could you identify the person we're talking of?"

"Haven't I to absolute satiety heard her described? I'll describe her for you in every particular."

"Don't!" I exclaimed with a promptness that made him laugh once more. I coloured at this, but I continued: "Did your servant introduce her?"

"He wasn't here—he's always away when he's wanted. One of the features of this big house is that from the street-door the different floors are accessible practically without challenge. My servant makes love to a young person employed in the rooms above these, and he had a long bout of it last evening. When he's out on that job he leaves my outer door, on the staircase, so much ajar as to enable him to slip back without a sound. The door then only requires a push. She pushed it—that simply took a little courage."

"A little? It took tons! And it took all sorts of impossible calculations."

"Well, she had them—she made them. Mind you, I don't deny for a moment," he added, "that it was very, very wonderful!"

Something in his tone prevented me for a while from trusting myself to speak. At last I said: "How did she come to know where you live?"

"By remembering the address on the little label the shop-people happily left sticking to the frame I had had made for my photograph."

"And how was she dressed?"

"In mourning, my own dear. No great depths of crape, but simple and scrupulous black. She had in her bonnet three small black feathers. She carried a little muff of astrachan. She has near the left eye," he continued, "a tiny vertical scar—"

I stopped him short. "The mark of a caress from her husband." Then I added: "How close you must have been to her!" He made no answer to this, and I thought he blushed, observing which I broke straight off. "Well, good-bye."

"You won't stay a little?" He came to me again tenderly, and this time I suffered him. "Her visit had its beauty," he murmured as he held me, "but yours has a greater one."

I let him kiss me, but I remembered, as I had remembered the day before, that the last kiss she had given, as I supposed, in this world had been for the lips he touched.

"I'm life, you see," I answered. "What you saw last night was death."

"It was life—it was life!"

He spoke with a kind of soft stubbornness, and I disengaged myself. We stood looking at each other hard.

"You describe the scene—so far as you describe it at all—in terms that are incomprehensible. She was in the room before you knew it?"

"I looked up from my letter-writing—at that table under the lamp I had been wholly absorbed in it—and she stood before me."

"Then what did you do?"

"I sprang up with an ejaculation, and she, with a smile, laid her finger, ever so warningly, yet with a sort of delicate dignity, to her lips. I knew it meant silence, but the strange thing was that it seemed immediately to explain and to justify her. We at any rate stood for a time that, as I've told you, I can't calculate, face to face. It was just as you and I stand now."

"Simply staring?"

He impatiently protested. "Ah! *we're* not staring!"

"Yes, but we're talking."

"Well, *we* were—after a fashion." He lost himself in the memory of it. "It was as friendly as this." I had on my tongue's point to ask if that were saying much for it, but I remarked instead that what they had evidently done was to gaze in mutual admiration. Then I inquired whether his recognition of her had been immediate. "Not quite," he replied, "for of course I didn't expect her; but it came to me long before she went who she was—who she could only be."

I thought a little. "And how did she at last go?"

"Just as she arrived. The door was open behind her, and she passed out."

"Was she rapid—slow?"

"Rather quick. But looking behind her," he added, with a smile.

"I let her go, for I perfectly understood that I was to take it as she wished."

I was conscious of exhaling a long, vague sigh. "Well, you must take it now as *I* wish—you must let *me* go."

At this he drew near me again, detaining and persuading me, declaring with all due gallantry that I was a very different matter. I would have given anything to have been able to ask him if he had touched her, but the words refused to form themselves: I knew well enough how horrid and vulgar they would sound. I said something else—I forget exactly what; it was feebly tortuous and intended to make him tell me without my putting the question. But he didn't tell me; he only repeated, as if from a glimpse of the propriety of soothing and consoling me, the sense of his declaration of some minutes before—the assurance that she was indeed exquisite, as I had always insisted, but that I was his "real" friend and his very own for ever. This led me to reassert, in the spirit of my previous rejoinder, that I had at least the merit of being alive; which in turn drew from him again the flash of contradiction I dreaded. "Oh, *she* was alive! she was, she was!"

"She was dead! she was dead!" I asseverated with an energy, a determination that it should *be* so, which comes back to me now almost as grotesque. But the sound of the word as it rang out filled me suddenly with horror, and all the natural emotion the meaning of it might have evoked in other conditions gathered and broke in a flood. It rolled over me that here was a great affection quenched and how much I had loved and trusted her. I had a vision at the same time of the lonely beauty of her end. "She's gone—she's lost to us for ever!" I burst into sobs.

"That's exactly what I feel," he exclaimed, speaking with extreme kindness and pressing me to him for comfort. "She's gone; she's lost to us for ever: so what does it matter now?" He bent over me, and when his face had touched mine I scarcely knew if it were wet with my tears or with his own.

VII

It was my theory, my conviction, it became, as I may say, my attitude, that they had still never "met"; and it was just on this ground that I said to myself it would be generous to ask him to stand with me beside her grave. He did so, very modestly and tenderly, and I assumed, though he himself clearly cared nothing for the danger, that the solemnity of the occasion, largely made up of persons who had known them both and had a sense of the long joke, would sufficiently deprive his presence of all light association. On the question of what had happened the evening of her death little more passed between us; I had been overtaken by a horror of the element of evidence. It seemed gross and prying on either hypothesis. He on his side had none to produce, none at least but a statement of his house-porter—on his own admission a most casual and intermittent personage—that between the hours of ten o'clock and midnight no less than three ladies in deep black had flitted in and out of the place. This proved far too much; we had neither of us any use for three. He knew that I considered I had accounted for every fragment of her time, and we dropped the matter as settled; we abstained from further discussion. What *I* knew however was that he abstained to please me rather than because he yielded to my reasons. He didn't yield—he was only indulgent; he clung to his interpretation because he liked it better. He liked it better, I held, because it had more to say to his vanity. That, in a similar position, would not have been its effect on me, though I had doubtless quite as much; but these are things of individual humour, as to which no person can judge for another. I should have supposed it more gratifying to be the subject of one of those inexplicable occurrences that are chronicled in thrilling books and disputed about at learned meetings; I could conceive, on the part of a being just engulfed in the infinite and still vibrating with human emotion, of nothing more fine and pure, more high and august than such an impulse of reparation, of admonition or even of curiosity. *That* was beautiful, if one would, and I should in his place have thought more of myself for being so distinguished. It was public that he had already, that he had long been distinguished, and what was this in itself but almost a proof? Each of the strange visitations contributed to establish the other. He had a different feeling; but he had also, I hasten to add, an unmistakable desire not to make a stand or, as they say, a fuss about it. I might believe what I liked—the more so that the whole thing was in a manner a mystery of my producing. It was an event of my history, a puzzle of my consciousness, not of his; therefore he would take about it any tone that struck me as convenient. We had both at all events other business on hand; we were pressed with preparations for our marriage.

Mine were assuredly urgent, but I found as the days went on that to believe what I "liked" was to believe what I was more and more intimately convinced of. I found also that I didn't like it so much as that came to, or that the pleasure at all events was far from being the cause of my conviction. My obsession, as I may really call it and as I began to perceive, refused to be elbowed away, as I had hoped, by my sense of paramount duties. If I had a great deal to do I had still more to think about, and the moment came when my occupations were gravely menaced by my thoughts. I see it all now, I feel it, I live it over. It's terribly void of joy, it's full indeed to overflowing of bitterness; and yet I must do myself justice—I couldn't possibly be other than I was. The same strange impressions, had I to meet them again, would produce the same deep anguish, the same sharp doubts, the same still sharper certainties. Oh, it's all easier to remember than to write, but even if I could retrace the business hour by hour, could find terms for the inexpressible, the ugliness and the pain would quickly stay my hand. Let me then note very simply and briefly that a week before our wedding-day, three weeks after her death, I became fully aware that I had something very serious to look in the face and that if I was to make this effort I must make it on the spot and before another hour should elapse. My unextinguished jealousy—that was the Medusa-mask. It hadn't died with her death, it had lividly survived, and it was fed by suspicions unspeakable. They *would* be unspeakable to-day, that is, if I hadn't felt the sharp need of uttering them at the time. This need took possession of me—to save me, as it appeared, from my fate. When once it had done so I saw—in the urgency of the case, the diminishing hours and shrinking interval—only one issue, that of absolute promptness and frankness. I could at least not do him the wrong of delaying another day; I could at least treat my difficulty as too fine for a subterfuge. Therefore very quietly, but none the less abruptly and hideously, I put it before him on a certain evening that we must reconsider our situation and recognise that it had completely altered.

He stared bravely. "How has it altered?"

"Another person has come between us."

He hesitated a moment. "I won't pretend not to know whom you mean." He smiled in pity for my aberration, but he meant to be kind. "A woman dead and buried!"

"She's buried, but she's not dead. She's dead for the world—she's dead for me. But she's not dead for *you*."

"You hark back to the different construction we put on her appearance that evening?"

"No," I answered, "I hark back to nothing. I've no need of it. I've more than enough with what's before me."

"And pray, darling, what is that?"

"You're completely changed."

"By that absurdity?" he laughed.

"Not so much by that one as by other absurdities that have followed it."

"And what may they have been?"

We had faced each other fairly, with eyes that didn't flinch; but his had a dim, strange light, and my certitude triumphed in his perceptible paleness. "Do you really pretend," I asked, "not to know what they are?"

"My dear child," he replied, "you describe them too sketchily!"

I considered a moment. "One may well be embarrassed to finish the picture! But from that point of view—and from the beginning—what was ever more embarrassing than your idiosyncrasy?"

He was extremely vague. "My idiosyncrasy?"

"Your notorious, your peculiar power."

He gave a great shrug of impatience, a groan of overdone disdain. "Oh, my peculiar power!"

"Your accessibility to forms of life," I coldly went on, "your command of impressions, appearances, contacts closed—for our gain or our loss—to the rest of us. That was originally a part of the deep interest with which you inspired me—one of the reasons I was amused, I was indeed positively proud to know you. It was a magnificent distinction; it's a magnificent distinction still. But of course I had no prevision then of the way it would operate now; and even had that been the case I should have had none of the extraordinary way in which its action would affect me."

"To what in the name of goodness," he pleadingly inquired, "are you fantastically alluding?" Then as I remained silent, gathering a tone for my charge, "How in the world *does* it operate?" he went on; "and how in the world are you affected?"

"She missed you for five years," I said, "but she never misses you now. You're making it up!"

"Making it up?" He had begun to turn from white to red.

"You see her—you see her: you see her every night!" He gave a loud sound of derision, but it was not a genuine one. "She comes to you as she came that evening," I declared; "having tried it she found she liked it!" I was able, with God's help, to speak without blind passion or vulgar violence; but those were the exact words—and far from "sketchy" they then appeared to me—that I uttered. He had turned away in his laughter, clapping his hands at my folly, but in an instant he faced me again with a change of expression that struck me. "Do you dare to deny," I asked, "that you habitually see her?"

He had taken the line of indulgence, of meeting me halfway and kindly humouring me. At all events to my astonishment he suddenly said: "Well, my dear, what if I do?"

"It's your natural right; it belongs to your constitution and to your wonderful if not perhaps quite enviable fortune. But you will easily understand that it separates us. I unconditionally release you."

"Release me?"

"You must choose between me and her."

He looked at me hard. "I see." Then he walked away a little, as if grasping what I had said and thinking how he had best treat it. At last he turned upon me afresh. "How on earth do you know such an awfully private thing?"

"You mean because you've tried so hard to hide it? It *is* awfully private, and you may believe I shall never betray you. You've done your best, you've acted your part, you've behaved, poor dear! loyally and admirably. Therefore I've watched you in silence, playing my part too; I've noted every drop in your voice, every absence in your eyes, every effort in your indifferent hand: I've waited till I was utterly sure and miserably unhappy. How *can* you hide it when you're abjectly in love with her, when you're sick almost to death with the joy of what she gives you?" I checked his quick protest with a quicker gesture. "You love her as you've *never* loved, and, passion for passion, she gives it straight back! She rules you, she holds you, she has you all! A woman, in such a case as mine, divines and feels and sees; she's not an idiot who has to be credibly informed. You come to me mechanically, compunctiously, with the dregs of your tenderness and the remnant of your life. I can renounce you, but I can't share you; the best of you is hers; I know what it is and I freely give you up to her for ever!"

He made a gallant fight, but it couldn't be patched up; he repeated his denial, he retracted his admission, he ridiculed my charge, of which I freely granted him moreover the indefensible extravagance. I didn't pretend for a moment that we were talking of common things; I didn't pretend for a moment that he and she were common people. Pray, if they *had* been, how should I ever have cared for them? They had enjoyed a rare extension of being and they had caught me up in their flight; only I couldn't breathe in such an air and I promptly asked to be set down. Everything in the facts was monstrous, and most of all my lucid perception of them; the only thing allied to nature and truth was my having to act on that perception. I felt after I had spoken in this sense that my assurance was complete; nothing had been wanting to it but the sight of my effect on him. He disguised indeed the effect in a cloud of chaff, a diversion that gained him time and covered his retreat. He challenged my sincerity, my sanity, almost my humanity, and that of course widened our breach and confirmed our rupture. He did everything in short but convince me either that I was wrong or that he was unhappy: we separated and I left him to his inconceivable communion.

He never married, any more than I've done. When six years later, in solitude and silence, I heard of his death I hailed it as a direct contribution to my theory. It was sudden, it was never properly accounted for, it was surrounded by circumstances in which—for oh, I took them to pieces!—I distinctly read an intention, the mark of his own hidden hand. It was the result of a long necessity, of an unquenchable desire. To say exactly what I mean, it was a response to an irresistible call.

RUDYARD KIPLING

*

The Bridge-Builders

(1898)

The fantastic in the stories of Rudyard Kipling (1865–1936) derives from the contrast between two worlds: the cultures of India with all the wealth of their religious and philosophical traditions and lifestyle, and the morality of the English, convinced they are building a new civilization in India and feeling the responsibility such a task entails as well as the anguish derived from the incomprehension of the Hindus and many of their fellow English. In Kipling, both worlds are the object of a profound knowledge and a profound passion.

Emblematic among his works is this story based on the chronicle of a technological enterprise, the construction of a bridge over the Ganges (the volume in which it appears is titled The Day's Work*), which conflicts both with the forces of nature and with the religion inspired by those forces—there is a visionary evocation of the gods of India. The dialogue among the gods, which we witness, is an ideological debate about the possible integration of both civilizations, in the sense that the much more ancient Hindu culture would be perfectly able to absorb English culture.*

THE LEAST THAT Findlayson, of the Public Works Department, expected was a C. I. E.; he dreamed of a C. S. I.: indeed, his friends told him that he deserved more. For three years he had endured heat and cold, disappointment, discomfort, danger, and disease, with responsibility almost too heavy for one pair of shoulders; and day by day, through that time, the great Kashi Bridge over the Ganges had grown under his charge. Now, in less than three months, if all went well, his Excellency the Viceroy would open the bridge in state, an archbishop would bless it, and the first trainload of soldiers would come over it, and there would be speeches.

Findlayson, C. E., sat in his trolley on a construction line that ran along one of the main revetments—the huge stone-faced banks that flared away north and south for three miles on either side of the river—and permitted himself to think of the end. With its approaches, his work was one mile and three-quarters in length; a lattice-girder bridge, trussed with the Findlayson truss, standing on seven-and-twenty brick piers. Each one of those piers was twenty-four feet in diameter, capped with red Agra stone and sunk eighty feet below the shifting sand of the Ganges' bed. Above them was a railway-line fifteen feet broad; above that, again, a cart-road of eighteen feet, flanked with footpaths. At either end rose towers, of red brick, loopholed for musketry and pierced for big guns, and the ramp of the road was being pushed forward to their haunches. The raw earth-ends were crawling and alive with hundreds upon hundreds of tiny asses climbing out of the yawning borrow-pit below with sackfuls of stuff; and the hot afternoon air was filled with the noise of hooves, the rattle of the drivers' sticks, and the swish and roll-down of the dirt. The river was very low, and on the dazzling white sand between the three centre piers stood squat cribs of railway-sleepers, filled within and daubed without with mud, to support the last of the girders as those were riveted up. In the little deep water left by the drought, an overhead-crane travelled to and fro along its spile-pier, jerking sections of iron into place, snorting and backing and grunting as an elephant grunts in the timber-yard. Riveters by the hundred swarmed about the lattice side-work and the iron roof of the railway-line, hung from invisible staging under the bellies of the girders, clustered round the throats of the piers, and rode on the overhang of the footpath-stanchions; their fire-pots and the spurts of flame that answered each hammer-stroke showing no more than pale yellow in the sun's glare. East and west and north and south the construction-trains rattled and shrieked up and down the embankments, the piled trucks of brown and white stone banging behind them till the side-boards were unpinned, and with a roar and a grumble a few thousand tons more material were flung out to hold the river in place.

Findlayson, C. E., turned on his trolley and looked over the face of the country that he had changed for seven miles around. Looked back on the humming village of five thousand workmen; up stream and down, along the vista of spurs and sand; across the river to the far piers, lessening in the haze; overhead to the guard-towers—and only he knew how strong those were—and with a sigh of contentment saw that his work was good. There stood his bridge before him in the sunlight, lacking only a few weeks' work on the girders of the three middle piers—his bridge, raw and ugly as original sin, but *pukka*—permanent—to endure when all memory of the builder, yea, even of the splendid Findlayson truss, had perished. Practically, the thing was done.

Hitchcock, his assistant, cantered along the line on a little switch-tailed Kabuli pony who through long practice could have trotted securely over a trestle, and nodded to his chief.

"All but," said he, with a smile.

"I've been thinking about it," the senior answered. "'Not half a bad job for two men, is it?"

"One—and a half. 'Gad, what a Cooper's Hill cub I was when I came on the works!" Hitchcock felt very old in the crowded experiences of the past three years, that had taught him power and responsibility.

"You *were* rather a colt," said Findlayson. "I wonder how you 'll like going back to office-work when this job 's over."

"I shall hate it!" said the young man, and as he went on his eye followed Findlayson's, and he muttered, "Is n't it damned good?"

"I think we 'll go up the service together," Findlayson said to himself. "You're too good a youngster to waste on another man. Cub thou wast; assistant thou art. Personal assistant, and at Simla, thou shalt be, if any credit comes to me out of the business!"

Indeed, the burden of the work had fallen altogether on Findlayson and his assistant, the young man whom he had chosen because of his rawness to break to his own needs. There were labour contractors by the half-hundred—fitters and riveters, European, borrowed from the railway workshops, with, perhaps, twenty white and half-caste subordinates to direct, under direction, the bevies of workmen—but none knew better than these two, who trusted each other, how the underlings were not to be trusted. They had been tried many times in sudden crises—by slipping of booms, by breaking of tackle, failure of cranes, and the wrath of the river—but no stress had brought to light any man among men whom Findlayson and Hitchcock would have honoured by working as remorselessly as they worked themselves. Findlayson thought it over from the beginning: the months of office-work destroyed at a blow when the Government of India, at the last moment, added two feet to the width of the bridge, under the impression that bridges were cut out of paper, and so brought to ruin at least half an acre of calculations—and Hitchcock, new to disappointment, buried his head in his arms and wept; the heart-breaking delays over the filling of the contracts in England; the futile correspondences hinting at great wealth of commissions if one, only one, rather doubtful consignment were passed; the war that followed the refusal; the careful, polite obstruction at the other end that followed the war, till young Hitchcock, putting one month's leave to another month, and borrowing ten days from Findlayson, spent his poor little savings of a year in a wild dash to London, and there, as his own tongue asserted and the later consignments proved, put the fear of God into a man so great that he feared only Parliament and said so till Hitchcock wrought with him across his own dinner-table, and—he feared the Kashi Bridge and all who spoke in its name. Then there was the cholera that came in the night to the village by the bridge works; and after the cholera smote the small-pox. The fever they had always with them. Hitchcock had been appointed a magistrate of the third class with whipping powers, for the better government of the community, and Findlayson watched him wield his powers temperately, learning what to overlook and what to look after. It was a long, long reverie, and it covered storm, sudden freshets, death in every manner and shape, violent and awful rage against red tape half frenzying a mind that knows it should be busy on other things; drought, sanitation, finance; birth, wedding, burial, and riot in the village of twenty warring castes; argument, expostulation, persuasion, and the blank despair that a man goes to bed upon, thankful that his rifle is all in pieces in the gun-case. Behind everything rose the black frame of the Kashi Bridge—plate by plate, girder by girder, span by span—and each pier of it recalled Hitchcock, the all-round man, who had stood by his chief without failing from the very first to this last.

So the bridge was two men's work—unless one counted Peroo, as Peroo certainly counted himself. He was a Lascar, a Kharva from Bulsar, familiar with every port between Rockhampton and London, who had risen to the rank of serang on the British India boats, but wearying of routine musters and clean clothes, had thrown up the service and gone inland, where men of his calibre were sure of employment. For his knowledge of tackle and the handling of heavy weights, Peroo was worth almost any price he might have chosen to put upon his services; but custom decreed the wage of the overhead-men, and Peroo was not within many silver pieces of his proper value. Neither running water nor extreme heights made him afraid; and, as an ex-serang, he knew how to hold authority. No piece of iron was so big or so badly placed that Peroo could not devise a tackle to lift it—

a loose-ended, sagging arrangement, rigged with a scandalous amount of talking, but perfectly equal to the work in hand. It was Peroo who had saved the girder of Number Seven pier from destruction when the new wire rope jammed in the eye of the crane, and the huge plate tilted in its slings, threatening to slide out sideways. Then the native workmen lost their heads with great shoutings, and Hitchcock's right arm was broken by a falling T-plate, and he buttoned it up in his coat and swooned, and came to and directed for four hours till Peroo, from the top of the crane, reported "All 's well," and the plate swung home. There was no one like Peroo, serang, to lash, and guy, and hold, to control the donkey-engines, to hoist a fallen locomotive craftily out of the borrow-pit into which it had tumbled; to strip, and dive, if need be, to see how the concrete blocks round the piers stood the scouring of Mother Gunga, or to adventure up-stream on a monsoon night and report on the state of the embankment-facings. He would interrupt the field-councils of Findlayson and Hitchcock without fear, till his wonderful English, or his still more wonderful *lingua-franca*, half Portuguese and half Malay, ran out and he was forced to take string and show the knots that he would recommend. He controlled his own gang of tacklemen—mysterious relatives from Kutch Mandvi gathered month by month and tried to the uttermost. No consideration of family or kin allowed Peroo to keep weak hands or a giddy head on the pay-roll. "My honour is the honour of this bridge," he would say to the about-to-be-dismissed. "What do I care for your honour? Go and work on a steamer. That is all you are fit for."

The little cluster of huts where he and his gang lived centred round the tattered dwelling of a sea-priest—one who had never set foot on black water, but had been chosen as ghostly counsellor by two generations of searovers all unaffected by port missions or those creeds which are thrust upon sailors by agencies along Thames bank. The priest of the Lascars had nothing to do with their caste, or indeed with anything at all. He ate the offerings of his church, and slept and smoked, and slept again, "for," said Peroo, who had haled him a thousand miles inland, "he is a very holy man. He never cares what you eat so long as you do not eat beef, and that is good, because on land we worship Shiva, we Kharvas; but at sea on the Kumpani's boats we attend strictly to the orders of the Burra Malum [the first mate], and on this bridge we observe what Finlinson Sahib says."

Finlinson Sahib had that day given orders to clear the scaffolding from the guard-tower on the right bank, and Peroo with his mates was casting loose and lowering down the bamboo poles and planks as swiftly as ever they had whipped the cargo out of a coaster.

From his trolley he could hear the whistle of the serang's silver pipe and the creak and clatter of the pulleys. Peroo was standing on the topmost coping of the tower, clad in the blue dungaree of his abandoned service, and as Findlayson motioned to him to be careful, for his was no life to throw away, he gripped the last pole, and, shading his eyes ship-fashion, answered with the long-drawn wail of the fo'c'sle lookout: "*Ham dekhta hai*" ("I am looking out"). Findlayson laughed and then sighed. It was years since he had seen a steamer, and he was sick for home. As his trolley passed under the tower, Peroo descended by a rope, ape-fashion, and cried: "It looks well now, Sahib. Our bridge is all but done. What think you Mother Gunga will say when the rail runs over?"

"She has said little so far. It was never Mother Gunga that delayed us."

"There is always time for her; and none the less there has been delay. Has the Sahib forgotten last autumn's flood, when the stone-boats were sunk without warning—or only a half-day's warning?"

"Yes, but nothing save a big flood could hurt us now. The spurs are holding well on the west bank."

"Mother Gunga eats great allowances. There is always room for more stone on the revetments. I tell this to the Chota Sahib"—he meant Hitchcock—"and he laughs."

"No matter, Peroo. Another year thou wilt be able to build a bridge in thine own fashion."

The Lascar grinned. "Then it will not be in this way—with stonework sunk under water, as the *Quetta* was sunk. I like sus-sus-pen-sheen bridges that fly from bank to bank, with one big step, like a gang-plank. Then no water can hurt. When does the Lord Sahib come to open the bridge?"

"In three months, when the weather is cooler."

"Ho! ho! He is like the Burra Malum. He sleeps below while the work is being done. Then he comes upon the quarter-deck and touches with his finger, and says: 'This is not clean! Dam jibboonwallah!' "

"But the Lord Sahib does not call me a dam jibboonwallah, Peroo."

"No, Sahib; but he does not come on deck till the work is all finished. Even the Burra Malum of the *Nerbudda* said once at Tuticorin—"

"Bah! Go! I am busy."

"I, also!" said Peroo, with an unshaken countenance. "May I take the light dinghy now and row along the spurs?"

"To hold them with thy hands? They are, I think, sufficiently heavy."

"Nay, Sahib. It is thus. At sea, on the Black Water, we have room to be blown up and down without care. Here we have no room at all. Look you, we have put the river into a dock, and run her between stone sills."

Findlayson smiled at the "we."

"We have bitted and bridled her. She is not like the sea, that can beat against a soft beach. She is Mother Gunga—in irons." His voice fell a little.

"Peroo, thou hast been up and down the world more even than I. Speak true talk, now. How much dost thou in thy heart believe of Mother Gunga?"

"All that our priest says. London is London, Sahib. Sydney is Sydney, and Port Darwin is Port Darwin. Also Mother Gunga is Mother Gunga, and when I come back to her banks I know this and worship. In London I did poojah to the big temple by the river for the sake of the God within. . . . Yes, I will not take the cushions in the dinghy."

Findlayson mounted his horse and trotted to the shed of a bungalow that he shared with his assistant. The place had become home to him in the last three years. He had grilled in the heat, sweated in the rains, and shivered with fever under the rude thatch roof; the lime-wash beside the door was covered with rough drawings and formulæ, and the sentry-path trodden in the matting of the verandah showed where he had walked alone. There is no eight-hour limit to an engineer's work, and the evening meal with Hitchcock was eaten booted and spurred: over their cigars they listened to the hum of the village as the gangs came up from the river-bed and the lights began to twinkle.

"Peroo has gone up the spurs in your dinghy. He 's taken a couple of nephews with him, and he 's lolling in the stern like a commodore," said Hitchcock.

"That 's all right. He 's got something on his mind. You 'd think that ten years in the British India boats would have knocked most of his religion out of him."

"So it has," said Hitchcock, chuckling. "I overheard him the other day in the middle of a most atheistical talk with that fat old *guru* of theirs. Peroo denied the efficacy of prayer; and wanted the *guru* to go to sea and watch a gale out with him, and see if he could stop a monsoon."

"All the same, if you carried off his *guru* he 'd leave us like a shot. He was yarning away to me about praying to the dome of St. Paul's when he was in London."

"He told me that the first time he went into the engine-room of a steamer, when he was a boy, he prayed to the low-pressure cylinder."

"Not half a bad thing to pray to, either. He 's propitiating his own Gods now, and he wants to know what Mother Gunga will think of a bridge being run across her. Who 's there?" A shadow darkened the doorway, and a telegram was put into Hitchcock's hand.

"She ought to be pretty well used to it by this time. Only a *tar*. It ought to be Ralli's answer about the new rivets. . . . Great Heavens!" Hitchcock jumped to his feet.

"What is it?" said the senior, and took the form. "*That 's* what Mother Gunga thinks, is it," he said, reading. "Keep cool, young 'un. We 've got all our work cut out for us. Let 's see. Muir wired half an hour ago: '*Floods on the Ramgunga. Look out.*' Well, that gives us—one, two—nine and a half for the flood to reach Melipur Ghaut and seven 's sixteen and a half to Lataoli—say fifteen hours before it comes down to us."

"Curse that hill-fed sewer of a Ramgunga! Findlayson, this is two months before anything could have been expected, and the left bank is littered up with stuff still. Two full months before the time!"

"That 's why it comes. I 've only known Indian rivers for five-and-twenty years, and I don't pretend to understand. Here comes another *tar*." Findlayson opened the telegram. "Cockran, this time, from the Ganges Canal: '*Heavy rains here. Bad.*' He might have saved the last word. Well, we don't want to know any more. We 've got to work the gangs all night and clean up the river-bed. You 'll take the east bank and work out to meet me in the middle. Get every thing that floats below the bridge: we shall have quite enough rivercraft coming down adrift anyhow, without letting the stone-boats ram the piers. What have you got on the east bank that needs looking after?"

"Pontoon—one big pontoon with the overhead crane on it. T' other overhead crane on the mended pontoon, with the cart-road rivets from Twenty to Twenty-three piers—two construction lines, and a turning-spur. The pile-work must take its chance," said Hitchcock.

"All right. Roll up everything you can lay hands on. We 'll give the gang fifteen minutes more to eat their grub."

Close to the verandah stood a big night-gong, never used except for flood, or fire in the village. Hitchcock had called for a fresh horse, and was off to his side of the bridge when Findlayson took the cloth-bound stick and smote with the rubbing stroke that brings out the full thunder of the metal.

Long before the last rumble ceased every night-gong in the village had taken up the warning. To these were added the hoarse screaming of conches in the little temples; the throbbing of drums and tom-toms; and, from the European quarters, where the riveters lived, McCartney's bugle, a weapon of offence on Sundays and festivals, brayed desperately, calling to "Stables." Engine after engine toiling home along the spurs at the end of her day's work whistled in answer till the whistles were answered from the far bank. Then the big gong thundered thrice for a sign that it was flood and not fire; conch, drum, and whistle echoed the call, and the village quivered to the sound of bare feet running upon soft earth. The order in all cases was to stand by the day's work and wait instructions. The gangs poured by in the dusk; men stopping to knot a loin-cloth or fasten a sandal; gang-foremen shouting to their subordinates as they ran or paused by the tool-issue sheds for bars and mattocks; locomotives creeping down their tracks wheel-deep in the crowd; till the brown torrent disappeared into the dusk of the river-bed, raced over the pilework, swarmed along the lattices, clustered by the cranes, and stood still—each man in his place.

Then the troubled beating of the gong carried the order to take up everything and bear it beyond high-water mark, and the flare-lamps broke out by the hundred between the webs of dull iron as the riveters began a night's work, racing against the flood that was to come. The girders of the three centre piers—those that stood on the cribs—were all but in position. They needed just as many rivets as could be driven into them, for the flood would assuredly wash out their supports, and the ironwork would settle down on the caps of stone if they were not blocked at the ends. A hundred crowbars strained at the sleepers of the temporary line that fed the unfinished piers. It was heaved up in lengths, loaded into trucks, and backed up the bank beyond flood-level by the groaning locomotives. The tool-sheds on the sands melted away before the attack of shouting armies, and with them went the stacked ranks of Government stores, iron-bound boxes of rivets, pliers, cutters, duplicate parts of the riveting-machines, spare pumps and chains. The big crane would be the last to be shifted, for she was hoisting all the heavy stuff up to the main structure of the bridge. The concrete blocks on the fleet of stone-boats were dropped overside, where there was any depth of water, to guard the piers, and the empty boats themselves were poled under the bridge down-stream. It was here that Peroo's pipe shrilled loudest, for the first stroke of the big gong had brought the dinghy back at racing speed, and Peroo and his people were stripped to the waist, working for the honour and credit which are better than life.

"I knew she would speak," he cried. "*I* knew, but the telegraph gives us good warning. O sons of unthinkable begetting—children of unspeakable shame—are we here for the look of the thing?" It was two feet of wire-rope frayed at the ends, and it did wonders as Peroo leaped from gunnel to gunnel, shouting the language of the sea.

Findlayson was more troubled for the stone-boats than anything else. McCartney, with his gangs, was blocking up the ends of the three doubtful spans, but boats adrift, if the flood chanced to be a high one, might endanger the girders; and there was a very fleet in the shrunken channel.

"Get them behind the swell of the guard-tower," he shouted down to Peroo. "It will be dead-water there. Get them below the bridge."

"*Accha!* [Very good.] *I* know; we are mooring them with wire-rope," was the answer. "Heh! Listen to the Chota Sahib. He is working hard."

From across the river came an almost continuous whistling of locomotives, backed by the rumble of stone. Hitchcock at the last minute was spending a few hundred more trucks of Tarakee stone in reinforcing his spurs and embankments.

"The bridge challenges Mother Gunga," said Peroo, with a laugh. "But when *she* talks I know whose voice will be the loudest."

For hours the naked men worked, screaming and shouting under the lights. It was a hot, moonless night; the end of it was darkened by clouds and a sudden squall that made Findlayson very grave.

"She moves!" said Peroo, just before the dawn. "Mother Gunga is awake! Hear!" He dipped his hand over the side of a boat and the current mumbled on it. A little wave hit the side of a pier with a crisp slap.

"Six hours before her time," said Findlayson, mopping his forehead savagely. "Now we can't depend on anything. We 'd better clear all hands out of the river-bed."

Again the big gong beat, and a second time there was the rushing of naked feet on earth and ringing iron; the clatter of tools ceased. In the silence, men heard the dry yawn of water crawling over thirsty sand.

Foreman after foreman shouted to Findlayson, who had posted himself by the guard-tower, that his section of the river-bed had been cleaned out, and when the last voice dropped Findlayson hurried over the bridge till the iron plating of the permanent way gave place to the temporary plank-walk over the three centre piers, and there he met Hitchcock.

" 'All clear your side?" said Findlayson. The whisper rang in the box of latticework.

"Yes, and the east channel 's filling now. We 're utterly out of our reckoning. When is this thing down on us?"

"There 's no saying. She 's filling as fast as she can. Look!" Findlayson pointed to the planks below his feet, where the sand, burned and defiled by months of work, was beginning to whisper and fizz.

"What orders?" said Hitchcock.

"Call the roll—count stores—sit on your hunkers—and pray for the bridge. That 's all I can think of. Good night. Don't risk your life trying to fish out anything that may go down-stream."

"Oh, I 'll be as prudent as you are! 'Night. Heavens, how she 's filling! Here 's the rain in earnest!" Findlayson picked his way back to his bank, sweeping the last of McCartney's riveters before him. The gangs had spread themselves along the embankments, regardless of the cold rain of the dawn, and there they waited for the flood. Only Peroo kept his men together behind the swell of the guard-tower, where the stone-boats lay tied fore and aft with hawsers, wire-rope, and chains.

A shrill wail ran along the line, growing to a yell, half fear and half wonder: the face of the river whitened from bank to bank between the stone facings, and the faraway spurs went out in spouts of foam. Mother Gunga had come bank-high in haste, and a wall of chocolate-coloured water was her messenger. There was a shriek above the roar of the water, the complaint of the spans coming down on their blocks as the cribs were whirled out from under their bellies. The stone-boats groaned and ground each other in the eddy that swung round the abutment, and their clumsy masts rose higher and higher against the dim sky-line.

"Before she was shut between these walls we knew what she would do. Now she is thus cramped God only knows what she will do!" said Peroo, watching the furious turmoil round the guard-tower. "Ohé! Fight, then! Fight hard, for it is thus that a woman wears herself out."

But Mother Gunga would not fight as Peroo desired. After the first down-stream plunge there came no more walls of water, but the river lifted herself bodily, as a snake when she drinks in midsummer, plucking and fingering along the revetments, and banking up behind the piers till even Findlayson began to recalculate the strength of his work.

When day came the village gasped. "Only last night," men said, turning to each other, "it was a town in the river-bed! Look now!"

And they looked and wondered afresh at the deep water, the racing water that licked the throat of the piers. The farther bank was veiled by rain, into which the bridge ran out and vanished; the spurs up-stream were marked by no more than eddies and spoutings, and down-stream the pent river, once freed of her guide-lines, had spread like a sea to the horizon. Then hurried by, rolling in the water, dead men and oxen together, with here and there a patch of thatched roof that melted when it touched a pier.

"Big flood," said Peroo, and Findlayson nodded. It was as big a flood as he had any wish to watch. His bridge would stand what was upon her now, but not very much more, and if by any of a thousand chances there happened to be a weakness in the embankments, Mother Gunga would carry his honour to the sea with the other raffle. Worst of all, there was nothing to do except to sit still; and Findlayson sat still under his macintosh till his helmet became pulp on his head, and his boots were over-ankle in mire. He took no count of time, for the river was marking the hours, inch by inch and foot by foot, along the embankment, and he listened, numb and hungry, to the straining of the stone-boats, the hollow thunder under the piers, and the hundred noises that make the full note of a flood. Once a dripping servant brought him food, but he could not eat; and once he thought that he heard a faint toot from a locomotive across the river, and then he smiled. The bridge's failure would hurt his assistant not a little, but Hitchcock was a young man with his big work yet to do. For himself the crash meant everything—everything that made a hard life worth the living. They would say, the men of his own profession . . . he remembered the half-pitying things that he himself had said when Lockhart's new waterworks burst and broke down in brick-heaps and sludge, and Lockhart's spirit broke in him and he died. He remembered what he himself had said when the Sumao Bridge went out in the big cyclone by the sea; and most he remembered poor Hartopp's face three weeks later, when the shame had marked it. His bridge was twice the size of Hartopp's, and it carried the Findlayson truss as well as the new pier-shoe—the Findlayson bolted shoe. There were no excuses in his service. Government might listen, perhaps, but his own kind would judge him by his bridge, as that stood or fell. He went over it in his head, plate by plate, span by span, brick by brick, pier by pier, remembering, comparing, estimating, and recalculating, lest there should be any mistake; and through the long hours and through the flights of formulæ that danced and wheeled before him a cold fear would come to pinch his heart. His side of the sum was beyond question; but what man knew Mother Gunga's arithmetic? Even as he was making all sure by the multiplication-table, the river might be scooping a pot-hole to the very bottom of any one of those eighty-foot piers that carried his reputation. Again a servant came to him with food, but his mouth was dry, and he could only drink and return to the decimals in his brain. And the river was still rising. Peroo, in a mat shelter-coat, crouched at his feet, watching now his face and now the face of the river, but saying nothing.

At last the Lascar rose and floundered through the mud towards the village, but he was careful to leave an ally to watch the boats.

Presently he returned, most irreverently driving before him the priest of his creed—a fat old man, with a grey beard that whipped the wind with the wet cloth that blew over his shoulder. Never was seen so lamentable a *guru*.

"What good are offerings and little kerosene lamps and dry grain," shouted Peroo, "if squatting in the mud is all that thou canst do? Thou hast dealt long with the Gods when they were contented and well-wishing. Now they are angry. Speak to them!"

"What is a man against the wrath of Gods?" whined the priest, cowering as the wind took him. "Let me go to the temple, and I will pray there."

"Son of a pig, pray *here*! Is there no return for salt fish and curry powder and dried onions? Call aloud! Tell Mother Gunga we have had enough. Bid her be still for the night. I cannot pray, but I have been serving in the Kumpani's boats, and when men did not obey my orders I—" A flourish of the wire-rope colt rounded the sentence, and the priest, breaking free from his disciple, fled to the village.

"Fat pig!" said Peroo. "After all that we have done for him! When the flood is down I will see to it that we get a new *guru*. Finlinson Sahib, it darkens for night now, and since yesterday nothing has been eaten. Be wise, Sahib. No man can endure watching and great thinking on an empty belly. Lie down, Sahib. The river will do what the river will do."

"The bridge is mine; I cannot leave it."

"Wilt thou hold it up with thy hands, then?" said Peroo, laughing. "I was troubled for my boats and sheers *before* the flood came. Now we are in the hands of the Gods. The Sahib will not eat and lie down? Take these, then. They are meat and good toddy together, and they kill all weariness, besides the fever that follows the rain. I have eaten nothing else to-day at all."

He took a small tin tobacco-box from his sodden waist-belt and thrust it into Findlayson's hand, saying: "Nay, do not be afraid. It is no more than opium—clean Malwa opium!"

Findlayson shook two or three of the dark-brown pellets into his hand, and hardly knowing what he did, swallowed them. The stuff was at least a good guard against fever—the fever that was creeping upon him out of the wet mud—and he had seen what Peroo could do in the stewing mists of autumn on the strength of a dose from the tin box.

Peroo nodded with bright eyes. "In a little—in a little the Sahib will find that he thinks well again. I too will—" He dived into his treasure-box, resettled the rain-coat over his head, and squatted down to watch the boats. It was too dark now to see beyond the first pier, and the night seemed to have given the river new strength. Findlayson stood with his chin on his chest, thinking. There was one point about one of the piers—the seventh—that he had not fully settled in his mind. The figures would not shape themselves to the eye except one by one and at enormous intervals of time. There was a sound rich and mellow in his ears like the deepest note of a double-bass—an entrancing sound upon which he pondered for several hours, as it seemed. Then Peroo was at his elbow, shouting that a wire hawser had snapped and the stone-boats were loose. Findlayson saw the fleet open and swing out fanwise to a long-drawn shriek of wire straining across gunnels.

"A tree hit them. They will all go," cried Peroo. "The main hawser has parted. What does the Sahib do?"

An immensely complex plan had suddenly flashed into Findlayson's mind. He saw the ropes running from boat to boat in straight lines and angles—each rope a line of white fire. But there was one rope which was the master rope. He could see that rope. If he could pull it once, it was absolutely and mathematically certain that the disordered fleet would reassemble itself in the backwater behind the guard-tower. But why, he wondered, was Peroo clinging so desperately to his waist as he hastened down the bank? It was necessary to put the Lascar aside, gently and slowly, because it was necessary to save the boats, and, further, to demonstrate the extreme ease of the problem that looked so difficult. And then—but it was of no conceivable importance—a wire-rope raced through his hand, burning it, the high bank disappeared, and with it all the slowly dispersing factors of the problem. He was sitting in the rainy darkness—sitting in a boat that spun like a top, and Peroo was standing over him.

"I had forgotten," said the Lascar, slowly, "that to those fasting and unused, the opium is worse than any wine. Those who die in Gunga go to the Gods. Still, I have no desire to present myself before such great ones. Can the Sahib swim?"

"What need? He can fly—fly as swiftly as the wind," was the thick answer.

"He is mad!" muttered Peroo, under his breath. "And he threw me aside like a bundle of dung-cakes. Well, he will not know his death. The boat cannot live an hour here even if she strike nothing. It is not good to look at death with a clear eye."

He refreshed himself again from the tin box, squatted down in the bows of the reeling, pegged, and stitched craft, staring through the mist at the nothing that was there. A warm drowsiness crept over Findlayson, the Chief Engineer, whose duty was with his bridge. The heavy raindrops struck him with a thousand tingling little thrills, and the weight of all time since time was made hung heavy on his eyelids. He thought and perceived that he was perfectly secure, for the water was so solid that a man could surely step out upon it, and, standing still with his legs apart to keep his balance—this was the most important point—would be borne with great and easy speed to the shore. But yet a better plan came to him. It needed only an exertion of will for the soul to hurl the body ashore as wind drives paper, to waft it kite-fashion to the bank. Thereafter—the boat spun dizzily—suppose the high wind got under the freed body? Would it tower up like a kite and pitch headlong on the far-away sands, or would it duck about, beyond control, through all eternity? Findlayson gripped the gunnel to anchor himself, for it seemed that he was on the edge of taking the flight before he had settled all his plans. Opium has more effect on the white man than the black. Peroo was only comfortably indifferent to accidents. "She cannot live," he grunted. "Her seams open already. If she were even a dinghy with oars we could have ridden it out; but a box with holes is no good. Finlinson Sahib, she fills."

"*Accha!* I am going away. Come thou also."

In his mind, Findlayson had already escaped from the boat, and was circling high in air to find a rest for the sole of his foot. His body—he was really sorry for its gross helplessness—lay in the stern, the water rushing about its knees.

"How very ridiculous!" he said to himself, from his eyrie—"that—is Findlayson—chief of the Kashi Bridge. The poor beast is going to be drowned, too. Drowned when it 's close to shore. I 'm—I 'm on shore already. Why does n't it come along?"

To his intense disgust, he found his soul back in his body again, and that body spluttering and choking in deep water. The pain of the reunion was atrocious, but it was necessary, also, to fight for the body. He was conscious of grasping wildly at wet sand, and striding prodigiously, as one strides in a dream, to keep foothold in the swirling water, till at last he hauled himself clear of the hold of the river, and dropped, panting, on wet earth.

"Not this night," said Peroo, in his ear. "The Gods have protected us." The Lascar moved his feet cautiously, and they rustled among dried stumps. "This is some island of last year's indigo-crop," he went on. "We shall find no men here; but have great care, Sahib; all the snakes of a hundred miles have been flooded out. Here comes the lightning, on the heels of the wind. Now we shall be able to look; but walk carefully."

Findlayson was far and far beyond any fear of snakes, or indeed any merely human emotion. He saw, after he had rubbed the water from his eyes, with an immense clearness, and trod, so it seemed to himself, with world-encompassing strides. Somewhere in the night of time he had built a bridge—a bridge that spanned illimitable levels of shining seas; but the Deluge had swept it away, leaving this one island under heaven for Findlayson and his companion, sole survivors of the breed of Man.

An incessant lightning, forked and blue, showed all that there was to be seen on the little patch in the flood—a clump of thorn, a clump of swaying creaking bamboos, and a grey gnarled peepul overshadowing a Hindoo shrine, from whose dome floated a tattered red flag. The holy man whose summer resting-place it was had long since abandoned it, and the weather had broken the red-daubed image of his god. The two men stumbled, heavy-limbed and heavy-eyed, over the ashes of a brick-set cooking-place, and dropped down under the shelter of the branches, while the rain and river roared together.

The stumps of the indigo crackled, and there was a smell of cattle, as a huge and dripping Brahminee bull shouldered his way under the tree. The flashes revealed the trident mark of Shiva on his flank, the insolence of head and hump, the luminous stag-like eyes, the brow crowned with a wreath of sodden marigold blooms, and the silky dewlap that almost swept the ground. There was a noise behind him of other beasts coming up from the flood-line through the thicket, a sound of heavy feet and deep breathing.

"Here be more beside ourselves," said Findlayson, his head against the tree-pole, looking through half-shut eyes, wholly at ease.

"Truly," said Peroo, thickly, "and no small ones."

"What are they, then? I do not see clearly."

"The Gods. Who else? Look!"

"Ah, true! The Gods surely—the Gods." Findlayson smiled as his head fell forward on his chest. Peroo was eminently right. After the Flood, who should be alive in the land except the Gods that made it—the Gods to whom his village prayed nightly—the Gods who were in all men's mouths and about all men's ways. He could not raise his head or stir a finger for the trance that held him, and Peroo was smiling vacantly at the lightning.

The Bull paused by the shrine, his head lowered to the damp earth. A green Parrot in the branches preened his wet wings and screamed against the thunder as the circle under the tree filled with the shifting shadows of beasts. There was a black Buck at the Bull's heels—such a Buck as Findlayson in his far-away life upon earth might have seen in dreams—a Buck with a royal head, ebon back, silver belly, and gleaming straight horns. Beside him, her head bowed to the ground, the green eyes burning under the heavy brows, with restless tail switching the dead grass, paced a Tigress, full-bellied and deep-jowled.

The Bull crouched beside the shrine, and there leaped from the darkness a monstrous grey Ape, who seated himself man-wise in the place of the fallen image, and the rain spilled like jewels from the hair of his neck and shoulders.

Other shadows came and went behind the circle, among them a drunken Man flourishing staff and drinking-bottle. Then a hoarse bellow broke out from near the ground. "The flood lessens even now," it cried. "Hour by hour the water falls, and their bridge still stands!"

"My bridge," said Findlayson to himself. "That must be very old work now. What have the Gods to do with my bridge?"

His eyes rolled in the darkness following the roar. A Mugger—the blunt-nosed, ford-haunting Mugger of the Ganges—draggled herself before the beasts, lashing furiously to right and left with her tail.

"They have made it too strong for me. In all this night I have only torn away a handful of planks. The walls stand. The towers stand. They have chained my flood, and the river is not free any more. Heavenly Ones, take this yoke away! Give me clear water between bank and bank! It is I, Mother Gunga, that speak. The Justice of the Gods! Deal me the Justice of the Gods!"

"What said I?" whispered Peroo. "This is in truth a Punchayet of the Gods. Now we know that all the world is dead, save you and I, Sahib."

The Parrot screamed and fluttered again, and the Tigress, her ears flat to her head, snarled wickedly.

Somewhere in the shadow, a great trunk and gleaming tusks swayed to and fro, and a low gurgle broke the silence that followed on the snarl.

"We be here," said a deep voice, "the Great Ones. One only and very many. Shiv, my father, is here, with Indra. Kali has spoken already. Hanuman listens also."

"Kashi is without her Kotwal to-night," shouted the Man with the drinking-bottle, flinging his staff to the ground, while the island rang to the baying of hounds. "Give her the Justice of the Gods."

"Ye were still when they polluted my waters," the great Crocodile bellowed. "Ye made no sign when my river was trapped between the walls. I had no help save my own strength, and that failed—the strength of Mother Gunga failed—before their guard-towers. What could I do? I have done everything. Finish now, Heavenly Ones!"

"I brought the death; I rode the spotted sickness from hut to hut of their workmen, and yet they would not cease." A nose-slitten, hide-worn Ass, lame, scissor-legged, and galled, limped forward. "I cast the death at them out of my nostrils, but they would not cease."

Peroo would have moved, but the opium lay heavy upon him.

"Bah!" he said, spitting. "Here is Sitala herself; Mata—the small-pox. Has the Sahib a handkerchief to put over his face?"

"Little help! They fed me the corpses for a month, and I flung them out on my sand-bars, but their work went forward. Demons they are, and sons of demons! And ye left Mother Gunga alone for their fire-carriage to make a mock of. The Justice of the Gods on the bridge-builders!"

The Bull turned the cud in his mouth and answered slowly: "If the Justice of the Gods caught all who made a mock of holy things there would be many dark altars in the land, mother."

"But this goes beyond a mock," said the Tigress, darting forward a griping paw. "Thou knowest, Shiv, and ye, too, Heavenly Ones; ye know that they have defiled Gunga. Surely they must come to the Destroyer. Let Indra judge."

The Buck made no movement as he answered: "How long has this evil been?"

"Three years, as men count years," said the Mugger, close pressed to the earth.

"Does Mother Gunga die, then, in a year, that she is so anxious to see vengeance now? The deep sea was where she runs but yesterday, and to-morrow the sea shall cover her again as the Gods count that which men call time. Can any say that this their bridge endures till to-morrow?" said the Buck.

There was a long hush, and in the clearing of the storm the full moon stood up above the dripping trees.

"Judge ye, then," said the River, sullenly. "I have spoken my shame. The flood falls still. I can do no more."

"For my own part"—it was the voice of the great Ape seated within the shrine—"it pleases me well to watch these men, remembering that I also builded no small bridge in the world's youth."

"They say, too," snarled the Tiger, "that these men came of the wreck of thy armies, Hanuman, and therefore thou hast aided—"

"They toil as my armies toiled in Lanka, and they believe that their toil endures. Indra is too high, but Shiv, thou knowest how the land is threaded with their fire-carriages."

"Yea, I know," said the Bull. "Their Gods instructed them in the matter."

A laugh ran round the circle.

"Their Gods! What should their Gods know? They were born yesterday, and those that made them are scarcely yet cold," said the Mugger. "To-morrow their Gods will die."

"Ho!" said Peroo. "Mother Gunga talks good talk. I told that to the padre-sahib who preached on the *Mombassa*, and he asked the Burra Malum to put me in irons for a great rudeness."

"Surely they make these things to please their Gods," said the Bull again.

"Not altogether," the Elephant rolled forth. "It is for the profit of my mahajuns—my fat money-lenders that worship me at each new year, when they draw my image at the head of the account-books. I, looking over their shoulders by lamplight, see that the names in the books are those of men in far places—for all the towns are drawn together by the fire-carriage, and the money comes and goes swiftly, and the account-books grow as fat as—myself. And I, who am Ganesh of Good Luck, I bless my peoples."

"They have changed the face of the land—which is my land. They have killed and made new towns on my banks," said the Mugger.

"It is but the shifting of a little dirt. Let the dirt dig in the dirt if it pleases the dirt," answered the Elephant.

"But afterwards?" said the Tiger. "Afterwards they will see that Mother Gunga can avenge no insult, and they fall away from her first, and later from us all, one by one. In the end, Ganesh, we are left with naked altars."

The drunken Man staggered to his feet, and hiccupped vehemently.

"Kali lies. My sister lies. Also this my stick is the Kotwal of Kashi, and he keeps tally of my pilgrims. When the time comes to worship Bhairon—and it is always time—the fire-carriages move one by one, and each bears a thousand pilgrims. They do not come afoot any more, but rolling upon wheels, and my honour is increased."

"Gunga, I have seen thy bed at Pryag black with the pilgrims," said the Ape, leaning forward, "and but for the fire-carriage they would have come slowly and in fewer numbers. Remember."

"They come to me always," Bhairon went on thickly. "By day and night they pray to me, all the Common People in the fields and the roads. Who is like Bhairon to-day? What talk is this of changing faiths? Is my staff Kotwal of Kashi for nothing? He keeps the tally, and he says that never were so many altars as to-day, and the fire-carriage serves them well. Bhairon am I—Bhairon of the Common People, and the chiefest of the Heavenly Ones to-day. Also my staff says—"

"Peace, thou!" lowed the Bull. "The worship of the schools is mine, and they talk very wisely, asking whether I be one or many, as is the delight of my people, and ye know what I am. Kali, my wife, thou knowest also."

"Yea, I know," said the Tigress, with lowered head.

"Greater am I than Gunga also. For ye know who moved the minds of men that they should count Gunga holy among the rivers. Who die in that water—ye know how men say—come to us without punishment, and Gunga knows that the fire-carriage has borne to her scores upon scores of such anxious ones; and Kali knows that she has held her chiefest festivals among the pilgrimages that are fed by the fire-carriage. Who smote at Pooree, under the Image there, her thousands in a day and a night, and bound the sickness to the wheels of the fire-carriages, so that it ran from one end of the land to the other? Who but Kali? Before the fire-carriage came it was a heavy toil. The fire-carriages have served thee well, Mother of Death. But I speak for mine own altars, who am not Bhairon of the Common Folk, but Shiv.

Men go to and fro, making words and telling talk of strange Gods, and I listen. Faith follows faith among my people in the schools, and I have no anger; for when all words are said, and the new talk is ended, to Shiv men return at the last."

"True. It is true," murmured Hanuman. "To Shiv and to the others, mother, they return. I creep from temple to temple in the North, where they worship one God and His Prophet; and presently my image is alone within their shrines."

"Small thanks," said the Buck, turning his head slowly. "I am that One and His Prophet also."

"Even so, father," said Hanuman. "And to the South I go who am the oldest of the Gods as men know the Gods, and presently I touch the shrines of the New Faith and the Woman whom we know is hewn twelve-armed, and still they call her Mary."

"Small thanks, brother," said the Tigress. "I am that Woman."

"Even so, sister; and I go West among the fire-carriages, and stand before the bridge-builders in many shapes, and because of me they change their faiths and are very wise. Ho! ho! I am the builder of bridges, indeed—bridges between this and that, and each bridge leads surely to Us in the end. Be content, Gunga. Neither these men nor those that follow them mock thee at all."

"Am I alone, then, Heavenly Ones? Shall I smooth out my flood lest unhappily I bear away their walls? Will Indra dry my springs in the hills and make me crawl humbly between their wharfs? Shall I bury me in the sand ere I offend?"

"And all for the sake of a little iron bar with the fire-carriage atop. Truly, Mother Gunga is always young!" said Ganesh the Elephant. "A child had not spoken more foolishly. Let the dirt dig in the dirt ere it return to the dirt. I know only that my people grow rich and praise me. Shiv has said that the men of the schools do not forget; Bhairon is content for his crowd of the Common People; and Hanuman laughs."

"Surely I laugh," said the Ape. "My altars are few beside those of Ganesh or Bhairon, but the fire-carriages bring me new worshippers from beyond the Black Water—the men who believe that their God is toil. I run before them beckoning, and they follow Hanuman."

"Give them the toil that they desire, then," said the River. "Make a bar across my flood and throw the water back upon the bridge. Once thou wast strong in Lanka, Hanuman. Stoop and lift my bed."

"Who gives life can take life." The Ape scratched in the mud with a long forefinger. "And yet, who would profit by the killing? Very many would die."

There came up from the water a snatch of a love-song such as the boys sing when they watch their cattle in the noon heats of late spring. The Parrot screamed joyously, sidling along his branch with lowered head as the song grew louder, and in a patch of clear moonlight stood revealed the young herd, the darling of the Gopis, the idol of dreaming maids and of mothers ere their children are born—Krishna the Well-beloved. He stooped to knot up his long wet hair, and the parrot fluttered to his shoulder.

"Fleeting and singing, and singing and fleeting," hiccupped Bhairon. "Those make thee late for the council, brother."

"And then?" said Krishna, with a laugh, throwing back his head. "Ye can do little without me or Karma here." He fondled the Parrot's plumage and laughed again. "What is this sitting and talking together? I heard Mother Gunga roaring in the dark, and so came quickly from a hut where I lay warm. And what have ye done to Karma, that he is so wet and silent? And what does Mother Gunga here? Are the heavens full that ye must come paddling in the mud beast-wise! Karma, what do they do?"

"Gunga has prayed for a vengeance on the bridge-builders, and Kali is with her. Now she bids Hanuman whelm the bridge, that her honour may be made great," cried the Parrot. "I waited here, knowing that thou wouldst come, O my master!"

"And the Heavenly Ones said nothing? Did Gunga and the Mother of Sorrows out-talk them? Did none speak for my people?"

"Nay," said Ganesh, moving uneasily from foot to foot; "I said it was but dirt at play, and why should we stamp it flat?"

"I was content to let them toil—well content," said Hanuman.

"What had I to do with Gunga's anger?" said the Bull.

"I am Bhairon of the Common Folk, and this my staff is Kotwal of all Kashi. I spoke for the Common People."

"Thou?" The young God's eyes sparkled.

"Am I not the first of the Gods in their mouths to-day?" returned Bhairon, unabashed. "For the sake of the Common People I said—very many wise things which I have now forgotten, but this my staff—"

Krishna turned impatiently, saw the Mugger at his feet, and kneeling, slipped an arm round the cold neck. "Mother," he said gently, "get thee to thy flood again. The matter is not for thee. What harm shall thy honour take of this live dirt? Thou hast given them their fields new year after year, and by thy flood they are made strong. They come all to thee at the last. What need to slay them now? Have pity, mother, for a little—and it is only for a little."

"If it be only for a little—" the slow beast began.

"Are they Gods, then?" Krishna returned with a laugh, his eyes looking into the dull eyes of the River. "Be certain that it is only for a little. The Heavenly Ones have heard thee, and presently justice will be done. Go now, mother, to the flood again. Men and cattle are thick on the waters—the banks fall—the villages melt because of thee."

"But the bridge—the bridge stands." The Mugger turned grunting into the undergrowth as Krishna rose.

"It is ended," said the Tigress, viciously. "There is no more justice from the Heavenly Ones. Ye have made shame and sport of Gunga, who asked no more than a few score lives."

"Of *my* people—who lie under the leaf-roofs of the village yonder—of the young girls, and the young men who sing to them in the dark—of the child that will be born next morn—of that which was begotten to-night," said Krishna. "And when all is done, what profit? To-morrow sees them at work. Ay, if ye swept the bridge out from end to end they would begin anew. Hear me! Bhairon is drunk always. Hanuman mocks his people with new riddles."

"Nay, but they are very old ones," the Ape said, laughing.

"Shiv hears the talk of the schools and the dreams of the holy men; Ganesh thinks only of his fat traders; but I—I live with these my people, asking for no gifts, and so receiving them hourly."

"And very tender art thou of thy people," said the Tigress.

"They are my own. The old women dream of me turning in their sleep; the maids look and listen for me when they go to fill their lotahs by the river. I walk by the young men waiting without the gates at dusk, and I call over my shoulder to the white-beards. Ye know, Heavenly Ones, that I alone of us all walk upon the earth continually, and have no pleasure in our heavens so long as a green blade springs here, or there are two voices at twilight in the standing crops. Wise are ye, but ye live far off, forgetting whence ye came. So do I not forget. And the fire-carriage feeds your shrines, ye say? And the fire-carriages bring a thousand pilgrims where but ten came in the old years? True. That is true, to-day."

"But to-morrow they are dead, brother," said Ganesh.

"Peace!" said the Bull, as Hanuman leaned forward again. "And to-morrow, beloved—what of to-morrow?"

"This only. A new word creeping from mouth to mouth among the Common Folk—a word that neither man nor God can lay hold of—an evil word—a little lazy word among the Common Folk, saying (and none know who set that word afoot) that they weary of ye, Heavenly Ones."

The Gods laughed together softly. "And then, beloved?" they said.

"And to cover that weariness they, my people, will bring to thee, Shiv, and to thee, Ganesh, at first greater offerings and a louder noise of worship. But the word has gone abroad, and, after, they will pay fewer dues to your fat Brahmins. Next they will forget your altars, but so slowly that no man can say how his forgetfulness began."

"I knew—I knew! I spoke this also, but they would not hear," said the Tigress. "We should have slain—we should have slain!"

"It is too late now. Ye should have slain at the beginning when the men from across the water had taught our folk nothing. Now my people see their work, and go away thinking. They do not think of the Heavenly Ones altogether. They think of the fire-carriage and the other things that the bridge-builders have done, and when your priests thrust forward hands asking alms, they give a little unwillingly. That is the beginning, among one or two, or five or ten—for I, moving among my people, know what is in their hearts."

"And the end, Jester of the Gods? What shall the end be?" said Ganesh.

"The end shall be as it was in the beginning, O slothful son of Shiv! The flame shall die upon the altars and the prayer upon the tongue till ye become little Gods again—Gods of the jungle—names that the hunters of rats and noosers of dogs whisper in the thicket and among the caves—rag-Gods, pot Godlings of the tree, and the village-mark, as ye were at the beginning. That is the end, Ganesh, for thee, and for Bhairon—Bhairon of the Common People."

"It is very far away," grunted Bhairon. "Also, it is a lie."

"Many women have kissed Krishna. They told him this to cheer their own hearts when the grey hairs came, and he has told us the tale," said the Bull, below his breath.

"Their Gods came, and we changed them. I took the Woman and made her twelve-armed. So shall we twist all their Gods," said Hanuman.

"Their Gods! This is no question of their Gods—one or three—man or woman. The matter is with the people. *They* move, and not the Gods of the bridge-builders," said Krishna.

"So be it. I have made a man worship the fire-carriage as it stood still breathing smoke, and he knew not that he worshipped me," said Hanuman the Ape. "They will only change a little the names of their Gods. I shall lead the builders of the bridges as of old; Shiv shall be worshipped in the schools by such as doubt and despise their fellows; Ganesh shall have his mahajuns, and Bhairon the donkey-drivers, the pilgrims, and the sellers of toys. Beloved, they will do no more than change the names, and that we have seen a thousand times."

"Surely they will do no more than change the names," echoed Ganesh; but there was an uneasy movement among the Gods.

"They will change more than the names. Me alone they cannot kill, so long as a maiden and a man meet together or the spring follows the winter rains. Heavenly Ones, not for nothing have I walked upon the earth. My people know not now what they know; but I, who live with them, I read their hearts. Great Kings, the beginning of the end is born already. The fire-carriages shout the names of new Gods that are *not* the old under new names. Drink now and eat greatly! Bathe your faces in the smoke of the altars before they grow cold! Take dues and listen to the cymbals and the drums, Heavenly Ones, while yet there are flowers and songs. As men count time the end is far off; but as we who know reckon it is to-day. I have spoken."

The young God ceased, and his brethren looked at each other long in silence.

"This I have not heard before," Peroo whispered in his companion's ear. "And yet sometimes, when I oiled the brasses in the engine-room of the *Goorkha*, I have wondered if our priests were so wise—so wise. The day is coming, Sahib. They will be gone by the morning."

A yellow light broadened in the sky, and the tone of the river changed as the darkness withdrew.

Suddenly the Elephant trumpeted aloud as though man had goaded him.

"Let Indra judge. Father of all, speak thou! What of the things we have heard? Has Krishna lied indeed? Or—"

"Ye know," said the Buck, rising to his feet. "Ye know the Riddle of the Gods. When Brahm ceases to dream, the Heavens and the Hells and Earth disappear. Be content. Brahm dreams still. The dreams come and go, and the nature of the dreams changes, but still Brahm dreams. Krishna has walked too long upon earth, and yet I love him the more for the tale he has told. The Gods change, beloved—all save One!"

"Ay, all save one that makes love in the hearts of men," said Krishna, knotting his girdle. "It is but a little time to wait, and ye shall know if I lie."

"Truly it is but a little time, as thou sayest, and we shall know. Get thee to thy huts again, beloved, and make sport for the young things, for still Brahm dreams. Go, my children! Brahm dreams—and till he wakes the Gods die not."

"WHITHER WENT THEY?" said the Lascar, awe-struck, shivering a little with the cold.

"God knows!" said Findlayson. The river and the island lay in full daylight now, and there was never mark of hoof or pug on the wet earth under the peepul. Only a parrot screamed in the branches, bringing down showers of water-drops as he fluttered his wings.

"Up! We are cramped with cold! Has the opium died out? Canst thou move, Sahib?"

Findlayson staggered to his feet and shook himself. His head swam and ached, but the work of the opium was over, and, as he sluiced his forehead in a pool, the Chief Engineer of the Kashi Bridge was wondering how he had managed to fall upon the island, what chances the day offered of return, and, above all, how his work stood.

"Peroo, I have forgotten much. I was under the guard-tower watching the river; and then. . . . Did the flood sweep us away?"

"No. The boats broke loose, Sahib, and" (if the Sahib had forgotten about the opium, decidedly Peroo would not remind him) "in striving to retie them, so it seemed to me—but it was dark—a rope caught the Sahib and threw him upon a boat. Considering that we two, with Hitchcock Sahib, built, as it were, that bridge, I came also upon the boat, which came riding on horseback, as it were, on the nose of this island, and so, splitting, cast us ashore. I made a great cry when the boat left the wharf, and without doubt Hitchcock Sahib will come for us. As for the bridge, so many have died in the building that it cannot fall."

A fierce sun, that drew out all the smell of the sodden land, had followed the storm, and in that clear light there was no room for a man to think of the dreams of the dark. Findlayson stared up-stream, across the blaze of moving water, till his eyes ached. There was no sign of any bank to the Ganges, much less of a bridge-line.

"We came down far," he said. "It was wonderful that we were not drowned a hundred times."

"That was the least of the wonder, for no man dies before his time. I have seen Sydney, I have seen London, and twenty great ports, but"—Peroo looked at the damp, discoloured shrine under the peepul—"never man has seen that we saw here."

"What?"

"Has the Sahib forgotten; or do we black men only see the Gods?"

"There was a fever upon me." Findlayson was still looking uneasily across the water. "It seemed that the island was full of beasts and men talking, but I do not remember. A boat could live in this water now, I think."

"Oho! Then it *is* true. 'When Brahm ceases to dream, the Gods die.' Now I know, indeed, what he meant. Once, too, the *guru* said as much to me; but then I did not understand. Now I am wise."

"What?" said Findlayson, over his shoulder.

Peroo went on as if he were talking to himself. "Six—seven—ten monsoons since, I was watch on the fo'c'sle of the *Rewah*—the Kumpani's big boat—and there was a big *tufan*; green and black water beating, and I held fast to the life-lines, choking under the waters. Then I thought of the Gods—of Those whom we saw to-night"—he stared curiously at Findlayson's back, but the white man was looking across the flood. "Yes, I say of Those whom we saw this night past, and I called upon Them to protect me. And while I prayed, still keeping my lookout, a big wave came and threw me forward upon the ring of the great black bow-anchor, and the *Rewah* rose high and high, leaning towards the left-hand side, and the water drew away from beneath her nose, and I lay upon my belly, holding the ring, and looking down into those great deeps. Then I thought, even in the face of death: If I lose hold I die, and for me neither the *Rewah* nor my place by the galley where the rice is cooked, nor Bombay, nor Calcutta, nor even London, will be any more for me. 'How shall I be sure,' I said, 'that the Gods to whom I pray will abide at all?' This I thought, and the *Rewah* dropped her nose as a hammer falls, and all the sea came in and slid me backwards along the fo'c'sle and over the break of the fo'c'sle, and I very badly bruised my shin against the donkey-engine: but I did not die, and I have seen the

Gods. They are good for live men, but for the dead . . . They have spoken Themselves. Therefore, when I come to the village I will beat the *guru* for talking riddles which are no riddles. When Brahm ceases to dream the Gods go."

"Look up-stream. The light blinds. Is there smoke yonder?"

Peroo shaded his eyes with his hands. "He is a wise man and quick. Hitchcock Sahib would not trust a rowboat. He has borrowed the Rao Sahib's steam-launch, and comes to look for us. I have always said that there should have been a steam-launch on the bridge works for us."

The territory of the Rao of Baraon lay within ten miles of the bridge; and Findlayson and Hitchcock had spent a fair portion of their scanty leisure in playing billiards and shooting black-buck with the young man. He had been bear-led by an English tutor of sporting tastes for some five or six years, and was now royally wasting the revenues accumulated during his minority by the Indian Government. His steam-launch, with its silver-plated rails, striped silk awning, and mahogany decks, was a new toy which Findlayson had found horribly in the way when the Rao came to look at the bridge works.

"It's great luck," murmured Findlayson, but he was none the less afraid, wondering what news might be of the bridge.

The gaudy blue and white funnel came down-stream swiftly. They could see Hitchcock in the bows, with a pair of opera-glasses, and his face was unusually white. Then Peroo hailed, and the launch made for the tail of the island. The Rao Sahib, in tweed shooting-suit and a seven-hued turban, waved his royal hand, and Hitchcock shouted. But he need have asked no questions, for Findlayson's first demand was for his bridge.

"All serene! 'Gad, I never expected to see you again, Findlayson. You're seven koss down-stream. Yes; there's not a stone shifted anywhere; but how are you? I borrowed the Rao Sahib's launch, and he was good enough to come along. Jump in."

"Ah, Finlinson, you are very well, eh? That was most unprecedented calamity last night, eh? My royal palace, too, it leaks like the devil, and the crops will also be short all about my country. Now you shall back her out, Hitchcock. I—I do not understand steam-engines. You are wet? You are cold, Finlinson? I have some things to eat here, and you will take a good drink."

"I'm immensely grateful, Rao Sahib. I believe you've saved my life. How did Hitchcock—"

"Oho! His hair was upon end. He rode to me in the middle of the night and woke me up in the arms of Morpheus. I was most truly concerned, Finlinson, so I came too. My head-priest he is very angry just now. We will go quick, Mister Hitchcock. I am due to attend at twelve forty-five in the state temple, where we sanctify some new idol. If not so I would have asked you to spend the day with me. They are dam-bore, these religious ceremonies, Finlinson, eh?"

Peroo, well known to the crew, had possessed himself of the inlaid wheel, and was taking the launch craftily up-stream. But while he steered he was, in his mind, handling two feet of partially untwisted wire-rope; and the back upon which he beat was the back of his *guru*.

H. G. WELLS

*

The Country of the Blind

(1899)

Herbert George Wells (1866–1946) is the most extraordinary inventor of stories in that extraordinary era in world literature that falls between two centuries. The inventiveness and precision of his imagination (which make him one of the fathers of "science fantastic") are accompanied by a transparent and fluid style and nourished by a sharp, firm, and clear morality. Many of his stories would occupy a distinguished place in an anthology dedicated to the invisible, mental fantastic that has its roots in images of everyday life. But it simply did not seem right to me to renounce a story that belongs to his more "spectacular" production and that is, without a doubt, one of his masterpieces.

"The Country of the Blind" is a great moral and political apology, worthy to be set alongside those of Swift, a meditation on cultural diversity and on the relativity of all pretensions to think oneself superior.

In the equatorial Andes, a village of Indians has remained isolated from the world for generations. All its inhabitants are blind. The children are born blind; the last old people who once enjoyed sight are dead: all have lost by now the memory of what it means to see. Their houses have no windows, no light, no colors. A man arrives from the outside world. They think he is handicapped, incapable of doing what they do, and they think he says meaningless things. The man imagines he will be their king, as in the proverb about the one-eyed man's being king in the land of the blind. But the proverb is wrong: in the land of the blind those who do not see are much stronger than the one who does. . . .

THREE HUNDRED MILES and more from Chimborazo, one hundred from the snows of Cotopaxi, in the wildest wastes of Ecuador's Andes, there lies that mysterious mountain valley, cut off from the world of men, the Country of the Blind. Long years ago that valley lay so far open to the world that men might come at last through frightful gorges and over an icy pass into its equable meadows; and thither indeed men came, a family or so of Peruvian half-breeds fleeing from the lust and tyranny of an evil Spanish ruler. Then came the stupendous outbreak of Mindobamba, when it was night in Quito for seventeen days, and the water was boiling at Yaguachi and all the fish floating dying even as far as Guayaquil; everywhere along the Pacific slopes there were land-slips and swift thawings and sudden floods, and one whole side of the old Arauca crest slipped and came down in thunder, and cut off the Country of the Blind for ever from the exploring feet of men. But one of these early settlers had chanced to be on the hither side of the gorges when the world had so terribly shaken itself, and he perforce had to forget his wife and his child and all the friends and possessions he had left up there, and start life over again in the lower world. He started it again but ill, blindness overtook him, and he died of punishment in the mines; but the story he told begot a legend that lingers along the length of the Cordilleras of the Andes to this day.

He told of his reason for venturing back from that fastness, into which he had first been carried lashed to a llama, beside a vast bale of gear, when he was a child. The valley, he said, had in it all that the heart of man could desire—sweet water, pasture, an even climate, slopes of rich brown soil with tangles of a shrub that bore an excellent fruit, and on one side great hanging forests of pine that held the avalanches high. Far overhead, on three sides, vast cliffs of grey-green rock were capped by cliffs of ice; but the glacier stream came not to them but flowed away by the farther slopes, and only now and then huge ice masses fell on the valley side. In this valley it neither rained nor snowed, but the abundant springs gave a rich green pasture, that irrigation would spread over all the valley space. The settlers did well indeed there. Their beasts did well and multiplied, and but one thing marred their happiness. Yet it was enough to mar it greatly. A strange disease had come upon them, and had made all the children born to them there—and indeed, several older children also—blind. It was to seek some charm or antidote against this plague of blindness that he had with fatigue and danger and difficulty returned down the gorge. In those days, in such cases, men did not think of germs and infections but of sins; and it seemed to him that the reason of this affliction must lie in the negligence of these priestless immigrants to set up a shrine so soon as they entered the valley. He wanted a shrine—a handsome, cheap, effectual shrine—to be erected in the valley; he wanted relics and such-like potent things of faith, blessed objects and mysterious medals and prayers. In his wallet he had a bar of native silver for which he would not account; he insisted there was none in the valley with something of the insistence of an inexpert liar. They had all clubbed their money and ornaments together, having little need for such treasure up there, he said, to buy them holy help against their ill. I figure this dim-eyed young mountaineer, sunburnt, gaunt, and anxious, hat-brim clutched feverishly, a man all unused to the ways of the lower world, telling this story to some keen-eyed, attentive priest before the great convulsion; I can picture him presently seeking to return with pious and infallible remedies against that trouble, and the infinite dismay with which he must have faced the tumbled vastness where the gorge had once come out. But the rest of his story of mischances is lost to me, save that I know of his evil death after several years. Poor stray from that remoteness! The stream that had once made the gorge now bursts from the mouth of a rocky cave, and the legend his poor, ill-told story set going developed into the legend of a race of blind men somewhere "over there" one may still hear to-day.

And amidst the little population of that now isolated and forgotten valley the disease ran its course. The old became groping and purblind, the young saw but dimly, and the children that were born to them saw never at all. But life was very easy in that snow-rimmed basin, lost to all the world, with neither thorns nor briars, with no evil insects nor any beasts save the gentle breed of llamas they had lugged and thrust and followed up the beds of the shrunken rivers in the gorges up which they had come. The seeing had become purblind so gradually that they scarcely noted their loss. They guided the sightless youngsters hither and thither until they knew the whole valley marvellously, and when at last sight died out among them the race lived on. They had even time to adapt themselves to the blind control of fire, which they made carefully in stoves of stone. They were a simple strain of people at the first, unlettered, only slightly touched with the Spanish civilisation, but with something of a tradition of the arts of old Peru and of its lost philosophy. Generation followed generation. They forgot many things; they devised many things. Their tradition of the greater world they came from became mythical in colour and uncertain. In all things save sight they were strong and able, and presently the chance of birth and heredity sent one who had an original mind and who could talk and persuade among them, and then afterwards another. These two passed, leaving their effects, and the little community grew in numbers and in understanding, and met and settled social and economic problems that arose. Generation followed generation. Generation followed generation. There came a time when a child was born who was fifteen generations from that ancestor who went out of the valley with a bar of silver to seek God's aid, and who never returned. Thereabouts it chanced that a man came into this community from the outer world. And this is the story of that man.

He was a mountaineer from the country near Quito, a man who had been down to the sea and had seen the world, a reader of books in an original way, an acute and enterprising man, and he was taken on by a party of Englishmen who had come out to Ecuador to climb mountains, to replace one of their three Swiss guides who had fallen ill. He climbed here and he climbed there, and then came the attempt on Parascotopetl, the Matterhorn of the Andes, in which he was lost to the outer world. The story of the accident has been written a dozen times. Pointer's narrative is the best. He tells how the little party worked their difficult and almost vertical way up to the very foot of the last and greatest precipice, and how they built a night shelter amidst the snow upon a little shelf of rock, and, with a touch of real dramatic power, how presently they found Nunez had gone from them. They shouted, and there was no reply; shouted and whistled, and for the rest of that night they slept no more.

As the morning broke they saw the traces of his fall. It seems impossible he could have uttered a sound. He had slipped eastward towards the unknown side of the mountain; far below he had struck a steep slope of snow, and ploughed his way down it in the midst of a snow avalanche. His track went straight to the edge of a frightful precipice, and beyond that everything was hidden. Far, far below, and hazy with distance, they could see trees rising out of a narrow, shut-in valley—the lost Country of the Blind. But they did not know it was the lost Country of the Blind, nor distinguish it in any way from any other narrow streak of upland valley. Unnerved by this disaster, they abandoned their attempt in the afternoon, and Pointer was called away to the war before he could make another attack. To this day Parascotopetl lifts an unconquered crest, and Pointer's shelter crumbles unvisited amidst the snows.

And the man who fell survived.

At the end of the slope he fell a thousand feet, and came down in the midst of a cloud of snow upon a snow slope even steeper than the one above. Down this he was whirled, stunned and insensible, but without a bone broken in his body; and then at last came to gentler slopes, and at last rolled out and lay still, buried amidst a softening heap of the white masses that had accompanied and saved him. He came to himself with a dim fancy that he was ill in bed; then realised his position with a mountaineer's intelligence, and worked himself loose and, after a rest or so, out until he saw the stars. He rested flat upon his chest for a space, wondering where he was and what had happened to him. He explored his limbs, and discovered that several of his buttons were gone and his coat turned over his head. His knife had gone from his pocket and his hat was lost, though he had tied it under his chin. He recalled that he had been looking for loose stones to raise his piece of the shelter wall. His ice-axe had disappeared.

He decided he must have fallen, and looked up to see, exaggerated by the ghastly light of the rising moon, the tremendous flight he had taken. For a while he lay, gazing blankly at that vast pale cliff towering above, rising moment by moment out of a subsiding tide of darkness. Its phantasmal, mysterious beauty held him for a space, and then he was seized with a paroxysm of sobbing laughter. . . .

After a great interval of time he became aware that he was near the lower edge of the snow. Below, down what was now a moonlit and practicable slope, he saw the dark and broken appearance of rock-strewn turf. He struggled to his feet, aching in every joint and limb, got down painfully from the heaped loose snow about him, went downward until he was on the turf, and there dropped rather than lay beside a boulder, drank deep from the flask in his inner pocket, and instantly fell asleep. . . .

He was awakened by the singing of birds in the trees far below.

He sat up and perceived he was on a little alp at the foot of a vast precipice, that was grooved by the gully down which he and his snow had come. Over against him another wall of rock reared itself against the sky. The gorge between these precipices ran east and west and was full of the morning sunlight, which lit to the westward the mass of fallen mountain that closed the descending gorge. Below him it seemed there was a precipice equally steep, but behind the snow in the gully he found a sort of chimney-cleft dripping with snow-water down which a desperate man might venture. He found it easier than it seemed, and came at last to another desolate alp, and then after a rock climb of no particular difficulty to a steep slope of trees. He took his bearings and turned his face up the gorge, for he saw it opened out above upon green meadows, among which he now glimpsed quite distinctly a cluster of stone huts of unfamiliar fashion. At times his progress was like clambering along the face of a wall, and after a time the rising sun ceased to strike along the gorge, the voices of the singing birds died away, and the air grew cold and dark about him. But the distant valley with its houses was all the brighter for that. He came presently to talus, and among the rocks he noted—for he was an observant man—an unfamiliar fern that seemed to clutch out of the crevices with intense green hands. He picked a frond or so and gnawed its stalk and found it helpful.

About midday he came at last out of the throat of the gorge into the plain and the sunlight. He was stiff and weary; he sat down in the shadow of a rock, filled up his flask with water from a spring and drank it down, and remained for a time resting before he went on to the houses.

They were very strange to his eyes, and indeed the whole aspect of that valley became, as he regarded it, queerer and more unfamiliar. The greater part of its surface was lush green meadow, starred with many beautiful flowers, irrigated with extraordinary care, and bearing evidence of systematic cropping piece by piece. High up and ringing the valley about was a wall, and what appeared to be a circumferential water-channel, from which the little trickles of water that fed the meadow plants came, and on the higher slopes above this flocks of llamas cropped the scanty herbage. Sheds, apparently shelters or feeding-places for the llamas, stood against the boundary wall here and there. The irrigation streams ran together into a main channel down the centre of the valley, and this was enclosed on either side by a wall breast high. This gave a singularly urban quality to this secluded place, a quality that was greatly enhanced by the fact that a number of paths paved with black and white stones, and each with a curious little kerb at the side, ran hither and thither in an orderly manner. The houses of the central village were quite unlike the casual and higgledy-piggledy agglomeration of the mountain villages he knew; they stood in a continuous row on either side of a central street of astonishing cleanness; here and there their parti-coloured façade was pierced by a door, and not a solitary window broke their even frontage. They were parti-coloured with extraordinary irregularity, smeared with a sort of plaster that was sometimes grey, sometimes drab, sometimes slate-coloured or dark brown; and it was the sight of this wild plastering first brought the word "blind" into the thoughts of the explorer. "The good man who did that," he thought, "must have been as blind as a bat."

He descended a steep place, and so came to the wall and channel that ran about the valley, near where the latter spouted out its surplus contents into the deeps of the gorge in a thin and wavering thread of cascade. He could now see a number of men and women resting on piled heaps of grass, as if taking a siesta, in the remoter part of the meadow, and nearer the village a number of recumbent children, and then nearer at hand three men carrying pails on yokes along a little path that ran from the encircling wall towards the houses. These latter were clad in garments of llama cloth and boots and belts of leather, and they wore caps of cloth with back and ear flaps. They followed one another in single file, walking slowly and yawning as they walked, like men who have been up all night. There was something so reassuringly prosperous and respectable in their bearing that after a moment's hesitation Nunez stood forward as conspicuously as possible upon his rock, and gave vent to a mighty shout that echoed round the valley.

The three men stopped, and moved their heads as though they were looking about them. They turned their faces this way and that, and Nunez gesticulated with freedom. But they did not appear to see him for all his gestures, and after a time, directing themselves towards the mountains far away to the right, they shouted as if in answer. Nunez bawled again, and then once more, and as he gestured ineffectually the word "blind" came up to the top of his thoughts. "The fools must be blind," he said.

When at last, after much shouting and wrath, Nunez crossed the stream by a little bridge, came through a gate in the wall, and approached them, he was sure that they were blind. He was sure that this was the Country of the Blind of which the legends told. Conviction had sprung upon him, and a sense of great and rather enviable adventure. The three stood side by side, not looking at him, but with their ears directed towards him, judging him by his unfamiliar steps. They stood close together like men a little afraid, and he could see their eyelids closed and sunken, as though the very balls beneath had shrunk away. There was an expression near awe on their faces.

"A man," one said, in hardly recognisable Spanish—"a man it is—a man or a spirit—coming down from the rocks."

But Nunez advanced with the confident steps of a youth who enters upon life. All the old stories of the lost valley and the Country of the Blind had come back to his mind, and through his thoughts ran this old proverb, as if it were a refrain—

"In the Country of the Blind the One-eyed Man is King."

"In the Country of the Blind the One-eyed Man is King."

And very civilly he gave them greeting. He talked to them and used his eyes.

"Where does he come from, brother Pedro?" asked one.

"Down out of the rocks."

"Over the mountains I come," said Nunez, "out of the country beyond there—where men can see. From near Bogota, where there are a hundred thousands of people, and where the city passes out of sight."

"Sight?" muttered Pedro. "Sight?"

"He comes," said the second blind man, "out of the rocks."

The cloth of their coats Nunez saw was curiously fashioned, each with a different sort of stitching.

They startled him by a simultaneous movement towards him, each with a hand outstretched. He stepped back from the advance of these spread fingers.

"Come hither," said the third blind man, following his motion and clutching him neatly.

And they held Nunez and felt him over, saying no word further until they had done so.

"Carefully," he cried, with a finger in his eye, and found they thought that organ, with its fluttering lids, a queer thing in him. They went over it again.

"A strange creature, Correa," said the one called Pedro. "Feel the coarseness of his hair. Like a llama's hair."

"Rough he is as the rocks that begot him," said Correa, investigating Nunez's unshaven chin with a soft and slightly moist hand. "Perhaps he will grow finer." Nunez struggled a little under their examination, but they gripped him firm.

"Carefully," he said again.

"He speaks," said the third man. "Certainly he is a man."

"Ugh!" said Pedro, at the roughness of his coat.

"And you have come into the world?" asked Pedro.

"*Out* of the world. Over mountains and glaciers; right over above there, half-way to the sun. Out of the great big world that goes down, twelve days' journey to the sea."

They scarcely seemed to heed him. "Our fathers have told us men may be made by the forces of Nature," said Correa. "It is the warmth of things and moisture, and rottenness—rottenness."

"Let us lead him to the elders," said Pedro.

"Shout first," said Correa, "lest the children be afraid. This is a marvellous occasion."

So they shouted, and Pedro went first and took Nunez by the hand to lead him to the houses.

He drew his hand away. "I can see," he said.

"See?" said Correa.

"Yes, see," said Nunez, turning towards him, and stumbled against Pedro's pail.

"His senses are still imperfect," said the third blind man. "He stumbles, and talks unmeaning words. Lead him by the hand."

"As you will," said Nunez, and was led along, laughing.

It seemed they knew nothing of sight.

Well, all in good time he would teach them.

He heard people shouting, and saw a number of figures gathering together in the middle roadway of the village.

He found it tax his nerve and patience more than he had anticipated, that first encounter with the population of the Country of the Blind. The place seemed larger as he drew near to it, and the smeared plasterings queerer, and a crowd of children and men and women (the women and girls, he was pleased to note, had some of them quite sweet faces, for all that their eyes were shut and sunken) came about him, holding on to him, touching him with soft, sensitive hands, smelling at him, and listening at every word he spoke. Some of the maidens and children, however, kept aloof as if afraid, and indeed his voice seemed coarse and rude beside their softer notes. They mobbed him. His three guides kept close to him with an effect of proprietorship, and said again and again, "A wild man out of the rocks."

"Bogota," he said. "Bogota. Over the mountain crests."

"A wild man—using wild words," said Pedro. "Did you hear that—*Bogota*? His mind is hardly formed yet. He has only the beginnings of speech."

A little boy nipped his hand. "Bogota!" he said mockingly.

"Ay! A city to your village. I come from the great world—where men have eyes and see."

"His name's Bogota," they said.

"He stumbled," said Correa, "stumbled twice as we came hither."

"Bring him to the elders."

And they thrust him suddenly through a doorway into a room as black as pitch, save at the end there faintly glowed a fire. The crowd closed in behind him and shut out all but the faintest glimmer of day, and before he could arrest himself he had fallen headlong over the feet of a seated man. His arm, outflung, struck the face of someone else as he went down; he felt the soft impact of features and heard a cry of anger, and for a moment he struggled against a number of hands that clutched him. It was a one-sided fight. An inkling of the situation came to him, and he lay quiet.

"I fell down," he said; "I couldn't see in this pitchy darkness."

There was a pause as if the unseen persons about him tried to understand his words. Then the voice of Correa said: "He is but newly formed. He stumbles as he walks and mingles words that mean nothing with his speech."

Others also said things about him that he heard or understood imperfectly.

"May I sit up?" he asked, in a pause. "I will not struggle against you again."

They consulted and let him rise.

The voice of an older man began to question him, and Nunez found himself trying to explain the great world out of which he had fallen, and the sky and mountains and sight and such-like marvels, to these elders who sat in darkness in the Country of the Blind. And they would believe and understand nothing whatever he told them, a thing quite outside his expectation. They would not even understand many of his words. For fourteen generations these people had been blind and cut off from all the seeing world; the names for all the things of sight had faded and changed; the story of the outer world was faded and changed to a child's story; and they had ceased to concern themselves with anything beyond the rocky slopes above their circling wall. Blind men of genius had arisen among them and questioned the shreds of belief and tradition they had brought with them from their seeing days, and had dismissed all these things as idle fancies, and replaced them with new and saner explanations. Much of their imagination had shrivelled with their eyes, and they had made for themselves new imaginations with their ever more sensitive ears and finger-tips. Slowly Nunez realised this; that his expectation of wonder and reverence at his origin and his gifts was not to be borne out; and after his poor attempt to explain sight to them had been set aside as the confused version of a new-made being describing the marvels of his incoherent sensations, he subsided, a little dashed, into listening to their instruction. And the eldest of the blind men explained to him life and philosophy and religion, how that the world (meaning their valley) had been first an empty hollow in the rocks, and then had come, first, inanimate things without the gift of touch, and llamas and a few other creatures that had little sense, and then men, and at last angels, whom one could hear singing and making fluttering sounds, but whom no one could touch at all, which puzzled Nunez greatly until he thought of the birds.

He went on to tell Nunez how this time had been divided into the warm and the cold, which are the blind equivalents of day and night, and how it was good to sleep in the warm and work during the cold, so that now, but for his advent, the whole town of the blind would have been asleep. He said Nunez must have been specially created to learn and serve the wisdom they had acquired, and that for all his mental incoherency and stumbling behaviour he must have courage, and do his best to learn, and at that all the people in the doorway murmured encouragingly. He said the night—for the blind call their day night—was now far gone, and it behoved every one to go back to sleep. He asked Nunez if he knew how to sleep, and Nunez said he did, but that before sleep he wanted food.

They brought him food—llama's milk in a bowl, and rough salted bread—and led him into a lonely place to eat out of their hearing, and afterwards to slumber until the chill of the mountain evening roused them to begin their day again. But Nunez slumbered not at all.

Instead, he sat up in the place where they had left him, resting his limbs and turning the unanticipated circumstances of his arrival over and over in his mind.

Every now and then he laughed, sometimes with amusement, and sometimes with indignation.

"Unformed mind!" he said. "Got no senses yet! They little know they've been insulting their heaven-sent king and master. I see I must bring them to reason. Let me think—let me think."

He was still thinking when the sun set.

Nunez had an eye for all beautiful things, and it seemed to him that the glow upon the snowfields and glaciers that rose about the valley on every side was the most beautiful thing he had ever seen. His eyes went from that inaccessible glory to the village and irrigated fields, fast sinking into the twilight, and suddenly a wave of emotion took him, and he thanked God from the bottom of his heart that the power of sight had been given him.

He heard a voice calling to him from out of the village. "Ya ho there, Bogota! Come hither!"

At that he stood up smiling. He would show these people once and for all what sight would do for a man. They would seek him, but not find him.

"You move not, Bogota," said the voice.

He laughed noiselessly, and made two stealthy steps aside from the path.

"Trample not on the grass, Bogota; that is not allowed."

Nunez had scarcely heard the sound he made himself. He stopped amazed.

The owner of the voice came running up the piebald path towards him.

He stepped back into the pathway. "Here I am," he said.

"Why did you not come when I called you?" said the blind man. "Must you be led like a child? Cannot you hear the path as you walk?"

Nunez laughed. "I can see it," he said.

"There is no such word as *see*," said the blind man, after a pause. "Cease this folly, and follow the sound of my feet."

Nunez followed, a little annoyed.

"My time will come," he said.

"You'll learn," the blind man answered. "There is much to learn in the world."

"Has no one told you, 'In the Country of the Blind the One-eyed Man is King'?"

"What is blind?" asked the blind man carelessly over his shoulder.

Four days passed, and the fifth found the King of the Blind still incognito, as a clumsy and useless stranger among his subjects.

It was, he found, much more difficult to proclaim himself than he had supposed, and in the meantime, while he meditated his *coup d'état*, he did what he was told and learnt the manners and customs of the Country of the Blind. He found working and going about at night a particularly irksome thing, and he decided that that should be the first thing he would change.

They led a simple, laborious life, these people, with all the elements of virtue and happiness, as these things can be understood by men. They toiled, but not oppressively; they had food and clothing sufficient for their needs; they had days and seasons of rest; they made much of music and singing, and there was love among them, and little children.

It was marvellous with what confidence and precision they went about their ordered world. Everything, you see, had been made to fit their needs; each of the radiating paths of the valley area had a constant angle to the others, and was distinguished by a special notch upon its kerbing; all obstacles and irregularities of path or meadow had long since been cleared away; all their methods and procedure arose naturally from their special needs. Their senses had become marvellously acute; they could hear and judge the slightest gesture of a man a dozen paces away—could hear the very beating of his heart. Intonation had long replaced expression with them, and touches gesture, and their work with hoe and spade and fork was as free and confident as garden work can be. Their sense of smell was extraordinarily fine; they could distinguish individual differences as readily as a dog can, and they went about the tending of the llamas, who lived among the rocks above and came to the wall for food and shelter, with ease and confidence. It was only when at last Nunez sought to assert himself that he found how easy and confident their movements could be.

He rebelled only after he had tried persuasion.

He tried at first on several occasions to tell them of sight. "Look you here, you people," he said. "There are things you do not understand in me."

Once or twice one or two of them attended to him; they sat with faces downcast and ears turned intelligently towards him, and he did his best to tell them what it was to see. Among his hearers was a girl, with eyelids less red and sunken than the others, so that one could almost fancy she was hiding eyes, whom especially he hoped to persuade. He spoke of the beauties of sight, of watching the mountains, of the sky and the sunrise, and they heard him with amused incredulity that presently became condemnatory. They told him there were indeed no mountains at all, but that the end of the rocks where the llamas grazed was indeed the end of the world; thence sprang a cavernous roof of the universe, from which the dew and the avalanches fell; and when he maintained stoutly the world had neither end nor roof such as they supposed, they said his thoughts were wicked. So far as he could describe sky and clouds and stars to them it seemed to them a hideous void, a terrible blankness in the place of the smooth roof to things in which they believed—it was an article of faith with them that the cavern roof was exquisitely smooth to the touch. He saw that in some manner he shocked them, and gave up that aspect of the matter altogether, and tried to show them the practical value of sight. One morning he saw Pedro in the path called Seventeen and coming towards the central houses, but still too far off for hearing or scent, and he told them as much. "In a little while," he prophesied, "Pedro will be here." An old man remarked that Pedro had no business on path Seventeen, and then, as if in confirmation, that individual as he drew near turned and went transversely into path Ten, and so back with nimble paces towards the outer wall. They mocked Nunez when Pedro did not arrive, and afterwards, when he asked Pedro questions to clear his character, Pedro denied and outfaced him, and was afterwards hostile to him.

Then he induced them to let him go a long way up the sloping meadows towards the wall with one complacent individual, and to him he promised to describe all that happened among the houses. He noted certain goings and comings, but the things that really seemed to signify to these people happened inside of or behind the windowless houses—the only things they took note of to test him by—and of these he could see or tell nothing; and it was after the failure of this attempt, and the ridicule they could not repress, that he resorted to force. He thought of seizing a spade and suddenly smiting one or two of them to earth, and so in fair combat showing the advantage of eyes. He went so far with that resolution as to seize his spade, and then he discovered a new thing about himself, and that was that it was impossible for him to hit a blind man in cold blood.

He hesitated, and found them all aware that he had snatched up the spade. They stood alert, with their heads on one side, and bent ears towards him for what he would do next.

"Put that spade down," said one, and he felt a sort of helpless horror. He came near obedience.

Then he thrust one backwards against a house wall, and fled past him and out of the village.

He went athwart one of their meadows, leaving a track of trampled grass behind his feet, and presently sat down by the side of one of their ways. He felt something of the buoyancy that comes to all men in the beginning of a fight, but more perplexity. He began to realise that you cannot even fight happily with creatures who stand upon a different mental basis to yourself. Far away he saw a number of men carrying spades and sticks come out of the street of houses, and advance in a spreading line along the several paths towards him. They advanced slowly, speaking frequently to one another, and ever and again the whole cordon would halt and sniff the air and listen.

The first time they did this Nunez laughed. But afterwards he did not laugh.

One struck his trail in the meadow grass, and came stooping and feeling his way along it.

For five minutes he watched the slow extension of the cordon, and then his vague disposition to do something forthwith became frantic. He stood up, went a pace or so towards the circumferential wall, turned, and went back a little way. There they all stood in a crescent, still and listening.

He also stood still, gripping his spade very tightly in both hands. Should he charge them?

The pulse in his ears ran into the rhythm of "In the Country of the Blind the One-eyed Man is King!"

Should he charge them?

He looked back at the high and unclimbable wall behind—unclimbable because of its smooth plastering, but withal pierced with many little doors, and at the approaching line of seekers. Behind these others were now coming out of the street of houses.

Should he charge them?

"Bogota!" called one. "Bogota! where are you?"

He gripped his spade still tighter, and advanced down the meadows towards the place of habitations, and directly he moved they converged upon him. "I'll hit them if they touch me," he swore; "by Heaven, I will. I'll hit." He called aloud, "Look here, I'm going to do what I like in this valley. Do you hear? I'm going to do what I like and go where I like!"

They were moving in upon him quickly, groping, yet moving rapidly. It was like playing blind man's buff, with everyone blindfolded except one. "Get hold of him!" cried one. He found himself in the arc of a loose curve of pursuers. He felt suddenly he must be active and resolute.

"You don't understand," he cried in a voice that was meant to be great and resolute, and which broke. "You are blind, and I can see. Leave me alone!"

"Bogota! Put down that spade, and come off the grass!"

The last order, grotesque in its urban familiarity, produced a gust of anger.

"I'll hurt you," he said, sobbing with emotion. "By Heaven, I'll hurt you. Leave me alone!"

He began to run, not knowing clearly where to run. He ran from the nearest blind man, because it was a horror to hit him. He stopped, and then made a dash to escape from their closing ranks. He made for where a gap was wide, and the men on either side, with a quick perception of the approach of his paces, rushed in on one another. He sprang forward, and then saw he must be caught, and *swish!* the spade had struck. He felt the soft thud of hand and arm, and the man was down with a yell of pain, and he was through.

Through! And then he was close to the street of houses again, and blind men, whirling spades and stakes, were running with a sort of reasoned swiftness hither and thither.

He heard steps behind him just in time, and found a tall man rushing forward and swiping at the sound of him. He lost his nerve, hurled his spade a yard wide at his antagonist, and whirled about and fled, fairly yelling as he dodged another.

He was panic-stricken. He ran furiously to and fro, dodging when there was no need to dodge, and in his anxiety to see on every side of him at once, stumbling. For a moment he was down and they heard his fall. Far away in the circumferential wall a little doorway looked like heaven, and he set off in a wild rush for it. He did not even look round at his pursuers until it was gained, and he had stumbled across the bridge, clambered a little way among the rocks, to the surprise and dismay of a young llama, who went leaping out of sight, and lay down sobbing for breath.

And so his *coup d'état* came to an end.

He stayed outside the wall of the valley of the Blind for two nights and days without food or shelter, and meditated upon the unexpected. During these meditations he repeated very frequently and always with a profounder note of derision the exploded proverb: "In the Country of the Blind the One-Eyed Man is King." He thought chiefly of ways of fighting and conquering these people, and it grew clear that for him no practicable way was possible. He had no weapons, and now it would be hard to get one.

The canker of civilisation had got to him even in Bogota, and he could not find it in himself to go down and assassinate a blind man. Of course, if he did that, he might then dictate terms on the threat of assassinating them all. But—sooner or later he must sleep! . . .

He tried also to find food among the pine trees, to be comfortable under pine boughs while the frost fell at night, and—with less confidence—to catch a llama by artifice in order to try to kill it—perhaps by hammering it with a stone—and so finally, perhaps, to eat some of it. But the llamas had a doubt of him and regarded him with distrustful brown eyes, and spat when he drew near. Fear came on him the second day and fits of shivering. Finally he crawled down to the wall of the Country of the Blind and tried to make terms. He crawled along by the stream, shouting, until two blind men came out to the gate and talked to him.

"I was mad," he said. "But I was only newly made."

They said that was better.

He told them he was wiser now, and repented of all he had done.

Then he wept without intention, for he was very weak and ill now, and they took that as a favourable sign.

They asked him if he still thought he could "*see*."

"No," he said. "That was folly. The word means nothing—less than nothing!"

They asked him what was overhead.

"About ten times ten the height of a man there is a roof above the world—of rock—and very, very smooth." . . . He burst again into hysterical tears. "Before you ask me any more, give me some food or I shall die."

He expected dire punishments, but these blind people were capable of toleration. They regarded his rebellion as but one more proof of his general idiocy and inferiority; and after they had whipped him they appointed him to do the simplest and heaviest work they had for anyone to do, and he, seeing no other way of living, did submissively what he was told.

He was ill for some days, and they nursed him kindly. That refined his submission. But they insisted on his lying in the dark, and that was a great misery. And blind philosophers came and talked to him of the wicked levity of his mind, and reproved him so impressively for his doubts about the lid of rock that covered their cosmic casserole that he almost doubted whether indeed he was not the victim of hallucination in not seeing it overhead.

So Nunez became a citizen of the Country of the Blind, and these people ceased to be a generalised people and became individualities and familiar to him, while the world beyond the mountains became more and more remote and unreal. There was Yacob, his master, a kindly man when not annoyed; there was Pedro, Yacob's nephew; and there was Medina-saroté, who was the youngest daughter of

Yacob. She was little esteemed in the world of the blind, because she had a clear-cut face, and lacked that satisfying, glossy smoothness that is the blind man's ideal of feminine beauty; but Nunez thought her beautiful at first, and presently the most beautiful thing in the whole creation. Her closed eyelids were not sunken and red after the common way of the valley, but lay as though they might open again at any moment; and she had long eyelashes, which were considered a grave disfigurement. And her voice was strong, and did not satisfy the acute hearing of the valley swains. So that she had no lover.

There came a time when Nunez thought that, could he win her, he would be resigned to live in the valley for all the rest of his days.

He watched her; he sought opportunities of doing her little services, and presently he found that she observed him. Once at a rest-day gathering they sat side by side in the dim starlight, and the music was sweet. His hand came upon hers and he dared to clasp it. Then very tenderly she returned his pressure. And one day, as they were at their meal in the darkness, he felt her hand very softly seeking him, and as it chanced the fire leapt then and he saw the tenderness of her face.

He sought to speak to her.

He went to her one day when she was sitting in the summer moonlight spinning. The light made her a thing of silver and mystery. He sat down at her feet and told her he loved her, and told her how beautiful she seemed to him. He had a lover's voice, he spoke with a tender reverence that came near to awe, and she had never before been touched by adoration. She made him no definite answer, but it was clear his words pleased her.

After that he talked to her whenever he could take an opportunity. The valley became the world for him, and the world beyond the mountains where men lived in sunlight seemed no more than a fairy tale he would some day pour into her ears. Very tentatively and timidly he spoke to her of sight.

Sight seemed to her the most poetical of fancies, and she listened to his description of the stars and the mountains and her own sweet white-lit beauty as though it was a guilty indulgence. She did not believe, she could only half understand, but she was mysteriously delighted, and it seemed to him that she completely understood.

His love lost its awe and took courage. Presently he was for demanding her of Yacob and the elders in marriage, but she became fearful and delayed. And it was one of her elder sisters who first told Yacob that Medina-saroté and Nunez were in love.

There was from the first very great opposition to the marriage of Nunez and Medina-saroté; not so much because they valued her as because they held him as a being apart, an idiot, incompetent thing below the permissible level of a man. Her sisters opposed it bitterly as bringing discredit on them all; and old Yacob, though he had formed a sort of liking for his clumsy, obedient serf, shook his head and said the thing could not be. The young men were all angry at the idea of corrupting the race, and one went so far as to revile and strike Nunez. He struck back. Then for the first time he found an advantage in seeing, even by twilight, and after that fight was over no one was disposed to raise a hand against him. But they still found his marriage impossible.

Old Yacob had a tenderness for his last little daughter, and was grieved to have her weep upon his shoulder.

"You see, my dear, he's an idiot. He has delusions; he can't do anything right."

"I know," wept Medina-saroté. "But he's better than he was. He's getting better. And he's strong, dear father, and kind—stronger and kinder than any other man in the world. And he loves me—and, father, I love him."

Old Yacob was greatly distressed to find her inconsolable, and, besides—what made it more distressing—he liked Nunez for many things. So he went and sat in the windowless council-chamber with the other elders and watched the trend of the talk, and said, at the proper time, "He's better than he was. Very likely, some day, we shall find him as sane as ourselves."

Then afterwards one of the elders, who thought deeply, had an idea. He was the great doctor among these people, their medicine-man, and he had a very philosophical and inventive mind, and the idea of curing Nunez of his peculiarities appealed to him. One day when Yacob was present he returned to the topic of Nunez.

"I have examined Bogota," he said, "and the case is clearer to me. I think very probably he might be cured."

"That is what I have always hoped," said old Yacob.

"His brain is affected," said the blind doctor.

The elders murmured assent.

"Now, *what* affects it?"

"Ah!" said old Yacob.

"*This*," said the doctor, answering his own question. "Those queer things that are called the eyes, and which exist to make an agreeable soft depression in the face, are diseased, in the case of Bogota, in such a way as to affect his brain. They are greatly distended, he has eyelashes, and his eyelids move, and consequently his brain is in a state of constant irritation and distraction."

"Yes?" said old Yacob. "Yes?"

"And I think I may say with reasonable certainty that, in order to cure him completely, all that we need do is a simple and easy surgical operation—namely, to remove these irritant bodies."

"And then he will be sane?"

"Then he will be perfectly sane, and a quite admirable citizen."

"Thank Heaven for science!" said old Yacob, and went forth at once to tell Nunez of his happy hopes.

But Nunez's manner of receiving the good news struck him as being cold and disappointing.

"One might think," he said, "from the tone you take, that you did not care for my daughter."

It was Medina-saroté who persuaded Nunez to face the blind surgeons.

"*You* do not want me," he said, "to lose my gift of sight?"

She shook her head.

"My world is sight."

Her head drooped lower.

"There are the beautiful things, the beautiful little things—the flowers, the lichens among the rocks, the lightness and softness on a piece of fur, the far sky with its drifting down of clouds, the sunsets and the stars. And there is *you*. For you alone it is good to have sight, to see your sweet, serene face, your kindly lips, your dear, beautiful hands folded together. . . . It is these eyes of mine you won, these eyes that hold me to you, that these idiots seek. Instead, I must touch you, hear you, and never see you again. I must come under that roof of rock and stone and darkness, that horrible roof under which your imagination stoops. . . . No; you would not have me do that?"

A disagreeable doubt had arisen in him. He stopped, and left the thing a question.

"I wish," she said, "sometimes—" She paused.

"Yes," said he, a little apprehensively.

"I wish sometimes—you would not talk like that."

"Like what?"

"I know it's pretty—it's your imagination. I love it, but *now*—"

He felt cold. "*Now*?" he said faintly.

She sat quite still.

"You mean—you think—I should be better, better perhaps—"

He was realising things very swiftly. He felt anger, indeed, anger at the dull course of fate, but also sympathy for her lack of understanding—a sympathy near akin to pity.

"*Dear*," he said, and he could see by her whiteness how intensely her spirit pressed against the things she could not say. He put his arms about her, he kissed her ear, and they sat for a time in silence.

"If I were to consent to this?" he said at last, in a voice that was very gentle.

She flung her arms about him, weeping wildly. "Oh, if you would," she sobbed, "if only you would!"

For a week before the operation that was to raise him from his servitude and inferiority to the level of a blind citizen, Nunez knew nothing of sleep, and all through the warm sunlit hours, while the others slumbered happily, he sat brooding or wandered aimlessly, trying to bring his mind to bear on his dilemma. He had given his answer, he had given his consent, and still he was not sure. And at last work-time was over, the sun rose in splendour over the golden crests, and his last day of vision began for him. He had a few minutes with Medina-saroté before she went apart to sleep.

"To-morrow," he said, "I shall see no more."

"Dear heart!" she answered, and pressed his hands with all her strength.

"They will hurt you but little," she said; "and you are going through this pain—you are going through it, dear lover, for *me*. . . . Dear, if a woman's heart and life can do it, I will repay you. My dearest one, my dearest with the tender voice, I will repay."

He was drenched in pity for himself and her.

He held her in his arms, and pressed his lips to hers, and looked on her sweet face for the last time. "Good-bye!" he whispered at that dear sight, "good-bye!"

And then in silence he turned away from her.

She could hear his slow retreating footsteps, and something in the rhythm of them threw her into a passion of weeping.

He had fully meant to go to a lonely place where the meadows were beautiful with white narcissus, and there remain until the hour of his sacrifice should come, but as he went he lifted up his eyes and saw the morning, the morning like an angel in golden armour, marching down the steeps. . . .

It seemed to him that before this splendour he, and this blind world in the valley, and his love, and all, were no more than a pit of sin.

He did not turn aside as he had meant to do, but went on, and passed through the wall of the circumference and out upon the rocks, and his eyes were always upon the sunlit ice and snow.

He saw their infinite beauty, and his imagination soared over them to the things beyond he was now to resign for ever.

He thought of that great free world he was parted from, the world that was his own, and he had a vision of those further slopes, distance beyond distance, with Bogota, a place of multitudinous stirring beauty, a glory by day, a luminous mystery by night, a place of palaces and fountains and statues and white houses, lying beautifully in the middle distance. He thought how for a day or so one might come down through passes, drawing ever nearer and nearer to its busy streets and ways. He thought of the river journey, day by day, from great Bogota to the still vaster world beyond, through towns and villages, forest and desert places, the rushing river day by day, until its banks receded and the big steamers came splashing by, and one had reached the sea—the limitless sea, with its thousand islands, its thousands of islands, and its ships seen dimly far away in their incessant journeyings round and about that greater world. And there, unpent by mountains, one saw the sky—the sky, not such a disc as one saw it here, but an arch of immeasurable blue, a deep of deeps in which the circling stars were floating. . . .

His eyes scrutinised the great curtain of the mountains with a keener inquiry.

For example, if one went so, up that gully and to that chimney there, then one might come out high among those stunted pines that ran round in a sort of shelf and rose still higher and higher as it passed above the gorge. And then? That talus might be managed. Thence perhaps a climb might be found to take him up to the precipice that came below the snow; and if that chimney failed, then another farther to the east might serve his purpose better. And then? Then one would be out upon the amber-lit snow there, and half-way up to the crest of those beautiful desolations.

He glanced back at the village, then turned right round and regarded it steadfastly.

He thought of Medina-saroté, and she had become small and remote.

He turned again towards the mountain wall, down which the day had come to him.

Then very circumspectly he began to climb.

When sunset came he was no longer climbing, but he was far and high. He had been higher, but he was still very high. His clothes were torn, his limbs were blood-stained, he was bruised in many places, but he lay as if he were at his ease, and there was a smile on his face.

From where he rested the valley seemed as if it were in a pit and nearly a mile below. Already it was dim with haze and shadow, though the mountain summits around him were things of light and fire. The mountain summits around him were things of light and fire, and the little details of the rocks near at hand were drenched with subtle beauty—a vein of green mineral piercing the grey, the flash of crystal faces here and there, a minute, minutely-beautiful orange lichen close beside his face. There were deep mysterious shadows in the gorge, blue deepening into purple, and purple into a luminous darkness, and overhead was the illimitable vastness of the sky. But he heeded these things no longer, but lay quite inactive there, smiling as if he were satisfied merely to have escaped from the valley of the Blind in which he had thought to be King.

The glow of the sunset passed, and the night came, and still he lay peacefully contented under the cold clear stars.

Permissions Acknowledgments

Grateful acknowledgment is made to the following for permission to reprint previously published material:

Angel Books: "A Shameless Rascal" from *Five Tales* by Nikolai Leskov, translated by Michael Shotton (Angel Books, London, 1986). Reprinted by permission of Angel Books.

Australian Literary Management: "The Dream" from *The Mysterious Tales of Ivan Turgenev*, translated by Robert Dessaix (The Australian National University, 1979). Reprinted by permission of Australian Literary Management.

John Calder (Publishers) Ltd.: "Wandering Willie's Tale" from *The Supernatural Short Stories of Sir Walter Scott*, edited by Michael Hayes [John Calder (Publishers) Ltd., London]. Reprinted by permission of The Calder Educational Trust, London.

Dedalus Limited: "The Story of the Demoniac Pacheco" from *Tales from the Saragossa Manuscript* by Jan Potocki, translated by Christine Donougher (Dedalus/Hippocrene, 1990). Translation copyright © 1990 by Christine Donougher. Reprinted by permission of Dedalus Limited.

Dover Publications, Inc.: "The Sand-Man" translated by J. T. Bealby from *The Best Tales of Hoffmann*, by E.T.A. Hoffmann, edited by E. F. Bleiler. Copyright © 1967 by Dover Publications, Inc. Reprinted by permission of Dover Publications, Inc.

Dutton Signet: "The Nose" from *Diary of a Madman and Other Stories* by Nikolai Gogol, translated by Andrew MacAndrew. Translation copyright © 1960, renewed 1988 by Andrew R. MacAndrew. Reprinted by permission of Dutton Signet, a division of Penguin Books USA Inc.

Faber and Faber Limited: "The Shadow" from *Hans Andersen: Forty-two Stories,* translated by M. R. James (Faber and Faber Limited, London, 1930). Reprinted by permission of Faber and Faber Limited.

Oxford University Press: "The Venus of Ille" from *The Venus of Ille and Other Stories* by Prosper Mérimée, translated by Jean Kimber. Copyright © 1966 by Oxford University Press. "The Very Image" from *Cruel Tales* by Villiers de l'Isle-Adam, translated by Robert Baldick. Copyright © 1963 by Robert Baldick. Reprinted by permission of Oxford University Press, Oxford, England.

A. P. Watt Ltd: "The Country of the Blind" from *The Country of the Blind and Other Stories* by H. G. Wells, (Oxford University Press, New York, 1996). Reprinted by permission of A. P. Watt Ltd., on behalf of The Literary Executors of the Estate of H. G. Wells.